'We look for medicine to be an orderly field of knowledge and procedure. But it is not. It is an imperfect science, an enterprise of constantly changing knowledge, uncertain information, fallible individuals, and at the same time lives on the line. There is science in what we do, yes, but also habit, intuition, and sometimes plain old guessing. The gap between what we know and what we aim for persists. And this gap complicates everything we do.'

Atul Gawande, *Complications: A Surgeon's Notes and an Imperfect Science*
New York: Metropolitan Books of Henry Holt and Company, 2002.

## Also by Gabriel Farago

# THE HIDDEN GENES OF PROFESSOR K

## Jack Rogan Mysteries Book 3

GABRIEL FARAGO

This book is brought to you by Bear & King Publishing.
First published 2016 © Gabriel Farago

The right of Gabriel Farago to be identified as the author of this work has been asserted by him in accordance with the Copyright Amendment (Moral Rights) Act 2000.

Cataloguing-in-Publication entry is available from the National Library of Australia: http://catalogue.nla.gov.au/

Title: The Hidden Genes of Professor K
Author: Farago, Gabriel Geza
ISBN: 978-0-9945763-4-7 (paperback)

Cover design and layout by Vivien Valk and Christopher Hammang.

Images used under licence from iStockphoto.com and Shutterstock.com

This book was inspired by, and is dedicated to, the many talented scientists who work at the Garvan Institute of Medical Research, in Sydney. In awe of nature, but not seduced by its beauty, or cowed by its terror, they are always on the lookout for inspired ideas to improve the journey of man.

To learn more about Garvan, what it stands for
and what it does, please visit
www.garvan.org.au

# Acknowledgement

Writing *The Hidden Genes of Professor K* was an ambitious project. For a layman, exploring subjects touching on cutting- edge medical research and complex science is never easy. The learning curve was both challenging and steep, and would not have been possible without the guiding hand of leading experts. A special thank you must therefore go to Professor Susan Clark, Head of the Genomics and Epigenetics Division at the Garvan Institute of Medical Research in Sydney, and Dr Peter Molloy, Senior Principal Research Scientist in CSIRO's Food and Nutrition Flagship, Sydney, for inducting me into the fascinating world of genomics and epigenetics. But this wasn't all. They patiently reviewed the relevant text to make sure I got the science right, didn't become lost in speculation, and kept at least one eye on what is realistic and achievable, based on what we know today.

Preparing a book for publication requires many skills; it is a team effort. I've been very fortunate to have a group of talented and dedicated specialists help me deal with the many challenges of a rapidly changing literary landscape. Without their professional support and advice, this book would not have seen the light of day. There are too many to mention, but a few definitely stand out.

First, Sally Asnicar, my editor. Her exceptional attention to detail and insights into the characters and the multi-layered storyline, have been invaluable in bringing this project to fruition.

Who says we don't judge a book by its cover? In a way we all do, especially when surfing the Net for inspiration of what to read. The talented Vivien Valk and Christopher Hammang have designed an imaginative cover that is true to the storyline, and captures the spirit of the book. Christopher is a scientific animation artist, creating visualisation of the microscopic inner space of life. He works as part of a multi- disciplinary research group, the Biological Data Visualisation team, led by Dr Sean O'Donoghue at CSIRO and the Garvan Institute.

And finally, it would be remiss of me not to mention my wife, Joan, literary critic, researcher, patient sounding board and cheerful travel companion—we visit all of the places mentioned in my books.

Thank you all for believing in me, and what I'm trying to achieve with my writing.

*Gabriel Farago*
*Leura, Blue Mountains, Australia*

# FOREWORD

We all stare into the darkness. There are things, many things, that we do not know about the world, or about ourselves. What makes us different from other animals, and sets us apart from each other, is the genetic material we inherit from our ancestors. Amazingly, however, the number and repertoire of conventional protein coding genes is similar across the animal kingdom. The rest of our genome was once dismissed as junk – a graveyard of evolutionary debris for which scientists could not attribute any purpose. However, it now appears that this DNA is in fact alive, transmitting. It is the cryptic code that orchestrates human development, empowers our thoughts, and perhaps even holds memories of experiences from generations past.

*The Hidden Genes of Professor K* combines imagination, history, and knowledge of the leading edge of medical science to weave an epic tale of greed and intrigue. It takes the reader into the recesses of the human psyche, the hidden corners of history, and the dark matter of the human genome. The secrets are all there.

*Professor John Mattick AO FAA,*
*Executive Director of the Garvan Institute of Medical Research, Sydney*
*(http://www.garvan.org.au)*

*The Hidden Genes of Professor K* is a thrilling medical mystery that incorporates new advances in genetic and epigenetic research to decipher the secrets of the past extracted from human DNA. Readers who were spellbound by Gabriel Farago's previous novels *The Empress Holds the Key* and *The Disappearance of Anna Popov* will be equally enthralled and captivated as they journey through the secrets of the past, and share the dreams of a visionary scientist with the power to change the future of medicine.

*Professor Susan Clark FAA,*
*Head of the Genomics and Epigenetic Division,*
*The Garvan Institute of Medical Research,*
*Sydney, Australia.*

*Dr Peter Molloy,*
*Senior Principal Research Scientist, CSIRO*
*Food and Nutrition, Sydney Australia.*

# THE HIDDEN GENES OF PROFESSOR K

GABRIEL FARAGO

# AUTHOR'S NOTE

Edwin Smith, a colourful character, is remembered for something he did one hot afternoon in a bazaar in Luxor, Egypt in 1862. He bought a papyrus that turned out to be one of the oldest medical texts in the world.

I first came across the Edwin Smith Papyrus some twenty years ago. I was studying Egyptology at the time, learning to read the hieroglyphs at night, because during the day I was a practising barrister and spent most of my days in court. Archaeology was my passion and has remained so to this very day.

Our professor used this unique text as an illustration of the extraordinary achievements of the Ancient Egyptians. The 4.6 metre long papyrus is written right to left in hieratic, a cursive form of hieroglyphs. Experts believe it was composed in about 1500 BC.

However, what is particularly fascinating about the papyrus is that it is now believed to be a copy of a much older text dating back to the Old Kingdom. And it doesn't stop there. Some scholars maintain that the true author of the text was none other than Imhotep, a remarkable renaissance man of the Old Kingdom who lived in around 2600 BC, and rose to high office under the pharaoh Djoser. Imhotep was a gifted architect, engineer, high priest and physician who, two thousand years after his death, was deified and became the god of medicine and healing. Centuries later, the ancient Greeks associated him with Asklepios, the god of medicine.

What makes this text so unique is the fact it describes forty-eight case histories based on rational anatomical, physiological and pathological observations, without looking at them through the eyes of magic, which was the accepted way to deal with disease, injury and trauma at the time.

Fascinated by the text, I immersed myself in the papyrus, which was translated by Breasted, an eminent Egyptologist, in 1930. That was how I came across case 46.

Case 46 deals with '*bulging tumours of the breast ... large, spreading and hard ...*' A more accurate description of breast cancer is difficult to imagine. For the first time in human history, the Emperor of Darkness – cancer – made its appearance in literature.

Every case study in the papyrus is followed by a discussion of its treatment except in case 46 for which, according to Imhotep, there was none.

Cancer is an ancient disease. Progress in medical research, especially in recent years, has been breathtaking. We have come a long way, yet have we come any closer to conquering this powerful, malevolent disease, or do we have to agree with Imhotep's prognosis 4500 years ago – that in many cases, there is no cure?

This question has been asked countless times through the ages and has plagued the medical profession for centuries. The search for an answer became the inspiration for this book.

*Gabriel Farago*
*Leura, Blue Mountains, Australia*

# CONTENTS

# PART I
## *MEMENTO MORI*

# Gordon Institute, Sydney:
# September 2011

Professor Kasper Kozakievicz – Professor K to colleagues because his name was almost impossible to pronounce – looked at the computer printout on his desk and smiled; the results were exactly as he had expected. A tremendous feeling of elation quickened his heartbeat, making his emaciated body tremble with excitement. Reaching for his chair to steady himself, he suddenly felt dizzy and weak. Stars began to dance in front of his eyes just before a bundle of sharp darts embedded in his brain. Moments later, his knees gave way and he collapsed to the floor.

Professor K had known for months he was dying. The cancer – a particularly aggressive one – had spread rapidly with relentless predictability. To an eminent research scientist, the prognosis was obvious: death was only a matter of time. Rather than subjecting himself to unpleasant and debilitating treatment to buy a few more feeble days, he had thrown himself deeper into his research, much to the dismay of his exasperated family, friends and colleagues. Only those who knew him well understood what he was doing, and why.

Ironically, the day he diagnosed his own cancer was the very day an unexpected breakthrough occurred in his research. From that day on, he knew he was getting close, very close. All he needed was a little more time – but time was running out.

Professor K opened his eyes. Darkness. He tried to move his fingers, but they wouldn't obey. Then slowly, a wave of excruciating pain reached his tortured brain as he regained consciousness and the darkness receded. Professor K knew exactly what was happening: death was standing at the door! Mustering the last of his remaining strength, he got unsteadily to his feet and fell into his chair. *My notes*, he thought, *where are my notes?* Trying not to panic, he searched his cluttered desktop for his research notes with shaking hands. Finding the little notebook under a pile of papers, he relaxed as a hint of a smile creased his wan face. Then, taking a deep breath, he reached for his pen and began to write like a man possessed.

On the other side of the globe, Dr Alexandra Delacroix was fast asleep in her Marseilles apartment, located next to the Université De La Méditerranée School of Medicine where she worked, when her mobile rang. She wasn't used to getting phone calls in the middle of the night, and sensed it must be something important. Instantly awake, she reached for the phone on her bedside table, peered at the incoming number and pressed answer. 'Do you know what time it is, Kasper?' she said sleepily.

'I do, Lexi,' replied the professor calmly. 'Please listen carefully, there isn't much time. I'm talking to you as a man who is about to die, but more importantly, I'm talking to you as a fellow scientist.'

Silence. Dr Delacroix had known about her mentor's illness for some time, but was unaware how far it had progressed. 'How bad is it?' she asked.

'I won't see tomorrow …'

'Go on.'

'I would like you to be my successor, so to speak.'

'What do you mean?'

'I think I've found a breakthrough in cancer diagnosis and treatment.'

Again, silence. Then, 'Across the board?'

'Quite possibly. It's groundbreaking.'

'Are you serious?'

'Absolutely!'

'My God, Kasper, *do you realise what you are saying*?'

'I do. There's still a long way to go with all the trials and such, but the proof is right here in front of me. But only you will understand my crazy notes and abbreviations, and how it all works.'

'What about Cavendish; isn't he next in line?'

'Cavendish is a plodder. Too much ambition, not enough talent. He's not in your league. This is far too important. I want *you—*'

'Because we've worked together before, you mean?' interrupted Dr Delacroix.

'Yes, and because of *who you are*,' said the professor, sounding weak.

'Speak up, Kasper, I can barely hear you,' said Dr Delacroix, raising her voice. For a while, all she could hear was heavy breathing on the other end of the line.

'I can't see any more,' said the professor, gasping for breath.

'Stay with me, Kasper!' shrieked Dr Delacroix. 'What do you want me to do?'

'It's all in my notes and the specimens. I've put everything into the safe here in the lab. This is the combination. Write it down: 12 … 48 … 62. Got that?'

'12, 48, 62,' repeated Dr Delacroix.

'Good,' sighed the professor, suddenly calmer. 'Will you be my intellectual heir, so to speak?'

'Yes.'

'Carry the torch; *promise?*' whispered the professor.

'I promise.'

'As my friend?'

'Yes.'

'Then you must hurry! A position is waiting for you here at the Gordon. It's all arranged.'

'And Cavendish?' Dr Delacroix asked again.

'Don't worry about him!'

Her mind racing, Dr Delacroix considered the implications. She would have to give up her position at the Institute for Structural Biology and Microbiology at the University and move to Sydney. The professor's offer was the opportunity of a lifetime. Cavendish could be a problem, but there was really nothing to consider. 'Can't you get some help?' she asked, concerned about her dying friend.

'It's Sunday morning; there's no one here. *And besides*,' whispered the professor, '*it's too late for that now. At least it hasn't been in vain …*'

'What did you say?' shouted Dr Delacroix, her eyes misting over. There was no reply; all she could hear was silence.

# Olympic Stadium, Moscow:
## September 2011

The gigantic, semi-circular stage erected inside the Olympic Stadium had been transformed into a haunted cemetery, complete with cobwebbed tombstones flanked by crying angels, sad-looking willow trees, live crows in cages and a large, pale moon, suspended from a mobile crane. Set against a backdrop depicting frightening ghouls and hooded monks, clever props and light effects completed the illusion. In front of the stage, a hundred thousand eager fans waited excitedly to hear the band. They began to chant 'Isis, Isis, Isis' as their idols walked on stage. Whipping up the crowd, the drummer began the introduction to their signature number – 'It's Time; come with us' – before the throbbing bass joined in and the guitars screamed into life. The Russian leg of Isis and The Time Machine's *Echoes from the Grave* World Tour had begun.

Transformed into an Egyptian goddess in her white silk robe and golden crown, Isis lay motionless in a glass coffin six feet below the stage. The hydraulics engineer adjusted the switches and waited for the signal from the stage manager. As the band was about to finish 'It's Time', the stage manager gave the nod. Slowly, the coffin ascended.

On the stage above, a large tombstone made of plywood and papier-mâché also began to rise, while green, smoke-like fog oozed out of the other tombs and covered the stage. As the glass coffin emerged from the open grave, the crowd became hysterical. The security guards in front of the stage barely managed to hold back the howling fans as Isis came into view. The guitars fell silent, and only the drummer continued with a mesmerising, blood-boiling solo.

On cue, the engineer flicked another switch and the glass lid of the coffin slowly opened. Suddenly, Isis came to life. First, she raised her arms, then her head. The guitars were back, playing 'Resurrection', the first track of The Time Machine's new studio album, which had shot to number one in twenty-eight countries since its release a month earlier.

Isis now stood up in the open coffin, took off her serpent crown and tossed it towards the jubilant crowd. Then she let the white robe slip from her shoulders, exposing her stunning, tattooed body. Wearing only a tiny black bikini studded with diamonds, her trademark black boots and fish-net stockings, Isis somersaulted out of the coffin – her acrobatic feats on stage were legendary – and began to sing.

Lola Rodriguez, Isis' fiery personal assistant, took the phone call and paled. Collecting her thoughts, she slipped the phone back into her pocket and began to look for the production manager. 'Where's Ed?' she asked, hurrying to the improvised change rooms behind the stage. The sound technician sitting in his booth pointed to some scaffolding supporting the five-storey high canvas backdrop. Ed Walker, the production manager, was keeping an eye on the stage through a small window cut into the canvas.

'Can I have a word?' shouted Lola, trying to make herself heard. The music was deafening.

'Not now, Lola, she's about to come off for a costume change,' replied the production manager, looking stressed.

'It's urgent.'

'Okay. What's up?' asked Ed. When Lola told him about the phone call, he was visibly shocked. 'Jesus, Lola, what are you going to do?'

'I have to tell her right now, what else?'

'Can't you wait until *after* the show?'

'Are you kidding? She'll eat me alive if she finds out I've held this back.'

'You're right. Good luck! Here she comes.'

Blowing kisses to her adoring fans, Isis strutted off the stage, her body covered in tiny beads of perspiration glistening like diamonds in the spotlight. Isis caught her breath, took a glass of iced tea from the waiting attendant and headed straight for her change room. The next five minutes were vital. During this short time, she would undergo a breathtaking transformation. Similar to a pit stop in a Formula One race, the costume team waiting for her knew exactly what had to be done. Every second counted.

Isis began her breathing exercises, swept into the tiny room and, standing in front of a large mirror, let her team go to work. Any interruption or distraction of any kind during this critical procedure was strictly forbidden.

Lola pushed past the frowning make-up artist and stood next to Isis. Isis watched her in the mirror and shot her a disapproving look that would have sent a grown tiger packing. 'I must speak to you privately …' began Lola haltingly, 'it's urgent.'

'What; now? *Are you out of your mind?*' hissed Isis. Lola insisted. Isis realised at once something was wrong. 'Everybody out,' she commanded curtly. 'Put my entry back three minutes and close the door.' Everybody stopped working and left the room. 'This better be good,' said Isis, carefully watching her personal assistant.

During the next sixty seconds, Lola recounted her earlier telephone conversation with the London police. Isis sat down on the make-up stool, her face ashen, and for a while didn't say anything. Her mind racing, she contemplated the consequences of what she'd just heard.

'What are you going to do?' asked Lola, conscious of precious seconds ticking by.

'I'll go back on and complete the show. As soon as it's over, you and I will fly to London. Get my plane ready—'

'What about Tokyo?' interjected Lola, 'The next concert is in three days.'

'Everything goes ahead as planned. I'll be there in time. Does anyone else know about this?'

'Only Ed.'

'Good. Now, send them all back in, and not a word of this to anyone; understood?' Lola nodded. Isis leant across to Lola and kissed her tenderly on the forehead. 'Thank you, Lola. I don't know what I'd do without you.'

Her cheeks glowing, Lola hurried out of the room. She lived for moments like this.

*Pegasus* – Isis' private jet – began its descent in preparation for landing. Lola walked to the back of the plane to wake her mistress. *'We're almost there,'* she whispered, gently touching Isis on the shoulder. Isis nodded, but didn't open her eyes. 'Your car will meet us on the tarmac. We should get to the hospital within the hour, London traffic permitting.'

Slumped into the back seat of her black Bentley, Isis was trying to prepare herself for what she sensed would be a life-changing ordeal. She hated hospitals with a passion, but worst of all was not knowing what had happened. They had been told so little. For someone used to being in control, uncertainty was torture. All she knew was that her parents, Lord and Lady Elms, had been attacked in their London home. Her father was dead and her mother on life support, not expected to live.

Two policemen from the Metropolitan Police met them at the designated side entrance to the hospital's casualty section and ushered them discreetly inside. Standing in the lift behind Boris, her Ukrainian wrestling-champion turned bodyguard who followed her everywhere like a shadow, Isis reached for Lola's hand and squeezed it. Isis had always found looking at the huge man's massive frame and bulging neck muscles reassuring, but not so this time. Boris could protect her from many things, but not from what she was about to encounter.

As she followed the policemen down a dimly lit corridor smelling of cleaning fluids and disinfectant, Isis tried in vain to calm herself. She could confidently go on stage and face a hundred thousand adoring fans, yet with each step her anxiety grew, fear clawing at her throat.

The softly spoken surgeon waiting at the end of the corridor explained with clinical efficiency that Lady Elms was conscious, but could slip away at any moment. 'She's waiting for you,' he said. 'That is what's been keeping her alive. I don't think she'll be able to speak anymore, but she wants to see you ...' Opening the door he added, 'I must warn you, her injuries are horrific.'

Isis nodded and went into the room alone.

At first, Isis thought there had been a terrible mistake. The person lying on the bed in no way resembled her mother. The face – mutilated beyond recognition – looked as if it had been attacked with a meat cleaver. Head turned towards the door, the person was staring at her with unseeing eyes. Then something happened: sensing her son's presence, Lady Elms' dying brain produced a final moment of clarity. Her mouth opened and the lips began to move, but there was no sound. However, coming closer, Isis thought she could hear something.

'*Georgie?*' whispered the mangled piece of flesh on the pillow. The face may have been unrecognisable, but there was no mistaking the voice.

'Mama!' cried Isis, falling to her knees next to the bed.

'I knew you would come. *Listen* ...' said Lady Elms, her voice barely audible. Exhausted by the effort, she kept staring at Isis. Her lips kept moving, unable to form words.

'Hush ... You must rest,' cried Isis, reaching for her mother's limp hand.

The touch of her son's hand seemed to revive Lady Elms. 'Great danger ... for you,' she warned. With her eyesight gone and blood filling her lungs, Lady Elms began to choke. '*My* ...' she whispered, her voice barely audible, '*our secret place ... hide and seek – remember?*'

'I do. But what—'

'Stars, hide your fires ...' With her last breath fading, the unfinished sentence turned into a final farewell from a loving mother leaving an inconsolable son to mourn her tragic departure.

The surgeon's trained ear heard it first: the alarm on the life support system had been activated. He burst into the room, followed by Boris and Lola. The furiously flashing lights on the monitors told him everything he needed to know: his patient was dead. Blood was still oozing out of Lady Elms' open mouth. Kneeling on the floor next to the bed, her cheeks covered in blood, Isis was sobbing uncontrollably. Sadly shaking his head, the surgeon walked over to the machine and turned it off.

# 1

*Calypso*, a former Russian icebreaker, was leaving Hamilton Island. It had spent the past five days cruising along the Great Barrier Reef on its way south to Sydney. Purchased for a pittance by Blackburn Pharmaceuticals from the Russian navy in the nineteen nineties, the massive ship had undergone a major transformation. The dilapidated, discarded icebreaker had become a state-of-the-art research vessel, its bulky exterior a clever disguise for the sophistication within. Equipped with cutting-edge communications technology rivalling that of the US navy, and laboratories that would have been the envy of many a university or teaching hospital, it ploughed the high seas as the floating boardroom and proud flagship of Blackburn Pharmaceuticals.

Alistair Macbeth, founder, managing director and major shareholder of the international pharmaceutical giant, was an enigma. Because he gave no interviews, didn't mix with his peers, had no fixed address and reported to no one, the press didn't know what to make of him. Shunning the limelight that went with his self-made billionaire status, he lived like a recluse on *Calypso* and ruled his massive pharmaceutical empire from his luxurious stateroom on board the vessel. Because so little was known about him personally – apart from the fact he was a paraplegic – speculation and rumour had filled the frustrating gaps left by missing facts. The press didn't mind; speculation and rumour were the grist of the insatiable tabloid mill, and the elusive Alistair Macbeth was a steady source of both. Annoyingly, the only thing missing was scandal.

His staggering wealth, power, influence and rugged good looks, periodically tempted hungry newshounds to pry into his affairs – usually with little success. Some had even tried to uncover his murky past, only to find smoke and mirrors thwarting their efforts at every turn. Macbeth fiercely guarded his privacy and knew how to protect it. If a curious journalist came too close to something he wasn't supposed to know, or in some way stepped over the line, Macbeth made sure he never did it again. This well-known cat and mouse game had gone on for years.

Macbeth surrounded himself with only the best. With several languages and a Harvard MBA on her impressive CV, Carlotta O'Brien was very good at what she did. As Macbeth's personal assistant, she had to be. Macbeth's demands and expectations were legendary. Confined to a wheelchair, he had become a man who rarely slept and never rested. His useless body had turned him into a cerebral creature with an extraordinary mind and a voracious appetite for work.

Carlotta knocked softly, and entered the stateroom. Macbeth was sitting in his wheelchair by the desk as usual. 'Adrian Cavendish for you,' she said, handing the satellite phone, which was encrypted with an untraceable number, to her boss. Macbeth waited until Carlotta had left the room before taking the call.

'You have something for me?' asked Macbeth.

'He's dead,' answered Adrian Cavendish, his voice sounding hollow.

'When?'

'The cleaner found him this morning in the lab.'

A hint of a smile creased Macbeth's face; so far, everything was going according to plan. 'When are you taking over?' he asked.

'There's a problem ...'

'Oh?'

'I will not be replacing him—'

'What?' interrupted Macbeth impatiently, 'Why not?'

'Apparently, he appointed someone else ...'

'You can't be serious! Who?'

'A French scientist. A former colleague of his. She's a leading expert in genomics. The CEO just told me.'

'Do you know who she is?'

'Yes. Dr Alexandra Delacroix.'

'But you assured me—'

13

'I'm just as disappointed as you are,' Cavendish cut in curtly.

*That's an understatement*, thought Macbeth, considering his options. Losing Cavendish at such a critical phase in this groundbreaking research project was a major blow. A breakthrough in cancer treatment could mean billions to Blackburn Pharmaceuticals. However, if it fell into the wrong hands – competitors, for example – it could cost the company a fortune. Blackburn Pharmaceuticals was the sole producer of a recently discovered drug that significantly slowed down the advance of the dreadful disease. It had taken years and many millions to develop, and was without doubt the company's top earner. If there were a breakthrough in prevention or reversal, the drug could become obsolete overnight. Macbeth had made his fortune by staying ahead of his competitors – at any cost – and silencing his critics. 'Do you have any idea how far he got?' he asked.

'Very close, that's all I know. He barely left his lab during the past few days. He worked like a madman. Alone, as usual.'

'He must have recorded his findings, surely.'

'He always kept meticulous records of everything he did.'

'Do you know where they are?'

'Usually, he kept his notes in a safe in the lab.'

'Well?'

'It's risky ...'

'I pay very well; you know that!'

'I'll see what I can do.'

'You'll have to do better do that, Adrian, before it's too late,' said Macbeth, steel in his voice, *'for all of us,'* he added quietly, and hung up.

The veiled threat wasn't lost on Cavendish. Macbeth was a master when it came to formulating an effective threat. He was also a master when the time came to carry it out. With so much at stake, there was no room for error.

Moments after Macbeth had hung up, Carlotta re-entered the room. 'I want you to find out everything you can about a Dr Alexandra Delacroix,' said Macbeth, holding up the satellite phone.

Nodding, Carlotta walked over to the wheelchair, took the phone from her boss' hand and left the room without saying a word.

## 2

The discovery of the dead professor in his lab that morning had sent the whole institute into a spin. The cafeteria was empty, young PhD students and researchers were walking around in a daze, and the corridors were eerily silent. The CEO had called an urgent board meeting and had locked himself in his office. The undertakers had removed the body and taken it to the morgue in the hospital next door. Professor K's personal physician had been notified and was on his way to examine the body and issue a death certificate.

Pacing nervously up and down in his lab, Cavendish was considering what to do. Making a copy and putting the notebook back in the safe wasn't an option. If the material was as valuable as he suspected, it was critical it disappear without a trace. The material could then safely resurface elsewhere, disguised as a new 'discovery' without arousing suspicion or being linked to Professor K's work in any way.

Macbeth's last words had triggered alarm bells that refused to stop ringing. Because Cavendish had always dealt with faceless intermediaries, he had no idea who he was doing business with. Neither Macbeth, nor Blackburn Pharmaceuticals had ever been mentioned. However, because the stakes were so high, and the money involved outrageous, he realised that serious pharmaceutical interests had to be present. Industrial espionage in scientific circles was not uncommon. He also realised he was playing a dangerous game that could not only cost him his career, but also send him to jail. In a strange way, however, he found the danger exciting, and the secrecy and cloak and dagger meetings in gay clubs exhilarating and empowering. And on top of all that, was the money …

The first approach had seemed harmless enough. Cavendish had met a young American in one of the gay bars he frequented. They had a brief affair, and his new lover introduced him to a friend – a South

African – who appeared to know a lot about Professor K's work. All of this happened shortly after an article by Professor K describing his groundbreaking work was published in *Nature* two years earlier. After that, one thing led to another. Lavish dinners in gay clubs and an all-expenses paid holiday for himself and his lover in an exclusive Fijian resort prepared the way.

At first, Cavendish supplied only little snippets of information about Professor K's research. The payments in return – always in cash – were outlandish and quickly had a significant impact on his lifestyle. After a while, Cavendish was put on a monthly 'retainer', which was more than double his salary at the institute.

After that, there was no turning back. Any significant piece of information attracted a six-figure 'bonus'. Scientists aren't well paid. The new car, a Bondi beach apartment, expensive clothes and holidays were all very easy to get used to. Cavendish's status and reputation in the gay community soared. Corruption had become a way of life.

Dr Delacroix's unexpected appointment came as a major blow. Professor' K's illness was no secret and his death not unexpected. However, Cavendish had been certain he would be the one to succeed him. The French interloper had changed all that. His cash flow and lavish lifestyle were now both under threat. Cavendish realised there was one last opportunity to make some serious money: he had to secure Professor K's notes and demand a big payment. He also knew that if he wanted to succeed in this, he had to act swiftly before things returned to normal. Confusion was always a good cover.

As a senior staff member, Cavendish had ready access to all the labs and offices in the institute. He used to visit Professor K's lab frequently, as they had worked together on many projects over the years and shared information. His presence in Professor K's lab, even on this tragic day, would therefore appear perfectly normal.

Carrying his notepad and a computer printout, Cavendish walked down the deserted corridor leading to Professor K's lab and stepped inside. A quick look around told him that the professor's notebook wasn't in its usual place on the workbench. It seemed unlikely he would have taken it home – which he used to do occasionally – because he had barely left his lab during the past week. *It has to be in the safe*, thought Cavendish, running his fingers nervously through his hair, *unless someone has already secured it!* He had watched the professor open his safe on many occasions and made a mental note of the combination. From time to time, the professor would change the combination according to institute policy. Cavendish had even helped him do it. They had often laughed about this. 'Who on earth could possibly be interested in a few notes?' the professor used to joke. 'I can hardly understand them myself.'

Cavendish walked over to the small wall safe, put on a pair of latex gloves and punched in the combination. The door opened with a beep. That's when he heard it: footsteps outside, approaching! Alarmed, he spun around and tried to busy himself with a few papers lying on the desk. *The gloves*, he thought, his heart beating like a drum, but it was already too late. The door, which he had left ajar, opened slowly.

'Good morning, Doctor Cavendish,' said the late professor's assistant, a young scientist named Akhil from Sri Lanka. 'Shall I come back later?'

'Give me a couple of minutes, I won't be long,' replied Cavendish, trying to appear calm. Smiling, Akhil withdrew. Taking a deep breath, Cavendish reached into the safe and pulled out Professor K's familiar notebook. Relieved, he slipped it into the pocket of his gown, closed the safe, took off the gloves and quickly left the lab. The fact he had just betrayed a dead colleague and stolen from his employer didn't cross his mind.

# 3

Jack Rogan looked at the army of waiting drivers holding up signs and was trying to find one with his name on it. Having experienced hair-raising trips to the Kuragin Chateau from Paris' Charles de Gaulle airport in the past, he had taken his publicist's advice and arranged a hire car to take him there this time. *Don't be silly, Jack, you're a celebrity now*, he remembered Rebecca Armstrong tell him sternly. *You can afford it; trust me.*

Remembering Rebecca's words brought a smile to his face. Not only was she his publicist and literary agent, she had taken over managing his entire life. Then again, he had to admit he did need some managing, especially after the Wizards of Oz – a notorious outlaw bikie gang – had burnt down his house and he had lost all his personal belongings. *Almost all*, he thought, smiling. Because his house didn't have a garage, his beloved MG was parked in the street at the time and had escaped the inferno. The material link with the past was all but gone and Rebecca had done a sterling job rebuilding his future. Jack didn't mind. In fact, he was looking forward to seeing his new penthouse on the harbour, which Rebecca had bought – sight unseen – and had furnished for him, for the first time.

Jack had spent the past year in New York rewriting his book, *The Disappearance of Anna Popov*, in preparation for publication. After the tragic events that led to Anna Popov's spectacular rescue in the Australian outback, Jack had discovered certain secrets of the past during his research which, had they been made public, could have destroyed the lives of people he held dear.

Torn between what was right and what would sell, Jack had made a courageous decision. The book would not be published. Anna's grateful parents were relieved. However, Jack's New York publishers were outraged and threatened to sue. Jack stood his ground. Then, unexpectedly, Countess Kuragin and Professor Popov – Anna's parents – changed their minds. They encouraged Jack to publish his book after all, provided he was prepared to leave certain sensitive parts out of it to protect the privacy of those most exposed. Jack accepted the compromise and threw himself into the task of rewriting the book. He had spent the past year in New York under the watchful eye of Rebecca, desperately trying to repair the damage to his reputation and his relationship with the hostile publishers.

Fortunately, success heals all. The much-awaited book was an overnight sensation and all was forgiven. Somehow, even the delay had worked in his favour. His reputation intact, Jack was once again the celebrated author and darling of the New York literary set.

With the exhausting book launch behind him, Jack had pleaded for a little time off and was on his way back to Australia. *You want to go for a month? Are you out of your mind?* he heard Rebecca complain after he had finished all the interviews. *Two weeks, that's it! I need you here!* They had settled for three and Jack was enjoying the freedom of being able to do his own thing for once. *No more book signings, no more TV shows, no dressing up*, he thought, *no shaving, no Rebecca! Bliss!*

Jack had decided to interrupt his trip back home to Australia to visit Anna and the countess. He wanted to deliver signed copies of his book to them personally; they deserved that courtesy. After all, it was *their* story. And besides, Jack was curious to see how Tristan was growing up. He hadn't seen any of them for almost a year. Emails and skyping just wasn't the same.

It was almost dark by the time the black hire car pulled up in front of the chateau. The countess had reopened her chateau as an exclusive boutique hotel, which had always been immensely popular with the super-rich looking for privacy and style and an opportunity to rub shoulders with a blue-blooded Russian countess.

As he got out of the car, Jack remembered the first time he and Rebecca had visited the Kuragin Chateau. The intimidating, liveried doorman had taken the two first-timers under his wing and inducted them into chateau etiquette. That was two years ago, Jack reminded himself. It had been the beginning of an extraordinary adventure leading to the sensational rescue of the countess' daughter, Anna. The recent publication of his book, which finally told the curious public what really happened after Anna disappeared from Alice Springs all those years ago, was the culmination of a long, exhausting journey.

The countess heard the car pull up and rushed outside. 'Here you are at last!' she said excitedly, kissing Jack on both cheeks, 'The famous author returns. Let me have a look at you. A little thinner than I remember,' she teased, linking arms with Jack. 'We'll do something about that! Dinner's waiting – come.'

'Why is it women always want to fatten me up?' remarked Jack.

'Because we are fond of you.'

'How's Anna, and Tristan?' asked Jack, following the countess into the foyer.

'Anna is in Paris; specialists ...' replied the countess with a hint of sadness in her voice. 'She's slowly improving, but Tristan hasn't stopped talking about you all week. And there's someone else here who wants to meet you ...'

'Oh? Who?'

'You'll see.'

As soon as Jack stepped into the grand foyer, he sensed something. Jack stopped and looked up. Tristan was watching him from the gallery above. Their eyes locked. *He has grown quite a bit*, thought Jack, watching the boy. *Quite tall for fifteen.* Then slowly – one step at a time – Tristan came down the stairs. Jack didn't move, nor did the countess. Reaching the bottom of the stairs, Tristan stopped without taking his eyes off Jack. Then suddenly, he ran towards him, threw his arms around him and hugged him tightly. *'I knew you would come,'* he whispered. *'You've stayed away far too long.'*

'You're right,' said Jack, gently stroking the boy's head. 'I had to finish the book. You know that.' Tristan nodded. 'Here, I have something for you.' Jack opened his duffel bag and pulled out two copies of his book. 'Fresh off the press and hand delivered. The first two copies in France, I believe. The French translation will be released next month.' With that, Jack took a bow and presented one copy to the countess, and the other to Tristan. Anna's striking painting, which had become the cover of the book, brought tears to the countess' eyes.

'That's quite a welcome,' said a voice from the other end of the foyer. Jack turned around and looked at the young woman slowly walking towards him out of the shadows. Her luxurious red hair shone like a beacon as she stepped into the circle of light.

'I'm not always this popular,' replied Jack, watching the woman with interest.

'That's not what I heard.'

'Oh?'

'Jack, I want you to meet my niece,' said the countess, turning to the young woman, 'Dr Alexandra Delacroix.'

After dinner in her private dining room, the countess excused herself and joined the 'paying guests', as she called them, for coffee and liqueurs in the music room. 'It's expected,' she explained. 'It won't take long.' Tristan had reluctantly gone back upstairs to finish his homework and Jack had to promise to come to his room later for a chat, man to man. This left Jack and Dr Delacroix momentarily alone at the dinner table.

'So, you are coming to Sydney,' said Jack, leaning back in the beautiful eighteenth-century dining chair. Jack had a good eye for antiques and lamented the loss of his own collection in the fire with a pang of regret. 'A bit unexpected?'

'Yes, Professor Kozakievicz – Professor K, as we used to call him – died suddenly and I'm to replace him,' she replied, a melancholy look clouding her eyes. 'He was a wonderful colleague and a true friend.'

*She's so young*, thought Jack, enjoying the closeness of the fascinating young scientist. 'And what exactly is it that you do?' he asked.

'I'm exploring the mysteries of the human genome.'

'Wow! Is that what Professor K was working on?'

'Sort of … He was on the cusp of an important discovery relating to cancer when he died.'

'What kind of discovery?'

'The professor's last words to me were that he had actually discovered a breakthrough in cancer diagnosis and treatment.'

'But that's extraordinary!' exclaimed Jack. 'And you are to carry on his work?'

'Yes.'

'You must be very good.'

Dr Delacroix didn't reply. Instead, she was watching the intriguing man she had heard so much about with interest. *He has green eyes*, she thought. *How unusual*. Jack's casual, self-effacing manner had put her instantly at ease and she enjoyed talking to him. In her line of work, meeting attractive men was rather difficult.

'Have you got somewhere to stay?' asked Jack, lowering his voice.

'Not yet.'

'Well then, why don't you help me explore my new penthouse, which incidentally, I've never seen. My literary agent – minder would be more accurate, I suppose – assures me it's very spacious. I'm returning to New York in three weeks, but you can stay as long as you like.'

Dr Delacroix burst out laughing. 'You're joking, surely.'

'No, I'm perfectly serious. I always wanted a research scientist as a flatmate.'

'Do you always invite women you've just met to share your apartment?'

'Only attractive ones,' bantered Jack.

'They warned me about you!'

'What, the incorrigible rascal bit? Surely, as a true scientist you wouldn't believe such scurrilous rumours?'

'Certainly not!'

'It's all settled then.'

'Let me think about it.'

'All right. Why don't we coordinate our flights Down Under and you can think about it along the way. How about that?'

Dr Delacroix held out her hand. 'Okay,' she said, a sparkle in her eye.

'Deal,' said Jack and shook her hand.

## 4

Isis had only one thing on her mind; to get out of the hospital as fast as possible. The horror of witnessing her mother's appalling death was taking its toll. She almost threw up in the lift and couldn't stop shaking. Afraid she might collapse, Boris held her tightly and Lola tried to wipe the blood from her pale cheeks with her handkerchief. Her mind racing, Isis was trying to come to terms with her mother's dying words, 'Stars, hide your fires.'

As soon as they stepped outside, Isis felt better. *Calm down and think*, she told herself as they hurried towards the waiting car. Boris opened the door and helped her get in.

'You okay?' asked Lola, handing Isis a bottle of water.

'I will be … in a moment.'

'What do we do now?'

Isis took a deep breath and looked at Lola sitting next to her. 'Ring my lawyer.'

'But it's four in the morning.'

'We are going straight to my parents' house. Tell him to meet us there.'

The quiet Chelsea street was cordoned off, the flashing blue lights of a dozen police vehicles casting crazy shadows across the wet pavement. Police officers wearing flak jackets and armed with machine guns patrolled the barricades, and commandoes dressed all in black guarded the entrance of the elegant Georgian mansion at the end of the street. Men in white overalls were examining a vehicle – all four doors wide open – parked in front of the house.

Before Lola could stop her, Isis hurried across to one of the police officers standing at the barricade. 'Who's in charge here?' she demanded curtly, her voice hoarse. 'I want to see the officer in charge!'

The police officer looked suspiciously at the breathless woman with dishevelled hair standing in front of him. 'He's a bit busy right now, luv,' he said. 'This place is off limits; better push off.'

'Don't patronise me! That's my parents' house over there. I am George Elms.'

'And I am Mickey Mouse. For the last time, get lost!'

Isis was about to vent her frustration and anger by hurling a barrage of abuse at the infuriating officer, when a man grabbed her from behind. 'Don't! Let me handle this, Georgie, please,' he said. 'I'm Sir Charles Huntley, solicitor,' continued the man, addressing the police officer. 'And this is my client, George Elms, son of Lord and Lady Elms ... Am I making myself clear?'

'Yes Sir,' replied the perplexed officer, sizing up the strange little man in front of him.

Shortish, overweight, in his middle sixties, Sir Charles had looked after George Elms' business affairs since his client's Eton days some twenty years ago. As Isis' solicitor, he was used to the unusual and the unexpected. 'I would like to speak to the officer in charge, please,' he said calmly.

'Wait here.'

Sir Charles turned to his client. 'What do you think you're doing, Georgie? Do you want to end up in the back of a police van under arrest? The press would have a ball! You look terrible, by the way.'

'Thanks, Charles,' said Isis, relieved to see her friend and confidant.

'What on earth has happened?' asked Sir Charles.

'My father was shot dead in the house and my mother died in hospital less than an hour ago.'

'Jesus! I'm so sorry! Anything else?'

'That's about all I know.'

'Then, let's fill in the gaps, shall we?' Isis nodded. 'And please let me do the talking – okay?'

'Okay.'

'And one more thing, George; you are *legally* a man – clear?' said Sir Charles.

'Yes, yes … we've been through this before; it's tedious.'

'It may be tedious to you, but people do get a little confused,' Sir Charles prattled on, trying to distract his obviously distressed client. 'You may be one of the highest paid rock stars on the planet, but you still have to live in the real world occasionally.'

'Yes, Charles.'

'This is one of those occasions; are you with me?' Isis nodded. 'Let's try and stick to the facts – okay? Isis is your stage name. You dress like a woman, you look like a woman, you *consider* yourself a woman, but you are George, Edward, Elms, *a man*. You do understand that, don't you?'

'I'm a woman trapped in a man's body, that's all. I can't help it if I was born with a dick …'

Sir Charles tried hard not to show his exasperation. 'Please, Georgie, not now! Do it for me?'

'Sure.'

'My God, you do lead a complicated life!'

'That's why I have chaps like you – to simplify things for me,' said Isis.

'I thought you were in Russia on tour.'

'Flew in last night, as soon as I heard.'

'Well, the private jet does come in handy after all … isn't that right, Lola?'

'It does come in handy at times,' Lola agreed.

'Tell me this is all a bad dream, Charles,' interrupted Isis.

'I wish I could. *Shush; here comes the officer in charge now,*' whispered Sir Charles, holding up his hand. '*Remember what I just told you.*'

'Daniel Cross, MI5,' said the man in the immaculate dark suit, holding out his hand.

'MI5? I thought this was a matter for the Metropolitan Police,' said Sir Charles, carefully watching the man.

'It is, but when a member if Her Majesty's Government is involved, as is the case here, we like to keep an eye on things – especially in these unsettled times. I'm sure you understand. Please follow me. Just you and your client, if you don't mind.'

'Sorry, Lola,' said Isis, following the man to an unmarked black van parked in a side street.

The man slid the door open and spoke to someone inside. Two men in suits jumped out and walked away. *Spooks*, thought Sir Charles. The inside of the van was full of electronic equipment, computer screens and wires.

Sir Charles and Isis sat down on a bench seat facing Cross. 'Allow me to introduce my client,' began Sir Charles.

'I know who your client is,' interrupted Cross. He reached for a slim manila folder, put it on his lap and opened it. 'I know you prefer to call yourself Isis, but I would prefer to address you by your real name, George Elms,' said Cross, looking at Isis. 'Do you mind?'

'Not at all.'

'Your personal assistant received a phone call from the London Metropolitan Police during your Moscow concert last night, informing her that your father had been killed, and your mother was dying.' Cross paused and turned a page. 'Your private plane landed five hours later in London, and you went straight to the hospital where you arrived at two-thirty in the morning. Your mother passed away at three-forty six—'

'I'm sure you have your reasons,' interrupted Sir Charles, the tone of his voice icy, 'but we already know all this.'

'I appreciate that; please bear with me. Lord Elms attended a cabinet meeting at three yesterday afternoon and then met with the PM in his office for about an hour,' Cross continued, undeterred. 'He was due to chair a committee meeting after that, and then give a speech at the French Embassy, followed by dinner.' Cross paused again – Sir Charles thought for effect – turned a page in his file and then continued. 'Apparently, Lord Elms felt unwell and asked his driver to take him home after the committee meeting. He arrived at his house at seven fifty-five. Lady Elms was at home alone last night; it was the maid's night off and the cook had left at around six after preparing dinner. We understand that the intruders entered the house from the back a few minutes later.'

'Are you suggesting that by coming home unexpectedly, Lord Elms *surprised* the intruders?' asked Sir Charles.

'It would appear so. We don't know exactly what happened in the house, except for this: at twelve minutes past nine precisely, the alarm went off inside the house. The security detail consisting of two officers sitting in an unmarked vehicle got out of the car and ran towards the house. They were both gunned down as they approached the front door. We believe the gunman fired from a window on the first floor.'

'And then?' asked Sir Charles.

'The getaway vehicle pulled up; a stolen courier van. Two men dressed in black wearing balaclavas got in, and the van sped off. It was found two hours later, burnt out just outside London.'

'What happened to my parents?' asked Isis quietly.

'Two security guards sent by the alarm company to investigate arrived at the scene first,' replied Cross, looking through the file. 'They were in the vicinity when the alarm went off. I have their statements right here. This is what they found: Two men with multiple gunshot wounds were lying on the stairs leading to the front door – dead. The front door was open.' Cross paused, letting the tension grow.

'Yes,' prompted Sir Charles, losing patience.

'Lord Elms was lying in the foyer, shot in the head at point blank range—'

'And my mother?' interrupted Isis, close to tears. 'What happened to my mother?'

'George, please,' said Sir Charles, placing a restraining hand on Isis' arm. 'Let's hear what Mr Cross has to tell us; all right?'

'She was tied to a chair in the study on the ground floor; alive, but badly injured.'

'*Badly injured?*' Isis almost shouted. 'Half her face was missing when I saw her in hospital.'

'That's right. Part of her face had been removed.'

'*Removed?* What on earth do you mean by that?' shrieked Isis.

'I understand how you must feel,' said Cross calmly, sidestepping the question, 'but these are the facts.'

'So far, all you've given us is a clinical account of what you *think* happened, but not a word about why, or who the perpetrators might be,' Sir Charles stepped in. 'Would you care to elaborate on this?'

'I was hoping your client might be able to throw some light on this question,' replied Cross, closing the file. 'Can you think of anything that could explain these events?' asked Cross, looking directly at Isis. 'Any threats against your parents; any enemies you can think of; anything out of the ordinary you may have observed recently? Anything at all that could be relevant, however far-fetched it may seem at the moment?'

'I don't know what to think right now,' replied Isis. 'I haven't seen my parents in months.'

Cross nodded. Isis didn't mention the fact that her mother had briefly regained consciousness just before she died and had spoken to her. This would remain a much treasured secret, not to be divulged to anyone. Isis realised that as matters stood, what her mother had told her with her last breath may well turn out to be the only clue to throw some light on the horror. Isis promised herself to leave no stone unturned to find out if that was so.

'You can see my client is upset,' interjected Sir Charles, not at all pleased by the change of tone. The 'briefing' was turning into an interrogation. As every experienced lawyer knows, the best thing to do in that situation is to say nothing.

'Is anything missing from the house?' asked Isis.

'Interesting you should ask that,' answered Cross. 'As far as we know at this early stage, no. The housekeeper has already confirmed this.'

'I think we should leave it there,' said Sir Charles, standing up. 'My client needs to rest.'

'Quite,' Cross stood up as well. 'You will be returning to Moscow?' he asked, turning to Isis.

'I'm in the middle of a sold-out world tour. We are giving a concert in Tokyo in two days; I intend to be there.'

'Grief must wait?' said Cross, the sarcasm in his voice obvious.

Anticipating an outburst, Sir Charles gripped Isis by the arm. 'Perhaps in your line of work you may not have noticed, but there are many shades of grief,' he said to Cross. 'You can reach my client through me, any time.' With that, Sir Charles handed Cross a business card, and opened the door.

'What an arrogant little prick,' said Isis, hurrying back to her car.

'The world is full of arrogant little pricks,' replied Sir Charles, trying to keep up. 'The secret is to know when and how to cut off their little balls. And this was certainly not the time, or the place to do it.'

For reasons she couldn't quite explain, Isis felt suddenly a lot better.

# 5

Jack knocked softly on Tristan's door, unsure if he was still awake.

'Come in, Jack,' Tristan called out from inside. Tristan was sitting at his desk, his copy of *The Disappearance of Anna Popov* open in front of him. 'I'm mentioned in the acknowledgements,' Tristan said excitedly.

'Well deserved. You've helped me with the book in more ways than you know,' said Jack. 'And you were very brave in allowing everything to go in; even the scary personal bits.'

'Thanks, Jack. I have something for you too. Here, have a look.' Tristan switched on his computer and turned the screen towards Jack. 'Watch.'

'What on earth is *that*?' asked Jack. Five half-naked, heavily tattooed men and a woman – obviously the singer, looking like a bird in a crazy costume – were performing on a huge stage. The music was deafening. 'Turn it down before the paying guests complain and leave.' As the camera swung around, a stadium filled with thousands of adoring fans – hands held up high – came into view.

'You mean you don't recognise them?' asked Tristan, shaking his head.

'I'm afraid this isn't exactly my ...'

'That's Isis and The Time Machine, the greatest rock band of our time, and you don't know ...?'

Jack shrugged. 'I have heard of them, of course ...' he lied. 'Why are you showing me this?'

'Because you and Isis are destined to meet. Your fate lines are intersecting,' said Tristan, turning off the computer. 'You have to prepare yourself.' Tristan took the DVD out of the slot and handed it to Jack. 'Listen to the music and try to understand it before it's too late,' he said, turning serious.

'All right,' said Jack, slipping the DVD into his pocket. 'And when will this meeting take place?' he asked, smiling incredulously.

'Soon; very soon. You don't believe me, do you?'

'It seems a little far-fetched, don't you think?'

'It's not what I think that matters; it's what I *see* …' retorted Tristan, looking at Jack with his large, dark, almond-shaped eyes.

*The Maori in him is becoming more prominent as he gets older*, thought Jack. *He's very good looking.*

Jack felt something ice-cold move slowly down his spine. Tristan's words reminded him of Cassandra, Tristan's Maori mother, a gifted psychic. *He's much better than I*, he remembered her saying. *He can glimpse eternity.* 'It's getting late,' said Jack, trying to shake off the disturbing memories.

'Be careful, Jack. There's real danger here,' warned Tristan. 'And remember, I can help you when the time comes. I always will.'

'I know that. Thanks,' said Jack, giving the boy a hug. 'Good night, mate. I'll see you in the morning before I leave.'

Despite being very tired, Jack couldn't go to sleep. He kept turning restlessly in his bed, unable to relax. Every time he drifted towards the sleep his exhausted body craved, Tristan's disturbing words would pull him back. Finally, bathed in sweat, Jack sat up, turned on the light and got out of bed. Slipping on a bathrobe, he opened the door of his room and peered outside. Silence.

Remembering a similar occasion during his first visit to the chateau, he decided to walk downstairs and visit the little chapel at the back. With that visit, the circle would be complete, he thought. However, one more thing remained to be done; he had to return something that belonged to the countess. Jack unzipped his duffel bag and took out Anna's photo the countess had kept on the altar in the chapel during all those lonely, painful years. She had given it to Jack, sealing the promise he had made that fateful night two years ago. It had accompanied him every step of the way along the dangerous and rocky path that had eventually led him to Anna.

'*I knew I would find you here*,' whispered the countess, standing in the shadows. Jack spun around, surprised.

'Katerina? You startled me. How long have you been here?'

'I've been watching you for a little while; I didn't want to intrude ...'

'I was just thinking how much has happened since the last time we stood here.'

'I was thinking the same thing,' said the countess, coming closer. 'You brought Anna back and gave me a family. I now have a beautiful grandson as well, and Tristan is like the son I never had. I'm forever in your debt.' Staring at Anna's photo Jack had put back on the altar, the countess was unable to hold back the tears any longer and began to sob. Overcome by a whirlwind of emotions, relief and gratitude merged with love and admiration for this rough diamond of a man who had brought back her only child from the dead. It was God's work, she knew that, and Jack was but an instrument of fate. 'You know Tristan is an extraordinary child with extraordinary powers ...' Jack nodded. 'He's worried about you. He's seen something ... frightening that concerns you.'

'He told me.'

'Don't dismiss it as adolescent fantasy; that would be a mistake.'

'I agree.'

The countess reached for Jack's hand and looked at him through teary eyes. 'Promise?'

'Promise.'

'Be careful, Jack. You are now part of this family. I hope you know that.'

'Thanks, Katerina. I will always remember that.'

'Love makes us vulnerable; I worry about you.'

For a while, they stood there in silence, watching the candles burning on the altar next to Anna's photo. 'How's Anna,' asked Jack, breaking the silence, '*really*?'

'She's a damaged human being trying to repair herself. Progress is slow,' replied the countess sadly. 'I don't think we can even try to imagine what she's been through. Despite all this, she's an excellent mother; she's very good with her little boy ...'

'But?'

'She lives in her own world ... However, her painting has flourished. Her work is in great demand, especially in Paris. Several prominent galleries are pursuing her with promises of exhibitions.'

'You must be very proud.'

'Of course, I'm happy for her.'

'Her treatment? How's that going?'

'She's under the care of the best specialists. Alexandra's mother has made sure of that. She's a leading neurologist, as you know.'

'Prognosis?'

'Non-committal. They all agree on only one thing: time. We have to give it time, that's all they say. I don't think they really know.'

Jack sensed something deeper was troubling the countess. 'There's more, isn't there?' he asked, squeezing the countess' hand.

'Very perceptive, as usual. Anna is much closer to Tristan than anyone else. They spend hours together while she paints, in silence. They talk to each other without speaking. It's quite extraordinary. Tristan has found a way of communicating with her that is beyond us.'

'Perhaps it was meant to be,' said Jack. 'Two troubled souls bound together by extraordinary events. I often thought about this while writing the book.'

'Perhaps ... You have never thought about a family of your own, Jack?' asked the countess.

Jack looked at her, surprised by the unexpected question. 'You mean, find a nice girl, settle down, a house with a large backyard for the dog; kids? Katerina, I've tried marriage; it's not for everyone, and it certainly wasn't for me,' Jack said, laughing.

'Never say never,' said the countess, wagging her finger. 'You won't be in your forties forever, Jack.'

'Marriage is definitely not for an adventure junky, as Rebecca likes to call me; we both know that.' The countess burst out laughing, grateful for the humour.

'How's Nikolai?' asked Jack.

'We are certainly getting along better since Anna's come back to us. He visits regularly, but I think he's punishing himself for having given up hope. As you know, he was convinced she was dead and lost to us forever. He now believes, in hindsight, that as a father he should never have lost faith. I don't think he can get over this.'

'Time heals all,'

'I hope you're right, for his sake.'

'I think I should go back to bed,' said Jack. 'Off to Sydney tomorrow; it's a long flight.'

'With Alexandra. Thanks for keeping an eye on her.'

'I don't think she needs me to keep an eye on her,' replied Jack. 'She strikes me as an exceedingly capable young woman.'

'Perhaps so. But it's still a new country, new job, new people … And you never know what's around the corner, do you?'

'I'll have to agree with you there,' said Jack, linking arms with the countess. 'But I've had enough excitement for a while, I can tell you.' Jack traced the little white scar on his temple with the tip of his finger. 'I'm planning to take it easy. A little sailing on the harbour is about all the excitement I can cope with at the moment.'

'Why is it that I don't I believe you?' asked the countess, trying to sound serious. 'I would like to; really, Jack, I would but …'

'Rebecca could answer that for you,' replied Jack.

'Oh?'

'Because – according to her, at least – I'm an infuriating, incorrigible rascal. Could that perhaps be the reason? What do you think?'

'I'm not going to answer that.'

# 6

As an entertainer used to gruelling schedules, Isis knew how to manage lack of sleep. However, the emotional strain of the past 24 hours was beginning to take its toll. Leaning against Lola in the back seat of the Bentley crawling towards the airport, Isis was trying to doze. London morning peak hour traffic was horrendous, as usual. Hovering in the foggy no-man's-land of an exhausted mind, she was unable to find the rest her body craved. Not quite asleep, but not entirely awake either, every time sleep beckoned, her mother's disfigured face would appear with alarming clarity. *Great danger*, Isis could hear her mother whisper ... *our secret place ... hide and seek – remember? What does it mean?* Isis wondered, over and over. Then suddenly, the disturbing image faded and Isis found herself back at Clarendon Hall, the Elms' family estate just outside Bath.

'Of course, that's it!' Isis cried out, suddenly wide awake. 'How stupid of me! *Hide and seek.*'

'Bad dream?' asked Lola, reaching for Isis' hand.

'No, a good one. We are going to Bath – now! Did you hear that?' Isis asked the driver. The driver nodded; Isis' moods and whims were legendary. 'Clarendon Hall; it's not that far. Ring the plane, Lola. We'll put our flight back.'

'What about Tokyo?' asked Lola, the scary spectre of a cancelled concert sending icy shivers down her spine.

'Don't worry, we'll make it, but only if we hurry.'

Clarendon Hall was built to impress. Over four hundred years old, it was constructed on a grand scale and set in magnificent grounds. The estate had served as the seat of the powerful Elms family for countless generations. Isis had spent most of her childhood there, until boarding school took her away and everything changed.

Isis hadn't been to Clarendon Hall for years. Staring dreamily out of the car window, she watched the familiar old oak trees lining the long driveway slip past as the car approached the huge manor house. Looking back, living at Clarendon Hall seemed like a distant fairytale. Grand staircases and long corridors filled with medieval armour, exotic hunting trophies and all kinds of weapons were the playground of a shy little boy growing up in a cold place, where the only warmth was the love of a lonely mother.

Lord and Lady Elms had lived separate lives throughout their entire marriage. Ten years older than his wife, Lord Elms had preferred to live in London, leaving Lady Elms to bring up their only child on the estate. The boy was her life.

News of the tragedy had already reached Clarendon Hall. Most of the remaining staff had spent their entire working life on the estate. Teary-eyed and looking old, Albert, the butler and Kate, the cook were waiting at the entrance. Both had known Isis since childhood.

Isis left Boris and Lola in Kate's care in the kitchen and excused herself. She told them she wanted to be alone with her memories for a little while. 'Don't take too long,' Lola reminded her, pointing to her watch. 'Take-off is at eight – remember? Any later than that, we've got air traffic problems.'

Returning to Clarendon Hall after all these years felt like visiting a museum where all the exhibits were exactly in the same place, only a little smaller and less imposing. Childhood memories were like that. Isis stood at the bottom of the huge staircase and looked up at the portraits of her bewigged ancestors staring accusingly, she thought, down on her from above. Then slowly, she walked up the marble stairs to the first floor.

Every house has a soul, especially one this ancient and with so many secrets and stories to tell. The stories were all still there, but only for those who knew how to listen. Isis' fascination with the occult and things supernatural had begun in this very place a long time ago. The Egyptian room at the end of the corridor had been her favourite. Filled with antiquities a museum would have been proud of, it was a magical place full of mystery and wonder. As she walked down the corridor, Isis remembered sitting on her mother's lap at the foot of a life-sized statue of the god Osiris, lord of the Underworld, listening to stories of the goddess Isis and her unlucky brother.

Isis opened the gilded door leading to the Egyptian room and looked inside ... everything was exactly as she remembered. The massive pink granite sarcophagus dominated the centre of the chamber with promises of immortality and a blissful afterlife. Tall statues of lion-headed goddesses and falcon-beaked gods stood guard along the walls, decorated with wonderful hieroglyphs – passages from *The Book of the Dead* – decipherable only by the initiated few. Rather than finding this place intimidating or frightening, Isis had found it a place of adventure and excitement, where the imagination of a young boy growing up on his own could run wild.

Over the years, the imposing stone gods had become friends, and the Egyptian room a place for a favourite game Isis used to play with her mother: hide and seek. However, this was not the conventional game where one player counted to thirty while the other hid somewhere. This was a game with a unique twist: it was played with a small golden ankh, a handled cross, the Egyptian symbol of life, which had to be hidden somewhere in the room while the other player stood outside in the corridor counting to thirty.

With so many exhibits to choose from, hiding the ankh was great fun. The art was to 'hide' it in plain view, but in such a way that it formed part of an exhibit and was therefore difficult to spot. The glass display cabinets containing jewellery and small ceremonial objects were favourite hiding places. Alternatively, it could be hidden inside one of the canopic jars, or wooden chests, or behind or on top of one of the statues. The more imaginative the hiding place, the better. During the game, clues were provided to guide the seeker. The more ingenious the clues and the longer it took one's opponent to find the ankh, determined the winner. While this was often a matter of opinion, debating the outcome was almost as much fun as playing the game.

The little golden ankh had become one of Isis' most treasured possessions. She had worn it around her neck since her childhood days and never took it off. The belt buckle of Isis, as some Egyptologists called the ankh, had become Isis' trademark and the symbol of her record label. It featured on all the merchandise and promotional material associated with the band and was even painted on the tail of *Icarus*, the band's customised Boeing 757, designed to fly the band around the world.

During one of these games, Isis had accidentally pressed one of the many eyes of Horus painted on the lid of a wooden chest shaped like a mummy. To the little boy's surprise, the back of the head opened up, revealing a concealed compartment the size of a small shoebox. Isis hid the ankh in the compartment and closed it. It had taken his mother three days and countless clues to find the correct eye to press. This hidden compartment was pronounced the ultimate hiding place, and George the overall winner of the game. The mummy's head became their 'secret place'. Occasionally, little presents would be waiting for George in there, or his mother would leave cryptic messages for him to decipher.

Once her eyes had become accustomed to the gloom, Isis walked slowly to the back of the room where the mummy-shaped chest stood in its usual place on a stone plinth. *This has to be it*, she thought, tracing one painted eye after another with the tip of her finger. Because all the eyes looked the same and she couldn't remember exactly which one activated the mechanism, she kept pressing each eye methodically, starting at the top of the head and working her way down to the chin with the false beard.

*Perhaps it isn't working any more*, she thought, becoming anxious. Then suddenly, the back of the mummy's head opened with a little shudder. Isis took a deep breath and looked inside. 'My God! *What is that?*' she whispered, surprise and disbelief clouding her face. Slowly, she reached inside and ran the tips of her shaking fingers along the smooth, gleaming surface of a strange object, its touch making the hairs on the back of her neck tingle with excitement. *It looks almost alive*, she thought. *Scary. And there's something underneath it … Letters?*

39

Isis had discovered something that had been hidden a long time ago for her to find when the time was right. The game was over, but this time there was no opponent, and no winner. Only questions.

As soon as the plane reached cruising altitude and had levelled out, Isis began to relax and sat down on her comfortable bed at the back of the plane. Boris was already asleep in his usual seat at the front, and Lola was working on her computer. All was quiet.

Isis switched on the reading light, reached for her handbag and pulled out the small bundle of letters she had found under the strange artefact inside the chest. *Whispers from the grave?* she wondered, untying the blue ribbon with trembling fingers. Yellowish and brittle, the small, neatly folded sheets of paper were almost transparent. There were no envelopes. Isis held one of the sheets up to the light and began to read:

*Dearest ...*

After she had finished reading the letters, Isis turned off the light, closed her eyes and for a while just lay there, quite still. *What does it all mean?* she asked herself, her mind racing. *Mamina! Mamina will know.* Feeling calmer, Isis reached for her satellite phone and dialled a familiar number.

# 7

Alexandra put down *The Disappearance of Anna Popov* and looked at Jack, asleep in his comfortable business class seat next to her. *Extraordinary*, she thought, closing the book. *He's without doubt the most exciting man I've met for a long time.* The chestnut brown hair – a little unkempt and a touch too long – and the five o'clock shadow on his relaxed face, gave the self-proclaimed incorrigible rascal a slightly roguish look. She had never come across anyone quite like him, although she had to admit that academic circles were not the ideal place to meet interesting men. Being attracted to someone has nothing to do with time, place or logic; it can happen in an instant, and for no apparent reason. All one needed was an opportunity, however fleeting. For a scientist who had spent most of her adult life in a research cocoon analysing data, this was a disconcerting realisation.

After a short, disastrous marriage to a Belgian biologist that had ended in an acrimonious divorce a year ago, Alexandra knew it was time to reassess her life. The offer she had received from her dying colleague and dear friend had come just at the right moment. She was ready for something new and, hopefully, exciting – not just professionally but personally.

As the only child of two eminent doctors, she had been destined for a medical career from an early age. Striving for excellence ran in the family. Her mother, as the younger sister of Professor Popov, a Nobel laureate, had become a leading neurologist. Her father, a brain surgeon, came from a long line of French doctors and was highly regarded for his work in pioneering new techniques in tumour removal.

Jack opened his eyes, looked at Alexandra and smiled. 'What did you think of it?' he asked, pointing to the book in her lap.

'I couldn't put it down.'

'That's what authors like to hear,' said Jack, sitting up. 'We always look for approval.'

'We all do. I particularly liked the – how do you say – "virtuosity" of your language.'

'Wow! I don't think I've ever had a compliment quite like that.' Jack looked at his watch. 'We must be almost there,' he said.

'Three more hours.'

'Have you made a decision?'

'About what?'

'Becoming my flatmate.'

'After what I've just read, I don't know. You're a dangerous man, Jack.'

'You think so?'

'Absolutely.'

'The answer's no, then?'

'No, it isn't. I accept.'

'*You do?* But I'm a dangerous man; you just said so. Why the sudden change of heart?'

'Because you are.'

'What? Dangerous?'

'Precisely.'

'Women!' said Jack, pulling the blanket over his head. 'I'll never work them out!'

'I think we should drink to that,' said Alexandra, laughing, 'if you are prepared to come out of hiding, that is.'

The first thing Jack always noticed about flying into Sydney from overseas was the light: brilliant, deliriously bright. There was no other place quite like it, especially when you called it home. First, the plane circled the city, giving them a splendid view of the sparkling harbour and the blue Pacific, and then approached the runway from the south. It was a perfect morning for a homecoming.

'I didn't quite believe you when you said you hadn't seen your apartment,' said Alexandra, following Jack to the concierge. Jack introduced himself and collected the keys. A magnum of champagne was waiting for him at the desk with a note from Rebecca, his literary agent. *Welcome home, Jack*, it said, *enjoy! P.S. I hope you like the little surprise in the lounge.*

'Top floor,' Jack said, holding up the keys. 'Let's go exploring.'

The penthouse occupied almost the entire floor, with a one hundred and eighty-degree view of the city and Sydney's magnificent harbour. 'Not bad,' said Jack, opening the sliding doors leading to the huge roof terrace. 'Must have cost a bomb.'

'You mean you don't know?' asked Alexandra, shaking her head.

'No, I have no idea.'

'I thought things like this only happened in movies.'

'Choose your bedroom; you're the guest.' With three large bedrooms, each with its own en suite, splendid views and access to the terrace, there were plenty to choose from. Alexandra chose the smallest one and left the master bedroom suite for Jack.

'I don't need all this,' said Jack, walking through the huge walk-in wardrobe. 'I always get into trouble with my clothes,' he joked, holding up his modest duffel bag. 'I believe in travelling light. Much to the exasperation of my agent, who always insists on buying me stuff to wear,' he added. 'Champagne?'

'At ten in the morning?'

'Why not? You've just moved in with a dangerous bloke – remember?'

'A *bloke*?' What's that?' asked Alexandra, whose English, while perfect – with a charming French accent – wasn't quite up to the finer points of Aussie slang.

'Someone who would call you a good lookin' sheila.'

'Is that what you would call me? A good looking *sheila*?'

'You bet.'

'Funny language.'

'Welcome to Oz. Let's have a drink, and I'll show you the surprise in the lounge.'

'I do like surprises.'

'Most sheilas do.'

'Does that remind you of something?' asked Jack, pointing to a painting on the wall in the lounge room. He opened a bottle of champagne, poured two glasses and handed one to Alexandra.

'Of course, it's on the cover of your book. How extraordinary. Is that the surprise?'

'It is. It was painted by your niece. Anna gave it to me,' said Jack. 'And my agent, who appears to be managing my entire life, has somehow managed to get it here. That's the surprise.'

'What's it about?'

'Well, you've just read the book. It's actually mentioned towards the end, in the epilogue.' Jack walked over to the painting and stood in front of it. 'This is the inside of the cave where I found Anna. Sitting on the floor here are the two Aboriginal women who cared for her, and this is Anna lying next to them. She was almost dead when I found her. And this is me in the shorts, right here, on my knees in front of her.'

'And what's that behind you?' asked Alexandra, pointing to a shadowy human skeleton floating through a shaft of light, away from the women.

'That's death leaving, as Anna put it.'

'Amazing. She captured a near-death experience, and the very moment of her rescue?'

'Yes.' *But it still reminds me of the adoration of the Magi,* thought Jack, *with only one king, bringing the gift of life after banishing death.* 'It's signed "Lucrezia" – here, see?'

'Her nom de plume of the paint brush, as I think you put it. Another example of your language virtuosity?'

'You have an excellent memory. I can see I'll have to watch what I say.' Jack topped up their glasses. 'Enough about me! Let's sit down. I want to ask *you* something.'

'What about?'

'Your work.'

'Oh? Fire away.'

'How does a geneticist as young as you, end up at the top of her field? I ask myself. From what Katerina told me, you're apparently one of the best. She's incredibly proud of you.'

'Don't believe everything my aunt tells you,' replied Alexandra, laughing.

'And why cancer research? It all sounds very esoteric and complicated.'

'Only to old blokes like you.'

'Thanks. Then why don't you enlighten this old codger? How did it all start?'

'All right. Have you heard of the Human Genome Project?'

'I have, actually.'

'What do you know about it?'

'It was a monumental international undertaking. It began in 1990, lasted thirteen years and cost three billion dollars.'

'And the aim was?'

'To discover all of the twenty to twenty-five thousand human genes.'

'And?'

'To determine the complete sequence of the three billion DNA sub-units?'

'You're right,' Alexandra replied, surprised. 'You seem to know a lot about this. The project was a great success and resulted in the first full reading of a human genome. It was hailed as one of the greatest achievements in the history of science and a milestone in the history of mankind.'

'And the results were announced jointly by President Clinton and the British Prime Minister, Tony Blair, in 2000,' Jack cut in.

'Not bad for an old bloke,' teased Alexandra, nodding appreciatively. 'The human DNA code has three billion letters. As researchers began to take a closer look at these letters in 2003, they found to their surprise that only one point five per cent of them actually carried instructions for genes. And inside this modest bundle, they identified twenty-five thousand genes. This was an extraordinary finding. What this meant was that man had the same set of genes as a *Caenorhabditis elegans*.'

'A what?'

'A humble, millimetre long, one thousand-cell roundworm.'

'I'm related to a roundworm? Great!'

'Don't despair. It soon became apparent that if this were so, then instructions for creating a human being must be encoded somewhere else within the DNA, which as you know is the physical substance that makes up a gene,' said Alexandra, becoming quite excited. 'Your genome is a code. It has three billion DNA letters, and there are two copies of that code, one from mum and one from dad; that's the unique *you*. And this is when things become really interesting—'

'Is that why you became involved in all this?' interrupted Jack.

'In a way, yes. I was a PhD student in Paris at the time. That's when I became Professor K's assistant. He was an extraordinary man and a close friend of my mother's. He was an iconoclast; an intellectual rebel who took nothing for granted and thought the answer in science was often to be found in the weird and the outrageous. He was right. To an impressionable, starry-eyed young student like me, he was like a god. He became my hero. He taught me how to think.'

'In what way?'

'Keep an open mind at all times, think laterally and don't be afraid to challenge dogma and be different. However, my interest in all this began well before I met Professor K.'

'Oh?'

'My father's hero was Aristotle, who – according to him at least – was one of the greatest thinkers of all time. I remember sitting on my dad's knee in our garden as a little girl, listening to stories about Aristotle, the acorn, and the egg.'

'Fascinating.'

'Don't laugh; it is. Did you know that Aristotle toyed with the idea of an acorn having within it a "plan" for an oak tree, and an egg containing the "concept" of a chicken?' Jack shook his head. 'When you step back from this and look at it carefully, what do you see?' asked Alexandra.

'The idea of a gene?'

'Exactly. It was the beginning of a two thousand three hundred-year journey, which reached its destination in 1953 with an epic discovery: the DNA double helix.'

'Compliments of Francis Crick.'

'Correct. Except that the "destination" was in fact just the beginning of a much bigger and more exciting journey – the search for the physical identity of the gene. Sitting there on my father's lap, I made up my mind then and there that I wanted to be part of that search,' said Alexandra.

'Amazing.'

'Another one of my father's favourite stories was about a monk and his peas—'

'Mendel,' interrupted Jack.

'Very good. And do you know why?'

'Obviously bored with monastic life, Gregor Mendel, a monk, turned to breeding peas, which was far more exciting. This was in the eighteen sixties. As you would expect, he was a man of iron discipline and great patience; you had to be if you wanted to be successful in breeding peas – right?'

'Absolutely. So far, I find your story far more interesting than my father's version. Go on,' said Alexandra, laughing, 'let's hear the rest.'

'After a lot of pea breeding, Mendel discovered that breeding was by no means arbitrary. On the contrary, he realised there were certain rules, quite precise ones that governed hereditary factors with mathematical precision. Mendel's hereditary factors later became known as …?'

'Genes,' answered Alexandra.

'A term coined by Wilhelm Johannsen, a Danish botanist, in his book *Elemente der exacting Erbichkeitslehre*, published in 1909.'

Alexandra looked nonplussed. 'Bravo!' she said. 'How do you know all this, Jack?'

'I wrote a series of articles on the Human Genome Project back in 2003.'

'You're an amazing bloke, Jack Rogan,' said Alexandra, holding up her empty glass. 'More champagne please.'

'And you are one clever little sheila,' said Jack, reaching for the bottle, 'who's chosen genomics. Why?'

'To integrate genomics into patient diagnosis and treatment.'

'Precision medicine?'

'Another time, please! Enough science for one morning, don't you think?' Leaning back in her comfortable leather chair, Alexandra looked at Jack. 'Are we going to have an affair?' she asked, lowering her voice.

Jack put down the bottle and looked at Alexandra. Their eyes locked and for a while, he said nothing. 'I hope so,' he said, sounding hoarse.

'I don't believe it,' said Alexandra.

'What?'

'You're blushing!'

'Nonsense.'

'Yes, you are.'

'It's the reflection from the windows; the sun ...'

'No, that's ... how do you say it in Aussie English, bull ...?

'Bullshit?'

'Yes; that's it.'

# 8

*Calypso* sailed through the Heads into Sydney Harbour just after sunrise and dropped anchor in front of the famous Taronga Zoo. Because of the vessel's size, there was no suitable berth available, and the converted icebreaker was assigned a mooring in the harbour usually reserved for visiting warships. Macbeth liked it that way. Contact with the shore would be by tender, and would give *Calypso* some distance from the curious press and prying eyes of the public.

Sitting in his wheelchair on the deck outside his stateroom, Macbeth was drinking in the fresh morning air. Sailing into one of the most beautiful harbours in the world at first light should have been exhilarating, but Macbeth had other things on his mind. Cavendish was turning into a potential liability and Macbeth was contemplating what to do about it. His Sydney agent had just reported in: Cavendish was becoming difficult. But it wasn't all bad news. Cavendish had secured Professor Kozakievicz's notes. However, realising his use-by date had arrived, he was behaving irrationally and had demanded an exorbitant payment for them.

Professor K's notes had to be obtained at any cost, so much was clear. But what to do about Cavendish? Macbeth pondered. It wasn't the money that troubled him; the problem was the man. Macbeth had used people like Cavendish before, many times. Being gay made Cavendish vulnerable, and it was his vulnerability that made him useful. Corrupting him had been easy. Distancing oneself from him could be difficult and risky. With the stakes so high, Macbeth couldn't afford any mistakes. Cavendish was a loose end who could very quickly turn into a loose cannon.

*No loose ends*, thought Macbeth, feeling better. He always felt better when he followed his instincts. 'Get Jan,' he said to Carlotta, who was standing behind him. Carlotta let go of the wheelchair and walked to the stern of the ship. She knew exactly where to find Jan, and what he would be doing.

Completing his second set of two hundred sit-ups on the helicopter pad covered in seaspray, Jan Van Cleef was going through his morning exercise routine. It was a gruelling program, which he had perfected many years ago. For a frontline commando in the British army, survival often depended on discipline and fitness. Decorated for bravery under enemy fire, he had been one of the rising stars until something went terribly wrong. He had entered the house of a suspected insurgent during a covert mission in Afghanistan, and mistakenly shot two elderly women and a young boy. The incident turned into a serious embarrassment for the British Forces, and if all else fails, a serious embarrassment needs someone to blame. Van Cleef, the decorated hero, was the perfect candidate. After an inconclusive court martial that neither convicted, nor exonerated, Van Cleef was quietly discharged. The army told him his services were no longer required. Disgraced and disillusioned, he had nowhere to go. For two years, he worked as a mercenary in South Africa, where he had lived as a boy. A bullet in the shoulder during an assignment in Zimbabwe brought all that to an abrupt end.

Wounded and down on his luck, Macbeth found him in a bar in Johannesburg. The army may have considered Van Cleef an embarrassment to be disposed of, but Macbeth saw him as a man of immeasurable value. Not only did he offer him a job, he gave him respect and a future. He made him his personal bodyguard and chief of security. The army had spent hundreds of thousands of pounds training him. Van Cleef was a decorated soldier with combat experience money couldn't buy. Used to loyalty beyond question, the devotion that had once belonged to the army and his comrades, now belonged to Macbeth. Van Cleef would gladly give up his life for the only man who believed in him. Macbeth realised that loyalty like that was beyond price.

'He wants to see you,' said Carlotta, watching Van Cleef's bulging neck muscles. Not many men can do fifty push-ups with only one hand. Van Cleef nodded, reached for his towel and wiped the sweat from his face.

'Where is he?'

'Outside; in front of his cabin.'

Tall and blond, with penetrating, cornflower-blue eyes and a powerful physique, Van Cleef looked more like a Dutch farmer from the Transvaal than the finely honed killing machine he really was. His school-boyish good looks were deceptive, disguising an extremely dangerous man in his early thirties. He reminded Macbeth of the beautifully engraved blade of a precious dagger: tempting to touch, but quick to draw blood from the unwary.

'We have a problem,' began Macbeth quietly. 'I have an important assignment for you I want you to handle personally. Don't use outsiders.'

'Yes, sir.' Van Cleef insisted on calling Macbeth sir. To him, he was his commanding officer. He felt more comfortable that way. He also insisted that all five 'security men' under his command – all former brothers-in-arms carefully chosen by him – did the same. To Van Cleef, discipline was the fabric that held them all together. It was the one thing he could always count on when things got tough.

'No weapons of any kind are to be used. If you can, make it look like an accident, but you don't have much time to prepare. It must happen tomorrow. Do I make myself clear?'

'Absolutely.'

'We have a reliable man on the ground; that should help. We'll stay right here in Sydney until the assignment has been completed. *Calypso* will sail as soon as you let me know that it's been done.'

'Understood.'

'Carlotta will brief you. That will be all.'

Without saying another word, Van Cleef turned and walked away. Macbeth watched him leave and smiled. *He almost saluted*, he thought, thanking his lucky stars he had such a man on his side.

# 9

*Pegasus* had begun its slow descent into Tokyo Narita Airport and was approaching the city in preparation for landing. Isis sat up in her bed at the back of the plane and looked around. 'What time is it?' she asked, massaging her stiff neck.

'You went out like a light and slept the whole way. We are almost there,' said Lola.

Isis felt calm and no longer so alone and lost in her grief. Just hearing Mamina's voice on the phone and speaking with her in Spanish had made her feel better. It had also helped her fall asleep and get the rest she so desperately needed. However, what she had been asked to do was puzzling, to say the least. It made no sense and only added to her confusion. Unconditional trust has always been Mamina's way, and this was certainly not the time to question her judgement. Isis reminded herself that somehow, in the end, everything Mamina suggested usually worked out for the best.

Isis got up and walked over to Lola. 'There's something I would like you to do for me,' she said, running her fingers playfully through Lola's short hair.

'Sure. How do you feel?' Lola savoured the caress and closeness of the one person on the planet she adored with every fibre of her being. Her love for Isis was unconditional; just to be near her was more than enough.

'Awful. Like a gutted fish. Somehow alive, but empty.'

'Are you sure you can do Tokyo tonight?' asked Lola, unable to hide her concern.

'Absolutely.'

'What do you want me to do?'

'Find out everything you can about this man.' Isis handed Lola a slip of paper she had torn out of her notebook.

'Who is he?'

'A famous writer.'

Lola knew better than to question Isis further. Instead, she turned to her computer and went to work.

# 10

Cavendish knew he was early. Sitting on a bar stool in the Blowhole, a bar popular with well-heeled, middle-aged gay men looking for adventure, he tried very hard to appear calm. The Blowhole had quite a reputation. It was one of the most unique establishments of its kind in the world. During the annual Sydney Gay and Lesbian Mardi Gras, the queue to get in just for a look around was a couple of hundred metres long. What made the Blowhole so popular was the fact it resembled a huge aquarium. All the walls, the bar and even the dance floor were made of thick plate glass. Large illuminated fish tanks concealed behind the glass opened up an underwater wonderland, with all kinds of exotic fish, coral, seashells, and even a wooden shipwreck with a skeleton and a treasure chest. Sitting at the bar, one had the feeling of being underwater. The couples embracing on the glass dance floor looked like ballet dancers floating on water, with menacing sharks cruising slowly past in a large pool beneath their feet. Danger was a powerful aphrodisiac.

'Hello, Daniel,' said a tall blond man standing next to Cavendish. He pulled up a barstool and sat down. 'Has Kevin explained everything?'

Cavendish looked at the younger man with interest. Kevin, his usual contact, had indicated that due to the large amount of money involved, his 'principals' needed verification. 'Yes,' he said, 'you want to see the material before—'

'You've got it with you?' interrupted Van Cleef.

'Yes.'

'Good. Let's have a drink first. There's no rush. What are you drinking? Is that an icebreaker?'

Cavendish nodded, and Van Cleef ordered two.

The evening was hotting up. Suddenly, the place was crowded, with standing room only. Sitting atop what resembled a huge ice cube, a bare-breasted, she-male disc jockey dressed as a mermaid turned up the volume. The music was deafening and the atmosphere electric. On top of another 'ice cube', two voluptuous she-males wearing only diamond-studded jockstraps were performing a pole-dance with a difference. Leaving little to the imagination, *The Blowhole* – the signature dance of the establishment – would have made a less jaded audience blush.

Van Cleef was enjoying himself; everything was going to plan – so far. The night before, he and one of his lieutenants had familiarised themselves with the unique layout and facilities of the club. The huge tanks and underwater feeding cages in the back, specially designed for sharks, suggested a unique plan. *Always let your surroundings dictate the approach, never the other way round*, was something Van Cleef never forgot. To make a hit look like an accident was an art, and Van Cleef was the Picasso of hit men.

There were a few basic rules: everything had to blend in and look logical and plausible – cause and effect. Ideally, the target should never be the only victim; confusion was the best cover. Suspicion and blame should always point *away* from the real perpetrator, to give the authorities someone or something else to seize upon. What Van Cleef had found in the club during the night ticked all the right boxes. All one had to have were nerves of steel and the courage to see it through. Van Cleef and his men had an abundant supply of both.

'We'll have to go out the back later, so I can have a closer look,' said Van Cleef, lifting his glass. 'Cheers.'

'Are you a scientist?'

'No.'

'Then I must warn you, the material is rather technical.'

'That won't be a problem.'

'Good.' Cavendish was starting to relax. The exciting man sitting next to him was sending his hormones wild.

'Do you come here often?' asked Van Cleef, putting his hand on Cavendish's thigh.

'I'm a regular. What about you?'

'My first time.'

'Do you like it?'

'Too early to tell.'

'Then let me show you round. The loos are particularly interesting. Everything is made of glass, even the urinals ...'

'All right. But first, can I have a quick look?' asked Van Cleef, his face like a mask. Cavendish unzipped his shoulder bag and let Van Cleef look inside.

'The professor's notebook?'

'Yes.' Van Cleef pulled out his iPhone, took a photo of two of the handwritten pages and sent the photo to the Blackburn lab in San Francisco. The scientists, who had been working on the Kozakievicz matter for over a year, would be able to confirm authenticity. Macbeth, a careful man, had insisted on this. Van Cleef was to wait for confirmation before going any further. 'As soon as I get the okay, we can go ahead,' said Van Cleef, holding up his phone.

'Clever,' said Cavendish. 'You have the money?' Van Cleef pointed to the backpack at his feet. 'A quick peek?'

'Sure.' As he opened the backpack, Van Cleef knew this was the right moment. Reaching into his pocket, he searched for the little capsule. Holding it carefully between two fingers, he pulled out his hand and quickly dropped the capsule into Cavendish's glass. The capsule dissolved instantly. *Five hundred thousand*, thought Cavendish, his heart beating like a drum. He had never seen so much cash before.

'A dance, until I get the go ahead? What do you say?' asked Van Cleef, handing Cavendish his glass.

'Why not?' Cavendish drained his glass and got up.

Van Cleef took Cavendish by the hand. 'Let's go.'

'Are you just going to leave that there?' asked Cavendish, pointing to the backpack on the floor.

'It's your money, unless the professor's book is a fake,' Van Cleef replied, laughing. 'Don't worry; no one's going to steal an old backpack – come.'

What Cavendish couldn't have known was the reason behind this cavalier approach: the man sitting to his right was one of Van Cleef's men. The backpack was perfectly safe ...

Van Cleef didn't find it easy to embrace another man like a lover and dance with him in a public place. However, if his work demanded it, he would play his part to perfection, and he did. In the unlikely event that the notebook was a fake, he would immediately withdraw. If not, everything would proceed as planned. Just before the music stopped, the phone in his pocket began to vibrate. He pulled out the phone and looked at the text message. '*We're on,*' he whispered into Cavendish's ear. '*One more dance to seal the deal?*'

'Why not?' said Cavendish, slurring his words.

Van Cleef knew the drugs would kick in soon. He could already feel the change in Cavendish's demeanour; he was unsteady on his feet. It was time to leave the dance floor. 'Come, let's go out the back,' he said, holding Cavendish firmly around the waist.

The dark, labyrinthine engine room of the club behind the huge fish tanks and all the machinery required to keep them going, was popular with regulars looking for a place to do drugs, or just fool around. Although strictly off limits, the management knew about this and did little to stop it. The maintenance staff looking after the tanks were in on it and enjoyed generous tips for 'turning a blind eye'. There were no CCTV cameras in this part of the club.

No one gave the two men walking into the back a second look. Locked in an intimate embrace and a little unsteady on their feet, they looked like all the other couples moving around in the dark. Drugs were the norm, cocaine the preferred poison. Cavendish was already delirious and Van Cleef had to hold him up and drag him along. Access to the large shark tank was at the end of the corridor. Two of Van Cleef's men were already there – waiting. A sizeable tip ensured no one would disturb them for a while.

'Here, look after this,' said Van Cleef, handing his backpack and Cavendish's shoulder bag to one of his men. 'The lock?'

'Removed.'

Van Cleef dragged Cavendish over to the steel feeding cage. Out of sight of the dance floor below, it gave access to the top of the pool. The grate covering the pool was usually only opened after hours at feeding time, and was secured with a padlock and chain. Looking down into the illuminated pool, Van Cleef could see several large sharks circling slowly below. Leaning over the pool was very popular with gay couples looking for a perfect setting for an illicit adventure: danger above, and danger below.

'Open it, quickly!' said Van Cleef. 'There isn't much time.'

Using both hands, one of the men lifted up the heavy steel trapdoor. Sensing movement in the feeding area above, the sharks came closer. Van Cleef was about to drop Cavendish into the tank, when he thought of something. 'Cut his hand,' he hissed. 'There, that rough edge will do.' The man standing next to him ran Cavendish's hand over the jagged steel until it began to bleed. Van Cleef knew at once that this was the masterstroke. Smiling, he watched the droplets of blood turn the water cloudy-pink.

The pain in his hand sent a warning signal to Cavendish's addled brain. He opened his eyes and stared at Van Cleef leaning over him. When he turned his head to look at his bleeding hand, he saw the sharks cruising past below him. Cavendish began to panic. Just before Van Cleef dropped him headfirst into the tank, he lashed out with his right hand and dug his fingernails deep into Van Cleef's wrist.

'Let's go, guys!' said Van Cleef, and quickly closed the trapdoor. As he turned to leave, he saw through the grate that one of the sharks had already ripped off Cavendish's right arm. The feeding frenzy had begun.

The couple nearest the bar on the dance floor saw it first; a human head floated into view under their feet. Eyes wide open, and with the contorted mouth frozen in a silent scream, it looked like something out of a horror movie or a ghost train ride. At first, the couple thought it was part of the setting, but when a shark shot out of the shadows and began to rip away the cheeks, they began to scream. Things turned ugly after that. Panic is like wildfire; once it starts, it's difficult to stop.

Several people died and many were injured during the stampede caused by the subsequent fire. To cover their tracks and create confusion, Van Cleef's men had started an electrical fire in the engine room on their way out. By the time the first police car arrived at the scene, hundreds of screaming patrons had already spilled out into the street with only one thought on their mind: to get away as far, and as quickly as possible. By the time the ambulances made it to the scene to treat the injured, and the fire brigade went inside to put out the fire and secure the building, Van Cleef and his men were already on board *Calypso*, preparing to leave the harbour.

# 11

Determined, unstoppable and like a human tsunami, the first wave of excited fans began streaming through the gates of the huge Makuhari Messe Arena. Isis and The Time Machine's Tokyo concert was due to start in one hour.

Isis sat at her dressing table, unable to hold still, which made it difficult for her make-up artist to apply the finishing touches. Lola was watching Isis in the mirror. 'Are you okay?' she asked, a worried look on her face.

'No, I'm not,' replied Isis, staring pensively into her own reflection. 'I'm getting too old for all this.'

'Nonsense!' Lola knew that the past forty-eight hours had put Isis under enormous strain. The horror of her mother's death, the long flights, the funeral arrangements, and the frustration of not knowing what really happened or why, was taking its toll.

However, what Lola couldn't have known was the real reason for Isis' disquiet was something quite different. Unable to get her mother's last words out of her mind, and haunted by what she had discovered at Clarendon Hall, Isis was nervously drumming her fingers against the top of her dressing table.

A prisoner of her enormous success, her every waking moment was planned and accounted for, yet she yearned to be somewhere else. She could hear the five musicians who made up The Time Machine warming up in their practice rooms, the familiar sounds momentarily bringing a smile to her weary face.

'See? That's better,' said Lola, putting her hand on Isis' shoulder. 'Now go out there and kick some ass!'

Isis lay in her glass coffin below the stage and listened to the roar of her Tokyo fans as The Time Machine finished the opening number. Usually, she would be going through her breathing exercises to help her focus on her imminent entry, but not so tonight. Suddenly it all became clear; Isis knew exactly what she had to do. Feeling calmer now, she felt the coffin begin to rise. *Resurrection*, she thought. *So be it. I'm ready.*

Concerned about Isis' state of mind, Lola watched anxiously as the lid of the glass coffin opened on stage. She needn't have worried. Somersaulting out of the casket to the roar of her adoring fans, Isis turned into the consummate professional she was. Usually, she would choose a face in the anonymous crowd somewhere close to the stage, and then perform for just that one person. This helped her tame the confronting crowd-beast and turn it into a personal encounter. That night, however, Isis performed for someone else.

Remembering the hide and seek games in the Egyptian room a long time ago, Isis reached for the little gold ankh she wore around her neck. *There are many shades of grief*, she thought, recalling Sir Charles' words. *'This is for you, mother,'* she whispered, and then delivered a performance the cheering fans would tweet about for years to come.

'I don't know how you do it,' said Lola, handing Isis a hot towel. 'That was amazing!'

Looking drained and exhausted, Isis wiped her face. 'What's next?' she asked.

Lola glanced at her notes. 'A short news conference in front of the stadium in half an hour – great publicity – and then a reception at your hotel given by the Tokyo division of your record label.'

'I'll wear the Marilyn Monroe dress,' announced Isis, stripping off. 'Japanese men like big tits, and mine aren't too bad. Let their eyes pop, and the tongues wag. You know what they say; if you've got it, flaunt it.' Isis looked around for her masseuse, who usually organised her shower routine after the concert and gave her a neck and scalp massage. 'Where's that girl?' she called out. 'Shower!' Lola followed Isis into the bathroom to continue the briefing. 'What have you found out,' asked Isis, enjoying the hot needles of water relaxing her muscles, 'about the author?'

'He's a fascinating guy.'

'Tell me about him.'

'He grew up on a remote farm in Queensland, Australia. His parents divorced when he was little and the mother returned to England. Life on the farm was hard. Years of drought, financial troubles, loneliness. At sixteen, he ran away from home and went to live with an aunt in Brisbane. His first job was sweeping floors and running errands at the local newspaper. That's where he fell in love with words—'

'How did you find all this out so quickly?' interrupted Isis.

Lola reached for a towel and dried Isis' back. 'He has a terrific website; it's all there,' she said. 'And then there was the feature article in *TIME* magazine a couple of years ago, "Man of the Year" ... I've got a copy for you right here.'

'What about his writing?'

'At nineteen, he moved to Sydney and became a cadet journalist. It all went from there ...'

'Anything about the occult?'

Lola followed Isis to her dressing table and let her team go to work. 'He wrote many articles about the occult, especially the Tarot,' she said. 'He's considered a bit of an authority in that area. He also writes about the Catholic Church and the supernatural. He likes controversy and isn't afraid to raise delicate topics and politically sensitive issues. He asks the big questions others are too scared to touch. He's a bit of a rebel, and a fighter.'

'Good.' *Just the man I need*, thought Isis.

'*The Disappearance of Anna Popov* is his second book. His first, *Dental Gold and Other Horrors*, was a great success. It even made it into the New York Times' bestseller list, and stayed there for weeks.'

'I remember. Wasn't that all about the Swiss banks and Nazi gold? He accused the banks of having illegally appropriated mega sums of money belonging to Holocaust victims – right?'

'Yes. It turned into a huge scandal with lots of red faces all the way to the top. He accused the Swiss government of trying to cover it up and pointed the finger at the Vatican for silent complicity. In the end, the pressure became too great and the banks capitulated. They opened their secret ledgers and offered compensation. And all of this because of a book, and a man brave enough to confront the establishment. It sold more copies than *The Da Vinci Code*. This guy's words are stronger than the sword!'

'Get it for me. I want to read it.'

'We really have to hurry,' said Lola, looking anxiously at her watch, 'the cameras are waiting.'

Isis stood up. 'How do I look?' she asked, examining herself in the mirror.

'Amazing!'

'This should give them something to write about, don't you think?'

'You bet.'

'You can never be too thin, or too rich. Now, who said that?'

'Wallace Simpson.'

'Or have too shapely an ass ...' said Isis, adjusting her bra.

'Enough! Go and dazzle the press!' said Lola, rolling her eyes.

Lola knocked softly and then opened the door to the presidential suite. 'You're up already,' she said. 'I only wanted to drop in the papers. The whole of Japan seems to have fallen in love with you.' Lola walked across the room and dropped the papers on the lounge. 'You haven't slept at all, have you?' she chided, looking through the open bedroom door. The huge California king-sized bed had obviously not been slept in.

Sitting on the floor with her eyes closed, Isis was doing her morning meditation. The breakfast, prepared by her chef who always travelled with her, was waiting on a trolley beside the bed. 'I was on the phone all night,' said Isis, without opening her eyes.

'Oh? I thought that was my job. Who to?'

'Charles.'

'Are you going to tell me what about?' asked Lola, sounding miffed.

Isis opened her eyes and rose to her feet. 'I will. In a moment,' she said. 'But first, let's have some breakfast. I ordered for both of us as you can see.' Isis pushed the trolley over to the dining table and turned around. 'Come here,' she said, reaching for the rose in the small crystal vase on the breakfast tray. Lola walked over to Isis and stood demurely in front of her like a schoolgirl standing in front of the headmistress. 'This is for you,' said Isis, handing Lola the flower. Then she bent slowly down and kissed her ever so tenderly on the mouth.

'*What have I done to deserve this?*' whispered Lola, tears sparkling in her eyes.

'You deserve it; trust me. You are always there for me. You don't question me, and you don't lecture me. Your loyalty is unconditional. It is in times of great pain and distress that we appreciate the people who really matter,' replied Isis, 'and believe me, you matter to me. I've been to hell and back these past two days. I should know.'

'*Thanks,*' whispered Lola.

'I asked Charles to make some inquiries for me. You know how well-connected he is.'

'Oh? What about?'

'Jack Rogan, the author you investigated for me.'

Lola looked up, surprised. 'Jack Rogan? Why?'

'Because you are going to meet him – in person – in a few hours.'

'I don't understand.'

'You will, in a moment. Please bear with me.' Isis reached for the orange juice. 'I want you to fly to Sydney this morning. *Pegasus* is ready and waiting.'

'You have been busy,' said Lola. 'But why Sydney? Our next concert is in Mexico City. My God, in three days! I have to—'

'Because Rogan's in Sydney right now and you have an appointment to see him,' interrupted Isis calmly, 'that's why. Charles tracked down his agent in New York and we found out a few unexpected surprises about his publisher that may come in handy …' said Isis, smiling. 'Serendipity.'

'No wonder you didn't get any sleep last night. But why are we doing all this?'

'You will deliver a proposal to him. It has to be done discreetly, with tact and, most importantly, face to face.'

Lola shook her head. '*A proposal?* What about?'

'Let's have some breakfast, and I'll tell you.'

# 12

Jack pulled up in front of the Gordon Institute and turned off the engine. He had promised to meet Alexandra after work and drive her back to his apartment. Watching Alexandra walk towards the car, Jack knew instantly that something was wrong. He got out of his MG and opened the passenger door. 'No red carpet on your first day at work?' he joked.

'No, more like a bed of nails. I need a drink. Can we go somewhere quiet? We have to talk.'

'I know just the place.'

For a while, Alexandra just sat staring out of the car window and said nothing, a dark frown creasing her brow.

'That tough – eh?' asked Jack, breaking the silence.

'It was a disaster.'

'In what way?'

'The professor's notes cannot be found. When I opened the safe in his lab, it was empty.'

'Could he have put them somewhere else?'

'Unlikely. He died in his lab soon after he spoke to me and gave me the combination to his safe.'

'What about his would-be successor? Perhaps he knows something.'

'He's dead.'

'*What?*' Jack swerved and almost hit the car next to him.

'He died last night in that gay nightclub incident we read about this morning. He was the one in the shark tank ...'

'Are you serious?'

'Yes. His name hasn't been released yet, but the CEO knew all about it.'

'Incredible! Where does that leave you?'

'Good question. I'm the black widow. I turn up a few days after the professor dies in his lab as his anointed successor, and the local guy who was hoping to take his place is tragically killed the day before I start work. And on top of all that, the professor's notes, which incidentally belong to the institute, go missing. A good start? What do you think?'

'None of this has anything to do with you. Surely they can see that.'

'It doesn't work that way. A research organisation is a closely-knit community. I'm viewed as an outsider who has parachuted into a top position. This breeds resentment, and boy could I feel that today.'

'Was anyone else present when you opened the safe?' asked Jack.

'No ... What are you getting at?'

'Nothing ... Did you tell anyone that the professor's notes were missing?'

'Of course. I went straight to the CEO and told him.'

'What happened then?'

'He called in Professor K's research assistant, a young scientist from Sri Lanka. He was about the only one who was pleasant to me today.'

'And?'

'He confirmed that Professor K always kept his notes in the safe.'

'Can you carry on the professor's work *without* his notes? What about that cancer breakthrough he was talking about?'

'I'm not sure; I doubt it. He said it was all in his notes. The fact that the notes are missing creates a big problem. He chose me because he believed I was the most qualified person to succeed him, and most importantly, I would understand what he was doing. In a way, my entire appointment rests on that. The stakes are very high here. There is something else you should know,' said Alexandra, lowering her voice.

'What?'

'Professor K used a form of shorthand when he made notes. I mean in a scientific sense. Abbreviations, formulas, references to articles and journals, things like that. I use the same shorthand. He taught me, you see. I'm sure that was part of the reason he had me appointed.'

'Are you suggesting that no one else would understand his notes?'

'Yes, I think that's right. And that's exactly what the assistant told the CEO. He couldn't follow the professor's notes, and he was his assistant! You must understand; these notes aren't formal records of what the professor was doing, like data and findings, stuff like that. Those things were meticulously recorded elsewhere on a daily, if not hourly basis. That's standard procedure. You leave a trail of everything you do. Every research scientist does that. These notes were different. Personal. Like doodling on a piece of paper, exploring possibilities, looking for connections, reaching into the unknown. *Ideas.* Most of the time, they were nothing more than speculation and conjecture. Hence the shorthand.'

'Creative stuff.'

'Precisely. The lifeblood of true research.'

'The difference between a plodder and a Nobel laureate?'

'Something like that. Every discovery, every breakthrough begins with an *idea.* Those notes were Professor K's book of ideas. I have one too.'

'The first few drops of an intellectual waterfall?'

'Well put, my creative wordsmith.'

'I like that. Here we are; my old sailing club. We can have a glass of wine on the terrace and I can show you my boat. How does that sound?'

'Sublime. If you wanted to distract me, you've succeeded. And how was *your* day?'

'Intriguing.'

'In what way?'

'Wine first; story later.'

'A man after my own heart,' said Alexandra, smiling for the first time that afternoon.

Sitting on the terrace overlooking the harbour, Jack told Alexandra about his surprise phone call from Rebecca. 'I know this will sound odd,' she had said, 'but your publisher has asked for a favour ... He wants you to meet someone tonight. At your place – it's important. The person in question, a woman, is flying in from Tokyo just to see you. That's all I know.'

'Is that all you were told?' asked Alexandra, sipping her wine.

'That's it.'

'What are you going to do?'

'Authors have to be cooperative when their publishers ask for something. Rebecca told me so, and I'm an obedient chap. We'll stay at home tonight, order some takeaway from a nice seafood restaurant I know and wait for the doorbell to ring.' Winking at Alexandra, Jack lifted his glass. 'Cheers.'

'What an exciting life you lead. I have obviously chosen the wrong profession.'

'Don't be too hasty. Excitement comes at a price. Take this here, for example ...' Jack pointed to a thin white scar, running from the corner of his mouth along the jaw to his right ear.

'What happened?'

'I surprised an intruder in my home a few years ago. This was the result. I mentioned it in my first book.'

'*Dental Gold and Other Horrors?*'

'I have more. Look at this,' boasted Jack, tracing a scar on his temple with the tip of his finger. 'Gunshot wound. You would have read about this one in *The Disappearance of Anna Popov.*'

'Of course, you were shot in the Wizard's crypt.'

'Spot on. My souvenirs of excitement; do you like them?'

'Oh yes! You are lucky. Nothing exciting like that ever happens in a scientist's life.'

'Stick with me, Dr Delacroix, and that may change,' said Jack, laughing.

'Is that an offer?'

'Maybe.'

Feeling relaxed after a few glasses of wine and a dozen oysters, Alexandra looked pensively across the sparkling harbour. Something

Professor K's assistant had said was bothering her and refused to go away. 'Why did you ask me if someone was present when I opened the safe?' she asked, looking at Jack.

'It occurred to me that it might have been a good idea to have someone with you when you opened it. Presumably, you were the only one who knew the combination?'

'We don't know that.'

'Still …'

'A witness, you mean?'

'I suppose so. If those notes are as important as you think and hold the key to a breakthrough … they could be invaluable.'

'There was something Professor K's assistant told me that's bothering me.'

'Oh?'

'He came to see me in the afternoon. We spoke about the missing notes and he mentioned in passing that he saw Dr Cavendish in Professor K's room on the very day the professor was found dead in his lab.'

'So?'

'Nothing unusual about that, except for the fact that he thought that the safe was open … but he wasn't absolutely sure about it.'

'Oh? Now that *is* interesting, don't you think?'

'Yes, I do.'

'And Cavendish is found floating in a fish tank the next day and the professor's notes have disappeared. Coincidence?' Jack felt something churn in his stomach. It was a familiar feeling. *Another story?* he thought.

'What do *you* think?'

'You really want to know?'

'Sure.'

'It's just a hunch.'

'Okay.'

'I think that the life of a certain geneticist I happen to know, is about to become very exciting.'

'I hope you're right.'

'Be careful what you wish for.'

# 13

The black hire car pulled into the driveway and stopped in front of Jack's apartment block. The driver got out and opened the back door. 'Please wait here,' said Lola, and walked over to the entrance. She pressed the penthouse intercom button, adjusted her hair and smiled into the camera.

'Good evening,' answered Jack.

'I'm Lola Rodriguez from Tokyo. I'm sorry it's so late, but the flight took a little longer than we thought. Turbulence.'

'I've been expecting you. Please come in. Top floor; I'll meet you at the lift.'

Jack stood in the hallway and listened to the lift come up. As it stopped and the doors began to open, the hairs on the back of his neck began to tingle. *Two stories in one day?* he thought. *There goes the holiday, I bet.*

The little woman standing in the lift reminded Jack of Cassandra, Tristan's mother. The resemblance was striking: the same short, raven-black hair – combed straight back – and the same piercing eyes, radiating mystery and danger. 'Mr Rogan?' said the intriguing guest, holding out her hand. *At least the voice is different*, thought Jack, shaking her hand. 'I'm Jack.'

'And I'm Lola. Thank you for seeing me.'

'Come in.'

Lola followed Jack into the apartment. Expecting Jack to be alone, she was surprised to find an attractive young woman sitting in the lounge room. *A complication*, she thought, her mind racing. *I can't offend him.* Used to dealing with the unexpected, Lola immediately adjusted her approach. She couldn't possibly ask the woman to leave. 'What a magnificent apartment,' she said breezily, 'and what a view!'

'This is Dr Delacroix,' said Jack, introducing Alexandra. Having sensed a flicker of unease and surprise in his mystery guest on finding

Alexandra in the room, he decided to come straight to the point. 'I don't know what brings you here, but whatever it is you wish to say to me, you can say in front of Dr Delacroix. Should that be of some concern to you?'

'I appreciate your candour, Mr Rogan, thank you. That won't be a problem.'

'Good. Please call me Jack. Drink?' Jack asked, indicating to Lola to make herself comfortable.

'Yes please.'

Jack walked over to the ice bucket and poured a glass of champagne for his guest. Sitting in a comfortable armchair, Lola collected her thoughts. For a while, no one said anything, the tension in the room rising by the second. Jack handed her the glass and sat next to Alexandra.

'Have you heard of Isis and The Time Machine?' asked Lola, carefully watching Jack. He sat up, as if a piece of ice had been shoved down the back of his shirt, and almost spilled his drink. *Tristan knew,* he thought. *How extraordinary!*

*He looks like he's seen a ghost,* thought Lola. *I wonder why.*

'It's a rock band; heavy metal,' replied Jack quietly.

'That's correct, and the lead singer is Isis. I'm her personal assistant. The group is currently on a world tour. The Tokyo concert was last night.' Lola paused, feeling her way. 'You may not be aware, but Isis' parents, Lord and Lady Elms, were attacked in their London home a few days ago,' she continued. 'Her father was shot dead by intruders, and her mother died as a result of horrific injuries sustained in the attack. Isis was present in hospital when her mother died.' Lola paused again, letting this sink in.

'That's terrible, I hadn't heard ...' said Jack.

'Lord Elms was a former chancellor of the exchequer. The official line at the moment is that Lord and Lady Elms were the victims of a home invasion gone wrong. However, Isis isn't convinced. She doesn't believe that was the case ...'

'Oh?'

'You must be wondering what all this has to do with you – right?'

'The thought had crossed my mind,' said Jack.

'I'm afraid that's how it will have to remain for the moment.'

'I don't follow.'

'Isis would have come to see you herself, if her commitments would have allowed her to do so. Unfortunately, the next concert is in Mexico City in three days' time, followed by Buenos Aires and then Rio. It's a relentless schedule that made it impossible for her to come. She and the band are on their way to Mexico as we speak. That's why she sent me instead.'

'But why?'

'I'm only the messenger, delivering an invitation …'

'*An invitation?*' said Jack, surprised. 'Please explain.'

'Isis would like to put a proposal to you – in person. I'm not privy to what it's about,' continued Lola, carefully watching Jack's reaction.

'So?'

'Because Isis cannot come to you, she would like you to accompany me to Mexico to meet her. Her private jet is waiting here at the airport. We could leave within the hour if—'

'You can't be serious!' interrupted Jack, unable to hide his annoyance. 'You want me to drop everything and just come with you? Halfway round the world to meet someone I don't know? This is ridiculous!'

Lola had expected something like this; things were quickly spinning out of control. She knew it was time to send the text message she had prepared earlier. Lola reached into her pocket and pressed the 'send' button on her phone. The message raced around the globe and reached Sir Charles, who had been waiting for it. Sir Charles rang Jack's publisher, who then called Rebecca.

'I know how this must look,' replied Lola calmly, taking her time, 'but please hear me out. I've been authorised to transfer two hundred thousand US dollars into your bank account.'

'What, just to keep an appointment with a busy rock star?' snapped Jack, his anger rising.

'Yes.'

'This is crazy!' Just then, Jack's mobile began to ring. Annoyed, he reached into his pocket to turn it off.

'I think you should answer that call,' said Lola, watching Jack carefully.

Surprised, Jack looked first at Lola, then at the screen. It was Rebecca. 'Please excuse me,' he said, and left the room.

'Is she still with you?' asked Rebecca.

'Yes, her name's Lola. Can you please tell me what's going on here? I've been asked to go to Mexico to meet a rock star.'

'Not just *any* rock star, Jack. *Isis*, a legend!'

'You haven't answered my question.'

'I don't know much more than you, except for this: your publishers want you to go along with it.'

'Why?'

'Just go and listen to what Isis has to say; that's all they're asking. There's no obligation and you get a fabulous fee. This is an opportunity of a lifetime, Jack. I know a dozen authors who would gladly sell their own mother to be in your position, yet here you are being *invited* to meet her and being paid handsomely for the privilege. Think, Jack! What have you got to lose – eh?'

'My holiday.'

'Jesus! Here's the deal: if you accept, I'll get you an extra week. How's that?'

'You really want me to go?'

'Yes. You're the one who keeps telling me that stories find you – right? Well, I think that a whopper of a story has just found you, buster. The question is, what are you going to do about it – eh? How's that for a challenge?'

'Okay. Two extra weeks.'

'*What?* I can't possibly—'

'You heard me,' interrupted Jack, 'two extra weeks.'

Silence.

'You're a tough bastard,' said Rebecca.

'No, I'm not. I'm an incorrigible rascal – remember?'

'Oh, for Christ's sake. All right, two weeks it is. Incidentally, is she pretty?'

'Who? Lola?'

'No, your new flatmate.'

'You *are* well informed,' said Jack, sounding a little sheepish.

'I'll take that as a yes. Looking after you is my job, Jack. Now go and tell Lola you'll do it and keep me posted. I'm dying to find out what this is all about.'

'You're not the only one,' said Jack and hung up.


'I'm intrigued,' said Jack, walking back into the room. 'How did you know?' He looked at Lola and held up his phone.

'I'm only the messenger,' replied Lola, sidestepping the question.

'Some messenger.'

'Well?'

'Give me ten minutes,' said Jack.

'To think about it?'

'No, to pack.'

# 14

Strapped into his seat behind Lola, Jack watched her prepare the jet for take-off. Fascinated by her ability to manipulate the aircraft's sophisticated controls, he listened to the instructions coming from the traffic control tower as the jet taxied slowly along the runway. With excitement and a little fear churning in his stomach, Jack felt like a co-pilot sitting in a fighter plane ready to take off and roar into battle. A few moments after the A380 in front of them had disappeared into the night, Traffic Control gave *Pegasus* permission to take off.

'Here we go,' said Lola, her hand on the throttle.

Jack had never before experienced such power in an aircraft. Pressed into his seat by the breathtaking acceleration of the jet, Jack felt a great sense of exhilaration gripping every fibre of his tense body. It was a wonderful feeling of being free. 'Wow!' Jack cried out, gripping the arms of his seat as the plane left the ground and rapidly began to climb.

As soon as the plane had reached cruising altitude and levelled out, Lola turned to the co-pilot sitting next to her. 'Okay, Joe, she's all yours,' she said, getting out of her seat. Jack did the same and followed Lola into the spacious cabin behind the cockpit.

'That was some ride,' said Jack, still on a high. 'You are full of surprises.'

'I'm glad you enjoyed it. Isis has two planes: *Icarus*, a big one for The Time Machine – crew and all – and then there's *Pegasus* here, her own private little beauty. It's one of the fastest and most powerful civilian aircraft in the world.'

'And you can fly it like a Top Gun. I'm impressed.'

Smiling, Lola shrugged. 'I never miss the take-off. I don't get the chance to fly that often any more. Would you like some supper? We have some great food on board,' she said, 'and you'll get to meet Hanna ...'

'This is Hanna, my assistant,' said Lola, introducing the young woman busying herself in the galley. 'She makes a splendid vodka martini; would you like one?' Jack noticed that the little dining table in front of the galley had been set for three, and a drinks trolley complete with ice bucket and flowers was standing next to it. Apart from the two pilots and the engineer in the cockpit, there was no one else on board.

'Sure.'

'Hanna comes from Israel,' said Lola, watching Jack's body language, well aware of the effect Hanna had on men. 'She's fluent in five languages. Mandarin, Russian and Japanese are her forte. She's invaluable when we're on tour.'

'I can imagine,' said Jack. *What a stunner*, he thought, watching Lola's assistant prepare his drink. Hanna had the classic looks of a catwalk model. Tall and slim, in her early twenties, she moved with an elegance and grace that was both enchanting, and exciting. Her short leather skirt, zippered at the front, showed off her long legs, and her waist-long, honey-honey blonde hair provided the perfect contrast to her olive complexion. But most striking of all were her blue eyes: almond-shaped and set a little too far apart, they gave her face an alluringly exotic look.

'Thanks for coming along, Jack,' said Lola, lifting her glass, 'and without having to be dragged. You made my mission easy.'

Smiling, Jack lifted his own glass. 'I'm not quite sure what I've let myself in for,' he said, 'but somehow, I seem to attract the unexpected. And besides, certain things are meant to be.'

'I know. I'm sure you won't be disappointed.'

What Lola couldn't have known was that the real reason behind Jack's quick decision and willingness to cooperate had nothing to do with her intriguing offer, or the arm-twisting from his publishers, or Rebecca's urging to go along with it all. The reason was Tristan.

Remembering Tristan's prophetic words – *you and Isis are destined to meet* – Jack watched Lola sitting opposite. The silver studs in her ears, her thin, yet deceptively strong and athletic body and the sultry look on her expressive face reminded him of Stieg Larsson's Lisbeth in *The*

*Girl with the Dragon Tattoo,* only a little older. *The lines on her face speak of suffering and loss,* thought Jack, looking into her huge, dreamy eyes, radiating intelligence and danger. 'Where did you learn to fly like that?' he asked.

'Sitting on my dad's lap in his biplane when I was about twelve,' replied Lola.

'You're kidding.'

'No. My father was an instructor in San Diego. Once flying gets into your blood, it never leaves you.'

'But you are a personal assistant to a rock star,' remarked Jack.

'It hasn't always been that way. I taught Isis how to fly. She's as passionate about flying as I am. She can fly this little baby like a pro. I gave her flying lessons; that's how we met. Then she bought her first plane and I became her pilot. That was about ten years ago and things went from there.'

'I have a confession to make,' said Jack, enjoying the company of the two fascinating women. With the martinis beginning to kick in, he started to relax.

'A confession? *Already?*'

'I know very little about Isis and The Time Machine ...'

'Don't feel too bad about it. The average age of our fan base is seventeen. I didn't think heavy metal would be quite your thing. You strike me more as a B&B.'

'A B&B? What's that?'

'A Bach and Beethoven man.'

'I do like that,' replied Jack, laughing. 'I've been called many things, but never anything quite so classy. But seriously, I would appreciate a little help ...'

'In what way?'

'I would like to know a little more about Isis and The Time Machine before I meet the star.'

'Did you hear that, Hanna? How would you describe Isis?'

'You are about to meet one of the most fascinating, talented, colourful, flamboyant, generous, and most importantly, incredibly intelligent persons on the planet,' said Hanna, handing Jack another martini.

'That's quite an introduction. Didn't you say that the average age of the fan base was seventeen?' said Jack, turning to Lola.

'Yes, yes, I know … I'm one of her biggest fans,' said Lola, 'and I was seventeen about twenty years ago. She's also impulsive, unpredictable and occasionally exasperatingly outrageous. That's why being with her is so much fun; it's never boring. Let me give you an example …' Lola paused and looked at Jack. She rarely felt at ease around men but to her surprise, not only did she find Jack incredibly attractive, she felt as if she had known him for years. It was a disconcerting realisation for someone who preferred the company of women.

'After we finished our flying lessons, Isis went on tour and I didn't really expect to hear from her again. Then early one morning, out of the blue, I received a phone call from her, asking me to come to Paris. She wanted to go shopping … for a plane!'

'What did you do?'

'I dropped everything, flew from San Diego to Paris and we bought the plane at an air show.'

'Just like that?'

'Yes. Here we were, two women on our own, dressed a little unconventionally as I remember – she was wearing her Greta Garbo outfit and I looked a bit like a rocker-chick in my bomber jacket – strolling arm in arm among all these corporate types looking at multimillion-dollar planes. I asked all the questions, which as you can imagine were quite technical and specific, until we found a plane she really liked. She told the sales team that she wanted to buy it. At first, no one took us seriously and they all laughed. But when she pulled out her chequebook, the penny dropped; they suddenly realised who was hiding behind the dark glasses, and everything changed. You should have seen them! Isis enjoyed herself. She likes to shock people. She offered me a job then and there and I became her personal pilot.'

'That's quite a story,' said Jack. 'I can't wait to meet her.'

'There is one more important thing you have to know about her,' said Lola, lowering her voice.

'Oh?'

'Isis is a man. At least she was born a man, George Elms, son of Lord and Lady Elms ...'

'Transgender?' said Jack, surprised.

'It's more complicated than that—'

'You won't be disappointed,' interrupted Hanna, clearing the table. 'You'll see when you meet her.' As she brushed past him, Jack could smell her perfume. 'Chanel,' he said. 'You're wearing Chanel.'

Hanna looked at Jack dumbfounded, making her large eyes appear even bigger. 'That's incredible!' she said, putting her hand on his shoulder. 'You're right.'

*Amazing guy*, thought Lola, watching Hanna, *she likes him.*

Lola stood up, put her arm around Hanna's waist and together they walked slowly to the back of the plane. 'Come, sit with us,' she said to Jack, pointing to a pair of comfortable leather lounges, 'and I'll tell you what sets Isis apart from everybody else.'

Feeling a little dizzy from Hanna's generous vodka martinis and the scent of her perfume, Jack followed the two women to the back of the plane and sat opposite them. 'Tell me,' he said.

'In the world of Isis and The Time Machine, reality takes on a different dimension,' said Lola.

'What do you mean?'

'Someone in her position can create her own reality. She opens the doors of the imagination through her music and her stage-presence, and she takes her audience with her on an extraordinary journey—'

'Like a time machine?' interrupted Jack, a sparkle in his eyes.

'A bit like that. All her fans have to do is to listen and follow; and millions do. She's not afraid of being different and she writes all her own material. That's one of the reasons for her tremendous success.'

'Is that how you see the world of Isis?' Jack asked Hanna, who had kicked off her high heel shoes and was snuggling up against Lola on the lounge.

'I would put it a bit differently,' Hanna said. 'The world of Isis is only limited by your imagination.'

'I've never looked at it that way,' said Lola, 'but Hanna's right. Her world has endless possibilities, and at this very moment, we are all part of it.'

Leaning forward, Lola took the swivel stick with the olive still attached out of her martini glass, and then ran it slowly up the inside of Hanna's thigh, leaving a trail of glistening moisture on her silky skin. Closing her eyes, Hanna moistened her lips with the tip of her tongue and, spreading her legs just a little, leant back further.

Lola looked at Jack and smiled. 'Endless possibilities,' she said, handing him the swivel stick. Then, turning towards Hanna, she unzipped the front of the young woman's skirt and began to play with her tiny lace G-string. '*You can get some sleep, Jack, or you can watch, or you can use your imagination ... and join in,*' she whispered, before kissing Hanna ever so gently on the mouth.

Jack woke with a start. He opened his eyes and looked around the cabin. The first thing he saw was his shirt lying on the floor next to his trousers and his shoes. Then it all came back to him. *Jesus,* he thought, rubbing his aching temples.

Lola and Hanna were sitting at the little dining table, eating breakfast. Noticing that Jack was awake, Lola walked over to him. 'Welcome to the world of Isis, Jack; imagination and endless possibilities – remember? You seem to have a robust supply of both. Good sleep?' she asked, handing him an orange juice. 'We're about to land; better get dressed.'

# 15

*Calypso* was sailing due north, hugging the New South Wales coast on its way to the Great Barrier Reef. An early riser, Macbeth was already at his desk. Lost in thought, he was carefully examining Professor K's handwritten notes in front of him. The entire little book had been scanned and emailed to the Blackburn laboratories in California for analysis, and Macbeth was anxiously awaiting a phone call from the scientist in charge. If those pages did in fact contain the breakthrough he was hoping for, they could be worth billions.

Macbeth was about to put the book back in the safe when his phone rang. It was the scientist from California. For the next ten minutes, Macbeth listened in silence to what the man had to say, and then slowly put down the phone. Looking out the window, he watched the rugged coastline glide past in the morning mist. Macbeth was used to dealing with the unexpected. In fact, he was at his best in a crisis, and if what the scientist had just told him was true, he was already in the middle of one.

Macbeth reached for Professor K's notes lying on his desk and slowly turned the pages. The small, spidery handwriting, the neat columns of numbers and strange-looking symbols and diagrams reminded him of Leonardo's drawings he had admired in the Vatican. The fact that none of it made any sense to him was not surprising. However, the fact it didn't make any sense to the scientists either, was a bombshell he hadn't expected. Macbeth closed the book and began to smile as the irony of it all began to sink in. By covering his tracks and tying up a potentially dangerous loose end, he had outwitted himself. The professor's notes were written in some kind of code. By having disposed of Cavendish, he had most probably silenced the only man who may have been able to help him break it. As the coastline disappeared again in the mist, Macbeth suddenly realised that this wasn't necessarily so. The professor had appointed a successor just before he died. If his notes did in fact hold the key to his discovery, which seemed more than likely, then his successor had to be able to read them. *Of course, that's it!* thought Macbeth. *That's why he appointed a former colleague and trusted friend instead of Cavendish.*

Feeling better, Macbeth rang for Carlotta. 'What have you found out about Dr Delacroix, the genomics expert?' he asked.

'Quite a bit,' said Carlotta. 'She's a prominent epigeneticist; high-profile. A lot has been written about her, mainly in scientific journals. We even have a recent photograph of her. I'll get my notes.'

'Please do that.'

For the next two hours, Macbeth locked himself into his stateroom with Van Cleef. He was formulating a plan. *Calypso* had already changed course and was steaming back towards Sydney; a simple phone call to the Gordon Institute had told him all he needed to know: Dr Delacroix had already taken up her position and was working at the institute.

As usual, Van Cleef didn't blink an eye when Macbeth outlined his daring plan. On the contrary, he came up with excellent strategic and tactical suggestions to make it work. Nothing seemed to faze him. 'Once again, timing is critical,' said Macbeth, playing with the two small steel balls in the palm of his hand, a nervous habit that helped him think. In a strange way, it compensated for his lack of mobility. 'And I don't have to tell you that nothing must link us to what we are about to do.'

'I understand,' said Van Cleef, feeling elated. His boss' plan had all the hallmarks of a military operation Van Cleef thrived upon: dangerous, challenging, and rewarding in a way no one but a professional soldier would understand. Macbeth could sense the excitement in Van Cleef. *He's straining at the leash*, thought Macbeth. *Like a pit-bull. I would hate to stand in his way.* 'Any questions?' he asked.

'Not at the moment.'

'Thank you, Jan, that will be all. Keep me informed.'

'Yes sir,' said Van Cleef, gathering up his notes.

*Dr Delacroix is in for a little surprise*, thought Macbeth, watching Van Cleef leave the room. He felt like a falconer who had just released his favourite hunting bird. He could already see it circling above, searching for its unsuspecting prey with deadly talons exposed, ready to strike. Like Van Cleef, Macbeth also thrived on danger and a challenge, except that in his case, all the action was in his mind.

Alexandra left the institute and decided to walk home rather than catch a taxi. Jack had shown her a shortcut through the beautiful Botanic Gardens. The extraordinary encounter with Lola the night before was still a blur. Everything had happened so fast. Alexandra had never met a man like Jack before. Within the hour, he had packed his duffel bag, given her the keys to his apartment and left for the airport with Lola. In a strange way, she missed him already.

Alexandra's second day at work had been a little better. Looking for clues about Professor K's discovery, she had spent the whole day poring over his institute records. Unfortunately, there was nothing there to suggest a breakthrough. However, Professor K had never been one to exaggerate. *It has to be in his notes*, she thought. *He would have tried to write everything down before he died. Damn!*

At first, Alexandra didn't notice the man following her. It wasn't until he was walking alongside her that she quickly looked at him. Tall, athletic, with a backpack casually slung over his shoulder and wearing a small straw hat and dark glasses, he looked like a tourist. 'Nice day at the institute, Dr Delacroix?' said the man without breaking his stride.

Alexandra stopped and looked at him, surprised. 'Have we met?' she asked.

'Not yet,' said the man, smiling. 'Please listen carefully; this is how it'll work.'

'What do you mean?' Alexandra was about to turn away and keep walking, when the man grabbed her hand, holding it like a vice.

Van Cleef knew that the next thirty seconds were critical. 'If you scream, or try to run away, I'll kill you. Please believe me; I've done it before,' he said. 'Is this a gun in my pocket here?' he continued,

84

placing her hand on his hip. 'What do you think?' Alexandra could feel something hard like steel. 'I carry a flick-knife in the other pocket, but you have to take my word for it. If you don't want to end up in a fish tank like Dr Cavendish, you will do exactly as I tell you. Clear so far?'

Frightened and confused, Alexandra looked around. There was no one nearby she could see. What she couldn't have known, however, was that two of Van Cleef's men were in fact just behind her, ready to assist Van Cleef if necessary. Her instincts and a quick assessment of the situation told her that the best option, at least for the moment, was to cooperate. *This is no crank*, she thought, her mind racing. *He knows who I am, and he knows about Cavendish.* The man radiated danger. 'What do you want?' she asked, her voice sounding hoarse.

'I can see we'll get on famously,' said the man, beginning to walk, but without letting go of her hand. 'For now, we are two friends strolling through the park. Try to look relaxed, and I'll tell you what I want you to do. If you do exactly as I say, you will not be harmed. Believe me, you are worth a lot more to me alive than dead. However, if you try something foolish, well, you already know the answer, don't you?' Alexandra nodded, but said nothing.

'Smile and wave to the concierge,' said Van Cleef, opening the door to the foyer of Jack's apartment block. Walking arm in arm, they passed the front desk on their way to the lifts. The concierge was busy on the phone and didn't even look up. 'I will kiss you now. Don't pull away, and try to look as if you enjoy it,' said Van Cleef as the lift doors opened. Going up in the lift, Van Cleef kissed Alexandra on the back of the neck like a lover, aware of the CCTV camera's searching eye above them. '*Not bad*,' he whispered, impressed by Alexandra's self-control, 'for someone whose entire life has just changed,' he added. 'You'll get through this, but only if you're strong and follow instructions ... '

*I mustn't underestimate this man*, thought Alexandra, standing quite still. Just then, the lift doors opened.

'Now, let's go inside and start packing, shall we?' said the blond man.

'Packing? Why?'

'Because you and I are going on a little journey. Why should Mr Rogan have all the fun – eh?'

# 16

Landing in Mexico City was a nightmare. They had to go into a holding pattern circling the city for more than an hour and wait their turn. Apparently, an American dignitary had just arrived, and the whole airport was in some kind of lockdown. When they finally touched down and were directed to taxi to a quiet corner far away from the terminal, the first rays of the morning sun were waking the 'city of palaces' built on top of the Aztec ruins of ancient Tenochtitlan.

'Welcome to Mexico City,' said the customs officer waiting for them on the tarmac. 'We've been expecting you.' When Lola replied in fluent Spanish and held up her passport, all formalities appeared to have been brushed aside, and they were ushered to a black Land Rover.

'Normally, Isis stays with the crew in one of the main hotels close to the stadium, but not this time. She's staying with … a friend,' said Lola. 'That's where we are going.'

'A friend?' asked Jack, watching the morning traffic choking the city with noise, frustration and toxic pollution so dense it made your eyes water.

'Yes, a close one. And her house … well that's something else. Not long now; we're almost there.'

The only thing visible from the busy road was an elaborate wrought iron gate, which opened all by itself as soon as they pulled into the driveway. Everything else was concealed behind high walls and lush, jungle-like vegetation. Jack noticed several CCTV cameras mounted on poles, watching them from above like birds of prey lining up for the kill. A security guard dressed in battle fatigues appeared out of nowhere and pointed to a wide garage door that also opened automatically as they approached.

'Most of the house is underground,' said Hanna, getting out of the car. She saw Jack looking at a rock wall lit up by spotlights at the back of the garage – huge, polished blocks of stone, irregular in shape, but fitting together so perfectly that it would have been impossible to push a razorblade between the blocks resting on top of each other.

'Aztec ruins?' Jack queried, running the tips of his fingers along the smooth surface of the polished stone.

'Yes. Tenochtitlan; what's left of it after the Spanish invaders razed it.'

'Amazing.'

'You ain't seen nothin' yet,' joked Lola. She pointed to a glass lift at the far end of the huge underground garage. 'Come; let me show you the rest.'

Set into the side of a small hill, the house was built directly on top of the ruins of an Aztec temple. The clever architecture incorporated the features of the ruins into the modern structure without altering, or in any way destroying their integrity. No restoration of any kind had been carried out. Ingenious glass panels and concealed lighting gave the house a surreal, almost stage-like appearance with stairways and corridors leading in all directions.

'The only thing missing are the high-priests,' said Jack, following Hanna into the lift. 'And the chanting of the faithful cowering before cruel gods expecting blood.'

'That may change,' said Lola, laughing.

'Is this a warning?'

'Maybe.'

'Here we are,' said Lola as the lift doors opened to reveal a large, cave-like chamber without windows.

Jack followed Hanna and Lola out of the lift and gasped. The huge room that had once been part of the temple forecourt was entirely lit by candles, sending crazy shadows dancing across the stone floor and conjuring up images of chanting priests and bloody sacrifices. Standing in niches cut into the stone walls, frightening looking gods – precious pre-Columbian artefacts – were staring disapprovingly, thought Jack, at him. It reminded Jack of another eerie place he had visited not long ago; the crypt where he had first met Cassandra and the enigmatic Wizard. However, here something was quite different and unexpected – the music.

'That's Isis,' said Hanna, pointing to the stunning woman standing in a pale circle of light.

'She's listening to baroque music? In this place?' said Jack, surprised.

'Lola was right; you're definitely a B&B.'

'Come, let me introduce you,' Lola said, as they approached.

'Superb,' said Isis, holding up an elaborate, helmet-like headdress made entirely out of multi-coloured feathers.

'Here, let me help you,' said her elderly, French dress designer, hovering like a protective crow over his creation. It was a perfect fit. Isis looked at herself in the mirror and nodded. 'Magnifique!'

Dressed head to toe in a tight-fitting costume inspired by the elaborate ceremonial cloaks and headdresses worn by Aztec priests, Isis looked like a goddess. Following the contours of her athletic body, the feathers and glass beads shimmered like precious stones in the candlelight.

Lola hurried across to Isis and kissed her on both cheeks. '*He's here*,' she whispered.

Isis took off her headdress, handed it to her designer fussing next to her and walked slowly towards Jack. *She's much older*, thought Jack, watching the tall woman come closer. The woman stopped in front of him, and for what seemed an eternity, just looked at him dreamily.

*He's much younger*, thought Isis, holding out her hand, *and very good looking*. 'Thank you for coming. Do you like the costume?' They shook hands.

'It's spectacular,' said Jack, a little taken aback by the unexpected question. 'Dress rehearsal?'

Isis smiled. 'Something like that. We are preparing for the highlight of our tour. Spectacular, you say? Good. You are the first one to see my new stage attire.'

'You like Bach? This is one of his solo cantatas – 'Ich will den Kreuzstab gerne tragen' – if I'm not mistaken.'

*This guy's good*, thought Isis. 'This may surprise you, but a lot of my music is based on classical principles,' she said. 'I listen to classical music all the time and try to learn from the masters.'

'It reminds me of Huitzilopochtli.'

'What does?'

'Your costume.'

It was Isis' turn to look surprised. 'Did you hear that, Jean-Paul?' said Isis, looking over her shoulder at her dress designer. 'Right again; that's exactly what it's modelled on. The Aztec god of war, sun and human sacrifice. And he was also the patron of Tenochtitlan, the ruins of which are all around us. And you, Mr Rogan are full of surprises.'

*She wants to play cat and mouse*, thought Jack. *All right by me.* 'And so are you,' he retorted, enjoying himself.

*More than you can possibly imagine*, thought Isis. 'Music, art and history all in one breath? I can already see we'll get on famously,' said Isis. 'Come, let's sit, and I'll tell you why I've invited you to come here.' Isis looked at Lola and shook her head. 'But only you,' she added quietly.

Realising they had been dismissed, Lola, Hanna and the ageing dress designer discreetly left the chamber.

'Let me show you something I know you'll find interesting,' said Isis. She took Jack by the arm and guided him towards the middle of the chamber. 'Here … do you know what this is?'

Jack looked at the exquisitely carved circular stone relief set into the floor. 'The Coyolxauhqui stone?' ventured Jack after a while.

'Bravo. Not many would know this. It's a replica, of course. The original was found in 1978 at the Temple Mayor site not far from here.' Isis sat down on a wooden bench facing the stone. 'Please.' Jack sat down beside her. 'It depicts Coyolxauhqui, a mythical being, decapitated and dismembered.'

'How gruesome.'

'Quite. According to Aztec mythology, Coyolxauhqui was a powerful magician. She was the daughter of Coatlicue and Mixcoatl and the leader of the southern star gods. She enticed her siblings to attack their mother, Coatlicue, the maternal earth deity, because she had become pregnant. When the time came for Coatlicue to give birth, Huitzilopochtli left his mother's womb and entered the world in full body armour and immediately killed Coyolxauhqui and her four hundred brothers and sisters.'

'A baby not to be messed with,' interjected Jack, a sparkle in his eye.

'Absolutely. This was retribution for having attacked their mother,' continued Isis undeterred. 'He then cut off Coyolxauhqui's head and threw it into the sky where it became the moon.'

Listening patiently, Jack was wondering where this was heading.

'You must be wondering why I'm telling you all this?' said Isis. Jack didn't reply. 'A few days ago, my parents were attacked in their home in London. My father was shot dead and my mother tortured. *Her face was mutilated beyond recognition* ...' Isis' voice trailed off. She paused, collecting her thoughts, staring pensively at the stone disc in front of her.

'I'm sorry,' said Jack, breaking the heavy silence.

'She spoke to me just before she died ...' Isis turned towards Jack and looked at him intently. 'I need your help.'

'In what way?'

'To make sense of what she told me.'

# 17

Sitting blindfolded between two of Van Cleef's men in the back of a speeding van, Alexandra was trying to come to terms with what had just happened to her. As soon as they had entered Jack's apartment, the blond man had confiscated her phone, put on gloves, and never left her side. Watching her every move, he had told her to pack everything that belonged to her. He even checked her passport and put it into his pocket. Alexandra had tried to engage him in conversation, but he wouldn't have any of it. He seemed to be totally focused on only two things: time, and his phone.

Speaking softly in what to Alexandra sounded like Afrikaans, he made several phone calls. As soon as Alexandra had finished packing, a man wearing a chauffeur's uniform came up to the apartment and took down her luggage to a waiting car. Following her abductor's instructions, Alexandra handed the keys to the apartment to the concierge for safekeeping. She told him that she would be going away for a few days, and that Mr Rogan would most likely be returning before she did. With Van Cleef standing beside her, she had no option but to play her part convincingly, and she did.

Van Cleef had every reason to be pleased with himself. He had completed his assignment with military precision and without harming his 'subject' in any way. However, what he was particularly proud of was the carefully constructed web of clues he had left behind, which would implicate Alexandra in her sudden departure. *A web of complicity*, as Van Cleef liked to call it. Always point the finger of blame at your victim if you can. That was the real genius in Van Cleef's work, which earned him the admiration of his men and his employer's praise and respect he so craved.

Instead of returning to Sydney Harbour, which might have looked a little odd, *Calypso* had pulled into Pittwater – a scenic waterway to the north of Sydney – and had dropped anchor behind Lion Island. The shore was only a few hundred yards away, and Sydney a short drive to the south. One of *Calypso*'s zodiacs was waiting in a protected cove, ready to take them back to the ship.

Van Cleef thanked his friend – a former brother-in-arms who had settled in Sydney and was running a security company – for his assistance 'on the ground'. Not only had the man provided the vehicles and all the logistical support needed to carry out the operation, but he had obtained invaluable intelligence about Alexandra and Cavendish. He had also acted as 'Kevin', the Cavendish go-between. Without his involvement, neither the Cavendish, nor the Alexandra operation could have been accomplished with such precision and in such record time. He was also well-connected with the local police.

Van Cleef was part of a worldwide network of former commandoes and mercenaries who had settled in various parts of the world and set up businesses usually associated with their former profession. They all kept in touch and assisted each other in various projects. This was a lucrative source of work that kept the old spirit and memories alive and bound them together.

'Thanks, Paulus,' said Van Cleef, patting his friend on his bald head for good luck, just as he used to do in Kabul. 'Your fee's already in your account. And a little bonus too,' he added, smiling.

'If you need anything else, you know where to find me. It's always a pleasure doing business with you,' said Paulus. 'There are only a few pros like us left.'

'You can say that again.'

'You were always one of the best,' said Paulus. 'Do you want to know why?' Van Cleef shrugged, and said nothing. 'Because you have no fear and use your brains; that's why.'

'Having no fear isn't such a good thing, my friend. Fear can protect you.'

'It can kill you too. We've seen it many times.'

'You're right. It's a fine line.'

'Sure is. Take care, and never lose sight of where it is.'

Within minutes, the zodiac had taken Van Cleef and his captive to the ship under cover of darkness. An hour later, *Calypso* passed the lighthouse at Palm Beach and left Pittwater, the whitewash from its powerful engines looking like a stairway to the moon, the only reminder it had ever been there.

'Welcome aboard,' said Carlotta, opening the door to a luxurious stateroom on the upper deck. Alexandra's luggage was already waiting inside. 'Mr Macbeth would like to see you in half an hour. I'll come and get you. I'm sure you'll find everything you need in here.'

Alexandra sat down on the huge bed, a thousand questions bombarding her exhausted brain. With denial, fear and curiosity taking turns to confuse her, she found it difficult to concentrate and think straight. *Be careful what you wish for*, she thought, remembering Jack's words, a wry smile creasing the corners of her mouth. *Excitement and adventure ... I think you just found it, girl! Just hope you live long enough to tell the tale.*

Alexandra took a shower to calm herself and put on fresh clothes. She was combing her wet hair in front of the mirror when Carlotta knocked and entered. 'Are you ready?' she asked. 'Mr Macbeth is waiting. Please follow me.'

It was well past midnight when Carlotta opened the door to Macbeth's stateroom. 'Dr Delacroix,' she announced, letting Alexandra walk into the cabin in front of her.

'Please leave us, Carlotta, and close the door,' said Macbeth, looking at Alexandra standing in front of him. 'You are much younger than I imagined,' he said. 'Your career and your reputation suggest someone older. Please take a seat.'

Alexandra tried to see the face of the man addressing her, but his wheelchair was in the shadows, the lamp on his desk the only source of light in the room. She had the impression that this was quite deliberate. Alexandra sat down in the chair facing the desk and crossed her legs. *She's very composed*, thought Macbeth, admiring the young woman's self-control, *and quite attractive. Brains and beauty.* For a while, Macbeth let the silence speak, the soft throb of the ship's powerful engines the only sound. 'I'm Alistair Macbeth,' said the man in the wheelchair after a while, 'chairman of Blackburn Pharmaceuticals, I'm sure you've heard of us. And in case you were wondering, you are on *Calypso*, the company's research vessel.'

Alexandra looked up, surprised. *So, that's the connection,* she thought. There wasn't a research scientist alive who hadn't heard of Blackburn Pharmaceuticals. The whole industry was in awe of Alistair Macbeth, its charismatic founder and man at the helm of the international juggernaut. Cavendish's sudden death and the professor's missing notes suddenly began to make sense. *But why has he brought me here?* she asked herself, unable to fit that perplexing piece of the puzzle into the emerging picture.

'What do you want from me?' asked Alexandra curtly.

Macbeth wheeled himself closer to his desk. He reached into one of the drawers, pulled out Professor K's notebook and placed it on the desk in front of him. 'I have something I know you want, and you have something I need.'

For a while, Alexandra just stared at the open notebook on the desk, her analytical mind refusing to accept what her eyes were clearly telling her. The familiar spidery handwriting and the peculiar diagrams, however, were unmistakable. And then suddenly, it all made sense. *He needs me because he can't follow Kasper's shorthand,* she thought, her spirits soaring. All wasn't lost; she had something to bargain with! 'You are right, I do want that notebook. It is the legacy of a dear friend and a genius,' said Alexandra quietly. 'The ideas and the recognition belong to him, but everything else belongs to his employer, the Gordon Institute—'

'You are mistaken,' interrupted Macbeth, a flash of anger racing across his face. 'It all belongs to me.'

'Be that as it may, isn't it all rather academic?' said Alexandra, sitting back in her chair.

'How so?'

'Let's not insult each other. I'm sure you know the answer to that as well as I do.'

Macbeth looked at Alexandra with renewed respect. It had been a long time since he had met a sparring partner of her calibre and ability. In his world, his word was gospel and only the reckless or the very brave would dare contradict him.

'All right; this is how it will work,' said Macbeth. 'You will translate the professor's notes into scientific language my researchers can understand. Once that has been done and we have confirmation from my team, we will evaluate the situation further. Clear so far?'

Alexandra realised there was only one way to deal with someone like Macbeth: with brazen confidence and total disregard for her own precarious position. Fear and cowardly cooperation would only be met with contempt. The wages of fear was death. It was an old story. Instead of agreeing with Macbeth, Alexandra began to laugh.

'You find this amusing?' snapped Macbeth.

'I find your arrogance amusing,' replied Alexandra calmly. 'What makes you so sure I will do your bidding? You steal the professor's work, you have his assistant – who must have been somehow involved – killed, you kidnap me and *command* me to deliver to you the only thing you cannot have. Yes, I think that's funny.'

*The woman is quite amazing*, thought Macbeth, realising a different approach was needed. He had to concede that so far, she had the upper hand and was winning. 'I don't think you quite appreciate the position you're in …' he began.

'Oh, I think I do,' interrupted Alexandra, trying to stay on the front foot. 'I think we can safely say I'm the only one who understands the professor's work and can make sense of it. You are obviously aware that he believed he had discovered a revolutionary breakthrough in cancer diagnosis and treatment that would change the way we look at and deal with that deadly disease forever. In my world and his, that's one of the holy grails of our time.' Alexandra paused, waiting for a response.

'Go on,' he said.

'If I give you what you want, what's there to stop you from feeding me to the fish, just as you've obviously done with Cavendish?'

'To begin with, you're worth a lot more to me alive than dead. Cavendish was foolish enough to step over the line; that's why he's no longer with us. You are far too smart for that.' Macbeth pushed his wheelchair out of the cone of light, and once again melted into the shadows. 'Here's my proposal: a top position is waiting for you in my organisation. You can choose the location. We have research centres in many countries. You will have the best equipment and the best people to work with. The recognition attached to your work belongs to you; reputation and fame in scientific circles would be guaranteed. I won't even mention money because that's too obvious. Suffice to say, the material rewards would be beyond your wildest dreams. In short, you come on board – forgive the pun – and work for me.'

'And all of this, I mean my sudden departure from the institute and my abduction, just go away? *This is fantasy!*'

'Not at all,' Macbeth contradicted her. 'Your sudden departure from the institute can easily be explained: you've only been there two days, and you haven't signed a contract yet.' Macbeth paused, watching Alexandra carefully.

*He knows that too*, thought Alexandra, trying to look calm.

'The only reason for your appointment was to carry on the professor's work – right? His notes have disappeared before you arrived; you are in no way implicated. The raison d'être for your appointment has disappeared with them. You owe the institute nothing.'

'And my abduction, how does that fit in? And if I were to join your organisation, how do we explain that?'

'That too is simple. You've been headhunted; it happens all the time. I like the term "headhunted", don't you? Many of our best scientists have come to join us that way.'

'And my abduction? I'm a prisoner here; let's not insult each other with niceties.'

'*Abduction?* What abduction? You are my guest. You have accepted my invitation to spend a few days on our research vessel to give you an opportunity to consider my offer. Leaving your apartment in a hurry is totally consistent with that. Simple. In these matters, time is always of the essence.'

Alexandra had to admit that Macbeth's proposal – while totally outrageous and corrupt – was as shrewd as it was clever. He offered her recognition and possible glory, and a lifestyle beyond her wildest dreams. All of it small change when compared with the staggering fortune he stood to make out of all this, should the professor's discovery become reality. By joining his organisation – obviously with a watertight contract to tie her in – all of her work would belong to Blackburn Pharmaceuticals. That would, of course, include Professor K's discovery, the key to which was most likely in the notebook on the table in front of him. Brilliant! She had no doubt Macbeth could deliver everything he had promised with a click of his fingers. She also realised she had little choice but to accept, for now. But not yet! 'I want to think about it,' she said after a while.

'Of course,' said Macbeth, sensing victory. 'You've had a busy day … and you must be starving,' he added, changing direction. 'We have an excellent kitchen and cellar on board.' Smiling, Macbeth paused. 'Perhaps you would like to take this with you …' he added, lowering his voice.

Alexandra looked at the bundle of papers Macbeth had pushed across the desk towards her. 'What's that?' she asked.

'A copy of the professor's notebook; just in case.'

'Just in case of what?'

'Just in case you decide to start work on it overnight.'

'Are you always that sure of yourself? What if I don't accept?'

'I'm sure there will be no need to consider that painful alternative.'

Just then, the door opened and Carlotta appeared on cue. 'Please take our guest back to her cabin, and make sure our chefs do not disappoint us,' said Macbeth. 'Good night, Dr Delacroix. It's a pleasure to have you on board.'

Taking her time, Alexandra stood up and looked in Macbeth's direction. '*We must always be careful what we wish for,*' she muttered, turning around. 'Good night, Mr Macbeth,' she added quietly and, without saying another word, followed Carlotta out of the room.

# 18

As soon as Carlotta had closed the door behind her and Alexandra found herself alone in her cabin, the enormity of what had happened during the past few hours began to overwhelm her. Her head spinning, she realised her entire life had suddenly changed and hung in the balance.

Lack of sleep and fear can quickly distort reality and lead to panic, and panic is the enemy of reason. Alexandra realised she had to resist this at all cost if she wanted to get through the dark moments and stay rational. Taking deep breaths to calm herself, she walked across to the little writing desk by the window and carefully placed Professor K's notes on the tooled leather top. *The solution to all of this is right in here,* she told herself, *I'm sure of it. All I have to do is find it. Think girl; think! And stay calm.*

Instead of throwing herself into the task, Alexandra decided to take another shower first. Temptation to delve into Professor K's mind resisted. She did some of her best thinking under the shower. Soon the needles of hot water caressing her face and neck had the desired effect; Alexandra began to relax, allowing clarity to return. Clarity brought hope, and hope banished despair.

Alexandra put on the robe she had found in the bathroom and, drying her wet hair with a towel until her scalp tingled, walked across to the little desk. Winding the towel around her head like a turban, she sat down and began to examine Professor K's notes.

By the time the first rays of the morning sun gave the foaming crests of the waves outside a pinkish glow, Alexandra knew exactly what she had to do.

Carlotta knocked on Macbeth's door and entered without waiting for a reply. She knew Macbeth, an early riser, would be sitting at his desk. She also knew he would be pleased to hear what she had to tell him.

'She wants to see you,' said Carlotta.

'Show her in,' said Macbeth, smiling. So far, all was going to plan; his plan.

'You're up early,' said Macbeth, watching Alexandra walk towards him.

'So are you.'

'I sleep very little.'

'I didn't sleep at all. Professor Kozakievicz's findings are extraordinary, just as I expected,' said Alexandra, choosing her words carefully. 'If it all stacks up, we may indeed have the breakthrough in cancer treatment the world has been waiting for. In fact, it could even change the way we look at cancer altogether.'

'Prevention?'

'Could be. And cure.'

'Are you suggesting the holy grail could be within reach, and we may finally be able to tame the Emperor of Darkness?'

'Possibly.'

'*Possibly?* Possibly doesn't sound like a breakthrough to me.'

'There's a problem.'

'Oh?'

'The material in the notes doesn't give us all the answers. It merely shows us the way. A lot more work is needed. Specific work.'

'I thought you were too smart to play games,' said Macbeth, steel in his voice.

'Let's not insult each other. I'm not playing games. That would certainly be foolish. Obviously, I can demonstrate what I've just told you and your scientists can verify the position. It's quite simple really. So, what could I possibly gain by playing games? After all I'm your *guest*, right?'

*Smart girl,* thought Macbeth, *she obviously has a plan.* Instead of becoming angry, Macbeth found to his surprise he was enjoying their duel of wits. A worthy opponent was rare in his world. 'And do you know what that specific work may entail?' asked Macbeth cutting to the chase.

'I do.'

'I thought so. Would you care to tell me?'

'All of Professor K's ideas and findings are based on certain changes in the tissue samples he's collected. He discovered a trend; the samples are the missing link. Without them, we cannot take the next step. He was close, very close, but couldn't pull it all together. That's what he wanted me to do, because he ran out of time.'

'And you could complete his work?'

'Yes, but only with the samples.'

For a while, Macbeth kept playing with the two steel balls in the palm of his right hand without saying anything. *Is she telling the truth, or manipulating me?* he wondered, looking straight at Alexandra. *Or is she clever enough to do both?*

'Do you know where those samples are?' he asked at last, breaking the silence, which was beginning to turn a little awkward.

'The professor hid them.'

'Why?'

'His notes aren't clear, but I think he didn't trust his assistant.'

Macbeth nodded. This did sound plausible.

'Do you know where?'

'The best way to hide a book is in the library – right?'

'What are you telling me?'

'They are buried somewhere in the freezers at the Gordon Institute with thousands of others.'

'Could you find them?'

'I believe so. He left clues …'

'Would you care to elaborate?'

'I would have to retrace his research, step-by-step, especially the experiments. They are all well documented in his notes, and there are other records at the Gordon that would help.'

'Could you?'

'Yes. We worked together before. I'm familiar with his methods and how he thinks – thought,' Alexandra corrected herself, sadness in her voice. 'But it would take some time and would obviously have to be carried out at the institute …'

*Very clever*, thought Macbeth. *The tables have turned and it all makes perfect sense. If she's telling the truth, the way forward is crystal clear.*

Macbeth realised another fresh approach with a new strategy was needed. 'Please join me,' he said, pointing to a table in the corner set for two. 'You must be hungry. We can discuss all this over breakfast.'

'You were expecting someone?' observed Alexandra.

'Yes; you.'

By the time Alexandra returned to her cabin, drained and exhausted, *Calypso* had already changed course and was heading south on her way back to Sydney.

# 19

Jack woke with a start. Rubbing his stiff neck, he turned his head and looked around. Nothing was vaguely familiar. Then slowly, everything came back to him. Dreamlike at first, but as the fog of sleep began to lift he remembered the long night flight from Sydney in The Time Machine's private jet, arriving in Mexico City and meeting Isis in the amazing underground chamber guarded by strange gods. Then he recalled the unexpected conversation with Isis, full of questions and surprises, in front of the Coyolxauhqui stone. *I promised to give her my answer in the morning*, thought Jack, looking for his trousers. *Better get going.*

Jack had tried to call Alexandra several times the night before without success. He reached for his phone on the bedside table, hoping for a message. Nothing. *Bloody time difference*, he thought, and blamed the lack of response on the unreliable Mexican mobile phone reception. Jack quickly got dressed and stepped out onto the terrace.

The sunlight was blinding. Shielding his eyes with his hand, he looked down into the garden. Isis and Lola were kneeling on mats in the courtyard below, their bodies contorted in a way that didn't seem possible. *Yoga*, thought Jack.

'I don't know how they do it,' said a soft voice from behind. Jack turned around and found himself looking at a striking, white-haired woman coming towards him with a glass in her hand. Some women radiate class and style regardless of age, commanding instant admiration from men, and envy from women half their age. Señora Gonzalez, well into her nineties, was one of those. 'I'm Dolores,' said the woman, her voice surprisingly deep, 'I thought you might like some guava juice.'

*The hostess*, thought Jack. *She must have been quite a beauty in her day.* Jack held out his hand. *Sad eyes though.* 'Jack Rogan.'

'I know who you are,' said the old lady, trying to smile. Jack noticed the sadness didn't leave her eyes. 'I've read your books.'

'Ah, reputation. Nowhere to hide. You know my soul then.'

'Perhaps just a little.'

Jack felt instantly at ease. 'What a magnificent home, Señora,' he said, changing the subject. 'When I woke up just then, I thought I must still be dreaming. That underground chamber ... full of treasures.'

'My late husband built the house fifty years ago. He was an archaeologist and an art dealer.'

Jack looked down into the garden.

Isis untangled her legs, arching her back like a subtle bow before rolling forward into a handstand. Standing momentarily quite still, her balance perfect, she made it all appear natural and easy. It was a feat of extraordinary strength and control.

'How do you know Isis?' asked Jack, watching the impressive exercise routine unfolding below. Lola was attacking Isis from behind with a lightning kick that would have floored a less experienced opponent. But not Isis. She sensed it coming and, sidestepping the lethal blow, reached out and took hold of Lola's ankle, her grip vice-like. Yoga had suddenly turned into hand-to-hand combat, reminding Jack of another bout in outback Australia not that long ago, where two deadly foes had tried to kill each other in the ring.

'Isis has one of the finest private collections of Mesoamerican art in the world. My late husband helped her put it together and sourced some of her best pieces.'

Isis wiped her face with a towel, put her arms around Lola and kissed her on the forehead. Then she looked up at the terrace, waved, and taking three steps at a time, ran up the stairs. 'And what have you two been talking about?' she said, catching her breath. She kissed Señora Gonzales on the cheek. 'Good morning, Mamina.'

'Mainly about you,' said Jack.

'He did all the talking,' added Señora Gonzalez, shaking her head. 'I told him nothing.'

'I believe you. You have to watch writers. They are very inquisitive,' said Isis, laughing, 'and most persuasive.'

'You thought it over, Jack?' asked Isis, after the maid had cleared the table. Jack noticed that Isis had only eaten fruit. 'I have to go to the stadium straight away,' Isis prattled on. 'Rehearsals for tonight's performance. A hundred thousand eager fans are waiting; I can't disappoint them. Relentless schedule. We won't have time to talk later.' Isis saw Jack glancing at Señora Gonzalez sitting opposite and smiled. 'I can see you are hesitating; no need to.' Isis reached for the old lady's hand and kissed it. 'Mamina and I have no secrets, Jack. Sooner or later, you'll find out why, so I may as well tell you right now.'

Looking a little puzzled, Jack sat back in his chair, but said nothing.

'But before I do, please let me know what you've decided.'

*Here we go again*, thought Jack, slowly folding his crisp napkin along its creases, *she wants a commitment before telling me the full story*. Jack always tried to take his time and choose his words carefully before making an important decision.

'You sent Lola with your plane halfway around the world to bring me here without giving me a rational explanation as to why you wanted to meet me so urgently. Yet for reasons I now cannot quite explain, I agreed to come along, and did. Then last night you gave me the briefest outline of what happened in London, which only raised more questions. You hinted that you had more to tell me later after I've given you my answer.' Jack placed the neatly folded napkin on the table in front of him. 'Looking at everything you've told me so far objectively, there's precious little for me to go by to make an informed decision.' Jack paused, and looked directly at Isis watching him from across the table. 'Please give me one good reason why I should drop everything and accept your proposal.'

'You're right,' said Isis. 'It's a matter of trust.'

'It's more than that,' Jack contradicted her, 'it's a leap of faith. That's what you are asking of me.'

'I suppose I am.'

'Why?'

'Because of what's at stake here. If you were to accept, you would step into my private world and I would have to show you corners of my life few have ever seen, or could possibly imagine. For this to work, nothing can be off limits. You have to admit that would be a leap of faith – by me – don't you agree?'

'It would,' Jack conceded. 'But why me?'

'Because of who you are.'

'But you don't know me.'

'Perhaps I do.'

'How can you say that? We've just met. We've barely spent an hour or so together so far, and you say you *know* me?' Jack shook his head.

'There are many ways to know a man; you of all people would understand that. Knowing someone has nothing to do with time. Dolores here understands that too, don't you?' said Isis, turning to Señora Gonzales.'

'Perfectly.'

'Are you prepared to let Jack into the hidden corners of your life, because that's almost certainly going to be necessary, should he accept?'

'I am,' said Señora Gonzales.

'I don't understand,' said Jack, looking confused.

'Oh, but you will.'

'How come?'

'Because our lives are intertwined, inextricably.'

'Can you enlighten me?'

'The woman who died in London so horribly the other day … was Dolores' daughter …'

'What?' Surprised, Jack almost shouted.

Isis reached for the old lady's hand again and began to stroke it, her touch gentle and full of love. 'Mamina is my grandmother,' said Isis, her eyes turning misty.

'I'm so sorry,' mumbled Jack, shaking his head. *Another moment of destiny*, he thought, remembering Tristan's words – *you and Isis are destined to meet ... How extraordinary!* Feeling a rush of excitement race to his head, Jack realised it was decision time. The familiar fork in the road. Things were moving at lightning speed, and time was quickly running out.

'Don't look so worried, Jack,' said Isis. 'A few words scratched into an old piece of discarded furniture you stumbled across on an abandoned farm sent you on quite a journey not that long ago – right? Look where it ended up; you found Anna. Against all odds. And then there was the old photograph buried in the ruins of that cottage after the bushfire; look what happened. Is this really all that different?'

'Point taken. You've obviously read my books; I'm flattered.'

'I judge a man by his deeds,' said Isis, 'and how he thinks. Jack the man, is displayed in his books for all to see. All one has to do is look.'

Taken somewhat aback, Jack shook his head. 'Interesting ... I never thought of my books in that way ... And then there's my publisher,' he added, 'I have commitments. I can't just—'

'I'm sure that can be resolved,' interrupted Isis, brushing the objection aside.

'It's not that simple, I have a—'

'It is; trust me,' Isis interrupted again.

'How can you say that?'

'We own the company.'

'You what?' exclaimed Jack. 'You own the publishing house I'm contracted to?'

'Yes.'

'That's a bit of a lightning bolt,' said Jack, trying to come to terms with what he had just been told. The implications were as far-reaching as they were surprising. Suddenly, the well-timed phone call from Rebecca made perfect sense. No wonder his publisher wanted him to go along with Lola's request. *Another puzzle solved*, he thought. *There's so much more behind all this. Be careful!*

Señora Gonzales sensed Jack's unease. He obviously had reservations and was getting cold feet. It was time to play her trump card.

'A moment ago, you asked for one good reason why you should accept our proposal,' she said, her voice sounding hoarse. 'I can give you one.'

'You can?' asked Jack. 'Then please do.'

Señora Gonzales took her time before answering, letting the tension grow. Then she mentioned a name Jack hadn't heard for a long time.

Jack just kept staring at the old lady, his face a mask of disbelief and confusion. 'I don't understand,' he said at last. 'What could he possibly have to do with all this?'

'Hidden corners of our lives,' said Señora Gonzales. 'That is all I can tell you, for now.'

*Another one of those watershed moments*, thought Jack, his mind racing. *Go forward, or walk away?*

'You thrive on a challenge, Jack, like I thrive on the energy generated by my fans,' said Isis. 'This is a leap of faith into the unknown for both of us. What will it be? Are we going to jump together?'

Jack looked first at Señora Gonzales, and then at Isis, the promise of excitement and adventure irresistible. 'Yes,' he said at last, holding out his hand, 'let's do it.'

# 20

*Calypso* dropped anchor in Broken Bay – a short distance north of Sydney – just before midnight on Sunday. Two hours later, Alexandra was back in Jack's apartment.

'You do know what to do?' said Van Cleef, putting Alexandra's small suitcase on the lounge next to her. It was more of a statement than a question, the tone cynical and patronising. Alexandra nodded. 'Let's go over it once more, just to make sure. You go to work in the morning after a lovely weekend away. Nothing happened. You find the professor's notebook in his laboratory among his papers and begin to work on the project that brought you here.' Van Cleef walked over to Alexandra and placed his hand on the back of her neck – the threat obvious – making her skin crawl. 'You report to us daily by email; understood?'

Alexandra nodded again. 'Don't disappoint us, Dr Delacroix. Mr Macbeth hates disappointments. Here's your passport, your phone and the good professor's notebook.' Van Cleef placed the three items on the coffee table. 'Ah, I almost forgot ...' Van Cleef paused for effect. 'There's a little surprise waiting for you in your bank account. Compliments of Mr Macbeth. Such a generous man. Look at it as an advance.'

Towering over Alexandra sitting on the lounge, Van Cleef squared his massive shoulders. 'And please remember,' he said, lowering his voice, 'we have eyes and ears everywhere.' Van Cleef turned around and slowly walked to the door. 'Good to have you on board, Dr Delacroix. Make sure it stays that way. Falling overboard can be very unpleasant, as Mr Cavendish recently found out. Disappointing Mr Macbeth has dire consequences, but a smart woman like you knows that already. Don't get up. I'll see myself out.'

For a while, Alexandra just sat there, hoping it had all been just a bad dream. However, Professor K's little notebook on the table in front of her reminded her it wasn't so. *What am I going to do?* Alexandra asked herself, feeling frightened and terribly alone. *Jack isn't here; I have no one.*

Running her fingers nervously through her hair, she kept staring at her phone. Suddenly, it looked like a lifeline. When in serious trouble, turn to the most resourceful person you know and you can trust. For Alexandra, the choice was as simple as it was obvious: Countess Kuragin, her aunt.

Feeling better, Alexandra picked up her phone, selected her aunt's number and pressed the button.

*Pegasus* circled Mexico City in a wide, spiralling arc, climbed quickly to its usual cruising altitude and then turned northeast on its way to London. Lola handed the controls back to the pilot, unbuckled her seatbelt and lifted herself out of the front seat. 'Thanks, Joe, twice in a couple of days is more flying than I managed in the last six months. She's all yours.'

Jack was sitting in the back of the plane going over his notes. He was trying to organise the little he had found out so far by putting pen to paper, an old habit. It wasn't much except for one curious thing: Señora Gonzales' cryptic parting words. 'If you look carefully, you may find the answers in the hotel on Place Vendôme,' she had said, squeezing Jack's hand, the sadness in her voice still ringing loudly in his ears. *What on earth did she mean by that?* He asked himself. *And how would she know?* Shaking his head, Jack wrote down *hotel on Place Vendôme* and went over his notes again. Slim pickings. This didn't trouble him too much; most of his assignments began that way, often with far less. Keeping an open mind and beginning with the obvious was the best way to start, and what appeared obvious here was to make contact with Isis' well-connected lawyer.

Returning to the scene of the crime as quickly as possible before the scent went cold was also imperative. Isis had put *Pegasus* and Lola at Jack's disposal, unconditionally. This was a luxury he wasn't used to.

'I have already contacted Sir Charles,' said Lola. 'He will meet us at the airport.'

'Excellent. We'll go straight to the Elms' residence where it all happened and start from there.'

'If they let us,' said Lola.

'What do you mean?'

'You'll see.'

Jack's mobile sitting on top of his iPad suddenly came to life, the familiar ring tone sounding surprisingly shrill and strange in the confines of the cabin, humming with the noise of the powerful engines. It was the first time his phone had rung in days.

'Alexandra!' said Jack, answering the phone. 'I tried to call you; did you get my messages?'

'Yes, just now. I …' Her voice faded away, banished by an annoying crackle and a monotonous buzzing noise. Jack held up his phone and shook it.

'We need to talk, Jack,' said Alexandra, drifting back. 'I'm in serious trouble …'

'What did you say?'

'Trouble; I need your help.'

'I can hardly hear you,' Jack shouted.

'Speak to Katerina; she'll explain.' Then the voice went dead and all of Jack's attempts to call back were unsuccessful. The plane was approaching a storm and passing through turbulence, wreaking havoc with the electronics. The pilot asked for all phones and devices to be turned off.

*That's it for now*, thought Jack, a worried look on his face. *I wonder what's happened.*

'What was all that about?' asked Lola, mixing another vodka martini.

'Not sure, but it didn't sound good.'

'Trouble with the girlfriend?'

'No, nothing like that. And she isn't my girlfriend.'

'Of course not.' Lola handed Jack his drink. 'Perhaps this will help?'

'It may, as long as I don't have to use the swivel stick.'

'Are Australian men always so timid?'

'I don't know what you're talking about,' said Jack, sipping his drink; his third. 'However, after what I've seen this morning, I would be risking life and limb …'

'You're not into Taekwondo, I take it?' Lola unbuttoned Jack's shirt.

'No, I leave that to the athletic women in my life.'

'Is that wise?'

'Absolutely. I know my limitations,' said Jack, feeling a little drowsy.

Lola ran the tips of her fingers slowly down Jack's chest. 'Is this safer, you think?' she asked, unbuckling his belt.

'I doubt it.'

'You like living dangerously?'

'Do I have a choice?'

'Not really.'

'Then why ask?'

'As Hanna isn't here, you should be able to take this in your stride.'

'I'll do my best.'

'You better. One kick could ruin you for life; remember that!'

'Ouch! Performance through intimidation?' said Jack.

'Something like that. The power of fear … can do wonders …'

'In what way?'

'To enhance a girl's pleasure, of course.'

'But one has to rise to the occasion …'

'Exactly,' said Lola, nibbling Jack's ear.

'And stand up for what you believe in.'

'Precisely. And what can I do to stiffen your resolve?'

'I'm sure you'll think of something.'

'You bet I will.'

Jack looked at his watch and calculated the time difference. *Should be about seven in the morning in France*, he thought, reaching for his shirt. *Time to call the countess.*

112

Careful not to wake Lola, Jack got up, walked to the back of the cabin and dialled the familiar number of the chateau. Jack had made an error; it was only five.

Countess Kuragin was asleep in her bedroom when her maid tapped her gently on the shoulder. 'The call you've been expecting, Madame,' said the maid. 'Mr Rogan is on the phone.' The countess got out of bed, put on her dressing gown and hurried to her study to take the call.

'Jack, where on earth are you?'

'Somewhere above the Atlantic on my way to London.'

'London? Why?'

'It's a long story.'

'You and your stories; what an exciting life you lead! I thought you were in Sydney on vacation. Never mind. This is serious, Jack. Alexandra called me last night; she's is in big trouble.'

'How come?'

'I'll tell you; just listen to this ...'

For the next half hour, Countess Kuragin recounted everything Alexandra had told her about her abduction and her extraordinary encounter with Macbeth on the *Calypso*.

'I can't believe you're telling me this,' said Jack, after the countess had finished. 'I only saw her a couple of days ago. This sounds like something out of a James Bond movie.'

'What are we going to do, Jack?'

'I can't go back right now.'

'She needs help – urgently.'

'I can see that. Let me think ... I have an idea ...'

'Don't take too long,' said the countess.

'Understood.'

'What would we do without you?'

'Leave it with me. I'll call you later. And tell Tristan ...'

'Tell him what?'

'He was right about Isis.'

# 21

Heathrow airport was chaotic as usual. Due to the heavy fog hovering over London like a malevolent blanket ready to smother the waking city, *Pegasus* had to join a host of other planes in a tight holding pattern for over an hour before finally being cleared to land.

Looking dapper in his customary dark navy pinstriped suit, crisp white shirt and polka dot bowtie, Sir Charles was waiting for them with his driver in the customs hall. 'I have bad news,' he said, shaking Jack's hand, 'We are not allowed to enter the Elms' residence as you requested. Off limits, I'm afraid; crime scene. Very hush-hush.'

Jack shrugged; he had expected something like that.

'However, I've some good news as well,' continued the ebullient Sir Charles. 'The officer in charge of the case will meet us in my office this morning for a briefing. He's MI5.'

'How did you manage that?' asked Lola, who obviously knew Sir Charles very well.

'I pulled a few strings, called in a couple of favours, made a subtle threat or two; the usual. But I must confess; it wasn't easy. As you can imagine, this is a very sensitive case and the authorities are very tight-lipped about everything. Cone of silence; hush-hush, so don't expect too much.'

'I never do,' said Jack, enjoying the ride in the comfortable back seat of Sir Charles' vintage Rolls Royce.

The bespectacled, middle-aged secretary gave Jack and Lola a stern, disapproving look as they followed Sir Charles into his inner sanctum. Located in an imposing building just around the corner from the Inns of Court, Sir Charles' office was a reflection of his clientele: exclusive, conservative, establishment, and very rich.

Sensing the secretary's disapproval, Jack gave her his best smile. '*Moneypenny of the Old Bailey, you think?*' whispered Jack, turning to Lola.

'*Behave yourself!*' hissed Lola, '*You make fun of her, she might poison our tea.*'

'What an exciting place.'

'Exciting? Dangerous more likely. Better look out.'

'Why should I worry when I have you to protect me?'

'*Hush!*'


*Great furniture*, thought Jack, admiring the splendid pieces adorning Sir Charles' huge office. Keenly interested in antiques and still smarting from the loss of his own collection when his house had been torched by a bikie gang the year before, Jack noticed such things.

Subdued lighting, Victorian mahogany bookcases crammed with leather-bound tomes, a grandfather clock ticking away in the corner, well-worn Chesterfields and a whiff of cigar smoke reminded Jack of another lawyer's chambers back in Sydney: Marcus Carrington QC's eccentric room. Three years earlier, Jack and Carrington had crossed paths in an extraordinary case involving a Nazi war criminal, secret Swiss bank accounts and Islamic terrorists.

*Marcus would feel right at home here*, thought Jack. *Except for the cricket.* Carrington's chambers were full of antiquities and ancient texts; Sir Charles, however, was obviously an ardent cricket fan. The walls of his office were lined with photographs of smiling cricket teams at Lords. Taking pride of place behind his massive, intricately carved oak desk was a glass case full of cricket memorabilia. Shiny cricket balls, floppy caps and cricket bats signed by the heroes of the game were Sir Charles' treasured reminders of past triumphs over the West Indies, the South Africans, and those annoying Aussies.

'Lords, 1994,' said Jack, pointing to one of the photographs near the door, 'the Aussies almost won the Ashes that year.'

'You're a cricket fan too?' said Sir Charles.

'My dad gave me a little cricket bat before I could walk … Apparently, to my mother's horror, I used to chew on it all the time. It gave me a taste for cricket, I suppose.'

'All right, you two,' said Lola, cutting short the exchange. She knew once Sir Charles started on cricket, there was no stopping him. 'Let's not forget why we're here, gentlemen?'

'We must have lunch in my club some time,' said Sir Charles, 'and have a chat about the game. No women allowed,' he added, lowering his voice. 'Last bastion.'

'You're on.'

'Splendid.'

As the grandfather clock chimed eleven, Sir Charles' secretary appeared and announced Daniel Cross, the officer in charge of the Elms' case.

*At least he's punctual*, thought Jack, sizing up the impeccably dressed man with an inscrutable face, shaking Sir Charles' hand. The body language was obvious; the man was here under protest. Cross had received a call from his superior officer the night before, telling him to go to Sir Charles' office for a briefing. 'Cooperate, but don't capitulate,' he was told. 'And find out what you can about this journalist chappie. We certainly don't want a curious newshound sniffing around, putting his nose into the investigation.' Cross knew exactly what that meant.

'Allow me to explain who Mr Rogan is, and why he's here,' said Sir Charles, introducing Jack.

'I know who Mr Rogan is,' said Cross, a hint of contempt in his voice. He turned to Jack and looked directly at him. 'You found Anna Popov last year,' he said, 'against all odds, I believe, and wrote a book about it; much anticipated and highly acclaimed. You succeeded where all the authorities failed. Are you hoping to do the same here, Mr Rogan?'

'Not at all,' interjected Sir Charles, before Jack could reply. 'Mr Rogan has been retained by my client, George Elms, as his representative. As you know, Mr Elms – Isis, as he is better known – is presently on tour, and is therefore unable to attend to this tragic matter personally. Obviously, my client wants to know what happened to his parents, and Mr Rogan is here to do just that on his behalf.'

'And to have you as his representative, Sir Charles, is not enough for your client?' Cross shot back.

'It is a choice my client made. I have to respect that, and I invite you to do the same,' said Sir Charles frostily.

Cross didn't like being put in his place, but he had his orders. 'I see,' he said. 'Lucrative pop concerts obviously have priority over family tragedy.'

'We all conduct our lives in different ways, Mr Cross. Is this a morality class, or are you going to brief us?'

'Before I can go any further,' said Cross, ignoring the rebuke, 'I need an undertaking from you all that what I'm about to tell you will be kept strictly confidential, and will only be disclosed to your client, Sir Charles, and no one else.'

'Understood,' said Sir Charles.

'I have no problem with that,' said Jack.

'And can we count on you as well, Miss Rodriguez?' said Cross.

'Certainly. I'm Isis' PA—'

'Confidante, bodyguard and pilot as well,' interjected Cross. He knew saying 'lover' might have taken things a little too far. He liked to put his subjects off balance by showing them just how well informed he really was. It made ensuring their cooperation so much easier.

'My client likes to surround himself with competent people,' said Sir Charles.

'I see we understand each other.' Cross reached for his briefcase. He opened it, took out a few photographs and placed them carefully in a neat row on Sir Charles' desk in front of him. 'In addition to what is public knowledge, this is something you may find interesting.'

Jack leant forward to get a better look. Taken from different angles, the photos showed the burnt out hulk of a vehicle parked in front of what looked like the ruins of an abandoned warehouse or factory.

'What are we looking at here?' asked Sir Charles.

'The getaway car, or what's left of it. It was found just outside London two hours after the alarm went off—'

'A stolen courier van; we already know this,' interrupted Jack, unable to hide his impatience.

'Quite,' said Cross. 'But what you don't know is what we found inside the vehicle.' Cross paused, letting the tension grow. 'Four men shot dead at point blank range.'

'The perpetrators?' asked Jack, surprised.

'It would appear so, but we cannot be absolutely certain at this stage.'

'Any IDs?' asked Lola.

'The bodies were almost completely obliterated by the fire. A lot of accelerant was used; professional job.'

'No IDs then?' said Sir Charles.

'We are working on it.'

'Does this rule out terrorists, you think?' said Jack.

'What makes you say that?' asked Cross.

'Terrorists carry out their own assignments, and then claim responsibility. What happened here is the opposite. Someone went to great lengths to distance himself from the crime and cover his tracks. A team of professionals was engaged here to carry out a specific task; complex and very well planned—'

'And were then almost immediately eliminated to make sure that no trail of any kind was left behind,' interjected Sir Charles. 'Very neat. An expensive, ruthless and carefully planned operation.'

'And a carefully planned operation like this has a purpose. This is not a random home invasion, or a burglary gone wrong,' said Lola.

'That is precisely what we think,' said Cross.

'Any ideas as to who and why?' asked Jack.

'I was hoping you or your client might be able to help us here.'

Jack shook his head, watching Cross carefully out of the corner of his eye. 'It's too early for that. Lord Elms held a high office in Her Majesty's Government,' continued Jack, changing direction. 'Was he involved in any specific project at the moment? I mean, working on something sensitive or controversial perhaps? Legislation; parliamentary committees; inquiries; anything like that?' Jack noticed a flicker of interest in Cross' demeanour. It only lasted for an instant, but it told him he was asking the right questions.

'I'm not at liberty to disclose that,' Cross answered curtly.

'Not very helpful,' said Jack, trying to provoke Cross into giving something away.

'But completely understandable,' Sir Charles stepped in, trying to diffuse the growing tension.

'I don't think we can take the matter much further at the moment.' Cross gathered up the photographs, slipped them into his briefcase and stood up. 'I'll be in touch, Sir Charles.' Cross turned to look at Jack. 'You might find cracking this nut a little harder and a little more dangerous than finding Anna Popov. If I were you, I would leave it to the experts, Mr Rogan. Good day.' With that, Cross left the room, closing the door quietly behind him.

'What an annoying little man,' said Lola.

'Spooks are like that,' said Jack. 'Full of self-importance, skulduggery and cloak and dagger stuff. I've seen it all before. But I believe he told us something important, albeit unwittingly.'

'What do you mean?' Sir Charles asked.

'An incident like this doesn't happen in a vacuum. I think the authorities believe it has something to do with Lord Elms' work, and so do I,' said Jack, thoughtfully rubbing the white scar on his temple. It was a habit he had developed after cheating death a year ago in the lair of a notorious outlaw bikie gang. 'If only we could find out ...'

'I may be able to help you there,' said Sir Charles.

'How?'

'I have friends in high places ... But enough of all this for now. You've had a long flight and must be tired. Are you going to stay at Georgie's place?' asked Sir Charles, turning to Lola.

'Yes, it's all arranged.'

'Would you care to join me for dinner this evening, Mr Rogan?' said Sir Charles, showing Jack and Lola to the door.

'Delighted.'

'Just you and me ... I have something to show you,' said Sir Charles, lowering his voice. 'I'll send the car round to pick you up.'

'Sounds intriguing.'

'It is; more than you can possibly imagine.'

# 22

Alexandra put down her handbag and looked around. Professor K's lab was exactly as she had left it on Friday. It felt strange starting an important new chapter in her career in the footsteps of a dead man, however great and admired he had been. Professor K's shadow was everywhere; she could feel it, touch it almost. Alexandra reached into her handbag, pulled out Professor K's little notebook and placed it on the desk in front of her.

*It's all in here*, she thought. *Ideas that can change the world crammed into a little notebook*. Alexandra ran the tips of her fingers over the well-worn cover and opened the book. The familiar, spidery handwriting of her friend and mentor brought a sad smile to her face. *I promised to carry the torch. I promised to be his heir*. Then she remembered her abduction and the strange, almost surreal late-night encounter with Macbeth in his cabin on the *Calypso*. *Did it all really happen?* she asked herself. Then a shadowy image of the blond man standing in front of her in Jack's apartment floated into her mind's eye. Powerful, threatening. *Don't disappoint us*, she heard him say, *Mr Macbeth hates disappointments*. Alexandra could still feel the touch of the man's hands on the back of her neck, the disconcerting sensation sending an icy shiver of fear rippling down her spine. *Remember, we have eyes and ears everywhere*. Part of her still refused to believe it had all really happened. However, the little notebook in front of her told a different story.

Alexandra looked up; someone was standing in the doorway.

'Are you ready, Dr Delacroix?' asked the young scientist from Sri Lanka she had inherited as her assistant. 'We are starting in ten minutes.'

'Yes; I'll be there in a moment,' Alexandra replied, grateful for the interruption, but embarrassed she couldn't remember the man's name. Her first two days at the institute were still somewhat of a blur. However, everything was slowly beginning to come back to her. The institute was holding a little memorial gathering in Professor K's honour in the auditorium that morning, and she had been asked by the CEO to say a few words. It would be a good opportunity for her to meet her new colleagues, he had said, and introduce herself. Alexandra had readily agreed, but that was before the turbulent events of the weekend that had changed everything by casting a disturbing shadow over her future.

*Behave as if nothing happened*, Alexandra heard her aunt, the countess, counsel her over the phone. *Everything must appear normal.* Jack had told her the same thing during their long telephone conversation earlier that morning, telling her that help was on the way. Unfortunately, he didn't say when or how. Nevertheless, just hearing his voice had been reassuring, even though he was half a world away. Jack's calm manner, unfazed by the amazing chain of events they had talked about, made sure she no longer felt quite so alone. Alexandra decided the best way to handle the situation was to channel all of her energies into her work and relegate all else to a back corner of her mind to be dealt with later.

Discipline and iron-willed self-control had seen Alexandra through many a crisis before. Taking a deep breath, she stood up, locked Professor K's notebook into the safe, and then took the lift down to the auditorium in the basement.

The auditorium was already packed and all the seats were taken. Several hundred scientists and staff had come to honour Professor K. The CEO saw Alexandra standing at the back and waved. Alexandra walked down to the podium and sat next to him.

'Thank you for doing this,' said the CEO, obviously pleased to see her. 'You seem to have known him better than anyone else.'

Alexandra nodded, finding herself suddenly thrust into the spotlight with a sea of faces looking expectantly in her direction. The speech she had planned and intended to prepare over the weekend should have been in her head by now, but it wasn't there. Alexandra knew she would be judged by how she conducted herself during the next hour. Her entire future at the institute hinged on it. Thankfully, she was an experienced public speaker who knew how to improvise. She decided to let her love and admiration for Professor K and her passion for her profession and his work do the talking.

The CEO gave a short speech first, then one of the directors of the institute said a few words, followed by two professors. Alexandra heard none of it. She was mentally preparing her own speech. It wasn't until the CEO returned to the lectern and introduced her that she realised it was her turn.

Walking to the microphone to give a speech can be a very long walk. But with each step, Alexandra felt calmer and a strange sense of peace descended upon her. *He's walking with me*, she thought, and suddenly everything became clear. She knew exactly what she would say.

'Ladies and gentlemen, because I've just arrived a few days ago, I really don't know any of you – yet,' began Alexandra. 'However, in a strange way we are all united by what has brought us here this morning. We are here to honour a man. Not just any man, but a man I'm sure all of us loved, respected and admired. To me, he was not only a true friend and mentor, but an inspiration.'

For the next half hour, Alexandra spoke about Professor K and his work with a passion and warmth – often sprinkled with humour – that had everyone in the room spellbound. She recalled funny stories, and sad ones, describing an extraordinary man with an extraordinary mind who had a vision for science and mankind.

'What sets a true scientist apart are certain special qualities. First and foremost, he must have a sense of adventure and love of the unknown. Exploring the mystery and wonder of life, understanding its beauty and its terror must be at the very centre of his being. Professor K certainly had all of these qualities, but he had a lot more: he had a vision ...'

Alexandra paused, searching for the right words. While her English wasn't that of a native speaker, her French accent gave her pronunciation an endearing quality. 'He believed that our generation would be the last generation to die of cancer,' continued Alexandra.

'He was convinced that those coming after us may die *with* cancer, but not *of* cancer. He believed that we are about to conquer the Emperor of Darkness, as he liked to call the ancient foe, and that a breakthrough was imminent. I firmly believe he was right.

'True genius never dies. It is passed on to others to follow and build upon. Professor K may have left us, but his ideas and dreams live on – right here in this very place he loved so much and where many of those ideas originated. Let him guide and inspire us. There's no better way to honour a fellow scientist.'

Momentarily overcome by emotion as she remembered her friend, Alexandra bowed her head and just stood there, motionless and silent, her striking red hair shining like a beacon. Then she turned away from the lectern and slowly walked back to her seat.

For a long moment, there was complete silence in the crowded auditorium, and then the room erupted in enthusiastic applause. What had begun as a sad and solemn occasion had turned into a celebration of an exceptional life and hope for a better future.

'Inspirational, Dr Delacroix,' said the CEO, escorting Alexandra back to the lifts. 'Good to have you on board.'

# 23

The Time Machine's London headquarters – 'Georgie's digs' – as Sir Charles liked to call it, turned out to be a converted nineteenth-century bond store right on the Thames, not far from the Tower Bridge. Complete with recording studio, offices, underground parking, resident staff, guest accommodation and a spectacular penthouse overlooking the river, it was The Time Machine's state-of-the-art nerve centre. It even had an in-house restaurant with seating for fifty, complete with twenty-four seven room service and a communications facility that would have made the BBC envious. Industrial chic at its very best. Functional, trendy, secure and totally original.

'I didn't quite expect this,' said Jack, standing next to Lola in the lift taking them to the top floor.

'You ain't seen nothin' yet,' joked Lola. 'Wait for the penthouse. We are staying in it.'

Silently, the lift doors opened.

'Wow!' Jack took in the breathtaking view of the London skyline. The penthouse – a two-storey, open-plan steel and glass cube – looked like an art gallery perched on top of an industrial complex. One part of the large space was divided by a huge canvas. Reaching from the marble floor to the glass ceiling two stories above, the painting reminded Jack of Jackson Pollock's *Blue Poles*. Other, smaller paintings were displayed along galleries linked by exposed glass stairs and steel bridges crisscrossing the open space, with the odd bronze bust of a Roman emperor or Greek philosopher thrown in to enhance the eclectic collection. In pride of place on a ledge just above the lift, a stunning Maori war canoe – complete with paddles – conjured up images of cannibals, bloody raids and brutal death.

'Isis likes to surround herself with art and curios,' said Lola. 'It inspires her.'

Jack looked at the massive reclining stone Buddha greeting them at the lift. *How on earth did they get him up here?* he pondered, shaking his head.

'Isis' suite is up there at the top; the guest accommodation is right here.' Lola opened a glass door. 'This is yours.'

'All of it?'

'Yes.'

'This looks like a Picasso,' said Jack, pointing to the painting above the bed.

'It is.'

'I should have guessed. First a shower, then a few phone calls.'

'Don't forget your dinner with Sir Charles. Better brush up on your cricket.'

'You reckon it'll be a test? Colonial boy from Down Under meets establishment in the Old Country?'

'Could be.'

'Do I have to wear a dinner suit?'

'I doubt it.'

'Good; I don't own one. Never have.'

Jack threw his duffel bag on the bed and began to unbutton his shirt. Lola walked over to him, put her arms around his neck and kissed him on the cheek. '*I like your style,*' she whispered. 'Now, let's have that shower together, shall we?'

'You're on, but only if you scrub my back.'

'What's it worth?'

'Why don't you come and find out?'

Sir Charles' chauffeur collected Jack at seven o'clock sharp and took him back to the office. Sir Charles had a small but comfortable flat on the floor above. He preferred staying in London during the week, as the family home was in the country. He left the running of the mansion to his wife and only went there on weekends. The small flat and his club were his domain. It was an amicable arrangement refined by forty years of marriage.

'We are dining here this evening; I hope you don't mind.' Sir Charles pointed to a table set for two by the dormer window overlooking the Old Bailey. 'More private that way,' he added. 'Scotch?'

'Yes, thanks. I didn't think you invited me here to talk about cricket.'

'No, I didn't. I have something to show you. Something quite extraordinary that may throw some light on what really happened.' Sir Charles paused, and lifted his glass. 'Cheers.'

'If you wanted to make me curious, you've succeeded.'

'What our pompous Mr Cross doesn't know is this: Just before Lady Elms passed away, she briefly regained consciousness and spoke to her son.'

Jack looked up, surprised. 'Oh?'

'A few words only, incoherent mostly, but she did manage to direct him to a secret hiding place at Clarendon Hall only she and Georgie knew about.'

'A hiding place? How intriguing. But why?'

'To find something,' said Sir Charles.

'What?'

'Hidden skeletons in the ancestral cupboard, is my guess. Every family has some.'

'What are we to make of it?' asked Jack.

'Not sure, but perhaps this will help.' Sir Charles pointed to his desk.

'What is it?'

'Isis calls it "whispers from the grave". See for yourself.'

Lola was still awake and working on her computer when Jack walked into the penthouse at three am. 'Did you pass the cricket exam? Must have been quite a night,' she said, pointing to her watch.

'It was, but not in the way you might expect.'

'I had no idea a bat and ball could be that exciting.'

'We didn't talk about cricket; not a word in fact.'

'Secret men's business?'

'In a way.'

'Care to tell me?'

'In the morning. If I don't get some sleep, I'll keel over.'

'Keeping a girl is suspense like that isn't nice ...'

'I'm buggered. Showering with you is very exhausting.'

'Is that a complaint?'

'Not as such.'

'That's a relief.'

There's a lot to take in ...'

'Not the party boy I thought you were,' teased Lola.

'I was reading all night. Using a magnifying glass most of the time ...'

'A little more interesting than cricket, I suppose.'

'I was trying to make sense of a puzzle. My eyes are burning and my head is spinning. Sir Charles' brandy didn't help,' added Jack, rubbing his stiff neck.

'Did you solve it?'

'No, I'm more confused now than I was at the start. Yet ...' Jack kicked off his shoes, 'I think Sir Charles knows a lot more than he's prepared to share.'

'What makes you say that?'

'Just a hunch. I think he was testing me.'

'How odd. Did you pass?'

'Not sure. I'm off to bed. By the way ... I have a surprise for you.'

'I like surprises.'

'You are going to meet a Russian countess and an extraordinary boy. Interested?'

'Absolutely. When?'

'Today. We're off to France in a few hours.'

# PART II
## *DE MEDICINA*

"Surgeons can cut out everything except cause."

*Herbert M. Shelton*

# Deep in the jungle, Yucatan Peninsula:
# 1355 AD

The drums stopped beating and the conch shell trumpets fell silent. Mesmerised, the worshippers watched in awe as the Tlacatecuhtli lifted his arms up high and looked up at the stars blazing in the night sky above. Even the jungle appeared to obey his command and for a moment, held its noisy breath.

'Let it begin,' said the Tlacatecuhtli, looking like a god in his resplendent cloak of ocelot skins and feathers. As warrior-priest, astrologer, healer and 'chief of men', he presided over all the important ceremonies in the land, especially human sacrifices.

Another priest wearing a tall helmet shaped like the beak of a bird of prey stepped out of the shadows, knelt down in front him and held up a basket. The Tlacatecuhtli lifted the lid, looked inside and smiled. He always felt a surge of tremendous excitement race through his veins every time he set eyes on the sacred skull. It was his link to the gods and the source of his power. He reached inside the basket and touched the skull with trembling fingers. Then, holding the heavy skull with both hands, he lifted it carefully out of the basket.

The worshippers gasped. Carved out of solid crystal and transparent like glass, the spectacular skull looked almost alive as the Tlacatecuhtli held it up for all to see. According to legend, the crystal skull was a gift from the gods, and the Tlacatecuhtli was its custodian.

The Tlacatecuhtli turned slowly around and, holding the crystal skull above his head, began the steep climb to the top of the stone pyramid looming large and ominous in the dark, like a stairway to an angry heaven. The worshippers began to chant, their voices rising like a prayer pleading with the gods to save their hero.

The altar at the top was surrounded by torches wedged into gaps between the large stones, sending flickering shadows gliding across the polished blocks like an army of ghosts rushing into battle to face the demons of the night.

The Tlacatecuhtli reached the narrow platform high above the impenetrable forest canopy and, catching his breath, looked around.

A naked young man – drugged and in a stupor – lay on the massive stone altar with his arms tied firmly to the slab. The Tlacatecuhtli walked over to him and carefully placed the crystal skull next to his head. *The living and the dead*, he thought, admiring the lifelike skull reflecting the dancing flames of the torches.

Everything needed for the procedure was laid out next to the young warrior on the slab, as tradition demanded. As an experienced healer, the Tlacatecuhtli knew exactly what was required. The large, black, razor-sharp knife fashioned out of obsidian – volcanic glass – sparkled like the eye of a malevolent demon waiting for a sacrifice. Usually, the demon would not have been disappointed. As chief priest in charge of sacrifices, the Tlacatecuhtli had used the knife countless times before to cut out many a living heart to appease the cruel gods lusting for human blood.

This time, however, he was facing a much more difficult and dangerous task. Instead of extinguishing life, he had to save one. And not just any life. He had to use his powers and his skills as a healer to save the life of the king's son – a celebrated hero. The young warrior had fought and won many a battle for his people and provided armies of defeated enemies needed to feed the bloodthirsty gods. And all of these captives had been sacrificed on the very same altar upon which he was now awaiting his own fate.

A terrible illness had struck him down the year before. His powerful body had almost withered away and something inside his head was sending him mad. Another priest, a famous magician, had opened up the young hero's skull, thereby easing the pressure on the brain caused by a large tumour. At first, all had seemed to go well. The young warrior recovered and quickly regained his strength. The people rejoiced. However, a few months later, the dreaded illness returned, more vicious than ever. This was seen as a sign that the gods were displeased. The magician was put to death.

The Tlacatecuhtli knew exactly what was at stake. If he failed to save the young warrior's life, he would forfeit his own. That was the law. However, unlike his hapless predecessor, he had a secret, powerful army of helpers – medicinal jungle plants – he could call upon to defeat the dreaded enemy inside the young man's head. With the help of sacred knowledge carefully guarded by the Tlacatecuhtli through the ages and handed down from generation to generation, he would succeed where the magician had failed. In the cruel world of the Aztecs, violent death and oblivion were never far away. Human life was cheap, and pleasing the gods was the only way to survive.

The Tlacatecuhtli let his splendid ocelot cloak slip from his shoulders and took off his headdress. He was ready to begin the operation. First, he reached for a torch and purified the knife with fire until it was almost too hot to touch. Then, holding the patient's shaved head with one hand, he slowly traced the outline of the previous incisions with the sharp tip of the knife and carefully applied pressure until he could feel the blade cut through the bone. The patient moaned and opened his eyes, staring unseeingly at his tormentor before his eyes rolled back and his mind retreated into the merciful darkness within.

Working quickly now, the Tlacatecuhtli completed the incisions. Then he folded back the skin, removed a square piece of bone and exposed the brain. The large tumour was right there in front of him. Normally, that would have been the end of the procedure, but not this time. The Tlacatecuhtli reached for a small stone bowl on the slab next to him. It contained a thick paste the colour of mud, which he spread evenly over the open wound with the tip of the knife. Satisfied, he applied another soothing salve and covered the head with large, medicinal leaves, which he tied together at the back of the patient's neck like a bandage. The operation was complete.

The Tlacatecuhtli rose, his naked chest covered in tiny beads of perspiration glistening like pearls, and held up the crystal skull once more for all to see. As the mighty roar of the jubilant worshippers rose like thunder from below, the Tlacatecuhtli glimpsed immortality, and for a fleeting moment, he felt like a god.

The wound healed and the king's son made a full recovery. Due to the secret paste the Tlacatecuhtli had applied, the tumour retreated and did not return. This momentous event was recorded in a sacred text, which was placed next to the crystal skull in a hidden chamber deep inside the pyramid. It was also commemorated with a relief cut into the stone altar that paid homage to the Tlacatecuhtli as one of the great healers of his time. It depicted the operation and a heart-shaped jungle plant, the root of which had been ground into a thick paste, which had killed the tumour and saved the young warrior's life.

# The Ritz, Paris: December 1940

Reichsmarschall Hermann Göring, Hitler's second-in-command, swept into the sumptuous dining room with his entourage of senior officers and was shown to the table reserved for the Germans. Since the occupation of Paris on 14th June 1940, the Germans had all but taken over the famous hotel on Place Vendôme and turned it into their headquarters.

Göring had commandeered the Imperial Suite and had it modified to cater for his rather eccentric needs. One of those modifications included the installation of a huge bathtub, not for aquatic pleasure – except perhaps with company – but, it was whispered, for medicinal reasons.

Göring was a morphine addict. He had desperately tried to kick his habit for years, regrettably without much success. He was always on the lookout for new cures. One of those cures included long baths, having his huge body submerged in the bathtub between injections. Professor Hubert Kahle, who invented the new 'wonder cure' for morphine addiction, was a frequent visitor to the Ritz. And so was Dr Erwin Steinberger, one of Göring's trusted personal physicians who was conducting certain secret medical experiments in the concentration camps, especially Auschwitz. Because Kahle's wonder cure had failed to deliver as promised, Göring had once again turned to Dr Steinberger for advice.

Göring enjoyed being on show. Pompous, a flamboyant dresser and natural showman with a flair for melodrama, he liked to surround himself with the social elite, especially beautiful women. And there was certainly no shortage of beautiful women frequenting the Ritz at the time. They were drawn to the German officers in their impressive uniforms like moths to a flame.

Power is an aphrodisiac, and the occupying forces had all the power in the world at their fingertips, and mountains of caviar and rivers of champagne to whet the appetite …

'Who is that over there?' asked Göring, pointing discreetly to a couple dining at the next table.

'A Mexican art dealer,' replied the maître d' in perfect German, 'and his charming young wife.'

'Ah … the man with the crystal skull?' said Göring.

'The very same,' said the maître d'.

'Excellent! Intrigue, a beautiful woman … and a stunning necklace. I want to meet them.'

'Certainly. I'll arrange it.' The maître d' smiled. Not only had he received a huge tip from the suave Mexican for seating him and his wife close to the German table in clear view of the Reichsmarschall, he would now most certainly receive an even bigger gratuity from the big man himself for arranging the introduction.

Göring's interest in the young woman was not her striking, head-turning beauty, but her exquisite necklace. Göring was obsessed with gems. He liked to surround himself with jewels, which he kept in a bowl next to his bed. There, in the privacy of his bedroom – dressed in outlandish kimonos, furs and opera gowns, and wearing earrings and heavy make-up – he would douse himself with perfume and caress his collection of treasured rubies, sapphires and diamonds like a lover.

Göring's fascination with precious stones was only overshadowed by a fanatical compulsion to acquire works of art. He collected art works like a man possessed and used to tour Paris with a retinue of art dealers and indiscriminately buy up every fine piece he could find, often offering a mere pittance. Of course, no one dared refuse him, and once he set eyes on something he had to have, nothing could stop him.

'Do you see that young woman over there?' said Göring, turning to Dr Steinberger seated next to him.

'What a beauty,' said Dr Steinberger, nodding appreciatively.

'And what a necklace,' said Göring. 'You and I will meet the charming couple after dinner.'

'The man with the crystal skull? What was all that about?'

'You'll find out.'

Used to Göring's whims, Dr Steinberger decided to go with the flow rather than ask for an explanation.

Mr Elminger, deputy director of the Ritz in charge of managing the German 'guests', took the Mexican couple over to the Reichsmarschall's table and introduced them. As the nephew of the hotel's Swiss president, Baron Hans von Pfyffer, he went to great lengths to appear scrupulously neutral. However, he kept a close eye on the Nazis, and made sure that the other guests in the hotel felt comfortable during these difficult and challenging times.

The Ritz was a hotbed of intrigue, espionage, clandestine liaisons, excesses, lust and betrayal. A dangerous cocktail, often with deadly consequences. Göring and Dr Steinberger stood up with military precision and welcomed their guests to their table. Elminger withdrew discreetly.

The young Mexican was delighted. He had tried for weeks to get close to the Reichsmarschall by spreading rumours about an extraordinary artefact – an ancient, Aztec crystal skull with magic powers – in his collection. Making contact with the well-connected rich in high places was the way he conducted his business. And there was no better place to do that than the Ritz.

As the son of a notorious Mexican revolutionary, he lived in self-imposed exile in France and rented a suite at the Ritz as a permanent guest with his wife, young daughter and a nanny. This was by no means unusual. Many well-heeled celebrities lived permanently at the Ritz. He was an art dealer, specialising in Mesoamerican artefacts, which he sold to rich collectors looking for the unusual and the exotic. If he could turn the Reichsmarschall into a client, the sky would be the limit.

Göring's weakness for women and jewellery was common knowledge at the Ritz, and the shrewd Mexican had used his beautiful wife and her breathtaking necklace as subtle bait. The door had been opened, the rest was now up to him.

After the obligatory small talk, the Reichsmarschall came straight to the point.

'You must tell us about that mysterious skull of yours, Signor,' said Göring. 'This place has been buzzing with rumours for days about its supernatural powers. I'm sure Dr Steinberger here would be most interested to learn more about it, and so would I.'

'Why don't you bring it down and show it to our friends, darling?' said the young woman, patting her husband on the hand.

'I could do that,' said the Mexican.

'What better way?' Göring agreed, enjoying himself. He lifted his glass and winked conspiratorially at the stunning beauty sitting opposite. Her husband excused himself and went upstairs.

'I've been admiring your necklace, Señora,' said Göring. 'It's spectacular. May I?' The young woman nodded and leant forward. Göring ran the tips of his fingers over the gleaming sapphires the size of ripe plums. 'Exquisite.'

'It belonged to my grandmother,' said Señora Gonzales. 'She lived in India for years.'

'A gift from a maharaja perhaps?' mused Dr Steinberger.

'Quite possibly, but she never told us.' Señora Gonzales reached for her champagne glass. 'Here comes José. You are in for a big surprise, gentlemen.'

The suave Mexican was a natural salesman, and deep down, a bit of a showman who used his Latin charm and his exotic wares to beguile the gullible. Handsome, likeable, and well informed, he knew instinctively how to appeal to potential clients, and at that moment, Göring was just that, albeit the most powerful and important one in the land.

He placed the beautiful box made of Cuban flame mahogany on the table in front of Göring. 'Please, open it,' he said.

Göring looked at the young woman. 'Why don't you open it, Señora,' he said, 'and surprise us?'

'As you wish.'

The young woman stood up and reached across the table. As she lifted the lid, the box came apart all by itself. A clever, concealed spring-operated mechanism folded down the front and the two sides of the box, leaving the back with the lid attached standing upright; the perfect backdrop for the amazing treasure within.

Göring gasped. Resting on a small blue velvet cushion in front of him was one of the most stunning objects he had ever set eyes upon. Carved out of crystal and transparent like glass, the beautifully proportioned human skull looked almost alive. Every anatomical detail, including the teeth was perfect.

'Incredible,' said Göring. Drawn irresistibly towards the skull, he stretched out his hand. 'May I?'

'Certainly,' said the Mexican, smiling. As soon as Göring touched the cool crystal with his fingertips and traced the eye sockets and the jaw, he knew he had to have the skull – at any cost.

'Tell us about it. Where does it come from? How old is it? Where was it found?' asked Göring excitedly.

'My father found it by accident during the Mexican Revolution in 1915. His unit was hiding in the jungle when one of his men came across a lost temple. My father was very interested in Aztec ruins and explored the temple, which was almost completely overgrown. The jungle had reclaimed it, you see. And there, in a hidden chamber, he found this skull and a fascinating text, an ancient Aztec codex, which you, Dr Steinberger, may find interesting.'

'Oh? In what way?' asked Dr Steinberger.

'Let me show you. It's right here.' The Mexican opened a small drawer set into the bottom of the box, pulled out a neatly folded piece of dry animal skin and placed it on the table in front of Dr Steinberger. 'The complete text was much larger. This is all that survived.' He unfolded the long, rectangular piece of skin covered in intricate, colourful illustrations, like a storybook. 'I've had the codex examined by experts in Mexico City, and they all agree this may in fact be the earliest record of a brain operation in Mesoamerica. It dates from around 1300 AD. They even gave it a name: *De Medicina*.'

'How fascinating,' said Steinberger, examining the illustrations with interest.

'You read it from right to left. As you can see, it follows the various stages of the operation. Here, in the first illustration, the naked patient is lying on a stone table, perhaps drugged; waiting. The man standing next to him – obviously the surgeon and most likely a priest – is holding a large knife, ready to begin. That's when things become really interesting ...'

'What do you mean?' asked Dr Steinberger.

'Have a closer look. Can you see something next to the patient's head?'

'Of course, it looks like ... Could it be?'

'It is,' said the Mexican, smiling. 'It's the crystal skull.'

'Astonishing. Perhaps watching over the patient with its magical powers?' suggested Dr Steinberger. 'Or guiding the surgeon's hand?'

'That's exactly what the experts thought. But it gets even more interesting.'

'In what way?'

'The next six illustrations show the opening of the skull with the knife, the removal of a piece of bone and so on. A detailed, step-by-step account of the procedure. However, then comes something surprising. This here.'

'What is that?'

'A picture of a plant. Not just any plant – a medicinal plant that grows in the jungle. The Aztecs used hundreds of different medicinal plants and herbs. In the next picture, the surgeon is holding a bowl in his left hand, and the knife in his right. In the last picture, he is covering the wound with leaves. And then here at the bottom is one more illustration. It shows the patient dressed as a warrior, now fully recovered, going into battle. The operation was obviously a success.'

'Astonishing,' said Dr Steinberger. 'Are you suggesting the plant was somehow part of the operation?'

'Absolutely. The experts are certain the bowl in the surgeon's hand contained a medicinal substance that was applied to the open wound. The preceding picture of the plant supports this and is consistent with Aztec iconography.'

'Amazing. Do you think it would be possible to identify, and perhaps find this jungle plant?'

'Yes. The illustration is very detailed and precise, and clearly shows the distinctive heart-shaped leaves of the plant. The plant has been identified. It is still being used for medicinal purposes by the natives in some remote areas.'

Momentarily overcome by a strange sense of excitement, Dr Steinberger reached for his champagne glass and looked pensively at the ancient text in front of him. A strong believer in destiny, he knew exactly what he had to do, and why.

# 24

St Pancras International was crowded as usual. The early morning train was very popular, especially with businessmen going to the Continent. The Eurostar to Paris was due to leave in five minutes.

'I told you we'd make it,' said Jack, catching his breath.

'Here's our carriage, slow coach,' said Lola.

'First class; very posh.'

Jack loved trains. Leaning back in his comfortable seat, he looked out of the window as the train slowly left the station. Soon the Eurostar would be travelling under the English Channel – one of the busiest shipping lanes in the world – reaching speeds of up to three hundred kilometres per hour. *Paris in three hours*, thought Jack, *bloody marvellous*.

'When are you going to tell me why we are going to France?' asked Lola. 'I'm sure it has nothing to do with your Russian countess and the wonder boy.'

'Yes … and no. It's the train actually,' teased Jack. 'I always wanted to travel on the Eurostar. Did you know it's one of the seven wonders of the modern world?'

'Says who?'

'The American Society of Civil Engineers.'

'Seriously, Jack, why France? Why the urgency? Why now? It has something to do with last night – right?'

'Before I tell you, I would like to ask you something.'

'Go for it.'

'When were you going to tell me that The Time Machine owns the company that publishes my books?'

Lola bit her lip and looked out the window. 'That wasn't up to me,' she said quietly, her unease obvious.

'And that phone call the night we met? It has bothered me from the beginning. I don't believe in coincidences.'

'All of that was before. I had to persuade you to come with me, get you over the line. Who told you?'

'Isis. In essence, The Time Machine is my publisher. How did all that come about?'

'As you can imagine, Isis has vast business interests. It's a global empire really. When we bought an American record label a couple of years ago, the publishing company was part of the portfolio we acquired. It's as simple as that.'

Jack nodded. The explanation made sense. *Another one of life's little ironies*, he thought. 'Isis also told me I could trust you with my life and there were to be no secrets between us. If we are going to be in this together, I need to know where I stand.'

Lola turned and looked intently at Jack. 'Yes, you can trust me with your life, and no secrets. You have to believe that.'

Jack nodded. 'Delving into the past can be very dangerous and judging by the little I've found out so far, the past we are trying to uncover could be about as dangerous as it gets. The passage of time doesn't make it less so. On the contrary, it can make it more lethal as the stakes of the present become higher. We've seen what happened to Lord and Lady Elms. Something like that doesn't happen in a vacuum. We are dealing with someone very resourceful, determined and utterly ruthless with much at stake, and no doubt a lot to lose. That's a deadly cocktail. Does that make sense?'

'It does.' Lola leant across and kissed Jack on the cheek.

'What was that for?'

'You know exactly what.'

'Sealed with a kiss?'

'You know a better way?'

'Suppose not.' Jack pulled his well-worn little notebook held together by a rubber band out of his pocket and opened it. 'What Sir Charles showed me last night, and what made my eyes burn and my head spin, was a bundle of old letters. And then there was something else I found particularly intriguing.'

'What?'

'Lady Elms' last words to her son.'

'She warned him and spoke about the hiding place …' interjected Lola.

'She did, but those were not her last words.'

'Oh? What else did she say?'

Jack reached for his notebook. 'According to Sir Charles, who spoke to Isis about this at the time and wrote it down, these were Lady Elms' last words: "Stars, hide your fires."'

'What does it mean?'

'Not sure … but I have a feeling it's important. Very important.'

Jack went on to tell Lola about the discovery of the letters in the secret hiding place at Clarendon Hall. However, he didn't tell her what else Isis had found hidden inside the mummy's head, not because he didn't trust her, but because he still didn't quite know what to make of it himself, or where it would fit into the unfolding story.

'I was there,' said Lola. 'Isis went up to the Egyptian room by herself. They must have been hidden in there, but she didn't say anything about the letters at the time.'

'Understandable. Everything was still very raw and moving quickly. Sir Charles kept the originals in his safe. I made some copies and took a few notes.'

'And?'

'Too early to tell,' said Jack, sidestepping the question. 'Some letters are incomplete and a few of the names, dates and places, and certain passages, have been blanked out completely. But we have a starting point. In fact, it was Señora Gonzales who gave me the first clue.'

'She did? In what way?'

'She told me I may find the answers in the hotel on Place Vendôme.'

'Fascinating. What does that mean?' asked Lola.

'Not sure yet, but I can tell you about the hotel.'

'You can?'

'The hotel on Place Vendôme is one of the most famous hotels in the world,' said Jack.

'It is?'

'Yes. It's none other than the Ritz.'

'Wow!'

'Marie-Louise and Cesar Ritz opened the doors of their lavish hotel in 1898. However, the period we are interested in is the war years, the forties, the hotel's most notorious, deadly and infamous period. Did you know that the Germans virtually took over the hotel in 1940 and made it their headquarters?'

'I had no idea.'

'And that Reichsmarschall Göring lived there during the German occupation? And so did Coco Chanel, Marlene Dietrich, and later, Hemingway and a host of other celebrities. The Duke and Duchess of Windsor gave up their palatial suite at the beginning of the war and Churchill and de Gaulle stopped coming. However, during the Nazi occupation the Ritz was a hotbed of intrigue, illicit affairs, espionage, treason and betrayal. It had it all.'

'Hold on. How come you know so much about this?'

'I wrote a series of articles for a London paper about the Ritz a few years ago – "The Mirror of Paris". I was a struggling freelancer at the time, but I actually made some money out of them,' said Jack, laughing.

'And the countess? Where does she fit into this?'

'She will help us.'

'How?'

'You'll see.'

Jack closed his eyes, enjoying the sense of speed as the train moved silently through the 'Chunnel' under the sea towards the French coast. The reason he had been late getting ready that morning wasn't a sleep-in, but phone calls.

Alexandra needed help, urgently, and the only way Jack could think of helping her was to turn to Jana and Marcus. After speaking to Alexandra and reassuring her, he had called Jana Gonski at The Hague.

Jana Gonski, a former Australian Federal Police officer, and Marcus Carrington QC, a barrister, had prosecuted Sir Eric Newman, a high-profile Nazi war criminal, three years before. Jack had shared an extraordinary adventure with them, which culminated in the publication of his bestseller, *Dental Gold and Other Horrors*. Marcus Carrington was now a judge sitting on the War Crimes Tribunal in The Hague, and Jana, who had left the police force, was his partner. Both had accepted Jack's invitation and were coming to the Kuragin Chateau for the weekend. *We are going to be together again*, thought Jack, smiling. *Fate? What else?* He was particularly looking forward to seeing Jana again.

Jack regretted his decision to hire a car and drive to the Kuragin Chateau almost immediately. The Paris traffic was as chaotic as ever, but luck was on his side. This time he took the correct turn onto the autoroute instead of getting lost and driving in circles around Paris, as he had done before. Two hours later, he could see the outline of the familiar chateau in the distance.

'I almost hit a peacock right here during one of my visits,' said Jack, as they crossed the bridge leading to the chateau. Remembering the funny incident with Rebecca Armstrong, his literary agent, sitting next to him on that occasion, brought a smile to his face.

'Not a bad pad,' said Lola, 'Isis would love this.'

'I'm sure she would like the countess as well. But you can judge for yourself.' Jack tapped the horn twice, put his hand out of the open car window and began to wave. 'That's her over there at the entry.'

# 25

Countess Kuragin was in her element. She put the finishing touches to the splendid floral arrangement in the middle of the dining table, straightened the candles in the silver candelabras, adjusted the crisp serviettes – making sure everything was perfection – and then stood back. *Excellent*, she thought. As an experienced hostess, she sensed that the dinner would have far-reaching consequences.

Her guests had gone to their rooms to get ready, giving her a little time to reflect on the events of the afternoon. Jack and Lola had arrived first. Tristan was blown away by The Time Machine poster signed by Isis – a rare collector's item – presented to him by Jack and Lola. He hadn't left Lola's side since and was bombarding her with questions about Isis and The Time Machine. This had given Jack and the countess an opportunity for a brief private chat.

Strolling arm in arm through the garden in the fading light of the late afternoon, Jack explained why he had invited Jana and Marcus, and outlined his plan to enlist their help in finding a solution to Alexandra's predicament.

Jana and Marcus had arrived late. An accident on the autoroute just outside Paris had delayed them for hours. After a brief introduction – it was their first visit to the Kuragin Chateau – they had gone straight to their room to freshen up. The drive from The Hague had been long and tiring. Dinner would therefore be the first opportunity for everyone to relax and talk.

The countess was a master of reading the mood of her guests, and then making them feel comfortable and at ease. With so much riding on the success of the evening, she was determined to make sure nothing was left to chance. A glass of vintage champagne was always the best way to begin an evening, and several chilled bottles were already waiting in the silver ice buckets on the sideboard. Satisfied, the countess straightened her dress, adjusted her hair and looked at the clock on the mantelpiece. Her guests were due in a few minutes. It was time to instruct the butler to open the champagne.

Seating dinner guests strategically at the dinner table was an art the countess had perfected over many years. Sitting next to, or opposite the right person could make the difference between a great evening and – God forbid – a boring, or embarrassing one. Her soirées and dinner parties were legendary and much sought after by the social elite who frequented the chateau.

Marcus, Jana and Jack had known each other for a long time. While she had heard a great deal about Jana and Marcus, and therefore knew of them through Jack's book, the countess had only met them in person for the first time that afternoon. Lola of course hadn't met anyone before, and Tristan who, as a special treat would be allowed to join them for dinner, only knew Jack.

'The people you are about to have dinner with,' said Jack, leading Lola into the dining room, 'are as close as I'll ever get to having a family.'

'You are lucky,' said Lola, 'and so am I. We both have families of choice. Isis and The Time Machine are my family.'

Jack handed Lola a glass of champagne. 'You're right. Let's drink to that,' he said, laughing. 'To choice, and family!'

'I'm sure you must all be wondering why I've arranged this weekend in such a hurry,' said Jack, after the dinner plates had been cleared away. Turning to the countess, he then asked her to outline what she had found out so far about her niece's baffling abduction and encounter with Macbeth on the *Calypso*. After the countess had finished, Jack spoke briefly about his surprise trip to Mexico to meet Isis, the megastar, and the extraordinary assignment to investigate the deadly attack on her parents.

'I don't know how you do it, Jack,' said Jana seated next to him. 'You must be some kind of adventure-magnet. While most of us lead ordinary lives, you find excitement and adventure around every corner.'

'Incorrigible rascals live dangerously.'

'Oh? Is that what it is?'

'Do I detect a hint of envy?' Jack was enjoying the familiar banter.

'Absolutely.'

'Then why don't we do something about it?'

'You have something in mind?'

Jack put down his serviette and looked at Marcus sitting opposite. 'We need your help, guys. You mentioned on the phone that you are about to go to Sydney—'

'Yes, Marcus wants to sell his house,' interrupted Jana. 'And besides, he desperately needs a break. He's worked on this dreadful trial for months: war crimes in Somalia. Shocking stuff. No time off.' What Jana didn't mention was another reason Marcus wanted to go back to Sydney: he was planning to leave The Hague and return to the Sydney Bar to resume his career as a barrister. He missed Sydney, and wanted to visit the graves of his wife and daughter killed in a terrorist attack in Egypt three years before.

'As you can see, I can't go back to Sydney right now to help Alexandra,' said Jack, 'but as you are both going ... I can't think of two better people to counsel Alexandra and advise her on how to deal with the situation – a judge, and a senior police officer. And you can stay in my new penthouse on the harbour,' added Jack, grinning, 'with Alexandra, who already lives there as my guest. That should work quite well, don't you think?'

Carrington looked at Jana. 'What do you think?' he asked. 'I can't go straight away, but you could.'

'Would you mind?' asked Jana, the promise of adventure lighting up her face.

'Not at all. I'll follow in a few days,' said Marcus. Jana had been quite restless for some months. Marcus was well aware of the reason: Jana desperately missed her job in the police force and found life at The Hague stifling. Jack's offer had therefore come at a good time. Marcus realised that the distraction and return to Australia would do Jana the world of good.

'It's all settled then?' said Jack.

'It is,' said Marcus.

The countess turned to Jana sitting on her right. 'Thank you,' she said, patting Jana on the arm. 'This is much more than I could have hoped for.'

The countess knew that somehow the best conversation always happened after dinner. Coffee and liqueurs for the ladies, and cognac for the gentlemen was served in the music room. Jana was talking with Lola, and Jack and Marcus had walked out onto the terrace for a private chat. Tristan had reluctantly gone to his room.

'It's really good to see you, Marcus. It's been too long. And thank you,' said Jack. 'You asked no questions and came.'

'You would have done the same.'

'Let me tell you why I really accepted this assignment,' said Jack. He took a sip of cognac, enjoying the mellow bite of the superb brandy warming his throat. 'It had nothing to do with the things I mentioned at dinner.'

'Oh? What then?' asked Marcus.

'A name.'

'How intriguing.'

'It's more than that. I asked Isis to give me one good reason why I should just drop everything and accept her proposal. That's when Señora Gonzales, her grandmother, stepped in and gave me a name.'

'What name?'

Jack took his time before answering, letting the tension grow. 'You'll find this hard to believe ... I still do.'

'Go on,' prompted Marcus impatiently.

'Sturmbannfuehrer Wolfgang Steinberger.'

For a while, there was stunned silence. Three years earlier, Jack and Marcus had exposed and prosecuted Sir Eric Newman, a notorious Nazi war criminal turned respected banker. Jack had written a bestseller, *Dental Gold and Other Horrors*, about it. Wolfgang Steinberger was Sir Eric Newman's real name.

'Are you serious? But he's dead. It's all over.'

'Is it? Evil has a long reach, even from the grave. We've both seen it before,' said Jack.

Marcus nodded. 'Did you question the lady about it?'

'Of course. But all she said was, "Hidden corners of our lives".'

'What do you make of it?'

'She has certainly read my book; she said so herself. As for the rest – don't know yet, but there has to be a connection. Obviously, it's all about Steinberger and his Nazi past.'

'Any ideas?'

'A few, but it's early days.'

'But you intend to find out?'

'Of course. That's what this assignment is all about.'

'Is that why you were approached in the first place, do you think?'

'I'm sure of it.'

'And you couldn't resist?'

'Could you?'

Marcus raised his brandy balloon. 'Perhaps not.' They touched glasses. 'Good luck!'

'And then there was this,' said Jack. He pulled his iPhone out of his pocket, called up a photo and handed the phone to Marcus. 'What do you make of this?'

'Wow! That's an Aztec crystal skull. Very rare. Did you take this?'

'I did.'

'Where?'

'Isis' solicitor showed it to me last night in his office. It belonged to Lady Elms, Isis' mother.'

'Amazing.'

Jack knew that Marcus, an amateur archaeologist specialising in Egyptology, was a fountain of knowledge when it came to religious practices, artefacts with mystical powers and the occult generally. 'What can you tell me about it?' he asked, carefully watching his friend, who couldn't take his eyes off the skull in the picture.

'A number of these skulls have surfaced over the years, especially during the nineteenth century. They are all quite famous, and some of them even have names like the Paris skull, the British Museum skull and perhaps the most controversial of them all, the Mitchell-Hedges skull. At first, they were thought to be genuine pre-Columbian Mesoamerican artefacts with mystical powers—'

'Thought to be?' interrupted Jack.

'Yes. Unfortunately, all the skulls that have actually been scientifically tested turned out to be fakes, most likely manufactured in Germany in the nineteenth century or even later.'

'How disappointing.'

'Perhaps, but fascinating nevertheless. Any more photos?'

'Yes. Just keep scrolling.'

'Ah. Is the jaw detached? You can't tell from the pictures.'

'Yes it is.'

'That narrows it down considerably.'

'How so?'

'The Mitchell-Hedges skull is the only one I know of with a detached jaw, and this one looks remarkably like it.'

'What do you know about it?'

'Anna Mitchell-Hedges was the adopted daughter of F.A. Mitchell-Hedges, a famous British adventurer. She claimed to have discovered the skull in a temple in Lubaantun in British Honduras, as it then was, in the nineteen twenties. It had a colourful life after that, I can tell you. Full of extravagant claims and controversy surrounding it, it became known as the Skull of Doom. Anna managed to make a good living out of it for years.'

'How did she do that?'

'She toured with the skull, gave interviews and charged a viewing fee. She also claimed to have been told by the few remaining Maya that the skull was used by the high priest to will death.'

'A snake oil saleswoman?' said Jack, laughing. 'Peddling the Skull of Doom?'

'A bit like that, I suppose.'

'What a story. This one here in the photo must have a story too.'

'Sure, and all you have to do, my friend, is find it,' said Marcus, raising his empty glass.

'I intend to.'

'But for now, why don't we find the bottle and have another brandy?' said Marcus.

'What a splendid suggestion.'

# 26

'How do I look?' Isis asked, casting a critical eye over her reflection in the dressing room mirror. The concert was due to start in ten minutes and a hundred thousand excited Mexican fans were waiting in the stadium for their idol to take to the stage.

'There is only one word for it, cherie: spectacular,' said Jean-Paul, who had designed the fabulous costume. 'You look like an Aztec princess.'

Isis adjusted the long feathers in her headdress and, satisfied with what she saw, turned around and began the breathing exercises she did before every performance.

'Five minutes,' said one of the technicians operating the sound system. Isis nodded, and started doing her squats.

Sensing the imminent start of the performance, the crowd began to chant: 'Isis; Isis; Isis!' Moments later, The Time Machine began to play the opening number, drowning out the roar of the crowd. It was time for Isis to get into her glass coffin.

Lying quite still and with her eyes closed, Isis waited for the coffin to rise. These were the moments she cherished most: the muffled roar of the crowd, the guitars screaming on the stage above and the throbbing, monotonous beat of the drums making her whole body tingle with excitement like a hit from a powerful drug, only stronger. It was a feeling like no other. A transfer of energy from adoring fans waiting for her arrival, to their idol about to deliver something none of them would forget.

Usually, Isis felt elated and could barely wait for the coffin to rise, her muscles tense and charged for her spectacular somersault entry, like a tightly coiled spring ready to explode into action. This time, however, she found it difficult to focus and was unable to shake off a feeling of dread. This was something she had never experienced before. Cold sweat began to pour down her face, smudging the elaborate make-up and her breathing became laboured. Feeling suddenly very cold, Isis opened her eyes. *A panic attack?* she thought, unable to stop her teeth from chattering. *Control yourself!*

Feeling a little better, Isis went through her breathing exercises once more to calm herself, her iron-willed discipline and self-control coming to her aid and serving her well. With only moments to go before the lid of the coffin was due to open under the spotlight, Isis felt suddenly dizzy and her head began to spin. '*Something is wrong,*' she whispered, barely able to move her lips as The Time Machine launched into 'Resurrection', her signature number indicating her entry. Then the coffin began to rise.

# 27

All was quiet in the chateau after the splendid dinner. Everyone except Jack and the countess had retired to their rooms some time ago. 'Nightcap?' said the countess, taking Jack by the hand. 'In the kitchen. We always seem to end up in there this time of night.'

Jack ran his fingertips along the polished timbers of the kitchen table, worn shiny and smooth by countless elbows of generations past. 'I love this old table and the stories it could tell,' he said and sat down facing the countess.

'About Russian winters and sleigh rides through enchanted forests?' said the countess, recalling their last late-night conversation in the very same place two years before. On that occasion, Jack had made a promise to find Anna. Against all odds he had succeeded, earning him not only the gratitude of a distraught mother, but a place in her heart and her family as well.

'Exactly.'

'Why is it that every time we come here – usually late at night – you help me?'

Jack shrugged, but said nothing. Deep down, under the easygoing larrikin-layer, Jack was actually reserved and quite shy. It was this hidden, endearing quality the countess loved so much about him. 'Thanks, Jack,' she said and reached for his hand.

'Perhaps this time you can help me in return,' said Jack.

'Oh? How?'

Jack told the countess about Dolores' cryptic parting words regarding the hotel on Place Vendôme.

'That's the Ritz,' interrupted the countess.

'Correct. And I was hoping you may know someone who could help me here. I'm particularly interested in the war years.'

The countess began to laugh.

'What's so funny?' asked Jack.

'I know just the person. You'll get on like a house on fire; trust me.'

'Oh? And who might she be?'

'A famous Russian ballerina. I can take you to her tomorrow if you like. She lives in a retirement home not far from here,' said the countess.

'See; what did I tell you?'

Jack saw a moving shadow near the open door out of the corner of his eye and turned around. Barefoot and in his pyjamas, Tristan stood in the doorway watching them. Something about the boy's demeanour made Jack uneasy.

'What's up, darling?' asked the countess. She stood up and walked over to Tristan.

'I couldn't sleep,' said Tristan, coming closer. 'I kept seeing this … image, over and over. And I heard—'

'What image?' interrupted Jack.

'Noise; crowds; sirens … I think Isis is in danger.'

'Hush now,' said the countess. She put her arm around Tristan's shoulder and stroked his burning forehead. 'You've been talking to Lola all night and I bet you listened to The Time Machine in your room. Am I right? And the Isis poster is hanging on the back of your door. You're excited, that's all. Come; sit with us. I'll make us all a hot chocolate and you'll sleep like a baby, you'll see.'

Ten minutes later, Lola burst into the kitchen, a haunted look on her face. 'That's where you are,' she said excitedly. 'I thought I could hear voices. Something terrible has happened …'

'What?' said Jack, almost knocking over his mug as he turned around to face Lola.

'I just had a call from Mexico …' Obviously distressed, Lola could barely speak. 'Isis collapsed on stage and has been taken to hospital. The concert's been cancelled. The crowd panicked. There was a stampede; several people died. It's a disaster!'

## 28

The *Calypso* was steaming north again towards the Great Barrier Reef, one of Macbeth's favourite places. He decided to stay close to the east coast of Australia for the time being. This would give him an opportunity to monitor Alexandra's progress at the Gordon, and be available to intervene at short notice if necessary, without arousing suspicion. With so much at stake, he thought this was definitely warranted.

Something about Alexandra made Macbeth feel uneasy. He couldn't quite put his finger on it, but her confident manner and sparkling intelligence told him she wouldn't be easy to control and manipulate. During their breakfast together, she had radiated independence and defiance. Compared with her, Cavendish had been an easy target. Macbeth realised there was only one way to make sure Alexandra was reporting truthfully and wasn't trying to deceive him. A reliable contact was needed on the inside. Someone had to keep a close eye on her activities at the institute and report back to him.

'Any progress?' asked Macbeth, playing with the two little steel balls in his left hand.

'Yes,' said Van Cleef. 'My Sydney contact is confident he has identified a suitable target. In fact, I believe an approach is imminent.'

'Who is the target?'

'Dr Delacroix's assistant. We've had him in our sights for some time. He was working with Cavendish ... he's now working with Dr Delacroix. A piece of luck.'

'What do we know about him?'

'He's Sri Lankan, a Tamil. Very bright and ambitious. He studied in England and took up a position at the Gordon three years ago. He has a wife and a small child. He also has a great weakness ...'

Macbeth looked impressed. 'Well done, Jan. Keep me informed.'

'Certainly. We should know more in the morning.' Van Cleef nodded and left the cabin.

Akhil Achari was watching the dealer intently, his face flushed with anxiety. He was counting the cards. He had been sitting at the blackjack table for hours and was down to his last three hundred dollars. Usually he had no problem concentrating, but not that night. Lady Luck had turned her back on him. Akhil had already lost one month's wages and was desperately trying to win it back.

Akhil looked at the two cards he had just received. *Hit or stand*, he thought, his mind racing. *Split, or take the risk and double down?* Double down allowed him to increase the initial bet by one hundred per cent. Akhil decided to double down. It was the wrong decision.

As Akhil stood up to leave the table, a man behind him put two hundred dollars into his shirt pocket. 'I've had a good run, mate. Take it and have another go,' said the man. All of his instincts told Akhil to return the money and walk away, but the little gambling demons in his head began to whisper seductively in his ear, urging him to stay.

The dealer looked at him, his face an inscrutable mask without expression. For an instant, Akhil wavered, his huge losses making his stomach churn. Then he sat back down and placed another bet.

Paulus put his hand on Akhil's shoulder and leant forward. '*There's more if you like*,' he whispered, and slipped another two hundred into Akhil's pocket.

## 29

Everyone was up early the next morning. With the Mexican rock concert disaster all over the news, there was no escaping the tragedy. The reports were unclear as to what really happened. However, six people had died in the panic that followed Isis' dramatic collapse on stage. Teary-eyed and obviously distraught, Lola was packed and ready to go. *Pegasus* was already in the air on its way to Paris to collect her and fly her back to Mexico City. Marcus and Jana had decided to leave as well and offered to drive Lola to the airport. The weekend that had started with such promise and good cheer the night before had lost its sparkle and was suddenly over.

Jana kissed the countess on the cheek. 'I should be on a plane to Sydney by tomorrow night at the latest,' she said. 'Don't worry about Alexandra, but you definitely have to watch this man,' she added, pointing to Jack standing in the doorway.

'I know,' said the countess and rolled her eyes.

'Beware of charming men.'

'Story of my life.'

Jack helped Marcus put the luggage into the boot. 'I may need to pick your brain about the crystal skull, Marcus,' he said.

'Nicely put. Any time, and thanks for letting us stay in your apartment. We'll look after Alexandra; don't worry. And the break will do Jana the world of good.' Marcus slapped Jack on the back. 'Stay in touch.'

Jack held the car door open for Jana. She put her arms around him and gave him a hug. 'Take care of yourself. I'll call you,' she said, and got into the car.

'Where's Lola?' asked Jack.

'Here she comes now,' said the countess.

Looking dejected, her eyes red from lack of sleep, Lola hurried towards them with a duffel bag slung over her shoulders. 'Last night was magic,' she said to the countess, 'then the sky caved in.'

'Any news?' said Jack.

'She's in hospital, that's all I know.'

'Call me as soon as you know more. In the meantime, I'll carry on unless—'

'You do that. Nothing's changed,' interrupted Lola.

Lola was about to get into the car when Tristan came running towards her out of the garden with a bunch of flowers in his hand. 'This is for you,' he said, handing the flowers to Lola. 'And this is for Isis.' Tristan held up a small Celtic cross carved out of whalebone. 'It belonged to my mother.'

Lola took the cross out of his hand, but before she could thank him, Tristan turned around and ran back into the house.

'Do you know what his mother said about him?' said Jack. Lola shook her head and slipped the cross into her pocket. 'He can hear the whisper of angels and glimpse eternity.'

With everyone gone, the chateau felt suddenly quite lonely. Jack sat on the terrace, deep in thought with a melancholy look on his face. He was going over the events of the past twenty-four hours. *How quickly things can change*, he thought. The countess watched him from inside. *He needs cheering up*, she thought.

'Are you coming?' said the countess.

'Are we going somewhere?'

'Of course. You are about to meet a Russian ballerina, remember?'

'Anastasia Petrova was already famous in her early teens,' said the countess as they drove through the ornate wrought iron gates. The exclusive retirement home, a converted chateau, was popular with well-heeled aristocrats and celebrities. 'She was one of the baby ballerinas of the Ballet Russe de Monte Carlo and later became a film star. She was also one of my mother's closest friends.'

'I can't wait.'

'You won't be disappointed.'

'And we are going to meet her because …?'

'She lived at the Ritz during the war.'

A nurse in a crisp uniform who seemed to know the countess well, welcomed them in the entry foyer and showed them to Madame Petrova's room on the ground floor. 'She's expecting you,' said the nurse and opened the door to a large room overlooking the manicured grounds.

Madame Petrova sat in a chair facing the open window. Elegantly dressed in a tight-fitting black dress and wearing a priceless string of baroque pearls and a pair of beautiful earrings that whispered '*Tiffany*', she certainly had presence; even in her nineties. 'Elegance and style are timeless' was her motto, and she certainly lived by it. Her snow-white hair was pulled back and tied in a neat bun, exposing a long, swan-like neck. Impeccable make-up accentuated her prominent cheekbones and made her almond-shaped, slightly slanted eyes look large, giving her an exotic, almost feline look.

'How wonderful of you to come, my dear,' said Madame Petrova in French, struggling to stand up with the aid of a walking stick she hated. 'I saw you arrive.'

The countess walked over to her friend and kissed her on both cheeks. 'I've brought someone who wants to meet you,' she said in English.

'A young man,' how exciting,' said Madame Petrova, switching to perfect English. 'Please come a little closer so I can see you.' She refused to wear glasses.

'He's a writer,' said the countess, lowering her voice. She knew that would excite her friend even more. She had a soft spot for writers.

'So, you want to know about the Ritz during the war,' said Madame Petrova after the maid had served petits fours and tea. 'It was without doubt the most exciting time of my life; exciting and dangerous …'

Madame Petrova paused, and let her eyes roam over the photographs on the grand piano next to her.

'What made it so dangerous and exciting?' asked Jack.

'The people. Especially the Germans. Here, have a look.' Madame Petrova pointed to the photographs on the piano, her fingers shaking. Jack noticed that her parchment-like skin was almost translucent.

'That's Reichsmarschall Göring with von Stulpnagel, the military commander of occupied Paris. Göring was crazy, but everyone was dancing around him, like moths drawn to a flame. And here, that's Canaris, head of the Abwehr, the German intelligence offices in Paris. He was a double agent.' Madame Petrova pointed to another sepia photograph. 'The man next to him is von Choltitz, a general. He was in charge during the last days of the German occupation. He defied Hitler and refused to burn Paris. As you can see, all of these photographs were taken at the Ritz. And look, over here, that's me standing next to Charles Ritz, Coco Chanel and Marlene Dietrich. You know what Charles used to say?' Jack shook his head. 'Luxury stains everyone it touches. And it certainly did.

'And then there were the writers. You would be interested in that,' said Madame Petrova, becoming quite animated. 'That's Jean-Paul Sartre and Simone de Beauvoir, Hemingway's drinking buddies. My God, we had some wild times together.' Exhausted by the memories of her youth, Madame Petrova slumped back into her chair.

'May I?' asked Jack, pointing to the photographs on the desk by the window.

'Go right ahead,' said Madame Petrova.

The photographs on the desk were much more recent. One in particular had caught Jack's eye. Two ladies in fur coats and a young girl were standing on the Tower Bridge in London. One of them was obviously Madame Petrova in her middle years. The other looked vaguely familiar, and Jack tried to remember where he had seen her before. 'Who is that standing next to you?' he asked, pointing to the photo.

'Show me, please.' Jack handed the photograph to Madame Petrova.

'Ah. That's a good friend of mine and her daughter. We met during the war. She too was living at the Ritz at the time.' As soon as Madame Petrova said that, Jack remembered where he had seen the woman before, the realisation making the hairs on the back of his neck tingle.

'Can you tell me her name?' he said, his voice sounding hoarse.

'Of course. That's Dolores Gonzales and her daughter, Mercedes. Why do you ask?'

Barely able to control his excitement, Jack began to question Madame Petrova about her friend.

'Please, not so fast,' interrupted Madame Petrova, holding up a shaking hand. 'If you live life in the rear-view mirror like I do, things become a little blurred.'

Obviously exhausted, Madame Petrova sank back into her chair again and looked suddenly quite frail. The sparkle ignited by her memories had gone out. All that remained was a little old lady, struggling with the present. 'The nurse will come any moment. It's time for my pills and my nap,' she said. 'The pills keep my body alive, but do little for my spirit.'

'We should go,' said the countess to Jack, quickly standing.

'But if you want to find out more about Dolores and our time at the Ritz, you should talk to my biographer,' said Madame Petrova.

'I didn't know you had a biographer,' said the countess, surprised.

'Oh yes, she lives in Paris and comes every Thursday. You may know her; she's quite famous.'

'Who is she?'

'Adrienne Darrieux.'

# 30

Boris, Isis' bodyguard, met Lola at Benito Juárez International Airport in Mexico City and took her straight to the hospital. Because Boris was a man of few words, Lola knew it would be pointless to question him about Isis' condition and what had really happened at the concert. Unable to sleep on the plane, Lola felt drained and exhausted, but concern and worry kept her going, running precariously on nervous energy.

'What's that?' asked Lola. She pointed to the huge crowd almost blocking their approach to the hospital.

'They've been here all night,' said Boris. 'Fans with candles, praying for Isis. There are thousands of them. There's even a little shrine by the entrance with a mountain of flowers.'

'Incredible.' Lola looked out the window at the multitude of silent faces staring back at her. What she saw reflected in those young faces moved her deeply. It was genuine grief and distress of a generation worried about its idol.

Police had cordoned off a narrow corridor leading to the hospital. Policemen on motorbikes patrolled the street and held back the excited crowd pushing against the barricades.

Being ushered through the maze of brightly lit corridors of the huge hospital with Boris by her side reminded Lola of another hospital visit not that long ago. On that occasion, Isis had rushed to her mother's bedside in London only to be met by horror and death. Lola hoped that this visit would be less traumatic and have a happier ending.

Boris spoke briefly to the security guard in front of Isis' room. The guard nodded, stepped aside and opened the door. Lola felt suddenly dizzy and weak, with needles of apprehension and fear churning through her empty stomach like shards of glass. *All hospitals smell the same*, she thought, the sickly-sweet smell of disinfectant and cleaning fluids assaulting her senses. Boris took her by the arm and gently guided her inside the silent, dimly lit room.

Her eyes closed, Isis was lying on an elevated bed with all kinds of tubes and monitoring devices attached to her arms and chest. Her pale face looked strangely serene and at peace. It reminded Lola of someone lying in state in some bizarre science fiction movie. *Oh my God*, thought Lola, tears blurring her vision. At first, she didn't notice Señora Gonzales and Hanna sitting in the shadows; watching. Then she felt someone put a comforting arm around her shoulders. It was Hanna.

'*How is she?*' whispered Lola.

'We don't know,' said Hanna, her voice quivering with emotion. 'She's in a coma.'

'What happened?'

'Let's go outside and I'll tell you.'

'I saw it all,' said Hanna. She handed Lola a glass of water and they sat down on a bench in the empty corridor. 'The coffin rose, the lid opened and Isis made her usual spectacular somersault entry but …'

'But what?' prompted Lola.

'She didn't land on her feet; she kept rolling and almost fell off the stage. And then, she just lay there. We ran over. I was one of the first to get to her. She was unconscious. Boris and I carried her backstage and called the ambulance.'

'And?'

'Examinations, specialists, tests and more tests. The doctors haven't told us much. I suspect they don't really know anything yet. I called Sir Humphrey and he's on his way.'

*At least that was good news*, thought Lola. Sir Humphrey, a trusted friend, was Isis' personal physician who had looked after her for many years. He lived in London. 'What next?' asked Lola, feeling a little better.

'We are waiting for a briefing.'

'I am so tired,' said Lola, resting her head against Hanna's shoulder. 'Maybe if I just close my eyes, I will fall asleep and it will all go away?'

'I wish,' said Hanna, tenderly stroking her friend's flushed cheeks. 'What do we do now?'

'The most difficult thing of all … We wait.'

Half an hour later, a nurse came and took them to a consulting room on the floor below. Boris and Señora Gonzales came with them. In the darkened room, a group of doctors were looking at X-rays on an illuminated screen. They stopped talking and turned around, the sudden silence adding to the tension in the room.

'I don't like this,' said Lola, squeezing Hanna's hand.

'I'm Professor Alvarez,' said a tall, white-haired man, standing next to the screen. 'I'm an oncologist. I'm afraid I have some bad news …'

'Please tell us,' said Señora Gonzales, her voice strong and steady. She stepped forward. 'I am her grandmother.'

'Certainly, Señora,' said the professor. 'I can do better than that. I will show you. Please come over here.' The professor picked up a ruler and pointed to one of the X-rays on the screen. All the X-rays were images of a human skull, but taken from different angles. 'This grey mass over here is a large tumour. It is pressing down on the brain – here.' The professor circled the grey blob with the tip of the ruler.

'What do you recommend?' asked Señora Gonzales, her voice no longer quite so confident and controlled.

'Normally, I would strongly advise we operate at once to remove it, but …' The professor stopped mid-sentence, collecting his thoughts, the silence in the room deafening. 'Unfortunately, this tumour is in a very precarious, dare I say hopelessly dangerous, location …' he continued at last.

'What are you telling us, Professor?' asked Lola.

'I've discussed this at length with my colleagues here … We have formed a view …' said the professor, a tinge of sadness in his voice he couldn't hide.

'*What view?*' whispered Señora Gonzales.

'We believe it is inoperable …'

# 31

Adrienne Darrieux, a well-known author and Paris socialite, was easy to track down. All the countess had to do was make a few phone calls. In her circles, everyone knew everyone or someone who did. Fortunately, Mademoiselle Darrieux was in Paris, and once she heard who wanted to talk to her, she instantly agreed to a meeting. She suggested they meet at La Closerie des Lilas on the Boulevard du Montparnasse, one of Europe's most famous historical literary cafes. Apparently, she was a regular there with her own table. Fame by association.

'I have to warn you,' said the countess, 'Mademoiselle Darrieux has quite a reputation.'

'Oh? In what way?' asked Jack. He was watching the diabolical Paris traffic edge past outside and thanked his lucky stars he wasn't driving.

'She's a man-eater. And once I mentioned your name ...'

'Should I be worried?'

'Oh, I think a man with your experience should be able to handle her.'

'I'm glad you think so.'

'She also considers herself somewhat of a literary identity.'

'Is she?'

'Yes, of sorts. She has written a number of very successful biographies. The one on Coco Chanel and Sarah Bernhardt did very well. And it is rumoured she's writing a book about the Ritz. That's why she's agreed to write Madame Petrova's memoirs.'

'How opportune.'

'And she's very flamboyant and likes to impress. I'm sure that's why she chose La Closerie des Lilas.'

'Is that why we are travelling in style?'

'Partly. It's a lot easier being dropped off than trying to park. Parking in Paris is virtually impossible.'

'And we'll make a good impression at the same time,' Jack said, laughing, 'by arriving in the family limo?'

'That too. Appearances are important. Especially in Paris.'

The countess had decided to take her late father's vintage Bentley and let François, the gardener who on rare occasions doubled as chauffeur, drive them to Paris instead of taking her own BMW.

'We are almost there,' said the countess as the car turned into the busy Boulevard du Montparnasse. Founded in 1808, the 'Garden of Lilacs' was once a carriage stop during the French Revolution. Its illustrious clientele included famous painters, writers and composers. Monet, Renoir and Whistler had been regulars and so had Balzac, Chateaubriand, Baudelaire and Oscar Wilde. Toscanini and Gershwin had almost called it home when staying in Paris.

Mademoiselle Darrieux saw the countess' car pull up outside and smiled as the chauffeur got out and opened the back door. To have such an important guest meet her at the café for lunch could only enhance her already considerable reputation in the eyes of the other regulars who would be witnessing the occasion. In her circles, being talked about was the oxygen of success; being ignored, social death.

Over the years, Mademoiselle Darrieux had perfected the art of being noticed. To ignore her was almost impossible. The fact that many laughed behind her back didn't seem to bother her. A flamboyant dresser in her late fifties – she admitted only to forty-something – she liked to show off her figure and considerable bosom by wearing daring dresses only worn by the reckless or the very brave, twenty or so years younger. She had never married; her relationships never lasted long, and she went through men faster than birthdays. However, her lovers became younger as she got older. Despite all this, she was well liked and respected as a serious and talented writer. Paris society embraced likeable eccentrics, and Mademoiselle Darrieux passed with flying colours – literally.

'That's her over there,' said the countess, following the maître d'
to Mademoiselle Darrieux's table in the busy brasserie.

'Oh my God,' said Jack, suppressing a smile.

Dressed in a stunning lilac, figure-hugging creation by Valentino
and a breathtaking hat that would have turned heads at the Ascot
races, Mademoiselle Darrieux gave them her best smile and ordered
champagne.

'What a splendid venue,' said Jack, admiring the classic décor of the
beautifully appointed room.

'The lobster tank and the grand piano have only been here since
the nineteen nineties, but you will find the names of famous patrons
inscribed on little plaques on the tables in the original piano bar,' said
Mademoiselle Darrieux. 'Hemingway once lived just around the
corner and came here often. He wrote about the café in *A Moveable
Feast*.'

'He also mentions it in *The Sun Also Rises*,' said Jack casually.

Mademoiselle Darrieux was impressed. 'Perhaps one day your
name will also appear on one of those plaques,' she said, patting Jack
on the hand.

'I doubt it. But you must show me the mirror.'

'What do you mean?' asked Mademoiselle Darrieux.

'Didn't Alfred Jarry, who wrote *Ubu Roi*, once discharge a revolver
into a mirror behind a lady here?'

'How do you know about that?' asked the countess, surprised.

'When I'm invited to dine with two charming ladies, I like to know
where I'm going. It could be a dangerous place ...' Mademoiselle
Darrieux and the countess burst out laughing.

'And didn't Jarry say to the lady after he fired the shots –
fortunately blanks – "Now that the ice has broken, let's talk"?' said
Jack.

'Exactly! Could this be a subtle cue?' said Mademoiselle Darrieux.

'Perhaps.'

'No shots, please.'

'I promise.'

'I understand you want to talk about the Ritz during the war years …'

'Yes, I do.'

'May I ask why? What's your interest?'

Jack had been expecting the question and was ready for it. 'I have been retained by a lady to investigate certain family matters …' said Jack, choosing his words carefully.

'Can you tell me her name?'

'Yes, but I would appreciate it if you could keep this confidential.'

'Of course.'

'Señora Dolores Gonzales. She lives in Mexico now, but she lived at the Ritz once … Madame Petrova and Señora Gonzales were close friends during the war.'

'Now, that is interesting …' said Mademoiselle Darrieux. 'I am actually writing a book about the Ritz, but please keep this under your hat.'

'Certainly,' said Jack. The countess nodded, watching the exchange with interest.

'In fact, I've recently done some research on Dolores Gonzales and her flamboyant art dealer husband, José. Did you know that José's father was one of the leaders during the Mexican Revolution? Quite a fanatic. Rumour has it José was interrogated and tortured by the German secret police during a scandal that rocked Paris and deeply affected all who lived at the Ritz at the time.'

'Scandal? What scandal?'

'You don't know?' said Mademoiselle Darrieux, surprised. 'The Scandal of the Crystal Skull. It was the talk of Paris in 1941, just after the occupation began.'

Jack looked thunderstruck. He reached for his glass and took a sip of champagne to give himself a little time to digest the implications of what he had just heard. 'Can you tell me about the scandal?' he said, trying to sound nonchalant.

'Of course. But before I do, you must promise me to come to one of my soirées …' said Mademoiselle Darrieux, lowering her voice.

'I'm not sure I ...'

'Mr Rogan would be delighted,' said the countess. She gave Jack a good kick in the shins under the table. 'Wouldn't you, Jack?'

'Delighted; absolutely,' said Jack.

# 32

Alexandra knew from experience that the best way to deal with the disturbing events of the past few days was to shut out distractions, resist the urge to speculate and focus on her work. Disciplined by nature and methodical by training, she immersed herself in Professor K's copious notes as she tried to piece together the cornerstones of his latest, groundbreaking research.

She attempted to do this by reconstructing his thoughts and ideas, hurriedly jotted down in his tiny, almost illegible handwriting during his final hours. It was obvious that Professor K had worked at a feverish pace, desperately trying to pass on what he had discovered and what he suspected, or hoped, the ultimate outcome might be.

There were obvious gaps in his reasoning, leaps of faith in some of his conclusions and often, it was impossible to separate facts from speculation. However, in the midst of all this noise, Alexandra was able to follow a golden thread of sound, inspired reasoning that meandered through the often confusing and exasperating maze of ideas. She called it the 'the trail of genius', which had set Professor K apart and made him so unique and admired by his peers.

Alexandra knew that cutting-edge research never moved in a straight line. There were always twists and turns, countless blind alleys, setbacks, intellectual quicksand and most dangerous of all, tempting solutions that more often than not, turned out to be false siren-calls luring the mind into error. Usually this happened with a Fata Morgana of promising answers that, under scrutiny, often turned out to be nothing more than illusion.

'Walking the tightrope of science' had been one of Professor K's favourite lines. Alexandra had never forgotten it, but more importantly, she herself had walked that precarious tightrope many times before. She knew exactly what it meant to look down into the abyss, and fall. She also knew what it took to pick yourself up again, climb back to the top, find your balance and continue.

173

'Doctor Delacroix, there is someone in reception to see you,' said Akhil Achari.

Alexandra looked at her assistant standing in the doorway, a puzzled look on her face. 'Do you know who?' she asked, suddenly feeling anxious. She certainly wasn't expecting anyone. Her assistant shook his head. 'I'll be down in a minute.' Alexandra put Professor K's notes back in the safe, took a deep breath to calm herself and walked outside to catch the lift to the ground floor.

George Papadoulis, a short, portly man with thinning black hair and thick, round glasses in old-fashioned tortoiseshell frames that gave him a somewhat comical, yet endearingly studious look, was waiting for Alexandra in reception.

'Forgive me, Dr Delacroix, for barging in like this to see you, but I saw no other way to get in touch,' said the little man, extending his hand. George Papadoulis turned out to be Professor K's accountant. He was also the executor of his Will, and it was in this capacity that he had come to see Alexandra. 'Could we perhaps go somewhere a little more private?'

Alexandra ushered her visitor into a small conference room next to reception. Papadoulis took off his glasses and began to polish them with his handkerchief. 'I am here to carry out Professor K's last wish,' he began, speaking quite softly. 'We had known each for several years and became good friends. He spoke often about you, always with affection, and held you in high regard.' Papadoulis opened his briefcase, pulled out a small parcel wrapped in brown paper and placed it on the table in front of him.

'Professor K came to see me a few days before he died ...' Papadoulis paused, his eyes misting over, 'and gave me this. He left it to you in his Will.' Papadoulis pushed the small parcel across the table. Alexandra looked at it and saw her name written across the top in Professor K's distinctive handwriting. 'He asked me to hand it to you in person, here at the institute, after you had taken up your new position. That's why I'm here. He was quite specific about this.'

'Do you know what's inside?'

'Not really, except for this: he said the contents of this little package had "the power to change the future of medicine and the journey of man". His very words.'

Alexandra felt an icy shiver tingle down her spine. 'Intriguing,' she said, and looked at the sad little man sitting opposite.

Papadoulis closed his briefcase and stood up. 'This concludes my mission,' he said. 'It has been a pleasure meeting you, Dr Delacroix. I know whatever Professor K has placed in your care, is in safe hands.'

Alexandra hurried back to her room, closed the door and put the little parcel on her workbench. She couldn't get those words, *it has the power to change the future of medicine and the journey of man*, out of her head. *I wonder what's inside.* She reached for a scalpel in her work tray.

First, she cut the piece of string and then made an incision in the wrapping paper along the sides of the parcel with her typical, surgical precision, careful not to damage anything inside. She used to do the same with Christmas presents, to the great amusement of friends and relatives. Then she folded back the paper.

On top of two small notebooks and an envelope that had her name written across it was a rectangular piece of what looked like parchment, or soft leather. Her curiosity aroused, Alexandra reached for the strange piece and carefully unfolded it. Fully opened up, the piece was quite long and covered in beautiful illustrations, reminding Alexandra of similar texts she had seen in museums. *Aztec*, she thought, running her eyes along the vivid illustrations. *A head operation; how amazing. How did he come by this, I wonder?* Then she reached for the envelope, opened it and began to read the letter.

*Dearest Alexandra*

*When you read this, all going well, you'll most likely be sitting in my chair at the Gordon. I'm sure you'll find what I'm about to tell you surprising, perhaps even a little confronting, but the truth is the truth and you of all people deserve – no – must know the truth …*

175

Teary-eyed, and overcome by emotion, Alexandra stopped reading for a moment as she remembered her dear friend and mentor reaching out to her from the great beyond.

For the next three hours, Alexandra kept reading with an intensity that made her cheeks glow with excitement. Unable to stop, she devoured first the letter with its astonishing revelations, and then the notebooks crammed with data. If only part of what they contained turned out to be scientific fact, then not only would they change the future of medicine, but also the journey of man.

Apart from her assistant asking her some questions connected with his work, Alexandra was only interrupted once that afternoon, by a phone call on her mobile. It was Jana Gonski letting her know she had just left Sydney airport, was on her way to the apartment and would be cooking dinner for them that evening. Suddenly, this phone call from a complete stranger she had only heard about, but never met, made Alexandra feel no longer so terribly alone.

# 33

Lola and Boris met Sir Humphrey at the Benito Juárez international airport and took him straight to the hospital. As the Elms' family physician, Sir Humphrey had looked after Isis' health since his school days at Eton. Lola knew it couldn't have been easy for a distinguished Harley Street specialist in his seventies like Sir Humphrey, to drop everything, get on a plane and fly to Mexico. Yet that was precisely what he had done, without question or hesitation.

'We don't know how to thank you, Sir Humphrey,' said Lola. 'We desperately need your guidance and advice. It's in times like these we find out just how fragile and vulnerable we are.'

'Quite. I've already spoken to the specialist in charge. A very competent and helpful chap,' said Sir Humphrey, patting Lola reassuringly on the hand.

'And?'

'I won't beat around the bush,' said Sir Humphrey, 'it looks serious.'

'How could this have happened so quickly?'

'Brain tumours can be very insidious. Harm by stealth, which makes them notoriously difficult to detect until it's almost too late.'

'Oh my God!' said Lola.

'Don't worry. We'll find a way to deal with this, you'll see. Isis is tough and I already have a few ideas ...'

Encouraged by Sir Humphrey's optimistic remarks, Lola sat back and stared out the window as the hire car crawled through the heavy evening traffic towards the hospital.

'How often did I tell you, Georgie; no more somersaults!' remonstrated Sir Humphrey, addressing his patient in the darkened room. Fully conscious, and feeling a lot better due to the heavy drugs that had been pumped into her, Isis looked at Sir Humphrey, a trusted old friend she had known her whole life. He was more like a favourite uncle you told things you didn't want your parents to know, than the family doctor who knew all your innermost secrets since you were a kid. A rare, kindred spirit she could trust without risk of being betrayed.

'It's really good to hear your voice after all the excited Spanish palaver round here,' said Isis. 'When can I get out of this place?'

'I knew you'd ask me that,' said Sir Humphrey.

'Well?'

'Not for a while, I'm afraid.'

'How bad is it?'

'Bad.'

'How bad?'

'Not too sure yet.'

'Come on … I know you too well. Tell me.'

'It's complicated …'

'Remember the day you taught me to play chess? You got bored talking to the vicar at dinner, and you and I went into Dad's study to have a game of chess? I think I was about eight or nine at the time.'

'Oh? How is this relevant?'

'Well, you told me the most important thing was to have a strategy.'

'All right; I get it. You've seen the X-rays?'

'I have.'

'You've seen the tumour?'

'Yes.'

'It must be removed.'

'They told me it can't be done.'

'There's a young surgeon in Boston who's pioneered a new technique. I think he could remove it, but it's risky.'

'How risky?'

'Very.'

'And if we don't operate?'

'Three months …'

'Then what are we waiting for?'

'That's my boy,' said Sir Humphrey. 'I'll arrange it. But you have to promise me one thing …'

'What?'

'No more somersaults. At least for the moment.'

'And how, do you suggest, I'm going to tell the thousands of fans waiting outside "no more somersaults"?' said Isis, enjoying the familiar banter. 'What about them?'

'I insist,' said Sir Humphrey, pointing a stern finger at his patient. 'Doctor's orders.'

'You drive a hard bargain.'

'You bet.'

'I'll be known as the Queen of Disappointments; you'll see.'

'That's a little harsh, don't you think?'

'Game of chess?'

'What? Now?'

'Why not? I'll ask Lola to get the plane ready, and in the meantime, you can see if my little grey cells are still working properly, as Hercule Poirot used to say. Diagnosis; Kasparov-style.'

Sir Humphrey began to laugh. His easygoing bedside manner was legendary, but actually had a serious side to it. While he was joking with his patient and engaging in light-hearted conversation, he was in fact assessing Isis' state of mind and making decisions about how best to deal with the crisis. This was a tried and tested technique he had perfected over many years. It had served him well on countless occasions, especially in situations of extreme stress.

In this instance, however, things were a little different. Because doctor and patient had known each other for such a long time, Isis was well aware of this strategy, and happily played along with it. The tables had been turned.

'You're on,' said Sir Humphrey. He took off his jacket, loosened his tie and sat down on the side of Isis' bed. 'I'm not sure my Mexican colleagues would approve of this.'

'Doctor and patient playing chess?'

'Yes.'

'Does it matter?'

'Not really. And besides, they all think we English are somewhat eccentric in any case.'

'Do they have a point, you think?'

'You tell me, Georgie,' said Sir Humphrey, laughing.

'The chess set is in the drawer over there,' said Isis, sitting up in bed.

'If I remember correctly, last time we played you ambushed my queen with a classic Kasparov ploy I taught you. You won't get away with it twice, I promise you.'

'We'll see,' said Isis, enjoying herself. 'You may not even notice it's happening.'

'Talk's cheap. Let's find out, shall we?'

# 34

Feeling relaxed and a little tipsy from too much champagne, the countess pulled down the armrest and let herself sink into the comfortable leather seat of the old Bentley. She had enjoyed the afternoon at La Closerie des Lilas and, to her surprise, she had also enjoyed meeting Mademoiselle Darrieux. The flamboyant socialite-writer with the fierce reputation had turned out to be far less self-possessed, and far more entertaining than the Paris social set gossip implied.

'Thank you, Katerina,' said Jack. He reached for the countess' hand, and kissed it gallantly.

'What for?' asked the countess, surprised by the unexpected gesture.

'For rescuing me from the velvet clutches of a social predator,' said Jack, laughing. You were right; Mademoiselle Darrieux is in a class of her own. The way you 'suggested' she meet me tomorrow at the Ritz and tell me all about the scandal in the very place where it all happened, was brilliant. At least now I won't have to attend one of her scary soirées. Thank you. You are a master tactician.'

'No one has called me that before,' said the countess, laughing. 'What did you think of her?'

'I quite like her. I think all this outrageous socialite stuff is a bit of an act, a front. Look, she's intelligent, witty, articulate, well-educated and fun to be with. Hardly the attributes of a flighty social butterfly. I think underneath the façade is a shrewd and astute woman, carefully observing and recording everything around her.'

'Very perceptive. Not bad for a country boy from Down Under. I completely agree with you. I like her too. Why do you think she's doing all this?'

'What? Almost intentionally making fun of herself and all that?'

'Exactly.'

'I think she uses it as a door-opener. And because people don't take her too seriously, they let their guard down and unintentionally allow her see things that would otherwise remain hidden. You said she was a successful author. A *biographer* – right? That's what writers do; they *observe*. She's in the people business. Do you remember what she called herself?'

'Tell me.'

'A connoisseur of human nature.'

'That says it all. I think you two will get on famously,' said the countess.

'We'll see. Tomorrow,' said Jack. 'Afternoon tea at the Ritz at three, to be precise. Could I borrow François and the Bentley? After all, appearances are important, especially in Paris. You told me so yourself.'

'And you don't want to disappoint Mademoiselle Darrieux.'

'That would be unforgivable.'

'In that case, you shall have the car and the driver.'

'Your blood's worth bottling,' said Jack.

'Another one of your curious antipodean sayings, no doubt,' teased the countess.

'You bet.'

Jack looked across the elegant square with its splendid classical buildings dating back to the Sun King days of Louis XIV. François was skilfully manoeuvring the big car through the heavy afternoon traffic towards number 15, Place Vendôme, one of the most famous hotel addresses in the world. One hundred and fifty-nine rooms of ultimate luxury, with a staff of six hundred to cater for every whim.

The back door of the car was opened as soon as the Bentley pulled up at the imposing front entrance. 'Welcome to the Ritz, Monsieur Rogan,' said the liveried doorman in perfect English. 'Mademoiselle Darrieux is expecting you in the Bar Vendôme. Please follow me.'

*I've been recognised without ever having been here; impressive*, thought Jack, and got out of the car. *Mademoiselle Darrieux is obviously a lady of considerable influence.*

It was impossible not to be impressed by the opulence and grandeur of the hotel's entry and foyer. The flowers alone were overwhelming. A pinnacle of classic elegance and style blending the beauty of nature with manmade craftsmanship and art.

The Ritz family sold the hotel to Mohamed Al-Fayed in 1979. Over the next ten years, the Egyptian tycoon spent two hundred and fifty million dollars renovating the tired icon. In August 1997, Princess Diana and Al-Fayed's son, Dodi, had dined in the famous Imperial Suite – once occupied by Göring – just hours before meeting their tragic end in the Pont de l'Alma underpass.

*Living history*, thought Jack, looking down the corridor on his left. He could imagine the Duke of Windsor with Wallace Simpson on his arm strolling towards the Ritz Bar for cocktails. *What an amazing place.*

Afternoon tea was already in full swing in the Bar Vendôme, a popular venue frequented by Parisian high society. Mademoiselle Darrieux's table was strategically positioned next to the grand piano, in clear view of the entrance and everyone else in the busy room.

If Jack thought Mademoiselle Darrieux's dazzling Valentino creation of the day before had been eye-catching, nothing could have prepared him for the spectacular outfit she had chosen for their afternoon meeting at the Ritz.

Lilac had been replaced by a yellow so bright, it would have made daffodils wilt in shame. However, Valentino's masterly hand had once again made sure that Mademoiselle Darrieux's figure was the hero to be admired with envy by women half her age. With her ample bosom sufficiently exposed to make even the most experienced waiter blush, Mademoiselle Darrieux had once again achieved her objective: she was impossible to ignore.

Trying hard not to laugh, Jack kissed his host on both heavily powdered cheeks, as instructed by the countess. *Mission accomplished*, he thought, and sat down. Jack didn't like being on show, but to have failed to follow this social ritual would have been an unforgivable faux pas only committed by bores and the socially inept.

Mademoiselle Darrieux pointed to the cocktail glass on the small table in front of her. 'You must try one of these,' she said, well aware that all eyes were on her and her handsome guest.

'Looks lethal,' said Jack.

'It is, but in a sublime way; trust me.'

'What is it?'

'It's called a "Rainbow", made famous by Frank Meier, a charismatic barman here at the Ritz Bar during the nineteen twenties and thirties. Yellow chartreuse, mint, anisette, cherry brandy, cognac, green chartreuse and kummel. Genius.'

'Sounds irresistible. I must have one.'

'You shall,' said Mademoiselle Darrieux. 'In fact, Meier was right here during the war. He was one of Göring's favourites. He even invented a cocktail for the Reichsmarschall; the "Stuka".'

'A dive-bomber, certain to obliterate the enemy?' quipped Jack.

'Something like that. Apparently, it was vile.'

'Fascinating. As a resident barman popular with the Germans, Meier would have known all about the scandal of the crystal skull?' said Jack, a sparkle in his eyes.

Mademoiselle Darrieux looked at Jack. 'I like your style,' she said, patting Jack on the hand, 'subtle, but persistent. I wonder, are you like that in all of your endeavours?'

'Only when I'm pursuing something exciting.'

'I like that even more.'

To his surprise, Jack was actually enjoying the light-hearted, flirty banter, and was warming to the flamboyant, outrageously dressed, eccentric woman sitting next to him. Her wit, good humour and sparkling intelligence left no room for awkwardness or embarrassment or, God forbid, boredom. An afternoon he had approached with some trepidation was turning into fun.

'In that case, could you please put this persistent pursuer out of his misery and tell him about the scandal?'

'I will, but first we must share a Rainbow. The pot of gold is always at the end. And besides, this story requires a stiff drink.'

# 35

It was almost midnight by the time the old Bentley finally crossed the moat leading to the Kuragin Chateau. Jack sat in the front chatting to François, who had patiently waited for him at the Ritz for hours without complaint. As it turned out, François had put the time to good use. He had arranged to meet an old friend, a lady, who was teaching at the Ritz-Escoffier School of French Gastronomy adjacent to the hotel. They had spent some time together – over a splendid dinner – in a private dining room where the celebrity chefs were trying out their new creations. Staff canteen à la Ritz.

Jack was certain that everyone would be fast asleep by now and quietly entered through a side door.

'The reveller returns,' said the countess, turning on the light. 'Afternoon tea until midnight? That's a record. You must have succumbed to Mademoiselle Darrieux's considerable charms is all I can think of,' teased the countess. 'You did kiss her on both cheeks as I told you? Perhaps you didn't stop there?'

'I'm not that brave. Powdered cheeks and perfume to make a rhino faint were enough for me, thanks. And besides, everyone was watching. You should have seen her outfit. The things I do to get a little information,' said Jack, shaking his head.

'I hope it was worth it.'

'Sure was.'

'Come into the kitchen and tell me all about it.'

'Boy, can this woman drink!' said Jack, making himself comfortable on the kitchen bench. 'First, she plied me with fancy cocktails that almost blew my head off, then she suggested we have dinner. Some posh restaurant at the Ritz.'

'L'Espadon? The Swordfish?'

'That's the one; I couldn't get out of it; sorry.'

'Poor boy. People with influence wait for months just to get a table … She was showing you off, that's all.'

'What do you mean?'

'Never mind …'

'She knows everybody, and the staff fawn over her like she owns the place. Tucker was great, and so was the wine. And after that, we ended up in the Bar Hemingway for more drinks. It was there she finally told me about the scandal.'

'The saga of the crystal skull?'

'Yes.'

'I can't wait.'

'You won't be disappointed.' Jack pulled his little notebook out of his pocket, slipped off the rubber band holding it together and put it on the table in front of him. 'What she told me was astonishing. I still find it difficult to get my head around it all, but I had the big surprise of the evening up my sleeve,' boasted Jack. 'She was speechless, I tell you. Lost for words. Well, momentarily at least.'

'How did you manage that?'

'With a photo. As you can imagine, it takes a lot to render Mademoiselle Darrieux speechless, but when I showed her the photo, she was gobsmacked.'

'The suspense is killing me,' said the countess. 'Why do you think I stayed up for you? *Tell me!*'

'All right. It's a great story. Only this one begins with a legend.'

'I can see where this is heading,' said the countess. 'We'll be here all night.' The countess pointed to the samovar on the kitchen table. 'Tea?'

'From my favourite tea urn warming generations?' mused Jack.

'It has heard more stories than you'll ever come up with.' Enjoying the intimacy of the moment, Jack opened his notebook. 'A long time ago,' he began, speaking slowly and putting on his best narrator's voice, 'somewhere deep in the jungle, an Aztec priest is about to perform a human sacrifice. Held down by four masked men, a young warrior is lying on the stone altar ready to have his chest cut open and his beating heart ripped out to placate the bloodthirsty gods. Drums are beating, priests are chanting, the faithful are watching. Holding a large knife in his right hand, the priest looks up at the stars, and then plunges the razor-sharp blade deep into the chest of the hapless warrior.

'Covered in blood, the priest reaches inside the open wound with his left hand, searching for the beating heart. This is something he has done many times before, only this time he cannot find the heart. Instead, he can feel something hard and smooth like stone, inside the man's chest.' Jack paused, letting the tension grow and reached for his teacup.

'And all this is relevant, I take it?' said the countess, raising an eyebrow.

Jack was enjoying himself. 'Sure is,' he said. 'Don't you want to know what the priest found inside the poor man's chest?'

'I'm sure you're about to tell me.'

'A present from the gods.'

'You don't say. What was it?'

Jack reached for his iPhone, called up a photo and pushed the phone across the table towards the countess. 'This.'

For a long moment, the countess just stared at the photo Jack had taken of the crystal skull in Sir Charles' study a few days before.

'Are you serious? What is this?' she said after a while, a puzzled look on her face.

'The Aztec crystal skull at the *heart* of the scandal that rocked the Ritz in 1941.'

'Pun intended?' teased the countess.

'And by the way, Mademoiselle Darrieux looked just like you did a moment ago when I showed her the photo – incredulous. Well, perhaps she was a little more surprised than you,' said Jack, laughing. 'Shocked, actually.'

'I don't understand,' said the countess. 'How does all this fit together?'

'Another cup of tea, and I'll tell you.'

Grateful to have an attentive confidante he could trust and who was prepared to listen, Jack told the countess everything he knew about the skull's extraordinary reappearance and discovery. He told her how Isis had followed the clues buried in her mother's last words and found the skull hidden in the Egyptian room at Clarendon Hall.

'But what about the scandal? Where's the connection?' asked the countess. 'Are you suggesting that somehow this is the legendary Aztec skull?'

'Not sure, but listen to this: Fast forward to January 1941,' said Jack. 'Dolores Gonzales, Isis' grandmother, stays with her husband, José, and her young daughter, Mercedes, at the Ritz in Paris. José, a Mexican art dealer, has a spectacular Aztec crystal skull in his collection, which he shows off to potential clients to attract business. Reichsmarschall Göring, who is living at the Ritz, hears about the skull and falls under its spell. He must have it at any cost. José doesn't want to part with it, but ultimately cannot refuse. Göring acquires the skull under the pretence that it is a present for Hitler who, as we know, was deeply interested in the occult.'

'And Mademoiselle Darrieux told you all this?' interjected the countess.

'Yes. As you know, she's writing a book about the Ritz during the war years and has done a huge amount of research on the subject. And besides, Madame Petrova was a close friend of Dolores Gonzales' at the time and played an important part in the scandal that followed. I have no doubt that's the reason Mademoiselle Darrieux is so interested in her.'

'How extraordinary. But what about the scandal?'

'Göring was obsessed with the skull and took it with him everywhere he went. It even sat on his table at the Ritz during dinner, grinning at his guests. Not only was the Reichsmarschall totally eccentric, he was a morphine addict, given to fits of rage and outlandish behaviour. A dangerous, unpredictable man with unlimited power.'

Jack paused and looked at the countess. 'And then it happened …' he said.

'What happened?'

'A couple of weeks after Göring acquired the skull from José – appropriated would be more accurate – it disappeared. Vanished without a trace. Göring used to keep it next to his bed in the Imperial Suite and when he woke up one morning, it just wasn't there. That's when all hell broke loose—'

'You don't say. This sounds more like a Shakespearian play …' interjected the countess.

'Wait. The best is yet to come,' said Jack, enjoying himself. 'Apparently, Göring appeared at the top of the stairs dressed in his silk pyjamas and a spectacular Kimono. Still in a morphine-induced fog from the night before, he began to scream and, brandishing a bejewelled baton, made all kinds of outrageous accusations.

'The Abwehr, the secret police, were called in at once to investigate the theft. Everyone was interrogated, the entire hotel was searched and, not surprisingly, suspicion fell on José and he became the prime suspect. Not the most careful or tactful man, he deeply resented having been parted from his prized possession by the high-handed Reichsmarschall, and openly complained about it to anyone prepared to listen.

'However, nothing was found. Infuriated, Göring and his henchmen continued to terrorise everyone at the Ritz. José was arrested and, it was rumoured, tortured, but to no avail. The skull had vanished.'

'What happened to José?' asked the countess.

'Don't know. That's where the trail suddenly goes cold, I'm afraid, for now …'

'And you are determined to do something about that; right?'

'Absolutely!'

'And what might that be?'

'Mademoiselle Darrieux and I have made a pact.'

'A *what*?'

'We have agreed to share information and find out what happened to the notorious skull after it disappeared from the Reichsmarschall's boudoir. Where did it go? Something so precious doesn't just disappear without a trace. The question is this: where was it during the past seventy years, and how on earth did it end up hidden in a mummy-case in the Egyptian room at Clarendon Hall?'

'Assuming of course it's the same skull,' interjected the countess.

'Sure, but it's so unique. And look at the circumstances and the people involved ... I have agreed to help her get access to the skull and perhaps even arrange an interview with Dolores Gonzales. That's my contribution. This could easily turn her book into a bestseller. She was on fire, I tell you.'

'Not just cocktail speak and unrequited passion?' teased the countess.

'Oh no. She knew exactly what she was saying.'

'So what's your next step?'

'Talking to Madame Petrova.'

'I thought you might say that. When would you like to see her?'

'In the morning? Don't look at me like that,' said Jack. 'That's what happens when you let an incorrigible rascal stay in your house.'

'I'm just beginning to find out what that entails,' said the countess, laughing. 'I only hope I don't regret it.'

'Never!'

# 36

Alexandra closed Professor K's notebook, took a deep breath and sat back, her head spinning. Then she reached for the letter addressed to her and read it again for the third time. *Extraordinary*, she thought. *Just when we think we know someone, we really don't know them at all.*

The material in the notebooks left to Alexandra in Professor K's Will explained the reasoning underpinning his groundbreaking research in painstaking detail that only she could understand. The professor's train of thought was unique and his methods unorthodox. He saw things differently, and it took a like-minded scientist to appreciate his ways. Alexandra was that scientist. She understood that the true scientist must not be dazzled by nature's breathtaking beauty, nor be cowed by its chilling terror. To know how, and why was everything.

Step-by-step, the copious notes, laborious calculations and often quite convoluted references and connections somehow pulled everything together with a clarity that was as compelling as it was obvious – if you knew how to read them and what to look for. Moreover, they appeared to contain much of the missing data supporting the professor's extraordinary findings, and neatly complemented the notes left for her at the institute.

To make sense, everything had to be considered together. Alexandra was sure this had been quite deliberate. Professor K, a cautious man, was fully aware of security and protecting his work. *Complexity made simple*, thought Alexandra, *and safe. Genius. If it works.* However, a lot still remained to be done. Then came the bombshell …

The letter went on the explain that the entire research and all of the sensational findings were the culmination of an inspired idea first conceived by Professor K's father – an eminent Polish doctor – in a German concentration camp during the war. Apparently, it had all begun with one curious case involving twins: the Abramowitz girls. And if that wasn't enough, there was more, a lot more. The other revelations, of a most personal kind, contained in the letter rocked Alexandra to the core ...

*Extraordinary*, she thought, suddenly feeling confused and exhausted. Since her meeting with Professor K's executor, Mr Papadoulis earlier that day, much had changed. She folded the letter carefully along its creases and slipped it back into the envelope. *Who could possibly have imagined all this? More questions after death than answers during life. Yet, here I am ... alone.*

Alexandra looked at her watch. *Jesus*, she thought, *Jana!* She crammed everything into her handbag, quickly locked the safe in her lab and headed for the door.

*She's late*, thought Jana. The simple stir-fry she was cooking for dinner was ready to go and the table was set. Jana poured herself another glass of wine and looked pensively out of the large panoramic kitchen window framing the Sydney Opera House and busy harbour below. It felt a little strange cooking for someone she hadn't met, but it felt good being back in Sydney on familiar turf.

Jana had missed Australia dreadfully and was looking forward to making contact with some of her old colleagues in the police force. However, what she had missed most of all was her career, which had come to such an abrupt and inglorious end during the Newman trial. Jack understood this, and his request for her help had come at a good time – for all concerned.

Jana heard the key turn in the front door lock and looked up. She turned down the music with the remote and walked to the lobby.

'I'm sorry,' said Alexandra, looking a little flustered. 'I lost track of time. It's been a turbulent day.'

They shook hands.

'Glass of wine?' said Jana, pointing to the kitchen.

'Absolutely. I can't tell you how good it feels to have you here. I've heard so much about you. From Jack of course ...'

'Real life is a little different, I'm afraid,' said Jana. 'And most of what I know about you, I've learnt from Jack and your aunt. A great fan, by the way. She sends her regards, and so does Jack. You seem to have had an interesting time since you arrived here ...'

'That's an understatement,' said Alexandra, feeling suddenly quite cold. 'I could certainly do with that wine.'

'I'm cooking Jack's favourite stir-fry. He taught me,' said Jana, laughing. 'He's a much better cook than I'll ever be. An absent friend joins us for dinner through his culinary prowess; that's Jack for you,' joked Jana. 'Let's eat first, and talk later.'

'You're on,' said Alexandra and followed Jana into the kitchen. 'I'm starving.'


The tasty meal washed down with a copious quantity of Jack's wine and Jana's easygoing manner made it possible for Alexandra to open up.

Barefoot and relaxed, they sat on the lounge, listening to jazz like old friends. Experienced in asking difficult questions, Jana took Alexandra through her abduction ordeal and the time she had spent on the *Calypso* as Macbeth's 'guest'.

'And you think Cavendish's death at the nightclub is somehow related?' asked Jana.

'I'm sure of it. Macbeth more than hinted that this was so. In fact, he used it as a clear warning. He was telling me he could reach me anytime, anywhere, and I believe him. He certainly has the power, the connections and the means. And besides, he had the professor's notebook right there in front of him. Tangible proof. He's the most chilling man I've ever met.'

'And the police know nothing of this?'

Alexandra shook her head. 'I doubt it. The papers said the fire was a terrible accident caused by an electrical fault in an overcrowded establishment, and that several patrons died during the panic that followed. Cavendish was one of them; that's all. And it all happened in a notorious gay club. There's a lot of homophobic feeling out there, if you know what I mean ...'

Jana nodded. 'And your involvement in all this? Why do you say you've been set up?'

'That's simple. It all has to do with Professor K's work. That's the reason I came to Australia in the first place, and that's the reason for my abduction and Macbeth's interest in me. No doubt about it. And let's not forget, Macbeth owns one of the largest pharmaceutical corporations in the world. We are talking mega dollars here. Influence and power on an almost unimaginable scale. With so much at stake, industrial espionage is rife.'

'Abduction and murder too?' interjected Jana.

'It would seem so,' said Alexandra. 'Greed and lust for power recognise no boundaries, moral or otherwise.'

'Is Professor K's work really that important?'

'It is, in more ways than I can explain right now.'

'Close to a breakthrough?'

'It would seem so.'

'How close?'

'Very.'

'Tell me about the money.'

'Well, it happened right here in this very room.'

'Oh?'

'Macbeth's blond thug with ice-blue eyes brought me back here and reminded me of where I stood, and what I had to do. He also reminded me of the consequences should I fail to cooperate … I was sitting where you are sitting right now, and he stood behind me. He put his hands on the back of my neck and began to squeeze, ever so gently. Then he told me that there was a little surprise waiting for me in my bank account. When I checked later, I saw that three hundred thousand dollars had been transferred into my account. You can see what they are doing, surely? It's very clever.'

'Tell me.'

'I arrive at the prestigious Gordon Institute as the anointed successor of Professor K, who has just passed away. He's on the brink of a spectacular breakthrough in cancer treatment that could make billions for a pharmaceutical company and revolutionise the way we deal with that dreadful disease. I take his place and continue his work. A few days later, I join the head of Blackburn Pharmaceuticals on his legendary ship and spend the weekend there as his guest. I'm seen leaving my apartment with a man who behaves like my lover and return two days later with him. It turns out that the man works for the company. The next day, I go to work as usual and continue my research at the Gordon.

'However, on the same day, three hundred thousand dollars is transferred into my bank account from an anonymous source, impossible to trace. The inference? Obvious, wouldn't you say? In return, I will pass information about my work to a source linked to Blackburn Pharmaceuticals. In doing so, I'm cheating on my employer by selling vital information potentially worth billions to a pharmaceutical giant. In short, I'm committing a serious crime. And if any of this gets out, I'm ruined. I will never work as a scientist again and will most likely end up in jail. How am I doing so far?'

Jana reached for the bottle on the table in front of her and refilled their glasses. 'Go on,' she said.

'*And what do you have to say for yourself, Dr Alexander?* I hear the prosecutor ask me in the dock. I then give my version of what happened. You've just heard it.' Alexandra reached for her glass, took a sip of wine and looked across to the Harbour Bridge. 'Now tell me honestly, which version would you believe?'

'We have a problem,' conceded Jana. 'But every problem has a solution. We just have to know where to look for it. But tonight is neither the time nor the place to do that. If I don't get some sleep soon, jetlag will turn me into a pumpkin, and pumpkins are notoriously unreliable. Let's see what the new day brings. And besides, I already have an idea …'

'Thanks, Jana,' said Alexandra, lifting her glass in salute. 'I cannot tell you what a difference just talking to you has made already. And I agree with you, everything looks different in the morning. And thanks for dinner; my turn tomorrow.'

'Not Heston Blumenthal-style, I hope,' joked Jana.

'Certainly not! When I cook, I leave science at the kitchen door.'

'Thank God for that.'

'Oh, I almost forgot,' said Jana. 'Jack sent you this.' Jana reached for a book on the coffee table.

'What is it?'

'*Dental Gold and Other Horrors*, the book that made Jack famous. Apparently, you haven't read it yet.'

'No, I haven't but I've heard a lot about it; thanks. A little bedtime reading, you think?'

'Perhaps ...'

# 37

Smartly dressed and wearing make-up and her favourite pearls, Madame Petrova was waiting for them in her room at the nursing home. For a woman well into her nineties, she looked remarkable. However, the nurse had suggested to the countess that a morning visit would be best, as Madame Petrova's concentration and attention span were better at that time.

The countess kissed her dear friend on the cheek.

'So, you've come to visit the old fossil again,' said Madame Petrova, laughing. 'It's hard to believe I once turned the heads of royalty just by walking into a room.'

'I can believe that,' said Jack, gallantly kissing Madame Petrova's hand.

'You are a wonderful liar, Mr Rogan, but please don't stop. Make-believe is better than despair.'

After the maid had served the obligatory coffee and petits fours, Jack decided to come straight to the point – dramatically. He called up the picture of the crystal skull on his iPhone and handed it to Madame Petrova. 'Do you recognise this?' he asked, watching her carefully.

Madame Petrova reached for the large magnifying glass with an ivory handle she used when reading, and had a look. Surprise; incredulity; confusion. The expression on the old lady's face told Jack all he had to know.

'Oh my God! How did you …? Where did this …? *The scandal of the crystal skull*,' whispered Madame Petrova. 'Now, that was something …' Transported by memories of a turbulent, distant past, it was obvious Madame Petrova was unsettled and beginning to drift.

'Mademoiselle Darrieux suggested I talk to you about it,' said Jack, anxious not to lose her train of thought. 'Because you—'

'You spoke to her?' interrupted Madame Petrova.

'Just as you asked me to,' said Jack.

'What would you like to know?'

Jack pulled his little notebook and a pen out of his pocket and sat back. 'Anything you can remember about the scandal would be most helpful,' he said, and looked expectantly at the elegant lady sitting opposite.

Enjoying the attention, Madame Petrova gave Jack a coquettish look and smiled. 'It was a long time ago,' she said, 'but it seems like only yesterday. We were all so young ...'

As often happens with old people, they may not remember that someone visited them an hour ago, but they can recall the past with extraordinary clarity and precision. This was certainly the case with Madame Petrova's recollection of the scandal at the Ritz seventy-odd years before. Animated by her memories, she recounted the events surrounding the scandal in surprising detail, including names, personalities, exact locations within the hotel and even conversations and rumours.

'What happened after José Gonzales was arrested?' asked Jack. 'What happened to his wife and daughter?'

'They remained at the Ritz,' said Madame Petrova. 'They had nowhere else to go, you see. That's when Dolores and I became friends; close friends. I lived at the Ritz at the time, and we all felt for Dolores and what happened to her and her poor husband. All of us living at the hotel were a bit like a family, including the staff.

'Göring was crazy, and very dangerous. Everyone was terrified of him, and all of us were potential suspects. No one felt safe. The theft of the skull almost sent the Reichsmarschall mad. I can remember terrible scenes in the lobby. Göring was shouting abuse at the Abwehr officers, calling them incompetent imbeciles and accusing them of deliberate failure to find the culprit and recover his precious artefact.'

Madame Petrova paused and took a sip of coffee from her tiny porcelain cup, her arthritic fingers shaking. 'That's when he called in the dashing young officer from Bavaria to take charge of the investigation.'

Jack sat up as if pricked by a hot needle from behind. He could feel the hairs on the back of his neck begin to tingle. It was a familiar sensation, a premonition, often heralding an unexpected revelation or surprise. 'Can you remember his name?' Jack asked, sounding hoarse.

'Oh yes; he was the brother of Göring's doctor. His name was Steinberger. Sturmbannfuehrer Wolfgang Steinberger, a most charming, devilishly handsome man.' Madame Petrova pointed to the piano. 'I think he's in one of the photos, right here. Let me show you.'

The countess and Jack left Madame Petrova's room soon after that. Madame Petrova had suddenly become very tired and confused, and reluctant to answer any more questions. The nurse suggested it would be best to continue the conversation another time.

'This is unbelievable,' said Jack, looking at the photograph he had borrowed from Madame Petrova. It showed an elegantly dressed young woman standing at the bottom of an imposing staircase – apparently somewhere in the Ritz – next to a tall young man wearing the distinct uniform of the notorious SS. It was difficult to make out the precise features of the man's face because the picture was quite small and the image a little blurred. However, there was something familiar about the officer in the photograph. His stance, the casual, almost arrogant confidence in the body language reminded Jack of another photo he had found in the ruins of a cottage destroyed by bushfire in the Blue Mountains in Australia three years before.

'The far-reaching tentacles of the past never cease to amaze me,' said Jack pensively. He handed the photo to the countess sitting next to him in the back of the Bentley, which François was driving. The countess had taken the old car because hers was being serviced. 'Quite often the important clues are right there in front of us,' continued Jack.

'What do you mean?' asked the countess.

'There's something odd about the way she's looking at the officer, don't you think? Look at the way he's holding her arm. What does that tell you?'

'Now that you mention it...' said the countess.

'What do you see?'

'Intimacy.'

'Exactly. Not quite what you'd expect in the circumstances, is it? The beautiful, vulnerable young wife of the man who had just been arrested and tortured by the Nazis, looking adoringly at the young SS officer?'

'What are you getting at?'

'There's a lot more to all this, and it all has to do with Dolores and Sturmbannfuehrer Steinberger, I'm sure of it,' said Jack. *Hidden corners of our lives*, he thought, remembering Señora Gonzales' cryptic reference to Steinberger at her house in Mexico.

'I see what you mean ...' said the countess.

'And wasn't it strange how Madame Petrova suddenly changed the subject and pretended to become confused when I questioned her about Dolores and the handsome Nazi? She didn't want to talk about it, and I think I know why.'

'Oh?'

'Because of her friendship with Dolores.'

'Fear of betrayal?'

'Something like that.'

'After all these years?'

'Sure. Friendship is a powerful bond. And let's not forget, Madame Petrova lives in the past,' said Jack.

'Then she's unlikely to tell you more.'

'I'm afraid you may be right. However, she did give us an important clue, perhaps unintentionally.'

'What about?'

'She let something slip just before we left. She told us that the skull was eventually recovered by Steinberger, and that Dolores was somehow involved. Do you remember what I asked her after that?'

'Yes. You asked her if that had happened before or after the photo was taken.'

'Exactly. And she answered without hesitation. She was certain it had happened well before the picture was taken. Doesn't that strike you as odd?'

'Why?'

'Well, the Nazi officer who apparently exposed the culprit and recovered Göring's precious treasure, and the woman who was somehow involved pose for a photo suggesting intimacy?'

'Good point … So, where to from here?'

'Not sure. Mademoiselle Darrieux doesn't appear to know much about Dolores either. That's why she's so keen to interview her. And what I find particularly intriguing is this,' said Jack, becoming quite animated, 'She knows about the skull affair, but I'm not sure she knows about Steinberger and what followed.'

'A dead end?'

'I don't believe in dead ends. In a way, this is just the beginning. I can sense it …'

'I may be able to help,' interjected François, who had of course overheard the conversation.

'In what way?' asked the countess, surprised.

'I have a friend who works at the Ritz. She's a teacher at the Ritz-Escoffier School right next to the hotel. I visited her yesterday while I was waiting. We had lunch. Her grandfather worked at the Ritz for many years, right through the war. She often speaks about him and his stories. He got her the job.'

'Is he still alive?' asked Jack.

'Not sure, but I can find out.'

'Could you?'

'Of course.'

Jack turned to the countess. 'See, there's no such thing as a dead end,' he said, patting her on the hand, 'only challenges. I think I'll leave this one to Mademoiselle Darrieux to tackle.'

'Now that you are partners?' interjected the countess.

'Exactly. She almost seems to live at the Ritz and knows everyone. Let's see what she can come up with. After that, it's definitely time for a little chat with Señora Gonzales. Hopefully, I'll have a few surprises for her.'

'I'm sure you will, Jack. Somehow, you never disappoint a lady …'

# 38

Akhil Achari hadn't left the blackjack table for hours. He was on a winning streak. Mesmerised, he watched the cards dance in the dealer's hands in front of him. Perfected by countless games, the dealer's fingers moved with elegant precision like the fingers of a concert pianist gliding expertly over the keyboard.

Paulus had been watching Achari for some time. The player sitting next to Achari picked up his chips and got out of his seat. *Time to make a move*, thought Paulus. He walked across to the table, sat down next to Achari and joined the game. 'Are you going to share some of your good fortune with us,' he said, turning to Achari, 'or are you too busy winning? You haven't been in touch ...'

'I can explain,' mumbled Achari, taking another card.

'Excellent. Now would be a good time. Look, here you go again. Another win. I suggest you call it a night and cash in before you luck runs out ... We need to talk.'

Reluctantly, Achari collected his chips and followed Paulus to the bar. 'A man came to see her yesterday at the institute,' he said. 'I was going to call you ...'

'What man?' asked Paulus.

'A stranger. She certainly wasn't expecting him. She hardly knows anyone in Sydney. They spoke for about half an hour in one of the conference rooms and then he left.'

'So?'

'He gave her something; a small parcel. I saw her bring it back to her lab and open it.'

'Do you know what was in it?'

'Not really, except for this: she sat at her desk all afternoon, reading. I can see her from my workbench through the glass. She seemed totally absorbed. I went in once to ask her a question, but she wasn't interested and told me to come back later. That isn't like her.'

'I expect there's a good reason you're telling me all this?' said Paulus.

'Sure is.'

'Enlighten me.'

'I got a good look at what she was reading. It was some kind of notebook or journal. It had a greenish cover. By itself, unremarkable, but I recognised the crazy diagrams and the handwriting ...'

'Oh?'

'Professor K's. I'm sure of it.'

'Have you seen that notebook before?'

'No; it looked quite different from the others.'

'Now that is interesting ...' said Paulus. 'Did you ask her about the visitor?'

'Yes.'

'What did she say?'

'That he was a friend of the professor, that's all.'

'Does this friend have a name?'

'I asked the receptionist ...'

'And?'

'I think my winning streak deserves to last a little longer, don't you agree?' said Achari, enjoying himself. For the first time, he felt he had the upper hand.

Paulus reached into his pocket, pulled out a wad of hundred dollar notes and put them on the bar in front of Achari. 'Does five thousand sound like a reasonable winning streak for a name?'

'George Papadoulis,' said Achari. 'And I have a little bonus for you ...'

'Oh?'

'He's an accountant,' said Achari, beaming. 'Here's his business card. He left it at reception.'

'Keep up the good work,' said Paulus and put another thousand dollars on the bar. 'And do keep in touch.'

'To keep up my winning streak, you mean?'

'Matter for you.'

Achari stuffed the money into his pocket, got off the bar stool and walked back to the gaming table.

# 39

François was in his element. He loved the old Bentley and enjoyed driving it, even if it meant having to manoeuvre the car carefully through the busy Paris morning traffic.

'Excellent lead,' said Jack. 'Thank you.'

'Mademoiselle Darrieux seemed happy,' said François.

'You can say that again,' said Jack, remembering the stunning Chanel chiffon creation that had greeted him that morning. The impromptu rendezvous to exchange information had turned into a high society adventure of stellar proportions, no doubt carefully stage-managed by the indefatigable Mademoiselle Darrieux herself. She had once again made sure she was the head-turning centre of attention. Jack was certain the whole of Paris considered them an item by now. The eager paparazzi waiting outside to get a photo of them leaving together only confirmed Jack's suspicions. Exhausted, but elated, Jack was on his way back to the chateau after a sumptuous champagne breakfast with Mademoiselle Darrieux at her favourite Paris café.

Despite being a long shot, Jack's intrepid new glittering socialite 'partner' had quickly tracked down François' contact – a delightful gentleman in his eighties – who had worked at the Ritz during the war as a bellboy. With access to every corner of the labyrinthine establishment, bellboys were the invisible eyes and ears of the hotel, and therefore a reliable source of information of the most secret and intimate kind.

The old man remembered the scandal of the crystal skull surprisingly well, and was able to provide some exciting new information and promising leads regarding Señora Gonzales and the Germans.

*This changes everything*, thought Jack, reaching for his little notebook. He was going over his notes again, trying to piece everything together, when his phone rang. It was Lola with some disturbing news. Isis had an unexpected turn during the night and was unable to travel to the US. The critical brain surgery was therefore, at least for the time being, off limits. Understandably, this had thrown everything into turmoil. Confined to bed under strict medical supervision in the privacy of her grandmother's home, Isis had requested an urgent meeting with Jack.

*Pegasus* was already in the air by the time Lola spoke to Jack. She was taking Sir Humphrey back to London and suggested Jack meet the plane in Paris on its return journey to Mexico. This gave Jack only a few hours to pack and get to the airport.

'Bad news?' asked François.

'It would appear so.'

Tristan walked into Jack's room and watched him pack his duffel bag. 'You are leaving,' he said, the disappointment on his face obvious.

Jack nodded. 'Isis …'

'I know.'

'How do you know?'

Tristan shrugged. 'Just do.'

Jack looked at Tristan. *He knows exactly what I'm thinking and how I feel*, thought Jack, *and what I'm about to say*. The special bond between them was growing stronger by the day.

'I know I promised,' said Jack. 'I'll make it up to you … soon.' Jack had promised to spend some time with Tristan during the school holidays and take him on a trip. That was a year ago. Somehow, something had always come up.

'Take me with you,' said Tristan.

'What? Now?'

'Yes. I can help you. You know I can. And I can help Isis too …' said Tristan, getting excited.

'Do I need help?'

'Yes, you do. Danger …'

'What are you saying?'

'I saw things again …'

'Katerina won't allow it,' said Jack, shaking his head.

'She will, if you ask her. Holidays have just started. There's no school for the next three weeks. We've nothing planned here.' Tristan pulled something out of his pocket and held it up. It was his passport. 'It's meant to be. I'm ready.'

For reasons he couldn't quite explain, Jack was pleased. The aura of calm confidence radiating from the boy had banished the apprehension he had felt about the unexpected trip and what would be waiting for him. His mind racing, Jack looked at Tristan. *Such a wise head on shoulders so young*, he marvelled. *Extraordinary.* 'I have to call Lola first...' said Jack.

Without saying another word, Tristan ran over to his friend and gave him a hug.

It was already dark by the time *Pegasus* landed. Tristan could barely contain his excitement as he watched the sleek plane taxi towards the terminal reserved for private jets. The countess had reluctantly given her permission for him to accompany Jack to Mexico for a few days. Lola had no objections and could see no reason why Tristan shouldn't come along. She too had sensed something special in the boy and remembered Jack's words: *He can hear the whisper of angels and see eternity.* With Isis facing the toughest challenge of her life, hearing the whisper of angels, she thought, might come in handy.

'You can sit next to me while we take off,' said Lola, putting on her headphones. 'Buckle up.'

'You will fly the plane?' said Tristan, his eyes as big as saucers.

'Only during take-off. I love the power of this little beauty.'

'How cool is that?' said Tristan, his cheeks glowing with excitement. He had a new hero – Lola – and couldn't wait to post something about her on Facebook for his schoolmates back home to feel envious about.

'Ready guys? Here we go,' said Lola gently pushing the throttle forward. The powerful engines whined into action as the plane began to move slowly away from its bay.

'Hold on tight, mate,' said Jack putting his hand on Tristan's shoulder from behind. 'You're in for the ride of your life.'

After take-off, Tristan pleaded with Lola to be allowed to stay in the cockpit with the pilots. This gave Lola and Jack an opportunity to have a private conversation in the back of the plane.

'I barely slept a wink since I left the chateau that morning,' said Lola, pouring Jack a drink. 'And after such an enchanting evening. That one phone call changed our lives. Isis in a coma with a brain tumour ... Who would have believed it? To me, she seemed invincible. It's been a nightmare ever since.'

'How is she?' asked Jack.

'Not well, I'm afraid. At first, Sir Humphrey was all upbeat and full of optimism. He reassured us and gave us hope. Stiff upper lip and all that. However, when Isis suddenly deteriorated, his mood changed. A trip to the US for that vital operation appears out of the question at the moment. Apparently, there's only one surgeon who can do it, and even that is debatable right now. We are trying to persuade him to come to Mexico to examine Isis.'

'Any luck?'

'We are working on it.'

'Who is looking after her now?'

'A whole team with a top specialist in charge.'

'And Sir Humphrey?'

'He had to return to London. Other patients; commitments. You know what scared me most?'

'What?'

'On the flight back to London, he looked a beaten man. He's known Isis all her life. I have never seen him like that. He looked ...'

'What?'

'*Defeated*,' whispered Lola.

'Come on ...' Jack realised it was time to change direction. 'Do you know why I've been summonsed? My investigation has barely begun. Why the urgency?'

'That's simple. Isis wants to know what happened to her parents, and why. She obviously feels that time is running out for her. She's become obsessed with the subject. And who can blame her?'

'So, it's all gloom and doom then?'

'It is, I'm afraid.'

'Then let's do something about it,' said Jack.

'How exactly?'

'By igniting the will to live.'

'What kind of match will you use?'

'Curiosity. I have information that will rock Isis to her core.'

'Of a positive kind?'

'Don't know; yet; it's too early to say. But what I do know is this: Once she hears what I have to tell her, she will not be able to rest until she gets to the bottom of it all and finds the truth.'

'Are you going to tell me about it?'

'Only in part. I think it would be only fair if Isis hears this from me first. However, I can tell you it all has to do with an ancient artefact, a beautiful Mexican woman, a dashing German officer and a spectacular scandal. The scandal of the crystal skull, no less.'

For a moment, Lola looked thunderstruck. 'Escorting Sir Humphrey back to London and bringing you over was only part of my mission,' she said quietly. 'Isis asked me to do something else for her.'

'Oh? What?'

'To bring something back with me she wants to have by her side – especially now.'

'And what might that be?'

'Let me show you,' said Lola. She walked over to her desk, opened an overhead locker and carefully lifted something out. As soon as Jack saw the wooden box, he knew instantly what it was.

# 40

Unlike Jana, who crashed as soon as her head hit the pillow, Alexandra couldn't go to sleep. Turning restlessly in her bed, she kept going over Professor K's letter again and again in her mind. *My God, those dreadful medical experiments with the twins*, she thought, *in the concentration camp!* Unable to banish the disturbing images floating into her mind's eye, she saw young girls lying on makeshift tables being operated on by Professor K's father and the notorious German doctors. Open wounds, children dying, rows of little glass bottles with tissue samples floating in formalin; leather-bound record books meticulously kept … scalpels and needles; blood; horror. The sickly-sweet smell of death.

Bathed in sweat, Alexandra sat up in bed. As soon as she turned on the light, the ghosts disappeared. Feeling better, she pulled Professor K's letter out of her handbag and for a while, looked at the creased pages.

She hadn't told Jana about the letter. Not because she didn't trust her, but because she needed more time to come to terms with what Professor K was telling her from beyond the grave. The man she had known and admired since her childhood was suddenly turning into a stranger with secrets. A new truth was threatening to destroy treasured memories of a dear friend and Alexandra was reluctant to let go. Searching for answers, she began to read, Professor K's familiar handwriting giving the letter in her hands a chilling presence:

*The spark of inspiration is never predictable. It can ignite an innocent train of thought that can change the way we look at everything, or lead to an insight with the most far-reaching consequences in the blink of an eye and in the most unexpected ways. The spark of inspiration can alter the course of medicine and change the destiny of mankind. I believe this has been the case with my work, and you of all people deserve – no – must know the truth. I don't say this lightly, but this is a story that has to be told.*

*If my work is to be understood for what it means and represents, it has to be viewed in its proper context and I must disclose where it all came from, and how it all began. To do otherwise would not only be unethical, it would be dishonest and could tarnish my work and reputation forever. This must not be allowed to happen and so I must speak for those who no longer have a voice, regardless of how painful the memories may be ... The warning finger of approaching death can be most persuasive ...*

*It all began a long time ago with a Polish doctor, an inspired idea, and a pair of young twins – the Abramowitz girls, Lena and Miriam – in a place of unimaginable cruelty and horror: a German concentration camp ...*

Alexandra put down the letter, her hand shaking, and looked pensively down into the dark harbour below. *He never spoke of this while he was alive. So, why now?* she thought, a strange feeling of premonition and dread gnawing at her insides.

*The man who conceived the idea and started it all was my father, Doctor Simon Kozakievicz,* Alexandra continued to read. *He was an expert on twins and was renowned throughout Europe for his research and discoveries, especially in understanding cancer. In 1942, he was deported from Krakow where he worked, and taken to Auschwitz with his wife and two young daughters.*

*The infamous Dr Mengele and his team of butchers was conducting secret medical experiments at Birkenau, a sister camp near Auschwitz. To give his work some credibility, Mengele liked to surround himself with talented Jewish doctors who had been deported and were on their way to the gas chamber. They were given a diabolical choice: they could work for him and carry out experimental operations and treatments that would have been unthinkable in any normal hospital environment and so keep themselves and their families alive, or they could refuse. The consequences were obvious. Usually, the doctors had family members in the main camp. They only survived there as long as the doctors cooperated. This was certainly the case with my father. His wife, his first wife that is, and two young daughters were at Auschwitz.*

*Mengele was picking his brains. He had an assistant, Dr Erwin Steinberger, an ambitious young surgeon who carried out most of the operations. Mengele and*

*Steinberger were obsessed with twins. They were convinced, as was my father, that the answer to why some people get cancer and some don't, and why some can fight it and survive and others can't, was to be found somewhere buried in the immune system and the genes of twins.*

*There is something else you should know. I've never told you this, but your mother and I were once lovers. We were both young students in Paris at the time. Part of five close friends; the gang of five …We were inseparable and had sworn to stay together forever. How life changes… There was of course Olga, your mother, her brother, Nikolai, Katerina and Zoltan, who was tragically killed in a nightclub fire. Sadly, that tragedy changed everything. We drifted apart and your mother met Pierre Delacroix, whom she later married.*

*After Zoltan died, and before Anna was born, Katerina married Nikolai Popov. You know the rest. What you don't know is that I've been in love with your mother ever since. Sadly, however, there's no future in the past. That's the real reason I never married. That and my work, I suppose, and you are … the daughter I never had …*

*How could I have been so blind, to see none of this?* thought Alexandra, tears welling in her eyes. *And Maman never spoke about any of this either. Yet now, here it all is.* Alexandra wiped the tears from her cheeks and continued to read.

*There are a few things I have to tell you about my father … He survived the war. His wife and two daughters did not. They were sent to the gas chamber just before the camp was liberated. Mengele went to ground and escaped. He fled to South America and died years later in Argentina. As for what happened to Dr Steinberger, things aren't that clear. Apparently, he too escaped. There have been rumours that he went first to Italy, where he was helped by the Vatican, and then just vanished …*

*In 1945, my father was in his prime. He was 42, well-known and respected in medical circles, even after Auschwitz, or perhaps because of it. A Swiss pharmaceutical company sought him out and gave him a job. He went to live in Switzerland and shortly thereafter, met my mother. I was born in 1949. As you know, I studied medicine at Heidelberg and followed in my father's footsteps. Medical research became my life.*

211

Alexandra folded the letter carefully along its creases and slipped it back into her handbag. Wide awake by now and too excited to go back to sleep, she reached for Jack's book, *Dental Gold and Other Horrors* that Jana had given her earlier, and began to read.

In the opening chapters, Jack explained how a letter sent to a Sydney newspaper by an old lady had started it all. The woman was claiming to have recognised the German officer in a photograph Jack had found in the ruins of a cottage destroyed by bushfire in the Blue Mountains. The shocking photograph had earlier been published in the paper, together with an article Jack had written about it.

When Alexandra read the name of the old lady in question, she sat up in bed with a jolt. *Coincidence, surely*, she thought, dismissing the wave of excitement washing over her as nonsense. Yet the feeling wouldn't go away. Instead of closing the book and going back to sleep, she continued to read, furiously turning the pages. By the time the first rays of the morning sun banished the darkness and gave the glass of the open windows a pinkish glow, Alexandra had finished the book. Exhausted, she closed her eyes, trying in vain to get her head around what she had just read. The implications, if true, were as far-reaching as they were astounding.

# 41

Tristan was in heaven. He hadn't left the cockpit throughout the entire flight. Just before landing in Mexico City, Lola even allowed him to hold the controls for a while, and showed him what to do. 'He's a natural,' she told the co-pilot. 'I could have him flying this little beauty in no time.'

Boris picked them up at the airport and drove them to the Gonzales villa.

Lola looked at Jack sitting next to her in the back of the car. 'You're very quiet,' she said.

'I may need your help,' said Jack.

'In what way?'

'It's a little delicate …'

Lola put her hand on Jack's knee and squeezed it, the gesture of intimacy and encouragement obvious.

'I don't know how I should handle Señora Gonzales,' said Jack.

'What do you mean?'

'The information I discovered just before I left is, to say the least, explosive, and it directly concerns Señora Gonzales. It could have far-reaching consequences of a very personal nature …'

'So, what's the problem?'

'Well, Isis is my client, so to speak, but it was Señora Gonzales who gave me the clue that pointed me to the information. In fact, it was because of that very clue that I accepted the brief in the first place. So, who do I tell first, or at all? Perhaps Señora Gonzales doesn't want Isis to know what I've discovered. But I have a duty to Isis. I just don't want to put my foot in it, that's all. Can you see my predicament? Once this information gets out, there's no way back.'

'Now, you've really got me intrigued,' said Lola. 'Leave it to me. I'll try to speak to Dolores and Isis separately before you see them.'

213

'Thanks.' Jack leant across and kissed Lola on the cheek. '*Look at those two,*' he whispered. He pointed to Tristan sitting in the front, chatting animatedly with Boris. 'Two strangers who've just met, or two buddies who have known each other for years? And I thought Boris was the quiet one.'

'Tristan's a special boy,' said Lola. 'I've never met anyone quite like him. He has a gift ... I'm glad you brought him along.'

'So am I.'

Isis had improved considerably during the night. The crisis had passed, at least for the moment. No longer confined to bed, she was sitting on the terrace soaking up a little sun under the watchful eye of her grandmother fussing over her. Lola had spoken to each of them, as promised. Isis and Señora Gonzales would see Jack together and hear what he had to report. Lola too, had been asked to be present.

As Jack walked up the stairs leading to the terrace from the garden below, he remembered the spectacular morning exercise routine he had witnessed during his last visit. When he reached the top of the stairs and looked at Isis sitting in a cane chair under a sun umbrella, he was shocked.

It was almost impossible to imagine that the frail-looking creature in front of him with the pale face and sunken cheeks was the same person who had engaged in a breathtaking acrobatic display of hand-to-hand combat with Lola just a short time ago. Her skin looked pasty, hair limp and without lustre, and her eyes had retreated into their sockets, making her protruding cheekbones look almost corpse-like.

*Jesus*, thought Jack, trying to appear his casual, easygoing self. 'No yoga this morning, I see,' he said cheerfully.

'Lola wasn't up to it,' said Isis, managing a little laugh, her first in days.

'That'd be right,' said Jack. 'All this jet-setting must be getting to her; no stamina.' He walked over to Señora Gonzales and held out his hand. Instead of shaking his hand, Señora Gonzales embraced Jack and kissed him on both cheeks. It was a gesture of genuine affection and a clear signal – *no secrets here.*

'Thanks for coming over, Jack,' said Isis. 'Here, sit with me ...' Isis patted the empty chair next to her. 'My world has changed a little since we saw each other last, and so have my priorities.' Jack was glad to see that Isis was as lucid and sharp as ever. Her mind had obviously not been affected. 'We have to talk. By *we*, I mean all of us here. Understood?'

'Absolutely,' said Jack, relieved.

'I appreciate your tact, Jack. Lola spoke to us earlier. Why don't we begin by letting you tell us what you've found out so far? All cards on the table. No holds barred; no secrets. I understand you have something important to share with us? But before you start, there's something else ... Lola, would you mind?'

Lola stood up and walked into the room opening onto the terrace. She returned moments later carrying the mahogany box and put it on the table next to Isis. Isis opened the lid, activating the mechanism that folded down the sides of the box to expose the spectacular artefact inside. 'I thought it was appropriate to have our friend here present. After all, he's an important player in this – right, Jack?'

When Jack looked at Señora Gonzales, he noticed that she kept staring at the sparkling skull, visibly shaken. Jack wasn't surprised. If only part of what he had discovered was true, Señora Gonzales' reaction was perfectly understandable.

'I am a storyteller,' began Jack, collecting his thoughts. 'I believe the best way to relay what I have found out so far, is to tell you a story. It is a remarkable tale spanning many decades. The characters are as colourful as the times they lived in were turbulent, and we have to look at the people and their actions in proper context. But I must warn you; I do not have all the answers – yet. Some of what I'm about to tell you is a little speculative, and I have to resort to conjecture to close some of the gaps because there are still too many questions left unanswered at this stage. However, the pieces of the puzzle are beginning to fall into place. The full picture is slowly taking shape.' Jack paused, and took a sip of his guava juice.

215

'It all began with a name and a clue given to me by Señora Gonzales right here, on this very terrace just over a week ago. The name? SS Sturmbannfuehrer Wolfgang Steinberger. The clue? The hotel on Place Vendôme in Paris; none other than the famous Ritz. However, there was a lot more, but I didn't appreciate the significance of the subtle connections at the time.

'When I met with Sir Charles in London, he gave me access to your late mother's letters and showed me this fascinating artefact here.' Jack pointed to the skull on the table next to him. 'The manner in which these items were discovered by you, Isis, are as remarkable as the items themselves. May I assume we are all familiar with this?'

'You can,' said Isis.

'That's where matters stood until Countess Kuragin introduced me to a dear old friend of hers ...' Jack paused and looked at Señora Gonzales. 'And a close friend of yours as well, I believe, Señora,' he continued. 'Madame Petrova.'

Señora Gonzales paled, but said nothing.

Jack then went on to describe his meetings with the Russian ballerina at the exclusive nursing home, and had them in stitches when he told them about the flamboyant Mademoiselle Darrieux and her antics. Jack did this quite deliberately. He was preparing the way for the bombshell to come with some levity.

'And then, when I thought I had hit a dead end and could go no further, I met a delightful old gentleman. Entirely by accident as it turned out. You may even remember him, Señora,' said Jack. 'His name is René Bardot, but he was known as *Petit Moineau* – "Little Sparrow" – at the time he worked as a bellboy at the Ritz during the war. He remembers you well, Señora. Apparently, he ran many an errand for you and ...' Jack reached into his pocket, pulled out a copy of the photograph he had borrowed from Madame Petrova and put in on the table next to the skull '... for the man standing next to you in the photo here,' said Jack, completing his sentence.

Isis picked up the photo, looked at it and then handed it to her grandmother.

'Sturmbannfuehrer Wolfgang Steinberger, I believe,' said Jack quietly.

'My God! How ... where on earth did you get this from?' stammered Señora Gonzales, her voice sounding faint.

'It stood on a piano in Madame Petrova's room, together with many other fascinating snapshots taken during the war. Shall I continue?'

'*Please do,*' whispered Señora Gonzales.

Jack outlined the whole story of the scandal, the theft of the skull and Göring's fury. 'Officially, the stolen skull was never recovered,' he said. 'Yet, here it is—'

'Provided it's the same one, of course,' interrupted Isis.

'Obviously. But I am quite sure it is; I'll explain why later. However, this is by no means the end of the story. In many ways, it's just the beginning,' said Jack.

'Extraordinary,' said Isis. 'You have been busy, and all of this in such a short time; amazing.'

'I have been lucky,' said Jack, turning towards Señora Gonzales. 'The leads appear to have found me in this case, and all I had to do was follow the breadcrumbs. However, I may need your help with the rest of the story, Señora,' he said, 'because the crumbs have become few and far between. Trampled into the ground by turbulent events. Please correct me if I get it wrong.'

Señora Gonzales nodded.

'This is how the story continues,' said Jack. 'A beautiful young Mexican woman is staying at the Ritz with her little daughter. Her husband has just been arrested by the Germans, accused of having stolen Göring's precious skull. The man is interrogated – robustly, I believe – but eventually released. Nothing has been proven. However, the man knows he has to get away from Göring's clutches as quickly as possible. Using his network of contacts – the French Resistance, it was rumoured – he leaves France in a hurry and returns to Mexico.

'Unfortunately, his escape has a price: he cannot take his wife and daughter with him. Left behind, they remain in France and continue to stay at the Ritz, under the same roof as the man who can destroy them at will, and would do so without hesitation, given the slightest reason to act. Ironically, that reason was right there under his very nose, so to speak, isn't that right?'

'*Yes,*' said Señora Gonzales.

'Enter, SS Sturmbannfuehrer Wolfgang Steinberger, a powerful, strikingly handsome man, who serves in the prestigious Leibstandarte SS Adolf Hitler, Hitler's personal bodyguard. Trusted by Göring and feared by everyone else, he was called in by the Reichsmarschall personally to investigate the theft.

'Thorough and ruthless, Steinberger methodically interrogates all the guests and the entire Ritz staff all over again, one by one. He succeeds where the notorious Abwehr, the secret police, has failed. While questioning one of the barmen, Steinberger discovers that the man is Jewish.

'Steinberger knows that the fear of pain is more powerful and persuasive than pain itself. Threatened with immediate deportation to a concentration camp, the barman capitulates and decides to talk ...'

Jack pulled his little notebook out of his pocket, took off the rubber band holding it together, and opened it.

'What Steinberger discovered, and where this discovery ended up, is perhaps the most intriguing aspect of the whole affair,' said Jack. 'The barman admitted his involvement in the theft of the skull and pointed the finger at José Gonzales as the instigator. He even told Steinberger where the skull was hidden and directed him to it.' Jack turned towards Señora Gonzales. 'Am I right, so far?' he said.

'*Yes,*' whispered Señora Gonzales.

'Now comes the really interesting part,' continued Jack. 'Instead of informing the Reichsmarschall of his discovery, returning the stolen skull and claiming the credit, Steinberger does something surprising – nothing. He keeps quiet about it all. In fact, he goes one step further. He covers it all up and silences everyone who knows about the affair. The barman disappears; case closed. In doing this, the Sturmbann-fuehrer has taken a huge risk. The question is, why? Perhaps you would like to tell us why, Señora,' said Jack, 'because so far, I've told you nothing new, have I?'

'I would like to speak privately to my grandson for a moment.' Señora Gonzales began to sob, unable to hold back the tears. She walked over to Isis. 'I'm so sorry,' she said. 'Forgive me. The truth can hurt more than we care to admit, and time alone cannot heal all. Hidden corners of our lives cannot stay hidden forever. Sooner or later, we must face the sins of the past. I only wish it wasn't so. You must believe me,' she said and slowly shuffled away. Surprised, Isis stood up and, leaning on Lola's arm, followed her grandmother into the room.

# 42

After a few minutes, a composed Señora Gonzales – walking arm in arm with her grandson – joined Jack on the terrace again. Lola followed soon after.

'Forgive me,' said Señora Gonzales. 'Often there's a lot more hidden in the dark corners of our lives than we realise or care to admit.'

Jack nodded. Lola shot him a meaningful look and sat down next to him.

'After my husband's arrest and all the dreadful accusations,' began Señora Gonzales, 'I didn't know what to do. People were afraid to talk to me. I was terrified, with no one to turn to for support or advice. I felt abandoned and terribly alone. I was so young; so inexperienced; so vulnerable. And then there was Mercedes, my little girl to think of … All too much.'

Isis reached for her grandmother's hand.

'Naïvely perhaps, or desperate more likely, I turned to the one man who I believed could help me,' continued Señora Gonzales. 'I pleaded with the handsome officer who held my fate in his hands to protect me. *No, I did more than that*,' whispered Señora Gonzales. 'Foolishly, I threw myself at him. Suddenly, I was no longer alone. Then one thing led to another and we became lovers. We fell in love, or so I thought at the time … I was wrong.' Señora Gonzales paused and stared at something in the distance only she could see.

'Looking back,' she continued, 'I don't think the dashing major was in love with me at all. He was *in lust* with me, relishing the power and control he had over me. Deep down he was a cold, ruthless man without pity or compassion. Blinded by love and gratitude, I suppose, I couldn't see any of this. Quite soon, however, I would – in the cruellest way imaginable.'

Señora Gonzales paused again, and pulled a handkerchief out of her sleeve. 'The precious skull retrieved by my husband – he didn't consider it theft because you cannot steal what is yours, he used to say – was hidden in a secret compartment in our suite at the Ritz. In hindsight, this was as reckless as it was foolish and put us all in danger, but José didn't see it that way. Several rooms at the hotel had secret compartments concealed behind the panelling. Only senior hotel management at the highest level knew about them. It was the way guests kept their valuables safe.

'Take Laura Mae Corrigan, for example, a glamorous widow and one of the richest women in America. She occupied the Imperial Suite until she was evicted by Göring, who took it over. She lived at the Ritz during the war and hid all her precious furs and jewellery in one of those secure places, well out of Göring's rapacious reach. Had he known about her treasures, he would have made her an offer impossible to refuse. Instead, the stunning jewels survived the German occupation safely hidden behind the armoire in Mrs Corrigan's dressing room. The whole place was a hotbed of skulduggery and intrigue, all of it under one roof. We were all sleeping with the enemy, literally speaking.'

Isis squeezed her grandmother's hand. It was a gesture of encouragement and support for someone she loved dearly, struggling to explain a painful past.

'If the major had exposed me, the consequences would have been severe. Not just for me, but also for my child and my friends, who were bound to be implicated somehow,' said Señora Gonzales.

'Göring was a ruthless madman, capable of anything. Little did I know that the major was the same, if not worse. He was consumed by ambition. Steinberger despised Göring and had an agenda of his own. It all had to do with breaking the French Resistance, and taking the credit for it.

'He did what he did, not to help me but out of ambition and spite. He didn't want to be the one who gave the crazy Reichsmarschall his exotic toy back. Instead, he kept a close eye on Göring and was reporting directly to Berlin on how Hitler's second-in-command was running the war in France. He was, in fact, Hitler's spy. Of course, I knew none of this at the time. I was young, naïve and in love.'

Isis glanced at her grandmother, a look of astonishment and surprise clouding her wan face. It was obvious she had heard none of this before. Señora Gonzales turned towards her grandson and said, 'It's easy to forget that even an old woman like me was young once ...'

'But there's more,' interrupted Jack. 'Isn't that so?'

'Yes, there is.'

'Shall I?'

'Please.'

'Steinberger and his brother, Erwin, Göring's physician, both stayed at the Ritz,' said Jack. 'The Sturmbannfuehrer closed the investigation and your affair blossomed, in secret. A few months later, he moved you into a lavish apartment close by and Petit Moineau, the bellboy, became your trusted go-between—'

'How did you find all this out?' interrupted Señora Gonzales, shaking her head. 'And so quickly?'

'A little sparrow told me. Would you care to tell us what happened next?'

Haunted by painful memories, Señora Gonzales covered her face with her hands. After a while she whispered, '*I fell pregnant,*' her voice barely audible.

'What?' cried Isis, her voice shrill and quivering with emotion. Lola walked over to her and put her hand on Isis' arm to calm her.

'I gave birth in the apartment,' continued Señora Gonzales. 'It was a difficult birth. Fortunately, the major's brother – a doctor – and a German midwife were present. Without them, I may not have pulled through. Mercedes had a beautiful little brother. Then everything changed.'

'In what way?' asked Jack.

'The major became cold and distant and kept away from me. He shunned me. I don't think a newborn baby fitted into his plans. He used the apartment for clandestine meetings. All kinds of agents were coming and going at all hours and kept reporting to him and his cronies. I think they were trying to infiltrate the French Resistance. I overheard conversations ...

'At first, I was confined to bed for quite a while. After that, I rarely went out. During this difficult time, I only had one friend who came to visit me regularly: Madame Petrova, the celebrated ballerina. Anastasia was wonderful. I think the only reason she was allowed to visit me was because of her liaison with one of the major's aides.

'Then the baby developed a fever and was rushed to hospital. The major's brother arranged it all. I was kept away and wasn't allowed to visit my son. It was as if I didn't exist. I was a virtual prisoner in the apartment. Miserable, unhappy and terribly alone.

'Soon after that, the major was recalled to Berlin. He had to leave Paris in a hurry and we had a dreadful row ...' Señora Gonzales paused, and kept staring vacantly into space.

'What about?' prompted Jack after a while.

'About me, us, the sick baby, what would happen to me and my daughter, the future ...'

'What did happen?'

'Just before he left, the major moved me back into the Ritz with Mercedes.'

'And the baby?'

Señora Gonzales covered her face with her hands again and for a while, just sat there in silence. '*I never saw my baby again,*' she whispered. 'I don't know what happened to him. The major told me to forget about the baby and never speak of the child to anyone if I wanted to live safely at the Ritz with my daughter. The threat was obvious, and he wasn't the kind of man you would cross.'

'And the crystal skull? What happened to it?'

'The major took it with him. He left Paris with his brother and I never heard from them again.'

'And then?' said Jack.

'Mercedes and I continued to live at the Ritz until the end of the war. So did my friend, Anastasia. Then the liberation came and my situation, and hers for that matter, became untenable.'

'In what way?'

'We were considered "horizontals", collaborators who had slept with the Germans and sided with the enemy. And in a way, I suppose, it was true. Fortunately, Anastasia had excellent connections. She was a survivor with a wonderful sense of humour. Do you know what she said to a self-righteous woman in the bar who accused her of being a traitor?'

'What did she say?' said Jack.

Señora Gonzales managed a little smile. 'My heart is French, but my ass is international,' she said. 'We left Paris soon after that and travelled to London. Then, with the help of friends, I got in touch with José in Mexico. He came over and we were a family again. My life improved after that ...'

'What a story,' said Lola, breaking the awkward silence.

'Did you hear from the major after the war?' asked Jack.

'No. Everything was so chaotic. I had no idea what happened to him, until I read your book and realised that Sir Eric Newman living in Australia was Sturmbannfuehrer Wolfgang Steinberger, the father of my lost child.'

'Is that why you asked Isis to get in touch with me?' asked Jack, quietly.

'That was certainly one of the reasons. After Mercedes was murdered and Isis discovered that dreadful skull hidden in the Elms' family home, I realised it wasn't over. The past was closing in, as it often does. Unexpectedly, and with a relentless momentum of its own. There are so many questions left unanswered, with many a dark thread linking us to the past. I believe everything here is somehow connected. The brutal murders, the skull's mysterious reappearance, your book, you, us – everything. I'm at the end of my life, but I must find out how, and why, before it's too late.'

'I understand,' said Jack.

'I hope you do. And I hope you will continue to help us find the truth.'

Jack closed his little notebook. 'I will,' he said.

'Regardless of danger?' asked Isis.

'I'm used to living dangerously,' said Jack.

'I know. *The Disappearance of Anna Popov* told us that. That's the other reason we approached you.'

Barely able to suppress his excitement, Jack realised that another great story had just found him, and all he had to do was to follow the breadcrumbs, and his gut.

# PART III
## *THE GREATEST DISEASE IN THE WEST*

'The greatest disease in the West today is not TB or leprosy; it is being unwanted, unloved, and uncared for. We can cure physical diseases with medicine, but the only cure for loneliness, despair, and hopelessness is love.'

Mother Teresa, *A Simple Path: Mother Teresa*

# Auschwitz: June 1942

SS Sturmbannfuehrer Wolfgang Steinberger opened the silver cigarette case presented to him by Himmler, lit a cigarette – Turkish, his favourite – and listened to the camp orchestra play a cheerful medley of Viennese tunes. Inhaling deeply, he enjoyed the familiar nicotine rush and prepared himself for the chaos that was about to erupt. The next train was due to reach the gates at any moment. It was thought that having music playing to welcome the terrified new arrivals packed like cattle sent to slaughter into the boarded-up, windowless carriages, would calm them and make them easier to control on arrival at the greatest extermination machine the world had ever seen.

The major's dog, a handsome Doberman, knew the routine and calmly watched the steam train roll slowly into the camp like a wheezing monster crawling into its lair. Soon, all hell would break loose.

After the wooden sliding doors were unlocked and opened by the guards, the major's men went to work. 'Juden raus!' they barked. 'Schnell; schnell! Rechts; links; schnell!' and began to herd the terrified wretches out of the foul carriages, as snarling dogs – fangs bared – pulled furiously on their chains. Women and children were lined up on the left, the men on the right. The selections were about to begin.

That morning, the major was only interested in one thing: twins. His brother, Dr Erwin Steinberger, was carrying out secret medical experiments with Dr Mengele at Birkenau, a sister camp next to Auschwitz, and they urgently needed more twins. Walking slowly along the crowded platform, the major looked at the sea of terrified faces staring at him.

*No luck with this lot*, he thought, when he noticed two young girls cowering behind a woman at the back of the long queue. The major stopped and pointed to the girls. 'Come here,' he said, the tone of his voice friendly. Slowly, the frightened girls came forward. It was impossible to tell them apart.

Dr Steinberger couldn't believe his luck. The Abramowitz twins, Lena and Miriam, were exactly what he needed. He had been looking for a suitable specimen for over a year, and had examined hundreds of twins in the hope of finding the right ones. The experiment he had been planning for so long could finally begin.

Dr Steinberger opened his briefcase and pulled out the precious Aztec codex he had bought in Paris the year before. *De Medicina*, he thought, carefully unfolding the long piece of animal skin with its beautiful illustrations, his fingers trembling with excitement.

'What do you think?' he said to Dr Kozakievicz, watching him from across the room. The only reason Dr Kozakievicz, a Polish Jew, was still alive was because of his extraordinary mind. As one of Europe's most gifted scientists – specialising in cancer – he had been highly sought after by universities, hospitals and pharmaceutical companies for years. Born in Krakow in 1902, he studied medicine in Heidelberg. There he met Sidney Faber, another Polish Jew, who lived in New York. Exceptionally bright, passionate and mutually fascinated by the old foe, cancer, the two young doctors became close friends. After finishing his studies, Faber returned to the US, where he became the first full-time pathologist at the Children's Hospital in Boston. Simon Kozakievicz returned to Krakow, where he continued his research into cancer and treating brain tumours. The two friends stayed in touch and exchanged ideas and research findings over the years.

Dr Steinberger knew this gifted doctor was in a league of his own and was determined to harness his talent and his knowledge to advance his own research and reputation. To ensure Dr Kozakievicz' unconditional cooperation, his wife and daughter had been kept alive in the camp. As long as he cooperated, they would remain that way.

The horrendous medical experiments at Birkenau were in breach of every moral code, and everything a decent, ethical medical practitioner stood for. Unscientific, capriciously experimental and cruel in the extreme, they explored fanciful and far-fetched theories, mainly aimed at proving the superiority of the Aryan race; it was the Hippocratic Oath turned upside-down.

Dr Steinberger, however, had a different agenda. Genuinely interested in science, he used the unprecedented opportunities the concentration camp offered to conduct medical experiments that in any normal university or hospital environment would have been unthinkable. He was looking for a cure for cancer, and would stop at nothing to pursue this aim in every way possible, regardless of the human cost involved.

Fascinated by the history of medicine and diseases, he firmly believed that the answer he was searching for might well be found buried in the past. For years, he had trawled through ancient texts and historical records looking for clues. And then, quite unexpectedly, he had stumbled across an ancient Aztec text in Paris. He was convinced that destiny and fate had guided him to *De Medicina*, as the codex was called, and that hidden in the text was the important clue he had been looking for, waiting to be discovered. He was about to find out if this was in fact so.

'Let's begin,' said Dr Steinberger. His tiny, twelve–year-old patient, head shaved and looking vulnerable and frail, lay on the crude operating table in front of him. Dr Kozakievicz would be assisting Dr Steinberger in reconstructing the very operation depicted in the ancient text. The operation, however, was only the first part of the experiment. The far more important, critical element would follow later.

When Dr Steinberger agreed to purchase the codex from José Gonzales, a Mexican art dealer, the year before, he had attached an important condition: Gonzales was to provide a sample of the medicinal plant depicted in the text as part of the bargain. Gonzales agreed and, true to his word, delivered the plant on his return from his next buying trip to Mexico.

Dr Steinberger, a meticulous and precise man, had obtained his young patients' medical records from a colleague in Prague. The records told him something quite unexpected, which excited him even more.

Lena's tumour, already well advanced, had been diagnosed the year before. However, at the same time, her twin sister, Miriam, also showed symptoms of a developing an aggressive tumour, but in its very early stage. Would both twins succumb to the disease and die, or would one be able to fight the cancer and live, just as depicted in the Aztec codex? And if so, how, and why?

Dr Steinberger firmly believed that the answer to these crucial questions was within his reach, and the operation he was about to perform would reveal all. If he was right, his place in medical history was assured, and the Swiss pharmaceutical company, which already followed his controversial experiments at the camp with interest, would pay a small fortune for the results.

Ironically, it had all come down to the healing power of a medicinal jungle plant known to the Aztecs for centuries and accidentally rediscovered in an ancient text sold as a curio by a Mexican art dealer in Paris.

'Ready?' said Dr Steinberger. Dr Kozakievicz nodded and handed him a scalpel.

# 43

Jana glanced at Alexandra walking slowly into the kitchen and smiled. *She looks like I feel*, she thought, remembering the two bottles of wine from the night before. Barefoot, pale, her hair dishevelled and wearing a creased pair of short pyjamas, Alexandra looked like a hungover reveller craving a pot of coffee after a long night on the booze.

'Shouldn't you be at work?' asked Jana, reaching for the coffee plunger.

'I would be, if it hadn't been for this,' said Alexandra. She put Jack's book on the kitchen bench.

'Oh? How come?'

'I read *Dental Gold and Other Horrors* – cover to cover – during the night. Barely slept a wink.'

'You are keen – why?'

'Jack would call it destiny.'

Jana looked at Alexandra and raised an eyebrow. 'Please explain.'

'What can you tell me about Lena Abramowitz?'

'Well, as it says in the book, she was the one who gave us the first solid lead. That's where it all began. She claimed to have recognised the SS officer in that dreadful photograph Jack found.'

'The photo of the officer holding the gun to the head of the naked young boy hanging by his ...' Alexandra didn't complete the sentence.

'Yes.'

'What else? How old would she be now, approximately?'

'Eighties, I'd say. A Holocaust survivor from Auschwitz. She was there as a young girl. Had the tattoos to prove it ...'

'Did she mention a twin sister?' asked Alexandra, her voice sounding hoarse.

'As a matter of fact, she did. Her sister died in the camp. Some dreadful operation ... Dr Mengele ... But how do you know this?' demanded Jana, surprised. 'That wasn't in the book; I'm sure of it.'

Alexandra reached into her pyjama pocket. 'Because of this,' she said, and put Professor K's letter next to Jack's book on the bench. 'This is a letter I received the other day from Professor K's executor. He came to the institute and handed it to me personally together with the professor's notebooks that were left to me in his Will.' Alexandra reached for the letter. 'Here, let me read something to you: "*It all began a long time ago with a Polish doctor, an inspired idea, and a pair of young twins – the Abramowitz girls, Lena and Miriam – in a place of unimaginable cruelty and horror: a German concentration camp*" ...'

Jana looked thunderstruck. 'Good God! This is unbelievable! Do you think she's the same – ?'

'Has to be. It all fits! Could she still be alive?'

'Sure. We only met her a few years ago ...'

'Can you remember where she lived?'

'Yes. In Rose Bay, a short drive from here. We could be there in twenty minutes. Is she that important?'

'She is, in more ways than I can possibly explain right now.'

'Destiny, eh?' said Jana, shaking her head. 'Jack and destiny ...'

'Would you mind if we were to go and see her?'

'What? Now?'

'Yes, please.'

'Why the urgency?'

'Let me put it this way: if she's still alive, she could be carrying the key to understanding one of mankind's most dreadful diseases in her genes ...'

'Are you serious?'

'Absolutely! It's all in the professor's notes.'

'Then what are we waiting for?' said Jana. 'Get dressed!'

Jana found the old block of flats without difficulty. She knocked on the door of the ground floor unit she had visited with Jack. There was no response. Jana knocked again and shook her head. 'I'm sorry,' she said to Alexandra standing next to her.

'Are you sure this is the place?'

'Quite sure.'

As Jana turned to leave, the door of the unit opposite opened just a little, and an old woman squinted at them from inside. 'You want Lena?' said the woman in a heavy, guttural European accent.

'Yes,' said Jana.

'She not here. Fell down stairs … hospital.'

'When was that?'

'Last year.'

'Do you know where she is?'

'Nursing home.'

'Do you know which one?'

'Wait here.' The woman closed the door.

Alexandra kept staring at the door, her heart beating like a drum. 'Do you think she's coming back?' she said, anxiously counting the seconds.

'Patience,' said Jana. 'Here she comes now; listen.' Slowly, the door opened again and a shaking hand appeared, holding a slip of paper.

'Thank you,' said Jana, taking the piece of paper from the old lady. The door closed again.

Jana stepped outside and read the address scribbled on the slip of paper in barely legible writing. 'I know the place,' she said. 'It's in Bondi, not far from here.'

'You are relatives?' demanded the matron at the reception of the dilapidated nursing home.

'We are; of a kind,' said Jana.

'Just in time, then,' said the matron brusquely. 'Follow me.'

'What do you mean?' asked Alexandra, following the woman down the dimly lit corridor reeking of cleaning fluids and urine.

'Lena's been in palliative care for a few days now; she's dying. I thought you knew.' The matron gave Alexandra a disapproving look. 'She's in there. Stay as long as you like. I'll be at reception.'

Jana could barely recognise the frail creature lying on the narrow bed in the corner of the tiny room. The curtains were drawn and a few fingers of sunlight were reaching hesitantly into the darkness as little reminders of a vibrant world outside.

*Waiting for death*, thought Alexandra, strangely moved, but feeling like an intruder into the final stage of a stranger's long and painful journey. Yet, if Lena were the surviving Abramowitz twin from Auschwitz, this was an opportunity she couldn't afford to miss.

Jana sat on the edge of the bed and reached for the old lady's hand. 'Hello, Lena; can you hear me?' At first, there was no response, but then slowly, the old lady turned her head and opened her eyes.

'Miriam?' she said, calling out her dead sister's name, her breathing shallow and her voice barely audible.

'No, it's me, Jana. Remember? We brought the major to justice, thanks to you. Sturmbannfuehrer Steinberger, from Auschwitz.'

Stimulated by memories of a painful past, something inside the old lady began to stir. Her cloudy eyes began to focus and she turned her head slowly towards Jana. '*Der Mann mit dem Hund. Arbeit macht frei!*' she whispered.

'Yes, the officer with the dog; that's him,' said Jana, gently squeezing the old lady's limp hand.

'Jana? Ah … Thank you, thank you …' The old lady closed her eyes and her voice faded away, the momentary recognition having drained away the little energy she had left.

'Well, what do you think?' asked Jana, turning to Alexandra standing behind her.

'It certainly appears to be her, but I have to be absolutely sure …'

'What do you mean?'

'This is very awkward; it's certainly not the time or the place, but this is too important.'

'What are you telling me?' asked Jana, looking puzzled.

'I would have to examine her.'

'Are you serious?'

'All I would have to do is look at her head. If this is indeed the Abramowitz twin from Auschwitz mentioned in Professor K's letter and the Auschwitz notes, then she would have a distinct scar on the top of her head.'

'I understand,' said Jana. 'Go ahead. I don't think she would mind.'

Alexandra walked over to the bed and began to stroke the old lady's head, the dispassionate, logical scientist in her wrestling with her humanity. Then, bending down, she parted the lady's hair. 'Here, look,' said Alexandra excitedly. A long scar running across the top of her head like a zipper on a lady's purse was clearly visible. Could you please take a photo of this?'

Jana pulled her phone out of her pocket and took a couple of close-ups of the scar. 'It's definitely her; can you believe it? No doubt about it!' said Alexandra, stepping back, the implications of what she had just seen making her feel dizzy.

'Is that it?' asked Jana.

'Not quite,' said Alexandra, her mind racing. It was obvious the old lady didn't have long to live and could slip away any moment.

'What do you mean?'

'I need a sample.'

'Are you serious? We cannot just—'

'A few strands of her hair would do. There, look.' Alexandra pointed to a hairbrush on the bedside table with a few white hairs caught in the bristles. 'What do you think?'

Jana looked pensively at the old lady in front of her. After all she had been through, especially in Auschwitz, Lena wouldn't mind, she thought. She wouldn't mind if medical science could somehow benefit from her ordeal and her sister's horrible death in Dr Mengele's obscene laboratory. Perhaps it could all be viewed as some kind of ultimate justice and vindication ... Jana paused. 'Go ahead. I think it's the right thing to do,' she said.

Alexandra looked at Jana gratefully, reached for the hairbrush and carefully pulled out a few hairs, one by one. Deeply moved, and with tears in her eyes, Alexandra bent down and kissed the old lady tenderly on the forehead. '*Thank you, Lena,*' she whispered, tears in her eyes, 'I'll make sure it hasn't all been in vain; I promise.'

# 44

From the moment they arrived at the Gonzales residence, Tristan had spent most of his time with Boris, his new friend. Lola had flown to Boston to collect the surgeon, who had finally agreed to come to Mexico to examine his famous patient, and Jack had locked himself into his room to plan his next move. He needed some quiet time to consider the new information provided by Señora Gonzales. Exhausted, Isis had retired to her suite to rest and prepare herself for the visit of the celebrity surgeon. This left Tristan momentarily alone to explore the extensive grounds of the villa, full of exotic treasures and surprises.

Señora Gonzales steadied herself, gripped the handrail and looked down into the candlelit temple chamber in the basement of her villa. *What a remarkable boy*, she thought, watching Tristan stand motionless in front of the statue of Huitzilopochtli. The bloodthirsty god looked threatening and strangely lifelike in the flickering candlelight casting wild shadows against the stone walls. 'So, there you are,' she said, and slowly walked down the narrow stone stairs towards Tristan. 'Isis would like to meet you. Come, she's waiting.'

'This place is silent, yet I can hear so much,' said Tristan without taking his eyes of the frightening god.

'What can you hear?'

'Chanting … and I can feel fear and see blood.'

'It's a little spooky down here, I agree,' said Señora Gonzales, trying to brush aside Tristan's strange remark.

'It's much more than that,' said Tristan. 'It's a window into the past, and I'm looking back through time …'

Señora Gonzales walked over to Tristan, who kept staring at the statue. *What an extraordinary thing to say*, she thought, taking Tristan by the hand. 'Come; let me take you to Isis.' Tristan turned away from the statue and looked at the elderly lady in front of him. 'But before I

238

do,' continued Señora Gonzales, 'I must tell you a few things about my grandson.'

They sat on the bench facing the Coyolxauhqui stone, where Jack had had his first real conversation with his new client.

'Isis is biologically a man,' began Señora Gonzales, 'but emotionally, intellectually and spiritually if you wish, a woman. He's a woman trapped in a man's body, but first and foremost, he's an artist. Does this make sense to you?'

'Perfectly,' said Tristan. 'When I meet someone new, I only look at their soul ...'

'And when you do that, what do you see?'

'It's hard to explain ... An aura. My mother taught me what to look for, and how to see. She had the gift ...'

'You must tell me about it sometime but for now, I must warn you, my grandson is very ill; a mere shadow of his former self, I'm afraid,' continued Señora Gonzales, trying to prepare Tristan – the adoring young fan – about to meet his idol. In doing so, she was unable to hide the pain and sadness in her voice.

'This doesn't change the soul ... I will meet the person, not the patient,' said Tristan.

Surprised by the remark, Señora Gonzales squeezed Tristan's hand. *He's trying to comfort me*, she thought. *Amazing!* 'Are you ready?' she asked.

'I am.'

'Then come.'

Isis, the consummate performer, had forced herself to get changed and put on some make-up before meeting Tristan. Greeting him as an invalid lying in bed was unthinkable, regardless of the circumstances.

'I look like shit,' she said, 'don't you think?' Isis examined the pale, listless image staring back at her in the mirror.

'Don't worry; he's only a boy,' said Hanna, helping Isis walk across the room to the lounge facing the terrace.

'Oh no. He's much more than that; wait and see.'

Wearing a spectacular blue Kimono – one of her favourites – instead of a dressing gown, and gold slippers with extravagant glass tassels, Isis had managed to momentarily transform herself. The frail, bedridden patient had once again turned into a seasoned performer. 'Show him in,' she said, letting herself sink into the soft cushions, her pose theatrical and relaxed.

Señora Gonzales opened the door to her grandson's bedroom and, sensing Tristan's hesitation, gently pushed him inside.

Tristan looked at Isis sitting on a lounge by the window, a shaft of sunlight pointing to her heart. He was trying to interpret the mixed messages assaulting his senses. Then their eyes met. Suddenly, Tristan felt an unexpected burst of pleasure-pain well up from somewhere deep inside, heralding the meeting of two kindred spirits in an eternity moment. It was an unfamiliar, disconcerting mixture of joy and sadness he hadn't experienced before. The starry-eyed boy meeting the megastar was wrestling with the ancient seer in his blood. Knowing too much can be as much of a burden as knowing too little. Tristan noticed that Isis was wearing the small Celtic cross he had sent her, on a leather thong around her neck.

'Jack tells me you can hear the whisper of angels and glimpse eternity,' said Isis, breaking the silence. 'Come; will you help me understand what that means?'

Señora Gonzales walked over to Hanna standing by the window. '*I think we should leave them alone, don't you?*' she whispered. Hanna nodded and followed Señora Gonzales quietly out of the room.

For the next two hours, Isis and Tristan were locked in deep conversation. Tristan only left the room after Isis had fallen asleep on the lounge, exhausted but comforted by the unexpected revelations of the eternity moment she had shared with another extraordinary soul.

# 45

After returning to London, Sir Humphrey had pulled off an almost impossible coup. By using his extensive network of worldwide contacts and calling in favours, he managed to persuade one of the busiest, most gifted and sought after surgeons in the US – if not the world – to fly to another country to examine Isis. But it hadn't been easy.

At first, he encountered a lot of resistance. The professor's inflexible minders, who guarded his diary with iron-fisted determination, told Sir Humphrey that travelling to Mexico to examine a patient, however famous, was out of the question. Professor Greenberg was far too busy to entertain such a ludicrous request. The fact the patient was dying and unable to travel didn't seem to matter.

The breakthrough came with a three million dollar donation for a new operating theatre and the offer to send a private jet to save time and make it all happen. The whole exercise would take up less than forty-eight hours of the good professor's precious time, travel included.

Out of options, Isis' medical team had reached an impasse. The specialists concluded that the tumour was inoperable; nothing further could be done. They were resigned to the fact that Isis had less than three months to live. Sir Humphrey refused to accept this – however sound and well-founded the diagnosis may have appeared at the time – and was pinning his hopes on the famous surgeon's legendary talents.

Professor Greenberg had recently pioneered new, revolutionary surgical procedures and techniques that allowed him to carry out complex operations previously thought to be impossible. Medical journals around the world were singing his praises and buzzing with articles about him and his ideas. At thirty-eight, he was hailed the 'new messiah' of surgery, and Isis was about to meet him.

Lola knocked softly and opened the door. Isis sat at her dressing table by the window and was putting the finishing touches to her make-up. 'He's here,' said Lola, watching Isis expertly apply her eye shadow with steady, experienced hands.

'What's he like?' asked Isis, scrutinising herself in the mirror. 'I still look like shit!'

'Don't be too hard on yourself. He's not here to see you perform.'

'You haven't answered my question.'

'Not at all what I expected.'

'In what way?'

'He's very young; looks like a schoolboy. He worked during the entire trip like a man possessed. I've never seen anything quite like it before … feverish. Workaholic, I suppose.'

'This is supposed to cheer me up? What's he doing now?'

'Conferring with your Mexican medical team. They are all here …'

'Good. And Sir Humphrey?'

'He's participating by video link from London.'

Isis stood up and began to parade up and down in front of the mirror to hide the fact she felt strangely nervous. An alien sensation for someone accustomed to performing in front of millions. 'Well, what do you think? Demure enough for an examination by a medical genius?' she said, her voice sounding hollow.

Dressed in a pair of tight-fitting black pants, high heels that would have made Madonna green with envy, and an electric blue Chanel blouse, Isis looked like someone who had just stepped off the catwalk.

'I suppose this would be a little too much,' she said, holding up an exquisite string of baroque pearls. 'What do you think?'

Lola tried in vain to suppress a smile. 'I'm sure he'll be impressed,' she said. She reached for Isis' hand and squeezed it. 'Don't worry. I think he's very good, and we should be grateful he's here …'

Feeling better, Isis bent down and kissed Lola on the cheek. 'You're right, I know. I'm just a little bit scared, I guess,' she said.

Surprised, Lola looked up. It was the first time she had heard Isis express such sentiments. As far as she was aware, fear had never before entered her boss' head, or her vocabulary. To see Isis afraid was unthinkable! The mere thought sent icy shivers of terror racing down Lola's spine. 'We'll get through this, you'll see,' she stammered, tears glistening in her eyes.

'That's what Tristan said …'

'Tristan? What has he to do with all this?' asked Lola, a puzzled look on her face.

'The boy can hear the whisper of angels …'

'You aren't making any sense,' protested Lola.

'Yes, I am. Would you like to know what the angels kept whispering in Tristan's ear when we met? Right here, in this very room only a little while ago?'

'Tell me,' said Lola, a little annoyed by what she considered a rather foolish and self-indulgent comment.

'It isn't my time … yet. Now, please fetch the good professor; I'm ready.'

'If my daughters knew that I'm standing here talking to you,' said Professor Greenberg, shaking Isis' hand, 'there'd be a riot at home, I tell you. They are ardent fans of yours. We have all your albums, and I know most of the lyrics by heart; I've heard them so many times. We've tried to attend one of your concerts for years, regrettably without success. Somehow, I've always been too busy—'

'Perhaps one day soon, we can do something about that,' interrupted Isis, sizing up the little man standing in front of her. He only came up to her chin, but she liked him instantly. Dressed in a pair of faded jeans, black sneakers and a Rolling Stones tee-shirt with Keith Richards in classical rocker-pose playing the guitar printed on the front, Professor Greenberg looked more like one of his young interns than the eminent surgeon he was.

A little unkempt and a little too long, his hair kept stubbornly curling around ears that were a little too big, giving him an endearingly loutish look, like an ageing student who has made the campus his home and career. The round, Harry Potter-style tortoiseshell glasses accentuated the prominent, slightly hooked nose that dominated his face.

However, his almost comical appearance and easygoing manner had a specific purpose: he was putting his patient at ease and carefully observing Isis' demeanour, mood and attitude generally. In short, the professor was conducting an examination without his patient being aware of it, or so he thought. In a way, he was doing exactly what Sir Humphrey had done for years, and Isis was onto him.

In Isis' case, a physical examination would have been pointless, and Professor Greenberg didn't believe in wasting time or going through the motions just for the patient's benefit. The extensive test results told him everything he needed to know. The only thing missing was the patient's persona, and Professor Greenberg was doing his best to find out all he could about that. 'Bedside espionage' he called it jokingly among colleagues and friends, and Professor Greenberg was the Sherlock Holmes of the infirmary.

'Well, how do I shape up?' asked Isis, a wry smile creasing her face.

'What do you mean?' said Professor Greenberg, a little taken aback by the remark.

'You've been analysing me since the moment we met. I recognised the signs, you see. Sir Humphrey, my physician, has done this for years. We often joke about it.'

'Oh. I didn't realise my methods were that transparent,' said Professor Greenberg, laughing. 'No matter. I can see we'll get on famously. So, let me cut to the chase, pun intended, and come straight to the point: I will tell you exactly what I think about your situation – I believe every patient deserves that. The only thing that requires a little tweaking and adjustment from case to case is *how* this should be communicated, and *when*. In your case, I think the direct approach is the right way to do this. The truth always looks best if we don't dress it up too much, don't you agree?'

Isis nodded, a lump in her throat. 'Shall we go and sit on the terrace? I love looking onto the garden …' Isis suggested, somewhat timidly.

'By all means,' said Professor Greenberg and followed Isis outside.

'Where are they?' asked Jack. Lola pointed to the terrace above them. 'Up there. Professor Greenberg wanted to see Isis alone.'

'Understandable.'

'She looked worried; I've never seen her like this.'

'Are you surprised? You heard what the Mexican doctors had to say—'

'They have all but given up,' interrupted Señora Gonzales. She reached for the decanter on the table and poured herself another glass of iced tea. 'But we haven't, have we?' she said softly, looking first at Lola sitting opposite, and then at Hanna. 'And you, Jack,' she continued, turning to Jack sitting next to her, 'don't know the meaning of that, do you?'

'You know me too well,' replied Jack, introducing a little humour and much needed levity into the conversation. He would have called it small talk distraction.

Señora Gonzales pointed to the far end of the garden. 'Just look at those two,' she said. Boris was seated on a stone bench playing the balalaika, the triangular-shaped instrument looking diminutive and fragile in his huge hands. Mesmerised, Tristan sat on the grass in front of him and listened intently. 'I haven't seen Boris play in years; extraordinary. That boy, Tristan, is truly remarkable …'

'He sure is,' said Jack. 'In more ways than you can possibly imagine. One day, I must tell you about his parents …'

'I've read your book …'

'*The Disappearance of Anna Popov?*' interjected Hanna.

'Yes,' said Señora Gonzales.

'There's certainly a lot about Tristan and his extraordinary parents in the book,' conceded Jack, 'but not all—'

'Look, here they come,' interrupted Lola, pointing to the stairs leading down into the garden from the terrace above. Relaxed and chatting casually, Isis and Professor Greenberg came slowly down the stairs. They looked more like two old friends than doctor and patient who had just met to discuss a crisis.

Señora Gonzales looked at Jack and nodded briefly, the signal obvious. Lola reached for Hanna's hand and squeezed it. Everyone was aware the moment of reckoning had arrived.

'I've asked David here to tell you all exactly what he just told me. That way, there can be no misunderstanding,' said Isis, introducing Professor Greenberg.

*First names already*, thought Jack, shaking the professor's hand. *Good sign.*

'Overall, I agree with your doctors here. Clinically speaking, their diagnosis is accurate, except in one fundamental respect,' began Professor Greenberg, looking suddenly much older. He took off his glasses and began to polish the lenses with his handkerchief. He did that often, especially when he was concentrating and collecting his thoughts. His vision temporarily blurred, it made him focus within. 'I don't believe the tumour is inoperable ...' he said calmly. Relieved, Lola squeezed Hanna's hand again. 'However ... before we become too excited, I must warn you that this doesn't solve our problem.'

'What do you mean, Professor?' asked Señora Gonzales, speaking softly.

'Despite its size and very precarious location in the brain, I'm confident that I can remove most of the tumour, but not all. If I were to do that, my patient would most likely die. Therefore, I have to leave some of the tumour behind, and that's the problem. Why? Because it will grow back; vigorously and quickly, I'm afraid.'

Stunned silence.

'So, what's the answer?' asked Señora Gonzales, finally breaking the awkward silence.

'I've been closely following a fascinating piece of research by a scientist in Australia of all places, which is right on this very subject ... Unfortunately, the scientist recently passed away without having completed his work ...'

'Professor Kozakievicz?' interjected Jack.

Professor Greenberg put on his glasses and stared at Jack, disbelief creasing his face. 'How on earth do you know this?' he asked, shaking his head. 'Are you a scientist?'

'No, I'm a writer. I happen know the scientist who has just

replaced him and is continuing his work: Dr Alexandra Delacroix,' replied Jack calmly.

'I know her!' exclaimed Professor Greenberg excitedly. 'She's brilliant! I thought she worked in France. I had no idea she …'

'It's all about genomics, isn't it?' said Jack.

'Yes. Epigenetics, to be more precise. In his most recent article, which I read again on the plane coming over here, Kozakievicz claims to have discovered certain hidden genes that, if stimulated by certain drugs, can direct the immune system to fight the tumour from within and make it disappear. Now, if this is right, the implications are staggering …'

'Such a drug exists?' asked Lola.

'You put your finger right on it. That's where matters become a little blurred, I'm afraid. Kozakievicz had hinted he knew the type of drug that could do this, and how. He even referred to the unique properties of a jungle plant, but he did caution that a lot more research needs to be done before we can be certain it really works. It all comes down to that. He did what every prudent scientist would have done in a situation like this – he was careful not to overreach.'

'So, what we need is time; is that what you are saying?' said Jack.

'Precisely, and I can provide that time by removing part of the tumour now. It isn't the whole answer; it is part of the answer. Can you see?'

'And would it help if Dr Delacroix were to become involved in this case?'

'Absolutely! In fact, there could be mutual advantages here. The more we know about this research and where it is heading, the better. Time is obviously of the essence here.'

'I'll talk to her.'

'Do you think she would be interested?' asked Isis, the anxiety in her voice obvious.

'Yes, I do.'

Isis glanced at Professor Greenberg sitting next to her. 'Do you believe in destiny, David?' she asked.

'I'm a surgeon …'

'And a surgeon has to have an open mind, yes?'

'Absolutely.'

'Well then … you've just seen destiny at work. Here, right now. Haven't you?'

For a while, Professor Greenberg just sat in silence and listened to the haunting melody floating across from Boris' balalaika. 'You may be right,' he said pensively. 'In any case, we'll find out soon enough.'

'And that boy over there can hear the whisper of angels and glimpse eternity,' said Isis, pointing to Tristan sitting in front of Boris.

'I don't follow,' said Professor Greenberg, smiling.

'You will, David, trust me, you will. One day soon.'

# 46

Alexandra asked Jana to drop her at the Gordon. 'I still can't believe we've just met Lena Abramowitz. It's sending a cold shiver down my spine. Something is reaching out of the past, guiding us and showing us the way. Astonishing. Do you believe in destiny, Jana?' she asked.

Jana shrugged. 'Jack does,' she said.

'Not very scientific, I know, but I think we may have made medical history this morning,' she said and jumped out of the car.

'That important, eh?' said Jana.

'Could be.'

'Jack would certainly call it destiny.'

'He may be right. I'm cooking tonight, remember,' said Alexandra cheerfully, and closed the door.

'No Blumenthal, please,' Jana called out, wagging her finger.

Alexandra and Jana had hit it off well. The instant rapport between them was quickly turning into a true friendship. Two like-minded women at a crossroads had found each other.

Alexandra hurried to her lab, unlocked the safe and took out Professor K's notebooks. Then she opened her handbag, reached into a side pocket and, careful to avoid contamination, pulled out the tissue with the few strands of Lena Abramovitz's white hair folded inside. When she placed it next to the notebooks, she noticed her fingers were trembling.

*The vision and the missing link finally coming together? Incredible! Proof perhaps*, she thought, feeling a little dizzy. *Could it really be? Only one way to find out. If Kasper's right, Lena's DNA sequence should give us the answer.* The recent acquisition by Gordon of an Illumina HiSeq X Ten machine made it possible to carry out this complex task right there on the premises, quickly, efficiently and at relatively low cost, which only a few years ago would have been fantasy. The sophisticated machine cost millions, and it was only by the generosity and support of donors and bequestors that the Gordon Institute had been able to afford such an expensive piece of high-tech equipment. Alexandra thanked her lucky stars: there were only a few places in the world where scientists had ready access to such a wonderful facility.

Akhil knocked on Alexandra's door and entered. 'The CEO was looking for you earlier,' he said. 'He would like to see you.'

Alexandra put the strands of hair into a small plastic container and handed it to Akhil. 'Please extract the DNA and prepare it for sequencing. It's urgent. I'll go and see the CEO.'

'I'll do it straight away,' said Akhil. He was tempted to ask a few questions, but thought better of it.

'Thanks,' said Alexandra and stood up. Something about Akhil made her feel uneasy. He was polite, but aloof. Efficient, like a robot, but without initiative or independent thought. He wasn't a man she could warm to. She had the feeling he was somehow watching her all the time, which was unsettling.

*Perhaps he resents my parachuting in here just like that*, she thought. Perhaps he just needs a little more time. However, rather than sharing her ideas with him and involving him in her research as one would normally do with an assistant, Alexandra decided to keep her distance, at least for the time being.

'The board was very impressed with the speech you gave at Professor K's memorial the other day, and so was I,' said the CEO, 'it was inspirational.'

'Thank you,' said Alexandra, acknowledging his compliment.

'As you know, our funding is heavily dependent on philanthropy. We have many generous donors and "Partners for the Future" who have made bequests in their Wills, leaving a lot of money to Gordon. We have regular functions here at the institute to keep them up to date and show them what we are doing. We always choose one or two of our prominent scientists to talk about their work. It's a great way to keep our donors engaged and motivated. There's nothing like meeting a dedicated scientist to create enthusiasm for a cause.'

'I understand,' said Alexandra, wondering where this was heading. 'It was the same at our institute in France.'

'I know this is short notice … but we would like to invite you to address our sponsors and tell them about Professor K's work. It would introduce you to that important group of supporters, raise your profile and, we believe, greatly benefit Gordon. Interested?'

'Sure.'

'There's only one little problem …' said the CEO.

'Oh? What?'

'The function is tomorrow.'

Alexandra went straight back to her lab, put everything on hold and began to draft her speech for the next day. There was no way she could have refused the CEO's request, short notice or not. In a way, she didn't mind. Having to focus on Professor K's work like that and put his ideas and vision into language a layman could follow and understand, was always an excellent way to strip away the noise and confusion that blurred the boundaries, and somehow seemed to accompany every complex research project.

In fact, Alexandra enjoyed the discipline and intellectual challenge of the task and realised it could substantially advance her position and standing at Gordon, not only among her colleagues, but also among the all-important donors who, as the CEO correctly pointed out, were the lifeblood of the institute that kept the lights on and the wheels of research turning. No money, no research. No research, no progress.

Alexandra was no stranger to preparing speeches. She had done so on many occasions and was a natural when it came to public speaking and delivery. She always tailored her speech to suit her audience in a way that spoke *to* them, not *at* them. The way she tackled this delicate task was to pick a friend – preferably not connected to science – and write a story about the subject specifically for that person. She would then reduce the story to bullet points, peel away unnecessary information and structure the speech accordingly, avoiding jargon and choosing concepts and language a layperson could easily understand. On this occasion, Alexandra chose Jana to be her sounding board and audience.

*To put Professor K's work into its proper context,* Alexandra began to write – she always prepared her speeches in longhand – *I have to take you on a little journey. We have to travel back to the 1940s and a place where atrocities were committed on an almost unimaginable scale: a concentration camp in Germany where life was cheap and morality as alien as kindness and compassion. A most unlikely place, one could argue, for an inspired idea that could alter the course of medicine and change the journey of mankind,* wrote Alexandra, recalling Professor K's letter. *Yet, that is precisely where it all began. Not with Professor K, of course – he wasn't even born yet – but his father, Dr Simon Kozakievicz, a brilliant Polish doctor who was deported to Auschwitz with his family in 1942.*

*Dr Simon Kozakievicz was renowned for his extraordinary cancer research before the war. His work involved mainly identical twins. He was convinced the way to defeat cancer was through the immune system. He used twins to learn how the immune system worked and why one twin was able to fight and survive cancer, when the other couldn't. This was quite a revolutionary idea, way ahead of its time.*

*After his deportation to Auschwitz with his family, he was forced to carry out certain secret medical experiments – with the notorious Dr Mengele in charge. Mengele was using him. The lives of the doctor's family depended on his cooperation.*

*Dr Kozakievicz survived the war; his family did not. After the liberation of Auschwitz, he went to Switzerland and joined a prominent pharmaceutical company. He remarried and had a son, Kasper; Professor K. Ironically, the horrible experimental operations at Auschwitz – carried out mainly on twins – provided a vital clue that later laid the foundations for the further development of his ideas … Medical research rarely moves in a straight line. Light can come out of darkness …'*

*That's it! Of course,* thought Alexandra, *how stupid of me! The dark matter! The junk! The answer is in the junk DNA!* She put down her pen, reached for one of Professor K's notebooks and immersed herself in his notes. Suddenly, all the confusing threads of thought and reasoning were beginning to come together like a picture in the clouds. Once you recognised the shape, the picture emerged with astonishing clarity. The notes, data and often confusing diagrams and connections were beginning to make sense. *It's all about genetics! Evolution!* Alexandra thought excitedly. *That's what Kasper, the iconoclast, was getting at. There's a difference between junk DNA and garbage! Junk isn't garbage. It has a function. Brilliant!*

By the time she closed the notebook and looked up, several hours had passed. Alexandra glanced at her watch. 'Oh … not again!' she cried out and reached for her phone. *No cooking tonight*, she thought. *I hope Jana doesn't mind.* First she called Jana, and then ordered a taxi and headed for the door.

# 47

'You look like the kitten that's just discovered the cream bowl,' said Jana as Alexandra burst into the apartment, her face flushed with excitement.

'I'm *so* sorry,' said Alexandra, following Jana into the kitchen. 'I completely lost track of time ... again.' She threw her keys on the kitchen bench, walked over to Jana and kissed her on the cheek. 'Thanks for this morning, and thanks for being so understanding,' she said.

'No problem,' said Jana, smiling. 'You're in charge of the wine, I'll finish the omelette. My next best dish in a rapidly dwindling repertoire. Your turn tomorrow.'

Alexandra opened the fridge and took out a bottle of New Zealand sauvignon blanc. 'You're on,' she said, opening the bottle and pouring two glasses, one of which she placed next to the stove for Jana.

'Tell me about your day,' Jana said, without taking her eyes off the pan.

Alexandra pulled a couple of crumpled pages out of her handbag, took a sip of wine and put them on the bench. 'It's been quite a day,' she said. 'You know when you've been wrestling with a frustrating conundrum for some time and then suddenly begin to *see* and everything falls into place?'

'A light bulb moment?' said Jana.

'Something like that. Well, that's what happened to me today. Quite unexpectedly. It was as if someone had handed me the key to Professor K's world. I put the key in the lock, opened the door and stepped inside ...'

'And what did you find?'

'Genius.'

'Oh? You must tell me about it, but not on an empty stomach. Set the table. This is almost done. Let's eat first and you can dazzle me with the good professor's genius after dinner. If you think a mere mortal like me is up to it,' teased Jana, a sparkle in her eyes.

Alexandra held up the crumpled pages. 'Don't worry; I've prepared a translation, of sorts. You won't have a problem,' promised Alexandra, 'I hope,' she added and refilled their glasses.

Alexandra devoured her omelette. She hadn't eaten anything all day. Jana did all the talking. She told Alexandra that she had spoken to Carrington on the phone and sought his advice regarding her abduction. He was due to arrive the next day and would advise her on what to do. 'Until then,' said Jana, 'we'll stay put and keep our heads down.' Jana pointed to the empty bottle. 'But that doesn't mean we have to stay sober. How about we open another one, and you tell me about your day?'

'You're on,' said Alexandra, feeling relaxed and no longer so concerned about her situation. Having someone like Jana staying with her and an experienced lawyer like Carrington arriving the next day, gave her peace of mind and confidence for the first time since her nightmarish ordeal.

Alexandra told Jana about the CEO's request and the speech she would have to give the next day. 'As you can imagine, a lot hinges on how I approach this, and how well I perform.'

'Sure. It's quite an ask at such short notice.'

'It is, but there's a lot more riding on this than that. I feel that the future of Professor K's entire work is at stake here …'

'In what way?'

'It's complicated. I've been invited to talk about his work, his groundbreaking research and, most importantly, his revolutionary ideas. I will have to *explain* what it's all about, under the spotlight. The eyes of the whole institute and its key supporters will be on this, looking for some kind of revelation about a legendary scientist and his legacy. A breakthrough of sorts is expected. I'm sure that's why I've been asked to do this tomorrow. If I fail to deliver … well …'

'Sounds tricky,' said Jana.

'It is. That's why I would like to ask you for a little favour,' said Alexandra.

'Fire away.'

Alexandra held up her crumpled notes. 'It all hinges on this.'

'Oh?'

'Professor K's work is complex to say the least. His extraordinary mind worked in different ways, sometimes impossible to follow and always difficult to understand. He suffered from an intellectual impatience of a most severe kind. He was an iconoclast; a rebel who took nothing for granted and was prepared to question everything. Yet, he had an unshakable trust in nature. He believed that nothing in nature has been put there capriciously or in vain. He believed in *purpose*. Often guided by instinct rather than accepted method, he took reckless shortcuts and jumped to extraordinary conclusions. Quite unscientific and unsupported at times, yet always with a sound reason and inspired, almost visionary insight. I've known him for years and worked with him closely, but even I found it often difficult to make sense of what he was getting at, until this afternoon that is.'

'Please explain.'

'I've been reading his notes for the past two days, trying to fit the pieces together and follow his reasoning in order to understand his explanations and findings.'

'And?'

'I was getting nowhere, but then something quite unexpected happened this afternoon. It's difficult to explain, but suddenly it all began to make sense. *I saw the connection.* If he's right, we are on the cusp of an extraordinary discovery and tomorrow, I have to talk about it.'

'I see. So, what's that favour you're asking?'

'I would like you to be my sounding board. Listen carefully to what I'm going to say. Play the devil's advocate. Question, probe. I've prepared an outline of what I'm going to talk about tomorrow. It has to make sense to the experienced, sceptical scientists examining every word and questioning every idea, and to the laymen who at best has only the vaguest notion of what a gene is and how DNA and RNA work, if he's even heard of them at all. This is a tightrope walk of a most delicate kind. A balancing act. One mistake … I feel that an exceptional man's work of a lifetime is at stake here. If I fail …'

'I understand.'

'Ready?'

Jana held out her empty glass. 'I am,' she said, 'but only if you fill up my glass.'

For the next hour, Alexandra delivered the speech she had prepared in the afternoon. She began by closely following her notes, but soon cast them aside and began to expand. Warming to the subject, she became passionate and spoke about Professor K's work with a conviction and clarity so gripping, it left Jana mesmerised and speechless.

'What do you think?' prompted Alexandra quietly after a while.

'Wow! I don't quite know what to say.'

'Don't be polite. What do you *really* think?'

'A tour de force of genomics. I've never heard anything quite like it—'

'But did it make sense?' interrupted Alexandra.

'It did, but my head's spinning. There's so much to take in.'

'I know. There's just no other way to somehow explain all this, I'm afraid.'

'I understand.'

'Any questions?'

'Quite a few. Let's go over it, step-by-step. But first, I need another drink.'

For Jana, the experienced policewoman, Alexandra's speech was like listening to expert evidence in court. To be effective, the subject matter had to be clear and easy to follow. Every member of the jury, regardless of background and experience, had to be able to understand it.

'You'll soon see from my questions where you have to provide more information and explain things a little better,' said Jana, leaning back into her comfortable chair. 'For someone like me, that is.'

'Exactly what I need,' said Alexandra. 'Go ahead.'

'I really liked the biographical background at the beginning,' said Jana. 'The reference to his father, the concentration camp, the horror of Auschwitz, the secret operations … fascinating stuff. It shows us Professor K, the man. No man is an island. Excellent, but I would keep it brief.'

'Point taken,' said Alexandra scribbling away on the crumpled page resting on her knee.

'Correct me if I'm wrong, but if I understood what you said, Professor K's revolutionary theory is a direct attack on accepted dogma …'

'It is. And that dogma states?'

'Help me here,' Jana said.

'DNA makes RNA; RNA makes protein. Compliments of Francis Crick, co-discoverer of the double helix, 1953. Think of a gene as a blueprint for constructing a complex engine. The blueprint is written in characters called DNA. RNA is a disposable copy of the blueprint that is used to build proteins in the noisy workshop of the cell. Proteins are the engine running life. Clear so far?'

'Absolutely. A gene is therefore a blueprint for the production of a protein? Is that right?'

'It is. But remember, there are many genes, each with its own blueprint, and all the blueprints taken together form our genome.'

'And instead of a complex engine at the end of the production line, you end up with a human being?'

'You got it.'

'But Professor K challenged that view?'

'He did. According to him, the gene blueprint contains a lot more information than previously thought. More information than is required to make protein. This view had the establishment rattled, I can tell you.'

'And what is that additional information all about?' asked Jana.

'That's the new frontier of molecular biology. We are just beginning to decode that information. You must understand, the volume is huge. Some call it garbage; others call it junk DNA.

Professor K called it a treasure trove of evolution accumulated over hundreds of millions of years, which must be *telling us something*. It may even contain the answers to many of the questions we are currently grappling with, such as how to cure or prevent cancer, for instance. Answers already provided by evolution and embedded right here in our genome, and all we have to do is try to understand what the "junk" is telling us. Decrypt it. That's what he believed and was working on just before he died.'

'How huge is huge?'

'Gigantic. And all of it is new stuff. It began with the completion of the genome project in 2001. Out of the three billion letters of our DNA, only about one point five per cent carries blueprints for proteins—'

'What about the rest? The ninety-eight point five per cent?' interrupted Jana.

'That's the really interesting question here, and Professor K had some quite specific ideas about that,' said Alexandra. 'The new dogma according to Kasper now states that DNA makes RNA, but only *some* of that RNA makes protein. Notice the difference?'

'Sure.'

Alexandra put her notes on the table and looked at Jana. 'And then we have exons, introns and splicing RNA. Ribozymes and Messenger RNAs,' said Alexandra. 'The complexity goes on and on, and so do the challenges and the excitement of new discoveries and possibilities buried in this new frontier. And it doesn't stop there—'

Jana held up her hand. 'Hold it right there! You've really lost me now. My head is spinning.'

'You're right,' said Alexandra, smiling. 'It's easy to get a little carried away here, but this is most helpful. Thank you. But enough for tonight. Why don't we sleep on it and continue in the morning? Early. Would you mind?'

'Not at all. Good idea. I find this absolutely fascinating.'

'Another favour?'

'Oh?'

'Would you mind coming along to my talk tomorrow as my guest? I need at least one friendly face in the crowd.'

'I would be delighted.'

'Excellent! It's all settled then,' said Alexandra, relieved. 'We'll iron out the creases in the morning.'

'Let's do that, Dr Delacroix,' said Jana and reached for her glass. 'A toast?'

'Why not?' said Alexandra, reaching for her own.

'To a visionary iconoclast, a maverick, rebel and genius. I give you Professor K. May his ideas flourish and change the journey of man.'

They touched glasses.

'*For the better*,' whispered Alexandra, tears in her eyes. 'To Professor K.'

# 48

Alexandra was the star attraction of the afternoon. The CEO and his team had 'marketed' her well, and everyone – from wealthy retirees to corporate donors – wanted to meet her.

As Alexandra walked up to the microphone, she felt confident and calm. The crowded room was no longer intimidating and the many inquisitive strangers she had met earlier no longer a distraction. Because she knew her subject matter intimately and was genuinely passionate about Professor K's work and vision, she found it easy to deliver her speech in a way that was both personal, and informative. Having rehearsed her approach with Jana earlier in the day and fine-tuned the pitch, was also of great help.

She spoke with affection about a man she had known all her life and admired deeply, and outlined his extraordinary research in a way that was easy to understand and had her audience spellbound. She peppered her talk with endearing anecdotes reaching all the way back to her teenage years that added a touch of intimacy and humour, making her audience laugh.

'Ladies and gentlemen – friends of the Gordon – without your generosity and support, this institute wouldn't be here, and exceptional scientists like the late Professor Kozakievicz would not be able to do what they do best: advance medical research, reduce – even prevent – human suffering and improve the journey of man. Thank you for this wonderful opportunity to speak to you about him. I hope I've been able to give you a little insight into the work of this extraordinary man and in a small way, share his vision with you.'

Once again, Alexandra was given a standing ovation. A beaming CEO thanked her publicly for an inspirational glimpse into a gifted mind, and hinted at possible advances and breakthroughs that may soon follow because if it.

Stepping down from the podium, the CEO took Alexandra by the arm. 'There's someone I would like you to meet,' he said, steering

Alexandra across the crowded auditorium. 'He just donated one hundred thousand dollars to the Gordon because of what you said. Congratulations,' continued the CEO, and lowering his voice, '*These are the people we need.*'

'How wonderful,' said Alexandra, genuinely pleased. 'Who is he?'

'A businessman. From South Africa.'

The mention of South Africa sent a cold shiver racing down Alexandra's spine, but she did her best to ignore it.

'Alexandra, this is Mr Van Dam,' said the CEO. Alexandra looked at the tall, blond man with piercing blue eyes, and paled. Smartly dressed in a light grey suit, her abductor was smiling at her. 'He wants to talk to you about your work. I'll leave you to it,' he added, gently pushing Alexandra forward.

'Great speech, Dr Delacroix; I've learnt a lot,' said Van Cleef. Alexandra bit her lip, but said nothing. She was desperately looking around the room, searching for Jana. 'As you can see, we are taking great interest in your work,' continued Van Cleef, 'and are happy to support it – generously. Of course, some reciprocation would be appreciated ...'

'What do you want?' hissed Alexandra.

'You haven't been entirely open with us, have you?'

'What do you mean?'

Van Cleef took a glass of wine from a passing waiter's tray and continued to smile at Alexandra. 'Here, let me show you.' He reached into his pocket, pulled out a pair of glasses and held them up. Both lenses were broken, but Alexandra recognised the distinctive tortoiseshell frames.

'What have you done to him?' she demanded, her voice sounding shrill.

'Keep your voice down and smile,' said Van Cleef calmly. 'Don't worry, Mr Papadoulis will be fine. Once the swelling goes down and the bruises heal.'

'Despicable monster ...'

'Hush, my dear. We don't want to alarm the other guests now, do we?' said Van Cleef, a threatening edge in his voice. 'After a little persuasion, Mr Papadoulis was most cooperative … He told us about a parcel he delivered to you the other day … Your inheritance. Left to you by the good professor, I understand … Notebooks. Naughty, naughty. You should have told us about it. I did warn you, didn't I? We have eyes and ears everywhere.'

Van Cleef took a sip of wine. 'Now listen carefully. This is what I want you to do. You will make a copy of every page, every line, and every word in those notebooks and leave the copies on your desk. Clear so far?' Van Cleef was enjoying himself. He was sending Alexandra a clear signal: he could reach her everywhere and even her place of work wasn't safe.

'What?' shrieked Alexandra.

'You heard me. And as a token of our goodwill and faith in you, a little bonus is already waiting in your account, compliments of Mr Macbeth. Such a generous and forgiving man. Please don't disappoint him again. Another payment will be made as soon as you provide us with the copies. Keep up the good work, Dr Delacroix. Better go now and look after your other guests. After all, you are a celebrity. I'll see myself out.' Van Cleef bowed, reached for Alexandra's hand and shook it.

Alexandra saw Jana talking to someone on the other side of the room. She hurried over to her and took her aside. '*He's here,*' she whispered, squeezing Jana's arm.

'Ouch! Who?' said Jana, surprised.

'My abductor!'

'What?'

'That's him over there by the door. The tall blond one.'

'Are you sure?'

'Absolutely!'

'Stay here and leave him to me,' said Jana, and made her way across the crowded room towards the exit without taking her eyes off the man. Van Cleef put his empty wineglass on a table by the door and left the room. Jana hurried after him. As she passed the table, she picked up the empty wineglass with a serviette and quietly slipped it into her handbag.

Van Cleef was waiting for the lift. He looked impatiently at his watch and kept staring at the indicator panel. Jana pulled her phone out of her pocket and, pretending to make a call, quickly took a couple of photos of him. Then she walked across to the lift and stood next to him. 'Quite something wasn't it?' she said.

'Sure was,' said Van Cleef, looking at his watch again.

'Your first time here?' Jana asked, noticing his heavy South African accent.

'Yes.'

'Mine too.' Then the lift doors opened and they got in. Jana continued to make small talk until they reached the ground floor.

'Got to dash,' said Van Cleef as soon as the door opened, and headed for the exit.

Jana had come across men like Van Cleef before, many times. *He radiates danger*, she thought, *just as Alexandra said. Annoyingly confident, and pedantically precise. Definitely ex-military.*

A black four-wheel drive was waiting outside with the engine running. Van Cleef got in and the car took off, but not before Jana got a good look at the number plate. *Cowboys never change*, she thought, smiling, and made a mental note of the number plate: I SPY 4U.

# 49

Jack pushed the pile of creased papers impatiently aside and, rubbing his tired eyes, sat back. The warm evening breeze caressing his face could do little to relax him. Searching for answers, he had worked through the whole afternoon without taking a break. Lola and Professor Greenberg were on their way back to Boston and Tristan had begged to be allowed to go along for the round trip. Persuaded by Lola and Señora Gonzales, who had been enlisted by Tristan to plead his case, Jack had reluctantly agreed.

*It's all somehow coming together*, thought Jack, looking out of the open window, the fading light casting long shadows across the terrace outside. The cryptic, hidden and often confusing clues gleaned from the letters he had copied in Sir Charles' office were finally beginning to make some sense. The next step was slowly emerging out of the maze of dead ends, false leads and speculation. A powerful, familiar gut feeling told Jack he was on the right track. However, one main clue central to it all was eluding him, despite being tantalisingly close.

*If only I had just a little bit more to go on*, he thought, staring at the piece of paper in front of him, *I could pinpoint where this came from. Damn!* Jack shook his head in frustration. Isis' mother had made sure that the sender's identity and address had either been obliterated, or torn off altogether. She had obviously gone to great lengths to conceal her lover's name and whereabouts. However, on the page in front of Jack, a tiny, yet valuable clue had been overlooked.

The letter had obviously been penned on some writing paper with an embossed name and address at the top that one would usually expect to find in one of the better hotels. Part of the page had been ripped off, but some of the cursive writing had been inadvertently left behind, and Jack had written it all down in his notebook.

Beginning at the top left hand corner of the page, the letters M . K . . U . O . GE were clearly visible. Then came a wide gap. At the top right, the letters . A . . O . I . could just be made out. At the bottom of the page where the signature had been torn out was a handwritten date. After playing with the letters and trying to fill in the gaps for over an hour, Jack finally gave up. He concluded that the first part must be a name – perhaps of a hotel – and the second an address of sorts. Jack closed his notebook. *It's no use*, he thought, *this is going nowhere.* It was time to speak to Señora Gonzales. Jack was certain she knew a lot more about the whole matter than she had revealed so far.

The fading light and excited chatter of the birds chasing the last meal of the day told Jack it was getting late. He stood up, stretched his aching arms and looked down into the garden below. Isis was asleep in a deckchair. Careful not to wake him, Señora Gonzales was draping a blanket over her sleeping grandson. It was an endearing expression of love and affection at a time of great uncertainly, anxiety and fear. Señora Gonzales looked up and saw Jack waving at her from the terrace. She tucked the blanket in under Isis' feet and slowly walked up the stairs towards Jack waiting for her at the top.

'I think I've gone as far as I can with the letters,' said Jack, pointing to the desk. 'Would you like me to tell you what I've pieced together so far?'

'I was hoping you would,' said Señora Gonzales.

'Once again, some of this is rather speculative, I'm afraid. There's just no other way to close some of the gaps, but a certain picture is clearly emerging. Here it is …' Jack walked over to the desk and picked up the bundle of letters. 'These are love letters,' he said, holding up the bundle, 'passionate, desperate, full of longing, desire and hope. The lovers are separated, perhaps by quite a long distance … I think we can safely assume that the letters were addressed to your daughter and that they have been sent by her lover … And I can tell you when they were written. Fortunately, one of them has a date: 13th March 1962. Please remind me how old Mercedes would have been then?'

'Twenty-two,' replied Señora Gonzales.

'And how long had she been married?'

'Two years. She married Lord Elms in 1960.'

'Tell me about Lord Elms. What was he like? How did they meet? How long had they known each other before they were married?'

'Lord Elms was one of the most eligible bachelors in England at the time. He was twelve years older than Mercedes. They mixed in the same social circles. Mercedes was quite a beauty; intelligent, popular, vivacious. She sparkled. He was rather reserved and quite shy, but well-connected and fabulously rich with huge estates in the country. Mutual friends introduced them ...'

'And they fell in love?' probed Jack, watching Señora Gonzales carefully.

'I know what you are getting at. Not entirely. My husband and I were very keen for Mercedes to marry well. She had refused several quite eligible suitors before and she was getting on in years for that era; girls married young in those days. People were beginning to talk ... These circles can be quite cruel and unforgiving. Time was running out for her, or so we thought.'

'What are you telling me?'

'We encouraged Mercedes to foster the relationship, and she did.'

'And Lord Elms?'

'He considered her a most desirable and suitable match, and so did his family. She ticked all the required boxes.'

'And love?'

Señora Gonzales allowed herself a dry laugh. 'Love wasn't one of the boxes. It was a match of the head, not the heart.'

'And you approved?'

For a while, Señora Gonzales looked at Jack, a shadow of sadness clouding her face. 'Yes, we did.'

'Was it a happy union?'

'You can't look into married people's hearts or bedrooms. And besides, shortly after the marriage, my husband and I returned to Mexico. I've lived here ever since.'

'But you corresponded, surely?'

'We did, of course, but letters can only tell you so much ...' Her reply was evasive, but it told Jack what he needed to know.

'Did Lord Elms have any particular interests? Did they travel, for instance?'

'As I said, he was rather reserved. British; typical establishment. But he did have one great passion …'

'Oh? What was that?'

'Hunting – big game. He even had a trophy room at Clarendon Hall. They travelled a lot. Africa mainly.'

'Do you know where in Africa?'

'Kenya. They always travelled to Kenya. Mercedes loved the place. She often sent me letters and postcards from Nairobi. She seemed so happy there … And they always stayed at some big lodge popular with the English.'

*Bingo!* thought Jack. *Of course!* Some of the missing letters at the top of the page had just been filled in.

'You know, you've just provided the missing link I've been looking for all afternoon.'

'I did?'

'Yes. These letters were sent from Nairobi, no doubt about it. Mercedes' lover lived in Kenya and was most likely involved in big game hunting, I'd say. There are various references in the letters to danger, adventure, living in tents and gazing at the stars. It makes perfect sense, and so does my next move.'

'And what will that be?'

'Going to Kenya, of course, to find out more. However, I can already tell you quite a bit about her secret lover.'

'You can?'

'Yes. He's articulate, well-educated with strong, distinct handwriting suggesting discipline and order. Also, he's widely read with a penchant for poetry. He freely quotes love poems. An English public schoolboy, I'd say.'

Señora Gonzales shook her head. 'Amazing,' she said. 'And you can tell all that just by analysing the letters?'

'Yes. I don't think we are far off the mark here. And then there's one more thing; it could be significant,' said Jack, leafing through the pages. 'I tried to arrange the letters in some chronological order. We only have one date, remember, but the content does generally suggest a logical flow.'

'I see.'

'I believe the letters were all written over quite a short period of, say, months – a year at the most. I think they were all written around 1962. And then suddenly, they stop.' Jack held up a piece of paper. 'I think this one here is the last letter; the tone and content strongly suggest this. No more pining and longing. Instead, we have hope, joy and euphoria. Interpretation? The lovers are about to be reunited!'

Señora Gonzales nodded, but remained silent.

'Did anything significant happen in Mercedes' life around that time?' asked Jack.

'Well, yes … she had a child; George was born in 1963. Needless to say, we were overjoyed. We were quite concerned that there were no children during the first years of the marriage … but then George came along.'

'And I suppose they stopped travelling?'

'Certainly. Once she had the baby, Mercedes' life changed. She didn't travel again.'

Jack turned serious. 'With her last breath, Mercedes directed Isis to the hiding place at Clarendon Hall where these letters were found. They must contain a major clue as to what happened to her and her husband. There has to be a *connection*, and let's not forget, she warned Isis of a serious, imminent danger. The only baffling thing is the crystal skull. I can't make any sense of it, can you?'

Señora Gonzales shook her head.

'You saw the skull for the last time when Sturmbannfuehrer Steinberger left Paris and took it with him. I think that was in late 1942 – right?'

'Yes.'

'And you have no idea what happened to it after that?'

'No.'

'Yet it turns up with the letters hidden at Clarendon Hall … extraordinary. There has to be a link. And Mercedes never spoke of it?'

'Never.'

'Can you think of an explanation? Anything at all?'

'No, I can't.'

'Then I will find out,' said Jack. 'And I know just the person to help me do that.'

'You do?' said Señora Gonzales, surprised. 'Who?'

'You'll be quite surprised when I tell you,' said Jack, enjoying the suspense. 'Hidden corners of our lives ...' he teased.

'Can't you tell me now?'

'Not yet. I have to make a phone call first, and then I'll tell you.'

Señora Gonzales shook her head. 'You are quite something, Jack Rogan. No wonder Isis is so fond of you ... Not even a little clue?'

'All I can tell you for now is this: it's a *she*; that's all.'

'That tells me nothing. Anything else? *Please?*'

'In a way, you've already met her ...'

Señora Gonzales looked at Jack. 'I have?' she said, confused.

'Yes, in one of my books.'

'How intriguing. And she will surprise me?'

'Oh, I should think so.'

# 50

Señora Gonzales woke with a start. She had fallen asleep in the chair next to Isis' bed. Rubbing her eyes, she looked at her watch: it was just after two. Isis was breathing regularly and the night nurse was sitting by the open window, reading. 'I'll go now,' said Señora Gonzales. 'I hope she'll be strong enough for the trip.' The nurse nodded.

Professor Greenberg had agreed to carry out the risky operation. However, there was one main logistical problem: he could only operate in his clinic in Boston and Isis was unable to fly, and to travel four and half thousand kilometres overland wasn't advisable either. To overcome the problem, it had been suggested that Isis travel by sea.

Hanna had already made the necessary arrangements and had chartered a suitable vessel to take Isis from the port of Heroica Veracruz in Mexico, to Boston. Isis would only have to travel four hundred kilometres by car to the coast to catch the boat. Professor Greenberg prescribed certain drugs to help take the pressure off Isis' brain and allow her to undertake the journey in relative comfort and safety.

As Señora Gonzales passed Jack's room on her way back to her own, she saw a circle of light under the door and could hear Jack talking. *He's still on the phone*, she thought, remembering their earlier conversation. Just then, the speaking stopped. For a while, Señora Gonzales stood there and listened. Silence. Overcome by curiosity, she knocked softly.

Jack opened the door and smiled. 'Don't you sleep at all?' he said.

Señora Gonzales shook her head. 'Curiosity has turned me into an insomniac,' she joked. 'It's all your fault.'

'Then let me make amends,' said Jack. 'Please come in. I have some encouraging news you'll find interesting …'

Señora Gonzales put her hand on Jack's arm and looked at him intently. 'We can all do with a little encouragement,' she said, and followed Jack into the room.

'The time differences are diabolical. That's why I had to make the calls now, but I've had some luck ...' said Jack, grinning.

'Are you going to tell me, or are you going to wait until this little old woman drops dead of curiosity?'

'I've just spoken to her,' said Jack, enjoying the banter.

'The woman I've already met in one of your books, and who can help you solve the mystery of the crystal skull turning up at Clarendon Hall?'

'The very same. Can you guess who that might be?'

'She's obviously connected to Steinberger ...'

'Correct.'

Señora Gonzales took her time before replying. 'His daughter?' she ventured quietly.

'Bravo! Yes – Dr Rosen. I knew you'd work it out.'

'Now we are really delving into hidden corners, aren't we?' said Señora Gonzales, a troubled look on her face. She sensed she was passing a point of no return. To stop now was unthinkable, to go back impossible, yet she was strangely afraid ... afraid of what she might find. 'You realise of course that Dr Rosen would be my son's half-sister; if he's still alive, that is,' she added sadly.

'I'm well aware of it. And that's our link of course; has to be. As you know, Dr Rosen is the head of the Rosen Foundation, doing wonderful work in some of the poorest countries in the world, especially in East Africa. She's an ophthalmic surgeon and fundraiser extraordinaire. She has restored the eyesight of countless unfortunates across the globe. She's quite something. We've shared some amazing adventures ... But you would have read about all that in the book. I've tracked her down, which wasn't easy – she travels a lot – and I've just spoken with her ...'

Señora Gonzales sat up with a jolt. 'You have?' she said. 'Where did you find her?'

'That's the really interesting bit, I suppose, especially in light of what we spoke about in the afternoon. Nairobi – remember?'

'I don't quite follow.'

'Dr Rosen is in Dadaab.'

'Where's that?'

'It's one the biggest refugee camps in the world at the moment. It's in Kenya, close to the Somali border.'

Señora Gonzales looked thunderstruck. *'Kenya again,'* she whispered. 'It's turning up everywhere ...'

'It is,' said Jack, and I'll find out why.'

'And how will you do that?'

'By going there, of course. Tomorrow, in fact. I've arranged to meet Dr Rosen at the camp. And I've already spoken to Lola – she just returned with a very tired Tristan. Apparently, it was quite a flight. They were delayed in Boston. Air Force One was in the area and all flights were grounded. That's why it took them so long to get back.'

Jack turned to Señora Gonzales. 'As long as Countess Kuragin doesn't find out about all this, I'm in the clear. If she does, she'll skin me alive,' lamented Jack, lowering his voice. 'I just hope the boy hasn't posted anything on Facebook! Otherwise ... Be that as it may, because Isis is travelling by sea to Boston, the plane isn't needed. So we are free to go; we are leaving in the morning.'

Señora Gonzales stood up. 'Then you must get some sleep,' she said. 'I firmly believe you were somehow meant to come into our lives, right now at this extraordinary time.'

'You may be right.'

Señora Gonzales stopped at the door and reached for Jack's hand. 'I cannot tell you what all of this means to me. I must find my son. Now, before it's too late. I must know what happened to him. Now, more than ever! You do understand, don't you?'

'I do.'

Señora Gonzales turned to Jack and kissed him tenderly on the cheek. It was a spontaneous gesture of genuine affection and gratitude by an old woman nearing the end of her life, yearning for answers about a past too painful to remember, but impossible to forget. 'Thank you,' she said. 'Now I must go to my own room and face my ghosts ... Sleep well.'

# PART IV
## DETEGO

'The path
to paradise
begins in
hell.'

Dante Alighieri; *Divine Comedy*

# 51

Sir Charles looked at his watch. *He's late*, he thought, trying to stay positive. He had arranged to meet his contact, a senior civil servant and good friend, at his club. He knew his friend was taking a huge risk in passing confidential information to him and Sir Charles was hoping he hadn't changed his mind.

To find out what Lord Elms had been investigating at the time of his death turned out to be almost impossible. The cone of silence that had descended upon the entire affair appeared impregnable. This had only hardened Sir Charles' resolve to pursue the matter.

Then Sir Charles had a lucky break: he discovered that his friend's department had worked closely with Lord Elms and his team just before he died and assisted him with certain research. Ironically, it was Daniel Cross of MI5 who had let this slip during one of their briefings. Sir Charles was hoping the subject matter of the research would throw some light on what Lord Elms had been working on, and why.

*Here he is.* Sir Charles stood up to welcome his friend.

'Sorry, Charles. Diabolical traffic,' said George Underwood.

Sir Charles and Underwood had met at Oxford many years ago and remained friends ever since. Underwood owed Sir Charles a big favour. A few years ago, Sir Charles had helped his son deal with a serious negligent driving charge that could have sent him to jail and cost him his career.

Sir Charles slapped his friend on the back. 'Don't worry, George. Scotch?'

'Please.'

Sir Charles liked the intimate atmosphere of his club. With privacy and discreet, attentive service assured, it was the perfect place to conduct a sensitive conversation well away from prying eyes and curious ears. It was obvious his guest thought so too, because he appeared to relax immediately. No doubt, the excellent scotch helped.

'We may be in luck,' said Underwood. He crossed his long legs and let himself sink into the comfortable leather Chesterfield. 'I checked all the records ...'

'And?'

'The pieces of an intriguing jigsaw puzzle are beginning to fall into place.'

Sir Charles ordered two more whiskies and waited until the waiter had withdrawn. 'Tell me.'

'You'll be surprised. I double-checked everything to make sure we were not mistaken.'

Sir Charles knew his friend was a cautious and meticulous man and therefore had no doubt that the information he was about to receive would be both accurate and reliable.

'Lord Elms was investigating the illegal dumping of toxic waste along the Somali coast in the nineteen eighties and nineties. I know this sounds odd, but the records are clear. We even had to delve deep into our archives to retrieve some of the stuff he requested.'

'That is strange,' said Sir Charles, sipping his scotch. 'The real question is, *why*? There has to be a lot more to all this. Otherwise, why all this secrecy and fuss about an issue that is now history?'

Underwood smiled. 'There is,' he said, lowering his voice.

'You know?'

'Perhaps. What I'm about to tell you is all based on Whitehall corridor- whispers, if you know what I mean ...'

'I sure do. So what are the corridors whispering about?'

'Apparently, Lord Elms digging up the past had a very specific purpose.'

'Oh?'

'It's all about the upcoming elections. You know the Conservatives are on the ropes and well behind in the polls – the papers are full of it. Losing government is a distinct possibility and most of it is due to the young, popular, charismatic Labour leader leading the charge.'

'So? What could all this possibly have to do with illegal waste dumping in Somalia twenty years ago?'

'A lot, as it turns out.'

'More corridor whispers?'

'Absolutely. You know there are no secrets in Whitehall, only rumours. Sooner or later, everything gets out … somehow. The trick is to separate fact from fiction and peel away exaggeration and gossip. If you can do that, you'll eventually find the truth, or at least part of it.'

'And you've been able to do that?'

'Perhaps. I can only be the messenger delivering the rumours. The rest is up to you.'

'Fair enough.'

'So, what are the rumours telling us?'

'It goes like this. For the Conservatives to have any chance at all of remaining in office, they somehow have to stop the Labour juggernaut. Apparently, they've tried to do this for years now, but the man at the helm has turned out to be exactly what his public persona suggests, and that is what makes him so appealing to voters. He's a young, talented, honest, squeaky-clean politician who gives voice to the masses who feel let down and ignored by years of Conservative rule and neglect. Tired of countless scandals and corruption, the voters are desperately searching for someone they can believe in and trust. He's a champion of the underdog. Public opinion reflected in the polls strongly suggests that in David Huntington, they have found their man.' Underwood sipped his scotch before continuing.

'So, the question for the government is this: What can be done about it? The answer? Simple. Discredit the man at the top and destroy his image. But you have to be careful. You have to do this convincingly, with overwhelming proof to support your allegations or the whole thing will backfire and blow up in your face, giving your opponents even more credibility and power. In short, you need the right man to undertake this extremely important and delicate task, and it would appear that Lord Elms – an ardent supporter of the government – was that man.'

'That's hardly surprising,' said Sir Charles. 'Lord Elms has been a Conservative power-broker for decades. He's guided at least two

Conservative PM's into office and kept them there. He was without question one of the most powerful, if not *the* most powerful and influential politician in the Conservative camp.'

'And very well-connected at the Palace. They say he had the Queen's ear,' said Underwood. 'Let's not underestimate that.'

'Correct. Politics was his life.'

'He was a king-maker all right, and then chose to be the power behind the throne. That's why he lasted so long. He held high office in the last two Conservative governments and was no doubt hoping to do the same, if this one got re-elected. If he could have pulled that off, it would have been quite a coup, right?' said Underwood.

'Coming from that far behind, sure,' said Sir Charles. 'However, that looks virtually impossible at the moment, wouldn't you agree?'

'Sure, but that was precisely what he was working on; to pull off the impossible. And this whole affair and the underlying strategy is classic Elms; Machiavellian, behind the scenes, ruthless, clever—'

'There is evidence of all this?' interrupted Sir Charles, sitting on the edge of his seat and hanging on his friend's every word. 'Lord Elms didn't strike me as a political dirt-digger.'

'I'm only the messenger, remember?' said Underwood, laughing. 'But we live in difficult times. GFC aftermath, immigration problems, talk of leaving the European Union ...'

Sir Charles shook his head. 'I don't know,' he said. 'I'm not convinced. It doesn't fit. What about that brutal attack on Lord Elms and his wife? MI5 are hinting that the Italian Mafia was somehow behind it all, which makes it even more baffling.'

'I heard that too, and it fits better than you may think.'

'Oh? In what way?'

'Do you know who the main player was in the illegal Somalian waste dumping enterprise?'

'Tell me.'

'The Calabrian Mafia.'

Sir Charles looked up, surprised. 'Now, that is interesting,' he said, 'but it still doesn't make sense.' Sir Charles shook his head. 'Assuming there is a connection, why would the Mafia carry out such a shocking, high-profile murder? Why murder a man who is making enquiries about something that happened twenty years ago? And why mutilate his wife? Doesn't add up.'

'Perhaps it does.' Underwood was enjoying himself. He had more startling information, but was taking his time revealing it. This was quite deliberate. He wanted to lead his friend step-by-step to the extraordinary conclusion he had come to. 'So, if you cannot effectively attack your political opponent, what do you do?' Underwood asked rhetorically. 'You attack those close to him and discredit your opponent by association – right? Provided you can establish a credible link,' added Underwood. 'Classic Elms.'

'What are you getting at?'

'I did some more digging and, it would appear, so did Lord Elms. Not much is known about Huntington's family and background. All the public knows is that he's well-educated, married to a doctor, lives in a modest house in Putney, has two children attending the local school, and has rapidly risen through the ranks and was propelled to the top by talent and hard work.'

'So?'

'This is a bit of a fairytale and only part of the story. Huntington wasn't born in the UK but abroad. He's an illegitimate child and was brought up by a single mother. He spent his early childhood in Africa and was later sent to an exclusive boarding school in Kent. In effect, he grew up without a father. His mother never married. Exceptionally bright and good looking, he studied law at Oxford and excelled at cricket.'

'Do we know who his father is?'

'Ah. Murky waters … but as usual, you are asking the right questions,' said Underwood, hinting that more was to come.

'Nice bio, but is this all really relevant?' interjected Sir Charles, the impatience in his voice obvious.

'Oh, yes it is. Please hear me out.'

'Sorry. Please go on.'

'After graduating top of his class with honours, Huntington could have had any job he wanted. But what did he do? He went into politics and there, almost from day one, the doors began to open and opportunities and advancement kept coming his way until he ended up as the youngest Labour leader in British history.'

'So?'

'This meteoric rise didn't happen all by itself,' said Underwood. 'Huntington had a mentor and a powerful backer who stood in the background pulling all the right strings and preparing the way for the golden boy. And that, my friend, is still very much the case today. Look; almost unlimited campaign funds, a sympathetic press moulding his public profile and praising his policies while at the same time attacking the government on all fronts? Almost too good to be true? How did he manage to do all this by himself without putting a foot wrong? The answer is, he didn't. He had help on an almost unimaginable scale and Lord Elms found out about it. He had discovered Huntington's Achilles heel and was gathering information for an attack. That's what he was working on when he was killed.'

For a while, Sir Charles sat in silence, digesting what he had heard. The implications of what his friend had just told him, if true, were staggering. 'How did you find all this out so quickly?' he asked.

'All I had to do was listen to the corridor talk. The walls are abuzz with all kinds of sensational gossip. And then I had a little bit of luck ...'

'Oh?'

'Lord Elms had only one trusted helper. A retired librarian called Maud.'

'And?'

'She likes to play bridge, and has one weakness ...'

'Tell me; I can't wait,' joked Sir Charles.

'Gin and Tonic. She even has a nickname: G&T. I have a close friend who plays bridge with her every Thursday night. They talked ...'

'What about?' asked Sir Charles.

'I'm only the messenger – remember?'

'Huntington's Achilles heel?'

'Ah. That's the real question here, right?' said Underwood.

'It would appear so. Do you know who this all-powerful, silent mentor standing in the shadows is supposed to be?' said Sir Charles, carefully watching his friend.

'I know enough for now, but not all of it, not yet. That's exactly what Lord Elms was working on when he died. A lot more still needs to be done before all the pieces fall into place. It's complicated, but we have enough to give it a go.'

'Well? Are you going to tell me?'

'Lord Elms' project had a name. A kind of slogan if you like, a rather curious one. In fact, there were two. In the beginning, his team referred to the project as *Detego.*'

'Any idea what that means?' asked Sir Charles.

'How's your Latin?'

'Ah ... *Detego* ... Something like uncover, reveal, lay bare?'

'Not bad. Try unmask.'

'Oh? Why that?'

'More corridor whispers, this time about MI5 and what was apparently found hanging around Lord Elms' neck after the attack—'

'No one said anything about that,' interrupted Sir Charles.

'True. It was all hushed up, but this is all rumour – remember?'

'So, what was it?'

'A Venetian carnival mask. And not just any mask. In fact, it was one of the most bizarre and recognisable masks.'

'Oh?'

'The Medico della Peste, the Plague Doctor mask. Originally, it wasn't a carnival mask at all, but something worn by physicians treating plague victims. It was thought to be a method of preventing the spread of that deadly disease.'

'How odd. A message?'

'Yes. A *memento mori,*' said Underwood. 'Latin for "remember you have to die". Classic Mafia. They like to leave something behind, as a warning.'

'Like a bloody horse's head in your bed?' joked Sir Charles.

'Something like that, but consider this: first we have Project *Detego* – unmask – but then the name changes …'

'Word games?'

'Lord Elms was a classical scholar. Each of his projects had a name. Quirky habit.'

'Hidden messages?'

'You're getting closer.'

'What's the new name?' asked Sir Charles.

'Stars, hide your fires.'

Sir Charles looked stunned. 'Now, that is interesting …' he said after a while.

'I suppose it is.'

'But not for reasons you may think,' said Sir Charles. 'Do you know what Lady Elms said just before she died; her very last words?'

'Tell me.'

'Her son was with her when she passed away. First, she told him that he was in great danger and then, just before she died, she said the cryptic words, "Stars, hide your fires". What do you make of that?'

'But that's incredible! There has to be a connection, surely. But what does it all mean?' said Underwood.

'That's for us to find out. Now, please tell me everything you know about Huntington's mystery mentor.'

Underwood held up his empty glass. 'One more scotch,' he said, 'and I will.'

# 52

'I've done more flying in the past two weeks than in the entire year,' announced Lola, climbing out of her seat. 'She's all yours, guys.' The two pilots gave her the thumbs up and took over.

'Can I stay here?' asked Tristan.

'Sure, as long as you leave some of the flying to the pilots.'

'We are doing navigation today,' said Tristan excitedly. 'I've prepared a flight plan and plotted our route across Africa to Nairobi. Here, have a look.' Tristan showed Lola his iPad. 'According to our airspeed and departure time in Mexico, we should be about here,' he said.

Lola shook her head. 'I can see where this is heading,' she said. 'I'll be lucky to get near the controls next time.'

'Thanks, Lola,' said Tristan and climbed into Lola's seat.

Jack sat in the back of the plane, poring over his notebook.

'Tristan is truly amazing, said Lola. 'He's like a sponge. He soaks up everything around him; doesn't forget a thing. He'll make an excellent pilot.' Lola sat next to Jack. 'Do you know what he did on the way to Boston?'

Jack closed his notebook. 'Tell me,' he said.

'He played chess with the good professor and they talked about comas and genomics.'

'Doesn't surprise me. Nothing about that boy surprises me.'

'Penny for your thoughts,' said Lola. She put her arms around Jack's neck and kissed him on the cheek.

'Careful now,' said Jack. 'This time, we are not alone …'

'Tristan won't leave the cockpit; trust me.'

'Temptress,' said Jack, and kissed Lola on the neck.

'Only kidding,' said Lola, pulling away.

'You know about everything I've discovered so far, except for this …' said Jack, enjoying the closeness of the exciting woman next to him.

'Oh?'

'Sir Charles called last night with some extraordinary news.'

'He did?'

'Two of the assassins have been identified. According to MI5, the whole affair is somehow connected to the Italian Mafia.'

'Are you serious?'

'That's the official word at the moment.'

'And Sir Charles, what does he think?'

'He's now almost convinced that it all has to do with Lord Elms' work. Apparently, he was heading an enquiry into a very sensitive subject that could seriously compromise some people in high places. So, it's all very political. And politics is a dirty business.'

'Wow! Do you know what it is?'

'Not yet. Sir Charles is making enquiries, discreetly. It's all very hush-hush with many vested interests at stake here. However, he's confident he's getting close and expects to have something in a few days. Until then, we'll just have to be patient, I suppose. In the meantime, our trip to Kenya could throw some more light on the subject.'

'You think it will?'

'Absolutely.'

'So, what's the plan?'

'To begin with, I want to make some enquiries about this here.' Jack opened his notebook and pulled out the letter with part of what he believed to be a hotel name at the top. 'If we can find this place, we could work backwards. Forty-odd years isn't such a long time. There's always something left behind, some trail to follow. Just look at Madame Petrova and the Ritz stories, and where that took us.'

'You are looking for Lady Elms' lover?'

'Yes. That's our link.'

'What else?'

'Meeting Dr Rosen, of course; extraordinary woman. We'll have to drive to Dadaab. She knows we are coming. You'll like her.'

'How far is that?'

'We should make it in about eight hours, I'd say. She's arranged for someone to meet us at the airport. That should make things easier.'

'You have been a busy boy. Drink?'

'Sure.'

'Isis was a lot better this morning,' said Lola, expertly mixing a martini. 'Far more confident. She believes in Greenberg and somehow, speaking to Tristan has really cheered her up. She wants to leave tomorrow. Get it over with as soon as possible. The boat is ready.'

'I meant to ask you. What's happening to The Time Machine business while all of this is going on?'

'Well, the crew went straight back to London, as you know,' said Lola, 'and all engagements have been cancelled indefinitely. However, record sales are soaring. I know this doesn't make sense, but the publicity guys and spin-doctors are doing an unbelievable job turning this into some kind of social media sensation. Everything's gone viral. Isis' 'mystery illness' has created enormous interest worldwide. Business is booming. We have some very talented and capable people working for us. It's an oiled machine all right. And believe it or not, Isis is keeping an eye on it all, even in her condition. Hanna has become her right hand for the moment and is doing an excellent job keeping her in the loop. Isis is making all the key decisions, as usual.'

'Do you ever wonder how people cope who haven't got the means or resources to do what Isis is doing?' pondered Jack.

'What prompted that thought?'

'Dadaab. I've been to camps like that before. You'll see misery and suffering on an almost unimaginable scale. The dark side of life can be very scary, especially in East Africa.'

'I know,' said Lola. She handed Jack his drink. 'We'll face that tomorrow. As for now, why don't we drink to Isis' recovery?'

'Sure. To Isis,' said Jack. They touched glasses.

Lola kicked off her shoes. 'Now, if we were alone, hypothetically speaking, you understand,' she said, running her toes up the inside of Jack's trouser leg, 'what might we be doing, do you think?'

'If you keep this up, you'll find out,' said Jack.

'Threat, or promise?'

'Your call.'

# 53

The long flight from Mexico to Kenya had been more difficult than anticipated. They had to skirt around a violent storm raging in Central Africa, which had caused fuel problems and delays. By the time *Pegasus* landed in Nairobi, everyone was tired and irritable, but glad to be once again on solid ground.

'I'm Kobo,' said a tall, athletic looking young African, an aid worker with Médecins Sans Frontières – Doctors Without Borders – as he followed the customs officials into the plane. 'Dr Rosen sends her regards. You are just in time.'

'What do you mean?' asked Jack, handing his passport to one of the officers.

'We are taking a delivery of medical supplies into Dadaab,' said the young man. 'That's our plane over there.' He pointed to a Fokker Friendship on the tarmac. 'We waited for you. You can come with us. Much faster and much more comfortable than the eight-hour road trip,' he added. 'But not quite as comfortable as this little beauty here. What a plane! But you couldn't land this on our dirt strip at the camp, that's for sure. Nor would you want to. How many of you are coming along?' Kobo prattled on.

'Three,' said Jack.

Kobo said something to the officer in a sing-song dialect with many clicks and unfamiliar sounds. The officer nodded and returned Jack his passport. 'My cousin,' said Kobo, grinning. 'All in order. We can go now; come.'

Jack looked at Lola standing next to him, the question on his face obvious. 'Our guys will look after the plane, no problem. The pilots know what to do,' said Lola. 'It's their job.'

'Then let's go.'

Tristan slung his duffel bag over his shoulder and turned to Jack. 'What a trip,' he said, his cheeks glowing with excitement.

'Just don't get used to it, buster,' said Jack. 'I can't promise you something like this every time …'

Tristan hurried after Kobo and fell in beside him. 'I'm Tristan,' he said, holding out his hand. 'You work for MSF?'

'I do.'

By the time they reached the other plane, which was just starting up its engines, Tristan and Kobo were locked in deep conversation. Kobo was carrying Tristan's bag and had his arm around him.

'Just look at those two,' said Jack, pointing ahead. 'Mates already. I suppose if we need to know something, we'll just ask Tristan and he'll find out, eh?'

'It's good to have him with us,' said Lola. 'Somehow, I feel safe when he's around. Silly, I know.'

The contrast between the opulent luxury of *Pegasus* and the stark, spartan interior of the ageing Fokker Friendship, a seasoned workhorse, couldn't have been more pronounced. Modified for transporting cargo, the few remaining seats had been bolted to the floor behind the open cockpit, and all kinds of exposed wires, tape, insulation and mesh dangled from the ceiling above, like a plastic curtain keeping out the flies in a country grocery store. However, worst of all was the deafening engine noise.

Tristan sat next to Lola in the front. With his nose pressed against the small window, he kept watching the monotonous brown landscape glide past below, hoping in vain to spot some wildlife.

Jack turned to Kobo sitting next to him. 'How big is the camp?' he asked.

'Actually, there are several refugee camps next to each other,' said Kobo. 'Hagadera, Kambios, Ifo … all are serviced by Dadaab, a UNHCR base. The camps were constructed in 1999 and were designed to house ninety thousand. However, in 2011 we had a terrible drought in East Africa and numbers swelled to almost five hundred thousand, making Dadaab the biggest refugee camp in the world at the time. Now we have about three hundred thousand, mainly refugees from war-torn Somalia. Still far too many. Disease, social problems, tribal violence and crime are out of control, but we are doing our best. Since 2013, voluntary repatriation of Somalian nationals has somewhat eased the situation, but progress is slow.'

'Any terrorist activity?' asked Jack.

Kobo squirmed in his seat, a clear sign of his unease, and appeared to take his time before answering the question. Jack noticed the change in his demeanour. 'Some,' said Kobo at last. 'Al-Shabaab mainly, a Somali rebel group. But we have more serious problems in the camps ...'

'Oh? What?'

'I think it's better if I let Dr Rosen tell you about that,' said Kobo, sidestepping the question. Jack nodded, sat back and looked out the window. He realised there was obviously no point in pursuing the matter further.

On its descent into Dadaab, the plane circled the sea of white tents set out in neat rows stretching all the way to the horizon and landed in a cloud of dust almost blotting out the blood-red disc of the setting sun. Shuddering alarmingly, the plane skidded to a halt, the silence almost deafening after the engines had been switched off.

Kobo unbuckled his seatbelt. 'Welcome to Dadaab,' he said. 'I'll take you to Dr Rosen.'

'I'm glad you know where we are going,' said Jack, sweat running down his neck and back in the oppressive heat of the approaching evening. He was trying to keep up with Kobo wending his way through endless dusty rows of white tents, the acrid smoke from countless cooking fires making his eyes water. 'Everything here looks the same.'

Kobo stopped and pointed to a large tent. 'That's Dr Rosen's surgery over there,' he said. A tall, grey-haired woman in a white coat stood next to an old man sitting on a chair in front of the tent. She was looking into his eyes and applying some ointment. A naked little boy with a bloated tummy sat on the old man's lap, playing with his beard. 'And that's Dr Rosen.'

'Hello, Bettany,' said Jack, walking up to her. 'I like your alfresco surgery ... African style.'

'You are here already,' said Dr Rosen. Her face lit up; Jack's familiar, easygoing banter bringing much needed humour into her camp-world of great suffering and despair. She wiped the old man's cheeks with cotton wool and said something to him in Somali that Jack couldn't understand. The old man got unsteadily to his feet, handed the little boy to a young girl standing next to him and hobbled slowly away.

Dr Rosen walked over to Jack and gave him a hug. 'Good to see you, Jack,' she said. 'Thank you, Kobo, for bringing this man to me. He and I have shared much ...'

*A little thinner, and a little older*, thought Jack, kissing Dr Rosen on the cheeks, *but otherwise her brilliant, remarkable self.* Jack introduced Lola and Tristan standing behind him.

Dr Rosen took off her white coat. 'Come inside and we'll have some tea,' she said. 'I'm dying to know what brought you here.'

After some polite chitchat, Lola sensed it was time to leave Jack and Dr Rosen alone to have an opportunity to talk in private. Pretending to be exhausted, she excused herself. Appreciating Lola's tact, Dr Rosen gave her a knowing smile and asked her assistant, a young Somali girl, to show Lola and Tristan to their tents.

'Scotch?' said Dr Rosen. Jack looked up, surprised. 'We may be on the outer edge of civilisation here, but we don't have to be uncivilised – right?' Dr Rosen walked over to one of the medicine cupboards in the corner of the tent and took out a bottle of Johnny Walker and two glasses. 'Medicinal,' she said, holding up the bottle.

'Of course. Make it a big one, please,' said Jack, laughing.

Dr Rosen cranked up her late husband's old gramophone and put on a record. 'So, what brings you here, Jack?' she asked, sipping her scotch. 'No one flies halfway around the world to a place like this without a good reason. You didn't say much on the phone, which is an ominous sign ...'

Appreciating her insight and candour, Jack sat back in his canvas deckchair and looked at Dr Rosen, Mozart's clarinet concerto playing softly in the background sounding strangely out of place.

'Your late father,' said Jack quietly.

Dr Rosen sat up with a jolt, a worried look on her face. 'But he's been dead for years …'

'But the past is very much alive,' said Jack.

'Please explain.'

Over several glasses of whisky, Jack told Dr Rosen how he had been approached by Isis, and why. He told her about Señora Gonzales and how the mention of Sturmbannfuehrer Wolfgang Steinberger's name had persuaded him to accept the assignment. He spoke about Madame Petrova, the Ritz and the scandal of the crystal skull. Step-by-step, he was bringing the conversation closer to the subject of real interest. He was carefully preparing the way for the disturbing revelation to come, which he knew would shock her.

'Firstly, did you know that your father had a brother, a doctor, who carried out secret medical experiments at Auschwitz?'

Dr Rosen paled, visibly shaken. 'Just before my father died, he called me to his bedside and we had a conversation. The first in years. I think I told you about it.' Jack nodded. 'He left a significant amount of money to the Rosen Foundation and told me that he was proud of my work and what my late husband had done.' Dr Rosen paused, collecting her thoughts. 'He also spoke of a brother,' she added quietly.

'This was the first time he had ever mentioned this. At first, I thought he must be confused and hallucinating. But he was perfectly lucid. However, I had no idea that his brother was a doctor … at Auschwitz.'

'Do you know what happened to him?'

'No. There was nothing in my father's papers about the brother. Apart from that brief conversation, the subject never came up.'

'Did your father mention anything else of a private nature during that conversation?'

Dr Rosen looked at Jack, surprised. 'No. What are you getting at, Jack? What else do you know?'

*Here comes the bombshell*, thought Jack, pouring himself another scotch. 'Your father had an affair with Dolores Gonzales in Paris. She had a son. He was born in 1942,' said Jack quietly.

'Are you certain about this?' said Dr Rosen, her voice barely audible.

'Yes.'

'Do you know what happened to him?'

'Only this: your father and his brother left Paris in a hurry in 1942 and took the baby with them. Mother and child were separated. That's the last thing Señora Gonzales, or anyone else for that matter, appear to know about the boy.'

'So, why are you here, Jack? Surely not just to tell me about some forgotten family history?'

'I've promised to find out what happened to the boy, but you're right, there's more, a lot more … But enough for tonight. It's getting late. Let's talk about it tomorrow.'

'That may be difficult,' said Dr Rosen.

'Oh? Why?'

'I too have made a promise … a promise to myself …'

'Care to tell me about it?'

'I'm leaving tomorrow, with Kobo. Early in the morning. We are going into Somalia. Not far; the border is quite close and the whole thing should only take a day. I have to find out about something terrible going on there. Something awful and deadly that affects the lives of many in a most brutal and horrendous way, if the rumours are accurate that is. We are talking here about greed, corruption in high places, misery, death and suffering on an almost unimaginable scale. Exploitation of the weak is nothing new, and we know all about that, don't we, Jack?'

'We sure do.'

Dr Rosen became quite agitated and Jack noticed she had tears in her eyes. 'And then there's something else, almost too shocking for words,' Dr Rosen added quietly, 'especially for a doctor like myself. Human nature at its lowest …'

'Tell me.'

'As this seems to be a night of extraordinary revelations, I will,' said Dr Rosen. 'But I must warn you, there's great danger involved here. Just knowing about this could put you at serious risk.'

*Another warning. How extraordinary*, though Jack, remembering Lady Elms' deathbed words to her son. 'I'm used to danger, and risk is no stranger to me,' he said, smiling.

'I know that. That's why I'm going to tell you.'

Over the next two hours, Dr Rosen told Jack what she had accidentally discovered during her work at the camp. It felt good to unburden herself and tell someone like Jack the whole dreadful story and her suspicions, and get his views.

With the bottle almost empty, the gramophone silent and the candle beginning to flicker in the lantern, Jack offered to accompany Bettany on her trip into Somalia the next day. A danger shared was only half a danger, he told her jokingly.

'Thanks, Jack,' said Dr Rosen, no longer feeling quite so alone. 'I'd like that.'

Jack thrived on a challenge. For him, the promise of adventure was the cherished reward for risks taken, and danger the icing on the cake that would become the subject of his next book. And there was more: Jack had a knack for trusting his instincts and following leads, however far-fetched and fanciful they might initially appear. He also believed in destiny.

# 54

Half asleep and with the warming, feel-good glow of the whisky still pleasantly clouding his brain, Jack dismissed the strange sound that had woken him as something coming from outside. But then, there it was again, only closer. A muffled kind of sobbing. *Definitely in here*, he thought, rubbing his stiff neck. He was much too tall for the narrow camp bed and had difficulty finding a comfortable position. The only other person in the small tent was Tristan lying on the bed next to him. Lola was sharing a tent with Dr Rosen's assistant. Wide awake by now, Jack sat up and looked at Tristan. *It's him*, he thought, *he's crying!*

Jack reached across and gently patted Tristan on the shoulder. *'What's wrong, mate?'* he whispered. The sobbing stopped. Silence. *Bad dream*, thought Jack, withdrawing his hand.

'They are crying,' said Tristan after a while.

'Who's crying?' asked Jack.

'The angels.'

'Why?'

'It's this place. I've never felt anything like it. This is a well of desperate souls. So many of them. They are all around us and they are drowning in their own pain. That's why the angels are crying.'

Jack had never heard Tristan speak like that. He must have glimpsed something really frightening. 'Come on, let's go outside,' he said, trying to break the spell. 'We can both do with a little fresh air.'

Outside it was much cooler. The cooking fires had died down, with only blinking embers remaining. They reminded Jack of a swarm of fireflies dancing off into the night. The camp was never silent. The daytime hum of activity had turned into a rhythmic, night-time whisper, like the heaving chest of a sleeping giant.

Jack pulled up two canvas chairs and they sat in front of Dr Rosen's surgery.

'You mustn't let this place overwhelm you,' said Jack. 'This is a sanctuary, a refuge where many amazing people do amazing things.

Take Bettany, for example. She works tirelessly to help those in need and has devoted her life to helping others. She's a healer. A very special one. There's a huge amount of love here, and compassion. You have to learn to see that.'

Tristan looked at Jack, surprised. He had never heard him speak like that before. Feeling better, he looked up at the stars and tried to identify the familiar constellations.

'I thought I could hear voices,' said Dr Rosen, stepping out of the shadows. 'You two should be asleep ...'

'Our young friend here had a bad dream ...' said Jack.

Dr Rosen understood at once. 'This place can get to you,' she said, taking another canvas chair and sitting next to Tristan. 'It gets to me every time I come here, which is twice a year. At first, I felt sadness, often even despair, but as I got to know the place better, I began to feel joy and hope. Wonderful things are being done here, the most important of which is to provide hope – to thousands. Just look at this place as one big hope factory.' Dr Rosen put her arm around Tristan. Tristan closed his eyes and began to relax. The love flowing from Dr Rosen towards him banished the dark thoughts that had so troubled him before.

'Take Ifra, my assistant for example,' continued Dr Rosen. 'She lost her entire family during the fighting in Somalia, but she radiates hope and compassion. She isn't much older than you. I'll ask her to show you around tomorrow. You will see this place in a different light, trust me.'

'Thanks,' said Tristan, and began to drift back to sleep in the chair.

For a while, Jack and Dr Rosen sat in silence and looked up at the stars blazing above them like a sea of diamonds reaching into eternity.

'Do you ever wonder ...?' Jack mused.

Dr Rosen pointed up at the night sky. 'How all this came about? The beginning of the universe from a single, primordial atom some twenty billion years ago? The big bang?'

'Yes. Did you know it was a Belgian priest – Georges Lemaître – who first proposed this in the nineteen twenties?' said Jack.

'And then Edwin Hubble observed that galaxies were in fact speeding away from us ...'

'Quite, and then came the discovery of cosmic microwave radiation—'

'By Penzias and Wilson,' interjected Dr Rosen.

'Leftover light from the big bang taking us back in time, perhaps to the very beginning.'

'But without giving us an answer to the big question ...'

'Which is?' asked Jack.

'The original cause of the big bang itself.'

'Something out of nothing? I don't buy it,' said Jack, shaking his head.

'Do you ever wonder how we ended up with a brain boasting one hundred billion neurons and one hundred trillion connections? That's more than all the stars in the universe,' said Dr Rosen.

'Wow! Staggering!'

'Sure is. Since life first crawled out of the primordial soup millions of years ago, it has come a long way. In the beginning, progress was slow and nothing much appeared to happen. Then, two hundred and fifty thousand years ago something occurred not far from here, in the Rift Valley in Ethiopia, which changed everything.'

'What?'

'An ape-man did something quite extraordinary.'

'He did?' said Jack.

'Yes. He picked up a lump of obsidian – volcanic glass – and split it. He now had a razor-sharp flint, which he attached to a long piece of wood. He now had a weapon, a spear for hunting. It all went from there. Two hundred and fifty thousand years later, a relatively short time, ape-man has become space-man.' Dr Rosen pointed to the sky above. 'Travelling up there. And all thanks to a grey blob of matter we still don't fully understand, weighing about a kilo and a half. Incredible, don't you think?'

Jack looked up at the stars again, the timeless beauty of the night sky filling him with awe. 'Stars, hide your fires,' he said. 'What did she mean by that, I wonder?'

'What are you getting at?' asked Dr Rosen.

'Lady Elms' last words to her son just before she died.'

'Don't you remember your Shakespeare?'

'Shakespeare?' repeated Jack.

'The full quote goes like this: "Stars, hide your fires; let not light see my black and deep desires". Macbeth. It's all about ambition.'

Jack sat up as if pricked by a hot needle from behind. 'Say that again!'

'Is ambition justified at all cost, or are we to accept fate and chance as our masters? That's the question. Classic Shakespeare,' said Dr Rosen.

'*Macbeth* ... How extraordinary!'

'Is it really?'

'It is in this case, believe me,' Jack said excitedly. 'I think you've just solved a puzzle that has confounded us since Lady Elms died.'

'I have?' said Dr Rosen, surprised.

'I spoke to Sir Charles, Isis' lawyer, yesterday. He's trying to find out what Lord Elms was working on just before he was murdered. All very hush-hush. However, the project had a name: Stars, hide your fires. Lady Elms uttered the same words just before she died. The question is, why? Dark ambition? This is all a little too much for me right now. I need some time to think.'

Dr Rosen reached across to Jack. 'A starry night of revelations?' she said, patting his arm. For a while they sat in silence again, marvelling at the stars and contemplating what had just been said.

Jack looked at Tristan. 'I think he's fallen asleep,' he said. 'The angels must have stopped crying.' Jack stood up, carefully lifted Tristan out of the chair and carried him back into the tent, returning moments later.

'What a remarkable boy,' said Dr Rosen. 'I read all about him in your book, of course. And about his parents ... He's special. I've come across only a handful of people like him over the years. They are wired differently. Emotionally, and some would say spiritually as well. It's both a gift and a curse.'

'He's special all right,' said Jack. 'His mother was a Maori clairvoyant. Not a day goes by he doesn't surprise me in some way. His insights are amazing ... He sees things differently. A kid with an ancient soul, and a lot more ...'

'I couldn't sleep, Jack,' said Dr Rosen, changing direction. 'I couldn't stop thinking about the things we spoke about earlier.'

'Understandable. Quite a lot to take in.'

'It's not just that. You asked me if I could remember anything, anything at all about the brother.'

'You said there was nothing.'

'But there is something ...'

'Oh? What?'

'I remember overhearing my father and his friend, Anton Hoffmeister, arguing on the veranda during one of his visits to Australia. We were all staying at our house in the Blue Mountains.'

'And?'

'They spoke German, of course, and Hoffmeister was shouting, *"Dein Bruder, immer dein Bruder"* – Always your brother. I'm almost certain this happened around the same time I found that dreadful photo in my father's study ...'

'Déjà vu,' said Jack. 'We are coming back to Hoffmeister again. The slippery Don Antonio from Buenos Aires who couldn't be trusted has re-entered the fray. He let us down big time once before, remember?'

'Sure did. Just before the court case started. Marcus was beside himself.'

'But it wouldn't do any harm to turn to him again to find out what he knows ...'

Dr Rosen shook her head. 'Do you really think he'll talk to you after all that's happened?' she said.

'Sure. Money turned him away from us, and money will bring him back; you'll see. Desperation and greed are very reliable. The main thing is to find out if he's still around. We must try to track him down, and I know just the man who may be able to do that.'

'Are you serious?'

'Absolutely.'

'Is it that important?'

'Could be.'

'Why, Jack? *Why have you come here?*'

'I'll tell you in the morning.'

Tristan was peacefully asleep inside, and Dr Rosen had gone back into her tent to get some rest before facing the challenges of the big day to come. Jack however, was too excited to go back to sleep. He had to tell someone about his discovery.

Sir Charles had spoken to him the night before and told him about a breakthrough. George Underwood, his contact, had made some remarkable progress. Not only had he discovered the name of Lord Elms' project whispered in the corridors of Whitehall – Stars, hide your fires – but he had also identified the subject matter of the Elms investigation. Lord Elms was investigating pharmaceutical companies at the time he died. But which one, and why, was still a mystery, and so was the meaning of the cryptic name given to his project. *Not any more*, thought Jack, composing his text message.

'*The penny dropped tonight, Charles*, typed Jack, *and all thanks to you and Shakespeare. Stars, hide your fires is part of a famous quote – "Stars, hide your fires; let not light see my black and deep desires". And do you know where it's from? Macbeth! And it's all about ambition. Think! Which pharmaceutical giant would you associate with Macbeth? Alistair Macbeth, Blackburn Pharmaceuticals; who else! Ask Underwood to start digging. Talk soon.*'

Feeling better, Jack walked into the tent and threw himself onto the narrow bunk. Moments later, he was fast asleep. He didn't hear the blip on his phone signalling an incoming message. It was a reply from Sir Charles:

'*Well done, Jack, you're a genius! Astonishing, but compelling. If Macbeth is our mystery man, all we have to do is find those black and deep desires … I'll speak to Underwood in the morning to start the ball rolling. Who says knowing the classics is old hat, eh?*'

## 55

Carrington was due to arrive in the evening after a long flight from London. Jana went to collect him from the airport and Alexandra was cooking the long overdue dinner. The unexpected encounter with her abductor at the institute had not only soured a most successful function and personal triumph, but had also rocked Alexandra to the core. She was seriously considering resigning and going back to France. Had it not been for Jana's reassurance and calm voice of reason, Alexandra would have been packing her bags right now. Instead, she immersed herself in something she loved to do: cooking.

Alexandra opened a bottle of red – a shiraz from the Barossa – and poured herself a glass. The warm, peppery taste of the smooth wine primed her palate for the familiar treat to come. *Perfect*, she thought. It was definitely the right wine for the dish she had chosen. Because Jana had told her that Marcus loved beef, Alexandra decided to cook Boeuf Bourguignon, one of her favourites. She knew the recipe by heart – her grandmother had taught her well – and enjoyed preparing the ingredients: *2 ½ tablespoons of olive oil; 1 large brown onion, finely chopped; 200g shortcut rindless bacon, halved lengthways and cut into 1 cm strips; a generous cup of red wine ...* Alexandra reached for the beef, a splendid piece of eye fillet, and began to cut it into five centimetre pieces.

The familiar routine reminded her of her grandmother's kitchen in her cottage just outside Paris. The treasured memories began to calm Alexandra. The excellent wine – her third glass – helped as well. With a sense of wellbeing washing over her, she relaxed and her mind began to wander.

She had spent many a school holiday at her grandmother's home in the country. From time to time, Professor K, who knew her grandmother well, came to stay for the weekend. Alexandra remembered sitting in the garden on balmy summer evenings, talking about mathematics – one of Professor K's favourite subjects – while mum and grandma were preparing dinner. She remembered how she struggled to understand Leibniz's notation and how her grandmother used to tease her about being more interested in the mysteries of the calculus than baking a cake.

Gottfried Wilhelm Leibnitz was a seventeenth century German philosopher and mathematician whose ideas had fascinated Professor K. In fact, Professor K was a closet computer nerd, obsessed with information technology, especially 'going digital', which he believed in some way helped him understand information storage and transfer in the genome.

As the mouth-watering aroma of frying onions drifted through the kitchen, Alexandra remembered something in Professor K's notes she had read the day before: the significance of 'junk' DNA. Professor K firmly believed that the huge amount of junk DNA in the human genome contained vital information accumulated over hundreds of millions of years of evolution, which if properly decoded, could provide answers and solutions to many of the fundamental questions taunting medical research. He also believed that the means to defeat the Emperor of Darkness – cancer – was buried somewhere in the junk DNA, and all science had to do was find it and unlock its potent secrets.

The hunt was on, and Professor K was stalking his elusive prey by carefully analysing certain specific tissue samples he had collected and studied for clues over the years. However, for the first time he had a new, powerful tool at his disposal: genome sequencing. And the amazing machine that could deliver a complete sequence with all of its three billion letters in less than a week was right here, literally under his feet, in the basement of the institute.

Alexandra reached for a wooden spoon and tasted the thick broth simmering in the pot. *Almost ready*, she thought, smacking her lips. Then her mind drifted back to Professor K's notebooks and the curious notations in the margin she had pondered the night before. They reminded her of something, but she hadn't been able to say exactly what – until now.

*Of course! The Leibniz Notation ...* 'That's it!' she cried out, and hurried to her bedroom to fetch her handbag. Impatiently, she rummaged through the confusing labyrinth littered with female paraphernalia and secrets, searching for a copy of some of Professor K's notes she had brought home with her.

Professor K had been a meticulous record-keeper when it came to documenting his work. The official records he kept at the institute followed all the required protocols according to the rules in minute detail. His notes, however, were quite different and even Alexandra, who was familiar with his methods and had worked with him for years, found it difficult to make sense of them and follow the reasoning underpinning the apparent confusion.

The Leibniz notations scribbled in the margin gave her an important clue. She was confident they somehow identified the samples kept at the institute he had been working on, and referred to the official institute register, linking the two records without disclosing this all-important information to the uninitiated, should his notes fall into the wrong hands. All Alexandra had to do was work her way through the mathematics involved to reach a number, which all being well, would correspond with the number of the target sample in the official institute register. Locating the sample in storage would then be easy. Alexandra was certain she was on the right track and would check the records at work in the morning. Professor K had thrown many a mathematical challenge à la Leibniz at her during the school holidays for her to ponder and solve. She was certain this was just another one of his little games he had loved so much.

*Typical Kasper; exasperatingly ingenious!* she thought, furiously working her way through the complex calculations, until a certain number appeared as the solution at the end. Another puzzling comment in Professor K's letter to her now also made sense ... *Remember Leibniz when you look for the tissue samples* ... Professor K was throwing her another challenge, just as he used to do in her grandmother's garden.

Alexandra heard the key turn in the lock and looked up. It was Jana. 'Smells good,' she said. 'All is forgiven. Let me introduce you to a very hungry man who's travelled halfway around the world for a good meal,' joked Jana, pointing to Carrington struggling with two large suitcases behind her at the door.

'Now, that's what I call pressure,' said Alexandra, shaking Carrington's hand. 'Table's set; dinner's in the pot; wine's opened. Let's eat.'

'A woman after my own heart,' said Carrington, following Alexandra into the dining room. 'What's for dinner?'

'Oysters, and Aussie beef,' said Alexandra, 'washed down with Barossa shiraz.'

'You beauty,' said Carrington. He reached for the bottle on the table and began to pour the wine.

# 56

Carrington stopped at the lichgate and looked into the silent cemetery. It had been four years since he had buried his wife and daughter. They had died right next to him at Luxor, torn apart by the senseless mayhem unleashed by terrorists in Egypt. He could still hear the screams of the wounded and see the mutilated bodies lying in pools of blood with gunfire raging all around.

Somehow, he had survived, but he had not been spared. Some people never stop grieving; they can't. Loneliness and regret can be a harsher sentence than years in a filthy Egyptian jail.

To escape the haunting memories and deal with his devastating loss, Carrington had decided to leave Sydney and the bar, and bury himself in new work. That was almost four years ago. He accepted an appointment at The Hague as a judge on the War Crimes Tribunal. However, his term was up, and it was time to come home.

In Jana, Carrington had found a loving companion who shared his pain and helped him rebuild his life. But deep down in his soul, nothing could replace the love he had shared with his wife and daughter, leaving an emptiness he had to face alone. Jana sensed this, and they had slowly drifted apart, hoping for a new beginning.

Carrington opened the gate and walked slowly along the silent rows of graves, some covered in fresh flowers, others overgrown with weeds of neglect, each step bringing him closer to the final resting place of his family. He had prepared himself for days for this visit but nothing could have prepared him for the moment he set eyes on the two identical graves under the rosebush he had planted.

With tears blurring his vision, he read the inscriptions on the headstones. First his wife's, then his daughter's, the finality of their untimely death stabbing at his heavy heart. As he bent down to place the flowers he had brought onto the graves, Carrington noticed his hands were shaking. Then, overcome by emotion, he stepped back and began to pray.

Carrington hadn't prayed in years, but Jana had taught him a little prayer she had learnt from her Polish mother:

*Love is always patient and kind.*

*It is never jealous.*

*Love is never boastful or conceited.*

*It is never rude or selfish.*

*It does not take offence and is not resentful …*

Feeling better, Carrington placed his hand briefly on each of the headstones and then walked slowly back to the gate. It was time to return to the world of the living and a fresh start. Carrington had kept his old chambers and was ready to resume his life as a respected QC at the Sydney bar. This would be his first day in his old, familiar surroundings and he was looking forward to making contact with his colleagues and friends.

Just as Carrington closed the lichgate behind him, his phone began to ring. He reached into his coat pocket and answered it. It was Jack. The reception was bad and Jack's voice sounded faint and distant, but his enthusiasm was infectious and Carrington was pleased to hear from him. After the solemn cemetery visit, it was just what he needed.

'I can't talk for long, Marcus. I tried to call you all morning, but the reception out here is very bad; satellite phone. I need a favour – urgently!'

'Where are you?'

'In a refugee camp in Kenya … I'll explain later.'

'What is it you need?'

'I want you to make contact with Anton Hoffmeister …'

Momentarily taken aback, Carrington said nothing.

'Are you there?' Jack shouted.

'Why?' asked Carrington.

'It's not over!'

'What isn't over?'

'The Steinberger Nazi affair …'

'I don't understand.'

'You will, trust me. Can you do this for me?'

'I'll try.'

'Thanks, Marcus. I'll call you.'

*That's Jack for you*, thought Carrington, shaking his head but feeling strangely rejuvenated. *I only left The Hague two days ago, and here he is, with a case for me already. Amazing!* Carrington got into his car and drove straight to his chambers in the city. Thanks to Jack, his first case back at the bar would most likely turn out to be a continuation of his last four years ago, the irony of it all bringing a fleeting smile to his weary face. Like Jack, Carrington didn't believe in coincidences ... only destiny.

# 57

Carrington was waiting for the rickety old lift to take him up to his Sydney chambers, when his phone rang again. This time it was Jana calling from Canberra. She was about to meet with George Cunningham, the Commonwealth Director of Public Prosecutions. Carrington had suggested Jana approach Cunningham to see if he could pull a few strings to get her old job back.

'Wish me luck, Marcus,' said Jana. 'I feel a little nervous.'

'You'll be fine, you'll see. You always got on well with him.'

Jana and Cunningham had worked on a number of high-profile cases in the past, which thanks to Jana's exemplary police work, had been hugely successful and significantly advanced Cunningham's career and reputation. Until the embarrassing photograph fiasco during the Newman trial four years ago, Jana had been one of Cunningham's most capable and trusted field officers. However, her fall from grace had been both memorable and spectacular. Shamed and compromised, her stellar career had come to a sudden end and Jana was forced to resign.

'Last time I was there was terrible ...' said Jana, remembering the humiliating photographs she'd had to face in Cunningham's office.

'I know, but that was ages ago, and now you have something to offer him ... I know Cunningham; he won't be able to resist, trust me. Don't even mention the job. The subtle approach is always best.'

'I hope you're right. And good luck with your first day back.'

'Thanks. I already have a brief of sorts, and you won't believe what it's about ...'

'Tell me.'

'Jack just called and asked for my help.'

'About Alexandra?'

'No. Ghosts from the past. Sturmbannfuehrer Steinberger ...'

'What? You can't be serious!'

309

'Apparently, the Newman matter isn't over yet.'

'Incredible. Got to run. I'm about to go in.'

'Good luck!'

Jana missed her old job dreadfully; Carrington's decision to return to the bar had only made things worse. She stood up, straightened her skirt and followed Cunningham's PA down the corridor.

Since his arrival from The Hague two days ago, Carrington had given Alexandra's situation a lot of thought. As they were all staying in Jack's apartment, discussing the matter had been easy. Jana decided to wait for Carrington and get the benefit of his vast experience before advising Alexandra what to do. As it turned out, this had been the right decision.

After questioning Alexandra at length about her abduction, Carrington was convinced she was not only telling the truth, but was correct in her assumptions, fears and conclusions, and would make a reliable and believable witness should it come to that.

Carrington agreed with Jana that Alexandra had to go to the police and make a statement. However, Jana and Carrington were at odds about when and how this should be done. Jana was of the view that Alexandra should approach the local police immediately. Carrington on the other hand, saw an opportunity. He knew Cunningham well and suggested that Jana take Alexandra's case directly to him and ask his advice on how best to approach the situation, before going to the local police.

It was a shrewd suggestion. If it turned out that Alistair Macbeth – the iconic head of Blackburn Pharmaceuticals – was in fact involved in fraud, industrial espionage, kidnap and murder in Australia, then this matter would quickly become a sensational case involving the Federal Police and the government. Thanks to Jana, who brought the matter to his attention in the first place, Cunningham would get the kudos for exposing an extraordinary crime and tracking down a high-profile international criminal. And as for Jana, she would have improved her prospects of re-employment to the point of certainty.

Knowing how the system worked was definitely an advantage, and there were only a handful of people in the country who knew the system as well as Carrington.

The PA knocked, opened the door and let Jana enter.

'It's really good to see you, Jana,' said Cunningham, extending his hand. He seemed genuinely pleased to see her. 'How was life at The Hague? I hear Marcus is going back to the bar. Good decision.'

After the initial polite chitchat, Jana came straight to the point. She told Cunningham that she had come to seek his advice on an important matter involving a friend. She then outlined Alexandra's predicament just as Carrington had suggested. Jana could see that she had the DPP's undivided attention. Coming from one of his former star officers, Cunningham knew that everything Jana told him had to be taken seriously, and he was certainly doing just that.

'This is truly extraordinary,' said Cunningham. 'And the police know nothing of this?'

'It would appear so,' said Jana.

'And Marcus spoke to her at length, you say?'

'He did. He's convinced she's telling the truth based on her accurate recollection of the recent events ...'

'You are right, of course; she must go straight to the police. However, let me make a call first. I'll let you know whom she should see ... I want this to be handled correctly from the start. Then make an appointment as soon as possible. Could Marcus go with her, do you think?'

'I'm sure he could.'

'Excellent.'

'And what about you?' asked Cunningham, walking Jana to the door. 'What are you doing now?'

'Looking around ...'

Cunningham understood at once. 'I'll see what I can do ...'

Jana smiled. The signal had found its mark. 'Thanks, I'd appreciate that,' she said.

'Good work, Jana,' said Cunningham, placing his hand on Jana's shoulder. 'I'm glad you came to me first. I'll be in touch.'

Jana gave Cunningham's receptionist her best smile on the way out. The meeting had gone exactly as Carrington predicted. Cunningham – an ambitious man – was hooked; Alexandra's predicament had come out of the shadows into the open, and Jana's prospects of re-employment had gone through the roof.

*Thanks, Marcus,* thought Jana, *you're a bloody genius!*

# 58

Jack stepped out of the tent and stretched his stiff back. It was just after sunrise and already quite hot. Tristan was still fast asleep inside and Jack didn't see any point in waking him, as the boy had to stay in the camp. *A little more sleep will do him good*, thought Jack. *Lola will look after him.*

'Here, put this on, Jack,' said Dr Rosen. She handed Jack a tee-shirt with the Médecins Sans Frontières logo printed on the back. Jack noticed that Kobo and Dr Rosen were each wearing one too. 'We are making a delivery of medical supplies and you are an MSF volunteer – understood?'

'Sure.' Jack pointed to the camera gear under Dr Rosen's arm. 'A spot of wildlife photography along the way?' he joked.

'I wish. Sadly, the photos we'll take today will have quite a different purpose.'

'Oh? What?'

'I'll tell you later; let's go.'

The route to the Somali border they had chosen was nothing more than a remote dirt track through dense bush frequented by migrating wildlife. They were avoiding the main road. Kobo was driving the old Land Rover and because he tried hard to miss deep potholes and rocks littering the track, progress was slow.

'We do this run regularly,' said Dr Rosen, almost choking on the dust rising up from the parched land around them. 'There's a small camp near the coast. It's a very sad place, as you'll see. It houses refugees too sick to travel. They are the unfortunates who couldn't make it across the border into Kenya and were left behind, mainly to die. There's a small clinic there run by a couple of nurses and a Somali doctor who visits from time to time, Dr Ina Cabdille Xasan, but we call him Dr Gaal. A wonderful man; he'll meet us there. As you can imagine, medicines – even basic stuff – are in short supply. That's where we come in. The border is officially closed, but everyone's turning a blind eye when we travel. Even the Somali warlords don't bother us, but fighting can erupt at any time. We have to be careful. But that's not the main danger ...'

'Oh?' said Jack.

'Our trip today is merely a cover ...'

'A cover for what?'

'Gathering information.'

Jack looked puzzled. 'Information? What about?'

Dr Rosen turned around and looked at Jack sitting in the back. 'I'll tell you,' she said. 'Every time we deliver medical supplies, we help out a little with treating the sick, especially the terminally ill. I run an eye clinic for a couple of hours before we drive back. That's when I first noticed it.'

'Noticed what?' said Jack.

'People with some horrific skin disease I have never seen before. Disfigured faces, blindness, open, weeping sores. Terrible stuff. As we found out later, these were the survivors. Many had died before reaching the camp, and they all appeared to come from the same region on the coast. We spoke to Dr Gaal about this and made some enquiries ...'

'And?'

'Tell him, Kobo.'

'Apparently, it's all to do with illegal toxic waste dumping along the Somali coastline. It has gone on for years and the people living on the coast have developed some dreadful illnesses. Deformed babies are common. Food and water have been contaminated. People have died by the thousands,' said Kobo.

'There are some powerful players involved here,' explained Dr Rosen, 'both local and international, and governments and organisations have looked the other way. This is one of the poorest countries in the world and one of the most vulnerable. However, as you can imagine, a lot of money is involved here and many shady people have made a fortune over the years. Corruption is rife everywhere.'

'How awful,' said Jack.

'However, we are going to meet some people today who want to fight back,' said Dr Rosen. 'Dr Gaal will take us to them. These are people who are determined to stop the exploitation of their country, whatever the cost. That's where the danger comes in. They want to show us something …'

'Show us what?'

'Evidence.'

'Who are these people?'

'That's the irony of it all,' said Dr Rosen. 'Pirates.'

By the time they finally arrived at the camp, thirsty and covered in dust, everyone was exhausted. The heat was unbearable and they had almost run out of water. The camp consisted of a few tents and a dozen or so hovels constructed mainly out of sheets of corrugated iron held together by rusty wire, empty oil drums and driftwood.

Two frightfully thin men sat in the shade under a tree, talking to a tall man wearing a stethoscope around his neck. A tiny, naked boy was coaxing a goat along a dirt track with a stick. Jack noticed that an open sore on the top of the boy's bald head was covered in flies. Otherwise, the camp appeared deserted.

'Where's everybody?' said Jack.

'Most of the patients here are too sick to come outside,' said Dr Rosen.

'Jesus.'

The man with the stethoscope turned around and waved. 'Good of you to come, Bettany,' he said, as he hurried towards them.

Dr Rosen introduced Jack. Noticing the concern on Dr Gaal's face, she took him aside. 'You can trust him with your life, Gaal. I vouch for him. Jack Rogan is a well-connected journalist and writer. He could be very useful to your cause.'

Dr Gaal nodded, relieved. 'We must hurry,' he said. 'If we don't turn up on time, they'll leave. It's not far.'

'Tell us about your contact,' said Dr Rosen, turning to Dr Gaal sitting in the back of the Land Rover.

'It's not often that one would turn to pirates in a humanitarian cause, but these pirates are different,' said Dr Gaal. 'Allow me to explain.'

Jack noticed that Dr Gaal was speaking perfect English with a pleasing, melodious accent. *Educated in England, I bet*, he thought, watching the fascinating man sitting next to him with interest. The shades of grey around the temples suggested a man in his fifties with rugged good looks and an expressive face pockmarked with traces of severe acne common in many Africans of his generation.

'It all began with fishing in the nineteen eighties before the outbreak of civil war in our country,' said Dr Gaal. 'The Somali fishing industry had great potential due to vast, unexploited marine stocks along our long, remote coastline. We had many promising joint ventures with foreign companies. The future looked bright. Then came the civil war. The central government collapsed and the Somali Navy was disbanded, leaving territorial waters undefended and open to exploitation. And that is exactly what happened.'

Dr Gaal became quite animated and spoke with passion, his long hands flying through the air every time he made a point. Jack noticed that each of the knuckles of his right hand had a small, star-like tattoo, which expanded every time he clenched his fist. 'The rape of our country had begun and continues to this very day,' continued Dr Gaal. 'Illegal fishing rapidly depleted the fishing grounds and foreign companies began dumping toxic waste into the sea just off the coast, further killing and contaminating marine life and the ocean floor. This continued throughout the eighties and nineties and became a highly organised and lucrative business for the corrupt, privileged few.'

Dr Gaal paused and looked out the window. 'We are almost there,' he said, giving Kobo directions. Suddenly the ground dropped away, opening up a splendid view of the ocean and the rugged coastline stretching as far as the eye could see. It was difficult to imagine the horrors described by Dr Gaal, lurking below the calm waters glistening below.

'Local fisherman saw their livelihood being systematically destroyed by foreign fishing trawlers plundering their fishing grounds,' continued Dr Gaal. 'Whole communities began to starve. And then came the sickness and disease … Then one day, the people had had enough and decided to fight back. And they did that the only way they knew how. They banded together and took to the sea. They became pirates, and you are about to meet one of them.' Dr Gaal pointed ahead. 'That's him over there.'

# 59

Jack looked down into the picturesque cove below. Apart from a small skiff with a powerful looking outboard motor and a man sitting on a rock nearby, smoking, the cove looked deserted. Jack didn't see the two men armed with machine guns guarding the beach until he came closer.

Dr Gaal waved to the man sitting on the rock. The man waved back, threw his cigarette into the water and stood up. 'That's Sharif,' said Dr Gaal. 'Come, let's meet him.'

Sharif, a young Somali of about thirty with a long scar running down his right cheek spoke briefly to Dr Gaal and pointed to the skiff.

'It isn't far. He will take us there in the boat,' said Dr Gaal.

Ten minutes later, they pulled into another small cove. Surrounded by tall cliffs on all sides, it was only accessible from the sea.

'Make sure you don't touch anything,' said Dr Gaal. 'Everything here is contaminated. Toxic waste.'

The two armed men jumped into the shallow water and pulled the skiff up onto the beach. Jack helped Dr Rosen climb out of the boat and followed the men on shore.

'In 2004, these rocks were battered by huge seas caused by the Indian Ocean tsunami,' said Sharif. 'The powerful waves scooped up heavy containers and drums filled with toxic and nuclear waste from the ocean floor and dumped them on the beaches all along the Somali coast.' Sharif pointed to the southern end of the small beach. 'Over there are four of the worst,' he said.

Jack and Dr Rosen walked over to the rusting containers partially buried in the sand. Keeping their distance, they looked at the cigar-shaped objects. 'Weird shape,' said Jack. 'They look like torpedoes, don't you think?'

Dr Rosen pulled her camera out of her bag and began to take pictures.

'These came from somewhere in Europe via Italy and were used for the disposal of toxic hospital waste,' said Dr Gaal. 'The Italian Mafia was very active in this wretched business at the time. There were many other containers, mainly drums scattered along the coast, which contained radioactive material. However, most of them were quickly collected and disposed of – buried somewhere inland, which only made things worse – no doubt by parties with vested interests trying to hide the damning evidence. By the time investigators arrived, the findings were inconclusive, and no doubt, bribes did the rest. No action was taken.'

Dr Gaal paused and looked pensively at the lethal containers, contemplating the misery they had caused. 'So nothing happened, except for this,' he said. 'People began to get sick up and down the coast here. Toxic material entered the water table and the food chain, poisoning the population and marine life. Horrible, previously unknown diseases began to appear. Babies were born with shocking birth defects and the incidence of cancer soared. Doctors were beginning to see more cases of cancer in one year than during their entire professional life.'

Dr Gaal turned to Sharif. For a while, they spoke animatedly in Somali. 'Sadly, this has continued to this very day,' continued Dr Gaal. 'You have seen some of the poor wretches in the camp we just came from. However, I'm afraid there's a lot more, and what we are about to show you is perhaps more shocking and despicable than anything you've seen so far.'

'What is he talking about?' asked Jack, turning to Dr Rosen.

'What I really came here to see. You'll be shocked all right, believe me.'

Ten minutes later they took off again, hugging the coast and travelling north at high speed. 'Where are we going?' shouted Jack, trying to make himself heard over the roar of the powerful outboard motor.

319

'Over there,' said Sharif, pointing to another beach a short distance away. Jack could just make out a small cluster of huts partially hidden by dense vegetation, scattered along the shore.

'What's that?' asked Jack.

'A camp for the dying,' said Dr Gaal, the sadness in his voice obvious.

They were met by a young woman in a nurse's uniform. She seemed to know Dr Gaal and Sharif well and Jack noticed that Sharif handed her something that looked like a wad of money.

Dr Rosen had brought some medical supplies with her in a plastic bag. Morphine mainly, which according to Dr Gaal, was desperately needed in the camp. This would explain Dr Rosen's surprise visit without, Dr Gaal hoped, arousing suspicion. MSF was well-known and highly regarded in Somalia for donating much needed medical supplies.

'Sharif's father was in here just recently,' said Dr Gaal. 'I've known Sharif for years. He brought me here to look after his dying father during his last days. That's when I discovered what's going on here …'

Dr Rosen shot Jack a meaningful look, but said nothing.

'This is a dangerous place,' said Dr Gaal, lowering his voice. 'Often, there are armed men here … If they show up, we must leave immediately. Don't talk to anyone. Just follow me. I've asked the nurse to show us around. For MSF to be interested in the camp is perfectly natural, and the much needed morphine should do the trick.'

Sharif's two armed men stayed with the skiff. Everyone else followed the nurse up the little hill to the huts in the bush above.

The nurse had two young assistants, two girls who giggled as they approached. Sharif seemed to know them and engaged them in conversation with Kobo in front of the huts.

'Most of our patients here are terminally ill; cancer mainly,' said the nurse, opening the door to the first hut. 'That's why we are always short of morphine. We had a huge increase in terminal cancer during the last few years in this area.'

Inside the crowded hut it was quite dark, and the smell was overpowering: urine; sweat; unwashed bodies; heat. Jack had to try hard not to choke. Once his eyes became accustomed to the gloom, he looked around. A dozen patients, men and women of all ages, were lying on narrow wooden beds lined up in a row along the wall with very little space between them. The smell reminded Jack of a leper colony he had once visited in South America: rotting flesh; decay; approaching death.

As they walked slowly past the pitiful row of beds, Dr Rosen noticed that each bed had a small wooden frame attached to one of the bedposts. The frames appeared to contain what looked like charts with neat columns of small, handwritten entries. *How curious,* thought Dr Rosen. *A chart for each patient ... in this place!* She made a mental note to have a closer look. *And a sophisticated medicine cupboard near the door. Possibly refrigerated! How odd!*

The nurse turned to Dr Rosen walking behind her. 'Most of the patients here are close to death,' she said quietly. 'We try to make their last days as comfortable as we can.'

The two other huts were almost identical.

Dr Rosen waited until they had stepped outside and the nurse was talking to Dr Gaal, before turning to Jack. *'Distract the nurse, please. I have to get back inside to look at something,'* she whispered. *'Do it – now!'*

Jack walked over to the nurse. 'Amazing place,' he said. 'How long has this facility been here?'

Dr Gaal looked at Dr Rosen and nodded. Dr Rosen turned around and slipped back into the hut. Jack and Dr Gaal took turns to ask questions, and kept a close eye on the door to the hut. It seemed like ages before Dr Rosen came back out. Thankfully, the nurse didn't appear to have noticed her absence.

'This is remarkable work you're doing here,' said Dr Rosen casually. 'We'll make sure you get some morphine on a regular basis.'

'That would be marvellous,' said the nurse.

'We better get going,' said Dr Gaal. He waved to Sharif, who was still talking to the giggling girls with Kobo, and then pointed to the skiff on the beach. They thanked the nurse for showing them around and walked down to the water.

They had almost reached the skiff when they heard excited shouting coming from the huts behind them. Two men, both Africans, were shouting at the nurse and the two girls, and kept pointing to the skiff. One of the men hit the nurse hard. The nurse fell to the ground and the shouting became louder.

'Ignore it!' shouted Dr Gaal, beginning to run. 'Let's get out of here. Hurry!'

Sharif ran towards his men who were pushing the skiff into the water. That's when gunfire erupted.

'Pin them down!' Sharif shouted in Somali. By now, Kobo had reached the boat and was holding it steady for the others to jump in. The two armed men trained their weapons on the huts and returned fire.

Sharif pulled his gun out of his belt and began to fire as well.

'Get in,' shouted Kobo, 'quickly!'

Sharif jumped into the boat, started up the engine and kept firing. The engine roared into life, and with everyone safely on board, they pushed off.

A group of armed men kept running towards a speedboat tied to a post on the far end of the beach, their intention obvious. Sharif assessed the situation and kept the skiff close to the shore. As they approached the speedboat, he turned to Dr Gaal sitting next to him. 'Here, take this,' said Sharif and handed the tiller to Dr Gaal. As they were about to pass the speedboat, he reached into the ammunitions box in the bottom of the boat and pulled out a grenade. A passionate cricketer since his early teens, Sharif stood up, steadied himself, took aim and then expertly bowled the live grenade towards the speedboat as they roared past. The grenade landed next to the fuel tank and exploded in a ball of fire, blowing the boat to smithereens. Before Sharif could sit down again, Dr Gaal was hit in the right arm.

By the time the smoke from the explosion cleared, the skiff had rounded the point, leaving their frustrated pursuers standing helplessly on the beach.

# 60

Dr Gaal was bleeding profusely. Dr Rosen was doing her best to administer first aid, which wasn't easy in the speeding boat. She had ripped off the sleeve of her friend's tattered tee-shirt and was trying to stem the bleeding.

'You've been lucky,' she said, tightening the bandage she had pulled out of her bag. 'The bullet only grazed your shoulder without causing any real damage. Flesh wound mainly; you'll live.' Unconcerned, Dr Gaal was grinning. He seemed almost proud of his injury.

Sharif looked at Dr Rosen sitting in front of him. 'As soon as we get to the camp, you must leave at once and get back to Dadaab,' he said. 'Cross the border as soon as you can. They'll try to find you, I'm sure of it, and it won't take them long to get here.'

'Who are these people?' asked Dr Rosen, her face and hair covered in sea spray.

'Tell you later,' shouted Dr Gaal from the back, 'And you must tell me what you've found in the hut …' Dr Rosen nodded and held on, her knuckles turning white.

It took them less than fifteen minutes to get back to the other camp. Sharif pointed to a fishing trawler bobbing up and down in the swell close to shore. It was obvious he was keen to get away. The trawler, captured from Indian poachers fishing illegally in Somali waters, was the 'mother ship'. The fast, manoeuvrable skiff with a powerful outboard motor was the 'attack vessel', which was used to intercept and board the target ships – classic Somali pirate tactics.

Wincing a little from the pain in his shoulder, Dr Gaal embraced his friend. 'We'll get them, don't worry. We owe it to your father and the others. Dr Rosen has a lot of influence … we can count on her.'

'Be careful, my friend,' said Sharif. 'Ruthless people do ruthless things.' Sharif waved to the others, climbed back into the skiff and, gunning the engine, raced towards the trawler.

'Would someone please tell me what all this was about?' asked Jack, after Sharif had left. 'Why were these guys attacking us? What's going on in that camp?'

'You put your finger right on it; something is definitely going on in the camp,' said Dr Rosen, 'and it's evil! Tell him, Gaal.'

'I first noticed something wasn't quite right during my visit to help Sharif's father,' said Dr Gaal. 'Firstly, the camp is run by some obscure charity called Help Africa United – HAU. I've never heard of it. They have an office in Mogadishu and employ the nurses. As you've seen, the main purpose of the camp is to help terminally ill patients to die. It's a palliative care camp of sorts. I've never seen one in Somalia before. With so many people dying and a country so much in need, it's an almost pointless concept—'

'Unless there's another purpose to this altogether,' interrupted Dr Rosen. 'A different agenda.'

'Quite. The next odd thing I noticed was that all the patients in the camp were suffering from cancer. Now this was really strange, I thought. People are dying here every day of all kinds of illnesses, so why only cancer patients? I didn't know it at the time, but that's the key to it all. Whoever is behind this is only interested in cancer.

'Then, during one of my subsequent visits, I came across a European doctor at the camp. He had come all the way from Mogadishu and was examining every patient. He had an assistant with him who took blood samples from each one. Everything was recorded. There were also some armed men with him, which I found quite strange. After they left, I questioned the nurse about all this. She didn't appear to know too much and assumed it was all part of the treatment provided by HAU. You've seen her. She isn't very bright, nor has she much experience.'

'So, what are you telling me, guys?' asked Jack.

'Someone is conducting clinical trials on these poor wretches,' said Dr Rosen. 'I've seen the medication. I don't know if you noticed, but each hut has a refrigerated medicine cabinet, and each bed has a chart with lots of detailed entries. It may not look like it, but this is a sophisticated laboratory for drug trials. With one big difference; instead of using mice, these people are using human beings!'

'Jesus! Are you serious?' said Jack.

'Absolutely! And here's the proof. Well, some of it anyway.' Dr Rosen opened her bag and pulled out a small bottle containing a yellowish liquid. The bottle had a label stuck to it with a few letters and numbers written in black ink. 'And I took photos of some of the charts,' said Dr Rosen. 'I think each patient had his own bottle of labelled medication in the cupboard, and a chart tied to his bed recording the relevant data. Simple and effective, if you know what you're doing and what you're looking for. And I think these people know exactly what they are doing. As we've just heard, they take blood samples from each patient, which are no doubt carefully analysed in some lab.'

'I agree,' interjected Dr Gaal. 'I'm sure when you find out what's in that bottle, you'll find the answer: a new cancer drug in the early stages of development being trialled on human beings. This would be unthinkable in just about any other part of the world,' said Dr Gaal sadly. 'But here, life is cheap. Almost anything goes if you have the money.'

'I still don't understand. Why would someone go to so much trouble to do this?' asked Jack.

'That's simple,' said Dr Rosen. 'It's all in the data. Clinical trials at this early stage can provide a tremendous shortcut ... years. You find out what works, and what doesn't, first hand. Not on mice, but on human beings! What would take years of painstaking research in a controlled laboratory environment using traditional methods, can most likely be achieved here in a fraction of the time using human beings suffering real illnesses. Armed with new, successful data supporting the findings, the pharmaceutical company that owns the drug can then submit it to the appropriate authorities say, in the US, and begin the necessary trials in the safe, traditional, accepted way. However, the outcome is already known. The drug company knows it works, and most importantly, it knows all the side effects. Why?

Because it has already been tried on countless hapless patients, and modified accordingly!'

'So, what's in it for the drug company?' asked Jack.

'Patents and lots of money,' said Dr Rosen. 'These human trials are a tremendous head start that gives the drug company the edge over its competitors. There are billions involved in this game, and whoever comes up with the next important drug that works, gets the prize. And there can be no greater prize than a cancer drug that works.'

'Unbelievable!' said Jack. 'And what about—' Jack was interrupted by shouting.

A breathless Kobo came running towards them with his hands in the air. 'Two jeeps full of armed men,' shouted Kobo.

'Where?' said Jack.

Kobo pointed to a cloud of dust hovering above the road a few kilometres away. 'Over there.'

'Leave now! Quickly!' shouted Dr Gaal. 'That way!'

'What about you?' said Dr Rosen. 'Come with us!'

'I can't ... I know this place well. I'll hide. Go! Now!' said Dr Gaal, holding his injured arm.

Dr Rosen quickly embraced her friend. 'Take care,' she said, 'and thank you for showing us all this. It was the right thing to do. I won't let you down!'

Kobo ran back to the Land Rover and started the engine. 'Get in! Here, take my gun.' Kobo handed Jack a high-powered hunting rifle that could have killed an elephant a hundred yards away. 'You know how to use it?'

'Yes.'

'If they come near us, aim for the tyres. The scope will give you the edge.'

'Right. Makes sense.'

'I also have a handgun. Here,' Kobo opened the glove box and gave his Beretta to Dr Rosen, 'you've used one before,' he said, smiling. Dr Rosen nodded. 'I know all the back ways around here,' continued Kobo. He turned off the road leading out of the camp and headed for the bush. 'With a bit of luck, they'll never find us.'

'I hope you're right,' said Dr Rosen, checking the gun. 'Let's get out of here!'

An hour later, when they thought they were safe and about to cross the border into Kenya, something caught Jack's eye. Movement. 'There,' he shouted, pointing into the bush. A jeep was coming towards them out of the trees, obviously trying to cut them off. Kobo turned left into a dirt track and accelerated. Then gunfire erupted from behind, a couple of bullets hitting the rear fenders.

'Keep your heads down, guys,' shouted Kobo, racing towards a creek. 'Jack, aim for the tyres. I must slow down to get across here.'

Jack turned around, steadied himself and positioned his gun, the powerful scope giving him a clear view. 'Stop the car now,' he shouted.

Kobo hit the brakes and the Land Rover skidded to a halt.

Jack took a deep breath, closed one eye and kept staring through the scope. '*Here they come*,' he whispered, watching the jeep race towards him. Remembering his days in Afghanistan as a war correspondent a few years earlier, where survival often depended upon how well you could handle a gun, he carefully lined up the hairs in the scope until the left front tyre was right in the middle. Then, holding his breath, he pulled the trigger. '*Got ya*,' he whispered, and lowered the gun.

The tyre exploded, ripped apart by the powerful bullet. The jeep lurched to the left, hit a small rock, became almost airborne and began to roll down an embankment towards the creek below.

# 61

It was already dark by the time they drove into Dadaab, exhausted, but strangely elated after their close escape. An adrenaline high, Dr Rosen had called it.

'How was it?' asked Lola, handing Jack a glass of water.

'You won't believe it when I tell you.' Jack gulped down the water and held out his empty cup for more.

'Why am I not surprised?' said Lola, smiling. 'You're an adventure … junkie!'

'How's Tristan?'

'I haven't seen him all day. He went off with Ifra this morning to explore the camp. They've become great buddies.'

'There's more danger here than we realise,' said Jack, lowering his voice. 'And we are right in the middle of it. We have to be careful.'

'Oh?'

'Dr Rosen thinks it best if we leave in the morning. She seems really worried, especially about Dr Gaal. There's a supply plane going back to Nairobi. She's coming with us. She has to talk to someone in MSF urgently …'

'You also look worried, Jack,' said Lola. She stood up, walked over to Jack and began to massage his stiff neck. 'Not like you. What's wrong?'

'At times I feel a little lost,' said Jack. Remembering his conversation with Dr Rosen early that morning about how far man had come in such a short time. He looked up at the stars. 'What we discovered in that camp just across the border from here is scary. I feel for Dr Rosen. She puts her whole life on the line here helping others, yet the ugly side of life is never far away, undermining everything she holds dear and believes in.'

'That's a bit morbid, isn't it?' said Lola. She bent down and kissed Jack on the back of the neck. 'Don't worry, Jack, you'll bounce back, you'll see. Guys like you always do.'

'Perhaps ... But if you'd seen what I have ...'

'I had a call from Hanna today,' said Lola, changing the subject. 'The boat is fantastic and they are on their way. Boston in a few days' time.'

'And Isis?'

'In good spirits, apparently.'

'At least that's good news.'

'Snap out of it, Jack,' said Lola, biting Jack on the ear.

Jack heard his satellite phone ring somewhere in the distance, the familiar ringtone a welcome intrusion into his dark thoughts. Because the battery had almost gone flat during the day, he had left the phone in the tent to recharge. Jack stood up and hurried inside to answer it.

'Marcus, what's up?' said Jack, pleased to hear the familiar voice on the other end of the crackling line. 'Any luck?'

'We've managed to track down Hoffmeister through his lawyers. He's fallen on hard times and is in some kind of nursing home for the poor in Buenos Aires.'

'At least he's still around. And ...?'

'The word is, he knows about the brother and can throw some light on the subject.'

'That's fantastic!' Jack almost shouted.

'Don't get too excited. You know how he behaved last time. He wound us up like puppets and then dropped us without hesitation.'

'Sure, but ...'

'He wants money. Lots of it.'

'How much money?'

'A hundred grand ...'

'Wow!'

'He's obviously desperate. But wait, there's more ...'

'Tell me.'

'He will only talk to Jana. He really liked her – remember? If she brings the money, he'll talk. He even hinted at some documents and gave us a clue. No doubt to whet our appetite.'

'What clue?'

'Curiously, just one word.'

'Tell me.'

'Africa.'

Momentarily taken aback, Jack didn't reply. 'Are you still there?' said Marcus. 'Does this mean anything to you?'

'Sure does! Look Marcus, this is really important. Could Jana go, do you think?'

'What, just fly to South America with a hundred grand in her handbag? What kind of client do you have?'

'A very rich one. Stay on the line, Marcus, I'll get some instructions.'

'I thought you were in some refugee camp in Kenya.'

'I am.'

'You never cease to amaze, Jack. I'll wait …'

Jack hurried out of the tent and spoke to Lola, who instantly authorised the expenses involved.

'Go ahead, Marcus! Ask Jana to take the first available flight to Buenos Aires and find out all she can about Steinberger's brother. This is urgent! We'll just have to take our chances with our slippery Don Antonio,' said Jack, 'but if he does know something, we could be on a winner. It's worth the risk. Just call me and tell me what you need, and we'll arrange everything from here. And tell Jana I owe her! And thank you! Great work, Marcus. I owe you too!'

'Stay safe, Jack,' said Carrington.

'I'll try.'

Jack switched off the phone and kissed it, the exuberant, almost childlike gesture bringing a smile to Lola's face. 'See what I mean?' she said. 'All it takes is a phone call, and you're back on top of the world.'

# 62

The phone call came in the early hours of the morning, but Carlotta decided to wake her boss immediately. She knew he would never forgive her if she didn't.

Macbeth, a light sleeper, sensed someone was in the room and propped himself up by his elbows. 'Something wrong, Carlotta?' he asked, instantly awake.

'A phone call from Mogadishu. It's urgent.' Carlotta handed Macbeth the phone.

'What is it, Johannes?'

'We have a problem.'

'Oh? What kind of problem?'

'An incident in Alpha Camp.'

'What happened?'

'Someone from Médecins Sans Frontières nosed around. Made enquiries…'

'And?'

'There was a shootout.'

'Jesus, Johannes; the guys should know better!'

'The south has always been difficult to control …'

'What else?'

'They got away by boat. We think some of the local pirates were involved.'

'What else?'

'Our guys captured one of them, a local doctor …'

'Come on, Johannes, this is like pulling teeth!'

'Their interrogation techniques aren't very sophisticated, but they did get some helpful information out of him before he—'

'Is he dead?' interrupted Macbeth impatiently.

'I'm afraid so.'

'Not very smart.'

'No.'

'So, what do we know?'

'A doctor working for MSF, a European woman and a couple of men, one of them also European, came to the camp and asked questions ...'

'Do we know who they are?'

'We are working on it.'

'Do we know *where* they are?'

'Yes. We believe they returned to Dadaab, where they came from.'

*At least that's good news*, thought Macbeth. *We have people there.*

'How much do they know?'

'Not clear. The questioning didn't get quite that far ...'

'I want you to drop everything and take personal charge of the matter. Is that clear?'

'Absolutely.'

'Go down there straight away. Use your contacts in Dadaab and find out more. I want to know everything about them; who they are, what they are doing, who they talk to, what they have for breakfast – everything! Understood?'

'Yes.'

'This has top priority. Pull out all stops. You know what to do. Results, remember? And keep me informed, day or night.'

'Understood.'

Macbeth pressed the bell next to his bed. Carlotta appeared almost at once. 'Ask the captain to prepare *Calypso* to set sail immediately and send Jan in.'

'Straight away.'

Feeling better, Macbeth lifted himself out of the bed and into his wheelchair. 'I'll be outside. Early breakfast.'

'I'll arrange it at once.'

Macbeth loved the time just before dawn and always felt somehow liberated out in the open air. Looking at the sea and the stars gave him a sense of freedom he rarely experienced sitting in his wheelchair. The movement of the ship also added to this seductive illusion and was one of the main reasons he lived on the ship. He also liked the anonymity and flexibility it gave him in conducting his complex affairs.

*So close and now this*, thought Macbeth, clenching his fists in frustration. He was certain that the quest that had begun seventy years ago with a chance discovery and an inspired idea by a man he had held dear, was tantalisingly close to reaching its destination.

The data from the Somali camps strongly suggested this. Incidents of recovery from terminal cancer were definitely on the rise; tumours were retreating and in some cases, disappearing altogether. However, the same baffling question remained: *why?* Why did patients suffering from the same cancer respond so differently to the drug? Why did a lucky few survive when most of the others died? To date, his army of scientists working on this project had been unable to come up with an answer. All the sophisticated modifications and refinements to the drug had so far been unsuccessful.

There was no doubt that the drug – an extract derived from the root of a rare jungle plant – did work spectacularly, but only in a few cases. So far, the many millions spent on research and brainpower by Blackburn Pharmaceuticals to find the answer, had failed. However, Macbeth was convinced that Professor K had come close to cracking this vital question just before he died and that his successor, Professor Delacroix, would do so soon. The challenge here was to secure the prize for Blackburn Pharmaceuticals, regardless of the cost involved, human or otherwise.

Feeling better, Macbeth watched the crew in the wheelhouse prepare the ship for departure. A new journey was a new beginning, and a new beginning brought challenges. For Macbeth, challenges were the stuff that made being so devastatingly disabled bearable and kept him motivated and alive.

Van Cleef arrived moments later. Woken by Carlotta, he had jumped out of his bunk, put on his tracksuit and was reporting for duty. Macbeth looked at the young warrior standing before him and smiled. 'Jan, I need you now more than ever,' he said. 'Look at it this way: we are in the middle of a campaign we must win at all cost …'

Van Cleef felt a familiar wave of excitement well up from deep within. It started in his gut and then tingled through every fibre of his body, making his muscles throb and yearn for action. It was a feeling he knew well, and its meaning was clear: he was about to go into battle.

'We have a serious problem in Somalia. We are about to sail for Mogadishu. I can no longer stay here to take care of things, but you can. You will be my eyes and ears here in Sydney. Work closely with Paulus. Needless to say, we'll be in regular contact, and you'll receive your instructions from me in the usual manner. Understood?'

'Absolutely! You can rely on me.'

'I know I can, just as I can rely on Johannes, who is already on his way to deal with the problem in Somalia.'

Johannes, Paulus and Jan had been brothers-in-arms for years. They had a bond only men who had saved each other from certain death many times over could share.

'You can count on Johannes,' said Jan.

'I know that too.'

'Now go and prepare your kit. We'll drop you off before we sail.' Macbeth held out his hand. This was a rare gesture and he could see that Jan kept staring at him, a startled look on his face. For what seemed a long moment, Jan stood perfectly still. Then he stepped forward like a soldier about to be decorated by his commanding officer, and shook his boss' hand.

# 63

To her surprise, Alexandra was beginning to feel quite at home in her lab at the Gordon. To share the same space her friend and mentor had worked in, and died in, just a short while ago, created not only a connection to the past, but a strange sense of continuity reaching into the present. When she added Professor K's handwritten notes to this, the sensation became even more real. There were moments when she felt his presence so intensely that she had to stop reading and look over her shoulder to make sure he wasn't standing behind her.

Many would have found retracing a dead man's thoughts and ideas disconcerting, intimidating even, but Alexandra didn't find it so. She had made a promise to a dear friend and intended to keep it.

Not only were the state-of-the-art facilities at the institute a pleasure to work with, but the Illumina HiSeq X Ten system available at the Gordon was the single most important tool helping her understand Professor K's work. Invented by Professors Balasubramanian and Klenerman of Cambridge University, Illumina dye sequencing had revolutionised medical research.

But the real breakthrough had only come a few months ago with the introduction of 'Capture Sequencing', a new gene sequencing technology. For the first time, Professor K had a unique window at his disposal, which allowed him to peer into the remote recesses of the human genome at a much higher resolution than ever before. Only a short time ago, this would have been considered science fiction.

Step-by-step, evidence supporting his revolutionary ideas was at last beginning to emerge out of the vast body of genes not coding for proteins that make up ninety-eight point five per cent of the human genome. Sadly, Professor K had run out of time. The Emperor of Darkness got to him just before he could put his hands on the prize that had eluded him for so long.

Alexandra realised that Professor K had been on a hunt for something quite unique at the time he died. He was stalking certain non-coding RNAs hidden somewhere in the genome, which he believed held the key to the breakthrough he had so desperately hoped for. He had discovered a number of long, non-coding RNAs that acted as oncogenes, and a growing number of these oncogenes appeared to be tumour suppressors. And somehow – in a way Alexandra couldn't quite understand yet – it all kept coming back to non-coding RNAs that could switch other genes on and off, as it had in the Abramowitz twins.

The Lena Abramowitz genome sequencing was well underway. Akhil, her assistant, had attached Lena's DNA molecules to primers on a slide. The next step was amplification of the DNA to allow the production of local colonies, which would prepare the way for the unique clusters technology to do its work.

However, the final results of Lena's genome sequencing were still almost a week away. This gave Alexandra time to immerse herself in the complexities and challenges of Professor K's notebooks and research papers.

Alexandra was beginning to make serious progress. Her hunch about the Leibniz notations scribbled in the margins had been correct. As she had suspected, the numbers turned out to be a code identifying the tissue samples stored at Gordon that Professor K had been working on. She was certain they were the signposts and markers he had left behind to show her the way. Alexandra was hoping they would ultimately lead her to the hidden genes he had been looking for, and the expected breakthrough he had mentioned just before he died.

There was more good news. Alexandra's much applauded talk the other day had raised her profile and standing at Gordon and had made her colleagues far more approachable. Alexandra knew that the most valuable respect – and the most difficult to earn – was the respect of your peers. Suddenly, Alexandra found herself included in meetings and activities, both professional and personal. The ice appeared to have melted.

However, the single most important development that had raised her spirits and made her feel at ease was Carrington's calm, analytical assessment of her precarious position vis-à-vis Blackburn Pharmaceuticals, and his sound advice of how to deal with it. In a way, Carrington and Jana had taken charge of the situation. They had both attended the meeting with the police the day before. Carrington had prepared Alexandra well. Instead of feeling vulnerable and finding the interview intimidating, she had approached it with confidence. She told her amazing story convincingly and provided information in a manner that was both impressive and believable.

They all thought the meeting had gone well, and the DPP's personal involvement certainly had its desired effect. Instructions from the top always make a difference. The senior officer placed in charge of the case had assigned one of his best men – Detective Sergeant Pasquale Moretti – to liaise with Alexandra and act as her contact point.

Alexandra dried her hands and picked up the phone.

'A Mr Moretti is in reception to see you,' said the receptionist. 'Meeting room 3 is available if you would like it.'

Alexandra took off her apron and safety glasses and hurried to the lift.

As soon as Moretti set eyes on the confident redhead coming towards him, he was smitten. He had a completely different picture in his mind of the famous scientist he had recently heard so much about. This tall, elegant young woman with striking red hair didn't quite fit the image of the brainy researcher he had expected to meet.

'I am Dr Delacroix,' said Alexandra. She extended her hand and smiled at the young man in the smart, dark suit standing in front of the reception desk. *Far too handsome for a policeman*, she thought.

As the only son of Italian migrants – his father was a greengrocer – Moretti had had to work hard to get to where he was. He had started work at the markets when he was just ten. He used to get up at four in the morning to help his father before school. By the time school started at nine, he had already done half a day's work. After school, he was back at the shop, helping his parents and doing homework at the back when things were quiet. Pasquale was the apple of his mother's eye, and she encouraged him to study hard and do well at school.

Because he was exceptionally bright and good at sport, he found it easy to excel. He won a scholarship and later went to university at night to study law. However, he had always wanted to be a policeman. He was one of only a few cadets who entered the police force with a law degree and soon became part of a new, well-educated breed of young officers advancing rapidly in a changing police force, hungry for brainpower to fight sophisticated crime.

'You will be pleased to hear that we've already made some progress since your interview,' said Moretti. He reached into his pocket and pulled out a small notebook.

*He's so young,* thought Alexandra, watching the confident officer sitting opposite with interest.

'The information provided by Ms Gonski has been most helpful. It isn't often we are provided with photographs and fingerprints of a suspect during a first interview,' said Moretti. 'And the quirky registration number of the car that picked him up,' added Moretti, smiling, 'was another good lead.'

Alexandra began to laugh. 'Taking that wineglass was rather clever,' she said. 'And then thinking of my passport cover ...'

'Quite. We've been able to lift excellent prints from both ...'

'That was quick. And?'

'Matching prints appear on both items. We can now link the man who handled the wineglass to your passport.'

'And what of the man?'

'There's no record of him in this country. Nothing. Just as we expected. He's like a phantom; appeared out of nowhere. Officially, he doesn't exist.' Moretti saw the disappointment on Alexandra's face. 'But that's not the end of it,' he added, lowering his voice.

'Oh?'

'The South African accent gave us an important clue. And so did his military bearing, Ms Gonski observed. It would appear she was right. While we couldn't find anything about him here, it was quite a different story in South Africa. We checked with our colleagues in Johannesburg.'

'And?'

'His name is Jan Van Cleef. Ex-army, just as Ms Gonski suspected. A notorious character. He has quite a record. Violence mainly. Now works as a mercenary … somewhere. We'll know more about him soon.'

'Wow! I wish my research would work that quickly,' said Alexandra.

'There's more,' said Moretti, enjoying himself.

'There is?'

'The car with that silly registration number – I SPY 4 U – is registered to a company called Universal Security with offices right here in Sydney in The Rocks. One of the principals is Paulus Koenig, another South African with a long record. He too is ex-army and a known associate of Van Cleef's.'

'I'm impressed,' said Alexandra. 'I certainly didn't expect this.'

'Ms Gonski did all the heavy lifting here,' said Moretti, dismissing the compliment. 'She handed the information to us on a plate. Incidentally, Ms Gonski was already a legend in the police force when I first joined. I attended several of her lectures.'

'Still …'

'We have made a good start, but that's all for the moment. We need more; a lot more.'

'I understand.'

'I've already spoken to Ms Gonski about this. I saw her this morning. As you know, she's flying to Buenos Aires tomorrow. When she comes back, we'll pick up the threads again and take it from there.'

Impressed, Alexandra smiled at Moretti.

'I've also spoken to Mr Carrington. You have influential friends, Dr Delacroix. I will be the contact point for all of you and will keep you informed.' Moretti reached into his pocket. 'Here's my card. Don't hesitate to call me, day or night.'

'Thank you,' said Alexandra, and put the card on the table in front of her.

'Have you been able to prepare copies of Professor Kozakievicz's notebooks as Van Cleef has asked you to do?'

'I have.'

'Please leave them on your desk this evening before you go home, but not all. Just a few pages.'

'Oh? Why?'

'To flush out Van Cleef. When he discovers that you've given him only a small part of what he asked for, he's bound to make a move. He obviously has an inside contact – right here. Men like Van Cleef are used to being in control and won't tolerate disobedience.'

*That's clever*, thought Alexandra. 'But what about me?' she said, the anxiety in her voice obvious. 'If there's someone on the inside as you suspect …'

'Don't worry, we are watching your every move. I'll never be far away,' said Moretti.

To her surprise, Moretti's reassurance made Alexandra feel a lot better. 'Will do,' she said. However, Moretti hadn't told her everything. He hadn't told her that the police surveillance team had installed cameras in her lab during the night and would be keeping an eye on her desk.

'Now, please consider this carefully. Is there anyone here at the institute you can think of who could somehow be implicated in this, or in any way linked to Van Cleef?'

At first, Alexandra hesitated. 'This stays strictly between us?' she said.

'Of course.'

'It's only a hunch, but there is something …'

Moretti looked at her, surprised. 'Please tell me,' he said and reached for his notebook.

# 64

Jana was one of those fortunate people who could, if necessary, sleep for a couple of minutes standing up in a bus. She therefore had no trouble sleeping right through the long flight crossing the Pacific to South America. She woke an hour before landing in Buenos Aires, alert and refreshed, and contemplated her good fortune.

A few days after arriving in Sydney, she had not only met with the DPP and prepared the way to get her old job back, but was unofficially working on what could turn out to be a sensational case with international implications involving the Australian government. The DPP had arranged for Alexandra to be interviewed by a senior NSW police officer Jana had worked with before. Not only that, but a small taskforce – *Operation Blowhole*, headed by Detective Sergeant Moretti – had been set up to investigate the matter. Cavendish's death had turned into a possible murder enquiry.

Relieved, and no longer feeling so vulnerable and alone, Alexandra had returned to work energised, and quite ready to continue her groundbreaking research following in the footsteps of her former mentor and friend. The CEO of the Gordon Institute had also been discreetly briefed by the police regarding the murder investigation and the spectre of a possible conspiracy to defraud Gordon of its research results.

Marcus too, had been fortunate. He had returned to the bar with a brief that could easily become the hottest case in town, and was well on his way to rebuilding his old practice. The DPP had retained him to examine all potential evidence in the unfolding Blackburn Pharmaceuticals investigation, and conduct any prosecution should it come to that.

*Jack, we owe you,* thought Jana, smiling. *The old rascal is at it again!* It was time to repay him and the long, tiring trip to Buenos Aires to interview Hoffmeister was part of that.

Hoffmeister's lawyers met Jana at the airport in Buenos Aires. The one hundred thousand dollars in their trust account Lola had transferred and the promise of a fat fee prepared the way for a meeting with their notorious client.

'Don Antonio, as he is known around here,' said the young lawyer sitting next to Jana in the car, 'has fallen on hard times. He's staying in a hostel for the poor run by nuns in a monastery just outside town. It will take us about an hour or so to get there. But I must warn you, it's not the most salubrious part of our city and we have to drive through some rough neighbourhoods ...'

Jana nodded. To refresh her memory, she went over Jack's email once again, summarising the main points she had to cover with Hoffmeister.

'Unfortunately, he had to sell his tango clubs to pay off his son's debts to the Colombian drug syndicate. You may remember this from last time?'

'I do,' said Jana. 'His son was on trial in Miami for drug trafficking.'

'Correct. He cut a deal and turned informer. He's due to be released from jail next year. This infuriated the Colombians and certainly didn't help Don Antonio here. The son is now all he has left. That's what keeps him going, and he desperately needs money.'

'You are familiar with our arrangements?' said Jana, closing her folder.

'I am. The funds are to stay in our trust account until you authorise their release. Don Antonio is confident he can demonstrate to you that he has the necessary information you seek and provide proof of its authenticity. Once he has done that, and you are satisfied, he will hand over the evidence and we'll be authorised to release the money to him.'

'Correct. Your client knows the interview is to be recorded?'

'Yes. He has consented to that.'

'Good.'

As an experienced interrogator, Jana was already preparing her questions and interview approach. Having met Hoffmeister before was a big help. It had been agreed that the whole interview would be recorded on video and Jana had brought all the necessary equipment with her. At least that way, Jack would have an opportunity to evaluate Hoffmeister's answers, body language and demeanour first hand. *Just like interviewing a suspect in police custody back home*, thought Jana. It felt good to have a challenging assignment again and be able to use her expertise and experience where it mattered.

The monastery had seen better days. Years of neglect had taken its toll. The roof of the bell tower had all but collapsed and a whole wing had been closed off years ago after a fire. What was left of the crumbling monastery was used to house the homeless and the destitute, and the nuns did their best with the little they had to look after the poor souls left in their care.

The nun at the gate spoke briefly to Hoffmeister's lawyer and pointed to a small courtyard overgrown with all kinds of weeds. At first, Jana thought there must be some mistake. The man who sat in the cane chair in front of a weather-beaten statue of the Madonna with a missing arm in no way resembled the suave Don Antonio she had met in the fashionable Buenos Aires tango club four years earlier. Gone were the good looks, the sharp clothes, the confidence and the arrogance. What Jana saw was a defeated shell of a man in his nineties with one foot in the grave. However, as she was soon to find out, looks can be deceptive.

As Jana came closer, the man took off his straw hat and looked up. 'Good afternoon, Miss Gonski,' he said. 'I hope you've been practising the tango steps I taught you.' As soon as Jana heard his voice, she knew it was Hoffmeister. The voice hadn't changed at all; nor had his mind. Hoffmeister was as lucid and alert as she remembered. 'Please forgive me if I don't get up.' Hoffmeister pointed to his legs and shrugged. 'As you can see, the past few years haven't been kind to me. But no matter; you didn't come here to talk about that, did you? You came to talk about Dr Erwin Steinberger ...'

'That's correct,' said Jana.

Hoffmeister said something to his lawyer in Spanish. The lawyer turned to Jana and told her to set up the video equipment.

Hoffmeister watched Jana adjust the camera. 'You look well,' he said. He'd always had an eye for attractive women. 'As I told you once before, you would make an excellent dancer ...' Jana ignored the remark. 'It would seem that my prayers have been answered,' continued Hoffmeister, undeterred. He pointed to the Madonna with the missing arm standing on a pedestal behind him. 'And you are the answer to my prayers.'

Jana looked at him through the camera, adjusted the focus, but didn't say anything. She wasn't quite sure if Hoffmeister was just joking, or toying with her. She knew it would be a mistake to underestimate the old fox. 'Who would have thought that the few scraps of paper in this rusty old box could come in so handy one day?' Hoffmeister held up a small tin and smiled into the camera.

*He's sending me a signal*, thought Jana.

'Are you ready?' said Hoffmeister. Jana nodded. 'Then let's begin. What would you like to know?'

'Everything you can tell me about Dr Erwin Steinberger.'

Hoffmeister put his straw hat back on and settled into his chair. 'This goes back a long time,' he said. 'The three of us – Wolfgang, his brother Erwin and I – were close friends. We grew up in the same village in Bavaria – Berchtesgaden – and went to the same little school in the mountains. Erwin was the eldest. He knew exactly what he wanted to do when he grew up; he wanted to be a doctor. Wolfgang and I had no idea ... Erwin was a brilliant student, very bright and full of promise. Not like us. When Wolfgang and I were skiing or climbing mountains, Erwin had his nose in books. We often teased him about this, but he just shrugged and kept turning the pages.'

For the next hour, Hoffmeister kept talking about the past. He could recall dates, names and places with astonishing detail and all

Jana had to do was change tapes to keep up with him. She hardly had to ask any questions because Hoffmeister was providing a precise, chronological account of three intertwined lives.

All went well until they reached the end of the war. Then things became tricky. Hoffmeister began to fidget in his seat and asked for the camera to be turned off. He wanted to speak to his lawyer in private.

*Here we go*, thought Jana, annoyed. *Just as we are getting to the important bits, he baulks. I know what he's doing ...* Jana turned off the camera and walked away, her displeasure obvious. Anticipating something like this, she had obtained approval from Jack to increase the money should it come to that and should the information on the table warrant such a move.

After a few minutes, Hoffmeister's lawyer came over to Jana. 'I'm sorry,' he said, looking a little embarrassed. 'I had no idea this was coming. I've been asked to show you this.'

'What is it?'

'A postcard from Africa; Nairobi. It has an address, a name, a signature and a date on the stamp here. As you can see, all relevant bits have been masked with some kind of tape ... My client will tell you all about this and hand over the postcard. He says it will answer all your questions and tell you everything you want to know about Dr Steinberger and what happened to him after the war.' The lawyer shrugged and showed Jana the postcard. 'But he wants more money ...'

'I didn't come all this way to play games,' snapped Jana.

'I understand.' The lawyer shrugged. 'As you can see, my hands are tied.'

*The old bastard's cleverly manoeuvred me into a corner*, thought Jana. *He knows I'll go for it!* She didn't like it, but there was only one way forward.

Jana walked over to Hoffmeister, who appeared to be dozing in the sun. In fact, he wasn't dozing at all, but watching Jana carefully out of the corner of his eye. 'Before we go any further, I would like a straight answer to the following questions,' demanded Jana.

Hoffmeister smiled and looked up. 'Fire away,' he said.

'Did you know that Wolfgang had an illegitimate child, a boy, who was born in France in 1942?'

'Yes.'

'Do you know what happened to Dr Steinberger after the war?'

'Yes.'

'Did he escape and leave Europe just like his brother, Wolfgang?'

'Yes.'

'Do you know where he went to live?'

'Yes.'

'Did he change his name like his brother, and do you know what name he used in his new life after the war?'

'Yes.

'Do you know what he did in Kenya?'

'Yes.'

'Do you know anything about an exotic Aztec artefact, a rare crystal skull?'

'I do.'

'Do you know what happened to the boy?'

'Yes.'

Jana looked carefully at Hoffmeister before asking the next question. 'And finally, can you substantiate all this?'

Hoffmeister took his time before replying. After a while, he held up the little tin and smiled at Jana. 'I can. And it's all in here.'

'How much more do you want?' snapped Jana.

'Fifty thousand.'

'Twenty.'

'Forty.'

'Thirty. Final offer,' said Jana.

'Done! Now, let's have a little break before we continue,' said Hoffmeister. 'All I can offer you is some water, but after our little heated exchange, you may find it refreshing.'

Jana clenched her fists in frustration, but managed a little smile. 'Excellent idea. Let's do that,' she said, and sat down on the little wooden stool next to her camera. 'I only hope you can deliver what you've just promised.'

# 65

Johannes knew the only way to properly investigate the disaster was to fly straight down south and visit Alpha Camp personally. Incidents like this had to be dealt with quickly, without letting the trail go cold.

As a seasoned campaigner and pilot with many years of combat experience in hotspots around the world, Johannes believed in travelling light. In his early fifties, powerfully built with broad shoulders and massive biceps kept supple by years of pumping iron, but completely bald with an earring in his left ear and a small dagger tattooed on the back of his neck, Johannes was an intimidating man. Despite his bulk, he moved with surprising agility and grace, like a jungle cat ready to pounce. He decided to take along only one of his trusted lieutenants, Abuukar, a senior member of the notorious Al-Shabaab rebel group. Al-Shabaab was well-connected and active in the south, which could come in handy, he thought.

The light plane that belonged to HAU – a subsidiary of Blackburn Pharmaceuticals – was always on stand-by, fuelled and ready to go. Registered in the Cayman Islands, HAU was impossible to trace.

Wearing his trademark battle fatigues, side-arms and aviator sunglasses, Johannes hurried across the tarmac, climbed into the plane and started the engine. He had already radioed ahead and asked for the body of the doctor to be brought to the camp. He knew that the nurse in charge had been badly beaten during a botched interrogation session. Johannes had made it clear she wasn't to be harmed any further, as he wanted to question her as soon as possible.

Trying to reconstruct what really happened after the event was always difficult and subject to error. Conflicting versions were the norm and considerable skill and experience were needed to piece together a likely scenario. It was therefore imperative to obtain as much information as possible from eyewitnesses to minimise speculation and serious mistakes.

It was almost dark by the time the plane touched down on the narrow dirt strip near the camp. The plane was met by a group of Somali youths no older than 17 or 18, all armed with AK-47s.

Johannes shook his head. 'That's what you get when you leave kids in charge,' he said to Abuukar standing next to him. 'Did you know about this?'

'No. They shouldn't be here. I'll find out what happened.'

Abuukar turned to one of the youths. 'Where's the nurse?' he asked.

'At the camp, waiting.'

'And the body?'

'Just arrived.'

'Take us to it; let's go.'

The body had been dumped on the beach. Johannes lifted up a corner of the bloodstained tarpaulin and winced in disgust. 'Jesus, look at this,' he said to Abuukar. 'They must have had some fun with this one.' The body was encrusted with dried blood and covered in flies. The stench was already unbearable. The right eye had been gouged out and the ears were missing. The whole face was badly bruised. 'And all for nothing, I bet. I just hope we can get more out of the nurse.'

Johannes turned to one of the armed youths watching him. 'Anything found on the body?' he asked. At first, the youth didn't reply and just stood there with his mouth open.

'Answer him!' snapped Abuukar. The youth reached into his pocket and pulled out a mobile phone.

Johannes held out his hand. 'Anything else? Last chance.'

The youth reached into his other pocket and pulled out a small wallet.

'Is that all?' said Abuukar. The youth nodded and handed both items to Johannes.

After questioning the nurse for half an hour, Johannes had found out everything he needed to know and was already planning his next move. 'We have a serious problem,' he said to Abuukar. 'We must act quickly before it's too late.' Johannes held up Dr Gaal's phone. 'This has been very useful,' he said. 'I want you to go to Dadaab as soon as you can.'

'No problem. And what do you want me to do when I get there?'

'Deliver a message and retrieve something for me. We have reliable contacts in the camp?'

'We do,' said Abuukar.

'Excellent. Come.' Johannes hurried back down the beach to the body. 'Get rid of the tarpaulin,' he said. Johannes pulled his razor-sharp army knife out of his belt and knelt down in the sand. 'The poor devil hasn't died in vain after all; watch.'

Dr Rosen hadn't slept a wink. The disturbing events of the previous day kept her awake all night. Every time she closed her eyes, trying desperately to fall asleep, the dying wretches left behind in the horror camp kept whispering to her, *Don't forget us … Don't forget us …*

Dr Rosen was pacing up and down in front of her tent and kept staring at the phone in her hand. It was just after sunrise. *The left column must be the blood pressure*, she thought, looking at the photos of the charts she had taken in the huts the day before. *The next one looks like quantities of sorts. Dosage of the drug administered on the day … must be.* The date was obvious, but the last column made no sense at all. However, the saddest entry was a number; the number of the patient. No name, just a number and the patient's gender and age. *Just like Auschwitz,* thought Dr Rosen. *We haven't learnt a thing!*

'You're up early,' said Jack, stepping out of his tent.

'We must try to get away as soon as possible,' said Dr Rosen. 'I feel very uneasy. We shouldn't have left Gaal behind. I'm worried about him.'

Jack put his arm around Dr Rosen. She looked at him gratefully, the comforting touch making her feel better. 'He knew the risks,' said Jack.

'Doesn't help. Thanks for coming along yesterday. I don't think we would have made it back without you. I must get that medicine bottle away from here,' said Dr Rosen, 'and to a secure lab for analysis. That's all we have apart from these charts here—'

'And our account of what we've seen, of course,' interrupted Jack.

'And the word of an African doctor and a pirate? Do you really think that would amount to much without some concrete evidence to back it all up? About a subject people would rather forget? Think about it, Jack! At times, I feel so helpless.'

A small boy with a runny nose walked up to Dr Rosen and just stood there, eyes cast to the ground.

'What's up, little one?' asked Dr Rosen, recognising one of her young patients. Jack noticed that the boy was holding a small parcel with both hands. Without saying a word, the boy handed the parcel to Dr Rosen and then ran away.

As soon as she touched the limp parcel, Dr Rosen felt a cold shiver rippling down her neck. Something quite heavy was wrapped in brown paper tied with coarse string.

'Payment for services rendered?' quipped Jack, 'From one of your young patients? And so early in the morning?'

Dr Rosen handed the parcel to Jack, a worried look on her face. 'Would you open it for me, please?'

Jack pulled off the string, unfolded the brown paper and looked inside.

'Good God!' he shouted and dropped the parcel. Dr Rosen let out a scream and stared at the severed hand lying at her feet in the dust. The little star-like tattoos on each of the knuckles left no doubt as to whose hand it was.

# 66

Dr Rosen tried to look away but couldn't. The severed hand on the ground in front of her – so vulnerable and surreal – held her gaze like a malevolent magnet; repulsive, yet impossible to resist. But when a swarm of flies settled on the bloody stump, the spell was broken. Feeling quite sick, Dr Rosen turned and hurried into her tent. Jack took a deep breath. Not knowing what to do about the hand, he quickly kicked some sand over it and followed her inside.

'What have we done, Jack?' stammered Dr Rosen, trying in vain to calm herself. 'This is spinning out of control!'

'You and Gaal have done what's right, that's all. Remember that.' said Jack. 'However, this changes everything ...'

Somewhere in the tent, Dr Rosen's mobile phone began to ring. At first, she tried to ignore it, but in the quiet tent it sounded like a siren. She walked across to her table, picked up the phone and answered it.

'You have something that belongs to us, Dr Rosen,' said a voice speaking in a heavy South African accent, but quite slowly as if to make sure that every word found its mark. The voice sounded dreamy and distant, yet chilling at the same time, and dangerous. Dr Rosen beckoned to Jack and held up the phone. Jack walked over to her and listened.

'Who is this?' asked Dr Rosen, her voice sounding hoarse.

'You took some medication out of the drug cupboard, didn't you? Don't deny it; the nurse checked. One of the bottles is missing. She was quite certain about this ... before she died ...'

'Who are you?' Dr Rosen almost shrieked.

'We want it back,' continued the voice, ignoring the question. 'The little boy you met earlier will come to your tent in five minutes to collect it. I hope for your sake he doesn't leave empty-handed. You already know how we deal with thieves ... Five minutes.' Then the phone went dead.

'They are right here, Jack. What are we going to do?' said Dr Rosen, feeling suddenly strangely composed. Now that the danger had a voice, it was out in the open and somehow no longer so frightening.

'We stay calm and we think. How much of the drug do you need to have it tested?'

'Not much. About a thimble-full should do it.'

'Where's the bottle?'

'In my bag over there. I packed it already to take with us.'

'Bring it over here, quickly!'

'What are you doing?'

'Isn't it obvious? We'll keep a little of the stuff for ourselves and hand the rest over. Get me a small container, please. Hurry!'

By the time the little boy came back to the tent, Dr Rosen was already waiting for him outside. She handed him the bottle, gave him a biscuit and sent him on his way.

'Now, let's get out of here,' said Jack. 'Collect your stuff and meet me at the plane with Kobo. I'll get Tristan and Lola. Act naturally, as if nothing happened.'

'I did warn you about this,' said Dr Rosen.

'You did; don't worry.' Jack patted his shirt pocket with the small glass container inside. 'We'll make sure this ends up in the right hands. Dr Gaal didn't die in vain, you'll see. We'll get those bastards!'

Abuukar watched the little boy come running towards him and smiled. He could see the bottle in his hands. Johannes' instructions had been very clear: Get the drugs back, do not approach, stay in the background and observe.

Once Johannes had realised that in Dr Rosen he was dealing with a high-profile identity with influence and international standing, he changed his approach completely. He sent her a clear warning, but using violence or force of any kind would not only be counterproductive, it could easily focus the international spotlight on the whole affair and give Dr Rosen's story credibility, which was the last thing he needed.

Instead, a more subtle approach was required. He would make sure that her story, if told, would lack credibility. Without proof, the whole matter would die down and disappear from the radar of public interest and scrutiny. Macbeth had already given instructions for the camp to be destroyed immediately. The drugs and precious records had been secured and the nurses silenced. Within a day or so, there would be nothing left, and it would appear as if the camp had never existed. 'Take the wind out of her sails,' Macbeth had told Johannes, 'and soon she'll be becalmed; you'll see.'

It was highly unlikely that Dr Gaal's death would be investigated by anyone. Southern Somalia was a lawless, dangerous place. There was fighting everywhere and people died every day. Violent death was nothing unusual. The doctor was just another casualty.

Johannes had carried out his instructions to the letter. However, he made one fatal mistake. He failed to investigate the other European who had accompanied Dr Rosen. There was nothing in Dr Gaal's phone records about him, nor had the nurse mentioned him. With all the attention on Dr Rosen, Jack had somehow fallen through the cracks as just another MSF volunteer who didn't feature in the bigger picture. It was a mistake that would cost Johannes and his boss dearly.

# 67

As soon as the Fokker Friendship became airborne and started to climb, Dr Rosen began to relax. Before leaving, she had forced herself to retrieve Dr Gaal's severed hand, wrap it in plastic and dispose of it in the field-hospital bio-waste container. This hadn't been easy for her, but she owed her friend that last bit of dignity and respect. Leaving the hand where it was, to rot in the sun, was unthinkable. Dr Rosen looked down upon the sea of white tents that was Dadaab, shimmering in the searing heat below like an apparition, and sighed. She was leaving with a heavy heart because she realised it was unlikely she would ever return.

Jack turned to Lola sitting next to him. 'As we are all together, I would like to raise something important,' he said. He had earlier filled Lola in on everything that had happened that morning. Tristan had gone to the front of the plane and was sitting behind the pilot and the engineer, talking shop.

'What about?' asked Dr Rosen, turning around.

Jack pulled the little glass container with the drug they had saved out of his shirt pocket and held it up for all to see. 'This here,' he said, 'is precious. It's all we have to show for what we've been through during the past 24 hours. It's what Dr Gaal died for. This is a silent witness, a direct link to the horrors we've seen at the camp. I have a suggestion …'

'Tell us,' said Lola.

'We have to secure this at all cost and get it to a lab for analysis as soon as possible.'

'Agreed,' said Dr Rosen.

'What would you say if we were to send it to the Gordon Institute in Sydney and ask Dr Delacroix to do the job? She's eminently qualified and currently working in this very field. And most importantly, we can trust her.'

'Great suggestion, but how do we get it there quickly and safely?' asked Dr Rosen.

'We need a reliable courier we can trust.' Jack put his arm around Lola. 'I know this is a big ask ... but could you take it?'

'What? Fly to Sydney? Now?' said Lola, surprised.

'Yes. We were going to approach Dr Delacroix and ask her to become involved in Isis' case – remember? You've met her; you could talk to her and explain the situation. I have to stay here and make some more enquiries unrelated to all this. You know what about, Lola ...' added Jack. 'Kobo has offered to assist me in that and has kindly invited me to stay at his house. In light of what happened this morning, I think it would be prudent for us to split up and be seen to be going our separate ways rather than giving the impression we're acting in concert. I'm sure we'll be watched ... This has suddenly become a very dangerous game. Bettany will stay at MSF headquarters in Nairobi and see what she can do about that shocking camp and what's been going on there. I would feel a lot better if Tristan were to be well away from here. He could go with you, Lola.'

For a while, everyone sat in silence, contemplating what Jack had just suggested.

'Makes sense,' said Dr Rosen, after a while.

'Looks like it's up to you, Lola,' said Jack.

'I suppose we could do the round trip in a few days,' said Lola.

'And you and Tristan can of course stay in my apartment,' added Jack. 'Marcus and Jana are staying there as well, and so is Alexandra. *Pegasus* isn't needed here at the moment. I'll need at least a few days here to sort things out ...'

'When do you want us to leave?' asked Lola.

Jack turned and spontaneously kissed her on the cheek, the exuberant gesture bringing a much needed smile to everyone's face.

'You're blood's worth bottling, luv,' said Jack. 'Straight away, if you don't mind.'

'Funny saying, but I get the drift,' said Lola, laughing.

# 68

Kobo lived in a humble shack on the outskirts of Nairobi with his two goats, a few chickens and a dog that took a shine to Jack and wouldn't leave his side. Jack felt instantly at home, because it reminded him of the Outback. The anonymity of the place was exactly what he needed. Kobo had lived in Nairobi all his life and Jack knew that his local knowledge and vast network of contacts would be invaluable for what he had to do.

*Pegasus* had just taken off on its long haul to Sydney, and Dr Rosen had settled into her room at MSF and was already talking to overseas agencies and prosecutors at The Hague about the sinister camp she had discovered in Somalia.

At first, Tristan pleaded with Jack to be allowed to stay. However, when Lola hinted at further flying instructions and the possibility of holding the controls along the way, Tristan was ready to go.

'Not a word of this to Katerina, you hear?' Jack reminded his young charge. 'This is strictly secret men's business. At least for now; is that understood? If she finds out I'm letting you fly halfway round the world by yourself, I'll be dead meat. You want me to stay alive don't you, mate?'

After a tight man-hug, Tristan was on his way.

Kobo, an excellent cook, grew all his own vegetables. He was busily preparing dinner in the tiny kitchen and swaying to the beat of African music blaring out of the tinny speakers of his vintage transistor radio on the windowsill. The mouth-watering aroma of a curry simmering on the stove filled the air with the promise of an excellent meal to come.

Jack sat on the rickety wicker chair in Kobo's veggie patch, which came right up to the back door, and opened his iPad. It was the first private moment he had managed to snare after their arrival in Nairobi.

The feverish activity to prepare *Pegasus* for departure and send Lola and Tristan on their way had taken up almost the whole day.

Jack had only briefly glanced at the video Jana had sent him from Buenos Aires during the night. It was only now that he was able to view the entire footage and give it the attention it deserved. Jack reached for the bottle of beer Kobo had handed him through the kitchen window earlier, settled back in his chair and pressed the play button.

*Is that really him?* thought Jack, as Jana's camera zoomed in on an old man with a straw hat sitting in the sun. But as soon as Jack heard the old man speak, all doubts disappeared. For the next hour, Jack sat glued to the small screen, hanging on Hoffmeister's every word. He only got up once to get his notebook from inside and ask Kobo for another beer. Then he watched the whole video again, stopping it from time to time to take notes.

*Incredible*, thought Jack. He turned off his iPad and closed his notebook, the staggering implications of what he had just witnessed racing through his head, throbbing with possibilities. The Hoffmeister interview, admittedly a longshot, surpassed all expectations. It had turned into a goldmine of events long past. *I owe you, Jana*, thought Jack, drifting back to the present.

It was almost dark, and a lot cooler. Kobo stuck his head through the open kitchen window. 'Dinner's ready,' he said. 'Come inside.'

'Do you recognise this place?' asked Jack, after Kobo had cleared away the plates. He turned the screen of his iPad towards Kobo and showed him a close-up of a postcard, front and back. It was the single most important item supporting Hoffmeister's extraordinary revelations about Sturmbannfuehrer Wolfgang Steinberger and his brother. It was the only piece of tangible evidence corroborating his story. *We bought this for thirty grand*, thought Jack. *It better be worth it.*

Kobo looked at the postcard. On the front was a picture of a large, bungalow-like building with wide stone stairs leading up to a sprawling veranda with latticework and an imposing entrance. The building was surrounded by exotic vegetation and a park-like garden.

There was a Nairobi address at the bottom. Kobo recognised the building at once. 'This is Mukuyu Lodge,' he said, pointing to the screen.

'What can you tell me about it?'

'It was very popular during the fifties and early sixties here in Nairobi. Wealthy tourists, mainly from England and America used to stay there before going on safari. It was a kind of exclusive country club for the rich.'

Jack smiled. This was exactly what Hoffmeister had said in the interview about the building on the postcard. 'Does it still exist?' Jack asked.

Kobo laughed. 'Oh no. It was pulled down long ago. We have a supermarket and a car park there today. Progress. I can show you if you like.'

Jack turned to the reverse side of the postcard. It was dated 25th October 1960, and addressed to Hoffmeister in Buenos Aires. The text, written in German, had been translated by Hoffmeister during the interview. It read:

*Dear Anton,*

*I have sad news. Life has taken a dark turn. Erwin was killed by the Mau Mau at the farm last week. We don't know exactly what happened, but the farm and the clinic have been burnt to the ground. Siegfried is safe and staying with me here in Nairobi. These are troubling times. I don't know yet what we are going to do, but at least we have the lodge. Siegfried is strong and a great support.*

*Greta*

Jack realised his next question was critical. 'Does the name Van Der Hooven mean anything to you?' he asked, watching Kobo carefully.

'Oh yes. The Van Der Hoovens were a prominent family here in Nairobi before independence. Kenyan nobility, if you like. Big landowners. They owned Mukuyu Lodge and ran safaris for rich tourists for years. Very exclusive.'

Jack's heart almost missed a beat. Once again, this corroborated what Hoffmeister had said about the Van Der Hoovens in the interview.

'So, there was Erwin Van Der Hooven, his wife Greta and Siegfried, their son,' said Jack. 'Is that right?'

'I'm afraid I don't know their names. I only know of the family. Everyone who lived here for some time knows about the Van Der Hoovens. But that's about all. We didn't mix in those circles. Africans were merely servants …'

'I understand. This has been most helpful, Kobo. Thank you. And your cooking is superb, by the way. My turn tomorrow, if you don't mind. You've got some fabulous veggies here. That has given me an idea already …'

After Kobo had gone to bed, Jack sat down at the kitchen table and watched the Hoffmeister video a third time. Now that Hoffmeister's account regarding Steinberger's brother had been largely substantiated, Jack was looking at the whole story in a different light. He decided to proceed on the basis that everything Hoffmeister had said was in fact true.

Jack slipped the rubber band off his notebook and carefully went over the notes he had made so far. He had tried to create a loose timeline by organising key events in chronological order:

1. *Steinberger, his brother Erwin and Hoffmeister grow up in Berchtesgaden, a mountain village in Bavaria.*

2. *Erwin, the bright one, is sent to study medicine at Heidelberg.*

3. *Wolfgang and Hoffmeister join the Hitler Youth, advance rapidly through the ranks and become prominent members of the Nazi Party. Wolfgang joins the Waffen SS and is admitted to the Leibstandarte Adolf Hitler, Hitler's elite bodyguard.*

*4. Encouraged by his brother, Erwin also joins the Nazi party. He meets Dr Mengele and later goes to Auschwitz to conduct controversial medical experiments.*

*5. Erwin meets Göring and becomes his personal physician.*

*6. Wolfgang and Erwin are both staying at the Ritz in Paris during the scandal of the crystal skull in 1941.*

*7. Wolfgang has an affair with Dolores Gonzales and covers up the theft of the skull.*

*8. Dolores falls pregnant by Wolfgang and gives birth to a boy in 1942.*

*9. Wolfgang and Erwin are ordered back to Berlin and leave Paris in a hurry. Wolfgang takes his son and the crystal skull with him. Mother and son are separated and Dolores never sees either Wolfgang, or her son ever again.*

*Enter Anton Hoffmeister* … thought Jack. He sat back, rubbed his tired eyes and opened another beer. The house was silent except for the dog snoring under the table. So far, most of what Jack had written down was background information already well-known to him from before and gleaned from the information recently provided by Señora Gonzales. However, all of it was relevant and preparing the way for the ultimate question; what happened after the brothers left Paris with the baby?

Jack had carefully jotted down Hoffmeister's answers to the questions put to him by Jana before she increased her offer:

**Question:** *'Did you know that Wolfgang had an illegitimate child, born in France in 1942?'*

**Answer:** *'Yes.'*

*Question*: 'Do you know what happened to Dr Steinberger after the war?'

*Answer*: 'Erwin left Auschwitz just before the collapse of the Third Reich in 1945 and made his way to Rome with his wife Greta and the boy. Erwin and Greta were a childless couple. Because Wolfgang couldn't look after the baby, they adopted the boy and brought him up as their own. Wolfgang was already in Rome waiting for them and prepared the way for their escape.'

*Question*: 'Did Erwin leave Europe just like his brother?'

*Answer*: 'Yes, he did. He stayed in the Vatican with Greta and the boy for almost a year under the protection of Cardinal Brandauer, an old friend, who made this possible by hiding them in a monastery.'

*Question*: 'Do you know where they went to live?'

*Answer*: 'Yes; Kenya.'

*Question*: 'Did Erwin change his name like his brother did, and do you know what name he used in his new life after the war?'

*Answer*: 'Wolfgang provided new identities for them all and obtained the necessary papers to back them up. The three of them – Erwin, Greta and the boy – travelled as a family under the name Van Der Hooven.'

*Question*: 'Do you know what Erwin did in Kenya?'

*Answer*: 'He bought a farm not far from Nairobi and established a clinic there to treat sick natives. However, this was only a cover. The real purpose of the clinic was to conduct lucrative medical experiments for certain Swiss pharmaceutical companies. He was testing new drugs and surgical procedures on patients without their knowledge or consent. Much the same as Auschwitz. His brother, Wolfgang, helped him set up the clinic and financed the venture. Apparently, it was very profitable.'

**Question**: *'Do you know anything about an exotic Aztec artefact, a rare crystal skull?'*

**Answer**: *'Yes. Wolfgang had it with him in Rome. He showed it to us many times. It was quite extraordinary. He said it belonged to the boy and should be given to him one day. He gave it to his brother to take with him into his new life.'*

**Question**: *'Do you know what happened to the boy?'*

**Answer**: *'Only vaguely. Apparently, he disappeared suddenly, not long after his father was killed. There were rumours that he too had been killed by the Mau Mau like his father. There were also rumours that he survived and was somewhere in hiding. No one was sure. Unfortunately, this was all too much for Greta. She died soon after. Some said of a broken heart, others that she took her own life. After that, there was no more contact.'*

Early the next morning, Kobo found Jack asleep at the kitchen table, slumped over his iPad and his open notebook, with the dog snoring at his feet.

# 69

Alexandra was an early riser, but not quite as early as Jana and Carrington. Despite having returned from Buenos Aires only the night before, Jana was already in the kitchen squeezing oranges and Carrington had gone on his morning run in the Botanic Gardens just below the apartment block.

'I just had a strange phone call from Jack in Kenya,' said Alexandra, walking into the kitchen.

Jana handed her a glass of orange juice. 'Oh? What about?'

'The connection was really bad, but he said that Lola was on her way here with Tristan. The plane had just taken off and would arrive later today.'

Jana looked at Alexandra, surprised. 'He isn't coming?'

'Apparently not.'

'How odd. Did he say why?'

'He only said that it was very important and that Lola would explain everything. Something about life and death, and apparently it somehow involves my work. That was it. He also said to tell you that Dr Rosen sends her regards.'

'Dr Rosen? Now, that is interesting …' said Jana. *Another blast from the past*, she thought. *First Hoffmeister, and now this. The Steinberger brothers and the Nazi past? What's going on here?* Jana shrugged. 'But then, we shouldn't be surprised. It's classic Jack,' she said. 'You never know what he's up to, and he likes drama and suspense.'

'He's quite a guy, isn't he?' said Alexandra.

'He sure is unique.'

'Like an incorrigible—'

'Rascal. Yes, that's it,' interjected Jana, laughing.

'What exactly is an incorrigible rascal?' asked Alexandra.

'A likeable rogue set in his ways, who knows he's a rogue and doesn't care. Does that make sense?'

'Sounds just like Jack.'

'Well then, there you have it. More juice?'

'Don't mind if I do. Thanks.'

*Pegasus* landed just after nine o'clock in the evening. Lola rang Alexandra from the airport and told her she was on her way. An hour later, she walked through the door of Jack's apartment with an excited Tristan by her side.

'A little different from our last meeting,' said Alexandra, 'but still surrounded by mystery. Last time you took Jack with you; this time you return without him.'

'A lot has happened since we last met,' said Lola, turning serious.

'You must tell us all about it,' said Carrington. 'Drink?'

'Thanks. Make it a stiff one, please.'

'I flew the plane, almost all the way here,' interjected Tristan excitedly.

'You did what?' said Jana.

'I flew *Pegasus*. Tell them, Lola.'

Alexandra shot Lola a disapproving look. 'Is that true?' she said.

'I'm afraid so. Tristan's a natural. He can actually fly the plane. Well, almost. With a little help from his friends in the cockpit.'

'Katerina will have a fit,' said Alexandra, shaking her head.

'We don't have to tell her. Please, Alexandra,' pleaded Tristan. 'This is secret aviator business. She doesn't even know we are here …'

*Jack needs his head read*, thought Alexandra. 'When I left France a short while ago, I was wishing for some excitement in my life,' she said. 'Be careful what you wish for, is all I can say!'

A couple of drinks later, Lola began to relax. She told them what had happened since they parted company at the Kuragin Chateau after that fateful phone call from Mexico. She told them about Isis' illness and the sea voyage to Boston, and explained how the clues and the twisted trail Jack was following had taken him to Kenya.

'My head's spinning,' said Alexandra. 'I'm confused.'

'Not surprising. It's all rather complicated,' conceded Lola. 'So much is going on here and only Jack knows all the facts and the bigger picture. I really think it would be better if you could wait a while. You should really hear this from him, not me. I only know bits.'

Suddenly, Lola looked quite exhausted. Overcome by fatigue, she sank back into her chair and for a while didn't say anything. Her eyes were almost closed.

'Makes sense,' said Carrington quietly, breaking the silence. 'But you still haven't told us why you've come here so suddenly.'

'A matter of life and death, I think you said, somehow involving my work?' interjected Alexandra. 'Remember?'

'Two reasons. Both involve life and death, in a way. The first has do to with this,' said Lola. She reached into her handbag, carefully pulled out a small plastic container and an envelope, and placed both items on the table in front of her. 'It's precious. According to Dr Rosen, a lot of suffering – even death – has gone into this. She wants to make sure it wasn't all in vain.'

'I don't understand,' said Alexandra, looking perplexed. 'What is it?'

'Some kind of experimental cancer drug, trialled illegally in a death camp in Somalia by a ruthless drug company,' said Lola, and pushed the container towards Alexandra. 'It's a long story. Jack and Dr Rosen discovered it accidentally. They were almost killed ...'

'I still don't understand,' said Alexandra. 'What has all this to do with me?'

'It's all in here,' said Lola. She reached for the envelope on the table and handed it to Alexandra. 'A letter from Jack to you. I'm sure he'll do a much better job explaining it all than I. Once again, I'm only the messenger,' said Lola, a wry smile creasing her weary face.

'You said there were two things ...' said Carrington, who had followed the exchange with interest.

'The second matter concerns Isis. Her operation in Boston isn't a cure. At best, it will only buy her a little more time,' said Lola close to tears. 'The tumour will return, unless—'

'Unless what?' interrupted Alexandra.

'Isis needs your help.'

'My help? In what way?'

'Professor K's work ...'

'Now you've really lost me,' said Alexandra, shaking her head.

'Please read the letter.'

'Why don't we continue this conversation in the morning?' said Carrington. 'Lola and Tristan must be exhausted. They've just flown halfway around the world to see us and deliver this.'

Lola looked at Carrington gratefully. 'I think that's a great idea,' she said, and got up.

'How long are you staying?' asked Jana.

'Not long. We were planning to return to Kenya as soon as possible to pick up Jack and Dr Rosen. Jack called me just before we landed. He sounded concerned. They have to get out of Nairobi, quickly ...'

'Did he say why?' asked Jana.

Lola pointed to the container on the table. 'It's all to do with this,' she said.

Alexandra put her arm around Lola. 'Come,' she said. 'Let me show you to your room. Tristan can sleep here on the couch. Let's see what tomorrow brings.'

Alexandra went to her room, closed the door and opened Jack's letter, his bold, familiar, handwriting bringing a smile to her face. For a while she looked thoughtfully at the little glass bottle she had taken out of the plastic container, and then began to read.

*Dear Alexandra*

*I don't quite know where to begin. So much has happened to both of us since Lola burst into our apartment in Sydney and I followed her to Mexico. However, strange as it may seem, all of it is somehow connected. I almost feel like a puppet on a string, manipulated by fate and compelled to play a part in a drama I cannot quite work out — yet. I recognise some of the other actors and parts of the plot seem familiar, but that's about all — for now.*

*Certain events of long ago, which I thought had been well and truly put to rest, have re-entered my life in unexpected ways and are closing in from all sides. There is a strange feeling of inevitability hanging over all of it, and I'm being swept along by what I can only describe as destiny … I'm not explaining this very well, am I? It's all a little too complicated at the moment and some of the pieces of the puzzle are still missing. So, instead of telling you more, I will focus on the most pressing matter that has brought Lola to you. She has very generously agreed to undertake this long journey for one reason only: to do the right thing and help the one she loves most; Isis.*

*Dr Rosen and I have accidentally uncovered what we believe to be a monstrous wrong that has caused unimaginable suffering to countless souls here in war-torn Somalia. To make sure that the world learns of this and the suffering hasn't been in vain, we need your help. But there is more, a lot more.*

*When you hear who appears to be behind it all, and where, and how it all began, you will refuse to believe what I am telling you and dismiss it all as fanciful speculation. I too have struggled to accept what I discovered, but the facts speak for themselves and cannot be ignored …*

Alexandra had to read the letter several times to make sense of it. She was desperately trying to piece together the often confusing snippets of information Jack had hurriedly crammed into the pages, to understand what he was trying to tell her.

Jumping from topic to topic – often without explanation – Jack took Alexandra on a breathtaking rollercoaster ride. He referred to Auschwitz and the horrible medical experiments. He mentioned Professor K's father and a Dr Steinberger, who ended up in Africa after the war, and suggested that she should look at the Hoffmeister video Jana had brought back from Buenos Aires. He called it a 'missile from the past, ready to explode and change the present.'

*How does Jack know all this?* Alexandra asked herself, nervously running her fingers through her hair. The extraordinary revelations, if true, were as far-reaching as they were astonishing. As Jack had correctly pointed out, the past was closing in from all sides. However, most disturbing of all, was the reference to Blackburn Pharmaceuticals and Macbeth.

*I did warn you*, wrote Jack. *Macbeth appears to be the spider sitting at the very centre of this deadly, complicated web. I don't know exactly how it all hangs together and works just at the moment, but I intend to find out; promise. I feel that I'm getting close, but it may come at a cost ... So, please consider my request in light of what I've just told you. We are poking a giant here, and poking a giant is never without danger. Huge interests are at stake. For that reason alone, I would completely understand if you don't want to get involved. Please think carefully before you decide and remember, once you come on board, there's no way back.*

Alexandra put down the letter and stared at the little glass bottle in front of her. *I have to give Lola my answer in the morning*, she thought. Then she picked up the letter and carefully read it once more. By the time she finished, she knew exactly what she had to do.

Lola could feel someone gently shaking her by the shoulder. At first, she refused to leave the cosy sanctuary of much needed sleep and tried to ignore the unwelcome intrusion, but the shaking wouldn't stop.

Lola opened her eyes. She could just make out a dark shape next to her pillow.

'*It's me,*' whispered Tristan, stroking her hair.

'What's wrong?' asked Lola and sat up. She turned on the bedside lamp and looked at Tristan.

'I saw something ...'

'Oh? What?'

'Jack and Dr Rosen ... bleeding.'

'What are you saying?'

Tristan looked at her with sad eyes. 'They are in great danger ...'

Lola knew better than to dismiss this as fanciful, adolescent nonsense. She reached for her phone and dialled Jack's number. There was no answer. 'Come here,' she said and held out her arms. Tristan bent down and Lola kissed him on the forehead. 'We'll leave first thing in the morning. Now, go back to sleep. I want you well-rested and alert; otherwise, no flying. Is that clear?'

'Absolutely,' said Tristan. Feeling better, he let go of Lola and went straight back to bed.

# 70

As expected, Kobo turned out to be very well-connected and resourceful. As he didn't own a car, he had borrowed a motorbike from his neighbour.

'What a beauty,' said Jack, admiring the vintage bike, a genuine Indian. 'I haven't seen one of these in years. My God! This is a 1943 Military Scout. An Indian classic! Would this have a few stories to tell …' Jack ran his hand over the handlebars of the powerful bike. This is worth a fortune. I know collectors who would give anything to own one of these, especially in the US.'

'You know about bikes?' said Kobo, surprised.

'A bit.'

'Want to ride it?'

'Could I?'

'Sure.'

Jack noticed that the bike had been slightly modified. A pillion seat and saddlebags had been added, but otherwise it looked original and in good condition.

Jack had retained Kobo for the duration of his stay in Kenya. He needed someone with good local knowledge to assist him in his investigation. Always short of money, Kobo willingly accepted. He was a bit of an opportunist when it came to work. However, he could turn his hand to almost anything. When he wasn't volunteering or doing odd-jobs for MSF, he would work as a cook or a guide on safaris. His extensive knowledge of the bush and engaging, easygoing manner made him popular and sought after by tour operators taking wealthy clients into the Masai Mara and Kruger National Park to see the Big Five. And most importantly, Dr Rosen had assured Jack that he could be trusted.

The surprising amount of information gleaned from Jana's Hoffmeister interview had given Jack an unexpected starting point.

He was ready to begin digging into the Van Der Hooven family history, and Kobo knew just the man to help him do it. Kobo had offered to speak to one of his cousins who worked in the local police.

'Another cousin?' said Jack, remembering the customs officer who had waved them through upon arrival, almost without looking at their papers. 'How many do you have?'

'Fortunately, quite a few,' said Kobo, laughing. 'And they all have good jobs in high places.'

'Lucky you. First stop, MSF,' said Jack. 'We'll pay Dr Rosen a visit to see how she's getting on. Especially after yesterday ...' Jack started the engine. It roared into life, making the old bike throb with power and the promise of speed. As soon as Kobo climbed on the seat behind him, Jack engaged the gear and took off, the aviator goggles giving him a distinctive, retro-look.

At first, he enjoyed the wind in his hair and the raw power of the old bike, but as soon as they approached the centre of Nairobi, the traffic became chaotic with no road-rules to speak of.

*This is scary*, thought Jack. He pulled over and stopped the bike. 'You better take over from here,' he said to Kobo. 'I'm not up to this.' Kobo grinned and they swapped seats.

Abuukar had been watching the MSF building all night. He was certain that Dr Rosen was still inside and hadn't left the compound. Hungry and tired, he kept moving his aching feet to stay awake. As he was the only one who knew what Dr Rosen looked like, he couldn't ask one of the other men to take over. However, when Kobo and Jack pulled up in front of the entrance, he instantly recognised them as the two MSF volunteers from Dadaab.

Abuukar turned to the young African standing beside him. 'Follow these two,' he said. 'As soon as they come out. I want to know where they go, who they talk to – everything. Don't lose them! Clear?' The young man nodded and got on his scooter. *Johannes will be pleased*, thought Abuukar.

Al-Shabaab, the radical Somali rebel group, had only a few young members in Nairobi. What they lacked in experience and leadership, they more than made up in zeal. Abuukar was well aware of this and allocated tasks accordingly. Al-Shabaab depended on HAU and people like Johannes for much needed cash and weapons and was therefore only too willing to do HAU's dirty work without questions asked. As allies of necessity, they complemented each other and were a force to be reckoned with. The only thorn in their side was some of the Somali pirates like Sharif, who had taken up the cause of the oppressed and the exploited, and troublemaking do-gooders like Dr Gaal and Dr Rosen. However, growing stronger by the day, they could no longer be ignored.

Dr Rosen was in a meeting with one of the senior MSF officials and sent word to Jack to come back later.

'Where's your cousin?' asked Jack, stepping into the searing sun outside.

'In the police station just around the corner,' he said. 'Let's go and talk to him.'

'Why exactly are we talking to a police officer?'

'He's much more than that; you'll see,' said Kobo, smiling.

Kobo had prepared the way. His cousin knew all about Jack and who he was. He was obviously delighted to make the acquaintance of a famous, best-selling international author who had arrived on a private jet, and was only too pleased to help.

'The Van Der Hoovens were a very powerful and influential family here in Kenya, especially before independence,' said Kobo's cousin, Rahim, a senior police officer approaching the end of his career. He worked in administration and was also an amateur historian who had written a book – *Thorny Road to Freedom* – about Kenya's long and bloody struggle for independence. 'They owned a lot of farmland and employed hundreds of Africans. In many ways, they pioneered safaris as we know them today,' said Rahim.

'When Erwin Van Der Hooven was killed by the Mau Mau in 1960, things began to change. He had been the driver behind everything the Van Der Hooven's had achieved and stood for. His death was seen as a great triumph for the Mau Mau and the independence movement at the time. It was held up as a victory against foreign landowners and colonial oppression, but there was a lot more to it than that ...'

Jack looked stunned. Kobo's cousin had turned out to be an almost inexhaustible source of information regarding the Van Der Hoovens. They featured prominently in his book as key players on Kenya's bumpy road to independence.

'I'm particularly interested in his son, Siegfried Van Der Hooven,' said Jack, watching the fascinating man sitting behind the desk with interest.

'That's quite a sad story,' said Rahim.

'In what way?'

'After his father was killed, Siegfried – then only about 18 – found himself as head of the family and at the helm of its vast business interests. He was an only child, you see. He was certainly thrown in at the deep end.'

'What about his mother? Didn't she step in?'

'No. Greta Van Der Hooven somehow always stayed in the background. She wasn't the social type, or a businesswoman.'

'How did her son cope?'

'He was a bit of a wild boy,' said Rahim, sidestepping the question. 'He preferred the company of the natives and loved hunting. He grew up with them on the family farm, he spoke their language, knew their customs and was at home in the bush.' Rahim took off his horn-rimmed glasses and began to polish them with his handkerchief, the perspiration on his bald head glistening like tiny glass beads. 'With independence approaching,' continued Rahim, 'instead of making arrangements to get out, as many of the English landowners did, he built up the safari business. He already had quite a reputation as a hunter and adventurer, and was very popular and sought after by wealthy tourists looking for African adventure and big game hunting. All went well until the scandal ...'

'What scandal?' asked Jack, leaning forward.

'The Elms scandal.'

'What?' Jack almost shouted. Both Kobo and Rahim looked at him, surprised. 'I'm sorry,' said Jack, settling back into his chair. 'It's just that ... I didn't quite expect this. What can you tell me about the scandal?'

'Siegfried Van Der Hooven was a very good looking young man. Blond, tall, with piercing blue eyes; very dashing and gregarious. And very popular with the ladies, of all ages ... They were attracted to him like moths to a flame. They saw reflected in him everything this exotic land had to offer: excitement, danger, adventure, sex. A heady cocktail. Then one day, Lord Elms, a passionate hunter, arrived from England with his new young wife. A frequent visitor to Kenya, he had gone on several safaris with Siegfried before. Lord Elms was much older than his wife and he treated her like a pretty, spoilt child. Apparently, the moment they set eyes on each other at Mukuyu Lodge, Siegfried and Lady Elms fell hopelessly in love.' Rahim paused, and glanced at Jack, watching him intently.

'To cut a long story short ... things ended badly.'

'In what way?'

'The young couple had an affair, right under Lord Elms' nose. The whole lodge knew about it except him. Then Lord Elms was suddenly recalled to London – he already held some high office at the time – and had to leave in a hurry. Lord and Lady Elms flew back to England, but Lord Elms promised to return as soon as he could to go on the safari he had missed out on—'

'When was that, do you know?' interrupted Jack.

'Around 1962. Early, I think.'

*That fits*, thought Jack, unable to hide his excitement. 'Then what happened?' he said, hoping there was more.

'All would have been forgotten if Lord Elms hadn't returned as promised. About eight months later, he came back with his young wife, and the lovers resumed their affair ... That's when things started to really go wrong.'

'In what way?'

'One evening, Lord Elms left the gambling table at the lodge early and discovered the young lovers *in flagrante* in his own bedroom of all places. They had become reckless. There was a terrible row and Lord Elms immediately made arrangements to leave the next day and return to England with his wife. That's when things went from bad to worse.'

'How?'

'The young lovers ran away together. The next morning, they were gone. They went bush, literally speaking.'

'How did Lord Elms take this?'

'Very badly. As you can imagine, the humiliation was devastating. He knew everyone here in Nairobi; the social elite, the officials – everyone. News spread like wildfire and turned into a huge scandal overnight. However, he put all the blame on the charismatic seducer.'

'What did Lord Elms do?'

'To return to England without his wife was unthinkable. He was determined to get her back. He put a search party together and went out into the bush to find her. The whole of Nairobi was talking about nothing else.'

'What happened?'

'After a week or so, he returned with his wife and left for England the next day.'

'And Siegfried? What happened to him?'

'There's been a lot of speculation about this for years …'

'What do you mean?'

'He disappeared.'

'What? Just like that?'

'The official word was that the couple was found hiding in a native village. When the search party closed in unexpectedly, Siegfried ran into the bush and hid.'

'What, leaving his lover behind to be captured by her angry cuckold of a husband? Doesn't sound like the dashing young adventurer, does it?'

Rahim shrugged. 'However, there were rumours ...' he said.

'What about?'

'That he was killed.'

'And?'

'There was no investigation. No one spoke to Lord or Lady Elms to find out what happened. They left in a hurry and never returned. It was said that those in charge covered everything up.'

'That's it?'

'Not entirely.'

'What do you mean?'

'There was also another rumour – a persistent one – that Siegfried had been captured by Lord Elms and was almost beaten to death.'

'And?'

'But had managed to escape and was somewhere in hiding.'

'Did anyone look into this?'

'His mother desperately tried to find out what happened, but all her attempts failed and fell on deaf ears. Officialdom closed ranks. She got nowhere.'

'Did you investigate this? For your book, I mean?' asked Jack.

'No. My book wasn't about that and it wasn't something you speculated about, if you know what I mean ...'

'What happened to the mother?'

'Not long after, Greta died and the Van Der Hooven family fell into obscurity. There were rumours she had taken her own life. No one has heard anything further about Siegfried since.'

'Is there anyone you can think of who could help me find out what really happened to him?'

'As a matter of fact, there is. I came across someone during my research who was a tracker in the search party. He's quite an old man now. Perhaps he can help you. Perhaps after all these years, he may be prepared to talk. I tried ... Kobo knows him. He doesn't live far from his place.'

Jack and Kobo stood up, ready to leave. 'Do you know anything about Dr Van Der Hooven's clinic?' asked Jack, almost as an afterthought.

Rahim looked up, surprised, a worried look on his face. 'How do you know about that?' he said.

'Old rumours …'

'A little bit of advice,' said Rahim, standing up.

'Oh?'

'Let sleeping dogs lie.'

## 71

'That was quite something,' said Jack, following Kobo out of the police station. 'I'm paying you a bonus for this one.'

Kobo beamed, obviously pleased with himself. 'I told you there was more to Rahim, didn't I?' he said.

'Do you know the man he mentioned?' asked Jack.

'No, but I know where he lives. It's on our way home; come.'

Just before they got on the bike, a man walked up to Kobo and spoke to him quickly in Somali.

'What was all that about?' said Jack.

'Tell you later. Let's go.'

Kobo turned off the main road and into a narrow dirt track leading into the bush. They had left the outskirts of Nairobi and were in a semi-rural area, not far from Kobo's place. Kobo didn't notice the scooter that had also turned off the main road and was following them.

To call the humble shack a home would have been an exaggeration. Built out of all kinds of materials obviously cannibalised from abandoned places nearby, it was more like some kind of improvised lean-to propped up by the trunk of a huge tree, than a structure fit for human habitation.

Jack's spirits sank as soon as he set eyes on the frail old man sitting on the ground in front of the shack. The man had his eyes closed and appeared to be asleep. *We'll be lucky to get something useful out of this one*, he thought.

'Stay here,' said Kobo, 'I'll talk to him. I doubt if he speaks much English.'

Kobo walked up to the old man and gently shook him by the shoulder. The old man opened his eyes and looked at him, his furrowed face expressionless. Kobo sat next to him and began to speak quietly in a dialect that sounded like some kind of sing-song with lots of lip smacking. Jack stood under the tree and watched.

The old man kept shaking his head. Kobo reached into his pocket and put a wad of notes into a chipped bowl in front of the man. The old man looked at the money and shook his head again. Kobo sighed, and put more money into the bowl.

*An African Hoffmeister*, thought Jack, unable to suppress a smile. *Some things are the same the world over.*

After a while, the old man began to speak, haltingly at first, but soon he became quite animated, and even raised his hand from time to time to make a point. Kobo just sat there and listened. He only interrupted a couple of times to ask a question. Then suddenly, the old man stopped talking and closed his eyes.

Kobo put a few more notes into the bowl and got to his feet. 'Come,' he said to Jack, and together they walked back to the bike.

'Any luck?' said Jack.

'Let's go home first, and I'll tell you.'

Kobo's dog greeted Jack like a long lost friend and wouldn't leave his side. Kobo went into the kitchen and returned with two beers. 'Cheers,' he said, and raised his bottle.

'Well?' said Jack, enjoying his first refreshing sip of the cold beer. 'Are you stringing this out on purpose, or do you want to get me drunk first, before letting me down gently?'

'I have some information you'll find most interesting,' said Kobo, grinning from ear to ear. 'You saw what happened. At first, he didn't want to talk, then came the usual thing. He asked for money …'

'And?'

'Rahim was right. The old man was part of the search party looking for Lady Elms. He was a tracker. They found the couple hiding in a small native village near the ruins of the Van Der Hooven farm. Siegfried knew the chief, and many of the young men there were his childhood friends. They put up a fight, with spears and clubs mainly. The search party was, of course, well-armed and killed a number of them. Siegfried was captured, tied to a post and badly beaten. The old man was sure they intended to kill him, but some of the young men hiding in the bush managed to cut him loose during the night and helped him escape. He got away. But the old man did say that Siegfried's injuries were so severe, he doubted he would have survived for long.'

'Was that it?' said Jack.

'Yes. That's all he had to say. Obviously there must have been a lot more to it all, but he wouldn't go any further. You heard what Rahim said. There was a cover-up and I'm sure everyone in the search party was somehow involved. Lord Elms would have paid handsomely for silence. That's how things concerning whites were resolved here at the time,' Kobo added quietly.

Jack held up his empty bottle. 'I need another beer,' he said. 'This definitely deserves another bonus. Great work, Kobo!'

Jack opened his notebook and quickly looked at the entries he had made during the day. While excellent progress had been made – especially with the old man hinting at a possibility that Siegfried may have survived – Jack found himself at a dead end.

*What if he did somehow survive? Where would he have gone? How would he have lived?* thought Jack, playing with his pencil. *Not even his mother seems to have known anything about this. He must have gone into hiding. How strange …* Jack closed the notebook. *Or perhaps he just died and this is as far as we can go. Perhaps this is it …*

Kobo saw the disappointment on Jack's face. 'Why don't we take a fresh look at all this tomorrow?' he said, and handed Jack another beer.

Kobo was enjoying himself. His client had just promised him another bonus and was preparing dinner. Jack loved cooking. He had just finished chopping the fresh vegetables from Kobo's garden and was expertly cutting some chicken into thin strips.

'Preparation; it's all in the preparation,' said Jack, turning up the heat under the wok. 'Now, some lemongrass and chilli. Voilà. Almost there. Get the plates!'

'I had word from Sharif earlier,' said Kobo, tucking into Jack's tasty curry. 'You remember the man I spoke to in front of the police station?' Jack nodded. 'One of Sharif's men. Sharif took Dr Gaal's death very badly. He's already hunted down two of the culprits. Al-Shabaab, just as we suspected. But there was something else ...'

'What?' said Jack.

'The camp's gone. Torched. Nothing left. A white South African was giving all the orders. A tough guy. Mercenary most likely.'

'We must have really spooked someone big time,' said Jack.

'Yes,' said Kobo, turning serious. 'And that worries me.'

'The hand?'

'That's part of it.'

'Anything else?'

'Just a hunch, but we have to be careful.'

'Sure.'

Kobo must have sensed something, because two armed men were hiding in the thick bushes nearby. One of them had a pair of binoculars and was watching Jack and Kobo through the open window. The other was cleaning his gun.

## 72

Someone was banging on the door of Kobo's shack, and excited voices could be heard coming from outside. It was just getting light when Kobo answered the door.

Woken by the commotion, Jack sat up in his bunk in the kitchen and kept rubbing his eyes. 'What's going on?' he said sleepily.

'Something awful; come!' Kobo was getting dressed.

'What?' said Jack, looking for his jeans.

'One of my neighbours just called in about the old man we visited yesterday. He's dead. Bashed to death.'

'Jesus!'

Kobo and Jack hurried outside, hopped on the bike and raced down the lane to have a look.

The old man was lying face down in a pool of blood in front of his hovel. The back of his head had been crushed and something grey and sticky-looking was oozing out of a large open wound covered in flies. Another old man and two women stood under the tree, watching.

Jack looked at the broken bowl at the old man's feet. The money was gone. 'Robbery?' he said.

'Don't know.'

'You don't think this has something to do with our visit?'

'Not sure,' said Kobo, shaking his head. 'Let's get away from here!'

'Shouldn't we report this?'

'Already been done. There's nothing more we can do for the poor wretch.'

Kobo felt suddenly uneasy. The violent death of the old man had unsettled him. Attacks like this were rare in the neighbourhood.

As soon as he stopped the bike in the laneway outside his cottage, Kobo knew something was wrong: the gate was open. *The dog*, he thought, *where's the dog?* Without fail, Kobo's dog would come running to greet him.

Kobo ran towards the house. 'Oh no!' he shrieked. The dog was lying on the doorstep, his head a bloody mess. Kobo bent down and picked up the limp little body and cradled it in his arms. Jack had to look away. Kobo carried his dead four-legged friend into the veggie patch and put him down gently under the tomatoes. 'Let's go inside and have a look,' he said to Jack, his voice sounding hoarse.

The whole place had been turned upside-down. Empty drawers, broken glass, clothes and kitchen utensils littered the floor.

'Whoever did this must have been in one hell of a hurry,' said Jack. 'We've been away for less than twenty minutes.'

'What does that tell you?' said Kobo.

'What do you mean?'

'Someone watched us leave.'

'You think there's a connection?'

'Yes.' Kobo turned and ran outside.

Jack was looking for his duffel bag. He found it in a corner under an upturned chair, its contents strewn across the floor. 'Shit! My passport! Gone!' he mumbled. 'How could I have been so stupid?' Usually, Jack never went out without his passport, wallet, notebook and phone. It was a golden rule he never broke whenever he travelled, except that morning. In a hurry to go and investigate the old man's death, he had left his passport and notebook behind.

*Fuck! The notebook and my iPad*, thought Jack, going through his things on the floor. *This is bloody serious!* Then he remembered the last thing he had done before falling asleep on his bunk. He had gone over some of his notes and listened to the Hoffmann interview again before turning off the light. Jack went down on his hands and knees and looked under the bunk. 'Gone!' he cried out. The iPad wasn't where he had left it the night before – tucked under the mattress – and his notebook was nowhere to be seen. *Jesus!* thought Jack, and banged his fist on the floor in frustration.

Feeling deflated, he got up, went outside and looked for Kobo. He found him pulling up floorboards in the chicken coop. 'What are you doing?' he asked.

'I don't keep anything valuable inside the house,' said Kobo. 'And this is the most valuable thing I own.' Kobo lifted a long metal container out of a hole under the floorboards.

Jack recognised the brown and green camouflage markings on the box at once. *Military issue. Weapons and ammo*, he thought.

Kobo opened the chest. 'I have a feeling we'll need this.'

'Impressive,' said Jack, looking at the arsenal of automatic weapons in the chest. 'How on earth did you get all this stuff?'

Kobo grinned. 'Better you don't know. Now, which one would you like?'

Jack chose a Beretta 92FS, and Kobo took the Glock G42 Gen4 pistol, his favourite. 'That should do it for the moment,' said Kobo. He took out some ammo, closed the lid of the metal box and, helped by Jack, lowered it back down into the hole under the floorboards. Then he placed the floorboards on top and covered them with straw.

'I meant to ask you,' said Kobo. 'Where did you learn to shoot like that? The way you took out that tyre the other day was pretty impressive.'

'Better you don't know,' said Jack, smiling.

'We can no longer stay here,' said Kobo, turning serious. 'We are obviously being watched. We should split up. Safer that way.'

Jack checked his gun. 'I agree,' he said. 'We must warn Dr Rosen. And I no longer have a bloody passport! Great.'

'Least of your worries,' said Kobo. 'Let's get out of here.'

# Part V

## 'Stars, hide your fires'

The mind is its own place, and in itself
can make a heav'n of hell, a hell of heav'n.'

John Milton; *Paradise Lost*

# 73

*Calypso* had taken on fuel and provisions in Perth and was crossing the Indian Ocean on its way to Mogadishu.

Macbeth controlled his impatience the way he always did, by keeping busy. With a worldwide, state-of-the-art communications network on board, he was never far away from where he wanted to be. Years of being confined to a wheelchair had taught him to become a 'cerebral man'. For him, action had long ago been replaced by mental activity. Being in control and a step ahead of the game was the reward for patience, and a disciplined mind operating without the usual distractions.

Macbeth opened the modified door of his stateroom, pushed his wheelchair out onto his private deck and watched the sunrise. This was his favourite time. He did most of his best thinking by watching the horizon bob up and down, and feeling the cool, salty air tingle on his face. There were few sensual pleasures in a life as restricted and confined as his.

Johannes had just reported in with some astonishing news. As expected, he had carried out his instructions to the letter: Alpha Camp was no more. Anyone who had anything to do with the project in the south had either been removed, or silenced. The clumsy, violent murder of the local doctor by the inexperienced young rebels had been blamed on fighting between local warlords.

All that had been the easy part; dealing with Dr Rosen and this new, unexpected development was a different challenge altogether. However, Macbeth had to admit that Johannes and his men had already shown some remarkable initiative in tackling the problem.

Macbeth looked at the bundle of pages that had just been emailed to the ship by Johannes from the HAU base in Mogadishu. The first two pages were photographs of an Australian passport of someone called Jackson Hannibal Rogan, journalist, born in Brisbane on 11th

November 1968. *That's one birthday easy to remember*, thought Macbeth. *A Scorpio born on Armistice Day.* The rest of the email consisted of a bundle of handwritten pages scanned from some kind of notebook. The brief message from Johannes was factual and to the point as usual:

*We kept Dr Rosen under surveillance in Nairobi as instructed. She received a visit from the two MSF volunteers who accompanied her to Alpha Camp. They were also placed under surveillance.*

*One of them is a local African known as 'Kobo' who works for MSF, the other a European called Jackson Rogan, a journalist. Rogan is staying in Kobo's house on the outskirts of Nairobi. We have been able to search the house in their absence to find out more about them, and have secured Rogan's passport, iPad and a notebook. Nothing else was taken. The relevant material has been scanned and is attached.*

*We thought the notebook could throw some light on Rogan's activities, as it appears to contain specific references to people, times, dates and places. The passport speaks for itself. Mr Rogan isn't going to travel far any time soon without it. The originals are here in Mogadishu.*

*I await your further instructions.*

The only thing Johannes didn't mention in his email was the old man's murder. He knew his boss wouldn't approve of what happened. Not because of the violence, but because he preferred a more careful, subtle approach. Macbeth hated anything that attracted unwanted attention. In the scheme of things, reasoned Johannes, it was highly unlikely he would ever find out.

Macbeth tucked the bundle of papers into the side of his wheelchair and buzzed his assistant. Carlotta appeared almost at once.

'Find out everything you can about this man.' Macbeth handed Carlotta the two pages of Rogan's passport. 'Same way you investigated

Dr Rosen. Surf the Net, use contacts; every detail is important here. I want to know everything about Mr Jackson Hannibal Rogan you can find.'

For the next hour, Macbeth immersed himself in the material received from Johannes.

He could feel something strange and sinister reaching out towards him from the past. People and places he hadn't thought of in years suddenly came to mind for no apparent reason. The notations in Rogan's notebook were pieces of an intriguing puzzle, which obviously had meaning and importance only to Rogan. Yet there were references and suggested links that somehow resonated with Macbeth, subconsciously at first, but becoming clearer and more meaningful the more he read.

The real shock came when he turned to the page with the Hoffmeister interview questions and answers. At times, Rogan's handwriting was difficult to decipher and the text hard to follow due to numerous changes and deletions. Macbeth had to go over the questions several times to make sense of the answers. However, what he read made the hairs on the back of his neck tingle and his heart beat a little faster.

*It can't be!* he thought, reading a particular name scribbled in the margin over and over. *It's just not possible!* Yet when he read on, more astonishing revelations came to light that ruled out both coincidence, and mistake. *Incredible! What is this man investigating? And why?* Macbeth asked himself over and over. *Who is this Jackson Rogan? What does he know?*

Macbeth looked across the heaving ocean, trying in vain to calm himself. For a while, he was unable to stop his hands from shaking. He knew nothing happened without a reason.

*Rogan; Rogan; Journalist ...* thought Macbeth, *why is this name suddenly familiar?* Macbeth closed his eyes. The rocking movement of the ship always helped him concentrate. Then, out of the recesses of his complex mind, a picture materialised and floated into his consciousness. It was the cover of a magazine with a face and a name.

Macbeth focused on the face. Slowly at first, but becoming clearer with each swaying movement of the ship, the blurred face took shape until it resembled the face in the passport photo. The writing too had become legible: *Jack Rogan, Man of the Year who never gave up.*

Macbeth opened his eyes. 'That's it!' he shouted. It was all coming back to him. *The Nazi gold book. Swiss banks; hidden bank accounts; Holocaust money*, thought Macbeth.

Macbeth pressed the call button on his wheelchair. Carlotta appeared within seconds. 'I know who he is,' Macbeth said excitedly. Carlotta looked at her boss, surprised. She rarely saw him so animated. 'He's a famous author. He was *TIME* magazine's 'Man of the Year' not long ago. Get Johannes on the phone straight away, and carry on with your research. I still want to know everything you can find about our Mr Rogan.'

'Certainly,' said Carlotta. She turned on her high heels and hurried back to her office.

# 74

Kobo dropped Jack off at the Médecins Sans Frontières HQ. Located in one of the poorer neighbourhoods of Nairobi, most of the time the dilapidated building wasn't occupied at all and served more as a warehouse than an office.

Kobo had arranged to stay with one of his cousins. He suggested to Jack they meet at a quiet restaurant just around the corner for dinner that night, to talk things over.

Jack caught up with Dr Rosen in her small room at the back of the building. She was writing a report and looked tired and uncharacteristically subdued.

'What's wrong, Bettany?' asked Jack.

'No one really wants to know about this,' said Dr Rosen, the disappointment in her voice obvious. 'I spoke to all my contacts. As soon as I mention Somalia, they run for cover. The place is just too dangerous, they say. Basket case, out of control. No one wants to take the risk of hostages being taken by the terrorists, or worse. What a world we live in.'

'Well, we must have rattled someone's cage big time,' said Jack, and told Dr Rosen about the murder of the old man and the break-in at Kobo's place. 'Kobo's certain we are being watched.'

'What do you suggest we do?'

'We must get away from here. I agree with Kobo; it's become too dangerous. I just spoke to Lola in Sydney. She will get here as soon as she can to pick us up. You can come with us, of course. I think that would be the best way. Until then, we keep our heads down and lie low. Could I stay here?'

'Sure. I'm sorry I dragged you into all this,' said Dr Rosen.

'I volunteered, remember?'

Dr Rosen managed a wry smile. 'Why is it that every time I hit a low you somehow make me feel better? And I'm about as low as you can get.'

'Jana would say it's what incorrigible rascals do best.'

'Ah. That must be it. How are your investigations coming along?' asked Dr Rosen, changing the subject.

'I was doing very well for a while, but then I hit a dead end.'

'You too? Care to tell me about it?'

'I can do better than that.'

'Oh?'

'I'll show you. This is what Jana sent me from Buenos Aires; watch …'

Jack opened his iPad and turned on the Hoffmeister video.

'This is amazing, Jack,' said Dr Rosen, unable to take her eyes off the screen.

'You pointed me in the right direction. We found Hoffmeister and money talked.'

'My uncle, Erwin Van Der Hooven, here in Kenya? Incredible!'

'The story rolls on,' said Jack. 'But then—'

'Siegfried?' interrupted Dr Rosen.

'Yes. Once Lord Elms brought his wife back to Nairobi and they returned to England, the trail goes cold. You heard what Hoffmeister said. Only speculation and rumours. And it's the same here. Not surprising, I suppose. Independence came soon after and everything changed. And besides, I can't stay here any longer and dig around in the past.'

'That's it then?'

'It would appear so.'

'I'm surprised to hear you say that, Jack. Not like you.'

Jack shrugged. 'Perhaps it's for the best. I was given some advice yesterday about all this.'

'What was that?'

'Let sleeping dogs lie.'

'They can still wake up and bite you.'

Jack closed his iPad. 'True. I'll keep that in mind. Kobo said we should stay inside and only go out if absolutely necessary. He was quite worried.'

'This place is very basic. There's no food here...'

'We'll go out and grab some dinner later. With Kobo. He'll come round and pick us up.'

Abuukar looked down the quiet street. He was watching the MSF building from across the road. Everything was in place; all he had to do was wait, and give the signal when the time came.

It was almost dark when Kobo pulled up on his bike and went inside.

'This is it, guys, you know what to do,' said Abuukar to one of his men standing behind him. 'Go!'

A few minutes later, Dr Rosen came out of the building accompanied by Jack and Kobo, and began to walk slowly down the street.

Abuukar raised his right hand. Within seconds, a scooter turned into the street followed by a dark van. As the scooter approached Dr Rosen, it appeared to hit the kerb, went into a spin and fell over. A girl was lying on the road, moaning. The dark van stopped behind her and the driver got out to have a look. Jack and Dr Rosen ran towards the girl, followed by Kobo. As Dr Rosen bent down to render assistance, three men jumped out of the back of the van.

Abuukar stepped out of the shadows, pressed his gun into Kobo's back and pulled Kobo's Glock out of his belt. '*I always wanted one of these,*' he whispered in Kobo's ear in Somali. '*Stand quite still and do exactly as I tell you, understood?*' Kobo nodded. '*Watch.*'

It was over within a few seconds. Jack was hit over the head from behind and dragged into the back of the van. One of the other men pulled a sack over Dr Rosen's head, picked her up like a ragdoll and carried her into the van. The driver jumped back behind the wheel and sped off. Uninjured, the girl stood up slowly, got on the scooter and disappeared down the dark street.

'Now I'll tell you exactly what I want you to do,' said Abuukar to Kobo. 'You'll wait here for fifteen minutes. Then you'll walk into the police station around the corner you appear to know so well and report what you've just seen. You'll tell them that you were held at gunpoint and made to watch as Dr Rosen and her journalist friend were abducted by Al-Shabaab. That's all. Understood?' Kobo nodded again. 'After that, I suggest you forget all about this and get on with your life. Clear?' Kobo nodded.

'Sorry about your dog,' said Abuukar, and remember, we are watching you. It would be a real shame to see a smart boy like you get hurt. Fifteen minutes.' Abuukar withdrew his gun and disappeared into the shadows.

'Well done,' said Johannes, who had observed everything standing in a doorway close by. 'Take them straight across the border and meet me at the airfield; clear?'

Abuukar nodded. 'No problem.'

'All going well, we should be in Mogadishu in the morning, and Al-Shabaab in all the headlines around the world.'

# 75

Al Jazeera was the first to broadcast the sensational news. Tipped off by local police, the Al Jazeera correspondent stationed in Nairobi filed his report during the night. By the next morning, the news was already racing around the globe:

*Terrorists kidnap world-renown doctor in Nairobi*, read the headline. *World-renown surgeon and philanthropist, Dr Bettany Rosen, head of the Rosen Foundation, and international best-selling author, Jack Rogan, were abducted at gunpoint last night, only metres from a Nairobi police station. Al-Shabaab, a Somali terrorist group, has claimed responsibility for the brazen abduction that has shocked the world and sent shivers of fear across Nairobi …*

*Pegasus* was travelling high above the Indian Ocean on course for Nairobi. Lola was sitting at her desk and Tristan was asleep in the back of the cabin. Lola first saw the headline as a newsflash on her laptop. Not trusting her eyes, she turned first to CNN, and then to the BBC. Both carried the same story. Details were sketchy, but the gist of the report was the same: Jack and Dr Rosen appeared to have been abducted in Nairobi by Al-Shabaab during the night.

'Good God,' mumbled Lola, running her fingers through her hair. 'What a disaster!' Lola closed her laptop and went to the cockpit to find out exactly where they were. The plane was due to land in Nairobi in just under three hours.

Suddenly, Lola felt terribly alone. She had just spoken to Hanna in Boston. Isis was in Dr Greenberg's clinic being prepared for her big operation. Sir Humphrey had arrived from London and was at her side. At least that was good news, thought Lola. With no one else to turn to, she knew she was on her own. Lola sat at her desk and stared blankly out of the small window. Her mind racing, she was trying to come to terms with what had just happened and how to deal with the crisis.

Woken by something, Tristan had been watching Lola for a while. 'What's wrong?' he asked, sensing Lola's unease. Lola walked over to him and sat down on the edge of his bunk. 'Please listen carefully,' she said. 'You and I will have to be strong and deal with this.' Lola then told Tristan what she had just heard on the news.

Tristan listened calmly without interrupting. 'I sensed something like this might happen,' he said after Lola had finished, 'but I refused to accept it. How foolish of me.' Tristan saw the distress on Lola's face and reached for her hand. 'Don't worry, as your new co-pilot, I will not let you down. Now, please turn on the news and we'll watch it again together. We must find out everything we can about what happened before we arrive in Nairobi and decide what to do.'

Surprised by Tristan's measured reaction to the dreadful news, Lola looked at him gratefully. *The boy is taking control of the situation*, she thought. *How amazing.* She no longer felt quite so alone.

Macbeth found waiting always difficult. For a man used to being in control, it was torture. Unable to go to sleep, Macbeth was sitting outside in his wheelchair in the dark. *Calypso* was ploughing through the huge waves of the Indian Ocean on her way to Mogadishu, the relentless monotony adding to Macbeth's frustration. If willpower alone could have propelled the vessel, they would have arrived days ago. As it was, there was still a long way to go.

Macbeth looked again at his watch. *They should have crossed the border by now*, he thought. Johannes had sent a brief text message to the ship advising his boss that the abduction had gone off without a hitch and they were on their way to the Somali border. That was eight hours ago. Macbeth knew that the HAU plane was waiting at an airfield near the border and would take the subjects to Mogadishu. He also knew there were many things that could go wrong. Until he heard from Johannes that they had safely arrived at the HAU base, the mission wasn't complete.

Carlotta didn't sleep either. She was sitting at her desk near the phone, waiting for Johannes' call. Used to emergencies like this, she knew exactly what was expected of her – nerves of steel and the patience of an elephant. Carlotta had both.

In the stillness of the night, the ringtone sounded more like an alarm than the muted buzz it was. Johannes was reporting in.

Carlotta hurried to Macbeth's stateroom. As soon as she saw the open door leading to the deck, she knew her boss was outside. Hearing footsteps behind him, Macbeth turned the wheelchair around and faced his PA.

'Johannes just called. Everything went according to plan,' said Carlotta. 'They are in Mogadishu.'

'Thank you, Carlotta,' said Macbeth. 'Now get some sleep.' Without saying another word, he turned his wheelchair around to face the heaving sea and kept watching the moonlit horizon, a sense of euphoria washing over him like an orgasm over newlyweds.

# 76

Jack had completely lost any sense of time. Exhausted and disorientated, he could barely move, the back of his head throbbing with excruciating pain. His hands and feet were swollen and hurting and the rope around his wrists and neck cut into his chafed skin, but worse by far was the raging thirst clawing at his parched throat.

They had been on the go for days it seemed. People around him were speaking in a strange tongue he couldn't understand. He couldn't see them either because he had been blindfolded since regaining consciousness after the abduction. Bruised all over, Jack had been tossed around for hours in the back of the van. Then came a plane ride followed by another uncomfortable trip in a van. More bruises. Finally, Jack was being dragged along by the rope tied around his neck like an exhausted dog on a leash, about to be put down.

Kobo was waiting impatiently for *Pegasus* to land. He knew every minute counted. His cousin had alerted him to the plane's imminent arrival. It was just after sunrise when the sleek silver bird touched down in Nairobi and began to taxi towards the terminal.

'Don't worry; Kobo will meet us, you'll see,' said Tristan casually.

'How can you be so sure?' asked Lola, the anxiety in her voice obvious. 'Perhaps he's been taken too?'

Tristan shrugged and kept preparing his duffel bag. 'Just know.'

Lola was desperately hoping for some news. The international news channels kept repeating the same story over and over without adding any further information or development. News teams from around the world were on their way to Nairobi to cover the sensational story and were already arriving in droves.

As soon as the cabin door was opened, Kobo stepped inside. Gone was the broad, cheerful smile that had greeted them only a few days before. This time, the haunted look on his face confirmed Lola's worst fears. 'We have to talk,' said Kobo, 'before you go outside and speak to anyone. My cousin is giving us a little time before he comes on board to check your papers.'

Kobo quickly recounted the abduction and what he had been instructed by Al-Shabaab to do. He also had some surprising news. 'I just heard from Sharif, our contact in Somalia who took us to the camp. Jack would have mentioned him?' he said.

'The pirate? He did,' said Lola.

'He's a bit more than that. Sharif was devastated by Dr Gaal's murder and has vowed to avenge his friend. He's very well-connected in Somalia, especially in the south. He has quite a following, with eyes and ears everywhere, even in Mogadishu. This could play into our hands—'

'Does he know anything?' interrupted Lola impatiently.

'He does. As we suspected, Jack and Dr Rosen were rushed across the border into Somalia. No surprises there, but what happened to them after that is interesting.'

'In what way?'

'Apparently, they were taken to a disused airfield not far from the camp we visited the other day. The camp's been completely destroyed; nothing left. An HAU plane was waiting there. That's the interesting bit. This no longer has anything to do with Al-Shabaab, if in fact it ever did.'

'What are you suggesting?'

'The people who ran the camp are behind all this,' interjected Tristan calmly, 'that's what it means. They've got Jack and Dr Rosen.'

'He's right,' said Kobo. 'They were taken by plane to Mogadishu.'

'Do we know where they are now?' Lola asked.

'Sharif believes they are being held somewhere in the HAU compound near Mogadishu harbour. An isolated and heavily guarded place.'

'In a lawless country,' said Lola, shaking her head. Kobo shrugged.

Tristan sat next to Lola with his eyes closed. 'They are in a dark place,' he said quietly. 'There are no windows. They are alone ... Fear ...'

'Where?' said Lola, turning to Tristan. 'What can you see?'

Tristan opened his eyes. 'Water. It's close to water,' he said.

Lola ran her fingers nervously through her short hair. 'What shall we do?' she asked. 'Any ideas? We are obviously wasting our time here.'

'We should fly to Mogadishu, right away. Sharif has men there who can help us. But we have to act quickly. We must leave at once. I could come with you ...'

'What about entering Somalia? Wouldn't that be a problem? Arriving in Mogadishu in a private plane like this?' asked Lola.

'My cousin can help us there,' said Kobo, 'and so can Sharif. But they need money ... US dollars. That's how things work in Somalia.'

'We can do that. Let's hear what your cousin has to say.'

'I'll get him,' said Kobo.


Jack could hear some kind of metal door creaking close by and felt the rope tighten around his neck. Someone was pulling him forward. Jack almost fell, but managed to regain his balance. Then the rope was removed, first from around his neck, then from his wrists. The door creaked again and appeared to close behind him with a dull thud.

Silence.

Jack began to rub is aching wrists. Then slowly, he removed the sweaty blindfold. Darkness. There was nothing to see, yet Jack sensed there was someone near him. 'Anybody there?' he said, his voice echoing through the chamber.

'Yes,' said Bettany, 'it's me.' Jack could feel a hand touching him from behind. He turned around, reached out and embraced a trembling Dr Rosen.

Moments later, a blinding flash of light banished the darkness. Still locked in an embrace, Jack and Bettany instinctively closed their eyes. Then, from somewhere above came a voice, sounding chilling and distant.

'Investigating matters that don't concern you can be very dangerous,' said the voice, speaking in a heavy South African accent.

'But then, you are no stranger to such matters, Mr Rogan, isn't that so? And neither are you, Dr Rosen.'

Slowly, one at a time, Jack opened his eyes and looked around, the bright light blurring his vision. They were standing in what looked like a metal box with a steel toilet in one corner. Jack guessed it was some kind of modified shipping container. Apart from two filthy mattresses on the rusty metal floor, the chamber was empty. A bright neon tube dangled from the ceiling, its harsh light bouncing off the polished steel walls like sparks from an anvil. The voice appeared to crackle through a speaker set somewhere into one of the walls.

'Who are you?' asked Jack.

Laughter. 'I'm the one who holds all the cards and tells you what to do.'

'What do you want?'

'For now, patience will do nicely. Someone wants to meet you and talk about your notebook …'

*Ah … Mystery solved*, thought Jack. *The old man's murder, the break-in and the abduction. All makes sense.*

Johannes was a master when it came to preparing subjects for interrogation. Uncertainty, disorientation and fear were his main tools. By the time his boss came face to face with the subjects, they would be ready and only too willing to cooperate and answer questions – truthfully. Johannes would make sure of that.

'Who wants to meet me?'

'You'll find out soon enough. Until then, you'll just have to enjoy my hospitality, I'm afraid.'

More laughter. Then suddenly, the speaker went dead and the lights went out.

## 77

It was just before sunrise when *Calypso* dropped anchor in a small bay popular with local fishermen, a short distance to the south of Mogadishu. For reasons of security, Macbeth didn't like bringing the ship directly into the harbour. The long journey across the Indian Ocean from Australia had been quite rough, and the calm waters of the sheltered bay were a welcome change.

While his extensive network of connections and generous bribes did provide some level of protection, in a volatile and dangerous country like Somalia, there were never any guarantees. A lawless place was always in flux, and no one knew that better than Macbeth, who had done business in that country for more than thirty years.

The HAU compound was only a short speedboat ride away and could be reached within twenty minutes. Jan's men were providing extra security by patrolling the decks of the *Calypso* day and night, and a zodiac with two armed guards was circling the ship at all times, allowing the men to keep an eye on the shore.

Macbeth was waiting for Johannes in his stateroom. He had asked him to come on board as soon as possible to present his report. Macbeth had carefully studied Jack's notebook and could hardly wait to meet the man who was so persistently prying into his past.

Carlotta's comprehensive research had given Macbeth a clear picture of Jack Rogan, the world-famous journalist and author, and Dr Rosen, the celebrated eye surgeon and tireless aid campaigner for the underprivileged poor in the Third World.

Macbeth, a master manipulator, was used to controlling people by catching them off guard. He did this by showing them a little of just how much he knew about them and their affairs, and then kept them guessing about the rest. Uncertainty and fear can be powerful tools, which often loosened the tongue in the most unexpected ways. Interrogating people from a position of strength had always produced surprising results quickly, and Macbeth was certain that his meeting with Jack and Dr Rosen would go the same way.

The material in Jack's notebook was touching on subjects and raising questions Macbeth thought had been buried forever. Long forgotten ghosts came floating towards him out of the shadows, demanding answers and reaching out for justice and retribution. Somehow, Jack had succeeded in delving into Macbeth's past life like no one else before. Many had tried, but none had succeeded. Macbeth was anxious to find out just how much Jack knew, and how he had managed to uncover so many of his carefully guarded secrets. For a man living in the shadows and obsessed with privacy, this was a major concern.

Macbeth couldn't believe his luck. To have Jack's notebook in front of him was an unexpected bonus, which only added to the excitement of the moment and gave him the upper hand. He would now be able to drill into Jack's head by using his own words and ideas, jotted down by him in his personal notebook meant for his eyes only. This was a rare opportunity Macbeth intended to exploit to the full.

Thanks to Kobo's cousin paving the way with a small river of US dollars, arriving in Mogadishu had gone much smoother than Lola expected. Sharif had met them at the airport and provided a few armed men to keep an eye on the plane around the clock. He had even found some basic accommodation for them close to the harbour. After that, things turned into a frustrating waiting game.

The HAU compound was not only heavily guarded, but completely enclosed by a high fence with razor wire and floodlights. Armed guards with dogs were patrolling the grounds day and night. Getting inside was therefore impossible, but Sharif had managed to position two of his men across the road from the compound to keep watch.

Sharif had received confirmation from his network of informers that Jack and Dr Rosen were being kept somewhere in the compound. That was the full extent of his intelligence until he received a phone call from one of his men early that morning.

'I can see them,' the man said excitedly.

'Are you sure?' said Sharif.

'Absolutely. They are being taken to a boat, right now!'

Sharif quickly made another call and alerted his men watching the compound from a boat in the harbour. 'Follow them, but stay out of sight. You know what to do.' Sharif then radioed one of his trawlers standing by off the coast and asked the captain to come into the harbour to pick him up.

'We may have something at last,' said Sharif, bursting into the room. Kobo and Lola looked up, surprised. 'What's happening?' she asked.

'They've been spotted,' said Sharif. 'They are on the move. Come, we'll meet my boat at the wharf. This is what we've been waiting for. Let's go!'

Macbeth had instructed Carlotta to allocate a cabin to each of his guests, as he liked to call them, to give them an opportunity to freshen up. A change of clothes was also to be provided. This had nothing to do with courtesy, but was part of a tried and tested strategy. It was all about tactics.

After their violent abduction and the harsh treatment Jack and Dr Rosen had received in Mogadishu, their arrival on board would herald a new beginning and in some way, it was just that. Macbeth was sending a clear signal of what life could be like if they cooperated. They already knew what could happen to them if they didn't. He wanted them to believe that the outcome was somehow in their hands, which was, of course, an illusion.

Macbeth liked to think he was in complete control and pulled all the strings. However, remembering Alexandra's stubborn and, he had to admit, successful defiance, brought a frown to his face. It only lasted for an instant and he dismissed the fleeting doubt as a sentimental lapse and immediately returned to the present. He rang the bell on his wheelchair. 'Send Johannes in,' he said to Carlotta. 'Let's hear what he has to tell us.'

Jack took off his filthy clothes and dropped them on the floor before stepping into the shower. He hadn't washed in days and feeling the hot needles of water caressing his back was bliss. Jack closed his eyes and tried to focus on the extraordinary events of that morning.

As soon as he set eyes on the *Calypso* anchored in the bay, everything began to make sense. This was the same ship Alexandra had been taken to in Sydney not that long ago. She too had been abducted, intimidated and questioned. The famous ship belonged to Blackburn Pharmaceuticals, and at the helm of that empire stood only one man. A powerful, enigmatic man who reputedly lived on board and never left the ship.

All the confusing and often incomplete snippets of information Jack had recently uncovered were somehow coming together, forming a complicated, but ordered pattern with purpose and design, like the intricate web of a deadly spider. And sitting in the centre of it all – sinister and dangerous and ready to devour his prey – was Alistair Macbeth.

*Stars, hide your fires; Let not light see my black and deep desires*, thought Jack. Could this be the man behind the attack on Lord and Lady Elms? Could he be the Machiavellian mystery backer and mentor of the young charismatic Labour leader in the UK? Was he the man involved with the Mafia and the illegal dumping of toxic waste in Somalia that had caused such misery to so many? Was this the man behind those dreadful medical experiments in that horror camp Dr Gaal had discovered? Jack had to admit that considered objectively as a whole, the evidence collected so far seemed rather compelling, and it all pointed to one man – Macbeth.

However, many big questions remained unanswered, but Jack sensed that all the confusing threads would come together when he met the man himself and that, he was certain, was imminent. *Once we find those black and deep desires*, thought Jack, *we'll know the answer to the ultimate question: who is this man? What drives him? Who is Alistair Macbeth?* He also sensed he was about to face a dangerous showdown of epic proportions that could easily cost him his life.

# 78

Carlotta knocked on Jack's cabin door and entered. 'Mr Macbeth would like to see you now. Please follow me,' she said.

'A little underdressed for the occasion, don't you think?' said Jack. He pointed to his cargo shorts and tee-shirt with the Blackburn logo on the front and smiled. The clothes were much too big. Carlotta raised an eyebrow, but didn't reply. *Tough broad, this one. No sense of humour*, thought Jack, and followed Carlotta out of the room.

Macbeth sat in his wheelchair by the open door. He had spent the past hour outside on his private deck, planning his approach. He would see his guests separately first, and then decide which way to proceed. The material in Jack's notebook had unsettled him more than he cared to admit. The past was closing in from all directions and the man he was about to meet was its messenger. *Why now?* he thought. *And why this man?* Macbeth always felt uneasy when he didn't have all the answers. However, he usually knew exactly where to look and how to find them.

'Our paths have crossed before, Mr Rogan, albeit indirectly,' said Macbeth, after Carlotta had left his stateroom. He was carefully watching the man in the ill-fitting clothes standing quietly by the door.

'You are obviously referring to Dr Delacroix's abduction and her detention on this very ship not long ago,' said Jack. 'Not a good start. She was a guest of mine in Sydney at the time …'

'That's a little harsh, Mr Rogan,' said Macbeth, enjoying the exchange. He liked nothing more than a worthy opponent and Jack appeared to be promising material, just as he had expected. 'She too was my guest and we had a little chat. Just as you and I are doing right now.' Macbeth pointed to a chair. 'Please, take a seat.'

'Ah, is that what you call it?' said Jack, playing along. It wasn't easy to spar with a man who held your fate in his hands and could make you disappear with the flick of his fingers. Jack had dealt with dangerous men before, but sensed that the man in the wheelchair was in a class quite of his own. Jack saw his notebook, iPad, passport and phone on the table in front of Macbeth. He realised then that this would be a contest of wits and that his future depended on how well he played the game. But there were no rules as such, and certainly no referee. The stakes were high, especially for him, and the material in his notebook represented the cards he had to use to stay in the game. And staying in the game was essential if he wanted to stay alive.

'Dr Delacroix – a very clever and sensible lady – and I came to an arrangement,' continued Macbeth undeterred. 'I only hope that we can do the same.'

'An arrangement, you say? How very interesting ...'

'We recruit scientists like her all over the world.'

Jack smiled. 'Recruit?' he said, the sarcasm in his voice obvious. *Blackmail and intimidation wrapped in buckets of money more likely*, he thought, but held his tongue.

*This guy is good*, thought Macbeth, enjoying himself. He wheeled his chair closer to his desk and pointed to Jack's notebook. 'Fascinating reading,' said Macbeth. 'I'm intrigued. Why is a man like you interested in my affairs, my life and my past? I cannot work it out, and that bothers me.'

Jack knew instinctively that trying to deceive Macbeth could be fatal. It was impossible to guess how much he knew and where the line was he couldn't afford to cross. Therefore, telling the truth, or parts of it, was the safest way forward.

'That's quite simple,' said Jack, leaning back in his chair. 'I was given an assignment.'

'An assignment? How fascinating. Would you care to elaborate?'

Jack wanted to appear as relaxed and detached as possible. However, his mind was racing as he tried to work out the best way to approach the question and deal with the man posing it. Whichever way he looked at it, this was a huge gamble and what was needed here was a good poker face, and nerves of steel.

'As you obviously know, I'm a storyteller,' began Jack, crossing his long legs. 'So, I'll tell you a story, but this story has several big holes in it at the moment. Much is still missing. However, I'm sure you could easily fill in the gaps and I would invite you to do just that. How does that sound?'

Momentarily taken aback, Macbeth looked at Jack. He was trying to work out if the relaxed man sitting opposite was joking, had lost his mind or was in fact, serious.

'You are imposing conditions?' snapped Macbeth at last, unable to hide his incredulity and annoyance, both of which were clearly reflected in his voice.

'I wouldn't call it conditions … Curiosity. I really want to know, that's all.'

'I don't have to remind you of your position …'

'No, you don't. So, what shall it be?'

*This guy is either mad, or extremely good*, thought Macbeth. He opted for extremely good. For a while, Macbeth played with the little steel balls in the palm of his hand, the sharp clicking noise the only sound in the room.

'All right, but there are rules,' said Macbeth. 'The price of deception and lies is very high on this ship. Do I make myself clear?'

'Perfectly. This works both ways?' said Jack, watching Macbeth carefully.

*Courageous and impertinent*, thought Macbeth, *not bad*. 'It does,' he said. 'I have no time for games.'

'Good. It would appear, neither do I.'

'Then fire away, Mr Rogan. Let's see how good a storyteller you really are.'

# 79

Sharif's men had followed the HAU launch all the way to the *Calypso* and watched Jack and Dr Rosen being taking on board. The notorious HAU flagship was a frequent visitor to Somali waters and well-known in Mogadishu. Most of the crew were recruited from fishing villages along the coast and Mogadishu served as a home port. *Calypso* usually took on fuel and supplies there and rotated the crew.

The 'mother ship', as Sharif liked to refer to his modified Indian fishing trawler, had dropped anchor among a cluster of local fishing boats within easy striking distance of the *Calypso*. From the outside, *AK-47*, as the trawler was called, looked like any other working vessel with nets and fishing gear scattered all over the deck. However, this was only a cover; below deck, it was a different story. Named after the most successful assault rifle ever made, *AK-47* was a floating arsenal. The experienced crew consisted mainly of disenchanted, battle-hardened veterans of the civil war that had raged for decades and decimated much of Somalia.

Sharif stood in the wheelhouse of *AK-47* and watched the *Calypso* through his binoculars. Everything appeared quiet on board. An open tender stacked high with all kinds of supplies in boxes, barrels and crates had pulled up alongside the ship and the crew was beginning to unload the cargo.

Sharif turned to Kobo standing next to him. 'I could get you on board,' he said. 'We know most of the men making the deliveries and a couple of crew members on board as well. Mainly girls doing the cleaning and working in the kitchen. If you could slip on board and make contact with them, we could find out what's happening. What do you think?'

'Good idea,' said Kobo. 'It's our best chance.' Kobo realised he was the obvious choice. He knew Jack and Dr Rosen, spoke fluent English and as a local African, would blend in well without arousing suspicion. The delivery of supplies was often chaotic and required a lot of manual labour. Restocking the ship took hours and involved a number of different suppliers and boats with their own crews.

'Could be dangerous,' said Sharif.

Kobo slapped his friend on the back. 'What else is new?' he said. 'Let's do it.'

Sharif turned to the captain and gave an order. Moments later, the powerful engines of the trawler throbbed into life.

Tristan had befriended Baashi, one of the young African deckhands, who had proudly taken him on a tour below to show him the weapons carried on board.

'We mainly use AK-47s,' said the young man, handing Tristan a gun. 'It's a little heavy, but very reliable. It fires every time. That's why our boat is named after it. Did you know that the AK-47 is on the Hezbollah flag?'

'No, I didn't,' said Tristan, handing the gun back. 'What are these?'

'RPGs – rocket propelled grenades. Maximum range five hundred metres, but you can easily take out a Humvee with these little beauties, or blow a very big hole into the side of a ship … very effective.'

'And what's this?' asked Tristan.

'Mortars. Russian, 82mm. They have a range of four thousand one hundred metres and a casualty radius of thirty metres in the open, and eighteen metres for troops on the ground. You could wipe out the whole bridge of the *Calypso* from right here.'

'Wow!' said Tristan, impressed. 'Have you been in any fighting yourself?'

Baashi grinned. 'I have,' he said proudly, and pointed to a long scar on his left arm.

Lola stepped into the wheelhouse. 'What's going on? Why are we returning to the harbour?'

'Because we have a plan,' said Kobo, smiling.

'What plan?'

Kobo pointed to the *Calypso*. 'I am going on board ...'

'The *Calypso*?'

'Yes. Sharif believes we have to act quickly. *Calypso* never stays in the port for long. Once she returns to sea, we'll lose her.'

'How will you get on board?' asked Lola.

'Easy. I will deliver some groceries to the ship. Trust me; it'll work. We know all the right people.'

Lola looked sceptical. Kobo took her aside. 'Are you sure you're up to this?' he asked, lowering his voice.

'What do you mean?'

'This could escalate very quickly ...'

'In what way?'

'Sharif has a score to settle with HAU and the *Calypso* ... He's a determined man and so are all the men around him. They are used to taking huge risks. And this boat is armed to the teeth. It could easily take out the *Calypso* ...'

'Come on ...' Lola shook her head.

'I'm deadly serious.'

'But Jack and Dr Rosen are on the ship.'

'I understand that, and so does Sharif; don't worry. You know what was going on at the camp I visited with Jack and Dr Rosen?'

'Yes, of course; Jack told me.'

'That's only part of the story.'

'Oh?'

'There are two more camps just like it along the coast. From time to time, patients from each of the camps were taken to the *Calypso*.'

'What for?'

'Further experiments. All of them were very ill and close to death. None has ever returned. The bodies were dumped at sea.'

'How awful.'

'Sharif's father was one of them. He died on the *Calypso* and his body was fed to the sharks. It was Dr Gaal who found out about this and told Sharif. Sharif took Gaal's death very badly and vowed to avenge him and his father. As you can see, this is a dangerous game and Sharif has his own agenda and score to settle. Rescuing Jack and Dr Rosen may be part of it, but I wanted you to see the bigger picture.'

'Understood. But what's the alternative?'

'Right now, I can't see any.'

'Then, what are we waiting for?'

'I was hoping you'd say that.'

# 80

Jack knew what every good storyteller knows: he had to capture his audience from the very first moment and then keep them hanging on his every word, interested and engaged. With only one daunting listener – Macbeth – as his audience, Jack knew this wouldn't be easy. There were also critical strategic considerations to think of, which made everything infinitely more complicated. Jack also knew his life could depend on how he told the story and how he 'traded' certain information to keep the man guessing, and give himself a chance to buy some time. This was going to be like running through a minefield, blindfolded.

'I was approached by a very famous rock star – Isis; The Time Machine – I'm sure you've heard of her?' said Jack. Macbeth nodded. 'She had a curious request. Isis wanted me to investigate a heinous crime ...' Jack paused and watched Macbeth watching him. His face gave nothing away. Jack couldn't read any reaction or even a hint of emotion on the expressionless face staring back at him. *Is this the man behind the murders?* thought Jack. *I wonder. Is this Lord Elms' Detego Man?*

'Isis' parents, Lord and Lady Elms, had been brutally attacked in their London home. Both died as a result of their injuries—'

'And this rock star approached you to investigate this?' interrupted Macbeth. 'Why? Why not leave it to the authorities?'

'That puzzled me too; I asked myself the same question. The answer, as it turned out, was as surprising as it was complicated. The first explanation was simple enough: Isis didn't trust the authorities to do a proper job – too many vested interests of a political kind were at stake here – she wanted an independent outsider to have a good look at what happened. Yet there was more; much more—'

'Why you? A journalist and an author? *An amateur?*' interrupted Macbeth again.

As Jack listened to the fascinatingly dangerous man in the wheelchair, something he had briefly thought of before, but dismissed

413

as too fanciful, again crossed his mind. Stronger this time, and more compelling than before, like a nagging little voice that couldn't be silenced and didn't want to let go. Images of two desperate young lovers running into the jungle, their eyes wide open with fear; the bloody face of a young man being savagely beaten; a faded postcard; Kikuyu Lodge; Kenya; the Hoffmeister video, and then a name – Siegfried Van Der Hooven, kept flashing across his mind's eye.

*Could this possibly be him? One and the same man?* whispered a little voice. *Destiny? Age fits. An invalid confined to a wheelchair? That too, could fit,* thought Jack. *My God, what if it's him? Long shot? Sure. Possible? Maybe. Worth a try? Absolutely!*

Jack made a spontaneous decision. *Flush him out,* he thought. *But how? Bait him! That's how. Arrogance and pride will do the rest.* For that to work, Jack realised he had to change focus and direction in telling his story. He was going to introduce another subject to entice his opponent out into the open. He knew this was a risky strategy, but definitely worth the gamble.

'Good question,' said Jack. 'I was about to turn down the offer, when something quite surprising happened. I'm tempted to call it an intervention of fate … I met an extraordinary woman – Señora Gonzales – in Mexico. You know her, surely.'

'Don't be absurd! Why should I?' Macbeth said, obviously annoyed.

'Are you seriously suggesting you've never heard of her?' *Unbelievable,* thought Jack.

'Do I have to repeat myself?' Macbeth shot back.

Jack shrugged, but refused to believe that Macbeth was telling the truth. Simple common sense suggested otherwise. 'The lady told me something that changed everything,' continued Jack, undeterred. 'She mentioned a name …'

'Is this remotely relevant? What name?' demanded Macbeth impatiently.

'Sturmbannfuehrer Wolfgang Steinberger.' Jack paused again, and watched Macbeth out of the corner of his eye. 'Does that name sound familiar?' he asked quietly.

*How could he possibly know about Steinberger?* thought Macbeth, his mind racing. *What is this man up to? How much does he know?* Macbeth hesitated before replying. It only lasted for an instant, but Jack had noticed it. 'Go on,' said Macbeth, his face as expressionless as before.

'Strangely, it all began with my book – *Dental Gold and Other Horrors* – as it turned out. Have you read it?'

'No.'

'Perhaps you should.'

'Why?'

Encouraged by what he had just seen, Jack decided to press on. 'Because it's all about Sturmbannfuehrer Steinberger ...' he said.

'So?' Macbeth demanded brusquely, a menacing edge in his voice.

'Please bear with me ...' Jack decided to change direction again and move away from the Steinberger subject to allow it to do its work. If it did have the relevance he suspected, then Macbeth would be unable to resist raising it again.

'MI5 seem to think the attack on Lord Elms and his wife was somehow connected with his work,' said Jack. 'Lord Elms was investigating something quite specific at the time he was killed—'

'This is becoming tedious,' interrupted Macbeth.

'You think so? Lord Elms was looking into the illegal dumping of toxic waste, right here in Somalia twenty or so years ago, which made certain people very rich.'

'So?'

'Would you know anything about that?'

'Should I?'

Jack hesitated for a moment. He had reached the fork in the road. Confronting Macbeth would mean crossing the line of no return and taking a huge risk. Jack was gambling with his life. He took a deep breath and said, 'Oh, I think so. MI5 are convinced that the attack on Lord Elms was a Mafia hit. And who was involved in arranging the massive illegal dumping of toxic waste?' Jack asked rhetorically. 'Operating in the shadows and conveniently solving a major problem for European governments? Lord Elms discovered who. The Calabrian Mafia.'

'Why are you telling me all this?'

'You know exactly why. "Stars, hide your fires; Let not light see my black and deep desires." Shakespeare; Macbeth. Ring any bells?'

*How does he know this too?* thought Macbeth. 'You speak in riddles,' he replied.

'Do I? It was you who arranged the Mafia hit on Lord and Lady Elms, isn't that so?' Jack pressed on. 'The only thing unclear to me in all this is, why? What was so important about all this, twenty years after the event? What else did Lord Elms discover? What were those black and deep desires? Would you care to tell me, or are you too afraid?'

'How dare you speak to me like that!' bellowed Macbeth, losing his temper for the first time.

'Facing the truth takes courage. We both know that you hold my life in your hands, yet here I am telling you all this. Have you got the courage to tell me what I'm missing in this story? I thought we had a deal, or are you too afraid?' taunted Jack again. 'Are you a coward?'

'Damn your impertinence!' shouted Macbeth.

Jack didn't respond, contempt clouding his face. For a while, Macbeth just stared at him without saying anything. No one had dared speak to him like that, ever.

Macbeth was trying to compose himself. 'All right, here's the deal,' he said calmly after a while. 'You realise I cannot let you live if you want me to reply.'

'This has been clear to me from the very start,' said Jack.

'Good. Then we understand each other. Your choice. You want me to go on?'

'Yes, I do.'

'You know what you've just done?'

'Sure.'

'You just signed your own death warrant.'

Jack shrugged. 'Then please, make it worthwhile,' he said.

'Oh, I will certainly do that. What would you like to know, Mr Rogan?'

'Everything.'

# 81

Sharif had arranged for Kobo to take the place of a crew member on the tender delivering supplies to the *Calypso*. The plan was for Kobo to slip on board and make contact with one of Sharif's men, a cook, working on the ship. There were also three young women on board servicing the cabins, who could help Kobo to find Jack and Dr Rosen. *AK-47* and her sister vessel, *AK-47-2*, had taken up strategic positions in close proximity to the *Calypso*, with camouflaged rocket launchers and mortars trained on the ship. Two zodiacs were also ready and could be dispatched at a moment's notice, with a well-armed boarding party who could reach the *Calypso* within minutes.

By instructing the captain to drop anchor in a nearby cove for security reasons instead of the main harbour, Macbeth had made a fatal mistake. He had unwittingly turned *Calypso* into a sitting duck, giving Sharif and his well-trained fighters the upper hand. They could easily take over the ship before help arrived from Mogadishu.

Kobo picked up a crate and carried it up the gangway. Two of Johannes' men, both South African mercenaries, stood on deck, watching the barefooted Africans unloading the tenders. 'Stupid kaffers,' said one of the men, 'just look at the bastards.' Restocking the ship at sea was tedious, boring and took hours.

The cook was expecting Kobo. He was organising the storage of fresh vegetables and waited for him in the kitchen.

'Put the crate over here and follow me,' said the cook, handing a box full of toilet paper to Kobo. 'Quickly; come!'

Below deck, the *Calypso* was a hive of activity with new supplies being delivered by the crew to various parts of the ship. 'This is Adna,' said the cook, pointing to a young woman pushing a trolley full of housekeeping gear along the corridor. 'One of us. She'll show you the way.'

'*Follow me*,' whispered Adna. She stopped her trolley in front of one of the cabins and busied herself with toiletries and towels. 'The

417

man you're looking for is in here. My friend will distract the guard over there.' The woman pointed with her chin to the far end of the corridor. 'When she does, I'll unlock the door and let you in; clear?'

'Clear.' said Kobo.

A young black woman was pushing her trolley towards them from the opposite direction. As she passed the guard – another surly South African – she tilted the trolley and all the cleaning gear fell on the floor.

'Stupid bitch!' shouted the guard. 'Look what you've done. Clean it up!'

As the angry guard turned his back to face the girl, Adna quickly unlocked the cabin and Kobo slipped inside, unnoticed.

'Does that answer all your questions,' said Macbeth, 'about those black and deep desires you mentioned earlier?'

Jack nodded, a stunned look on his face. *Unbelievable*, he thought, trying to come to terms with what Macbeth had just told him. While he had been on the right track all along, nothing could have prepared him for the full picture. The implications of what he had heard, if true, were staggering. And he couldn't think of any reason for Macbeth to lie. He was far too proud and arrogant for that.

'I think it's my turn now,' said Macbeth. He opened Jack's notebook. 'I have a few questions of my own.'

'Go ahead. But let me warn you …'

'Oh? A warning? What about?' asked Macbeth, surprised.

'You too are crossing a point of no return, just like I've just done.'

'You don't say,' said Macbeth, the sarcasm in his voice obvious. 'Surely with different consequences?'

'Perhaps. Knowing too little can be frustrating, but knowing too much can be devastating,' said Jack, ignoring the remark. 'It's the genie in the bottle. Once it's out, there's no way back. I think you may find this to be one of those occasions.'

'I'll take that chance,' said Macbeth.

'What would you like to talk about?'

'Sturmbannfuehrer Wolfgang Steinberger, an ancient crystal skull and a video tape.'

'Could Dr Rosen join us?' asked Jack.

'Why?'

'Because she's a major player in all this.'

'You surprise me again.'

'Oh, this is just the beginning ...'

'Very well.' Macbeth rang the bell on his wheelchair. Carlotta appeared almost at once, as usual. 'Please bring Dr Rosen up.'

'Now you've really piqued my interest,' said Macbeth after Carlotta had left the stateroom.

'You will not be disappointed,' said Jack. He sat back in his chair, trying to look relaxed but in fact, he was preparing himself for the performance of his life.

Just like Jack, Dr Rosen had also been given some fresh clothes: a pair of ill-fitting shorts and a *Calypso* tee-shirt that was much too big for her.

'I've been looking forward to meeting you for a long time, Dr Rosen,' said Macbeth. 'I've followed your work with interest for years. We have much in common.'

*If only you knew*, thought Jack.

'I doubt that very much,' said Dr Rosen quietly. 'Complete disregard for human life and suffering are far removed from what I believe in and what I do.'

'Our methods may differ, granted, but the end result is the same,' Macbeth shot back. 'You would be aware that Blackburn Pharmaceuticals has pioneered more drugs relieving human suffering and revolutionised how we deal effectively with disease than almost anyone else on the planet.'

'Perhaps, but at what cost?'

'A discussion for another time perhaps? For now, let's agree to disagree. You are here because Mr Rogan has requested you should hear what he has to say. However, you should know that he has made a fateful decision,' said Macbeth, a chill in his voice.

419

'Oh?'

'He has traded information for his life.'

'Are you serious?'

'Deadly.'

Dr Rosen shot Jack a meaningful look.

'And that may well apply to you too,' continued Macbeth, 'should you decide to stay and listen to what he has to say.'

'I'll stay,' said Dr Rosen.

'Very well. As you've already found out, meddling in matters that do not concern you can have serious consequences. And you, Dr Rosen, have been very busy doing just that.'

'Addressing a monstrous wrong isn't meddling; it's something every decent human being would do; instinctively, and without hesitation,' retorted Dr Rosen. 'But perhaps you do not understand that.'

'Tell me, Mr Macbeth, you have obviously no hesitation in pursuing your goals at any cost. You will do whatever it takes to succeed – right?' interjected Jack.

'You already know the answer to that.'

'Does that include killing your own flesh and blood?'

'I don't follow,' said Macbeth.

'You will, trust me.'

'Again, you speak in riddles, Mr Rogan.'

'Perhaps you should hear this from someone else; someone who has firsthand knowledge of the matters you are so interested in.'

'Please elaborate.'

'You've seen the references to the Hoffmeister video in my notebook? Quotations?'

'Yes, I have. And some cryptic references to Sturmbannfuehrer Steinberger and a certain crystal skull. Fascinating. These are some of the things I want you to tell me about.'

'The Hoffmeister video can do that much better than I,' said Jack calmly. 'You can watch it right now if you like. In private would be best. No distractions that way ...'

'You are full of surprises, Mr Rogan.'

'The video's on my iPad, which you have in front of you. It's quite long. My password is Eureka.'

'Very well.'

Macbeth pressed the bell on his wheelchair. 'Carlotta, would you please return our guests to their cabins?'

As soon as Macbeth was alone, he opened Jack's iPad, called up the Hoffmeister video and pressed the play button.

'Could Dr Rosen stay in my cabin for a while?' asked Jack, following Carlotta and the guard downstairs. 'Or are we to be segregated?'

'I don't see why not,' said Carlotta. She knew the cabin would be locked and there was a guard outside at all times.

'What's going on, Jack?' asked Dr Rosen as soon as they were alone in Jack's cabin.

'Macbeth is playing a deadly game. I've never come across anyone quite like him. He's an insane genius living in an upside-down world of his own making. He was behind the attack on Lord and Lady Elms, just as we suspected. He admitted it.'

'But why?'

'That's the really interesting bit—' Jack was interrupted by a noise coming from his bathroom. '*There's someone in there,*' he whispered and pointed to the door.

They watched the bathroom door open slowly and held their breath.

'*You?*' said Jack. 'How on earth—'

'*Shhhh.*' Kobo raised his index finger to his lips, and stepped into the room. 'Listen carefully; there isn't much time.'

## 82

Macbeth closed Jack's iPad and stared out the window, the last question put to Hoffmeister ringing loudly in his ear: '*Do you know what happened to the boy?*' He could also hear the answer: '*Only vaguely. Apparently, he disappeared suddenly, not long after his father was killed. There were rumours that he too had been killed by the Mau Mau like his father. There were also rumours that he survived and was somewhere in hiding. No one was sure. Unfortunately, this was all too much for Greta. She died soon after. Some said of a broken heart; others that she took her own life …*'

*Incredible!* thought Macbeth. When your whole view of the past is suddenly crushed by a different reality, emotions run wild and confusion reigns. Wolfgang, Erwin and Anton. Three voices from the past; two dead, one still alive, and reaching out to him through Jack the messenger. *I wonder what else he knows.* Macbeth turned his wheelchair away from the table and rang the bell.

As soon as they heard the key turn in the lock, they stopped talking.

'*Fifteen minutes, remember,*' hissed Kobo and darted into the bathroom. Jack looked at the door. It was Carlotta and the guard.

'Mr Macbeth would like to see you,' said Carlotta. Jack and Dr Rosen stood up. 'Not you; only Mr Rogan.' Jack made eye contact with Dr Rosen, pointed quickly to his watch, and then followed Carlotta out of the cabin.

For a man who thrived on action, waiting was torture. Sharif lit another cigarette and reached for his binoculars. Everything appeared calm and normal on the *Calypso*. Sharif put down the binoculars and looked first at his watch, and then his phone on the chart table in front of him. *He should have called by now*, he thought. *Everything is ready. We should be going now!* A successful raid relied on surprise. Sharif realised that each passing minute put the entire plan in jeopardy.

'What's wrong?' asked Lola, sensing Sharif's unease.

'Nothing, I hope, but we can't be sure.'

Then the phone rang. It was Kobo.

'He's in and has made contact with Jack and Dr Rosen,' said Sharif, relieved. 'They are ready for us. We are going in fifteen minutes!'


'You were absolutely right, Mr Rogan,' said Macbeth after Carlotta had left the cabin. 'Once the genie is out of the bottle, there's no way back. For you, or for me. You do understand that, don't you?'

'Perfectly,' said Jack. He quickly looked at his watch again. *Ten minutes*, he thought.

'What was he like?' asked Macbeth.

'Who?'

'Wolfgang Steinberger.'

'In a way, he reminds me of you. When I met him, he was Sir Eric Newman, a respected banker living in Sydney,' said Jack. 'A new name, new identity, new life. He had become a powerful and successful man, but the past had caught up with him. He was put on trial for war crimes. It's all in my book. As I said before, you should read it.'

'What happened to him?'

'He had a stroke in court in the middle of the trial. The case was closed. He died a few weeks later …'

'Do you believe in destiny, Mr Rogan?'

'Oh yes. Do you?'

'You have to ask? How else can we explain this fascinating encounter? Here, right now. You and me. We are instruments of fate …'

Jack looked at Macbeth intently. 'Then please answer this for me: *Are you Siegfried Van Der Hooven?*' he asked.

'What do you think? You must have given this a lot of thought,' said Macbeth.

'I have. Maybe I should ask another question first before I give you my answer. It's a question I've wrestled with for quite some time. I believe it's a question only Siegfried would know how to answer.'

'Go ahead.'

'How did the crystal skull end up with Lady Elms, and why?'

'Let's see … There are a number of possibilities. Perhaps the most plausible answer is this: her young lover gave it to her as a token of his love and devotion. It was his most treasured possession and he wanted her to have it.'

'Yes, that makes sense. It answers the *why*, but not the *when*,' said Jack.

'Does that really matter?'

'I think it does.'

'All right. According to your notes, the young lovers run away. The jilted husband is in hot pursuit, determined to get his wife back. He finds them hiding in a native village somewhere in the bush. The young man is caught and terribly beaten. The distraught young woman is convinced her husband has killed her lover in a fit of jealous rage and returns with her husband to England,' said Macbeth.

'So?'

'What if her lover isn't dead? What if he has somehow survived and later sends her a signal, a message only she would understand? Something personal and totally unique?'

'Interesting; go on,' said Jack.

'He sends her the crystal skull as proof that he's alive and asks her to join him.'

'Not bad,' said Jack. 'But we know she didn't.'

'Not every story is a fairytale with a happy ending,' said Macbeth, the bitterness in his voice obvious.

'I understand this is all hypothetical,' said Jack, playing along. 'But it doesn't end there, does it? Allow me to continue the story. Hypothetically, of course.'

'Go ahead.'

*Here it comes*, thought Jack, taking a deep breath. *I wonder how he'll take this.* 'The young woman returns to England with her angry, estranged husband. She soon discovers she's with child — *her lover's child!*' Jack paused, letting the bombshell find its mark.

'This is nonsense!' blustered Macbeth, almost shouting.

'Hypothetical, perhaps, but not nonsense. Please hear me out. Her husband knows the child isn't his, but a divorce is out of the question in their circles. To avoid a scandal, they pretend the child is theirs and go on living separate lives.'

'What about the crystal skull?' asked Macbeth. '*The message?*'

'I'm coming to that. When the young mother receives the crystal skull, she's both overjoyed and devastated. It tells her that the father of her child is alive, but she knows she cannot leave and join him. She has a child and a very powerful husband who will stop at nothing to save face. He has done so once before. She hides the skull and tries to forget—'

'She doesn't tell the father about the child?' interrupted Macbeth, raising his voice again.

'No. She cannot.'

'Because she doesn't love him anymore?'

'No ... *because she does!*'

'Is this still hypothetical, or do you have some proof? I have to know!' demanded Macbeth.

'If you kill me, you'll never know.'

'A clever ploy to stay alive?'

'No, it isn't.'

'I don't believe you.'

Jack glanced at his watch again. *Two minutes*, he thought.

'You keep looking at your watch,' said Macbeth. 'Why? Is time running out, you think?'

'Perhaps it is,' said Jack. 'But not necessarily for me.'

'Oh, really?'

'Let me show you something,' said Jack.

'Go ahead.'

'It's outside.'

'All right.' Macbeth turned his chair around and wheeled himself to the open door. 'What is it?'

'Do you see that boat over there?' said Jack, pointing to *AK-47*.

'What of it?'

'Let's call it a vessel of destiny. In exactly two minutes, the rocket launchers and mortars behind those fishing nets will attack your ship.'

Macbeth paled. 'You're bluffing,' he said. He pressed the button on his wheelchair, pulled a gun out of a side pocket and pointed it at Jack.

'We'll see soon enough,' said Jack.

Carlotta appeared almost instantly. 'Get Johannes; quickly!' barked Macbeth. 'Now!'

'Straight away,' said Carlotta and hurried out of the cabin.

'A little concerned?' said Jack.

'Not really.'

'You should be,' said Jack, laughing, and kicked the gun out of Macbeth's hand. The gun went off, the bullet missed. Moments later, the first grenade hit the wheelhouse. A steel door flew off its hinges and all the windows exploded, sending a shower of glass raining into the sea below. The second grenade punched a large hole into the portside of the ship just above the waterline, and started a fire in the kitchen.

The two girls in the corridor outside Jack's cabin were ready. As soon as they heard the first explosion, they went into action. One of them began to scream and turned over her trolley in front of the guard. The second hit the surprised guard over the head with a steel pipe from behind and then quickly unlocked the door to Jack's cabin. The girls pulled the unconscious guard inside and closed the door.

# 83

Jack had just picked up Macbeth's gun when Johannes burst into the cabin with one of his men. Jack pointed the gun at Macbeth and walked over to the wheelchair. 'Gentlemen, drop your weapons and kick them over here,' he said calmly, holding the gun at Macbeth's head. 'Now listen carefully.'

'Do as he says,' hissed Macbeth.

'There are two boats out there with enough firepower aimed at this ship to sink it. You've already had a little taste of what they can do. If you look outside, you'll see that a boarding party is on its way and will reach the ship at any moment now.' Jack looked at Johannes, who was obviously in charge. 'Order your men to assemble on deck, unarmed, and with their hands in the air. Clear?' he said.

Taken completely by surprise, Johannes looked bewildered and uncertain.

'Now lie face down on the floor and put your hands on the back of your heads where I can see them,' continued Jack. His time in Afghanistan as a war correspondent had taught Jack how to deal with tense situations involving firearms, and dangerous men.

Macbeth had assessed the situation much faster than Johannes. He understood the seriousness of the predicament he was in. He also understood that to get out of it, he had to keep calm and negotiate. This required diplomacy, not force. 'Do it!' he bellowed. *This would never have happened with Jan in charge*, he thought. *Too late.*

Out of earshot, Johannes spoke quickly in Afrikaans into the microphone around his neck. All of his men on the ship were radio-connected and could be reached at all times. As the enormity of what was happening began to sink in, Johannes realised that having to surrender to a bunch of ignorant kaffers one hundred metres from the shore and just a short distance from the HAU HQ would mean the end of his career. He would become the laughing stock of his comrades. He was determined to do everything in his power to prevent this from happening, even if it meant going against his orders. This had suddenly become a matter of self-preservation and honour, which went far beyond protecting his employer and following his wishes. His reputation was on the line, and for a man like Johannes, reputation was everything.

Johannes knew he could rely on his men. Their loyalty was beyond question. As the senior mercenary on board with a fierce reputation and many years of combat experience behind him, the men looked up to him. Instead of telling them to do what Jack had asked, he ordered them to take out the boarding party as soon as they set foot on the ship. He also told the captain to prepare the *Calypso* for sailing and have the helicopter ready for immediate take-off. Johannes wasn't going to let a bunch of fucking kaffer pirates take over the ship on his watch. He was preparing for battle, not surrender.

'What now, Mr Rogan?' asked Macbeth.

'Call Carlotta and tell her to bring Dr Rosen and the man in my cabin up here at once. Unharmed, or … and not a word about any of this; clear?'

Macbeth did as he was told.

'Now please call Dr Rosen. I want to talk to her.'

'Here,' said Macbeth, and handed the receiver to Jack.

Jack spoke briefly to Dr Rosen and put down the phone without taking his eyes off the men on the floor.

'What do we do now?' asked Macbeth.

'We wait,' said Jack cheerfully.


Carlotta knew something was wrong the moment she turned into the corridor leading to Jack's cabin. The guard wasn't there! She hurried to the cabin and was about to try the door, when it opened from the inside. A tall black man stood in the doorway, pointing a gun at her. 'In here, quickly,' said Kobo.

The guard, still unconscious, was lying on the bed, his hands and feet tied to the posts with bed sheets. The two girls had done an excellent job. Kobo had instructed them to stay in the cabin, lock the door and keep an eye on him. 'Any trouble, use the pipe,' he said, and followed Carlotta and Dr Rosen outside.

Macbeth's stateroom was on the upper deck, which was strictly off limits to the crew and unauthorised personnel. It only took them moments to reach it. While chaos and confusion reigned below after the surprise attack, the upper deck was deserted. Carlotta opened the door and entered, followed by Kobo, his gun at the ready.

'Sharif will be pleased when you tell him about this,' Jack said to Kobo and pointed his gun to the two men lying on the floor. 'Mr Macbeth here will enjoy meeting him. They'll have much to talk about, don't you think?'

'I doubt it,' said Macbeth.

'Oh, but you will,' Jack contradicted Macbeth.

'What on earth about?'

'His father. I believe he died right here on this very ship not that long ago … part of your medical experiments.'

Kobo picked up the guns from the floor in front of Macbeth's wheelchair and handed one to Dr Rosen. 'I know you can use this,' he said, a broad grin on his face, 'but watch these bastards like a hawk.' Then he reached for his phone and called Sharif.

Sharif's men jumped into the zodiac and were about to push off, when Lola jumped in after them. 'I'm coming with you,' she said to Sharif.

'Not a good idea,' said Sharif, holding up his AK-47. 'You have to know how to use one of these … Better stay here with the boy.'

'I've been using guns on our farm back home since I was five,' scoffed Lola, 'and I can do hand-to-hand combat like a US Marine. Can you see that helicopter over there?' Lola pointed to the *Calypso*. 'That's a Robinson R44 on the landing pad. Can you or one of your men fly it?'

'Of course not.'

'But I can. Think about it.'

'All right; hop in. And better take this.' Sharif handed Lola his handgun, a Glock. 'And keep your head down!'

'If she's going, I'm coming too,' shouted Tristan, excitedly waving his hands.

'No way, buster!' said Lola. 'You are staying right here with Baashi, and that's final! Let's go and kick some ass, Sharif!'

The boarding party from *AK-47-2* reached the *Calypso* first. The men ran up the temporary gangway suspended by steel cables from above, their assault rifles at the ready. As soon as they set foot on deck, they came under fire from all sides. Two of the men were killed instantly. Another dived overboard and two of his comrades managed to take cover and return fire.

As Sharif's zodiac approached the *Calypso*, they could hear gunfire coming from above. Sharif knew at once something was wrong. This wasn't the reception he had expected.

'Let's go,' said Sharif. He checked the grenades dangling from his belt and jumped onto the swaying gangway. 'You stay behind us,' he said to Lola, 'until we clear the deck.'

'Okay.'

The firefight on deck was fierce. Sharif's men, all experienced raiders, spread out and took cover. They knew exactly what to do. Two of the men climbed along the side of the ship just below the deck towards the bow. They would try to outflank the enemy and attack from behind. Sharif rolled one of his grenades across the deck to flush out the fighters. The grenade exploded with a bang so loud that it almost split the eardrums. Sharif could see movement near a doorway and fired. One of Johannes' men was hit in the chest and collapsed on deck. Another man tried to pull him inside and was shot in the shoulder. *Two down*, thought Sharif, and lobbed another grenade towards the door.

The fire in the kitchen was spreading. The cook and his assistants desperately tried to douse the flames, but failed. The heat was becoming unbearable and they had to retreat. When two large tins of cooking oil caught fire, the flames became unstoppable and raced towards a gas cylinder attached to one of the large stoves. The cylinder exploded.

The force of the explosion was so powerful it enlarged the hole in the side of the ship, forcing the steel plates below the waterline apart. Water gushed into the ship, flooded the floor of the kitchen and cascaded down into the engine room. With fire spreading rapidly above and tonnes of water rushing in below, *Calypso* was doomed.

Tristan heard shooting and explosions coming from the *Calypso* and could see flames leaping through a large hole in the side of the ship just above the waterline.

'The ship is on fire!' shouted Tristan, pointing to the burning vessel. The flames appeared to be spreading. The glass in two of the portholes further up exploded and hungry flames shot outside, feasting on the oxygen.

'We can't just stay here and watch, Baashi,' said Tristan. 'We must do something! I can see things … and feel …'

'There's a dingy at the back,' said Baashi excitedly. He too was disappointed. For him, having to stay behind was torture. He desperately wanted to be part of the action. 'What the hell; let's go!' he said, and quickly lowered the dinghy into the water.

# 84

'What's that?' asked Jack.

'Fire alarm,' said Macbeth. 'They've set my ship on fire! Black scum!' he fumed. 'We've got to get out of here!'

Then a voice boomed through the microphones. 'Abandon ship; abandon ship!' repeated the voice with chilling monotony as the siren tone became more urgent.

'Abandon ship, for Christ's sake!' shouted Macbeth, squirming in his wheelchair. 'Can't you hear?'

Jack looked at Kobo. 'I'll go down and try to make contact with Sharif,' said Kobo. He checked his gun and hurried out of the cabin.

Johannes realised he had to do something. To lie helplessly on the floor while the ship was on fire and his men were fighting below, putting their lives on the line, was unthinkable. He was prepared to risk his own life to change that.

Inch by inch, he moved towards Dr Rosen standing closest to him until he was within striking distance. The shrill sound of the siren appeared to be distracting everyone. Jack felt the floor tilt ever so slightly to the right and the deck began to shudder and groan under the stress. *The ship's listing,* he thought. *It must be taking on water! We're sinking!*

Then suddenly, Johannes made his move. He twisted his body to the left, grabbed Dr Rosen's ankle with his right hand and pulled it towards him. Dr Rosen lost her balance, dropped her gun and fell on top of him. Johannes put his left arm around Dr Rosen's throat in a stranglehold like a wrestler and used her as a shield. Before Jack could react and shoot, Johannes was already moving towards the door. He almost stepped on Dr Rosen's gun and quickly kicked it towards his comrade lying on the floor. By then, it was too late; Jack couldn't fire without the risk of hitting Dr Rosen.

Dr Rosen's gun was now within easy reach of the other man. He rolled to the right and picked it up. Jack saw the movement out of the corner of his eye, turned, and fired. The man's head exploded in a bloody mess just as Johannes disappeared through the door.

In the corridor outside, everything was quiet. Johannes let go of Dr Rosen's throat, hit her hard in the chest with his elbow and ran. Dr Rosen fell against the wall, hit her head and slid to the floor, dazed and bleeding.

Jack backed towards the open door to have a look. Dr Rosen was lying on the floor, blood oozing out of a cut above her left ear; otherwise, the corridor was deserted. Jack quickly grabbed her under the arms and pulled her inside without taking his eyes off Macbeth, and shut the door.

'How are you?' asked Jack.

'All right, I think,' said Dr Rosen, her speech slurred as she tried to sit up.

'Now it's just us,' said Jack, pointing his gun at Macbeth. 'What a difference a few minutes can make, eh?'

'Let's be sensible. Get me out of here and we'll settle this,' said Macbeth. 'Name your price.'

'I'll think about it, but first, I want a few answers,' said Jack.

'What do you want to know?' growled Macbeth.

'I'll tell you—'

'I have a question of my own,' interrupted Dr Rosen.

'Go ahead,' said Jack.

'I visited that dreadful camp of the dying. Terminal cancer patients one and all, receiving the same experimental drug treatment on their way to the cemetery. I saw the records. Tell me, is that how Blackburn Pharmaceuticals conducts drug trials? Causing such suffering to find a way to prevent it?' Dr Rosen looked Macbeth in the eye. 'How do you justify it, or is it all just for profit? Anything goes. Is that it? I want to understand. I *need* to understand.'

'That's confidential,' snapped Macbeth.

'Does that really matter now?' said Jack.

'I suppose not.'

'Well?'

'All right. I'll tell you,' said Macbeth.

*Calypso* was beginning to list noticeably to port and the fire was advancing with alarming speed, devouring everything in its path. Most of the crew had jumped overboard by now and were being picked up by fishing boats circling the sinking ship. The fighting, however, hadn't let up. Sharif's men were now attacking from two sides. Thanks to Sharif's grenades, they were gaining the upper hand, but due to the chaos and confusion, progress was slow.

Sharif saw Kobo first and waved. Keeping his head down, Kobo crawled across the deck to reach his friend.

'There isn't much time,' said Kobo, trying to catch his breath.

'Where are they?' asked Sharif.

'Upper deck. In Macbeth's cabin.'

'And Macbeth?'

'He's there too.'

'Then let's go.'

A speedboat full of heavily armed men – HAU reinforcements from Mogadishu – turned into the bay and raced towards the burning ship. Anticipating such a possibility, *AK-47-2* had positioned itself near the entry and opened fire with heavy machine guns. The men in the boat were torn apart by a hail of bullets just before their speedboat exploded, sending a plume of blue-black smoke high into the brilliant sky.

Lola hurried after Kobo and Sharif and caught up with them near the stairs leading to the upper deck. 'I'm coming with you,' she said, checking her gun. 'Can you hear it?'

'What?' said Kobo.

'The chopper. Someone has just started the helicopter.'

Baashi and Tristan ran up the gangway. Tristan recognised Lola's voice and caught a glimpse of her at the opposite side of the deck just before she disappeared around the corner. Dodging bullets, Tristan ran after her. 'Wait for me!' he shouted.

Lola froze and then turned around. 'You? Here? Are you out of your mind?' she hissed, barely able to speak.

'You'll need me,' said Tristan. 'Jack and Dr Rosen need us; up there. We must hurry!'

'Stay behind me; both of you,' ordered Lola and hurried after Kobo and Sharif.

As they passed one of the cabins, the door opened. One of Johannes' men stepped into the corridor and opened fire with his handgun. Sharif was hit, but only in the arm. Honed by years of hand-to-hand combat practice, Lola's reflexes worked like lightning. Before the man could take aim again and fire, she raised her gun and shot him between the eyes, blowing the back of his head away.

'You can come on our raids any time,' said Sharif, impressed. He had never seen a woman shoot like that before.

'You are bleeding,' said Kobo.

'It's nothing,' said Sharif, grinning. 'Upstairs; hurry!'

# 85

*Calypso* was sinking fast. The water had almost reached the main deck and the stern was already under water. Time was running out. Carlotta burst into Macbeth's cabin, breathless, her voice shrill. 'The chopper's waiting,' she shouted. 'If we don't leave right now, it's too late!'

'We aren't going anywhere,' said Jack calmly.

'You are crazy!' exclaimed Carlotta, her eyes wide with fear. She kept staring first at the gun in Jack's hand, then at the dead man on the floor.

'Not yet, anyway,' said Jack, 'because—' He was interrupted by a commotion in the corridor outside. 'We are waiting for this man here,' Jack finished, and pointed to Sharif standing in the doorway.

'Go! Now!' said Sharif to Jack. 'Hurry! Leave him and his death ship to me. Take the helicopter. There's room for you all. Lola and Tristan are waiting outside with Kobo. Move!'

'Lola and Tristan? Here?' said Jack, surprised.

'Yes. I've waited a long time for this … Hurry!' said Sharif.

'You can't do that!' shouted Macbeth. 'You can't leave me here with *him*!'

'Oh, yes I can. Destiny and fate, remember? In the end, we live and die by what we do, and who we are. And we both know who, and what you are, don't we?' Jack hit back. He quickly snatched his notebook from Macbeth's desk, slipped the gun into his pocket and picked up Dr Rosen from the floor. 'Put your arm around me, Bettany,' he said. 'Let's go.'

'Rogan; no!' shouted Macbeth.

Jack stopped at the door and looked at Macbeth. 'Here, have a good look. For someone who's achieved so much, you know so little. Say goodbye to your sister here, and think about the son you've never met and the woman you had killed who loved you. You've lost, Macbeth. It's over!'

Jack turned to Sharif. 'Thank you my friend, and good luck. One less villain like this in the world is something to celebrate. Until the next time,' he said, and helped Dr Rosen out of the cabin.

'Damn you, Rogan. Go to hell!' shouted Macbeth.

'You, much sooner than I, Siegfried,' said Jack, 'count on it,' and hurried down the corridor.

The noise outside was deafening. Tilting alarmingly to one side, the helicopter was ready to take off, its rotor blades churning up the air like a wild storm at sea. Lola sat at the controls, Tristan in the seat beside her. Kobo was pointing a gun at the pilot lying on the deck in front of him.

'Hurry, Jack,' said Kobo. 'Get in, before it's too late!'

'What about you?'

'I'm staying. Sharif and I have unfinished business here ...' said Kobo, grinning.

Johannes stood behind a winch and watched the helicopter getting ready to take off. Most of his men had been killed or wounded in the firefight. Those who could had jumped overboard to save themselves. Two had drowned. For Johannes, abandoning ship wasn't an option. Instead, he would stop the helicopter and kill everyone on deck. Right now.

He was so focused on what was happening in front of him that he didn't notice the man creeping up from behind. Johannes raised his machine gun and was about to pull the trigger when he felt something hard pressing against the back of his head.

'Put down the gun,' said Baashi, 'or I'll blow your head off.'

Johannes froze, not wanting to believe what was happening. His gun was pointing at Kobo. He knew he could kill him easily before the man standing behind him could pull the trigger. *Die a little later, or die now with honour and kill the fucking kaffer?* Johannes pondered. He made a split-second decision and pulled the trigger. Hit in the chest, Kobo collapsed. Baashi pulled the trigger too and blew Johannes' head apart.

'Oh my God!' shouted Jack, looking over his shoulder. He lifted Dr Rosen into the helicopter and ran back to Kobo, convulsing in a pool of blood. Kobo's eyes were turning glassy, but somehow he managed a crooked smile. '*Go, my friend,*' he whispered, blood gushing out of his mouth and a huge hole in his chest. The terrified pilot got up, ran across the deck and dived overboard.

Jack looked at the chopper. Lola and Tristan were madly waving at him from inside. Then the deck moved again and Lola had to take off to prevent the chopper from sliding sideways and turning over. Water from the stern had almost reached Jack by now and he had to wade through water to reach the chopper hovering a few feet above the pitching deck. Only an experienced pilot like Lola could have attempted such a risky manoeuvre. Leaning out of the open door, Tristan reached out to Jack, struggling below. Jack managed to climb on top of one of the chopper's skids, grabbed Tristan's hand and pulled himself inside. Without Tristan's help, he wouldn't have made it. Lola smiled at Jack, pulled out the throttle and took off.

'There – look!' said Tristan, and pointed excitedly to the sinking ship below. Lola turned the chopper around to give them a better view. Sharif and Baashi were pushing Macbeth's wheelchair across the flooded deck towards the handrail. Carlotta ran after them, obviously distressed and gesticulating wildly.

Macbeth had been strapped into the wheelchair with some kind of chord wound around his chest and was unable to move. Now up to their knees in water, Sharif and Baashi lifted the wheelchair onto the handrail. Sharif looked up at the chopper hovering above, waved with one hand and then pushed Macbeth and the wheelchair into the deep water.

Carlotta jumped in after him. For an instant, the wheelchair appeared to float away from the sinking ship, but before Carlotta could get hold of Macbeth, the forces of the deep reached up from below and sucked Carlotta, Macbeth and the heavy chair down into the darkness.

Macbeth and Carlotta drowned well before the wheelchair sank to the sandy bottom and came to rest next to a large container full of toxic waste.

Sharif and Baashi threw away their guns, jumped overboard and swam towards the zodiac coming to pick them up. Moments later, *Calypso*'s bow disappeared below the waves and the sea was calm again.

Lola could see Mogadishu airport below. *Pegasus* was parked on the tarmac next to the main runway. She had earlier radioed ahead and told the pilots to prepare the plane for immediate departure. Ignoring the frantic instructions coming from the control tower, Lola put the chopper down next to *Pegasus* and turned off the engine. This was contrary to all safety regulations, but she didn't care. Instead, they all climbed out quickly and ran towards *Pegasus*.

'We're just about there,' said Jack, helping Dr Rosen up the stairs.

'Why is it that every time we do something together, it almost ends in disaster?' said Dr Rosen, holding on tight.

'Travelling with incorrigible rascals is like that, I'm afraid,' said Jack, almost hitting his head as he ducked through the narrow door into the plane. 'You should know this by now.'

Lola secured the door behind him and hurried past Tristan to the cockpit. 'I want to talk to you,' she said, pointing an accusing finger at Tristan. Tristan knew what was coming and was ready.

'Don't be too hard on him,' said Jack. 'Without him, I wouldn't be here.'

'And without Baashi shooting that man, none of us would have made it,' said Tristan. 'That's what I saw, and that's why Baashi and I couldn't stay behind. It was meant to be, can't you see?'

'He always has an answer, doesn't he?' said Lola, shaking her head.

'Tell me about it,' said Jack.

*Pegasus*' powerful engines roared into life and the plane began to move forward. Minutes later, they were in the air – high above Mogadishu – and then turned north heading for London, their destination.

## 86

Nothing could have prepared them for the media frenzy at Heathrow. Dr Rosen had called her contact in the United Nations from the plane and told her what happened. She was hoping to ignite some interest in the Somali atrocities she had discovered, which before her abduction, had so frustratingly fallen on deaf ears. Sensing a unique opportunity to go public with the Somali horror camp incident as part of a sensational news story unfolding across the globe, her UN contact had tipped off the media. Dr Rosen didn't mind and agreed to hold a press conference with Jack upon their arrival in London.

Jack looked at Dr Rosen sitting next to him in the plane. 'Are you sure about this?' he said, well aware of what could be waiting for them.

'I know it'll be rough going, but if it's the only way to draw attention to what's happening in Somalia, it's worth it.'

Jack nodded. 'I understand.'

'I'm sorry to drag you into this,' continued Dr Rosen, 'but I do believe we must face the media together, don't you think?'

'I suppose so. But I'll stay in the background. This is your story.'

Jack could visualise his New York publicist eagerly rubbing her hands together. 'All publicity is good publicity, Jack,' she used to lecture him. 'Remember that!'

'Will you help me deal with the press? You know a lot more about this than I do.'

Jack glanced at Dr Rosen. She looked vulnerable and a little scared, he thought. After what they had just been through, it was hardly surprising. However, Jack knew that Dr Rosen was a fearless warrior with a cause, and he was determined to help her in the battle to come.

'I think I know how we should handle this,' said Jack. He pulled his treasured little notebook out of his pocket and began to write.

'You got it back!' said Dr Rosen, pointing to Jack's familiar notebook held together with the rubber band.

'You didn't think I would leave without it?' Jack shook his head. 'No way! My iPad and phone may be at the bottom of the sea, but not this.' Somehow, Jack's easygoing manner and irrepressible humour made Dr Rosen feel suddenly better.

'So, what's the plan, Jack?'

'I'll tell you …'

Sensational news of the audacious Somali pirate attack and the sinking of the *Calypso* was already racing around the globe. Rumour that the enigmatic head of the Blackburn Pharmaceuticals empire had gone down with his ship had gone viral. This was big news. And then, to find that Dr Rosen's abduction was somehow part of it made the story irresistible.

However, Jack's involvement was still a bit of a mystery to the eager press, but it was generally assumed he had been assisting Dr Rosen in breaking the story, and that was why he too, had been abducted.

Every major news channel was trying to get a piece of the action, and the action was unfolding at Heathrow Airport with the arrival of *Pegasus*, Isis' private jet with The Time Machine's famous logo prominently painted on its sides. This alone made the story even more exciting and intriguing to the hungry newshounds sniffing a major coup.

After they were cleared by the British authorities, Jack and Dr Rosen were ushered by security staff into a hall where the press was waiting. Every major TV channel and newspaper was represented, with dozens of cameramen and journalists jockeying for position in the crowded hall.

Jack had left Tristan in Lola's care. They were ushered through a side exit to a waiting car and were already on their way to The Time Machine studios. Jack and Dr Rosen would catch up with them there after the press conference.

'My God, Jack, look at them,' said Dr Rosen. She was trying to shield her eyes with her hand from the glare of the flashes from countless cameras pointing at her. 'Did you expect this?'

'I did, I'm afraid.'

Jack stepped up to the microphone and held up his hand. He was a storyteller and he would tell the waiting press a story they wouldn't forget in a hurry.

The room fell silent and all eyes were on the man in the baggy, ill-fitting shorts and bloodstained Blackburn Pharmaceutical's tee-shirt.

'Ladies and gentlemen, only hours ago, Dr Rosen and I went through a horrific ordeal. It is only because of luck and the bravery of others we are standing here to tell the tale. And this is a tale that has to be told now. You will see why in a moment,' said Jack. Suddenly, it was so quiet in the crowded hall that all one could hear was the clicking of the camera shutters. 'However, there are conditions …'

'What conditions?' shouted someone at the back.

'I will tell you what happened to us after our abduction by Al-Shabaab in Nairobi four days ago, and how it ended. But first, Dr Rosen will make a brief statement. She will tell you about a terrible discovery we made in Somalia. We are convinced that this discovery was the reason behind our abduction and the extraordinary events that followed. As you can imagine, both of us are still somewhat in shock. Therefore, neither Dr Rosen nor I will take any questions; that will be for another time. We would ask you to respect that. And no interruptions please. Thank you.' Jack turned away from the lectern. 'Dr Rosen …'

Dr Rosen had presence. She stepped forward with confidence and adjusted the microphone, her hand shaking. *This is for you, Gaal*, she thought. *It wasn't in vain.*

'Ladies and gentlemen, Mr Rogan and I have agreed to meet with you now – moments after our arrival – because we have discovered something in Somalia the world has to know about. You are the eyes and ears of the world, and if we don't speak up, the atrocities will go on, the vulnerable and the weak will continue to suffer in silence, and the dead will have died for nothing because no one cares. And why is this so? Because no one knows, and those who should, don't want to. We are here to change that.'

Dr Rosen was a charismatic speaker who knew how to engage her audience. She spoke with a passion that had everyone in the room spellbound, hanging on her every word. She described the horrible skin diseases and deformities caused by exposure to years of illegal toxic waste dumping in graphic detail. She spoke of social destruction, hopelessness and pain of an entire generation in a way that had many an eye turn misty.

'Sad and tragic as all of this is, ladies and gentlemen, it is not the reason I am talking to you now. I'm here to tell you about something far worse: the ugly side of human nature that somehow believes the end justifies the means, whatever the cost.' Dr Rosen paused, ran her fingers through her hair and looked at something in the distance only she could see.

'It is what Mr Rogan and I discovered in a secret camp in Somalia,' she said quietly after a while, 'that brings us here. What we discovered will shock you. But what will shock you even more is to learn who was behind it all, and why.'

Dr Rosen then went on to describe what she found at the camp, and what had been going on there. She spoke of their narrow escape, Dr Gaal's violent death and how his severed hand had been sent to her at Dadaab as a warning. Overcome by emotion, she had to stop several times, before she was able to continue.

Cross knew he would be late. He was stuck in traffic and cursed the fact that MI5 had only just received word of the impromptu press conference at the airport. Aware of the potentially far-reaching consequences should Jack decide to speak about certain sensitive subjects currently under investigation, he had been instructed by his superiors to shut it down – discreetly – and without causing a scandal or embarrassment to the government.

Cross realised his career could be on the line if he failed. He had called Sir Charles and asked him to meet him at the airport as a matter of urgency. He was hoping Sir Charles would be able to persuade Jack to fall into line without causing a fuss.

The wild card was Dr Rosen. Cross had no idea how much she knew or what her involvement was in all this. However, her international reputation and standing made her a powerful voice that couldn't be ignored or easily silenced. It also made her difficult to control.

Sir Charles arrived first. He entered the crowded hall full of journalists and stood at the back. He had just caught the last part of Dr Rosen's stirring speech and the spontaneous applause that followed, when Cross tapped him on the shoulder. 'You have to stop him,' said Cross, breathless, his face flushed.

'Why?'

'We have reason to believe Mr Rogan has certain sensitive information touching on national security and is about to reveal it to the press. I don't have to tell you what the consequences would be if he does.'

'That's gobbledegook!' said Sir Charles, unimpressed.

'Will you talk to him, or do I have to arrest him?'

'What? Here? Now? In front of the press? You're bluffing!'

'I have my orders.'

Sir Charles had just heard about the sinking of the *Calypso* and the wild rumours circulating about Macbeth and Blackburn Pharmaceuticals. He was well aware of the financial turmoil that was likely to cause in stock markets around the globe. He knew of course about the abduction, but was as surprised as anyone else to find that Jack and Dr Rosen had turned up in London out of the blue and were holding a press conference.

He looked at Cross. *Macbeth and the black and deep desires*, he thought. *He suspects Jack has discovered who was behind the Elms attack, and why. That's it! Has to be! No wonder he's worried.* However, the lawyer in Sir Charles told him to be careful. 'I'll see what I can do,' said Sir Charles, and pushed past the cameramen to get to the front.

Jack had just taken the microphone from Dr Rosen, when he saw Sir Charles waving at him in the crowd.

Sir Charles walked up to Jack and took him aside. '*If you want to stay out of jail, not a word about the Elms attack and the Macbeth connection; clear?*' he hissed.

Jack nodded. 'I wasn't going to talk about that.'

'Good. Don't. *MI5 is watching!*'

As Sir Charles moved away, Jack stepped back to the microphone and continued.

Sir Charles made eye contact with Cross and nodded. Cross moved to the front with two of his men. He would pounce as soon as Jack strayed into dangerous territory. However, he was desperately hoping he wouldn't have to do that.

# 87

The door to Jack's room was open. Lola looked inside and saw that Jack had his eyes open. 'The sleeping prince awakes,' she teased and walked into the room.

'What time is it?' asked Jack, rubbing his eyes.

'Four p.m. The next day. You slept almost 24 hours. Coffee?'

'You bet.'

'Where's Bettany?'

'Next room. She's been on the phone for hours.'

'And Tristan?'

'Downstairs, with the guys in the studio. Mixing sound.'

'That'd be right.'

'Sir Charles has rung several times. He wants to talk to you – urgently.'

'I feel like I've been trampled on by elephants. I'll hit the shower. That should help.'

'You may need a little more than that,' said Lola. 'I'll get the coffee.'

Jack stood under the hot shower and let his mind wander. What happened after the news conference was still a bit of a blur. He remembered sitting next to Dr Rosen in the back of Sir Charles' car and being dropped off at The Time Machine studios. After that, it was bed; sleep; bliss.

Jack knew that exhaustion can distort reality and the mind can play tricks on you and turn off to cope. It had happened to him before, in Afghanistan. His body always responded in the same way: craving sleep. After that, he would quickly recover and return to normal. *I'm starving*, thought Jack. *Good sign*, and turned off the water.

'That's a lot better,' said Lola, who had returned with much needed coffee for Jack. 'You almost look like yourself again. Amazing what a shower and a shave can do.'

'Thanks, Lola,' said Jack. He adjusted his bathrobe, walked over to her and kissed her gently on the cheek.

'What for?'

'Everything. You're one hell of a girl. That helicopter ride was truly amazing. We wouldn't be here without you. I had this strange dream, over and over.'

'What dream?'

'I was standing on the deck of the *Calypso*, waste deep in water and unable to move. I looked down into the deep and saw bodies floating up from below. One of them was Macbeth, still sitting in his wheelchair. He kept staring at me. Then came Carlotta, eyes bulging and her mouth wide open in a silent scream. Dr Gaal was next. His right hand was missing. It was floating along next to him, a trail of blood clouding the water. Then more bodies. They came from everywhere. I wanted to look away, but couldn't.

'Then along came Kobo. He shot the gunman who was about to shoot me in the head, but was himself shot. Then Tristan reached out to me with his hand and pulled me up, but the ship was sinking and we had nowhere to go. Then suddenly, there was a helicopter, hovering above us. You were at the controls and tried to land, but there was only water ...'

'Snap out of it, Jack, and have some coffee,' said Lola. 'Better call Sir Charles. He was on the phone again a moment ago. And while you think about that, here are today's papers. You and Dr Rosen are all over the front pages.'

Lola handed Jack a pile of papers and he glanced at the headlines: *Horror crimes against humanity … Secret death camps in Somalia exposed … Blackburn Pharmaceuticals accused of illegal drug trials …*

*Well done, Bettany*, thought Jack and put the papers back on the table. *The sensation-genie is out of the bottle. You have the ear of the world.*

Jack called Sir Charles after Lola had left the room. 'You enjoyed our little news conference, I hear,' he said.

'I did,' said Sir Charles, 'but what I enjoyed most of all was to see that little weed of a sleuth shake in his polished boots. You really had

Cross worried there for a while. Every time you mentioned Macbeth, he began to squirm. Well done! You certainly got your message across. The newspaper coverage is sensational. And you didn't let anything slip about Lord Elms ... smart man!'

'Thanks, Charles. We have to talk.'

'Sure, but first we should meet with Cross. He's been badgering me with calls all day. He wants to talk to you.'

'I bet he does. What do you think?'

'We should go along with it and see what we can get out of him,' Sir Charles suggested shrewdly. 'We are in a strong position. He's worried and on the back foot. You never know, perhaps we could even trade information ...'

'Arrange it.'

'When?'

'As soon as you can. Let's strike while the iron's hot!'

'That's my boy,' said Sir Charles, and hung up.

When Sir Charles called to arrange a meeting, Cross indicated that Sir Reginald Holloway, his boss, would attend. This was highly unusual and could only mean one thing: the subject matter was of the utmost importance. Sir Charles and Sir Reginald went back a long time and had crossed paths, and swords, many times.

'Hello Reggie,' said Sir Charles, walking into the dimly lit conference room at MI5. 'How's your golf?'

'Lousy. I hardly get to play these days. It's people like you who keep me off the green.'

'In that case, we won't keep you long,' said Sir Charles cheerfully. 'And you can get back to your putting.'

'I can see we understand each other, as usual,' said Sir Reginald. 'Drink?'

'Scotch, thank you,' said Jack and took a seat.

'Let's get down to business, shall we?' said Sir Charles. 'First, our conditions.'

Cross was about to say something, but Sir Reginald held up his hand. Cross sat back in his chair and said nothing.

'We tell you what we know, and you tell us what you know. We sense you are holding back, we walk out. Mr Rogan hasn't signed the Official Secrets Act. He's an Australian citizen and has come here in a spirit of cooperation to assist you. He hasn't committed any crime, or broken any law. You have no right to hold or interrogate him. You do that, the press will be down on you within the hour. Clear so far?'

Cross looked at his boss. Sir Reginald nodded. 'Absolutely,' said Cross.

'Intimidation or threats do not work with us. I'm sure you know that by now, Mr Cross. So, let's start at the very beginning, shall we?'

'Very well. Who will begin?' asked Sir Reginald.

Jack put down his glass. 'I will,' he said. 'Let's go back to where it started: the attack on Lord and Lady Elms.' Jack paused and looked at Cross. '"Stars, hide your fires". Does that mean anything to you, gentlemen?'

Sir Reginald lit a cigarette. 'Before we answer that, here are my conditions,' he said, inhaling deeply.

'Oh? And what exactly do you mean by that?' asked Sir Charles, a little taken aback.

'Bring him in, Cross,' said Sir Reginald, enjoying the nicotine rush. Cross stood up and left the room. He returned moments later with a very worried looking George Underwood, the senior civil servant who had helped Sir Charles crack the Elms mission and its connection to the government.

'George has, of course, signed the Official Secrets Act,' said Sir Reginald quietly, 'and so has everyone working with him. George has passed classified information to you, Charles. Stars, hide your fires? He's admitted it. And that puts you in the frame as well.'

Thunderstruck, Sir Charles was unable to look his friend George, who was now seated directly opposite, in the eye. 'Your conditions, Reggie?' he said after a while.

Sir Reginald was enjoying himself. 'Quite simple, really,' he said. 'You tell us everything you know about this whole affair, and we'll do the same. You hold something back, George will not only lose his job, but he'll be charged and go to jail. For how long would you say, Charles? Twenty years?' said Sir Reginald. 'You go to the press with this, or leak any information, the same thing happens. So you see, George's fate is in your hands, gentlemen.'

Sir Charles looked at Jack. 'What do you think?' he asked.

'Do we have a choice?'

'Not really. Unless you want to send George down, or walk away.'

'I have one condition of my own,' said Jack.

'Tell us,' said Sir Reginald. He liked the plucky Australian.

'I must be allowed to tell my client, Isis, Lord and Lady Elms' son, and a few of his associates about all this.'

'Understood,' said Sir Reginald. 'But the same conditions apply. If there's a breach of our understanding, George suffers the consequences. And you already know exactly what that means. Fair enough?'

'Fair enough,' said Jack.

Sir Reginald looked at Sir Charles. 'What about you?' he said.

'Agreed,' said Sir Charles.

'Now, let's talk about Stars, hide your fires, shall we?' said Sir Reginald. 'I always liked Shakespeare. So full of hidden meaning and open to interpretation.' He reached for his silver cigarette case and lit up. 'Go ahead, Mr Rogan, let's hear yours.'

# 88

Isis had surprised everyone, including Sir Humphrey, who hadn't left her bedside since his arrival in Boston, with her stoic attitude and positive approach to the risky operation. Even Dr Greenberg was surprised. He had expected what he called 'irrational last minute jitters', when most of his patients about to face the operating table were prepared to accept certain death rather than go under his knife. Somehow, Isis appeared to be different, but all was not as it seemed.

The face radiating confidence was in fact a mask. Years of rigorous training and discipline – especially before a performance – had equipped Isis well. She knew how to suppress her emotions and control her fears. Deep down, however, she was terrified and what Greenberg was about to tell her, would almost push her over the edge.

Encouraged by Isis' apparent calm and rational approach to the operation, Greenberg decided to tell her more about the complex procedure than he would normally disclose to other patients. To have Sir Humphrey – Isis' trusted friend and physician – present, was another important factor, and Greenberg had a special role for him in mind. A pioneer at heart, Greenberg was constantly on the lookout for innovation and ways to improve his surgical techniques.

The close relationship and excellent rapport between Sir Humphrey and his patient had given him an idea. Greenberg would ask Sir Humphrey to participate in the operation and Greenberg was about to tell his patient and her physician exactly what he had in mind, and why.

'I like to start early,' said Greenberg cheerfully, sitting down on the edge of Isis' bed. 'Around six a.m. And I have to warn you, the operation will take several hours.' Isis had expected this and wasn't surprised. 'This is a complex operation requiring many diverse skills. It's a team effort. I will introduce you to the team tomorrow morning before we start. They're a terrific bunch. You'll like them.'

'Excellent,' said Sir Humphrey.

'What music would you like?' continued Greenberg. 'I always play music during the operation. It calms the spirit and focuses the mind.'

'Does it matter what I like?' asked Isis.

'Of course it does. It is the effect it will have on you that counts.'

'I don't understand,' said Isis. 'I will be—'

'Awake, of course. I need you fully awake and alert during certain parts of procedure. Without that, I cannot operate. I thought Sir Humphrey would have …'

Stunned silence. Isis looked at Sir Humphrey and paled. 'Is this some kind of joke?' she said quietly.

'Far from it; it's the only way,' said Greenberg.

Sir Humphrey looked slightly sheepish. 'We were going to discuss this later this evening,' he said.

'Now you don't have to.' Greenberg reached for Isis' limp hand. 'Cheer up, my friend, you won't notice a thing. The good news is, the brain cannot feel pain. And besides, your head will be safely secured in a steel brace. It works a bit like a vice because you have to be perfectly still, you see. The slightest movement could be fatal. But you will have to talk to us.'

'What do you mean?' asked Isis, becoming more and more alarmed.

'Because your tumour is in such a – how will I put it? – delicate position near the cortex, I will have to be guided by you to some extent, or more precisely, by your brain functions.'

'What?' Isis almost shouted.

'By hearing you talk to me, I know what function of the brain is being activated, and that helps me find the best way to go in and remove the tumour without causing damage.'

'My God,' said Isis, suddenly feeling quite sick.

'This is usually the point when most of my patients want to run away,' said Greenberg. 'Understandable. But not you – right? Of course not,' he said, laughing, and turned to face Sir Humphrey standing behind him. Sir Humphrey knew all of this was part of

Greenberg's revolutionary operating technique. It was the main reason he was able to attempt operations other surgeons would consider too risky and walk away from.

Not only was engaging the patient and talking to him during the operation part of this technique, but Greenberg believed the subject matter of the conversation was even more important, as it would activate quite specific parts of the brain in certain ways, which in turn gave him important pointers and clues of how to proceed. In fact, Greenberg had discovered this while playing music during his operations. Sir Humphrey realised that only a genius like Greenberg could come up with such an idea and use it effectively to save lives.

'I would like you to participate in the operation, Sir Humphrey,' said Greenberg. 'I hope you'll agree.'

'In what way?' asked Sir Humphrey, surprised.

'Because you know Isis so well and she trusts you, you would be the best person to talk to her during the operation. Interested?'

'Certainly, if Isis agrees.'

'Fine by me,' croaked Isis.

'What would you like us to talk about?' Sir Humphrey asked.

'Chess. I saw you play chess here this morning and that gave me the idea …'

'What do you mean?' asked Sir Humphrey.

'I want Isis to concentrate. I want her to focus. To be fully absorbed by the subject matter, like solving a puzzle, or a complex mathematical problem. Does that make sense? Can you think of something like that?'

'Oh yes, I can,' said Sir Humphrey. He pointed a finger at Isis. 'Do you remember the famous games we used to play? Without a board?'

'Sure,' said Isis. 'But that was years ago.'

'Tell me about it,' said Greenberg.

'Sir Humphrey taught me to play chess when I was a boy. As part of my training, he made me memorise famous games. It was a lot of fun.'

'What, all of it? All the moves?' asked Greenberg.

'Absolutely. In chess, thinking ahead, anticipating and planning your moves far in advance and working out possibilities is everything. So we used to memorise famous games and play them by heart. Without a board. Just calling out the moves. Well, the first ten or so, and then it was on. After that we did our own thing.'

'Amazing. What a feat! Could you do this now?' asked Greenberg.

'I don't see why not,' said Isis.

'All right,' said Sir Humphrey, warming to the idea. 'Which game would you like?'

'How about the 1981 Kasparov v Fedorowicz game?' said Isis. 'It was all over in 34 moves.'

'I knew you'd choose that,' said Sir Humphrey. 'It was your favourite.'

'That's right. Queen's Indian Defence ...' said Isis.

'Petrosian Variation,' added Sir Humphrey. 'Inspirational.'

'Quite so.'

'Excellent!' said Greenberg, getting excited. 'What do you think, Sir Humphrey?'

'Sure, we could do that, if it helps.'

'It certainly would,' said Greenberg. 'That's exactly what I want her brain to do. Fight the enemy on the chessboard while I attack the enemy within. Concentration, focus, excitement. Perfect!'

'This could turn into quite a tournament,' said Isis, feeling suddenly much better. The idea of playing mental chess with her old mentor and friend while her brain was being operated on appealed to her. The idea was endearingly bizarre.

Greenberg stood up to leave. 'That only leaves the music ...' he said.

'Bach,' said Isis. 'I love Bach Cantatas.'

'So do I,' said Greenberg. 'You got it!'

'What about the prize?' said Isis, a sparkle in her eyes.

'What do you mean?' asked Sir Humphrey.

'Well, every tournament must have a winner and a prize.'

'Obviously,' said Greenberg, turning serious.

'Oh? What will it be then?' asked Isis.

Greenberg walked to the door and turned around. 'Can't you see? Your life, of course. See you in the morning, gentlemen.'

## 89

Carrington had missed his old chambers and eccentric colleagues more than he cared to admit. He even missed Cyril Archibald QC, his old rival and sparring partner. Archibald had defended Sir Eric Newman, a notorious Nazi war criminal, in a sensational trial a few years before, which had become the subject of Jack's hugely successful book – *Dental Gold and Other Horrors*. Carrington had also missed MacDougall, his crusty, cantankerous old clerk and was looking forward to his quirky ways of running the floor.

Leaving Sydney and the bar had been an escape, a way to deal with the grief that had threatened to overwhelm him at the time. Losing both his wife and daughter in that dreadful terrorist attack in Egypt three years ago had seemed almost too much to bear. Somehow, running away and accepting The Hague appointment seemed the only way to cope with the unspeakable tragedy.

Carrington ran his hand along the edge of the familiar mahogany bookcase filled with Egyptian artefacts, papyri and manuscripts in Latin and Hebrew, and looked up at the bronze busts of Roman emperors and bearded philosophers staring down at him from above. *Good to be back*, he thought, and sat down at his desk.

The files he had requested from the police regarding the Blowhole fire had been delivered and Carrington was anxious to begin his review of the case and examine the evidence as instructed by the DPP. Even if only part of what Alexandra had told him was correct and Macbeth and his thugs were somehow behind it all, this could quickly become one of the most explosive and sensational cases to land on his desk in years.

Carrington realised this was exactly what he needed and was ready to do what he did best: looking at a case with an open mind; assessing the evidence rationally; taking nothing for granted; questioning everything, even the obvious; and then examining every minute detail

– however remote or trivial it may appear at first glance – to get to the truth. He firmly believed that the truth was hidden somewhere in every case and all one had to do was have a good, hard look. However, many knew how to look, but few knew how to *see*.

The volume of material was massive. The case was still being prepared for the coroner and a hearing wasn't expected for weeks. Some of the forensics reports were outstanding and some of the patrons who had been at the club at the time of the fire, still had to be tracked down and interviewed. It seemed to Carrington that the case lacked direction and had stalled. This often happened in difficult cases. He had seen it many times before.

If Alexandra was right about Cavendish and he was in fact murdered at the club and the fire deliberately lit to cover it up, then it made sense to begin with Cavendish. Carrington looked for the autopsy report. *Ah, Dr Penelope Ritter. Excellent*, he thought, opening the report. Carrington had run several cases involving Dr Ritter and knew her well. He had cross-examined the pathologist with the fierce reputation many times and respected her opinions and impeccable methods.

Carrington began to read the report and carefully examined the photographs of the charred remains. Burnt beyond recognition, Cavendish's body had been identified through dental records and a distinctive signet ring. *How could that be?* he wondered, and began to sift through the many photographs until he found what he was looking for: photos of a perfectly preserved right hand. Instead of ploughing through the long report full of jargon and pedantic detail, Carrington decided to cut to the chase. He reached for the phone and called Dr Ritter.

'You're in luck, Marcus,' said Dr Ritter. 'Lunch break. Fancy a sandwich?'

'You're on. Where?'

'Usual place across the road in, say, fifteen minutes?'

'Done. See you there,' said Carrington and hung up.

Dr Ritter's office was next to the historic sandstone Sydney Hospital, just around the corner from Carrington's chambers.

'Thanks for seeing me straight away, Penelope,' said Carrington, shaking Dr Ritter's hand. 'Let's have some lunch.'

'I heard you were back, Marcus. It's good to see you. How can I help you?'

'The Blowhole case, Cavendish autopsy,' said Carrington.

'You are looking into it?'

'The DPP has asked me to, unofficially.'

'Ah.'

'You'll hear about it soon enough; this is now a possible murder enquiry, but please keep it to yourself for the moment.'

'What? They believe Cavendish was murdered?'

Carrington shrugged. 'What did you find?'

'You read the report?'

'In part.'

'This is a bizarre case. I examined a badly burnt body with a missing head and severed arm. Death was by drowning in the fish tank. The head and the arm were bitten off by sharks after death. The head was also badly burnt and so was the arm. The hand was missing.'

'Death by drowning, a badly burnt body and a missing hand?' said Carrington.

'I know it sounds weird, but this is what appears to have happened: Cavendish was high on drugs—'

'I read the toxicology report,' interrupted Carrington. 'An interesting cocktail of drugs, but mainly ice.'

'Correct. Cavendish falls into one of the large fish tanks and drowns. He is then attacked by sharks. His head is ripped off and so is his right arm. Then a fire breaks out in the club. Panic. The fish tank explodes in the heat, the water runs off, leaving the body behind to be consumed by fire.'

'Then how do we end up with a perfectly preserved right hand?' asked Carrington.

'Ah, that's the really fascinating bit. How do you think it survived the fire,' said Dr Ritter, 'virtually intact?'

'No idea.'

'It was protected from the fire, because …'

'Please just tell me,' said Carrington, 'the suspense is killing me.'

'It was inside one of the sharks.'

'You're kidding.'

'No; perfectly serious.'

'Let me get this straight. One of the sharks bites off Cavendish's hand and swallows it before the tank explodes?'

'You got it. The shark was surprisingly intact, hardly burnt at all. When I opened it, I found the hand with the ring inside its stomach.'

'Incredible.'

'Could Cavendish have been pushed into the water?'

'Sure. But that's a matter for the police and the coroner. Apparently, no one saw anything. No evidence and certainly nothing to suggest this from the autopsy. You must understand, there was panic in a crowded nightclub. A stampede; ugly stuff. First, body parts floating in a fish tank with sharks in a feeding frenzy, and then the fire. You can imagine what was going on. But now you tell me this is a possible murder investigation and not some kind of horrible accident. How come?'

'Can't say too much; too early. But let's assume this for the moment: Cavendish is high on drugs, is pushed into the tank and drowns. Could there have been some sort of struggle before he fell in?'

'Sure, but I certainly can't tell from what's left of him.'

'What about the hand?'

'What do you mean?'

'I know it's a long shot, but did you examine the fingernails?'

'Of course. You mean for some evidence of a defensive struggle, something caught under the nails perhaps?'

'Exactly. How many cases did we run with DNA extracted from some tissue fragment trapped under the fingernails, and then nailed the suspect with it?'

'Several. I did find some. It's all in my report. However, there was just no reason to look for anything specific in this case.'

'I completely understand. But the line of enquiry has changed and now suggests a possibility of murder. A favour?'

'You want me to have another look?'

'Could you? Unofficially at this stage. We don't want to rock the boat unnecessarily, do we?'

'For you, Marcus, I'll do it. Coming home present.'

'Thanks, Penelope. I owe you.'

# 90

Sir Humphrey looked at Isis propped up in bed, her head covered in bandages. *Thank God, she's sleeping,* he thought. *She looks like a mummy. She'd like that.* The operation had lasted close to seven hours and had been far more complicated and risky than anyone had expected. The awkward position of the tumour had pushed Greenberg and his team to the edge. Sir Humphrey had talked Isis through several famous chess games to keep her focused and alert until he was so exhausted, he could barely speak.

Sir Humphrey's admiration for Greenberg's exceptional surgical skills had risen to new heights. He was convinced there wasn't another surgeon alive on the planet who could have attempted such an operation. Overcome by fatigue, he pulled up a chair and sat down. He was drifting towards much needed sleep, when he heard the door open behind him.

'I thought I'd find you here,' said Greenberg. He walked over to the bed and looked at his sleeping patient for a while without saying anything. 'We almost lost her, you know,' he said. 'Between the defending bishop and the attacking knight. It was the most dangerous part of the operation. A millimetre each way could have made the difference between life and death. I wasn't sure which way to go until she made her next move. Her brain responded and suddenly it all became clear. I had to turn to the left, and I did. Had I gone the other way, well …'

'And without the operation?' asked Sir Humphrey.

'Five weeks; perhaps eight. The tumour was a monster. You saw it. Very aggressive. But she's a fighter.'

'Prognosis?'

'I got most of it, but not all. Just couldn't go there; she would have died on the spot. It will come back.'

'How fast?'

'I wish I knew, but we've certainly given her a little more time. A few months.'

'And then?'

Greenberg shrugged. 'We can't do this again.'

'So, where to from here?'

'You won't find the answer in my knife, but in genomics.'

'The Kozakievicz research you spoke of?'

'Yes. Dr Delacroix and her work. We have to defeat the tumour from within.'

'You think that's possible?'

'Kozakievicz thought so. He was a strong believer in immunotherapy.'

'It's a race against time then?'

'I'm afraid so.'

'There are a few more moves left in this game, David,' said Sir Humphrey, 'and we never give up.'

'I saw that during the operation. And Rogan is one of your white knights?'

'He is, and young Tristan is the other. But Dr Delacroix is the undisputed queen of this game.'

'Good,' said Greenberg.

'How quickly will Isis recover now?'

'Quite fast. For a while, she will almost feel her old self again. Until it comes back …'

'The Emperor of Darkness?' said Sir Humphrey.

'Yes. He doesn't like anyone threatening his deadly domain.'

'Then we'll just have to find a way to defeat him.'

'How?'

'With the help of our queen, we can defeat the emperor.'

'Dr Delacroix?'

'Yes. And don't underestimate the white knights … Watch this game, David.'

'This sounds more and more like an episode of Lord of the Rings,' joked Greenberg.

'Orcs and elves, evil wizards and dragons?'

'A bit like that. Only we have tumours and genomics, surgeons, white knights and an evil emperor,' said Greenberg, laughing. To enjoy a little levity after a traumatic day was refreshing. 'And we both know the prize waiting at the end of that tournament, don't we?'

'Yes, we do. Life,' said Sir Humphrey, turning serious again. 'When can Isis travel, do you think?'

'Soon.'

'I want to take her back to London. Home.'

'Good idea. And I want her out of hospital as soon as possible. Infection is always a big danger. Hospitals are not a good place for recovery,' said Greenberg.

Sir Humphrey stood up. 'What you've done, David, borders on miraculous,' he said, extending his hand. 'Thank you.'

'There are no miracles in surgery, only courage, imagination and luck. I too want to defeat the emperor. If I can in some way help you do it, that would be reward beyond my wildest dreams. Perhaps there's still a little part this pawn can play in your game?' joked Greenberg.

'Oh, I should think so. Pawns can be very dangerous. The emperor's on notice. He better look out.'

'You bet!'

## 91

Because news coverage in Somalia was haphazard at best, and Van Cleef hated television and didn't read the papers, news of the audacious pirate attack and the sinking of the *Calypso* hadn't yet reached him. He was therefore unaware that his boss was dead, and was still following his instructions with dogged determination.

Van Cleef stepped out of the lift and looked for the blackjack table. *Problem gamblers are so predictable*, he thought. *You always know where to find them.*

Ashari was winning. He had been playing blackjack for hours and couldn't believe his luck. He was ten thousand ahead. However, he was beginning to make the mistake many gamblers make when they are on a winning streak: increasing the bets.

Van Cleef put his hand on Ashari's shoulder from behind. Annoyed, Ashari looked up. 'Call it a day,' said Van Cleef, 'before Lady Luck turns her back on you.'

'Mind your own business,' snapped Ashari.

'It is my business. Kevin couldn't come; he sent me instead …' said Van Cleef quietly. 'And keep your voice down. The bar; now!' Van Cleef withdrew his hand and walked across to the bar. Ashari nodded to the dealer, picked up his chips and left the table.

*Dr Delacroix was right*, thought Moretti, watching Ashari follow Van Cleef to the bar.

'You've got something for me?' said Van Cleef, and ordered a drink. Ashari pulled an envelope out of his pocket and put it on the bar. Van Cleef opened it and looked inside. 'Don't fuck with me. Where's the rest?' he barked.

'That's all there was. That's what she left on her desk,' said Ashari.

Van Cleef watched Ashari carefully. 'If you are playing games …'

'That's all there was,' repeated Ashari timidly.

*It's not him*, thought Van Cleef. *He hasn't got the balls. It's the bitch!*

'All right, you can go back to the table and lose it all, for all I care.' Van Cleef slipped the envelope into his pocket and climbed off the bar stool. 'We'll be in touch.'

'What about my money?' asked Ashari.

'You get it when you deliver the rest,' snapped Van Cleef. Ashari was beginning to annoy him.

'But …'

Van Cleef put his arm around Ashari's shoulder and bent down until their faces almost touched. '*You heard what I said*,' he whispered. 'Now piss off.'

'I have something that may interest you,' said Ashari.

'And what might that be?'

'I think she's gone to the police …'

'What makes you say that?' asked Van Cleef, frowning.

'I overheard things …'

'What things?' demanded Van Cleef.

'Rumours. Chatter in the common room over coffee, stuff like that. There are no secrets in a place like ours.'

*Makes sense*, thought Van Cleef. 'Anything else?' he said.

'She seems different towards me. Something's changed …'

'You're not just making this up. I warn you …'

'Definitely not. I'm concerned … my position …'

'No need to be. We'll handle the matter. Nothing's changed.' Van Cleef reached into his pocket, pulled out a wad of cash and stuffed it into Ashari's shirt pocket. 'Go and enjoy yourself and leave the rest to us,' he said. Then he turned away and walked to the lift.

Van Cleef tipped the doorman and got into the black Range Rover waiting in front of the busy casino entrance. 'We have a problem, Paulus,' he said.

'Oh?' said his buddy and pulled away from the kerb.

'I think she's gone to the police.'

'But you're not sure?'

'No.'

'Leave it to me; I'll find out. I have contacts.'

'I knew I could rely on you,' said Van Cleef, relieved.

'All part of the service. Cocky bitch,' said Paulus. 'What do you want to do about it?'

'If it's true, we'll teach her a lesson,' said Van Cleef.

'What's on your mind?'

'I want to put the fear of God into her. I'm sure between us we'll come up with something to do the trick, don't you think?'

Paulus looked at Van Cleef and grinned. 'Oh, I should think so. And I know just the place for some fun the lady isn't going to forget in a hurry.'

'What kind of place?'

'A little bit of Sydney history directly beneath our office. It's the reason I bought the property and we operate our business from there. I'll show you.'

'You are full of surprises,' said Van Cleef, feeling better.

'Just like the good old days in Joburg, eh Jan?'

'Sentimental bastard,' said Van Cleef and slapped his friend on the back.

# 92

Moretti knew Alexandra's routine well. So did Van Cleef. In the morning, she would catch a cab from Jack's apartment to work. She ate all her meals there during the day, and then called United Taxis for a cab to take her home in the evening. The time would vary, depending on her workload, but she didn't depart from her routine. Carrington had advised her not to go out by herself for the time being, just to be on the safe side. This suited Alexandra well, as she was totally committed to her work and happy to spend every spare minute in her lab exploring Professor K's research. In addition, Moretti had arranged for his team to keep watch around the clock. One of his officers was always close by, keeping an eye on Alexandra, day or night.

Paulus was aware of this and it severely limited his options, but he had a plan. 'We'll do it tonight,' he said. 'It's all arranged.'

'How?' asked Van Cleef.

'Quite simple, really. I'll tell you,' said Paulus, laughing. 'Get ready.'

At 8 o'clock that evening, Alexandra phoned United Taxis as usual and ordered a cab to take her home. She asked for the taxi driver to call her as he approached. This normally took only a few minutes. Alexandra locked away her papers in the safe, reached her handbag and headed for the lift. She would wait for the taxi in the lobby downstairs as she did every evening.

Paulus sat in the cab just around the corner from the institute, waiting for the call. Universal Security owned several cabs through overseas subsidiaries that couldn't be traced, and Paulus had arranged to take the place of one of his drivers. As he knew the staff allocating the fares at United Taxis well, and had always looked after them generously, it had been easy for him to make sure he would get the fare in question. And besides, he was the closest cab available, so all would look normal and routine. No questions would be asked, nor suspicions aroused. Talking to the cops was a no-no in any event; taxi drivers and call staff were a closely-knit unit and looked out for each other.

The call came in at three minutes past eight. Paulus started the engine and called Alexandra's mobile. 'Taxi for Dr Delacroix,' said Paulus, 'I'm just pulling up.'

'Thank you, I'll come outside,' said Alexandra and walked to the door.

Moretti's officer on duty that night saw the taxi arrive and started the engine. He would follow the cab all the way to Alexandra's apartment block and then park just outside the entrance for the night. Normally, there were two of them, but his partner had called in sick at the last minute and he was therefore on his own.

As soon as the taxi pulled up, Alexandra stepped outside, got into the back seat and gave the driver her address.

'There's been an accident,' said Paulus. 'I've just driven past it. We'll go down Elizabeth Street to avoid the congestion, if you don't mind.'

'Sure. Thanks,' said Alexandra. She opened her bag, took out her notebook and went over some of the entries she had made in the afternoon.

*Another South African*, she thought, recognising the accent.

The traffic going down Elizabeth Street towards Circular Quay was heavy as usual. It was late-night shopping and the sales were on. Cars were inching slowly forward, trying to manoeuvre through the congested lanes. A black four-wheel drive began to change lanes in front of the officer's car and pushed in. Then another car did the same and he found himself hemmed in without being able to see the taxi in front. *Shit*, thought the officer, drumming his fingers against the steering wheel in frustration. *He can't go anywhere; we're all in the same crap.*

Paulus looked into the rear-view mirror and smiled. All was going to plan. Van Cleef was in the car just behind him, with another one of their vehicles between him and the officer hemmed in with nowhere to go.

*Another South African*, thought Alexandra. *South African?* She looked at the powerful looking man driving the taxi and for reasons she couldn't quite explain, began to feel uneasy. Then she looked at the photograph with the driver's ID displayed at the top of the windscreen and paled. The photo in no way resembled the driver. She knew instantly something was wrong.

'This is so slow. I've changed my mind,' she said. 'Please let me out as soon as you can. I'll walk from here.'

*Perfect*, thought Paulus. 'No problem,' he said. 'How about just over there in front of David Jones? I could stop briefly at the entrance.' Paulus couldn't believe his luck. This was the prearranged spot he would have stopped the taxi in any event, to give Van Cleef an opportunity to drag Alexandra out of the cab and then disappear with her into the crowded department store.

'Fine; thank you,' said Alexandra, pulling out her purse. 'How much?'

'Twenty will do just fine.' Paulus put on the indicator and let it blink just three times. This was the agreed signal for Van Cleef to get ready.

Paulus stopped the cab and Alexandra opened the back door. Van Cleef jumped out of the four-wheel drive behind her and ran forward. He grabbed Alexandra by the arm, dragged her into the department store and disappeared into the crowd. The taxi moved forward again in the line of traffic. It had all happened in the blink of an eye.

The officer following behind just caught a glimpse of Alexandra and a man walking into David Jones together. *Jesus*, he thought, *it's her!* He stopped the car and, leaving the engine running, got out and ran after them. Before he could reach the entrance to the department store, a burly guy – one of Paulus' men – bumped into him on the crowded footpath and knocked him to the ground. By now, horns were blaring and the traffic was at a standstill. Holding his aching shoulder, the officer got up and looked around, searching for Alexandra, but all he could see were eager late-night bargain-hunters flooding into the store for the sales.

# 93

Alexandra's first reaction was to scream for help, but one look at Van Cleef towering over her made her hold her tongue. The grin on his face was as threatening and sinister as a Hieronymus Bosch painting, she thought, but what frightened her most were his ice-blue eyes; expressionless, cruel windows into a dark soul.

'We meet again, Dr Delacroix,' said Van Cleef, holding Alexandra's arm in a vice-like grip as he made his way through the crowded store towards the exit on the opposite side. 'You know the drill by now. If you scream, I'll have to silence you. Do exactly as I say, and you'll be fine.' Alexandra had no doubt that Van Cleef meant what he said and would carry out his threat without hesitation. 'As soon as we step outside, a car will pick us up. No struggle. Just get in; clear?' Alexandra nodded. 'Now smile as if you're enjoying yourself. You are happy to see me again. After all, I'm a generous donor – right?'

Rubbing his aching shoulder, Moretti's young officer burst into the store and just caught a glimpse of Alexandra near the exit. He began to push furiously through the crowd towards her. Another one of Paulus' men was just behind him. As he passed one of the glass promotion display cases filled with little perfume bottles, he pushed the officer into it. The young man lost his footing and fell into the display. The glass case toppled over and crashed to the marble floor, sending a lethal spray of glass splinters flying in all directions. The crowd began to scream and security guards came running. By the time the officer got up – his cheeks and forehead bleeding profusely – Alexandra had disappeared. Still in a daze, he pulled out his mobile and called Moretti to give him the bad news.

Moretti was furious. Despite all of his precautions and careful planning, he had been outwitted. Alexandra had been whisked away from right under his nose in the middle of the busy peak hour! The unthinkable had happened. Moretti immediately contacted his men watching the Universal Security premises in The Rocks. He was told the lights were on, the office was still open, but everything was quiet.

The car carrying Van Cleef and Alexandra in the rear seat was now crawling through the heavy traffic. Van Cleef handed Alexandra a beanie. 'Put this on and pull it down over your eyes. And tuck your hair in.' he ordered. Van Cleef didn't want a red beacon sitting next to him in the car.

'Where are you taking me?' croaked Alexandra.

'Mr Macbeth is very disappointed,' said Van Cleef, ignoring the question. 'He's been so generous, and how have you repaid him? You sent me a few miserable pages of the professor's notes instead of the full set I asked for. And then what did you do? You went to the police. I thought you were smarter.'

'It's not quite as simple as that. What do you want from me?' asked Alexandra.

'Mr Macbeth hates disappointments. But most of all, he hates disloyalty. We think it's time for … a little obedience lesson.'

'An obedience lesson? What on earth do you mean?'

'It's a surprise …'

Alexandra didn't like the sound of that. 'What surprise?' she said.

'If I were to tell you, it wouldn't be a surprise, would it? Patience. You'll find out soon enough.' *If only she knew what we have in mind*, thought Van Cleef, *she'd freak out for sure.*

It wasn't often that Moretti, a resourceful man, was at a loss what to do. Things had gone spectacularly wrong and he didn't even know where to begin to reverse this devastating setback. There were no leads. He could already hear the laughter of his colleagues and see the finger-pointing and disapproving looks of his superiors.

*Where would you take her?* he asked himself over and over. *Somewhere safe and familiar. But why take her at all?* The abduction had been meticulously planned – like a military operation – with precision and daring that had caught Moretti and his men off guard. *Bugger!* Then the phone rang in his pocket. It was one of the officers keeping watch in The Rocks.

'A car just pulled up in front of the garage,' he reported.

'Can you see who's inside?'

'No.'

'Don't approach; stay out of sight and keep me informed.'

'Understood.'

Van Cleef's car came to a halt. 'Here we are,' said the driver. Alexandra slowly raised her beanie until it sat just above her left eye. She turned her head to look out of the window. The car was facing a large garage door, which was opening slowly. Van Cleef was talking to the driver sitting in front of him and appeared momentarily distracted.

*Now!* thought Alexandra. She quickly opened the car door and dropped something on the footpath. Van Cleef responded like lightning. He turned around, grabbed Alexandra by the collar of her jacket and pulled her roughly towards him. 'Going somewhere?' he said. 'I think not. Definitely time for an obedience lesson.' He reached across and closed the car door.

Moretti was on his way to the department store to sort out the fiasco. Things were going from bad to worse. Caught in heavy traffic, he was impatiently drumming his fingers against the steering wheel. *The Rocks? Makes sense,* he thought. *Their turf; familiar and safe, and only a few minutes away. Could be it. Fingers crossed.* Then his phone rang again. It was the same officer who had called earlier.

'You won't believe what just happened,' said the officer, barely able to speak. He appeared excited and out of breath.

'Calm down,' said Moretti. 'What happened?'

'As the car was waiting in the driveway, someone tried to get out, but was pulled back in.'

'And?'

'Then the car drove into the garage and the door closed behind it.'

'Is that it?'

'No.'

472

'Come on!'

'Moments later, I observed a woman walking her dog along the footpath. As she walked past the garage she stopped, bent down and picked something up.'

'Get to the point, man!'

'I went over to see what it was.'

'And?'

'She found something extraordinary. It's right here in front of me.'

'For Christ's sake, what is it?'

'Dr Delacroix's ID from the institute.'

'Jesus!'

'What do you want me to do?'

'Absolutely nothing! I'm on my way.'

## 94

Moretti walked up to the unmarked police car parked in the shadows and knocked on the driver's window. The officer behind the wheel opened the window and looked up at his boss. 'Anything I should know?' asked Moretti.

'Nothing's happened,' said the officer. 'Not since we found this.' He handed Moretti Alexandra's Gordon Institute ID through the window. Moretti looked at the ID in the plastic sleeve with the cord still attached. Normally, Alexandra would wear the ID around her neck all day, as it opened security doors and activated the lifts at the institute.

'Good work. The boys in black will arrive soon.'

'Tactical Response is coming?' said the officer, surprised.

'Yes. When they do, ask them to stand by and call me. I'm going in.'

'You're going inside? Alone?'

'Yes. Don't let anyone leave, especially by car. And keep a close eye on that garage over there. Is that clear? Not a mouse moves, in or out, without me knowing about it.'

'Yes, sir.'

'If anyone should arrive, stay away and let them go in.'

'Got it. Good luck.'

The registered office of Universal Security was an unassuming, tastefully restored, three-storey sandstone terrace built in the eighteen eighties. Moretti knew he was taking a considerable risk, but instinct and gut feeling told him to go in now, before Tactical Response arrived. He knew once that happened, all hell would break loose, and he wanted to get a 'feel' for the place and gather as much intelligence as possible. The element of surprise was a powerful tool he had used often. Tactical Response could be very effective, but was never subtle.

Moretti walked up the few well-worn steps leading to the entrance and pressed the intercom button. Aware of the curious eye of the security camera watching from above, he looked up at it and smiled.

The intercom crackled into life. 'How can I help you?' asked a female voice.

Moretti held up his police ID towards the camera. 'Letting me in would be a good start,' he said.

'Do you have an appointment?'

'I don't believe I need one. Please open the door.'

Silence.

*I bet there's some feverish activity going on in there*, thought Moretti. 'I will count to three, and then we'll break down the door,' he said calmly. 'Such a beautiful door; shame. One ... two ...' The buzzer sounded. Moretti pushed the door open and walked inside.

'I'm sorry,' said the young woman coming towards Moretti, her high heels clicking on the polished timber floor, 'I didn't expect anyone this late ...' Impeccably dressed in a designer suit, she looked more like a hostess welcoming guests to a cocktail party than a receptionist working late for a security firm tucked away in The Rocks under the Harbour Bridge.

Tastefully furnished with antiques, paintings and comfortable leather chairs facing a marble fireplace, the reception exuded elegance and style. In contrast, the ultra-modern reception desk with its glass display cabinets showing off the latest state-of-the art surveillance gear reminded the visitor where he was, and why he had come to Universal Security. A clever blend of old and new. Conservative expectations meets cutting-edge technology.

The young woman gave Moretti her best smile. 'What can I do for you?' she asked.

'I'm Detective Sergeant Moretti. I would like a word with Mr Koenig,' said Moretti. 'It's quite urgent.'

'He isn't here, I'm afraid.'

'I can wait.'

'I'm not sure—'

'Please call him,' interrupted Moretti. 'I'm sure Mr Koenig will be most interested to hear what I have to say.' Moretti turned towards a large painting hanging on the wall next to the fireplace. 'Brett

Whiteley? Very nice,' he said, and made himself comfortable in one of the leather chairs. It was obvious he wasn't going anywhere.

'Coffee?' said the young woman.

'Yes please; black.'

Ten minutes later, Moretti received a call from his officer outside. 'I SPY 4U just pulled up,' said the officer. Moretti smiled. The gamble was paying off.

Moments later, Moretti heard footsteps in the hallway.

'You said it was urgent, Detective Sergeant,' said Paulus in his heavy South African accent, 'I came as soon as I could. What can I do for you?'

*Tough guy*, thought Moretti, sizing up the broad-shouldered, bullet-headed man in the leather jacket walking towards him. Moretti stood up. 'Can you tell me where you were during the past two hours, Mr Koenig?' asked Moretti.

Paulus looked at Moretti, surprised. It wasn't a question he had expected. 'I was on an assignment. For a client,' said Paulus, recovering quickly.

'Can you be a little more specific?'

'I'm afraid not. Confidentiality and discretion are essential aspects of the work we do. We guarantee it, and our clients expect it. I'm sure you understand …'

*He's good*, thought Moretti. It was time to try a different tack. 'Very well. We have reason to believe that a Mr Van Dam is here on the premises. Right now. I would like to talk to him.'

'Van Dam, you say? Never heard of him,' said Paulus, feigning surprise. 'There's no one here apart from Natasha and me.'

'Is that so? You might know him under a different name: Jan Van Cleef. Does that help, perhaps?' Moretti pressed on, undeterred.

Paulus shook his head. 'No.'

'But you spent two years in jail with him in Johannesburg … Does that jog your memory?'

Paulus gave Moretti a withering look. 'No. You're mistaken.'

Just then, Moretti's phone began to ring in his pocket. 'Forgive me, I have to take this,' he said, and answered the phone.

'The boys are here,' said the officer outside.

'Send them in; now!' said Moretti.

'We can easily resolve this,' said Moretti, turning to Paulus.

'Oh? How?'

'We search the premises; simple.'

'Now, hold on—' protested Paulus, but was interrupted by a loud noise coming from outside.

Reduced to splinters, the front door flew off its hinges and four commandoes dressed in black – faces covered by balaclavas and guns at the ready – stormed into the room. 'Don't move!' said the officer in charge.

Moretti held up his hands. The commandoes stopped in their tracks. 'I will ask once more, Mr Koenig. Is Jan Van Cleef here?'

'I've already answered that,' said Paulus, a defiant look on his angry face. Moretti began to feel uneasy. This wasn't the reaction he had expected. *What makes him so confident? Is he just gambling, or is there more to all this? What is it I cannot see here?* he wondered. Doubts and nagging uncertainty began to claw at his stomach, but he had reached the point of no return.

Moretti reached into his pocket to make sure that Alexandra's ID card was real and still there. *Concrete evidence*, he thought, feeling better.

'So, what you are saying is this: apart from the young lady over there and yourself, there's no one else on the premises. Is that right?' he said, repeating his earlier question.

Paulus sat back in his chair and smiled, his smug confidence infuriating. 'That is exactly what I'm saying.'

'You don't mind if we have a look around then?'

'Go right ahead,' said Paulus. 'Do you mind if I call my lawyer?'

Moretti turned to the officer in charge. 'You heard the man. Go!' The commandoes fanned out and rushed to the back to search the building.

Paulus appeared to be enjoying himself. He had made careful preparations for a moment just like this. Foresight and planning were about to pay off. He was used to pressure and knew how to handle it.

He had been in tighter corners before and knew what was needed to get out of them: balls and nerves of steel, and he had plenty of both. He also knew that the best defence was often attack. *I'll teach this little prick a lesson he won't forget in a hurry*, he thought.

'I hope you know what you're doing, Detective Sergeant,' said Paulus, smiling. Then he reached for his mobile and called his lawyer.

# 95

Jana looked at her watch again and frowned. It was 11:30 p.m. and still no word from Alexandra. Alexandra had told her at breakfast that she would be home at her usual time and hadn't called to say she would be late. But most worrying of all was the fact she wasn't answering her phone.

Jana realised that Alexandra got easily carried away with her work and lost track of time, but not like this. She called Alexandra's mobile again. Still no answer. Seriously concerned by now, Jana dialled Moretti's number.

As soon as Jana heard Moretti's voice, she knew something was wrong. Dismayed, she listened to what he had to say. 'You can't be serious. How could this have happened?' she said.

'I know,' said Moretti quietly, sounding dejected.

'Jesus, Pasquale, you've got to find her!'

'We are doing everything we can. We'll get a search warrant first thing in the morning and then take the place apart, brick by brick.'

'And until then?'

'We seal off the place and keep watch around the clock. There are no other leads.'

'Where are you now?'

'In The Rocks. In front of Universal Security.'

'That's just ten minutes from here. I'm on my way.'

'Wait …' said Moretti, but Jana had already hung up.

Jana turned into the quiet street and parked her car. Then she crossed the road, walked up to Moretti's four-wheel drive and got into the back seat. Jana instantly recognised the familiar signs of exhaustion and fatigue: the bleary eyes, stubble, the crumpled shirt, loosened tie, and the seat littered with empty, disposable coffee cups.

Jana saw Alexandra's ID Moretti had told her about on the dashboard in front him. 'I don't understand it,' he said. 'Here, have a look.' Moretti handed the ID to Jana. 'She was right here. There's just no other rational explanation for this. She dropped it. Yet we searched every inch of the place – nothing.'

'No other exits? At the back perhaps?'

'Nothing. There's a small backyard, but that wall of rock directly behind the terrace blocks everything. We couldn't find a thing. Whoever was in the car that drove into the garage earlier, just vanished. No wonder Koenig was so cocky. He knew … And then he added insult to injury …'

'In what way?'

'He called his lawyer. An arrogant bastard. He arrived with a barrister in tow, a QC, while we were still searching. He lodged a formal complaint—'

'To be expected, surely,' interrupted Jana.

'You're right, but what came next wasn't.'

'Oh?'

'Koenig instructed him to settle for an apology and a new door.'

'You're kidding.'

'No. He said he didn't want any fuss, apparently because of his clients.'

'Did you believe him?'

'Of course not. He just wanted us out of there.'

'What did you do?'

'I ate humble pie and apologised. The boys secured the door and left. I expect I'll get a bill in due course.'

'Smart move, Pasquale,' said Jana. 'It couldn't have been easy.'

'What do you think? But we'll be back in the morning. No one just disappears without a trace. There's something in that building we've missed, or just couldn't find because it's cleverly concealed. After all, these guys are in the security business. Pros.'

'What are you suggesting?'

'A hidden cellar, an underground passage, perhaps something in the rock behind the terrace, a tunnel or another exit. There's so much high-tech stuff in there you could launch a satellite with it. Something like that, or they just got away. Somehow. But I doubt it. This was all carefully planned and professionally executed. Why bring her here if this wasn't the right place?'

'Good point,' said Jana, running her fingers over the ID. 'And the proof's right here in our hands. If it weren't for that … I would say there's been a huge mistake.'

'And I wouldn't have barged in like that in the first place,' said Moretti. 'We're right back to where we started.'

'Not quite,' said Jana. 'Just hold on … Let's think outside the square for a moment.'

'Oh? What's on your mind?'

'The Markovich case I was working on five years ago. Right here in The Rocks. Drugs; a sophisticated lab producing ice on a large scale. We worked on it for months and came up against a similar problem.'

'What do you mean?'

'All the leads and all the information we received pointed to one particular place. Come to think of it, that too was an old terrace not far from here. Just around the corner from The Hero of Waterloo hotel, which is right there.' Jana pointed down the street. 'When we went in, there was nothing. No drugs, no lab, no cash. Everything had vanished into thin air, or so we thought. Until we received a tip-off.'

'Tell me about it.'

'The entire drug operation had gone underground. Did you know there's a whole network of tunnels right here in The Rocks? Links to its colonial past. Take the tank stream, for instance. It was Sydney's original water supply, then it became a sewer and finally an underground stormwater drain. It's still there. Not far from here. They even have tours. And there are disused rail tunnels and "ghost platforms" under the city and its parks. The rail network was never completed, mainly due to the Great Depression and World War II. The tunnels were converted into bomb shelters during the war and then abandoned and closed. But they are still there.'

'So, what are you telling me?'

'Back to the Markovich case. After the tip-off, we went back and had a closer look. That's when we found it.'

'Found what?'

'A well-concealed trapdoor in the backyard leading down into a secret world of tunnels and chambers chiselled out of the rock. The Markovich brothers, Zoran and Zac, operated a sophisticated lab and drug distribution business down there. There even a tunnel leading all the way down to the harbour, which isn't far away. The drugs were picked up at night by boat right under the Harbour Bridge. Daring, original, and very effective. It had worked for years but it wasn't a new idea.'

'What do you mean?'

'Back in colonial days, it was rumoured that a secret tunnel ran from the cellar of The Hero of Waterloo over there, down to the harbour. Apparently, it was used by rum smugglers and press gangs. Get the would-be sailor drunk in the bar, drop him down a trap door into the cellar and then drag him through the tunnel to the harbour. By the time he woke up, he found himself working on a clipper bound for London. In fact, the Markovich tunnel linked up with it, if I remember correctly.'

'Is it still there?' asked Moretti excitedly.

'Sure. It was blocked off with steel bars and stuff; some of it was even bricked up, but it's all still there. In fact, you could get into it from The Hero of Waterloo cellar. All the tunnels are somehow connected.'

Moretti's gut was telling him something. No longer feeling sorry for himself, and tired of licking his wounds, he reached for his mobile and made a call.

'What was that all that about?' asked Jana.

'I asked for backup. I told them to bring bolt cutters, crowbars and a portable oxyacetylene torch. We are going in.'

'In where?'

'The cellar of The Hero of Waterloo, of course. Let's go.'

# 96

'Well done, gentlemen, thank you,' said Paulus and pressed the remote control button to open the garage door. He had to let his lawyers out through the garage because the front door had been boarded up by Moretti's men. 'I think the eager boys in blue have had their wings clipped and fingers burnt a little tonight, don't you think?'

'They may be back,' warned Cyril Archibald QC, his barrister. 'Be careful. No one likes to lose face.'

'I have nothing to hide,' said Paulus.

'If they do come back, you know what to do,' said the solicitor. 'Call me.'

'They are still here,' said Archibald as they walked into the quiet street outside. 'I bet those two cars over there are police.'

'I'm sure they are,' said Paulus. 'I can sleep easy then. No burglars tonight.'

The lawyers hurried across the road and jumped into the solicitor's car.

'Confident chap, isn't he?' said Archibald. 'A little reckless perhaps?'

The solicitor shrugged. 'Good client. Never questions a bill and always pays on time,' he said, and drove off.

Paulus watched the car disappear down the street. Then he turned around slowly, walked back inside and closed the garage door.

The large control panel in the garage not only operated the sophisticated alarm system inside the building, it activated the many CCTV cameras that kept a watchful eye on just about every corner of the property.

Paulus looked at one of the monitors showing a section of the street outside and smiled. *The cavalry has returned to barracks, but a few foot soldiers have been left behind to keep watch*, he thought. *Cops are so predictable.*

Paulus was pleased with himself. The sophisticated setup inside the Universal Security building had come through an unexpected police raid with flying colours. Careful planning and foresight had once again paid off. It was time to have a little fun.

Paulus activated a number of alarm zones in the building and then punched a code into one of the panels. A section of the concrete wall at the back of the garage began to recede silently into the rock. Then he walked through the narrow opening and punched another code into a panel on the other side. The concrete wall moved again and silently slotted back into position.

As he walked along the damp, dimly lit tunnel lined with concrete, Paulus remembered the enormous effort – no expense spared – that had gone into creating this hidden, sophisticated underground complex. While having an office and showroom in The Rocks – a predominantly tourist area – may have been a radical move, it made perfect sense for a business as diversified as Universal Security. Paulus stopped in front of another panel set into a steel door and pressed a few buttons on the pad. The door opened and he stepped into the 'dungeon', as it was known at Universal Security.

Hewn out of the virgin rock, the dungeon was a small chamber divided into two. At one end was a stage illuminated by coloured spotlights. On the other, a jumble of cameras, cables and video equipment.

A rock wall almost covered in human skulls provided the backdrop. Each skull had a candle burning inside, which sent eerie shadows dancing across the stone floor. Rusty chains and an assortment of medieval torture instruments dangled from hooks set into the ceiling, conjuring up images of pain, torn flesh, screams and death. Amy Winehouse's haunting *Back to Black* was playing in the background. The dungeon was a cleverly designed film set used for shooting extreme bondage movies for the lucrative Asian and Middle Eastern markets.

Centre stage stood an ingenious wooden contraption bristling with lots of sharp spikes, hooks and nails. Invented by the Inquisition, it had been used effectively by zealous monks to extract confessions –

mainly from hapless women accused of witchcraft – by inflicting excruciating pain, mainly in, and around the genitals.

Alexandra sat astride – legs pulled wide apart – on what looked like a medieval rack. Her wrists were tied to iron rings set into the rock wall behind her and her feet to wooden stakes bolted to either side of the strange contraption. Hooked through the throat, a ghastly human head made of wax sat on top of each stake. Eyes bulging and covered in mock blood, the heads were reminiscent of a macabre display in Madame Tussaud's. Apart from a red ball-gag stuffed into her mouth, Alexandra was completely naked. Her face was streaked with runny make-up and tears, and her sweaty red hair pulled back and dishevelled, but her humiliated body radiated defiance.

'I can see the fun has already begun,' said Paulus. He waved to Van Cleef and the man operating the camera at the far end of the chamber. 'Where's Igor?'

A huge man built like a weightlifter stepped out of the shadows. 'Over here,' he said. Still wearing a tight-fitting black latex mask that covered his face, and leather belts with chains that criss-crossed his hairy chest, Igor looked like a medieval torture-master straight out of some silent horror movie. 'Just getting dressed,' he said, laughing. 'I've done my bit. It's Jan's turn, if he wants to have a go.'

Paulus walked over to Alexandra and looked at her. 'Brains and a good body,' he said, nodding appreciatively. 'The Japanese love big tits. And a genuine redhead to boot; in every department. The Arabs will go wild.' Unable to speak or make any kind of sound because of the nauseating gag in her mouth, Alexandra stared at Paulus, the look in her eyes hurling daggers of contempt at her tormentor that would have made an attacking cobra recoil in fear. 'You've already met Igor then. I hope he's been gentle. But then, he's such a big boy, isn't he? And so hairy.'

'Come, have a look,' said Van Cleef, adjusting the video camera. Paulus walked over to him and watched the replay.

'Good God, Igor, what have you done to the lady?' asked Paulus, laughing. 'My goodness, she'll never be the same again.'

'Jan's idea. He thought she'd like something a little different ...'

'Great ass,' said Paulus. 'Not bad for a scientist sitting in a lab all day, don't you reckon, guys? What a waste!'

Everybody laughed.

'I think we have enough,' said Van Cleef, turning serious. 'We better get her back home.'

'You're right,' said Paulus and switched off the camera. 'This makes *Deep Throat* look like a movie fit for nuns.'

Van Cleef walked over to Alexandra and placed his right index finger on her throat. 'So that there's no misunderstanding,' he said quietly, beginning to push ever so gently, 'here are the rules: You step out of line, or in any way fail to do exactly what we ask, the video will be released on the Internet. YouTube, social media, the lot. We might even place it on the official Gordon Institute website.' Van Cleef paused, licked his finger and then ran it slowly further down. First, he circled Alexandra's left nipple, then her right, and then moved down to her naval. 'An intelligent woman like you,' he continued, barely touching her skin, 'will appreciate the serious consequences should that happen. This is not a game. I'm sure you know this by now and you also know what we can do with you ... and to you.' Van Cleef paused again and ran his hand along the inside of Alexandra's thigh – making her skin crawl – and down her right leg until he reached the rope cutting into her ankle. 'This is your last chance, Dr Delacroix. Please don't disappoint us,' he said, and began to untie the rope.

## 97

Patrick O'Mara, the publican, was still doing the till in the bar when Moretti knocked on the front door of The Hero of Waterloo. *Another bloody drunk*, thought the burly Irishman, annoyed, and ignored the unwelcome interruption. He poured himself another Irish whiskey and continued to count the money. Moretti knocked again. This time the knocking was louder and more urgent.

'We're closed. Fook off!' shouted O'Mara in his guttural Irish accent and walked over to the glass door to have a look.

Moretti held up his ID. 'Police. Open up,' he said.

O'Mara unlocked the door. Stunned by the number of police officers armed with all kinds of implements streaming into the bar, he stood aside and watched.

'Apologies for the late intrusion,' said Moretti, 'but this is important. We need to get down into your cellar. Now!'

'All right.' Remembering a similar situation a few years before, O'Mara went behind the bar, opened a drawer and took out a bunch of keys. As an experienced operator in the liquor business, he knew that cooperating with the police was always a good idea. 'Come with me,' he said.

'I remember you,' said Jana, following the publican to the stairs. O'Mara looked at her. 'I remember you too,' he said. 'The Markovich raid.'

'That's the one,' said Jana. 'This is something similar and we need your help.'

'No problem. Let's go down.'

The spacious cellar under the historic pub – classified by the National Trust – dated from the mid-eighteen hundreds. Built by George Paton, a Scottish stonemason, using convict labour and sandstone from the nearby Argyle Cut, it was a precious window into Sydney's convict past. Reminders of the colonial days were everywhere.

If one looked carefully, the chisel marks of the convicts who had carved the sandstone blocks were still visible. At the far end of the cellar was the narrow entry to the notorious smugglers' tunnel. In the middle of the damp room stood a large wooden table with chairs and benches facing a huge fireplace. Iron pots, bottles and even shackles and chains littered the stone floor. Reminders of brutal colonial times long gone.

O'Mara threw the bunch of keys on the table and looked at Jana. 'You said you needed my help,' he said. 'What's on your mind?'

'As I remember it, you used to know the tunnels down here very well.'

'Sure, but a lot's changed since then.'

'In what way?' interjected Moretti.

'Well, after the Markovich raid, many of the tunnels were blocked off and the old exits bricked up, especially those down by the harbour.'

O'Mara pointed to the tunnel entry. 'As you can see, we put in an iron grate to secure our entry here just as we were told to, and—'

'How far does this tunnel go?' interrupted Moretti.

'Quite a ways, but I haven't been in there in years,' said O'Mara.

'Could you show us?'

'Sure.' O'Mara picked up the bunch of keys and walked across to the grate. 'I know one of these will open the lock. The Markovich brothers got off, didn't they?' he said, fumbling with the keys. 'Bloody shame. They were rogues, them boys.'

'Unfortunately, you're right,' said Jana. 'Insufficient evidence. They were only convicted of some minor offences and went in for a year or so. The ones who did real time were their associates who were caught red-handed, right here. Usual story, I'm afraid.'

'The Markovich brothers used to drink here all the time.'

'What; Zac and Zoran?'

'Yes, after they got out. They joined the bikies and came here often with their mates.'

'The Wizards of Oz,' said Jana.

'That's them. Their leader, the Wizard, was an evil bastard. Huge. Used to get into fights all the time. Bad for business. But he had a great voice,' O'Mara prattled on. 'Used to sing when he was pissed; opera mainly. Ha. We were glad to see the back of them though when they finally left and found another place to pull apart.'

*Incredible. Echoes of Anna Popov all over again. Here ... now*, thought Jana, remembering Jack's latest book. *If Jack could only hear this. Six degrees of separation* ... 'You do know what happened to the Wizard?' she said.

'I read something in the papers a while back ...'

'He met a horrible end.'

'I'm not surprised. You live bad, you die bad ... Ah, this one fits,' said O'Mara, and turned the key in the rusty lock. The grate squeaked open, revealing a narrow passage leading down into the darkness of the smugglers' tunnel.

Moretti turned to the Police Rescue crew standing around the table. 'Wait here, guys. We'll go in and have a look,' he said, and followed O'Mara and Jana into the tunnel.

Van Cleef waited impatiently for Alexandra to get dressed. Shaking uncontrollably, and still in shock, she fumbled clumsily with her clothes. For reasons he couldn't quite explain, Van Cleef felt suddenly uneasy. He had an uncanny sixth sense for detecting danger. It had saved him many times in the past. 'Hurry up,' he said, eager to get away. Helped by Igor, the young cameraman was packing away the video gear.

Van Cleef turned to Paulus. 'What next?' he snapped.

'We get out of here,' said Paulus. 'Through the special back door I showed you the other day. Our friends watching the front will be none the wiser, trust me. One of our cars is always parked in the back lane. Then we put our new film star here into a taxi and send her home; simple. And we both know she'll keep her mouth shut; won't you, my dear?' said Paulus, looking at Alexandra. 'Otherwise ...'

'I hope you're right,' said Van Cleef.

Paulus slapped his friend on the back. 'Why so glum all of a sudden?' he said. 'Cheer up. Everything's gone like clockwork.'

'This is it,' said O'Mara. 'That's as far as we can go.' He pointed to a brick wall blocking the narrow passage in front.

'What's behind this?' asked Moretti.

'The rest of the old smugglers' tunnel leading down to the harbour.'

'Anything else?'

'Yeah. The tunnel dug by the Markovich gang. It used to link up with it a little further down to give the gang access to the harbour. That's why this was blocked off.'

'Stay here. I'll get the guys,' said Moretti.

'What are you going to do?' asked Jana.

'Knock down the wall, of course, and see what's behind it.'

The brick wall was a flimsy, hastily erected affair. Using sledgehammers and crowbars, it took the crew only minutes to make an opening large enough for a man to crawl through.

'This is the old entry to the Markovich tunnel,' said O'Mara, pointing to a bricked-up opening to his right on the other side of the wall. Moretti noticed it appeared to be pointing towards the Universal Security premises further up the road.

'Well, what do you think?' asked Jana.

'Not bad for a hunch,' said Moretti. 'So far so good. When there's nothing left, follow your instincts.' Moretti turned around. 'Okay guys, you know what to do.'

Paulus was leading the way, his powerful torch lighting up the tunnel ahead. Still in a daze and unsteady on her feet, Alexandra stumbled along behind him. Igor and the cameraman had to steady her a couple of times to prevent her from falling. Van Cleef brought up the rear.

'Did you hear that?' said Van Cleef from the back. 'Stop! Listen!'

Paulus stopped. 'What? I can't hear a thing,' he said.

'Knocking … there,' said Van Cleef.

Silence.

'I can't hear anything either,' said Igor.

'You are imagining things,' said Paulus.

The tiny hairs tingling on the back of his neck and the perspiration running down his chin told Van Cleef otherwise. 'No, I'm not!' he said. Every fibre in his tense body told him to turn around. 'We should go back.'

'Nonsense,' said Paulus. 'We are almost there. Let's go.'

Moretti had reached a low section in the Markovich tunnel. To go any further, he had to get down on his hands and knees and crawl forward through the rubble. 'What's this?' he said, shining the torch up ahead. The tunnel appeared to be opening up again into what looked like an intersection.

'What can you see?' asked O'Mara.

'Looks like another tunnel. Here on the right.'

'I don't remember this,' said O'Mara. 'Must be new.'

Moretti turned off his torch. 'Shh! Did you hear that?' he said.

'What?' said Jana, coming up behind him.

'Voices!'

Moretti crawled forward and looked around the corner. That's when he saw it: a light was coming towards him out of the darkness. 'Not a sound! Get back and don't move. And keep your heads down. Someone's coming!' he hissed and reached for his gun.

# 98

Moretti held his breath and let Paulus walk past. Then he jumped to his feet, walked up to him from behind and dug the muzzle of his gun into his back. 'Freeze!' he shouted. 'On your knees; now!'

Caught completely by surprise, Paulus stopped in his tracks.

Jana stood in the shadows with O'Mara by her side and let the Police Rescue officers run past. 'You two,' said one of the officers pointing his gun at Igor and the cameraman, 'on your knees.'

Van Cleef reacted like lightning. Years of training had honed his reflexes and ability to assess the unexpected and make snap decisions. His mind racing, he turned around and began to walk slowly out of the circle of light and away from the commotion because he knew nothing attracts the eye more than movement. Van Cleef felt suddenly his old self again. Uncertainty had been replaced by danger. He could handle danger.

Van Cleef remembered passing a ledge under the ventilation duct moments before. For some reason, he had made a mental note of it. There was just enough light drifting across from the torches in the tunnel to make out shapes in the gloom. Running by now, Van Cleef reached the ledge, looked up and smiled. *Perfect*, he thought, and lifted himself up onto the ledge with one, easy, fluid move. The ledge was just wide enough for him to lie down. There was more good news: the suspended duct, which ran along the ceiling all the way to the exit, had enough clearance under the tunnel roof for him to crawl along without being seen from below.

Jana saw Alexandra leaning against the sandstone wall opposite, disorientated and confused. She hurried over to her. Alexandra saw her coming. Overcome by relief and sobbing, she collapsed into her arms.

Moretti handcuffed Paulus kneeling in front of him. 'We meet again, Mr Koenig,' he said. 'And so soon. We have unfinished business – remember? For the last time, where is Van Cleef?'

'I want to call my lawyer,' said Paulus.

'He was just behind me,' said Alexandra, who had overheard the question.

'Search the tunnel – quickly!' said Moretti to the other officers crawling out of the smugglers' tunnel behind him.

Ignoring the commotion below him in the semi-dark, Van Cleef kept doggedly crawling along the ventilation duct towards the concealed exit at the far end of the tunnel. Paulus had proudly shown it to him the day before and explained how it operated.

Moretti hurried along the tunnel in the opposite direction until he reached the concrete wall behind the garage and could go no further. *Nothing*, he thought. *Damn! Where is he?*

'He must have gone into here,' said one of the officers, pointing to the steel door with the flashing green light on the panel.

'Get Koenig!' barked Moretti.

Holding him by his handcuffs, one of the officers dragged Paulus along the tunnel towards Moretti.

'Now, are you going to open this, or do we have to break it down?' said Moretti.

'Go to hell,' hissed Paulus. 'I want my lawyer.'

'A little cooperation would go a long way for someone in your position.'

'Fuck off!'

'All right, guys, go to work, and take this lowlife and his cronies outside.' said Moretti. 'I want this opened as quickly as possible.'

'This will take a while,' said one of the Police Rescue officers, examining the door. 'We need to cut through the metal here with the torch. Tricky job.'

'Call me when it's open, but don't go inside. And search the rest of this tunnel, every inch of it. I'll be in the pub upstairs.'

'Some of us are lucky,' joked the officer, and went to work.

Jana and Alexandra were sitting in the bar. The publican had poured them a large whiskey each and was having one himself. Alexandra had a blanket wrapped over her shoulders, but was still shivering. Jana took Moretti aside. 'You'll be shocked when you hear what happened to her,' she said, lowering her voice.

'I can imagine,' said Moretti.

'I doubt it. She was—'

'Later,' interrupted Moretti. 'She's safe, that's all that matters for now. Catching Van Cleef has top priority. He's got to be somewhere down there. It's a bloody fortress full of electronic stuff, and that arrogant bastard still thinks he's calling the shots. Well, in a way he is, but not for long. We've sealed off the place. Van Cleef can't get away. It's only a matter of time, but I still feel uneasy. Until we catch him …'

'They were leaving,' interjected Alexandra. 'They were going to put me in a taxi and send me home … I want to go home; please.'

'Don't worry. The guys are searching the rest of the tunnel right now,' said Moretti. 'If there's an exit, they'll find it.' Moretti looked at Jana. 'Why don't you take Alexandra home,' he said, lowering his voice. 'I don't want to put her through more … '

'No medical examinations? Evidence?'

'No. We can interview her in the morning and she can make a statement then.'

'Good idea,' said Jana. 'She has to get away from here, but I'll come back. Marcus is at home, he'll look after her. I'm sure he'll attend the interview with her as well.'

'Excellent. I'll ask one of the guys here to drive you home. Go.'


Paulus, Igor and the cameraman were under arrest and on their way to the station. The rest of the tunnel had been thoroughly searched. Except for another steel door set into the concrete wall at the far end, no exit or escape route of any kind had been found. No one thought of checking the duct running along the ceiling. From below, it appeared innocent enough.

*Dead end?* thought Moretti. *Can't be!* He was certain that an exit of sorts was behind that door. However, that would have to wait. Cutting open the other door turned out to be far more difficult than expected and was taking its time. *Where is Van Cleef?* Moretti pondered, over and over. Becoming increasingly agitated, he was nervously pacing up and down in front of the bar.

'You keep that up, you'll wear a hole into the carpet,' said Jana, walking back into the pub.

'Back already?' said Moretti.

'I've been thinking ...' said Jana.

'Oh?'

'When we raided the Markovich compound and the gang's tunnel, we discovered a secret escape route ... It's difficult to orientate yourself down there, but it could be the same one.'

'Perhaps, but for now all we have is a dead end. A steel door set into the concrete wall at the end of the tunnel. I left an officer there, just in case. No one's going through that door. Until we break it down, we won't know.'

'Perhaps we will ...' said Jana.

'What do you mean?'

'I think I can show you where the Markovich tunnel used to come out into the street. I arrested one of the Markovich brothers – Zoran – as he was climbing out, trying to get away.'

'What? Do you think you could find the place?' asked Moretti.

'I think so. Let's have another look and see where the tunnel ends. It could give us a clue.'

'Definitely worth a try. I hate waiting. Let's go down.'


Van Cleef had reached the end of the duct and was lying perfectly still just above the young officer guarding the exit. This was a complication he hadn't expected. Everybody else was busy at the other end of the tunnel, trying to break down the door to the dungeon.

Tired and bored, the officer was sending text messages on his iPhone. The distraction was exactly what Van Cleef needed. Silently, like a deadly spider stalking a hapless fly, he slid down from the duct until his feet touched the ground. Then, looking at the young man in front of him, he worked out the best way to kill him. Taking a deep breath, he struck. Moments later, the young man was convulsing on the ground – already dead – his neck broken and twisted, his phone still in his hand, a text message from his girlfriend awaiting a reply.

Van Cleef stepped over the dead body and quickly punched a code into the panel. The door opened with the promise of freedom and escape.

# 99

Moretti knew something was wrong. The back of the tunnel was in complete darkness. *Where's the guy?* he thought, and began to run.

The young officer was lying on his back, eyes open wide, blood oozing out of the corner of his mouth. 'Jesus,' said Moretti and knelt down to feel his pulse. 'Dead. His gun's gone!'

'When?' asked Jana, catching up to Moretti.

'Moments ago.'

'Van Cleef?'

'Who else?'

'How?'

'Don't know, but I'm sure he's gone through this door. Over here, guys,' shouted Moretti, raising the alarm. As he waved his torch about, his eyes fell on the ducting above.

'Look at this,' said Moretti, pointing his torch at the duct. 'That's how, I bet! While we were busy searching the tunnel down here, we failed to look up there. Too late! He's one step ahead of us again. What a mess.'

'And now he has a gun,' said Jana.

'What about that Markovich exit? Do you think you could find it?'

'I think so. Certainly worth a try.'

'Forget the other door, guys, work on this one,' shouted Moretti as the Police Rescue officers came running. 'Break it down, any way you can! He's just killed one of ours.' Moretti turned to Jana. 'Let's go,' he said, 'I only hope we're not too late.'

Van Cleef felt elated. For him, killing was the ultimate thrill. It ran through every fibre of his body and gave him a sublime feeling of invincibility and power. He had pulled off an almost impossible escape right under the noses of his pursuers. Macbeth would be proud of him. The gun too, felt good in his hand.

Van Cleef feared only one thing: failure. He slipped the gun under his belt and began to climb up the ladder attached to the wall of the narrow shaft leading to the street above.

Moretti and Jana ran out of The Hero of Waterloo. 'As I remember it,' said Jana, we were tipped off about the gang's escape route and the hidden exit. It was in a small side alley just behind the hotel. I think it was a dead end.'

'Come, let's have a look. I don't have to tell you what's riding on this,' said Moretti, fidgeting nervously beside Jana.

'You don't,' she said, concentrating. 'The street had lots of trees, just like that one over there.' Jana pointed to a small side street, a dead end, with lots of cars parked in front of a row of terraces.

One of the cars caught Moretti's eye; a black four-wheel drive. 'Have a look at this,' he said excitedly.

'What?' said Jana.

Moretti pointed to the number plate. 'I SPY4U 2. Does this remind you of something?'

'A getaway car? We must be in the right place,' said Jana. Then it was all coming back to her. The raid; the manhole on the side of the footpath; the gunfight and the arrest.

'Here, I think this is it,' said Jana. She pointed to what looked like an ordinary Sydney Water manhole cover next to the footpath.

'I hope you're right,' said Moretti.

'What do we do now?'

'We hope and we wait. Over here, out of sight. Behind the car under the trees.'

Van Cleef reached the top of the ladder and smiled. The car keys were exactly where Paulus had left them the day before. Set into the concrete next to them was another control panel with a flashing green light. It operated the steel trapdoor leading into the street outside. *The code*, he thought, *what was that code?* Van Cleef had a mental block. He could clearly remember the code for the tunnel door below, but after that, everything just went blank as he tried to think about the trap door above.

*Shit! What was it?* Desperately trying to remember, he punched in several combinations, his fingers shaking, but all to no avail. Think man, think, he admonished himself, refusing to consider the consequences of failure. To be trapped at the exit was unthinkable. He could already hear the crew working on the door below. *It was just like the other code, except for the end digits*, he thought, and tried again. Nothing. Desperate by now, he kept punching in more combinations. Still nothing. Then the penny dropped. *Of course*, he thought, *that's it:* ISPY4U2DAY. With a purring hum, the round trapdoor above him clicked open.

'There, look,' said Moretti.

'What? I can't see a thing,' said Jana, her eyes watering from the strain.

'The trapdoor. It's opening!'

'Wishful thinking …'

'No! Look!'

Moretti was right. First, the manhole cover began to lift slowly, then it opened up completely and a head began to appear.

Van Cleef sucked in the cool, fresh air and looked around. Apart from a streetlight at the end of the lane, all was dark and quiet. *Perfect*, he thought, and lifted himself out of the hole.

'*Get ready*,' whispered Moretti, pulling his gun out of the holster. '*As soon as he opens the car door, we move.*'

'*Okay*,' Jana replied.

Van Cleef closed the manhole cover and pressed the button on the car keys. A beep and a flashing light told him all he had to know: in a few seconds, he would be gone. Elated, he hurried over to the car and opened the driver's door.

Moretti stepped silently out of the shadows from behind and pressed his gun against the back of Van Cleef's neck. At the same time, he pulled the gun out of Van Cleef's belt and handed it to Jana. 'Don't even think about it,' said Moretti. 'Nothing would please me more than to blow your head off. Raise your hands where I can see them and kneel – now!'

Van Cleef did as he was told.

'Jana. Handcuffs; here,' hissed Moretti, handing her his handcuffs but without taking his eyes off Van Cleef. Jana stepped forward and handcuffed Van Cleef from behind.

'Now, lie down,' ordered Moretti.

Again, Van Cleef obeyed without a word. He knew this wasn't the time to do anything foolish. His chance to make a move would come later, he was sure of it.

'Keep him covered,' said Moretti to Jana and made a phone call asking for urgent reinforcements.

Moretti saw a deep scratch on Van Cleef's right wrist and smiled. 'I bet I know where that nasty scratch came from,' he said, leaning over Van Cleef.

'I don't know what you're talking about,' hissed Van Cleef.

'Oh, I think you do,' Moretti contradicted him. 'A struggle in a nightclub? Does that perhaps ring a bell?'

Silence.

'Ah, nothing to say? When the pathologist looked under Cavendish's fingernails, she found some flakes of skin. We have an excellent DNA sample. I bet when we compare it with yours, we might be in for a little surprise. What do you think? Perhaps even another murder implicating Mr Macbeth, your employer?'

More silence.

'But then again, it's all a bit academic, isn't it?' continued Moretti, enjoying himself. 'Now that he's *dead* ...'

Van Cleef said nothing, but his body went suddenly tense. Moretti smiled. 'You'll be facing the music all by yourself, mate, and it isn't a pretty tune. An Australian prison for the rest of your life? Oh ... Perhaps you haven't heard the news yet? After all, you've been so busy abducting people and killing policemen ... The Blackburn Pharmaceuticals ship was attacked by pirates in Somalia yesterday and went down, taking Mr Macbeth with it into the deep. *He's dead,*' whispered Moretti.

'Lies! You must think I'm stupid,' barked Van Cleef.

'Jana, why don't you Google today's papers on your phone and show the headlines to our friend?' Moretti wanted to keep Van Cleef busy and engaged until reinforcements arrived.

Jana called up *The Sydney Morning Herald* and put her iPhone down on the grass next to Van Cleef's face where he could see it. *Flagship of Pharmaceutical giant sunk by Somali pirates; Reclusive billionaire goes down with his ship*, read the headlines. Van Cleef kept staring at the screen without saying anything.

'It's the end of the road, Van Cleef,' said Moretti. 'And about bloody time too. Filth like you—'

Moretti was interrupted by laughter and shouting coming from one of the terraces behind him. The front door opened and a group of young revellers – obviously drunk – staggered out into the street with bottles in their hands. One of them spotted Van Cleef lying on the footpath with Moretti and Jana standing over him.

'What the fuck are you guys doing over there?' asked one of the men, his speech slurred. Two women walked into the lane. One bent over the gutter and was sick.

'This is a police operation,' said Moretti, 'stay back!'

'Oh yeah?' said one of the other men. 'Did you hear the man, guys? He says he's a fucking copper. And I'm Mickey Mouse, looking for my car. I left the bloody thing somewhere right here. Perhaps you can help me find it, Mr Policeman?'

Laughter.

'Stay back!' said Moretti, aware the situation could quickly get out of hand.

Van Cleef realised this was his chance. The distraction was a godsend; exactly what he needed. 'Help me,' he shouted.

One of the young women limped over to him – she had lost one of her shoes – and looked at him. 'Poor bastard. Come over here, guys,' she shouted and then was sick again. Jana walked over to her and tried to calm her. 'Fuck off!' screamed the woman, her brain addled by party drugs. Her friends came running over to see what was going on.

501

Van Cleef knew this was it. He had to make a move before reinforcements arrived. With the unexpected commotion and confusion erupting all around him, he knew Moretti wouldn't take the risk and fire his gun. Clenching his teeth, Van Cleef rolled over onto his back like a caged tiger and, lifting his right leg, kicked Moretti in the knee. It was a mighty blow, sending Moretti staggering backwards. By the time Jana turned around to see what was happening, Van Cleef was already sprinting down the street, cheered on by the rowdy crowd.

# 100

Van Cleef realised if he could make it to the street corner without being shot, he would have a real chance of getting away. *Almost there*, he thought, running like a madman.

Moretti steadied himself, his knee throbbing with pain, and lifted his gun. He shut out all the excitement erupting around him and took aim. As Van Cleef ran through a cone of light under the lamppost at the end of the lane, Moretti had a clear line of sight and fired. Van Cleef heard the gunshot behind him and felt a searing pain in his thigh, but he didn't slow down. He turned the corner and sprinted into the street just as the second shot echoed along the lane.

*Damn!* thought Moretti. *Missed!* and ran after him.

A minibus pulled up in front of the entrance to the famous Sydney Bridge Climb, a popular tourist attraction. A group of excited Japanese tourists got out of the bus and went inside to prepare for their dawn climb. It was 4:30 a.m.

The blood running down his trouser leg and the excruciating pain confirmed Van Cleef's worst fears: the gunshot wound was serious. Ignoring the pain was easy, but he knew the blood loss could be fatal. With his hands firmly tied behind his back, he was unable to stem the flow. Then he saw lights in the distance, and people going into a brightly lit building directly under the Harbour Bridge. For a man on the run in his condition, crowds were a much safer place than a deserted street in a quiet neighbourhood.

Van Cleef ran through the door and looked around. Inside, the hall was packed with eager tourists looking forward to their Bridge Climb adventure they had booked months before. They would wait for sunrise at the top of the famous Sydney Harbour Bridge and enjoy the spectacle of a lifetime. The first group had already changed into the obligatory grey overalls and was walking along a narrow passage above the entrance.

Van Cleef was very good at assessing situations quickly. Going back outside wasn't an option; his armed pursuer would be coming through that door any moment. With people now screaming and staring at him, hiding wasn't an option either. There was therefore only one way to go: follow the route of the famous Bridge Climb leading onto the Harbour Bridge, and take your chances.

Moretti turned the corner and looked around. Nothing. *Where the hell did he go?* he wondered, and began to jog down the deserted street. *In there, I bet,* he thought, as he approached the Bridge Climb entrance. Van Cleef always did the unexpected.

Moretti pushed past the eager visitors and burst into the crowded hall. Screams coming from above told him all he needed to know: Van Cleef was on a narrow, suspended walkway directly above him. He was pushing his way through a group of terrified tourists towards a gate that marked the beginning of the climb. A guide stepped forward, held up his hand and tried to stop him. A devastating head-butt from Van Cleef flattened the hapless young man who collapsed onto the floor, blood gushing from a deep cut above his eyebrow. Then more screams as Van Cleef disappeared through the gate leading outside.

'Stand back! Police!' shouted Moretti holding up his ID. Taking three steps at a time, he ran up the stairs. 'Where does this go?' he asked another guide who was helping his injured colleague.

'Outside; the approach to the bridge, the pylon and then up the arch,' said the guide.

'Jesus!' said Moretti. 'Anybody else out there?'

'No. This is the first group.'

'Thank God,' said Moretti, and darted through the gate.

Jana called Moretti on his mobile. 'Where are you?' she asked. 'Tactical Response has arrived and is looking for you.'

'On the Bridge Climb,' said Moretti, trying to catch his breath.

'What? Are you serious?'

'Deadly. Van Cleef's been shot. He's limping and bleeding badly, but he's just begun to climb up the arch with his hands tied behind his back. He's struggling, but he's right here in front of me and I'm not far behind him.'

'Shall I tell the guys to take up positions?'

'Do that. They should have an excellent view of all this from below. This will be a sunrise to remember,' said Moretti, and hung up.

Van Cleef's mind was in overdrive. Beginning to feel dizzy from severe blood loss, he knew he couldn't keep up the punishing pace for long. He looked over his shoulder and saw Moretti – gun in hand – closing in from behind and realised his situation was hopeless. He was effectively trapped on the bridge with nowhere to go, especially in his condition. But for him, surrender wasn't an option. And besides, he'd just killed a policeman. *You'll spend the rest of your life in an Australian jail,* he heard Moretti say. *You'll face the music all by yourself because Macbeth is dead ... Macbeth is dead ...*

With his feet beginning to feel like lead and white sparks dancing in front of his eyes, Van Cleef kept losing his balance, but was doggedly dragging himself up the hundreds of steps leading to the viewing area at the top. The early morning traffic crawling across the deck of the bridge below had almost come to a standstill. Drivers cursed in frustration as they did every morning, oblivious to the drama unfolding above.

'Stop right there! It's no use,' shouted Moretti, 'there's nowhere to go.'

'Go to hell,' shouted Van Cleef, and kept climbing.

The pain in Moretti's swollen knee was so severe by now he could barely walk. He stopped to catch his breath and looked across the still harbour and out to sea.

Suddenly, the horizon to the east began to glow as the promise of a new day lifted the veil of the night. Hesitantly at first, but quickly gaining strength, the first rays of the morning sun began to rise out of the sea, illuminating the top of the arch of the Harbour Bridge.

Jana stood next to one of the Tactical Response commandoes watching Van Cleef through the scope on his gun. 'Look at that,' she said. 'Isn't it beautiful?'

'Very unsteady on his feet. Losing a lot of blood,' said the commando flatly, ignoring her remark. '*What is he doing?*'

'I can't see; too far away.'

The commando handed Jana his binoculars. 'Try this,' he said.

Van Cleef reached the top of the arch and stood under the huge Australian flag moving gently in the morning breeze. Barely able to stand upright, he was leaning against the handrail to steady himself and appeared to be watching the sunrise.

Moretti too, had almost reached the top by now. He was pointing his gun at Van Cleef and was slowly climbing the last few steps to the top. 'It's over,' he said, panting. 'Sit down. You need medical attention, and soon.'

Van Cleef didn't reply and kept staring out to sea. Suddenly, he lifted his right leg up high and over the handrail. Then, with his foot balancing on a narrow ledge on the other side, he lifted the other leg over as well. Within seconds, he managed an almost impossible feat for someone so weak, and whose hands were tied behind him: he had climbed over the handrail and was standing precariously on a narrow ledge one hundred and thirty-four metres above the harbour.

'He's going to jump,' said the commando.

'I think you're right,' said Jana, mesmerised.

'Stay where you are,' shouted Van Cleef.

Moretti stopped in his tracks, put his gun back in its holster and looked at Van Cleef.

'You were wrong about one thing,' said Van Cleef.

'Oh? In what way?'

'I won't be spending the rest of my life in an Australian jail.'

'Fair enough,' said Moretti. 'Better that way.'

For a long moment, Van Cleef kept staring at the rising sun like a man facing a firing squad. Then he let go of the handrail behind him, stood perfectly still for an instant, and then began to fall forward.

'There he goes,' said the commando, and lowered his gun. Jana held her breath and watched Van Cleef plunge headfirst into the dark waters of the harbour below, barely missing a ferry full of early morning commuters on their way to work.

# 101

The PM went over the questions one more time. Then he closed the dossier, looked across to Westminster Abbey and smiled. *This should do it*, he thought. Two things mattered in politics more than anything else: timing, and luck. With the election only weeks away and all the headlines dominated by Dr Rosen's surprise press conference and the extraordinary revelations regarding Blackburn Pharmaceuticals and its activities in Somalia, the timing was perfect. The only potential embarrassment was the MI5 investigation implicating Blackburn Pharmaceuticals and Macbeth in Lord and Lady Elms' murder. However, Macbeth's unexpected death might just be enough to put the matter to rest, reasoned the PM. With so much at stake, it was worth the gamble.

Successful politics is always a delicate balancing act, and no one understood that better than the PM. It was now up to him to establish a credible link between Macbeth and Huntington – the infuriating Leader of the Opposition who couldn't put a foot wrong – without implicating Lord Elms. Exposure of what Lord Elms had been working on just before he died, and why, could quickly turn into political dynamite that could easily blow up in the government's face. It now came down to tactics, and the PM was a master tactician.

He picked up the phone and asked his secretary to come in. 'Please have this delivered to Mr Huntington as soon as possible,' he said, and handed the dossier to his secretary. The dossier contained a series of questions the PM would ask in parliament the next day. To maximise the damage, the PM had decided to give Huntington advance notice of what was about to happen. This was certainly not a matter of courtesy; it was a matter of strategy. If he could achieve his objective without having to expose his sources to scrutiny and possible attack, so much the better.

The carefully crafted questions didn't refer to Lord Elms or the recent tragedy. Instead, they focused on the notorious pharmaceutical giant, Macbeth's murky past, and his relationship with the Labour Party and its leader. However, the most devastating blow would come from a single piece of paper the PM had attached to the questions. It was a photocopy of a document discovered by Lord Elms a few days before he was murdered. The document was like a deadly missile. The PM was confident it would not only hit its target, but obliterate it.

Huntington looked up, annoyed. 'What is it?' he demanded. He didn't like to be interrupted when he was preparing for Question Time.

'This just arrived from the Prime Minister,' said his PA, and placed a folder marked 'Urgent and Confidential' on the desk in front of her boss. Huntington looked at it, surprised. In all his years as Leader of the Opposition, this had never happened before.

Political instinct is a curious creature. One either has it, or not. Something about the folder made Huntington feel uneasy and the hairs on the back of his neck tingle. 'Thank you,' he said without taking his eyes off the document. The PA took this as a dismissal and headed for the door. As soon as she had left the room, Huntington opened the folder, and paled.

*Questions the Prime Minister will be asking in Parliament tomorrow:* read Huntington.

*1. Has the Labour Party received any political donations – directly or indirectly – from Blackburn Pharmaceuticals or Alistair Macbeth?*

*2. Has the Leader of the Opposition received any benefit or support –directly or indirectly – from Blackburn Pharmaceuticals or Alistair Macbeth?*

*3. Has the Leader of the Opposition ever met with Alistair Macbeth, or had any dealings with him personally?*

In shock by now and trembling, Huntington read how Alistair Macbeth had allegedly made a fortune out of illegal toxic waste disposal in Somalia during the nineteen eighties and nineties, which had caused untold misery to the local population and killed thousands. He learned how this highly profitable venture had been brokered by the Calabrian Mafia ... His vision blurred, Huntington took off his glasses and sat back to digest the enormity of what he had just read.

Then, taking a deep breath, he finished reading the questions and turned the page. For a long while, he just stared at the document pinned to the front page, his fingers shaking.

Two hours later, Daniel Huntington shocked the nation. Overwhelmed by another man's black and deep desires, he fell on his sword and resigned.

# 102

Jana walked into the rundown Bondi nursing home and asked to see the matron. She had received a phone call early that morning, telling her that Lena Abramowitz had passed away during the night.

'She died peacefully,' said the matron. 'Would you like to see her? She's still in her room. Will you be making the funeral arrangements?'

'There's no one else?' asked Jana.

'Not that we're aware of. A Jewish charity arranged her admission here and a couple of volunteers came to visit her from time to time, but apart from that ...'

'I see. Yes, I will make the arrangements.'

'Good. Just come to see me when you're ready,' said the matron, and pointed down the corridor. 'You do remember her room?'

Jana nodded. 'Yes, I do,' she said.

Jana stopped in front of Lena's room, a sense of apprehension washing over her. She remembered the first time she had visited Lena Abramowitz with Jack in her shabby little flat in Rose Bay three years ago. On that occasion, they had shown her that horrible photograph of the SS Major and the pitiful, naked boy. That had been the beginning of an extraordinary journey of discovery and revelation, lifting the curtain on unspeakable suffering and monstrous wrongs of the past. Jack's famous book – *Dental Gold and Other Horrors* – dealt with some of it, but there was more; so much more ...

*This is the end of an era*, thought Jana, *and the end of a sad and tragic life. The horrors Lena would have witnessed in Auschwitz* ... Jana remembered the recent Hoffmeister interview in Buenos Aires. *And we thought the Steinberger saga had been closed ... Somehow, evil never dies ...*

Jana opened the door and quietly entered the room.

Lena Abramowitz was lying in her bed, a small posy of flowers in her bony hands. She looked fragile, but at peace. For a while, Jana stood by the bed and just watched the old lady. Then, overcome by the sadness of the moment and the finality of it all, she began to pray: 'Love is always patient and kind. It is never jealous. Love is never boastful or conceited …'

Jana heard someone knocking softly and turned around to see the door open and a woman enter the room. 'Matron told me I would find you here,' said the woman. 'You are Jana?' Jana nodded. 'I'm Pastor Caroline. Do you mind if I come in?'

Jana welcomed the interruption. 'Please do,' she said, wiping tears from her cheeks.

'I was with Lena when she died,' said the pastor. 'She was very coherent and lucid right to the very end. I speak German, you see. She spoke about Auschwitz and her sister Miriam, and the operations … She spoke about the Nazi major with the dog, and the trial. She spoke about you …'

'Me?' said Jana, surprised.

'Yes. You and your friend brought the Sturmbannfuehrer to justice,' she said. 'And that's why she wanted you to have this.' The pastor reached into her pocket and pulled out a small silver locket on a chain. 'She wore it around her neck,' said the pastor, handing the locket to Jana. 'She said you would know what it was.'

Jana opened it. Inside was a tiny photograph of two identical looking young girls in ponytails, and a lock of blonde hair.

Jana met Alexandra at the Gordon for coffee later that morning. Alexandra had insisted on going straight back to work after her ordeal, to continue her research. She thought that keeping busy would be the best way to cope with what she'd been through in the past two days.

'How did it go?' asked Alexandra. 'You look sad.'

'She's at peace. I've made funeral arrangements. There's no one else. Marcus and I will pay for it.'

'May I contribute?' said Alexandra. 'I would really like to.'

'Sure.'

'Moretti came to see me. You just missed him.'

'Oh?'

'Akhil, my assistant, has been arrested.'

'That's hardly a surprise. Moretti came to tell you this?'

'No, he came to apologise … He feels somehow responsible for what happened,' said Alexandra.

'That's nonsense, surely,' said Jana.

'Not the way he sees it. I was his responsibility. He had to keep me safe, he said, and he failed.'

'Wow!'

'There's more,' said Alexandra, 'and it's really interesting.'

'Tell me.'

'You know what he said? Apparently, when forensics examined the video equipment they discovered that everything had been wiped … The recording of my …' Alexandra faltered, then she whispered, *'It's gone. Disappeared.'*

'Just like that? Do you believe him?' asked Jana, lowering her voice.

'That it's gone – yes. As to how – no, not really. I think he wiped it. It was his way to make amends. He almost hinted … He wanted to spare me, I'm sure of it. The stuff was really unimaginable. Grotesque, brutal, degrading in the extreme …' said Alexandra. 'Having to watch it say, in court, would be unthinkable.'

'Decent chap,' said Jana, nodding her head. 'Rare.' Skipping the almost mandatory medical examination after Alexandra's ordeal suddenly made sense.

'Moretti also said that this would have no bearing on the prosecution. He had enough evidence to convict the guys several times over. And with Van Cleef dead …'

'That's great. You deserve this. I too have something to tell you,' said Jana. She reached into her handbag and pulled out Lena's locket.

'What's this?' asked Alexandra.

Jana handed her the locket. 'Open it,' she said.

Alexandra held up the lovely piece. 'How beautiful. Where did you get it from?'

'Lena left it to me,' said Jana, her voice quivering with emotion.

'Oh?' Alexandra opened the locket and looked inside.

'My God! Is that what I think it is?'

Jana nodded.

Alexandra could barely suppress her excitement. 'The Abramowitz twins? A lock of hair? Miriam's?' she said.

'I think so.'

'Do you realise what this means?'

'Tell me.'

'We can now sequence the genome of the other twin.'

'Is that important?'

Tears in her eyes, Alexandra stood up, and embraced Jana. With all the pent-up emotions of the past forty-eight hours bursting like a dam, Alexandra began to sob. *'More than I can possibly explain right now,'* she whispered and kissed Jana on the cheek.

# 103

Jack knew he was being watched. With the whole country in turmoil after the Labour leader's shock resignation, it was hardly surprising. Sir Charles' advice had been brief and to the point: 'Better lie low for a while, Jack, or better still, get out of Britain until things settle down a bit. Toppling the Opposition is enough excitement for the time being … Everyone's a little jumpy here. I've already told Isis that this is definitely *not* the right time to come home. MI5 is a little trigger-happy and the newshounds are already in a frenzy. We don't want to throw another juicy bone to the salivating pack, do we?'

'Good point,' agreed Jack. He welcomed the friendly advice because he was about to take Tristan back to France in any event. Jack closed his notebook, stepped out of his room and went looking for Lola. He found her hunched over her computer by the huge window overlooking the Thames, her favourite place in The Time Machine's apartment. 'I have an idea …'

Lola pushed her keyboard aside and looked expectantly at Jack.

'I've been thinking …' he said.

'Oh? What about?'

'How best to complete my assignment.'

'I don't follow …' said Lola.

'Somehow, I have to get everyone together in one place …'

'Why?'

'So I can tell them what we've found out. They should all hear it at the same time to avoid misunderstandings and confusion. That's really important here. Remember what Isis said?'

'What?' said Lola.

'No secrets.' Jack held up his notebook. 'It's all in here. All the threads. I believe I now have everything needed to pull them all together to complete the picture and solve the puzzle. And what a puzzle it is.' Jack shook his head. 'Quite unbelievable. This should really happen sooner rather than later. Especially in light of recent events here, in Sydney and in Somalia.'

'Is that really necessary? Everybody coming together, I mean.'

'It is.'

'Who should be there?'

'Isis of course, and Señora Gonzales; the two central players. Then you and Hanna, Sir Charles and Sir Humphrey, naturally. Dr Rosen, if she can spare the time. She too may be glad to get out of the limelight for a while. The countess and Tristan would be there already … Alexandra and Jana would be good, but that's unlikely. Tyranny of distance.'

'You've obviously thought of something. What's on your mind?'

'Well, things are a little bit hot around here and Sir Charles definitely doesn't want Isis to come back just now. So, why don't we speak to Countess Kuragin and see if we can rent her chateau for a while? It's big enough to accommodate everyone. It's geographically convenient and totally private. It could even be a great place for Isis' recuperation for a while. I'm sure she'd like that. What do you think?'

'Excellent idea, Jack. Let's get on to it straight away.'

'Why don't you speak to Isis and I'll call the countess,' said Jack. 'Let's see what reaction we get.'

Early the next day, Jack caught the Eurostar to Paris with Tristan and Dr Rosen. Lola had flown to Mexico to pick up Señora Gonzales before collecting Isis and Hanna in Boston on her round trip to Paris.

As expected, Countess Kuragin had embraced Jack's request with enthusiasm and delight. She immediately cancelled all other engagements and was looking forward to welcoming everyone to her chateau. The hostess in her was already in overdrive. Jack, Tristan and Dr Rosen would be the first to arrive and the countess had sent François to meet them at Gare du Nord, the train station in Paris. The others were due the next day.

Jack looked at Tristan sitting next to him. 'We have to get this right, you understand,' he said, the tone of his voice conspiratorial.

'Oh? What exactly?'

'Our story. Your holiday with me … If Katerina gets wind of what we've really been up to, you can forget your next trip, mate.'

'She already knows,' said Tristan, casually brushing Jack's concerns aside.

'What are you talking about?'

'Katerina and Lola have been in contact all the time. She knows exactly where we've been, and what we've been doing. There's nothing to worry about.'

'I see,' said Jack. 'And you knew this all along?'

Tristan shrugged.

'Great. I'm just the dummy in the middle,' said Jack.

'No. You're much more than that,' said Tristan, grinning. 'You're an incorrigible—'

'Just shut up,' interrupted Jack, and looked out the window.

'Sulk if you must, but I thought you'd be pleased.'

'For Christ's sake!'

'All right; I get it.'

The welcome Jack and Tristan received at the chateau was a little overwhelming. The whole household was buzzing with excitement and Countess Kuragin was overseeing everything personally. Flowers in every room, a string quartet for the evening and a dinner menu fit for royalty were just the beginning. To have everyone come to her home was a treat she hadn't expected, and to have a megastar like Isis staying indefinitely as her guest was something the whole district would talk about for months. *Never a boring moment with Jack*, she thought, *and Tristan is doing cartwheels.*

'Aren't you pleased now that Katerina already knows everything?' said Tristan.

'What are you getting at?' asked Jack, feigning disinterest.

'Can't you see? No grilling for either of us, no endless questions, no recriminations … only hugs and kisses. We can do no wrong. Thank you, Lola!'

'All right. You may have something there,' conceded Jack. 'Now, please keep out of the way for a while. François just pulled up. I have to talk to Sir Charles before the others arrive. Isis will be here in a couple of hours. That should keep you happy – right?'

Sir Charles and Sir Humphrey had arrived on the Eurostar together and François picked them up from the station. Sir Humphrey had gone to his room to freshen up and Sir Charles was in the library on his own. He was enjoying a glass of champagne and reading *The Times* he had brought with him, when Jack walked in.

'Splendid idea, Jack, to bring everyone here,' said Sir Charles. He put down the paper. 'It's a madhouse at home. Here, have a look.'

'I've seen it,' said Jack. He took the champagne bottle out of the ice bucket and topped up Sir Charles' glass.

'This whole affair needs some time to settle down. Huntington's resignation has virtually handed the election to the government on a plate. People are screaming for answers.'

'So, Stars, hide your fires was a success?' said Jack. 'Post-humously?'

'Resounding. Here, I have a present for you,' said Sir Charles. He reached into his coat pocket, pulled out an envelope and put it on the table in front of Jack. 'From a very grateful George Underwood. Something for your briefing session tonight ...'

Jack opened the envelope. It contained only one piece of paper, neatly folded in half. He pulled it out of the envelope and read it, disbelief and surprise clouding his face. 'Is that what brought Huntington to his knees?' said Jack quietly after a while.

'What do you think?' said Sir Charles, and raised his glass. 'Stars, hide your fires, indeed. In this case, they appear to have ignited an unstoppable inferno. Cheers!'

# 104

'Well, do you like it?' said Isis, examining herself in the mirror.

'Stunning, as usual,' Lola reassured her. It was the first time Isis had displayed any interest in her appearance since the operation. Accentuated by a blonde wig that would have made Lady Gaga jealous, her tight-fitting black pantsuit by John Galliano – one of her favourite designers – showed off her figure to perfection.

'At least I still have my curves,' said Isis. She smoothed down the sides of the pantsuit and held up a pair of black trousers. 'Or do you think the black culottes with a Chanel blouse would look better? I'm certainly not wearing a bloody dress. Formal dinner or not,' she said.

Lola walked over to Isis and kissed her on the cheek. 'Don't fret; you look great. And please remember, you're among friends here.'

Isis took off her wig, her shaved head making her suddenly appear much older. 'Look at this train wreck,' she said, tracing the long, zipper-like scar running down the back of her skull with the tips of her manicured fingers. 'At least we're in the transformation business, appearance wise. I no longer know who I am,' continued Isis, shaking her head. 'Perhaps tonight will change that,' she said quietly. 'Come on, let's do make-up and see if we can turn this train wreck into the Orient Express – eh?'

Watched over by Lola and Señora Gonzales, Isis had slept during most of the flight, which was exactly what Dr Greenberg had hoped for. She had arrived refreshed and in good spirits at the Kuragin Chateau in the afternoon. Feeling instantly at home in the fabulous suite on the first floor, with a great view down into the park-like gardens, she enjoyed the warm welcome extended to her by the countess. With an instant rapport springing up between them, they had liked each other at first sight and got on like old friends. And then, of course, there was Tristan, radiating exuberance and teenage adoration, which was as endearing as it was irresistible. Isis certainly didn't mind. It was precisely what she needed after her Boston ordeal.

Señora Gonzales, on the other hand, felt tired and apprehensive. She had only spoken to Jack briefly after her arrival, but what he told her filled her with dread. Part of her desperately wanted to know, and part of her desperately wanted to forget. She had hurried to her room after their arrival to collect her thoughts and to rest.

Unable to have a nap, she examined the past and tried to prepare herself for what Jack would reveal in the evening. All he had said was that he had found the answers to most of the questions ... She tried to get more out of him, but he had politely refused, reminding her of their arrangement. Señora Gonzales knew exactly what he meant. She had set the rules in place herself.

Exhausted, Señora Gonzales closed her eyes and floated back to that painful time at the Ritz during the war. Having her child taken from her in such a brutal way is something no mother can forget. *Has Jack really found out what happened to my baby?* she wondered, drifting into a restless slumber. *Will I be content when I finally know what happened, or will my heart bleed again?* Then she saw long forgotten faces and heard familiar voices reaching out to her from a turbulent past.

First, the handsome SS Major who had swept her off her feet was smiling at her from the top of the stairs at the Ritz, and calling her name. Then came Göring, chatting excitedly with Coco Chanel and Sarah Bernhardt in the fabulous dining room filled with Germans. Finally, she saw her friend, Anastasia Petrova, flirting with a dashing young officer at the bar, telling him that her heart was French, but her ass was international ...

Señora Gonzales sat up with a jolt; someone was knocking on her door. It was Lola coming to take her down to dinner. Isis walked up to Lola from behind. 'Let's go down together, Mamina,' she said. 'I have the feeling that tonight will change us all.'

'As you wish,' said Lola and stepped aside.

Always conscious of appearances and maximum impact, Isis, the consummate performer, couldn't help herself. She linked arms with her grandmother and guided her towards the stairs. Together they would make an entry worthy of a megastar.

Downstairs, the evening was already in full swing. A string quartet was playing softly in the background and pre-dinner drinks were being served in the elegant salon facing the garden. The floral arrangements the countess had ordered from the village were stunning, giving the evening a festive touch, like a special occasion to be celebrated with family and friends in the intimacy of a beautiful home.

Countess Kuragin, an experienced hostess, knew exactly how to make her guests feel relaxed and at ease. She made sure that Sir Charles and Sir Humphrey were comfortably seated next to Hanna. Two elderly gentlemen and a ravishing young woman were always a good mix and an excellent way to keep the conversation lively and sparkling. Copious quantities of vintage champagne would do the rest and François made sure that no one had an empty glass.

Jack and Dr Rosen were chatting on the terrace. *Far too serious,* thought the countess, looking at their faces. *Definitely in need of some lighthearted distraction.* She took a silver tray with an assortment of delicious canapés from the waitress and walked outside. 'You must definitely try one of these,' she said. 'Foie gras in puff pastry; an old Russian recipe from my aunt. Delicious.'

The countess needn't have worried. Distraction was on its way. Slowly, one step at a time, Isis and her grandmother came walking down the stairs. For an instant the conversation stopped, as everyone watched. *Two remarkable women approaching an evening of destiny together,* thought Jack, and followed the countess across the room to greet them.

The dinner was a sumptuous affair. Coquilles St Jacques and freshly shucked oysters, followed by honey-roast confit of duck with sour cherries, prepared the way for a crème brûlée that Escoffier would have been proud of. The countess had instructed François to raid the wine cellar for something special, and he did. A 1982 Château Latour à Pomerol, and a spectacular 2009 Château Margaux blended perfectly with the main course. Impressed by the vintages, Sir Charles – a serious wine connoisseur – was delighted. The evening was off to a good start.

The countess realised the meal was merely preparing the way for the main event of the evening – Jack's briefing – and had structured the dinner accordingly. As the hostess in charge, she was able to control the evening and guide her guests. After the dessert plates were cleared away, she suggested they all go into the music room next door for coffee and liqueurs. Tristan, who as a special treat had been allowed to join them for dinner, said goodnight; he was taking his new friend Boris to meet Anna in her studio.

With all eyes on him and anticipation growing by the second, Jack knew it was time to begin.

# 105

Jack walked over to a large TV screen set up in front of the grand piano. 'You may be wondering,' he said, 'what something so obviously out of place is doing here in this beautiful music room.' Jack pointed to the TV. 'Actually, tonight it will take centre stage. Why? Let me show you.' Jack looked at his watch. *Just gone six a.m. in Sydney*, he thought, and turned to face François standing behind him. 'It's time,' he said. 'Let's start.'

Everybody in the intimate room was comfortably seated around the elaborate marble fireplace, with a good view of the TV. Countess Kuragin had arranged this quite deliberately because she knew what was coming. To accommodate its sophisticated clientele, the chateau was equipped with the latest video conference facilities. Jack had the same setup in his Sydney apartment for conference calls with his publishers and editor on the other side of the globe. François made a quick phone call and turned on the TV.

First, a picture of a modern living room appeared. Brilliant sunshine was streaming through large open windows, and water could be seen sparkling in the distance. Then slowly, the camera turned slightly to the left, showing three people seated around a coffee table facing the camera with Anna's striking painting on the wall behind them.

'Good morning, Sydney,' said Jack. 'Can you see us?'

'We can,' said Alexandra, waving. 'Good evening. We hope you've had a lovely dinner.'

Jana and Carrington waved too. 'The reception is excellent,' Carrington said.

'What a splendid idea,' said Sir Charles to Sir Humphrey sitting next to him.

Isis held her grandmother's hand and kept staring at the TV screen, but said nothing.

*Skype on steroids*, thought Lola. *Clever*. She locked eyes with Jack and nodded, her approval obvious. Once again, Jack had surprised everybody. Despite the tyranny of time and distance, he had managed to bring everyone together. Once he had made the necessary introductions and explained who everyone was, his anticipated briefing session could begin.

'Firstly, a big thank you must go to Katerina for opening her wonderful home to us at such short notice,' said Jack, pointing to the countess sitting next to Lola and Hanna in front of him. 'And for a most memorable dinner that made us all feel so welcome and relaxed.' Jack bowed to the countess to a round of polite applause. 'Without her,' continued Jack, 'we wouldn't be here. And without all of us coming together, right now, here, in one place, I wouldn't be able to tell you about the extraordinary things I've discovered, and the events – and the people – who played a part in making it all possible.

'As many of you have directly participated in those events and contributed to the discoveries, I will call on some of you, if I may, to give your own account of what happened, and why. That way, we'll make sure that nothing is lost or overlooked and authenticity and accuracy are preserved in every way possible. This is essential if we are to uncover the truth, which is often cleverly disguised, hidden, or simply too far-fetched to be believable.'

Having set the parameters, Jack the storyteller was in his element and ready to begin. The story he was about to tell had all the hallmarks of a riveting tale of war crimes, deception, greed, intrigue and murder, but also of selfless love, heartache and joy, where destiny and fate had ensnared lives in a complex web, resulting in a drama of Shakespearean proportions that was bound to keep any audience spellbound and glued to their seats to the very end.

In many ways, however, it was much more than that. It was a reflection of real life and real people, and Jack was about to disclose what he had discovered about some of those people, tucked away in hidden corners of their lives.

'On the way here, I thought long and hard about how I should begin,' said Jack. 'To do this story justice and put everything into proper context, we have to travel back a few years and revisit a devastating bushfire in the Blue Mountains just outside Sydney, and a photograph discovered by accident. This is it here ...'

Jack held up a copy of the shocking photograph of the SS Major, his Doberman, and the naked boy hanging from a tree. 'This is where it all began. In the ruins of a cottage destroyed by that fire. Those of you who have read my book – *Dental Gold and Other Horrors* – would be familiar with all this. It was the beginning of another extraordinary journey, which culminated in the exposure and trial of a notorious Nazi war criminal – Sir Eric Newman, alias Sturmbannfuehrer Wolfgang Steinberger, the man in this photograph. Jana was the investigating police officer and Marcus the barrister who conducted the trial in Sydney. And the person who gave us the first important clue in the investigation and showed us the way, was Lena Abramowitz, an Auschwitz Holocaust survivor. I mention her here because in a surprising twist, she features again in a most amazing way in our story. But for now, let's focus on Sturmbannfuehrer Wolfgang Steinberger, and how the mention of his name persuaded me to take on this extraordinary assignment.' Jack paused and turned to Señora Gonzales. 'Perhaps you would care to tell us, Señora, why I was approached by Isis, your grandson, in the first place?'

'Go on, Mamina, do as he asks,' said Isis, squeezing her grandmother's hand in encouragement. 'It's important.'

Señora Gonzales nodded. 'I read Jack's book when it hit the bestseller list,' she said. 'When I discovered that the respected Australian banker, Sir Eric Newman, was none other than the notorious Sturmbannfuehrer Wolfgang Steinberger I knew a long time ago, I was in shock. At first, I thought there had been some mistake, but the more I read, the clearer things became. This was definitely the same man. For months, I desperately tried to forget all about this and bury the ghosts of the past, but they wouldn't let go. Then came my daughter's shocking murder ...' Señora Gonzales covered her face with her hands. '*Hidden corners of our lives* ...' she whispered, beginning to sob.

'I can take it from here,' said Isis, coming to her grandmother's assistance. 'I was with my mother when she died. Her injuries were so horrific, her face so disfigured, I could barely recognise her. Just before she passed away, she told me I was in great danger and mentioned a secret hiding place in our home only she and I knew about. Her last words were, "Stars, hide your fires"—'

'As you will see, these fateful words – "Stars, hide your fires" – will take on a special significance later in the story,' Jack interjected. 'In fact, without those words, and without the discoveries Isis made in that secret hiding place, this story would never have been told and the truth would have remained hidden, perhaps forever. It's often the little things, a word, perhaps even just a gesture, the casual mention of a name or a place that give us that vital little clue ...' Jack looked at Isis. 'Could you please tell us what you found in that secret hiding place?'

'I went from the hospital where my mother died, straight to Clarendon Hall in Kent, the Elms family residence where I grew up. There, hidden in an ancient wooden chest in the Egyptian room, I found something quite extraordinary,' said Isis, her voice barely audible.

'What did you find?' prompted Jack.

'A bundle of letters, and ...'

'What else?'

'Lola, would you mind?' said Isis. 'This won't take long.'

Lola stood up and hurried out of the room. Moments later, she returned with a beautiful wooden box, which she placed on a small table in front of Jack.

'May I?' said Jack. Isis nodded. Jack activated the concealed mechanism by pressing a button. The box opened, revealing the magnificent crystal skull, reflecting the light of the candles flickering on the mantelpiece behind them. The scene reminded Jack of another occasion not that long ago, when he and Jana had replaced the missing piece of a pharaoh's beard on a statue during an auction in London. 'I feel a bit like a magician,' said Jack. He pointed to the skull in front of him, glowing like a watching demon.

'It was the discovery of this extraordinary artefact that triggered the chain of events that has brought us here tonight,' said Jack. 'Would you care to explain how that came about, Señora Gonzales?' said Jack.

'When Isis told me about the crystal skull she had discovered and what my daughter had told her just before she died – the warning – I realised it was far from over. The past was once again closing in and I had to do something …' Señora Gonzales paused again and looked at Isis.

'Tell them, please,' said Isis.

'I had to find out what happened during the war in Paris all those years ago. Or, at the very least, I had to try.'

'What did you do?' asked Jack.

'I asked Isis to contact you and ask for your help.'

'Why?'

'*Because of your book* …' whispered Señora Gonzales. 'You exposed Steinberger and found out who he really was. Perhaps you knew more. Perhaps you could find out what happened to …' Overcome by emotion, Señora Gonzales began to choke.

'I think we should take a little break,' suggested Jack. He walked to the sideboard and poured a glass of water. Then he sat down next to Señora Gonzales. 'Are you all right?' he asked, and handed her the glass.

'Thank you, Jack. I will be in a moment. I wouldn't miss this for the world.'

# 106

Carrington turned the sound off and poured some orange juice for Jana and Alexandra during the short break Jack had suggested. 'He's doing a marvellous job,' said Alexandra. 'A born storyteller.'

'He is that,' Jana said. 'But as you'll soon see, there's always a lot more to Jack's stories than meets the eye. Deep down he's a very shrewd and perceptive operator with an uncanny instinct and ability to uncover the truth.'

'Well put,' said Carrington. 'I'm sure we're in for a few surprises before this is over.'

'I can't wait,' said Alexandra. 'Isn't Isis absolutely fascinating? And her grandmother – in her nineties? What do you make of her?'

'She's obviously at the centre of it all,' said Carrington. 'I would really like to know how Steinberger fits into all this and how Jack managed to find out about it.'

'Remember the Hoffmeister interview? That should give us a clue,' said Jana.

'Sure, but where's the connection? The link between Steinberger and his brother, and Señora Gonzales and Isis?' said Carrington, shaking his head.

'Knowing Jack, I'm sure we are about to find out,' said Jana. 'Here he is. Looks like he's ready to continue.'

Carrington waved at the camera and turned the sound back on.

'After Señora Gonzales mentioned Sturmbannfuehrer Steinberger's name and I accepted the assignment,' said Jack, 'she gave me an important clue. She hinted that a good place to start looking into those hidden corners would be at the hotel on Place Vendôme, none other than the famous Paris Ritz. And that is exactly what I did.'

Jack then went on to talk about how Countess Kuragin introduced him to her old friend, Anastasia Petrova, the famous Russian ballerina, and the extraordinary information he discovered about the years she

527

had spent at the Ritz during the war. He spoke of the scandal of the crystal skull, Göring's eccentric tantrums and the ballerina's close friendship with Señora Gonzales. He entertained his audience with his flirtatious adventures involving the flamboyant Mademoiselle Darrieux, and had them in stitches when he told them how he tried to resist her amorous advances without offending her. He explained that he did all that by following what he called 'breadcrumbs of destiny', to guide him through the confusing maze of information unfolding all around him.

'The real breakthrough came in two ways,' continued Jack. 'First, there was the information I gleaned from the letters Isis found at Clarendon Hall, pointing to Africa – Kenya, to be exact. Then came Dr Rosen with her childhood memories of Anton Hoffmeister visiting her father in the Blue Mountains.

'When we found out that Hoffmeister was still alive and Jana agreed to fly to Buenos Aires to interview him, things began to take on a momentum of their own.' Jack turned towards the TV screen. 'Jana, could you please give us a brief account of what happened during that interview?' he said.

'Sure,' said Jana. 'We knew Hoffmeister was a greedy rogue. Devious, and unreliable. He had played an important part during the Newman trial that caused us much embarrassment. But we also knew that he could have valuable information. He had known Steinberger and his brother since childhood. They had joined the SS together and collaborated during, and after the war. We thought it was worth the gamble.' Jana went on to describe her meeting with Hoffmeister at the old monastery and how she managed to acquire that important postcard from Nairobi, which provided the next crucial link in the investigation.

'This is it here,' said Jack. He held up a copy of the postcard for all to see. 'It cost a hundred thousand dollars for the interview, and a further thirty thousand just for this old postcard. But it was worth it, because without it, we wouldn't be here. It was the breakthrough I had been looking for. It pointed the way to Nairobi and the Van Der

Hooven family. The significance of this will become apparent in a moment. However, before I tell you about that, we have to take a step back.'

Jack needed some time to collect his thoughts. He reached for his brandy balloon on the piano behind him and took a sip of cognac.

'Let's pause for a moment and take stock,' he said. 'Most of what I've told you so far, you would have heard before. However, I feel it is important to revisit how it all began and how we arrived at this point. Allow me to recap: Lord and Lady Elms are brutally murdered in their home in London under suspicious circumstances four weeks ago. The official line of enquiry by the London Metropolitan Police and MI5 – that this was some kind of home invasion gone wrong – isn't accepted by Isis or Sir Charles. They don't trust the authorities.' Jack paused and looked at Sir Charles. 'They don't believe the matter will be properly investigated and suspect some kind of cover-up,' continued Jack. 'The only question is, why? Determined to find out, Isis decides to commence her own independent investigation and contacts me.

'For entirely different reasons, Señora Gonzales also suspects that there is a lot more behind the murders. When she learns about her daughter's hidden letters, her last words to Isis, and especially that crystal skull, her worst fears are confirmed: The past is closing in.

'But what exactly does that mean? What are those hidden corners of her life she keeps referring to? By talking to her friend, Anastasia Petrova, I discovered a great deal about those hidden corners. I found out what happened at the Ritz during the war. It all began with the scandal of the crystal skull and ended with Señora Gonzales being abandoned by the dashing German officer who held her fate in his hands. Not only was Sturmbannfuehrer Wolfgang Steinberger her lover and the father of her illegitimate child, he was the one who so ruthlessly took that child from her, never to be seen, or heard of again.'

Jack paused again and looked at Señora Gonzales watching him intently. She couldn't take her eyes off him and was hanging on his every word. 'Until now,' added Jack quietly. 'I believe that I have found out what happened after Steinberger left Paris with the baby and the crystal skull. I know what happened to the child and how all of this is connected to the Elms murders. Would you like me to continue, Señora?' asked Jack.

For a long moment, Señora Gonzales looked at Isis sitting next to her and then nodded her head.

'Very well,' said Jack. 'Some of you may find what I'm about to tell you difficult to believe, but the truth is the truth, whichever way we look at it. The past cannot be changed, nor can the truth be denied. I was approached by Isis to find out what happened to her parents, and I agreed to do just that.' Jack pointed to his notebook on the table in front of him. 'I believe I have the answers right here,' he said.

'As Señora Gonzales correctly suspected, those answers are inextricably intertwined with people and events of the past. Her past. What happened at the Ritz during those dramatic days during the war, set a chain of events in motion that marched on relentlessly for decades, and sent ripples of discord far into the future, with tragic consequences that will surprise and shock you.' Jack looked at Isis. He was trying to gauge her reaction, but couldn't see any.

'However, this discovery wasn't without danger and it did come at a price,' he continued. 'The ferryman has to be paid. Always. Dr Rosen, Lola and I almost lost our lives in Somalia a few days ago.' Jack didn't mention Tristan because he didn't want to frighten the countess. 'Several people died along the way, some in horrific circumstances. The forces of destiny are most powerful and cannot be resisted. Their reach is as long as their memory is relentless. At best, we can only hope to understand them and try to make sense of what is happening, and why—'

Jack was interrupted by a sudden commotion in front of him. Señora Gonzales pressed her right hand against her chest, her breathing laboured and heavy. Sir Humphrey rushed to her side. 'Some water please,' he said, and opened the top buttons of her blouse.

Feeling better, Señora Gonzales looked at him gratefully and drank some water. '*Angina*,' she whispered.

'A little too much excitement …' said Sir Humphrey, reaching for her wrist to feel her pulse.

'I think another little break may be in order,' said Jack.

'Excellent idea,' said the countess. 'Coffee everyone?'

## 107

The countess went to the conservatory at the back of the chateau, which she had converted into a studio for Anna, to see if Boris would like some coffee. When she opened the glass door, Tolstoy, her Labrador came to greet her. The countess stopped, patted her dog on the head and took in the remarkable scene.

Anna stood in front of her easel, painting as usual. Billy, her little boy, was fast asleep in his cot next to her. Tristan sat in the shadows, watching Boris play his balalaika. The familiar, melancholic folk tune reminded the countess of long Russian winters, and sleigh rides through the snow with her grandparents. The countess walked over to her daughter, looked at the painting and gasped. 'Anna, how did you—?'

Anna pointed to the iPad on the table next to her with a close-up of the crystal skull displayed on the illuminated screen.

'It's mine,' said Tristan. 'I took the photo and showed it to Anna. She said the skull had soul.'

'Amazing, darling,' said the countess, stroking Anna's short hair. 'You've certainly captured its soul.'

'You think so, Mama?' said Anna, looking at the countess. 'It's one of the most beautiful things I've ever seen, or touched.'

'You saw it?'

'Yes. Jack showed it to me this afternoon and told me its story. It came out of the jungle. A long time ago, as a gift from the gods. I'm painting the story – see? Tristan asked me to paint it. A gift for Isis …'

Boris stopped playing and walked over to the countess. 'Tristan saw something disturbing,' he said quietly. 'Just before you came in.'

'Oh? What?'

'Why don't you ask him?'

The countess looked at Tristan. 'What did you see?' she asked.

Tristan seemed reluctant to answer. 'Death,' he said, a troubled look on his face.

'Where?'

'Right here.'

The countess felt a cold shiver race down her spine. 'Nonsense,' she said. 'You've been looking at the crystal skull here a little too closely, I suspect.'

'I felt it too,' said Anna calmly, and applied some more green paint to the jungle plants forming the exotic background in the striking picture. Illuminated by a shaft of sunlight from above, a naked man wearing a spectacular headdress made of coloured feathers held up the crystal skull to the light with both hands, like an offering to the gods.

Anna stepped back from the easel. 'The skull needs more work,' she said. 'The eye sockets look dead, yet when I touched them they felt very much alive. They were telling me things ... You don't need eyes to see. I have to give it more soul, don't you think?'

The countess knew her daughter lived in a world of her own. This was especially so when she painted. Most of the time only Tristan could communicate with her, but on a different level. Remarkably, they did this without speaking. He and Anna had a special bond.

The countess realised it was time to leave. 'Don't stay up too late,' she said, and kissed Anna on the cheek. 'And that goes for you too, young man.'

*Someone will die tonight*, thought Tristan. Anna heard him and nodded ever so slightly. 'We won't, Mama,' she said, and resumed work on the skull.


Señora Gonzales appeared to have recovered her composure and was looking expectantly at Jack. 'Before we can go any further, Sir Charles has something to tell you,' said Jack. 'Charles, please ...'

Sir Charles walked up to the TV screen so that everyone could see him and stood next to Jack. 'Jack will shortly talk to you about Lady Elms' last words – "Stars, hide your fires" – and what they mean,' began Sir Charles. 'A number of high-ranking civil servants in Her

Majesty's Government put their careers and reputations on the line to help us find out what those words represented. The tragic murder of Lord and Lady Elms involves matters of national security at the highest level, implicating certain people in high places.

'One man in particular, a close friend of mine, was instrumental in passing classified information to me, which helped us find out what happened to Lord and Lady Elms, and why. This was discovered by MI5. Jack and I met with the man in charge of Her Majesty's Secret Service after Jack's spectacular press conference the other day, which appears to have, well, spooked the spooks ...

'We gave an undertaking not to disclose any of the information we've uncovered regarding Lord and Lady Elms' murders to anyone except those in this room, and that includes our friends in Australia. However, we are only permitted to do this if all of you respect the undertaking Jack and I have given. Any breach could have serious consequences. Not only would several people be severely compromised and their careers shattered, but a number of them, including my friend, would go to jail for a very long time. Needless to say, my own reputation and future are on the line here. So, before Jack can continue, we would ask each of you to give us your word you will not disclose any of this to anyone, especially the press. May I assume that this is acceptable?'

Everyone nodded and mumbled their agreement.

'Over to you, Jack,' said Sir Charles, and went back to his seat.

'I will now tell you an extraordinary tale spanning more than seventy years,' said Jack. He looked at Señora Gonzales. 'The story begins in Paris in 1942. Sturmbannfuehrer Steinberger and his brother, Erwin, leave Paris together and take Señora Gonzales' baby and the notorious crystal skull here with them.' Jack pointed to the crystal skull on the table in front of him. 'Señora Gonzales is left behind to fend for herself and her young daughter, Mercedes. The baby is taken in by Dr Steinberger and his wife, Greta – a childless couple who live in Vienna – and brought up as their own. The boy is given a name – Siegfried – and the necessary papers are arranged by his father. Siegfried becomes part of the family.

'Then, something really interesting happens,' continued Jack. 'Dr Steinberger joins the infamous Dr Mengele in Auschwitz and together, they carry out medical experiments using prisoners in the death camp. Dr Steinberger is particularly interested in twins, and cancer—'

'This is unbelievable!' interrupted Alexandra.

'I'm sorry. What is?' asked Jack, glancing at the TV screen.

'Dr Simon Kozakievicz, Professor K's father was there too! At the same time. Working with Mengele in Auschwitz!'

Stunned silence.

'How do you know this?' asked Jack, surprised.

'It's all in a letter Professor K left me. I have it right here. Wait …' Alexandra hurried to her room and returned with the letter moments later. She held it up to the camera to show the signature. 'Let me tell you what it says …'

Alexandra quickly summarised Professor K's letter with all the surprising revelations. She told them how his father survived the war and went to live in Switzerland after the liberation of Auschwitz, to work for a pharmaceutical company. She spoke about his research, his second marriage and his new family. She explained how his son, Kasper, followed in his father's footsteps and carried on his work in cancer research and became one of the leading scientists in his field.

'Serendipity,' said Jack quietly, shaking his head. 'This is a night full of surprises. Now let me tell you what happened to Dr Steinberger and his family after the war. They went to Italy and spent the next year hiding in a monastery in Rome under the protection of the Catholic Church. Wolfgang was there too and prepared the way for their escape and new lives abroad.'

'We discovered all that during the Newman trial,' interjected Carrington, who had been listening intently. 'Wolfgang had access to Nazi money in Switzerland and arranged the escape of many high-ranking SS officers, especially to South America. Anton Hoffmeister was one of them. Wolfgang himself travelled to Australia as Erich Neumueller, and began a new life in Adelaide with help from the

Vatican. He later changed his name to Eric Newman and became a successful banker.'

'And his brother, Erwin, went to live in Kenya under the name Van Der Hooven. He bought a farm just outside Nairobi,' continued Jack, 'and established a clinic there. However, this was no ordinary clinic. He continued to carry out medical experiments on sick natives. He was testing certain drugs – without their knowledge or consent, of course – just as he had done in Auschwitz.'

'What happened to the boy?' asked Señora Gonzales quietly.

'He grew up on the farm. A very handsome boy, apparently, who spent a lot of time with the natives in the bush. All went well until 1960. Then disaster struck.'

'What happened?' asked Señora Gonzales, her voice quivering and faint.

Jack held up the copy of the postcard from Nairobi. 'Here, listen to this,' he said. 'This postcard was sent by Erwin's wife, Greta, to Anton Hoffmeister in Buenos Aires. It is dated 25th October 1960:

*"Dear Anton*

*I have sad news. Life has taken a dark turn. Erwin was killed by the Mau Mau at the farm last week. We don't know exactly what happened, but the farm and the clinic have been burnt to the ground. Siegfried is safe and staying with me here in Nairobi. These are troubling times. I don't know yet what we are going to do, but at least we have the lodge. Siegfried is strong and a great support."*

'It's signed "Greta",' said Jack. 'After this, Hoffmeister lost contact with Greta and her son. But the picture on the postcard here provided a valuable clue.' Jack pointed to the house on the front of the postcard. 'Mukuyu Lodge,' he said. 'That's where I picked up the Van Der Hooven trail in Nairobi and found out something extraordinary about Siegfried. His affair with—'

Jack was interrupted by the sound of someone opening the door at the back. It was Boris, a little out of breath and with a puzzled look on his face. Everyone turned around to look at him.

'Please forgive the intrusion, Countess,' said Boris, looking quite embarrassed, 'but you should come and see this.' Jack and the countess excused themselves and followed Boris out of the room.

# 108

The countess could hear her dog barking well before they reached the conservatory. Boris held the door open and let her and Jack walk inside. Anna stood exactly where she had left her just a short while ago: in front of her easel, painting. Tristan stood next to her, looking intently at the painting with Tolstoy barking excitedly behind him.

'Shh, Tolly,' said the countess, trying to calm the excited dog. 'What's going on?'

'You've just missed it,' said Anna without taking her eyes off the painting.

'Missed what?' asked Jack.

'The skull was glowing ... telling me how to give it soul.'

The countess looked at Jack and shrugged. 'You don't say,' she said.

'It really did. I saw it just now,' said Tristan. 'And this plant here took on a peculiar shape – look, like a heart.' Tristan pointed to the painting. 'This is it here.'

'Exactly,' said Anna. 'And all I had to do is paint what I saw, and then the glowing stopped because I got it right – see?'

'Really?' said the countess, shaking her head.

'I saw it too,' said Boris. 'It happened exactly as she says ...'

'Tolly saw it as well and got quite excited, didn't you boy?' said Tristan. He turned around and patted the dog's head. Tolstoy sat and nuzzled up against his thigh.

'Don't look at me like that, Jack. I know what you're thinking. It happened ...' said Tristan.

'I believe you,' said Jack, 'but not all of us can see what you can.'

'I know,' said Tristan, 'but Anna can, and so can Boris.'

'Painting looks great,' said Jack, changing the subject.

'You like it?' said Anna.

'I do.'

'What do you like about it?'

'It's got soul,' said Jack.

Anna turned around. 'You're teasing me,' she said and dabbed Jack on the cheek with her brush, leaving a little green dot behind.

'Does this mean I'll glow in the dark now?'

'Only if you turn into a skull.'

'No chance.'

'Philistine.'

Jack turned to the countess. 'Let's go back. Philistines are obviously not welcome here,' he said, laughing, and headed for the door.

'What did you make of all that?' asked the countess on their way back to the music room.

'Not sure. All I know is that Anna and Tristan have a special gift, and a unique bond. They are spiritual beings. I would never dismiss what they say, or see for that matter, as nonsense.'

'Thanks, Jack.'

'Does that help?'

'A little.'

'Anna looks well.'

'She's getting better; day by day,' said the countess. 'The treatment in the Paris clinic has done wonders. We are grateful for that. She's back home now.'

'You think this was weird? Wait until you hear what I'm about to tell them in there,' said Jack and opened the door for the countess. 'It will make a glowing skull pale into insignificance.'

'Can't wait.'

'What happened?' asked Sir Charles as Jack and the countess walked back into the room.

'Storm in a teacup,' said Jack. 'Sorry about the interruption. I was telling you about Mukuyu Lodge and how I managed to pick up the Van Der Hooven trail again in Nairobi.'

Jack looked at Isis. 'I thought very carefully about this again. What I'm about to say now will affect you, Isis, most of all, but your grandmother as well. Profoundly. Things will get very personal, I'm afraid, and could be quite upsetting. So, I must ask again. Would you like me to continue, or would you like to talk to me privately first?'

'Please go on,' said Isis. 'Everyone here has been part of the journey so far and deserves to know. Are you comfortable with this, Mamina?'

'I am,' said Señora Gonzales.

'You have your answer, Jack,' said Isis.

'So be it. After her husband's murder and the sacking of their farm and the clinic by the Mau Mau, Greta went to live at Mukuyu Lodge in Nairobi with Siegfried. Their lodge was very popular, especially with the British, and Siegfried, an accomplished hunter and guide, took wealthy tourists on safari. The Van Der Hooven safaris were legendary and Mukuyu Lodge was the social hub of Nairobi and the safari capital of the world at the time.

'This was another clue. Señora Gonzales had previously told me that Lord Elms had one great passion: big game hunting. As it turned out, he had been a regular visitor to Kenya for years, and always stayed at Mukuyu Lodge when going on safari. Another piece of the puzzle had fallen into place. Suddenly, a picture began to emerge, and the letters Isis found at Clarendon Hall began to make sense.'

Jack held up a bundle of papers. 'These are all love letters. Any reference to the sender's identity – like a name, or an address – had been carefully removed, except for a few subtle clues. However, there can be no doubt that these letters were sent to Lady Elms by her lover.'

Jack paused and ran his fingers through his hair. He was preparing himself for what came next.

'A few months after Erwin Steinberger was killed, Lord Elms visited again. This time, however, he didn't come alone. He brought his lovely new wife, Mercedes, with him. As soon as Siegfried and Mercedes set eyes on each other, it was love at first sight,' said Jack quietly. 'And not just any love, but a passion that appeared to overwhelm and consume them both.'

'No! This cannot be!' cried Señora Gonzales. 'You must be mistaken! My daughter and her ...' Stony-faced, Isis squeezed her grandmother's hand, but didn't say anything.

'Yes, half-brother,' Jack cut in. 'Your son. A cruel, ironic twist of fate, perhaps, but true nevertheless. And it doesn't stop there, I'm afraid,' Jack pressed on. 'There's more to come ... much more.'

Now that some of the most devastating cards were on the table, Jack thought it best to reveal the whole pack. Quickly and accurately, so as not to prolong the pain this was certain to cause.

He spoke of the young lovers' reckless affair, right under the nose of Lord Elms, the proud, newlywed husband. He explained when and how the love letters originated and why they were sent. 'It might have ended there,' said Jack, 'if Lord Elms hadn't returned to Nairobi for another safari. But that was exactly what he did later the same year. And this was, of course, what the young lovers had been pining for. The letters clearly reflect that. They resumed their affair with reckless abandon and became careless.

'Then the inevitable happened: the affair was discovered by Lord Elms, resulting in a huge scandal the whole of Nairobi was talking about. To escape his wrath, the young lovers went bush. Literally speaking. Determined to get his young wife back and avoid the ultimate humiliation of losing her, Lord Elms mounted a search party and went after them.'

Jack paused, the silence in the room deafening.

'How did you discover all this?' asked Isis, her voice hoarse.

'From eyewitnesses and other reliable sources.'

'An accurate account then?'

'I believe so—'

'What happened to them?' interrupted Señora Gonzales, finding it difficult to breathe.

'The search party found them hiding in a native village in the bush. Lord Elms brought his wife back to Nairobi and immediately returned to England.'

'And Siegfried?' asked Carrington, who had been following the extraordinary revelations with great interest.

'This is where accounts differ and the story becomes a little vague,' said Jack. 'Apparently, he was caught by the Elms search party, savagely beaten and left for dead. Some thought he had been killed, but no one I spoke to was absolutely sure. Despite his mother's desperate attempts to find out what happened to him, Siegfried Van Der Hooven vanished and was never heard of again. Greta Van Der Hooven died soon after, and the Van Der Hooven name and fortune disintegrated and sank into obscurity.'

'Was that the end of it?' asked Carrington.

'Far from it. In many ways, it was just the beginning. The beginning of a new, tragic chapter with far-reaching consequences.' Jack looked at Señora Gonzales. 'Did you know any of this?' he asked. Señora Gonzales shook her head. 'Then what I'm about to tell you will shock you even more. When Mercedes returned to England with her estranged husband, she discovered she was pregnant—'

'Oh my God!' cried Señora Gonzales. She pulled a handkerchief from her skirt pocket and pressed it against her mouth.

Sir Charles turned to Sir Humphrey. 'This is incredible,' he said. 'If—'

'Are you suggesting that Siegfried was the father?' Isis interrupted, articulating the question on everyone's mind.

'Yes,' said Jack. 'You see, the reason no children came along during the first two years of the marriage was due to one simple fact: Lord Elms was impotent—'

'How do you know this?' interrupted Isis.

'Sir Humphrey confirmed …'

Isis kept staring vacantly into space as the implications of what she had just heard began to sink in. Suddenly, many things that had happened during her childhood and teenage years began to fall into place and make sense. The cold, estranged relationship between her parents; the often cruel, distant father; the doting mother, showering her with love; boarding school from an early age …

Jack sensed the growing tension in the room and decided to press on as quickly as possible and reveal all.

'You may remember I told you at the beginning that there were three separate parts to this story. All related to what happened just before Lady Elms died. So far, you've heard about the letters. Now I must tell you about this here.' Jack pointed to the crystal skull.

'Well aware of the rumours regarding Siegfried and what had happened to him after he was caught, Mercedes was certain he had been killed. Pregnant, and desperately unhappy, she resumed her life as Lady Elms at Clarendon Hall. To avoid a humiliating scandal and hide his embarrassing impotency, Lord Elms decided to bring up the child as his own. A divorce was unthinkable. No one was to know the child wasn't his. A healthy boy, George, was born. From then on, Lord and Lady Elms effectively lived separate lives.'

Jack turned towards the TV screen, certain that Carrington would be hanging on his every word. 'This brings me to the second part of my investigation,' he said, 'the crystal skull. So, where does it fit into all this? Hoffmeister told us that Wolfgang Steinberger had it with him in Rome and gave it to his brother when they parted company in Italy and went their separate ways. It was something that belonged to the boy, he told his brother, and should be given to him one day. That day came when Erwin was killed. Greta gave the precious skull to Siegfried to remind him of his father. It became a distraught boy's most treasured possession.

'The next part is a little speculative,' continued Jack, 'but we can safely assume that Siegfried would have shown his precious skull to Mercedes at Mukuyu Lodge. She must have been aware of it and known what it represented and what it meant to her lover. Why? Because of what happened next.

'A few years later, Lady Elms received an anonymous parcel. It contained only one item.' Jack pointed to the crystal skull on the table next to him. 'A beautiful wooden box with the crystal skull inside; nothing else. No letter, not even a note; nothing. However, Lady Elms knew exactly what it meant. It was a sign, a message telling her that the father of her son was alive!'

'Come on,' interjected Carrington, the sceptical barrister in him unconvinced and demanding to know more. 'How can you possibly know this is true and not just fanciful speculation?'

Jack turned back to the TV screen and dropped the bombshell. 'Because the person who sent the parcel told me so himself,' he said.

Stunned silence again.

'Are you serious?' said Carrington.

'Absolutely. And this brings me to the third part of my investigation: "Stars, hide your fires"; Lady Elms' ominous last words …'

*I need a drink*, thought Jack. He reached for his empty brandy balloon on the piano, and looked at François. François nodded and walked over to the sideboard to get the cognac bottle.

# 109

'Throughout my investigation, I became more and more convinced of one thing,' said Jack. 'What Lady Elms told her son moments before she died was of the utmost significance and could provide the answer to what happened to her and her husband. As it turned out, this was correct. I've already told you about her letters and the crystal skull. That leaves only those cryptic words, "Stars, hide your fires". What did they mean? Why had Lady Elms chosen those words as her last? Actually, it was Dr Rosen who provided the vital clue. I will never forget that moment.' Jack paused and looked at Señora Gonzales again, watching him intently.

'We were sitting in front of Dr Rosen's tent in Dadaab – the refugee camp in Kenya, near the Somali border – when I mentioned those words and speculated as to what they could mean.' Jack turned to Dr Rosen. 'Bettany, would you mind telling us what happened?'

'Jack had just spoken to Sir Charles on the phone and received some important news regarding the Elms' murder investigation in London—'

'That's correct,' interrupted Jack. 'Charles had just told me that he had met with a friend of his – a senior civil servant – who had provided some important confidential information regarding the Elms affair.'

'Forgive me for interrupting,' said Carrington, 'but what exactly was that important information about?'

'Charles told me that MI5 was convinced the Calabrian Mafia was behind the brutal attack.'

'How can that possibly be?' asked Isis.

'At first, I asked myself the same question,' said Jack, 'but then things began to fall into place. Apparently, it all had to do with Lord Elms' work. What he had been working on just before he died.'

'Did you find out what that was?' Carrington asked, unable to resist asking the question on everyone's lips.

'I did. Lord Elms was investigating pharmaceutical companies …'

'And the Mafia was somehow interested in this?' said Carrington, almost cross-examining Jack.

'Yes.'

'Why?'

'Because of something that happened in the past,' said Jack. He looked at Dr Rosen. 'Would you mind taking it from here, Bettany?"

'As I was saying before, Jack told me about Lady Elms' final words, "Stars, hide your fires", and pondered what they could possibly mean. That's when I told him …'

'Told him what?' interjected Isis, confusion and impatience reflected in her voice.

'That it was a famous quote from Shakespeare,' said Dr Rosen. '"Stars, hide your fires; let not light see my black and deep desires".'

'And this was helpful?' said Carrington, pursuing his would-be witness in the hypothetical witness box on the other side of the globe.

'It sure was,' said Jack, 'because it gave me that all-important, final clue to make the connection.'

'What connection?' demanded Carrington.

'Charles, would you mind answering that?' said Jack.

'Not at all. The quote is significant in two ways: first, where it comes from, and second, what it's about.'

'Please explain,' said Isis quietly, shaking her head.

'The quote is from Macbeth, and speaks about black and deep desires …'

'I still don't see the connection,' said Carrington.

'You will in a moment,' said Jack. 'Charles, please?'

'All of Lord Elms' projects had code names. It was a well-known, somewhat eccentric habit of his. Initially, his investigation was called Project *Detego*, which means something like "unmask" in Latin. Sometime later, however, it changed. He changed it to Stars, hide your fires. Why? Because he had *unmasked* the identity of the party he had been searching for. He was now investigating the affairs of a major international pharmaceutical company at the time he was killed. But which one, we didn't know, until Lady Elms' last words gave us a clue: Macbeth. Alistair Macbeth is synonymous with Blackburn Pharmaceuticals, the company Lord Elms was looking into.'

Stunned silence, again.

'But even if all this is correct, where's the connection?' demanded Carrington, cutting to the chase.

'The best way to answer that is by continuing Siegfried's remarkable story,' said Jack quietly. 'You'll remember he was left for dead somewhere in the bush near Nairobi after he was captured and beaten by Lord Elms' thugs. However, after that, the trail went cold. No one seemed to know what really happened to him, until those breadcrumbs of fate I've been talking about showed me the way …'

'Come on, Jack,' prompted Carrington, unable to hide his impatience. 'Please, just tell us.'

'As you would have already guessed from what I told you about the crystal skull, Siegfried did, of course, survive and I know what happened to him. Why? Because I met him and he told me all about it himself—'

'You met him! Is he alive?' interrupted Señora Gonzales, her voice trailing off.

'Forgive me, Señora, if I don't answer that straight away,' said Jack. 'This story must be told a certain way. Siegfried suffered some dreadful injuries at the hands of Lord Elms' men. Someone less fit and strong wouldn't have survived. He was taken in by the natives of the village he had visited since childhood, and was slowly nursed back to health. However, this did come at a price, a high one. He became … a paraplegic—'

'Good God!' interrupted Señora Gonzales.

'If this alone wasn't amazing enough, what happened after is even more remarkable,' continued Jack. 'Siegfried knew he couldn't show himself in Kenya, not even to his mother. The British authorities had closed ranks and hushed up the whole affair by colluding with all those involved to protect the Elms name and bury the truth, no questions asked. So, what did he do? He reinvented himself. He left

Siegfried Van Der Hooven behind in the village, presumed dead, and with the help of his African friends, he made his way to Somalia and a new life. A truly astonishing one ...'

Jack paused again, searching for the best way to break the next part of the story and looked at Señora Gonzales, the anguish on her face reflecting the pain of a desperate mother yearning to learn the fate of her lost child. Then he looked at Isis. *This will change her life*, he thought, *I know it would change mine*, and pulled the pin on his information grenade.

'Siegfried changed his name. He became Alistair Macbeth, one of the most powerful and influential business tycoons of our time. The man who almost single-handedly built Blackburn Pharmaceuticals, the multinational giant, while sitting in a wheelchair.'

'Incredible!' said Carrington, shaking his head.

'*You are talking about my father, here?*' whispered Isis, looking dumbfounded and confused. She looked at Señora Gonzales sitting next to her, searching for answers, but couldn't find any. She was just as stunned and stared stony-faced into the distance, trying to come to terms with what she had just heard.

'It's incredible, all right,' said Jack. 'But it doesn't stop there.'

'What do you mean?' asked Carrington.

'Alistair Macbeth's black and deep desires, were just that: black and deep ...'

'Please explain,' said Jana.

'Initially, Macbeth made a fortune out of the illegal dumping of toxic waste in Somalia. This was arranged and brokered by the Calabrian Mafia, the feared Ndrangheta. Several European countries desperate to solve the politically sensitive problem of toxic waste disposal which, incidentally, included radioactive material, were only too willing to deal with the Mafia – no questions asked – and pay handsomely for a convenient solution. A crime of expediency. And Macbeth was only too happy to provide that solution at the expense of a whole, impoverished and corrupt country and its hapless, desperately poor population. He then used his huge wealth to acquire pharmaceutical companies around the world until he had built up a vast conglomerate, which became Blackburn Pharmaceuticals, the giant we know today.'

'And you met him, you say?' said Carrington.

'Yes.'

Jack then went on to describe what he and Dr Rosen had discovered in Somalia, the horrible, secret drug trials, their abduction in Nairobi and how they had ended up on the *Calypso* as Macbeth's prisoners. 'That's when I confronted Macbeth and he told me all about his past.'

'Why did he do that?' asked Carrington.

'Because he had us in his power, completely. I'm sure he was going to kill us and make us disappear, just as he had done with many others. He was a man who loved that power. The power over life and death. He played with us – like the Roman emperors played with the gladiators in the arena – by holding our lives in his hands. Like the evil Lord Dracula needed blood, Macbeth needed power to stay alive. He savoured every moment of telling me exactly who he was, and what he had done, and why. But he wasn't alone. I too had something to tell him that put some big cracks into his private world. I showed him the Hoffmeister interview. But more on that later—'

'I still don't understand,' interrupted Carrington. 'How is all this connected to the Elms murders? Are you suggesting that Macbeth was somehow behind it?'

'Yes, I am.'

'Are you serious? Why?'

'Because of those black and deep desires ...'

'Would you care to explain?'

'I think Sir Charles could do this much better than I,' said Jack. 'Charles, would you mind?'

# 110

Sir Charles stood up, adjusted his bowtie and walked over to the TV screen so that everyone could see him. 'All of you would have heard about the recent events that rocked Britain: the surprise resignation of David Huntington, the charismatic Labour leader?' began Sir Charles. 'You may also know that he was the clear front-runner in the upcoming elections and was tipped to become Britain's next, and youngest ever, Prime Minister. I'm sure you are asking yourselves why I am telling you this. The reason is simple: David Huntington's shock resignation is directly related to those black and deep desires Jack has been telling you about.'

Jana looked at Carrington sitting next to her. '*Can you believe this, Marcus?*' she whispered.

Carrington shook his head. '*This is better than Shakespeare,*' he whispered back, his eyes glued to the screen. '*You could write a play …*'

'What I'm about to tell you,' continued Sir Charles, 'are some of those sensitive matters involving national security I spoke of earlier, and the reason I had to ask you to respect the undertaking Jack and I had to give in this murky affair to keep out of trouble. You will see in a moment just how sensitive and potentially explosive these matters really are.' Sir Charles kept adjusting his bowtie, a nervous habit that somehow helped him focus when tackling difficult subjects.

'The reason Lord and Lady Elms' murders attracted so much secrecy and the attention of MI5 at the highest level is simply this,' continued Sir Charles. 'At the time of the attack, Lord Elms was investigating certain matters involving David Huntington, the Leader of the Opposition, on behalf of the government. This was entirely politically motivated and designed to discredit Huntington and the Labour Party. The aim? Simple. To cause maximum damage just before the election, thereby seriously undermining Labour's chances of winning. In fact, you could say that Lord Elms was digging up the dirt on Huntington and, as you'll see in a moment, he was very successful in doing so. That is what cost him his life.'

'Are you suggesting, Sir Charles, that Macbeth was somehow implicated in this?' interjected Jana.

'Yes, but he was more than that. He was both; the instigator and the target.'

'I don't understand,' said Carrington.

Jack turned to Sir Charles standing next to him. 'May I?' he said.

'Of course.'

'Charles and I met with the head of MI5 the day after our impromptu press conference at the airport you would have all seen on TV the other day,' said Jack. 'You will recall, that was all about our abduction and the horrors we discovered in Somalia implicating Blackburn Pharmaceuticals, the sinking of the *Calypso* by the pirates and Macbeth's dramatic death. Sensational stuff, and as it turned out, political gold for the Conservative government. You will see why in a moment.'

Overwhelmed by what she had just heard, Señora Gonzales covered her face with her hands and began to sob.

Carrington looked at Jana. 'This is getting better by the second,' he said under his breath. 'Jack and his adventures …'

'After Charles and I gave the undertaking we spoke of to MI5,' continued Jack, 'we exchanged information. This is the full, murky story … warts and all.' Jack paused, the silence in the room deafening.

'As Charles just told you, Macbeth was both the instigator and the target, albeit indirectly. The government had suspected for a long time that Huntington had a powerful backer standing behind him in the shadows, watching, and shaping his career. And not just any backer, but someone who could manipulate the press at will, provide unlimited campaign funds, silence opposition to Labour policies and ideas and create a powerful image and a public persona with huge appeal to the electorate. And most importantly, that mystery backer could do all this well away from prying eyes, by staying in the background and under the radar of scrutiny and accountability. In short, someone was grooming the man for a historic election victory and the highest office in the land by carefully paving the way for the Labour darling who couldn't put a foot wrong, because most of the usual obstacles had been carefully removed.

'Understandably, the government wanted to expose this and approached Lord Elms, a trusted supporter of the Prime Minister and one of the most powerful political figures in Britain, to undertake this highly sensitive, and politically dangerous task. Project *Detego* – unmask – remember? Lord Elms was going to *unmask* Huntington's secret backer and, hopefully, discredit Huntington by association. At least, that was the strategy because, it was assumed, such support didn't come for free. There had to be a catch, a payback of sorts and Lord Elms had to find it.

'Lord Elms, a brilliant, well-connected strategist, worked mainly alone and without leaving too many footprints. However, we believe most of the missing pieces have now been found, and a clear picture of his activities has emerged.

'When he began to dig deep into certain highly confidential toxic waste disposal arrangements during the nineteen eighties and nineties, Lord Elms knew he was getting close. He also knew he was treading on some important and powerful toes. The Calabrian Mafia, for instance, and those in high office who had done business with them at the time, and profited handsomely from it.

'By now, Lord Elms was following a clear trail and began investigating certain pharmaceutical companies. That's when the name of his project changed from *Detego* to Stars, hide your fires—'

'Are you suggesting Lady Elms knew about this?' interrupted Carrington.

'She must have,' said Jack. 'Otherwise, why would she have used those exact words? And let's not forget, by linking that dreadful attack on her and her husband with precisely those words, she pointed the finger at those responsible. And as it turned out, she was absolutely right.'

'What do you mean?' asked Isis.

'MI5 discovered very soon after that the Calabrian Mafia was somehow behind the attack. We know this for two reasons. Firstly, the attackers left something behind. Quite deliberately, as a warning ...'

'No one told us about that!' interjected Isis. 'What was it?'

'A message; a *memento mori*. A mask. And not just any mask, but a most bizarre and recognisable mask, the Venetian Medico della Peste, the Plague Doctor mask. It was hanging around Lord Elms' neck when he was found shot dead in his home.'

'A warning, you think?' said Carrington.

'It would appear so, and a signature. Classic Mafia,' interjected Sir Charles.

Jack continued. 'The second reason was this: Once the bodies in the burnt out getaway van had been identified, it soon became apparent that the Mafia was indeed involved. However, the hitmen were executed within hours of the attack.'

'To frustrate any further investigation, you think?' asked Jana. 'To cover the trail and protect those behind it all?'

'Very likely, because the attack had gone spectacularly wrong,' said Sir Charles.

'What do you mean?' interjected Carrington.

'Allow me to answer that,' said Jack. 'According to MI5, the attack was originally intended as a warning, not an execution. We know that Lord Elms arrived home unexpectedly and surprised the intruders. They panicked and killed him as they fled the scene. This had not been the plan—'

'Then what was?' interrupted Isis.

'To disfigure Lady Elms' face in her home and leave the Medico della Peste mask behind as a warning and a clear message to Lord Elms and those behind him to drop *Detego*. Instead, he was killed and his wife mortally wounded in the botched attack, and he ended up wearing the mask himself as the Medico della Peste.'

'Lord Elms, the Plague Doctor having fallen victim to the very disease he was trying to expose?' speculated Carrington. 'Something very contagious. Political pestilence perhaps? How ironic!'

'Could be,' said Jack. 'The warning was supposed to be all about exposure. If Lord Elms didn't stop and persisted with his enquiries, the whole affair would blow up in the government's face, causing even more damage to its already very slim chances of re-election. That was the obvious threat.'

'This is absolutely right,' said Sir Charles. 'This was a political gamble at the highest level. Bold; risky; desperate. The attack was intended to stop Lord Elms and signal to the government that its smear campaign to discredit Huntington had been discovered and would be exposed – no doubt through a sympathetic press – causing a major scandal and embarrassment to the government.'

'This is all getting a little too much for me,' said Isis, shaking her head.

'Understandable,' said Sir Charles.

'Something puzzles me here, Jack,' said Isis. 'If Macbeth was indeed behind all this, and he was that mystery backer dabbling in British politics as you suggest, answer me this: *why?*'

Jack had been expecting the question and was prepared for it. However, he knew he had to tread lightly as one more rather devastating revelation was still to come. Well aware that Señora Gonzales had perhaps endured as much as anyone in her position could be expected to cope with in one night, he realised he had to choose his words carefully.

'We are coming back to those black and deep desires,' said Jack. 'To put it another way, *revenge* and *ambition.*'

'In what way?' asked Isis, the heavy make-up no longer able to mask the strain on her wan face. Despair was beginning to show as her world was crumbling all around her.

Lola reached for Isis' hand and held it tight. It felt cold and limp. *Just like her heart*, thought Lola, *I fear* ...

'Revenge first,' said Jack. 'The handsome young man almost beaten to death by the jilted husband of his lover, had somehow survived, but as a cripple, abandoned by the love of his life and stripped of everything he held dear. He keeps himself alive by nurturing one burning desire: revenge. He vows to avenge the terrible wrong done to him by Lord Elms and the Establishment that had helped him do it, and allowed him to get away with it and cover it up. The British.

'Next: ambition. Fast forward fifty years. The abandoned, penniless cripple has turned himself into one of the most powerful business tycoons on the planet and is ready to strike. He has two things in his sights: Lord Elms, and the British Establishment. He plans to destroy them both.

'However, just before he's quite ready, something unexpected happens. Incompatible with destiny, Macbeth's meticulous planning is intersected by fate. Lord Elms begins his secret investigation and uncovers what had been carefully hidden for decades, thereby raising the spectre of something Macbeth fears most ... exposure.

'After that, things begin to go wrong; very wrong. First, the ill-fated attack. Lord and Lady Elms were not supposed to have been killed. In fact, without the Elms investigation, the attack wouldn't have taken place at all. For Macbeth, just killing Lord and Lady Elms would have been far too lenient a fate. He had something much more subtle and cruel in mind. He wanted to destroy their lives and dreams just as they had destroyed his. He wanted them to *know* who had done it, and why. And in David Huntington, he had the perfect tool to achieve his darkest desires ... all of them. How? I'll tell you. Through an exquisite plan of revenge that would have made the story of the Count of Monte Cristo look tame.'

'Please explain,' said Carrington.

'Macbeth plotted to achieve all this by crushing Lord Elms' dream of a third successful Conservative government brokered by him. For decades, Lord Elms had been a highly successful king-maker, standing behind two successful Conservative prime ministers. By ending his long, illustrious political career through one of the most devastating election defeats since the war, Macbeth would make sure that this defeat would become Lord Elms' legacy and what he would be remembered for in history.'

'Come on, Jack, facts please, not speculation,' interjected Carrington, unable to help himself.

'I know how this must look,' said Jack, 'but please bear with me. You will not be disappointed; promise. In order to fully appreciate what I'm about to tell you, please keep this in mind: I confronted Macbeth on the *Calypso* in person about all this. This was just a few days ago. I showed him the Hoffmeister interview with all its far-reaching implications. Macbeth too, had to come to terms with some quite earth-shattering revelations. To begin with, he found out about Wolfgang Steinberger, his real father, and discovered that Erwin and Greta weren't his parents at all … Then came Dr Rosen. Remember, she was a prisoner on his ship at the time, just like me and he was going to obliterate us both. I asked Macbeth if he was prepared to kill his own flesh and blood. That's when he realised that the very person who had exposed his secret medical experiments in Somalia, was in fact family! And if that wasn't enough, he had to deal with another cruel, ironic twist of fate: Mercedes, the love of this life he had killed in such a brutal way, had been his half-sister! That's quite something to get your head around, even for someone like Macbeth. But then came the killer blow …'

'What do you mean by that?' asked Isis.

'I told Macbeth that he had a son … *you*, Isis. He had no idea, you see. At first he didn't believe me, but when I began to explain, the irony of it all began to dawn on him. Blinded by black desires, he had killed the mother of his love-child. A child conceived during the happiest time of his life.'

'We understand all that,' interjected Carrington, getting impatient again, 'but the Huntington bit still doesn't make sense. Surely you can see that.'

'Perhaps this will help,' said Jack. He pulled a piece of paper out of his pocket and held it up. 'This is without doubt the most brilliant part of Macbeth's plan. Dark genius. It combines revenge and ambition in a devastating blow designed to crush Lord Elms and the government at the same time.'

'What is it?' asked Isis.

'This is what Huntington was shown by the Prime Minister the other day. This is the reason Huntington resigned ...'

Silence.

'Come on Jack, what is it?' Carrington probed, realising that his would-be witness might be getting the upper hand after all.

'In a way, this is what killed Lord and Lady Elms ...'

'Please, Jack,' pleaded Isis.

'It's a copy of a birth certificate issued in South Africa in 1965 ...'

'Yes?' prompted Jana.

'Macbeth had an affair with a young white nurse who looked after him in Somalia.' Jack paused, taking his time. 'This document proves that Macbeth is David Huntington's father,' he said quietly, and once again held up the document for all to see.

Moments later, Señora Gonzales collapsed and had to be carried up to her room. Sir Humphrey gave her a sedative. He tried to give Isis one too, but she refused. She told him that sleeping would be more terrifying than staying awake to deal with the implications of what had just taken place. Drained and exhausted, everyone went to their rooms. Isis, however, was determined to stay with her grandmother. The evening that had started with such excitement and anticipation, had turned into a revelation of black and deep desires of the most devastating kind.

Jack could feel something touching his shoulder and heard someone talking. Reluctant to leave the much needed sanctuary of sleep, he tried to ignore both, but the voice wouldn't go away. There it was again. 'Jack, wake up, please,' he heard someone say over, and over. This time, however, the voice sounded familiar. Jack opened his eyes and looked at Lola leaning over him.

'Something terrible has happened,' she said.

Jack sat up, instantly awake. 'What?'

'Señora Gonzales just passed away.'

'Oh my God! I'm so sorry. It was all too much! Perhaps I should have ...'

'Don't, Jack. There's nothing you could, or should have done differently,' said Lola, putting her arms around Jack to comfort him. That's when she noticed he was crying. 'Come on, Jack, she was ninety-four ...'

'I know; still ... How did Isis ...?'

'You can imagine ...'

'Where is she?'

'In the chapel. With Dr Rosen and the countess.'

Jack put on his tracksuit, slipped on his shoes and went downstairs with Lola, their footsteps cutting through the eerie silence. He stopped in front of the familiar chapel door, unsure whether to go inside. Memories of another late-night visit to the chapel came flooding back. On that occasion, he had made a promise to a distraught mother to find her lost daughter. This time, however, he was about to visit a grieving grandson whose world had just fallen apart, mourning the loss of someone he held very dear. 'I don't know ...' said Jack.

'Go to them,' said Lola, gently pushing Jack towards the door. Slowly, Jack opened the heavy door and looked inside.

Isis and Dr Rosen sat side by side in the front pew, two candles burning next to Anna's photo the only light in the chapel. The countess was kneeling in front of the altar with her head bowed, praying.

'Come in,' said Isis without turning around. 'Please, sit with us.' Jack went to the front with Lola and sat down next to Isis. 'I'm so sorry,' he said. 'Perhaps I should have—'

'There's no need to apologise, Jack,' interrupted Isis. 'No regrets, please. Mamina was finally at peace, thanks to you. The pain of knowing what happened was much kinder than the anguish of not knowing at all. She would have died a long time ago, except for that. She had to know. Now, she was ready.'

Isis looked at Jack. 'Words can never express how grateful I am for what you and Lola have done. Painful as it is, the truth is precious. I may have lost my entire family, but I have found someone special I didn't know I had and, most importantly, I found the truth.' Isis turned to Dr Rosen and kissed her tenderly on the forehead. 'You know what Mamina's last words were, Jack?'

'Please tell me.'

The countess stopped praying and turned around to listen.

'"*If we don't believe in something greater than ourselves*",' whispered Isis, '"*we are destined to remain forever small*". Sound familiar?'

# PART VI
## *KALM 30 AND DEMEXILYN*

"The life is so short,
and the craft so long to learn."

*Hippocrates*

# Kuragin Chateau: three months later

Isis desperately needed closure. She had ignored Sir Humphrey's advice to avoid long flights, and had taken her grandmother back to Mexico for burial. This was to keep a promise made a long time ago to lay her to rest next to her husband, José, in the family crypt on their estate. In honour of the lady she had admired and loved so dearly, Lola had insisted on flying *Pegasus* all the way to Mexico herself.

Shocked by Señora Gonzales' sudden death, everyone had left the chateau the next day, needing time and distance to reflect on Jack's extraordinary revelations, and an evening none of them would ever forget. Jack had agreed to accompany Isis to Mexico to attend Señora Gonzales' funeral. He understood that Isis wanted him by her side to help her come to terms with the new reality he had uncovered, and which had so dramatically changed her life forever.

After the funeral, Isis took Jack to the Coyolxauhqui Stone where they had first met, and asked him a favour. She asked him to write a detailed account of everything he had discovered, leaving nothing out. Jack sensed that feeling empty and terribly alone after her grandmother's death, Isis needed him, and would do everything she could to keep him close. He was right. Isis offered him something she knew he wouldn't be able to resist: to write her biography. At first, Rebecca – Jack's literary agent, publicist extraordinaire and self-appointed minder – couldn't quite believe it and reminded him that this was an opportunity of a lifetime he couldn't afford to miss. And then, of course, there was the matter of his publishing house … Jack had readily accepted the assignment and thrown himself into endless interview sessions with Isis. For Isis, this was the cathartic experience she so needed, to help her understand what had happened to her and her family.

A few days after the funeral, Isis returned to the Kuragin Chateau, which would become her home away from home during her recovery. Sir Humphrey had advised against going back to the inevitable stress and glaring publicity of London, and welcomed the decision. Countess

Kuragin was delighted and willingly opened her home. Isis, Lola and Jack had become members of her household, and in some way, her family. Tristan had gone back to school and was living the dream. Isis, the megastar, was staying at his home with Jack, his closest friend and mentor, who was quickly turning into the father he never had. Boris and François had become good mates – an unlikely match. Boris was teaching Tristan to play the balalaika, and François promised him driving lessons, soon. Several times a week, they even cycled to school together, and Boris, the gentle giant, had become a popular curiosity with Tristan's school friends.

Anna too, appeared to be changing for the better. She had become more animated and outgoing and had formed a close bond with Isis. They were communicating in a way and on a level only Tristan could relate to and understand. Jack called it the language of intuition, reserved for the gifted few.

Jack and the countess sat in the garden and watched Isis and Anna through the open conservatory doors. Anna was painting as usual, and Isis was sitting next to her, composing the next hit by The Time Machine on a portable electronic keyboard. She was working on her new album, and watching Anna paint helped her concentrate and inspired her creativity.

The countess turned to Jack. 'You do know of course what they all have in common?' she said.

'What do you mean?'

'Pain. They are all sharing pain – Anna, Tristan … Isis.'

'What an extraordinary thing to say.'

'Perhaps. But think about it …'

'I've never looked at it that way,' said Jack. 'They are different, no doubt about it. But pain?'

'Not just any pain. Lonely pain; the worst kind. They've all been to the edge and looked down into the abyss.'

'Haven't you?'

'Not like them.'

'Because you had your faith?' speculated Jack.

The countess looked at him, surprised. 'How incredibly perceptive of you,' she said. 'Yes, I believe you're right. Even in my darkest hour, I was never alone. They were. That's the difference.'

'How do you know this?'

'I can feel it. But enough of that.' The countess turned around and pointed to a bundle of papers tied together with string on the table in front of Jack. 'What's that?' she asked.

'A present. For Isis.'

'And the ice bucket and the champagne? At ten in the morning?'

'You'll find out in a moment. Here she comes now.'

Wearing a pair of flared, white linen culottes and matching blouse accentuated by a sky-blue silk scarf and a pair of bright red earrings that would have made a nightclub singer proud, Isis looked as if she were about to have lunch with the Great Gatsby. Her hair, which had slowly grown back, was still very short. Combed straight back, it suited her strong features. The large, tortoiseshell sunglasses reminded Jack of Sofia Loren with Cary Grant by her side in some schmaltzy nineteen fifties romance.

'Are we celebrating something?' asked Isis. She pointed to the champagne in the ice bucket and sat down next to Jack.

'We are,' said Jack, and expertly popped the cork.

'What's the occasion?'

Jack reached for the bundle of papers and handed it to Isis. 'You.'

'You finished it?' Isis said excitedly.

'It's a draft. Needs more work, but good enough for you to read and tell me what I've got wrong.'

'I can't wait. And you've included everything? All the recent stuff?'

'I have.' Jack poured the champagne. 'A toast.'

'Wait. Here comes Lola,' said Isis.

Lola stepped out of the conservatory and came walking towards them. 'Was that a champagne cork I heard just now?' she said, laughing.

'You've obviously got bubbly-ears with acute alcoholic hearing,' said Jack and handed Lola a glass.

'All right, Jack, what are we drinking to?' asked the countess.

Jack turned to Isis and lifted his glass. 'To an extraordinary life,' he said. 'Not that long ago, we both took a leap of faith into the unknown and jumped, together. Little did we know where that would lead us. Now we do.'

'To an extraordinary life,' repeated the countess and touched glasses with everyone.

'Thanks, Jack. I too, have a little surprise,' said Isis, turning serious. 'Lola, would you mind?'

Lola stood up, hurried into the chateau and returned moments later with an envelope.

'This is for you, Jack,' said Isis.

'For me?' Jack looked up, surprised.

Isis motioned to Lola. 'Give it to him.'

Lola handed Jack the envelope. He opened it and looked inside. 'What is this?' he asked.

Isis was enjoying herself. 'A share certificate. From now on, you can publish your books without having to worry about deadlines, demanding publishers, or pushy editors. Why? Because you own a big chunk of the company. Cheers!'

After they had finished their second bottle, Isis excused herself. Feeling pleasantly tipsy and content, she picked up Jack's manuscript and went to her favourite spot in the garden – a small gazebo overlooking the duck pond – and began to delve into her past.

'She looks happy,' said Jack.

Lola reached for Jack's hand and squeezed it. 'You make her happy,' she said. 'You make everyone happy, because you care. It's a gift. Never lose it.'

'No chance. Incorrigible rascals never change. I've been told countless times—'

'Here we go,' interrupted the countess, shaking her head. 'Somehow, he always falls on his feet.' The countess held up the envelope. 'Just look at this. Let's go inside and have some lunch; I'm starving.'

Half an hour later, they heard a scream coming from somewhere in the garden. Boris and Jack got up from the table and hurried outside to have a look. One of the maids – hands in the air and shouting – came running towards them from the direction of the duck pond. *Isis*, thought Jack, and began to run.

Isis lay face down on the wooden floor inside the gazebo, with pages of Jack's manuscript scattered all around. An overturned wicker chair had crushed her sunglasses and was resting on the back of her legs. '*Good Lord*,' whispered Jack and knelt down next to her to feel her pulse. 'Alive!' he said. 'Let's carry her inside; quickly!'

First, Boris turned Isis over and then gently lifted her up.

'Take her inside. I'll call an ambulance,' said Jack, and ran back to the chateau.

The ambulance arrived twenty minutes later. Her breathing shallow, and looking pale, Isis was still unconscious when the paramedics went to work.

'I'll go with her,' said the countess. 'You follow with François.'

The paramedics radioed ahead to alert the hospital, put Isis into the back of the ambulance and raced off, the blaring sirens shattering the stillness of the afternoon and sending the waterbirds ducking for cover.

# 111

Sir Humphrey caught the first available Eurostar to Paris and arrived at the hospital late that afternoon. He had already phoned Dr Greenberg in Boston, who had then spoken to the French oncologist in charge at the Paris hospital.

Isis was in intensive care. Lola saw Sir Humphrey first. She ran over to him and threw her arms around him. 'Thank you,' she said, tears in her eyes.

'That bad?' asked Sir Humphrey, trying in vain to appear cheerful and composed. What he had found out so far wasn't good news. The deadly tumour was back. More aggressive than ever.

Sir Humphrey walked over to the countess and extended his hand. 'I'm so sorry, Countess, that we have to meet under such trying circumstances. Where's Jack?'

Lola pointed to a door at the end of the corridor. 'Inside, with Isis.'

'They let him stay?'

'You know Jack. They sent us outside, but he charmed his way back in.'

Sir Humphrey shrugged, excused himself and walked over to the nurse standing in front of the patient's door.

Jack was sitting in a chair next to Isis' bed in the darkened room. A nurse was adjusting some of the tubes connected to various monitoring devices humming in the background, the green lights throwing an eerie glow across the bed.

Sir Humphrey put his hand on Jack's shoulder and squeezed it. 'Breathing normal; heart rate okay; resting. Good,' he said.

'Heavily sedated.'

'To be expected.'

'We didn't expect this. She was doing so well.'

'It's an insidious monster.'

'Where to from here?' asked Jack, the sadness in his voice obvious.

'I'll talk to the oncologist – first class chap, know him well – and we'll see.'

'Then what?'

'We knew this was coming …'

'So soon?'

'You never know with tumours. Stress isn't good, and the long flights didn't help either.'

'What are you saying?'

Sir Humphrey shrugged, but didn't reply.

'There must be *something* we can do,' said Jack, raising his voice.

'There is. Come outside and I'll tell you.'

Lola and the countess looked expectantly at Jack and Sir Humphrey as the two men came out of the room.

'How is she?' asked Lola.

'As well as can be expected,' replied Sir Humphrey. 'She'll get better with the drugs, for now. But it will only be temporary, I'm afraid.'

'What are you saying?' shrieked Lola, close to tears.

The countess reached for Lola's hand. 'Can she come back home?' she asked.

'I expect so. In a few days.'

'Then what?' demanded Jack.

'Then it's all up to Dr Delacroix, I'm afraid.'

'What do you mean?' asked Jack.

'I spoke to Greenberg just before I left London. As you know, he's been in regular contact with Dr Delacroix and her groundbreaking research, and so have I.'

'And?' prompted the countess.

'She's apparently getting close; very close …' said Sir Humphrey.

'What does all this mean?' asked Lola.

'More surgery isn't an option, we know that. The only way we can hope to fight this malevolent, aggressive disease is with medication. A radical, new immunotherapy drug like the one Dr Delacroix is working on—'

'How much time do we have?' interrupted Jack.

'Difficult to say …'

'Jesus,' said Jack. 'It's a race against time, then.'

'It is, and a lot more, I'm afraid.'

'You said earlier there was something we could do?'

'There is.'

'What?'

'Go and talk to Dr Delacroix and see where she's up to. Even in an early experimental stage, the drug could be useful. Perhaps we could try it to see …'

'Are we that desperate?' asked Jack, lowering his voice.

'I'm afraid so. Our medicine cupboard is bare.'

When Jack looked at Lola standing next to the countess, he noticed she was crying. Jack looked away, a tide of sadness washing over him. It only lasted for an instant and was banished by a decision he had just made. 'I'm leaving in the morning,' he said, feeling better.

'I thought you might,' said Sir Humphrey. 'It's our only chance to stop the Emperor of Darkness.'

'We'll defeat the bastard; just you watch.'

The next day, Jack caught the first available commercial flight Down Under. Lola had to stay behind to assist the countess in caring for Isis at the chateau and keep *Pegasus* ready, just in case. A competent nurse had already been engaged who would oversee Isis' day-to-day care. Sir Humphrey would liaise with the French doctors, keep a close eye on medical issues and stay in touch with Jack and Dr Greenberg in Boston.

During the long flight to Sydney, Jack read Isis' biography he had just completed, in its entirety for the first time. If he hadn't been part of the more recent events, he would have dismissed the entire work as fanciful fiction.

*The last chapter hasn't been written yet*, he thought, closing his laptop. *I'll be buggered if it's to be set in a bloody cemetery!*

# 112

Alexandra kept staring at the genome sequencing results of the Abramowitz twins on her screen. *It's all in here*, she thought, *I know it is!* Alexandra had barely left her lab during the last three months because she knew she was getting close.

As the samples extracted from the strands of hair had contained hair follicles with sufficient DNA, it had been possible to prepare libraries for both Lena and Miriam for genome sequencing. Alexandra realised that in some way, this was the crucial missing link Professor K had been looking for. While identical twins had been used extensively in the past to understand the impact of inheritance and environment – nature vs. nurture – on differences in general health and risk of disease, Professor K had focused on differences that might be due to epigenetic switching on or off of genes. *It's the differences in immune function that matter here*, thought Alexandra, *that's the key. But how does it all work? And most importantly, why?* She reached for her notepad and began to read what she had been able to establish so far:

- *Genome sequencing of the Abramowitz girls has revealed that both twins suffered from Li Fraumeni syndrome, which can lead to cancers, including brain cancer.*
- *The genomes of twins should essentially be the same, except for mutations that will occur during life in some cells.*
- *However, the genomes can have 'epigenetic' differences that arise during development, and are then carried through life.*
- *There are two possibilities: these differences can either be in modifications of chromosomal proteins, or of the DNA – DNA methylation.*
- *DNA methylation is often involved in switching genes off.*
- *Lena's immune system was able to fight the tumour and make it regress, while Miriam's continued to grow aggressively and ultimately killed her. WHY?*

Alexandra was reaching for her pencil to make a correction, when her phone rang. It was the receptionist downstairs. 'Mr Rogan is here to see you,' she said.

'What?' Alexandra almost shouted, surprise and disbelief creasing her brow. 'Can't be!'

'He's standing right here in front of me,' insisted the receptionist.

Alexandra closed her notepad and hurried to the lift.

Jack had come straight from the airport to see her. He was leaning casually against the front desk and chatting with the receptionist. His luggage – a small duffel bag – was on the floor next to him.

'I don't believe it!' said Alexandra, throwing her arms around Jack. 'What on earth brings you here so suddenly?'

'Sad news, I'm afraid. Isis …'

'Oh. Come up to my lab and tell me all about it.'


'So, this is the Aladdin's cave where it all happens,' said Jack, looking around as they entered the lab.

'Yes. This was Professor K's lab. It's virtually unchanged.'

'Except for its new occupant.'

'Succession works like that, I suppose. I stepped into his shoes, in more ways than one. That was the easy bit. Stepping into his head has been a little more difficult as it turns out.'

Jack quickly explained Isis' sudden deterioration, her collapse at the Kuragin Chateau and the dire prognosis.

'So, why have you come,' asked Alexandra, 'so suddenly, and unannounced?'

'Isn't it obvious? After all that's happened, you are our only hope.'

Alexandra shook her head. 'You can't do this to me, Jack,' she said.

'No choice, I'm afraid. Time's running out.'

'I'm not ready. I've already told Greenberg and Sir Humphrey there's still a long way to go.'

'Isis can't wait.'

'What do you expect me to do? I'm not a magician,' Alexandra shot back.

'Try. Improvise. Anything. What you've done with Professor K's work so far is gob-smacking, I'm told. Everyone's talking about it.'

Alexandra shook her head. 'Gob-smacking?' she asked.

'Aussie slang for breathtaking.'

'How's a French sheila supposed to know that – eh?' said Alexandra, continuing the banter.

'You've got a point there. Why don't you show me where you're up to,' said Jack, changing direction.

'All right.'

'And please keep it simple. I don't have a PhD in biology.'

'This is how it goes. It all comes back to the Abramowitz twins. Lena's immune system was able to fight the tumour and make it regress, while Miriam's continued to grow aggressively and ultimately killed her. The question is, *why?* Why wasn't Miriam able to fight the tumour? Professor K had come up with a possible answer: One copy of the non-coding RNA gene had been epigenetically silenced, thereby reducing its activity and consequently her immune system's surveillance of cancer cells—'

'And this didn't happen to Lena?' interrupted Jack.

'It did. The very same thing happened to her as well—'

'But wasn't Lena cured? The Auschwitz operation?' interrupted Jack again. 'She lived for another seventy odd years.'

'Yes. Both twins had brain cancer, and both were operated on, but only one survived and was cured. The Auschwitz notes are quite clear about this. They were among Professor K's papers – remember?'

'How, and why?' asked Jack.

'That's the ultimate question here, and that was precisely what Professor K was working on when he died. He believed that Lena was cured with the help of a compound extracted from that Mexican jungle plant Dr Steinberger had obtained from José Gonzales in Paris.' Alexandra reached for a glass phial on her desk and held it up. 'This here.'

'Is that what Lola brought back from Kenya for you? The stuff from the experiments in that dreadful Somali death camp we discovered?'

'Not quite. I have substantially modified the compound to make it more effective, and so had Professor K. However, the composition of the drug from Somalia gave me an important clue, which was a big help. Essentially, it's very similar, reaching right back to Auschwitz and what Professor K's father used on Lena, only it's stronger and more refined, I suppose. Miriam didn't receive any drug treatment and she succumbed to the tumour.'

'How does this compound work?'

'Ah. That's what those dreadful experiments in Somalia were all about. It appears to work in some cases – spectacularly – and fails miserably in others. This was also what Professor K was wrestling with just before he died. He wanted to know why that was so, and what could be done about it. Macbeth's scientists were doing the very same thing.

'Are you suggesting that Blackburn Pharmaceuticals and Professor K were working *on the same problem?*'

'Yes. Only their methods were vastly different. Blackburn Pharmaceuticals were using real people, Professor K was using mice and his intuition. And it would appear that he was winning.'

'How?'

'Just like his father before him, he had a hunch that turned into an inspired idea.'

'Oh?'

'He developed more active forms of the compound extracted from the Mexican medicinal plant and experimented on mice. He even gave the compound a name – Demexilyn, would you believe. A new drug based on a Mexican jungle plant extract with demethylation properties. A play on words; clever. I have painstakingly reconstructed the experiments described in his notes and examined the tissue specimens he concealed here in the lab. The results are clear. They have shown that this compound is not only able to prevent growth of gliomas – brain tumours – in mice, but it can also inhibit the growth of a number of different types of cancer. The compound was stimulating immune T-cells to recognise and destroy cancer cells. In short, it was mobilising the body's own defence mechanism.'

'But that's fantastic, isn't it?' said Jack.

'In mice, Jack. In mice,' Alexandra reminded Jack.

'So?'

'Let me explain where Professor K was up to just before he died.'

'Please.'

'For years, he had carefully studied "non-coding" RNAs.'

'What's that?'

'RNA copies from parts of the genome that do not code for proteins.'

'What, the junk DNA? The 98.5%?'

'Spot on. And by carrying out new in-depth "next-generation" sequencing of RNA from different types of cells, Professor K had been able to identify an RNA with an unusual structure found only in immune T-cells that are important for fighting cancer.'

'And that was important?'

'Oh, yes. This RNA was encoded by a gene – let's call it gene X for the moment – located hundreds of thousands of bases away from the nearest gene known to code for a protein. Needless to say, Professor K was intrigued by this and began to experiment. He made "knockout" mice.'

'What on earth are knockout mice?' asked Jack, shaking his head.

'Mice in which one copy of the gene had been deleted. These mice seemed healthy and normal, except that they were very susceptible to cancers, which grew rapidly and they were unable to suppress.'

'And this was significant?'

'Yes. Absolutely. When Professor K examined the T-cells of these mice, he found that expression of a number of genes was altered, especially a protein-coding gene, DD1alpha, which played an important role in suppressing recognition of cancer cells. The new gene X was located on the same chromosome – Chromosome 10 – as DD1alpha, but more than two hundred thousand bases away. And *this* brings me to Professor K's last experiment that had so excited him. In fact, he had the results of that experiment in front of him when he called me just before he died.'

'Incredible! And you were able to reconstruct all of this?'

'Yes. From his notes. It wasn't easy, I can tell you.'

'So, what was that last experiment all about?'

'He tested the effect of that new compound – Demexilyn – on mouse and human immune T-cells in culture right here in his laboratory. And I've just done the same.'

'And?'

'The results were surprising, to say the least. Demexilyn activated expression of the newly discovered gene X and blocked expression of DD1alpha, making the T-cells much more potent in fighting cancer.'

Jack held up his hands in defeat. 'Stop right there! You've lost me. This is far too complicated for a bloke like me.'

'Bloke? All right.' Alexandra reached for a small notebook on the table in front of her. 'This is the last entry in Professor K's notebook. I believe he wrote it in a great hurry just before he died. His writing is barely legible. This is what it says:

"Abramowitz puzzle: Why did the tumour kill one twin and not the other? Their genomes were the same and both carried the same mutation in the P53 gene that fuelled their tumours. Possible solution? What if they had epigenetic differences?"'

Alexandra paused, and looked at Jack. 'If Professor K was right, then the next sentence is the inspired idea I mentioned earlier; his genius.'

'What does it say?'

'This: "*If so, then the difference had to be something that responded to Demexilyn, the extract from the Mexican medicinal plant*".'

'Do we know what that difference is?' asked Jack.

'Professor K believed it had to be the new RNA gene X. That's what could have cured Lena. She was able to defeat her cancer with the help of a revitalised immune system, and this was made possible by gene X, which had been switched on by Demexilyn. This process activated the body's own defence system against cancer and destroyed it.'

'Wow! Will we ever know if he was right?'

'Yes, we will.'

'How?'

'Because of a critical test that unfortunately eluded Professor K.'

'And you can perform?'

'Yes.'

'My God! When?'

'Tomorrow.'

# 113

Isis sat in a comfortable wicker chair on the terrace overlooking the Kuragin Chateau garden. François had brought her home from the hospital that afternoon, and just smelling the fresh evening air rising from the pond and listening to the hum of the insects felt like hope after those horrible few days in intensive care. However, Isis realised hope was but an illusion as she remembered that dreadful hologram the director of cancer imaging had shown her on his computer screen earlier that day. In hindsight, Isis almost regretted having insisted on being present at the briefing arranged by Sir Humphrey. It had been a most terrifying experience.

Isis had seen her cancer, which had rapidly spread to various parts of her body, including her lungs and bones, in stunning, three-dimensional detail. There were now several tumours putting pressure on her brain. The Emperor of Darkness was advancing with relentless determination, preparing for his final triumph.

Sir Humphrey walked over to his patient, and sat down next to Isis. He had desperately wanted to spare her from the horror of viewing her own approaching death, but his headstrong patient had insisted.

'How much time have I got?' asked Isis.

'Difficult to tell …'

'Don't beat around the bush.'

'You saw …'

'Not long then. But I'm a fighter; you watch!'

'I know you are. And we have a white knight talking to our queen Down Under – right now.'

'Dr Delacroix. Have you heard from Jack?'

'Yes.'

'And?'

'The research is at a critical stage.'

'When will we know?'

'Tomorrow.'

'And then?'

Sir Humphrey shrugged. 'Uncharted waters, I'm afraid,' he said.

Isis reached for the wooden box on the small table next to her and opened it. With the last rays of the setting sun caressing the gleaming crystal, the spectacular skull seemed to come to life. 'The Emperor of Darkness better get ready for a fight, then,' said Isis, smiling for the first time since her return.

'I couldn't have put it better myself,' said Sir Humphrey. 'Let's go inside and join the others. It's getting a little chilly out here.'

Unable to sleep, Alexandra kept tossing restlessly in her bed. Feeling hot and clammy, she sat up and looked again at the clock on the bedside table. It was four in the morning. She realised that the test scheduled for later that day was not only critical, but a watershed moment in her life. It was the culmination of a long sequence of extraordinary events bringing together the work and vision of several gifted people, who had each made it their life's work to improve the journey of man.

Jack was peacefully asleep next to her. *He's like a child*, she thought, watching Jack and envying his ability to switch off. Telling Jack all about her ordeal had been both liberating and cathartic, and jumping into bed together after the dinner he had prepared for her as a surprise, had seemed the most natural thing to do. Jack – a good listener and experienced lover – had sensed Alexandra's needs, and knew exactly how to banish loneliness and make her feel wanted. The paralysing blemish had been removed.

Jana and Marcus had moved out weeks ago and were looking for a house to buy. Thanks to the spectacular success of 'Operation Blowhole', Jana had re-joined the Federal Police and been given her old job back. Marcus had landed the hottest brief in town, and was preparing the case for the prosecution. This had left Alexandra by herself in Jack's apartment, which had quickly become her home. She didn't mind living by herself, even after the traumatic events leading up to Van Cleef's spectacular bridge-jump suicide, but having Jack around felt good.

Alexandra reached for her dressing gown and tiptoed out of the room to make some tea. She knew going back to sleep wasn't an option. Instead, she would go over the notes she had prepared for the critical test to make sure nothing had been overlooked. She also had an idea for a name for that new gene, should it turn out to be as groundbreaking as Professor K had believed it would be.

Jack stood in the doorway and watched Alexandra. Hunched over the kitchen table, she was reading her notes, her concentration making her oblivious to anything going on around her. It was just after sunrise, and the still waters of the harbour below reflected the first light of the new day, making the striking sails of the Opera House glow in hues of pink and mauve. Jack walked over to Alexandra, kissed her gently on the neck and looked over her shoulder. She turned around, surprised, and smiled.

'KALM 30? What's that?' he asked, reading the scribbled letters in kthe margin.

'Every new discovery needs a name. This is a name for a new gene. If Professor K was right, then this hidden gene has the power to change medicine and the journey of man.'

'Wow! What does KALM stand for?'

'K for Kozakievicz; A for Abramowitz; L for Lena and M for Miriam. KALM.'

'Clever. And 30?'

'The twins were born in 1930, and so was the gene.'

'Brilliant!'

'You like it?'

Jack nodded. 'So, that's how it works,' he said. 'Full-on hanky-panky at night, followed by a little sleep, and then up at first light to tackle the challenges of another day in the lab. I don't know if I can keep up with this. More tea?'

Alexandra raised an eyebrow. 'Hanky-panky, you call it? Unable to keep up?' she said. 'I expected a little more from such a dangerous bloke.'

'French sheilas …'

'Is that a complaint?'

Jack held up his hands. 'No! Definitely not.'

'Good. You had me a little worried there,' said Alexandra, laughing.

'Tell me about this test.'

'This is it; crunch time. Today we'll find out if Professor K was right. We are lifting the curtain to find out what's hidden behind it and the DNA of the Abramowitz twins should provide the answer. Extraordinary, isn't it? After all these years and everything that's happened, it all comes down to this.'

'Destiny?'

'Yes, I think you're right.'

'The test?'

'I believe we have just enough DNA left from the hair samples to perform it. We have to read the methylation code on the DNA.'

'How do you do that?'

'First, we treat the DNA with sodium bisulphite, a chemical, then we amplify the DNA that regulates the new RNA gene – KALM 30, and read its methylation sequence. If this works, we should have all the answers.'

'And this could help Isis?'

'I believe so.'

'How?'

'By treating patients like Isis with Demexilyn, we could switch on this amazing new gene – KALM 30, and thereby activate the body's own defence against cancer.'

'And this could fight the cancer even at an advanced stage?'

'No reason why not. I've seen spectacular new immunotherapy drugs like Keytruda and Yervoy do just that in a few months. It's almost miraculous, but it works. They attack and destroy cancer cells, and Demexilyn could do the same, perhaps even a lot better. However, I believe we'll have to "tailor" the drug – its dose and application – to each patient's needs. That's the key. This has become clear to me from the Somali trials. The drug has to be slightly modified from patient to patient to make it work. Professor K realised this from the beginning. Blackburn Pharmaceuticals did not. That's why they failed. And Professor K also knew how the drug could be customised to make it more effective.'

'How?'

'Through personalised medicine. The way I see it, we would have to sequence each patient's genome to ascertain the precise dose, composition, strength, etc. of Demexilyn application to make it work effectively. Otherwise, it could be effective in some cases, but not in others. Hit and miss, just as it did in Somalia. But fortunately for us, it appears to have worked for Lena, just as it did for the young Aztec chief in the *De Medicina* codex. That was luck. We need more. All going well, we should know for sure later today exactly how, and why it all works.'

'So, the Somali drug we brought back did help?'

'Hugely. It was another important piece in the puzzle, which pointed us in the right direction and provided a massive shortcut. In some way, it worked like a crude clinical trial, telling us where we had to go.'

'Incredible. But before we could help Isis with this drug and activate this new wonder-gene, we would have to sequence her genome to make it work?'

'Yes. That's right.'

'How long would that take?'

'About a week. Why?'

'Give me a second,' said Jack and hurried out of the kitchen. He returned moments later with a small ivory box in his hand. 'Here, this is for you,' he said and handed the box to Alexandra. 'From Isis.'

'What is it?'

'Open it.'

Alexandra opened the box and looked inside. 'Hers?' she asked.

'Yes. Hair, complete with follicles. I'm a fast learner – see?'

'You're an amazing guy, Jack Rogan,' said Alexandra.

'Not really, just an attentive sorcerer's apprentice.'

'I'm getting a little confused here. I thought you were a dangerous bloke?'

'Most sorcerer's apprentices are.'

'I give up,' said Alexandra, holding up her hands. 'Give me genomics any time; much simpler, I tell you.'

Sir Humphrey, an early riser, was enjoying breakfast with Countess Kuragin on the terrace when his phone rang. It was Jack.

'I hope I'm not too early, but we wanted you to be the first to hear this,' said Jack.

'Oh? What have you got for me?'

'Hope … Here's someone who can explain this much better than I – Dr Delacroix.' Jack handed his phone to Alexandra.

'I just received the results of the test we spoke of, Sir Humphrey,' said Alexandra, the excitement in her voice obvious.

'And?'

'The amplification of the DNA from Professor K's new gene – we gave it a name: KALM 30 – has been successful, and we were able to read its methylation sequence.'

'That's great news!' exclaimed Sir Humphrey.

'It is. When we had a close look at the sequence, all the pieces of the puzzle began to fall into place. In the DNA from Miriam's hair, one copy of the KALM 30 gene was methylated, but in the DNA of the survivor – Lena, who had successfully fought her brain cancer, both copies of the gene were completely free of methylation and would therefore have been active and able to fight the disease. That's why she was cured and lived well into her eighties.'

'Extraordinary!' said Sir Humphrey. 'And do we know how that happened?'

'Yes, we do. It's all thanks to Demexilyn, the new drug. The reason Lena was able to successfully fight her cancer was with the help of this drug. What it did was to switch on Professor K's hidden gene – KALM 30 – and this activated the body's own defence against cancer.'

'Fantastic! This new drug works then?'

'Everything we've done so far tells us it does, and this crucial test with the Abramowitz twins' DNA has shown us exactly why, and how.'

'Congratulations! What an extraordinary result! This is a game changer! A new immunotherapy drug with the power to change the way we treat cancer!'

'Early days, Sir Humphrey ... But we'll soon see,' said Alexandra trying to curb Sir Humphrey's enthusiasm.

'Where does that leave Isis?'

'I'm working on it. We have already started extracting her DNA for sequencing. After that, we'll see.'

'Are you confident?'

'I am. Even at this early stage, I believe the drug is virtually ready to go. Isis may well become our first patient ...'

'My God; I hope so!'

# Mexico City: one year later

Jack looked at his watch. 'Where's Isis?' he said. 'Shouldn't we get going?'

'She's visiting Dolores' grave ...' said Lola.

'Oh.'

'This is a big day for her.'

'Sure. Have you seen the crowd outside?'

'I've never seen anything quite like it. There must be thousands of fans just in front of the gates. Everything's ready; we'll leave in a minute.'

Isis' 'Thank You' concert in Mexico City – her first since her recovery, and the beginning of her Cristal Skull Tour – had been carefully choreographed for maximum impact. Isis would leave the Gonzales residence with The Time Machine, and be driven to the stadium in a fleet of convertible vintage cars. The procession would enter the stadium one hour before the performance was due to begin, and do a lap of honour while local bands were entertaining the huge crowd lucky enough to have scored tickets to the rock concert of the decade. Isis had invited Jack and Lola to ride with her in her car. They would then join the others waiting at the stadium, and watch the performance in reserved seats right in front of the stage.

'Well, what do you think, guys?' said Isis, strutting into the room, fussed over by Jean-Paul, her ageing French dress designer. He was doing his best to put the finishing touches to her spectacular costume, and tried desperately to keep up with her. It was the same tight-fitting, Aztec-inspired bodysuit she had worn during the aborted concert a year before, which had ended so abruptly with her dramatic collapse on stage.

'Not bad for someone who just a few months ago looked like a dead man walking,' joked Jack. 'Beg your pardon; dead girl walking.'

'Thanks, Jack. You certainly know how to pay compliments.'

'It's true. Seeing you here like this, is nothing short of a bloody miracle.'

After analysing Isis' DNA sequence and interrogating the results, Alexandra had refined the Demexilyn compound to switch on the newly discovered KALM 30 gene and sent it into battle to defeat the Emperor of Darkness that was killing Isis. Jack had taken the drug back to France, and Sir Humphrey arranged to have it administered in a private clinic close to the Kuragin Chateau run by an oncologist he knew well. Almost immediately, the results were spectacularly successful. Not only did the tumours stop growing, but they began to retreat at a breathtaking rate. Twelve months later, Isis was cancer free. After the Gordon Institute had registered appropriate patents to protect the discovery, Alexandra – now a professor – published her findings in *Nature*, which sent the entire medical fraternity into a tailspin, and drug companies clamouring for part of the action, worth billions.

Lola walked over to Isis and embraced her. 'I would kiss you, but I don't want to destroy your make-up,' she said, tears in her eyes.

'*Thank you, Lola*,' whispered Isis, '*for everything*,' and kissed Lola ever so gently on the forehead. 'Come on, guys. Let the show begin!'

The jubilant crowd lining the route from the home Isis had inherited from her grandmother to the stadium was estimated at two hundred thousand, with more gathered in the side streets. TV cameras positioned strategically at every corner transmitted the spectacle to a worldwide audience of millions.

Isis' publicity-machine had done a remarkable job in promoting the event. *Dead Girl Walking* – The Time Machine's new album based on material Isis had composed during her recovery – had shot to number one in more than thirty countries. Her biography bearing the same name, and completed by Jack during the same period, was due to be released worldwide at the end of the concert. Bookstores around the world were waiting for the signal to open their doors.

Tristan sat next to Countess Kuragin in one of the front rows reserved for Isis' guests. He could barely contain his excitement as he watched the procession of cars pass by a few metres in front of him.

The crowd was on its feet, chanting 'Isis', and Tristan thought he could see his idol waving to him as her car drove slowly past.

'Did you see her waving?' said Tristan, pointing to the cars. Sarah, the stunning blonde girl sitting in front him – one of Dr Greenberg's daughters – nodded and continued to scream. Dr Greenberg had brought his wife and two teenage daughters to the concert to celebrate an extraordinary journey in which he had played a crucial part. However, he was still struggling to come to terms with Isis' recovery.

Sir Humphrey looked at Greenberg sitting on his left. 'A little different from the operating theatre?' he said.

'Not really,' replied Greenberg. 'Excitement; chaos; anticipation. Just like one of my ops.'

'What do you think about that, Professor Delacroix?' asked Sir Charles.

'Sounds about right. Soon, surgeons like him will be obsolete,' joked Alexandra, winking at Sir Charles.

'Your wonder-drug will make plastic surgeons out of us all, you think? Facelifts instead of tumour removal?' said Greenberg.

'Would that be such a bad thing?'

'Not at all,' said Greenberg, playing along. 'I'm ready for a new challenge. I suspect, however, that some of those faces could be quite scary ...'

Isis was going through her breathing exercises backstage, just as she had always done before every concert. Hearing a hundred thousand adoring fans chanting her name outside, wasn't something she had expected to experience ever again just a few months ago. She had been to the edge of her grave and looked inside, only to be pulled back moments before falling in. This had provided some extraordinary inspiration for *Dead Girl Walking* – which she had composed as her legacy at the Kuragin Chateau, not expecting to live.

'How do you feel?' asked Lola, watching Isis doing her squats.

'Exhilarated.'

'Now, remember what Sir Humphrey said ...'

'Yes, yes, I know. No funny moves.'

'This is resurrection, not genuflection – remember?'

'I get it. I won't be kneeling in front of the Almighty, begging for admittance – yet,' joked Isis. 'Now, tell the boys I'm ready to show the world that Isis is very much alive!'

As soon as the lights went out and the stadium was plunged into darkness, the excited crowd fell silent. Then suddenly, a lonely drum began to beat, and a beam of light moved slowly across the dark stage until it came to rest on a tall man wearing a spectacular helmet made of feathers, and a long ocelot cloak. 'Let it begin,' said the man, his deep voice echoing across the stadium.

Another man, wearing a striking helmet shaped like the beak of a bird of prey stepped out of the shadows, knelt down in front of him and held up a basket. The tall man lifted the lid, looked inside and smiled. Then he reached into the basket and touched the crystal skull with trembling fingers and, holding it with both hands, lifted it carefully out of the basket. Laser lights projected the amplified image onto large screens set up all around the stadium.

The crowd gasped.

Followed by a beam of light and looking like an Aztec god, the tall man turned slowly around and, holding the crystal skull above his head, began the steep climb to the top of a pyramid looming large and ominous behind him in the dark, like a stairway to an angry heaven.

'I'm glad we came, aren't you?' said Carrington to Jana sitting next to him. Jana reached for Carrington's hand.

'You have to pinch yourself, don't you? So much has happened, yet here we are. This is real!' Jana sensed that Carrington would be thinking of another fateful performance a few years ago in Luxor – Aida – which had ended in bloodshed and unspeakable horror; the terrorist attack that had killed his wife and daughter. 'I know what you're thinking,' said Jana, squeezing Carrington's hand. 'This is a celebration of life, Marcus.'

'I know. Look!'

Isis, her eyes closed, was lying on a stone altar on top of the pyramid bathed in green light, and was listening to the lonely drumbeat echoing through the stadium below. Never before had she felt so alive, every passing second a precious gift she had not expected. The tall man reached the top of the pyramid, walked over to the stone altar, knelt down and carefully placed the crystal skull next to Isis' head. The drumbeat stopped, plunging the packed stadium into sudden silence, the tension in the crowd growing with every heartbeat.

Then suddenly, out of the darkness, The Time Machine's guitars screamed into life and began to play 'Resurrection', Isis' signature song. First, Isis slowly lifted her right hand and pointed to heaven. Then she sat up and turned towards the crowd who were now chanting 'Isis, Isis!' below her, as laser lights came on, casting lifelike jungle images across the pyramid.

Unable to resist one of her signature moves, Isis somersaulted off the altar and began to sing.

During the brief interval, Alexandra felt her phone vibrate in her pocket. She was about to turn it off, but changed her mind and answered the call.

'Professor Delacroix?' said a voice, speaking in an unfamiliar accent.

'Yes …'

Moments later – looking pale and a little shaken – Alexandra slipped the phone back into her pocket and turned to face Jack sitting next to her.

'You look like you've seen a ghost,' said Jack. 'What was that all about?'

'A call from Oslo.'

'Oh?'

'*I have just been nominated for the Nobel Prize for Medicine,*' whispered Alexandra, barely able to speak. '*It's not right; it belongs to Kasper …*'

Jack threw his arms around Alexandra. 'Nonsense!' he said, 'it belongs to *both of you*. Congratulations. Not bad for a French Sheila …'

Before Alexandra could reply, the lights went out and the crowd began to cheer again, celebrating a precious life saved by an inspired idea, and the ingenuity of man.

# A Future to Look Forward to...

You have probably just finished reading The Hidden Genes of Professor K and I hope you enjoyed reading it as much as I have enjoyed researching and writing it.

Writing a medical thriller about the fascinating world of genomics was inspired by the amazing research being carried out right here, at the Garvan Institute of Medical Research, in Sydney.

You may have noticed that my book is dedicated to the many talented scientists who work here to improve how we diagnose, treat and ultimately, prevent some of the major diseases of our time.

Writing *The Hidden Genes of Professor K* was an ambitious project. For a layman like me, exploring subjects touching on cutting-edge medical research and complex science is never easy, and would not have been possible without the guiding hand and generous help of leading experts.

There has probably never been a more exciting time to be a research scientist than right now. Progress is breathtaking, the possibilities endless, breakthroughs come almost daily, and the speed of progress is head-spinning. Advances in technology are making the unthinkable possible, and what would once have taken two scientists several years of painstaking work, can now be done by a machine overnight!

I firmly believe that we are about to open a treasure-trove of knowledge buried in our genome right here, inside us all, that will transform the future of medicine and the journey of man.

The introduction to the book by Professor Mattick, executive director of the Garvan, begins with the words: *We all stare into the darkness.* I thought a lot about this sentence and would like to add this to it: As we stare into the darkness, something extraordinary is now happening. A shaft of light is slowly banishing the darkness and lifting the curtain of ignorance.

What is that light? It is the dawn of a new era of medicine as we explore that treasure-trove of evolution hidden in our genes. The secrets are all there for us to find, and with the help of dedicated scientists and institutes like this, we will do just that.

These are incredibly exciting times. If you would like to be part of this adventure, and find out more about how thriller-fiction is rapidly becoming science-reality, then may I invite you to visit the Garvan website at www.garvan.org.au Perhaps you may even like to become part of the Garvan family and join me in becoming a partner for the future and make a real difference? You can! Hope to see you there!

*Gabriel Farago MA., LL.B.*
*Director*
*Garvan Research Foundation*
www.garvan.org.au

# SECRETS OF PROFESSOR K:
# GARVAN MYSTERY CHALLENGE

Now that you've read The Hidden Genes of Professor K, I have a little surprise for you I'm sure you will enjoy. What is it? An invitation!

I would like to invite you to discover the secrets of Professor K by participating in the exciting **'Garvan Mystery Challenge'**. Intrigued? I'm sure you are! Just paste the link below into your browser and enjoy the ride!

https://professork.online

You're in for quite an adventure with a few lovely surprises to entertain you along the way.

*Gabriel Farago*

# MORE BOOKS BY THE AUTHOR

The Jack Rogan Mysteries Starter Library
The Empress Holds the Key
The Disappearance of Anna Popov
Professor K: The Final Quest
The Jack Rogan Mysteries Box Set Books 1-4

So, what exactly is a STARTER LIBRARY? I hear you ask. Well, it's a way to introduce myself and what I do to new readers, and create interest in my writing. How? By providing little insights into my world, and the creative process involved in becoming an international thriller writer.

The Starter Library consists of four short books:

**1.** Letters from The Attic - a delightful collection of auto-biographical short stories;

**2.** The Forgotten Painting - A multi-award-winning Jack Rogan Novella;

**3.** The Kimberley Secret - a much-anticipated prequel to the Jack Rogan Mysteries series;

**4.** The Main Characters Profile, which provides some exciting background stories and insights into the main characters featured in the series.

The Jack Rogan Mysteries Starter Library is available right now, and can be downloaded for FREE by following this link:
https://gabrielfarago.com.au/starter-library2/

In 2013, I released my first adventure thriller–The Empress Holds the Key.

## The Empress Holds the Key

A disturbing, edge-of-your-seat historical mystery thriller

## Jack Rogan Mysteries Book 1

**Dark secrets. A holy relic. An ancient quest reignited.**

Jack Rogan's discovery of a disturbing old photograph in the ashes of a rural Australian cottage draws the journalist into a dangerous hunt with the ultimate stakes.

The tangled web of clues—including hoards of Nazi gold, hidden Swiss bank accounts, and a long-forgotten mass grave—implicate wealthy banker Sir Eric Newman and lead to a trial with shocking revelations.

A holy relic mysteriously erased from the pages of history is suddenly up for grabs to those willing to sacrifice everything to find it.

Rogan and his companions must follow historical leads through ancient Egypt to the Crusades and the Knights Templar to uncover a secret that could destroy the foundations of the Catholic Church and challenge the history of Christianity itself.

Will Rogan succeed in bringing the dark mystery into the light or will the powers desperately working against him ensure the ancient truths remain buried forever?

*The Empress Holds the Key* is now available
on my website at this link:
https://gabrielfarago.com.au/my-books/

Encouraged by the reception of The Empress Holds the Key, I released my next thriller–The Disappearance of Anna Popov—in 2014.

# THE DISAPPEARANCE OF ANNA POPOV

A dark, page-turning psychological thriller

## Jack Rogan Mysteries Book 2

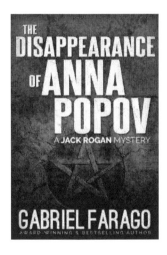

**A mysterious disappearance. An outlaw bikie gang. One dangerous investigation.**

Journalist Jack Rogan cannot resist a good mystery. When he stumbles across a hidden clue about the tragic disappearance of two girls from Alice Springs years earlier, he's determined to investigate. Joining forces with his New York literary agent, a retired Aboriginal police officer, and Cassandra, an enigmatic psychic, Rogan enters the dark and dangerous world of an outlaw bikie gang ruled by an evil master.

Entangled in a web of violence, superstition, and fear, Rogan and his friends follow the trail of the missing girls into the remote Dreamtime-wilderness of outback Australia where they face their greatest challenge yet.

Cassandra has a secret agenda of her own and uses her occult powers to conjure up an epic showdown where the stakes are high, and the loser faces death and oblivion. Will Rogan succeed in finding the truth, or will the forces of evil prevail, causing untold misery and destroying even more lives?

*The Disappearance of Anna Popov* is now available
on my website at this link:
https://gabrielfarago.com.au/my-books/

My fourth book, *Professor K: The Final Quest*, was released in 2018. Here's a short sample to pique your interest:

# PROFESSOR K: THE FINAL QUEST

An action-packed historical medical mystery

## Jack Rogan Mysteries Book 4

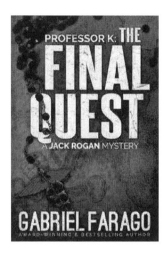

**A desperate plea from the Vatican. A kidnapped chef. An ambitious mob boss. One perilous game.**

When Professor Alexandra Delacroix is called in to find a cure for the dying pope, she follows clues left by her mentor and friend, the late Professor K, which lead her on a breathtaking search through historical secrets, some of them deadly.

Her old friend Jack Rogan must step in to assist while also searching for kidnapped Top Chef Europe winner Lorenza da Baggio.

He joins forces with his young friend and gifted psychic, Tristan, a dedicated mafia hunting prosecutor, a fearless young police officer, and an enigmatic Egyptian detective on a perilous hunt for a notorious IS terrorist.

Together, they stand off with the head of a powerful Mafia family in Florence and uncover a network of corruption and heinous crimes reaching to the very top.

Will Rogan and his friends succeed in finding Lorenza and curing the pope, or will the dark forces swirling around them prevail in their sinister plots?

*Professor K: The Final Quest* is now available
on my website at this link:
https://gabrielfarago.com.au/my-books/

# THE JACK ROGAN MYSTERIES BOX SET

## Books1-4

*The Jack Rogan Mysteries Box Set* is now available
on my website at this link:
https://gabrielfarago.com.au/my-books/

# ABOUT THE AUTHOR

Gabriel Farago is the international, bestselling award-winning Australian author of the Jack Rogan mysteries and thrillers series for the thinking reader.

As a lawyer with a passion for history and archaeology, Gabriel Farago had to wait for many years before being able to pursue another passion—writing—in earnest. However, his love of books and storytelling started long before that.

'I remember as a young boy reading biographies and history books with a torch under the bed covers,' he recalls, 'and then writing stories about archaeologists and explorers the next day, instead of doing homework. While I regularly got into trouble for this, I believe we can only do well in our endeavours if we are passionate about the things we love. For me, writing has become a passion.'

Born in Budapest, Gabriel grew up in post-war Europe and, after fleeing Hungary with his parents during the Revolution in 1956, he went to school in Austria before arriving in Australia as a teenager. This allowed him to become multi-lingual and feel 'at home' in different countries and diverse cultures.

Shaped by a long legal career and experiences spanning several decades and continents, his is a mature voice that speaks in many tongues. Gabriel holds degrees in literature and law, speaks several languages and takes research and authenticity very seriously. Inquisitive by nature, he studied Egyptology and learned to read the hieroglyphs. He travels extensively and visits all of the locations mentioned in his books.

'I try to weave fact and fiction into a seamless storyline', he explains. 'By blurring the boundaries between the two, the reader is never quite sure where one ends, and the other begins. This is of course quite deliberate as it creates the illusion of authenticity and reality in a work that is pure fiction. A successful work of fiction is a balancing act: reality must rub shoulders with imagination in a way that is both entertaining and plausible.'

Gabriel lives just outside Sydney, Australia, in the Blue Mountains, surrounded by a World Heritage National Park. 'The beauty and solitude of this unique environment,' he points out, 'gives me the inspiration and energy to weave my thoughts and ideas into stories that in turn, I sincerely hope, will entertain and inspire my readers.'

*Gabriel Farago*

# CONNECT WITH GABRIEL

**Website**
https://gabrielfarago.com.au/

**Goodreads**
https://www.goodreads.com/author/show/7435911.Gabriel_Farago

**Facebook**
https://www.facebook.com/GabrielFaragoAuthor

**Twitter**
https://twitter.com/Gabriel_Farago

Made in the USA
Monee, IL
25 June 2021